DIG TO THE DEATH

Books in the Jake Tyler Series

In the Dark of the Sun

Under a Hard Blue Sky

Dig to the Death

Also by Mykel Hawke

The Quick and Dirty Guide to Learning Languages Fast

Hawke's Green Beret Survival Manual

Hawke's Special Forces Survival Handbook

Family Survival Guide (with Ruth England Hawke)

Foraging For Survival (with Douglas Boudreau)

Surviving Extreme Weather (with Jim N.R. Dale)

KIM MARTIN
MYKEL HAWKE

DIG TO THE DEATH

A JAKE TYLER NOVEL

PIXEL DRAGON PRESS

For information, email: authors@martinandhawke.com.

First Pixel Dragon Press U.S. trade edition May 2024

Published and printed in the United States.

Book Design by Kim Martin
Cover Image: Jim Niakaris

martinandhawke.com

ISBN: 978-0-9829316-8-4

ACKNOWLEDGMENTS

An enormous amount of research and resources go into our thrillers, beginning long before the first word and continuing throughout the creative process. So, as always, we begin by offering our profound appreciation for those who have so generously given their time, knowledge, expertise, and support. We hope we have applied the input and feedback accurately and in the best way possible.

With the interest of those new to our Jake Tyler series in mind, you should know that there are spoilers that reference previous books in the series. For this reason, while each book can be read as a stand-alone novel, you may enjoy them more by reading in sequential order.

THANK YOU…

Phillip Gonzales, as ever, for the providing the serendipity that brought us together in a friendship and partnership of nearly three dec-ades, as well as in this great endeavor.

Paul Jiménez Caro and Gaël Brose for enduring friendship, not to mention always availing themselves for subject matter help.

We owe a tremendous debt of gratitude to our friend, Stephen Humphreys, a major inspiration for this book. He is doing amazing work with his organization, American Veterans Archaeological Recovery (AVAR), which we enthusiastically support. Thank you, Stephen, for your kindness and for taking the time out of a packed schedule of fieldwork and associated commitments to guide us through the archaeology, and also for sharing the ways in which you apply it to benefit and enrich the lives of veterans. Also, special appreciation for Operations Manager, Mackenze Burkhart, BA, RA; and the rest of the AVAR staff.

We have other esteemed archaeologists to thank, including Yiorgos Kalomoiris, Scientific Director, IDAology Project, and Joanne M. Murphy, Professor of Aegean Archaeology, Archaeological Methods and Theory; both for helping us get our footing, so to speak.

An absolute mainstay in our Greek navigation—in more ways than one—was our friend, George Malakos, sailing captain extraordinaire with Alternative Sailing. No matter the challenge, minor or major, he patiently (and often passionately) educated and enlightened in sailing and all things Greek. Thanks also to Matt Barrett, for the introduction.

Ongoing thanks and respect for our friend, Nir Kalron, of the Maisha Group for being the inspiration behind Nash Remington and *Habari*. Stay safe and keep up your important work!

In Costa Rica: Jake and Callie's home base in Dominical, thank you to the owners of the beautiful Casa Serendipia for the use of their villa; Jesse and Karen Maurer for the use of Punta Gabriela.

Muchas Gracias, Alvaro Cedeño (all the best on your new life path!), Abraham Mendez Venegas, and all of the *Guardavidas* Costa Ballena who provide an invaluable service in protecting the beaches and those who enjoy them, also the dynamic Tara Tiedemann, Viva Adventures; enormous thanks to Beth Sylver for going above and well beyond in all the legwork...you rock, *chica*! Thank you to Beth's accomplice in our special event planning and accommodations, Michael Witte of Roca Verde; Hacienda Barú's tree climbing guide, Pedro Porras. And to Jack Ewing, the OG, ambassador of Dominical, guide, storyteller, and dear friend, much gratitude. We hope you guys enjoyed your cameos!

In Greece, Turkey, and elsewhere in the Mediterranean: Ntaiana Katakouzinou of Psara Travel; Eleni Karagiorgi of Spitalia; Angeliki Zannikou of the Chios Chandris Hotel. Very special thanks for the assistance and generosity of time from Ioannis Arampatzis, Police Colonel of the Chios Police Directorate, not only for guidance in local law enforcement but also, in Chios; Alessandro Lattanzio, the Semeli Hotel and Baos, Mykonos, for being absolutely stellar in his hands-on participation (and hope you enjoyed your cameo appearance!); Aziza Mammadova and Deniz Akaltan, the Yalikavak Marina, for providing so many essential details of your spectacular facility and location; Isil Yalcin, for her considerate assistance with Turkey.

Great friends and always helpful and supportive: Martine Villeneuve, of the Danish Refuge Counsel; Dr. Lanice Jones, *Médecins Sans Frontières*.

In the Air: Our wonderful friend, Gulfstream Captain Grady Montgomery, for sharing the world along with his expertise, and truly one of the nicest people on the planet; Tom Aniello and Brian Mead, Pilatus Aircraft, for all the assistance with flying the PC-12 NGX; pilots Thomas Vander Vellen and Simon Canning, for always availing themselves for random questions and scenarios; Dimitra Kiriakopoulou, Universal Aviation Greece and Sissy Coucouvinou, Goldair Handling, for the help in navigating FBOs.

On the seas: Aaron Amick, Sub Brief; H. I. Sutton, Covert Shores, both for their help with undersea cables and superyachts; Ben Dinsmore, who is always up for anything seafaring; Fernando Cadena Duque, for diving guidance; Yioryos Raptis, Amaso Dive Center, Ikaria, for providing technical diving support as well as assistance with localities; Lindsay Lyon, Ocean Guardian, for Jake's shark protection and who is always so kind; Xerxes Matten, sailor and world traveler, who more than knows his way around superyachts; Annita Sima and Panos Zois, Technohull, for assistance with those amazing RIBs.

For the Tech: Joe Ailinger Jr., Teledyne FLIR, for continuing to provide key support for all their cutting-edge tech and gadgets employed by Jake and Remington; Drew Smith, of the veteran-owned Lone Star Drone, for some great conversations about drone operation; Adam Bennett, HawkEye 360, for explaining that amazing technology; Deviant Ollam, security penetration specialist (and lockpicker), for sharing some of his cool tricks.

Other Key Assistance: Blaine Campbell, for CheyTac; Karl Stone, Team O'Neil Rally School, for help with some hardcore driving.

Special thanks to Scott Bohlinger, Regional Director International NGO Safety Organization, for discussions about the Middle East, Turkey, and regional conflicts, among other things. Ivan Kovalev, for all kinds of tactical support and background.

We thank several confidential sources for input and scenarios involving rare-earth minerals, polymers, and missiles.

Good friends Billy and Stacy Ray, the best kind of daydream believers—they don't give up.

In these fraught and perilous times when the scary what-if's become the what is…

Blessed are the peacemakers.

DIG TO THE DEATH

PART ONE

VISION OF A GENTLE COAST

1

WHAT HE DID NEXT had brought him to the spot where he now stood, on the beach down from the hills near his home, his nerves firing unlike they might have on any of the innumerous battlefields he'd fought, his heart pounding in his chest, his breath catching in his lungs. A few yards away, waves from the Pacific Ocean were rolling in and flattening in a lacy froth as the tide began to recede, the sky turned serenely blue after a brief afternoon rain. Seabirds seemed to swoon drunkenly through the gossamer clouds.

His eyes slid to the right, welling with emotion as he took in the vision of the woman beside him…and then, the moment was shattered by a supersonic vector that tore by the left side of his head like a ripped seam in the atmosphere, followed fractions of a second later by a distant crack. The concussive force sent him reeling sideways, stunning him momentarily, his cheek and jaw and teeth vibrating as if a beehive had split apart inside his face.

Dizzily, Jake Tyler instinctively lunged, surrounding Callie with his body and propelling them both away from where they'd been standing. He raised an arm and gestured emphatically to the group of people seated just in front of the palm trees, commanding them to move. Chairs raked across the sand, tipping sideways or upending as everyone scrambled in startled confusion, heads twisting back and forth in bewilderment bordering on mild concern. With the music and their absorption in the present, most had barely registered the sound.

Into Callie's ear, Jake urged, "Go with Eddie and Curran," nudging her toward the two men who had sprung from their chairs and rushed over.

Even as he was moving toward the tree cover and issuing instructions, Jake was peering up into the hills, searching for the point of origin. Beside him, another man said, "There, white structure."

"Yeah," Jake replied, "I think that's it."

Neither had to discuss what they were going to do; they knew each other's actions and reactions from a credo and methodology practiced over years of operational fraternity and personal friendship.

Together, they took off running.

FROM HIS PERCH UP in the hills, the man lay prone atop an octagonal platform raised over a multistory luxury estate, surrounded on all sides by rainforest.

Punta Gabriela is a popular vacation rental, often occupied by whole families or large groups, and encompasses several villas, a VIP owners suite, and a penthouse. Its amenities include a large pool, an indoor-outdoor bar, a zip line, and even a private helipad, on which the man had been set up since daybreak. During the peak tourist season—the "dry" months of November to April—this property was typically booked solid, but it was the shoulder season and the man's preliminary legwork had revealed that the place would be closed for a week or so while routine maintenance and painting were done, which was certainly fortuitous as that time covered the date he needed. Even better, the owners would be out of town for the duration. It had then just been a matter of cozying up to the foreman of the work crews and making a little side arrangement; in exchange for a day's pay—plus some extra *colones* for the boss— the man could have the whole place to himself for that particular day. A nice deal for the workers who, in essence, would be paid for a day without working.

This day.

For the past several weeks, in preparation for the day, the man had submersed himself into the funky little *pueblucho*, scouting the layout, the locals, the lifestyle, and finding it a little too laid back for his taste, the people a bit too friendly. With his dark hair and skin, he blended in well with the *Ticos,* but he could have easily been just another *turista,* wearing shorts and flip-flops and t-shirts printed with graphics of sailfish and surfboards and *Pura Vida Costa Rica* logos. But he was not here to vacation, he was here for his objective, and finding this place with its stunning 180-degree views overlooking his mark was golden.

Prior to that, he'd explored the roads, the businesses, the beaches. And he had done intensive recon on the residence of his target. With the target away for several weeks, the man's surveillance had been focused on the property itself and the staff managing it. Early on, he'd determined that the security measures and systems were impressive, though potentially breachable, at least during the day. He had proved it by doing just that, and enjoyed every moment of it.

On that occasion, he had looked down at his target's beautiful little woman as she'd blinked up at him from their pool with the shock of one seeing some kind of...what? An apparition? He'd found her reaction strange, but it did not matter. Initially, he considered formulating a contingency plan using her for leverage, but everyone was so damned protective of her it would have been near impossible. She never went out, and the one time she had, at the beach before his home visit, he had spooked her so badly that he was sure his whole op had been compromised. Fortunately, that wasn't the case, but he knew then its success was going to be more of a challenge than he had anticipated.

Just how much of a challenge became apparent when, upon the target's return home, the man could never get a bead on him anywhere. His target was abundantly cautious in town and intensely vigilant at home.

So when the man learned of this event, he'd known it was the best opportunity he would have and, in all likelihood, his one window.

He had spent the day before analyzing the terrain between his hide and the beach, estimating the distance and elevation, keeping an hourly log of temperature and humidity and winds. This morning, as the staging was being assembled and arranged on the beach below, he watched through the optics of his Steiner M7Xi 4-28x56 ballistic scope, twisting the turrets to make a few adjustments and then letting the IFS automated system of calculators and sensors do the rest.

The afternoon rain shower had sent him inside the house for a while, where he'd made himself at home, taking care to maneuver around the painting apparatus and supplies. He foraged in the downstairs gourmet kitchen which, in anticipation of the staff's hiatus had been depleted of fresh produce and proteins, but a check of the walk-in freezer rewarded him with an artisan-style pizza. He microwaved it, plucked a can of Coca-Cola from the Sub-Zero refrigerator, and carried it all upstairs to the penthouse suite. Sprawled on the king-size bed, he watched a soccer match between Deportivo Saprissa and Límon on a big-screen TV, where the *Caribenos* of Límon appeared to be getting their asses handed to them. As he enjoyed his pizza—a tasty combination of rich tomato sauce, local *queso fresco,* ham, mushrooms, and arugula—he ogled the opulent décor of the suite, furnished in light and dark caramel tones of leather and ornately carved wood, the recessed ceiling mirroring the shape of the helipad just overhead.

Stuffing the last of the pizza in his mouth and draining the can of Coke, he saw that the rain had stopped and the skies were clearing. Time to get back to the op. He headed to the roof.

ONCE AGAIN, THE MAN had laid flat on his stomach, the long gun positioned on its bipod in front of him. He had revised his earlier settings to accommodate the atmospheric changes left in the wake of the rain, noting the reversal in direction and tempo of the breeze, which caused him to second-guess his windage analysis. He held out his kestrel, and compared its readings to those of the scope, finding them almost identical. The humidity also bothered him, sometimes causing his visualization to swim as perspiration moistened his forehead and creeped into his eyelids. But he had watched and waited, and when the moment had come—his target centered in the reticle—he'd taken the shot.

The rifle bucked into his chest, the brass casing popping out by his elbow. He wiped his brow.

As soon as he'd fired, he expected to see his target drop to the ground, but that wasn't what happened. And people were clearing the beach in a hurry.

"*Hijo de puta!*" he hissed, immediately flipping the bolt handle to chamber another round. He swore again. *"Mierda!"*

It was too late, his target was also leaving the beach—but not before being joined by another man, both of them looking up toward his hide and then taking off at a run. He had to get the hell out of here.

That was why you often heard "one shot, one kill," he thought. That was the one shot and it did not kill.

The man hurriedly folded the gun's buttstock, removed the suppressor, and picked up the expended casing, putting everything in a BlackHawk drag bag which he zipped up and slung over his shoulder. Then he descended from the helipad, sprinted across the top balcony, and continued down the stairs to the rear patio where his rented motorcycle was parked. He hopped on the Honda XRE300, slapped his helmet on and took off so suddenly and with so much acceleration that the bike almost surged from beneath him. He swung around the side of the big mansion and then sped up to the road that would take him down to the coastal highway.

IN THE TREES, JAKE and his friend ran along the path to the Roca Verde hotel, the soles of their shoes thumping across a wood-slatted walkway, almost tripping over a black dog languishing lazily on the other side. They rounded the corner of the open-air restaurant, where Jake's charcoal-gray Jeep Rubicon sat in the shade of a tall coconut palm, and stopped. Exchanging looks, both quickly fumbled to undo the brass buttons on their dark green Class A's, Jake fishing his Outlaw Fugitive TAC sunglasses from a pocket of his before removing it and tossing it to the back seat.

Behind the wheel of his Jeep, Jake exited the short drive and turned right onto Route 34.

The Costanera Sur highway stretches for 130 miles of Pacific Coast between Oratina in the north and Palmar in the south. Close to the middle of that span, it clings to the shoreline of the beach towns that make up Costa Ballena in Puntarenas province.

From the passenger seat, Jake's longtime friend and combat comrade studied Jake's face through his Oakley shades, but neither spoke. Jake watched the road as dense forest climbed to his left, thick foliage on his right.

Nash Remington, his copper hair fade-tapered to a short textured top, a trim beard and mustache around his mouth and jaw, wore a tailored khaki button-up shirt and chinos, and seeing the tropical-print Tommy Bahama shirt that had been underneath Jake's dress uniform jacket should have made him smile. Instead, he grimaced inwardly, thinking about what had almost just happened to the man wearing it.

They were barely a minute from Roca Verde when Jake remarked, "That place should be coming up right—"

Before he could finish, a man on a motorcycle flew from a road on the left, hitting the highway in front of them so hard and fast the bike launched a few feet into the air, the rider's haunches leaving the seat and then bouncing back down, his legs flying out to the sides.

"Fuck!" Remington yelled, bracing himself with a hand on the Jeep's dash.

Jake stomped the brakes, bringing their vehicle to a jarring halt, the motorcycle rider fighting to gain control of his machine and swerving across the two-lane—just as a semi with a bright red cab came chugging around the bend.

2

CONFRONTED WITH THE HONDA XRE300 flying out from the hillside road, the driver of the Cascadia freightliner blared his horn but was in no position to stop in time, so he must have been greatly relieved when the bike cleared his path. The semi continued its northbound travel at a moderate and steady speed and soon disappeared, motoring northward. But Jake and Remington saw what happened in its wake, the motorcycle and rider swerving and skidding from in front of the truck to the second lane, hitting the embankment and going airborne over the coastal side of the highway. The rider's helmet popped off, from beneath which a dark-haired ponytail flipped straight up.

"Shit," Jake muttered, and pulled his Jeep onto the shoulder.

Both men sprang from the vehicle and stepped around a stand of bamboo lining the roadway's edge. Peered down into a wild mix of balsa and qualmwood trees and dense foliage, the sound of ocean waves audible somewhere on the other side. They began to carefully negotiate the incline, grabbing onto tree trunks and roots and plant stalks. Everything was wet and slippery from the rain, the ground bumping at their backs as they slid downward, branches lashing their arms and faces. The temperature was in the comfortable seventy-degree range, but the humidity was high and they quickly began to sweat with the exertion.

"God, how steep is this?" Remington asked after a few minutes.

"It goes almost straight down," Jake said, and felt one of his feet losing traction. Tommy Hilfiger boat shoes were sporty but not the ideal choice for climbing. He managed to wedge the loose foot in the crevice of a ficus tree limb before resuming his descent.

They had only progressed a short way before the slope seemed to fold under itself, a cavern of greenery filling the void. Through a narrow gap in the cover, some thirty feet below, they could just make out a massive shelf of jagged rock with surging waves all around it. Nowhere to be seen was the wreckage of a motorcycle or the body of its rider. No sound of an engine throttling or fading out, no human sounds at all.

Anchoring himself to another part of the massive tree, Jake wiped dirt from his face and said, "I don't know how he survives this…do you?"

"Hell no," Remington replied. "But where is he? Where is the wreckage?"

Jake looked down, saw nothing but trees and brush and rocks and water. He gazed at the water, trying to estimate the depth. "The tide is going out, but I suppose he could have bounced off and gone in. Still…" He looked around again. "Surely he didn't get out. Surely."

Remington did not respond.

"Godammit," Jake blurted. He glanced to his right and left. "We could go back up, get farther down and find a place that's not quite as steep."

Remington shook his head. "Naw, that guy's a goner. Even with the helmet, no way he makes it. I know you want to find out who he was, and I certainly do, but honestly, I've got to think he's being swept out to sea. You know he flew off that bike, probably even before impact."

Jake blew out a breath. "Okay, I'll call it in and let the police sort it out. And I guess it's possible he wasn't even the guy."

Remington made a snuffling sound. "Tearing down that hill like some kind of damn Evel Knievel? He was the guy."

They made their way back to the highway, brushing and stomping dirt and mud from their clothing and shoes, and got into the Jeep. Jake knew the small force of local police and called the captain, who was programmed into his phone. He provided coordinates for the accident and asked to be contacted if the rider or motorcycle was recovered. He did not tell the policeman anything about what had happened on the beach prior to the accident. The last thing he needed was for the OIJ to become involved; the *Organismo de Investigacion Judicial* are the Costa Rican equivalent of the U.S.'s FBI, and Jake remembered all too well the frustration he'd endured on being detained by their investigation when a local cop had been killed at his home months ago. Jake understood their protocols and appreciated their thoroughness, but the OIJ had taken up hours of time he desperately needed.

U-turning to the northbound lane of the highway, Jake noticed a green sign at the entrance to the hillside road. It had a graphic of a toucan and read: THE VILLAS AT PUNTA GABRIELA, LUXURY IN THE JUNGLE. "I don't believe it," he said. "This is the place I tried to book for you guys. Never been there, but it was highly recommended. Couldn't get it, though."

"That's the place with the helipad?" Remington asked.

"I think so, yeah."

"How in the hell could that guy be able to use it in broad daylight?"

Jake drove up the steep road and pulled in to the front of the resort property, gazing inquisitively through the Jeep's windshield at the big elegant house. Like so many of the grand estates here—like his, in fact—it had been built right in the middle of rainforest and high up enough to maximize the ocean views. Made of sand-hued concrete and stone and native hardwoods, the entrance was covered by a portico with dark, carved wood doors. Off to one side, a silver Mercedes passenger van was backed in next to a white Toyota truck displaying the resort's toucan logo, both late models and spotlessly clean. Several ATVs sat nearby. There were no other vehicles, and Jake wondered if there was another parking area for guests somewhere on the grounds.

He and Remington emerged from the Jeep and strolled to the entry doors, where they found a printed notice. Reading it, Jake said, "I guess this is how he did it, also why I wasn't able to book it. They're closed for maintenance." He reached out and tried the door handles, but they were locked.

Remington said, "Let's see if we can find a way up top and hope the guy left us something."

They followed the wide stone walkway to the right, which led to the rear of the house and continued down past the swimming pool to three detached villas. They saw no one, not any staff, not any work crews and, of course, not any other vehicles or guests. There was a flat stillness to the lack of personnel and activity around this plush and well-appointed place. The lower-level patio had a bar, which had been covered with tarps, and the glass doors to the house were sheathed in plastic taped around the edges. Jake tried those, too, finding them also secured. Balconies on each of the two upper levels were accessible by stairs going up the right side, which they took, checking each level and then climbing to the top where they found another set of stairs to the helipad.

There, they stood in the middle of the octagonal landing platform, which was a concrete pad framed on all sides with multiple rows of wood planks. It took only a few minutes to determine that nothing had been left behind.

A somber silence built between Jake and Remington. This guy, the shooter, was a pro. He had found a perfect perch, had taken advantage of an opportunistic situation, and used an event where his target was vulnerable.

Neither men spoke for a few minutes, both taking in the spectacular view that spanned rainforest and highway and beach and ocean from an elevation of over three hundred feet. The sun had penetrated the shroud of clouds and mist and, from this distance, it cast a sheen that was like stardust over the water. The view was much like that from Jake's villa, and he felt a hollow ache begin to spread in his gut. His eyes locked on the spot where, just a little while ago, he had been standing with Callie.

God, what if instead of missing me, he hit her?

Beside him, Nash Remington was watching Jake's face, could read the anguish in his friend's dark eyes. Saw him gulp, rake a hand through his black hair, and glance down to deflect the show of emotion. Softly, Remington asked, "You okay, brother?"

Jake swallowed again but did not say anything. He couldn't.

Remington said, "Come on, let's get back."

WHEN THEY RETURNED TO the beach, a man their age, dressed in a white cotton shirt in a micro dot pattern and tan chinos, was waiting for them. Through aviator-style sunglasses, he looked from Remington to Jake and held out his hand, revealing a shiny copper object one and a half inches long and pointed at the tip. It looked like a miniature missile.

Both stared at it for a few charged seconds and then Remington proclaimed, "Holy shit, a four oh eight."

The man with the bullet in his hand was Efron Kipnis and, with his slight build, low-key demeanor, brown hair worn short and precisely cut, he looked more the part of a high-tech geek, or maybe a think tank wonk, than the former Mossad operator who worked with Nash Remington. He had been one of several from *Habari*, Remington's security logistics company in Nairobi, who had taken part in an African mission from which Jake had just returned a few weeks ago. Kipnis actually did handle the technical aspects of Remington's operations, everything from cutting-edge tactical equipment and systems to intel management, but Jake had seen the man's combat skills up close and, to say he could handle himself was putting it mildly.

"That's affirmative," said Kipnis. "FBG."

Jake was regarding them quizzically, his mind working to place the significance of the bullet's caliber.

"As in fucking big gun," Remington clarified.

And then Jake got it, his eyes widening. "A fucking CheyTac."

The gun to which they were referring was an elite sniper rifle used by the British SAS and a few other special forces units, the .408 caliber cartridge being the telltale clue. It was arguably the best rifle of its class, which was that of extreme long range, and had recorded kills from over a mile away, its rounds traveling at a rate of three thousand feet per second.

Remington's olive-green eyes held on Jake and he said, "My man, somebody seriously wants you dead."

"Looks that way," Jake agreed soberly.

Just before Jake's departure from Africa, Remington had given him troubling intel from Kipnis about a contract posted on the Dark Web. While Jake had been on that mission, Callie had seen a man at home—once on the beach and once as she was emerging from the pool—a man who, apparently, looked exactly like Adonís Valentín, a cartel kingpin Jake had killed in Colombia. Jake was 100 percent certain Valentín was dead, but having been abducted and viciously violated by the man for the duration of her captivity, Callie suffered from endless nightmares in which she still saw him, and she had been convinced the man she'd seen was Valentín. Because there had been a price on Jake's head the entire time he'd been operating in South America, before leaving for Africa Jake had fortified the security at his villa. But on learning about a new hit out on him and the man, whoever he was, that had so easily gotten close to Callie, he wondered if he'd ever have enough security without turning his home into a fortress, which he was not about to do. When Remington and his guys had arrived a few days ago, they had conducted a comprehensive review of everything, enhancing what they could and, for the most part, finding it all solid. But a sniper was not really something you could anticipate or be totally secure from, no matter what measures were put in place.

Remington tilted his head toward the Punta Gabriela helipad visible over the treetops in the distance. "What do think, Kip? Seven or eight hundred meters? Not too many could make that shot from that height and angle."

"I could," Kipnis said confidently. "But you're right."

"And that guy almost did make it," Jake said. He stared up at the helipad. "Damn, I wish we could have at least IDed the guy."

"Did you see him?" Kipnis asked.

"In a blur," Jake replied, and told him what happened. "I wish I at least knew if he was the guy Callie saw, or worse, another guy." Before he could say anything else, his iPhone beeped in his ear. Tapping his Bluetooth device, he said, "Eddie, yes, I'm back. No, stay where you are. Is Callie okay?" He listened for a minute, then asked, "Everybody else? Okay, good. Just hang tight. We'll be there in a few." He ended the call and looked back to Remington and Kipnis.

Kipnis said, "While you guys were gone, Luther, Kean, Kent, and I checked the entire hotel property and about a klick each direction of the road. You're good to go." He paused, eyed Jake. "That is, if that's what you want to do."

Remington put a hand on Jake's shoulder. "We got you, no matter what."

"Well, nothing's changed," Jake said succinctly, "but then again, it *has*." He glanced away, pinched at his eyes.

"I know, man. I know. Just tell me what you want to do next."

Jake inhaled and sighed heavily. He consulted his watch, a Garmin tactix Charlie, and saw that it was just past three thirty. "I have to have a conversation."

Remington offered a solemn acknowledgment and then looked him up and down, a thin grin sliding onto his face in spite of the tension. "One thing I can tell you…you need to get cleaned up before you have that conversation."

Jake checked out his soiled shirt and pants, nodding. "Guess it's a good thing we took those jackets off."

ROCA VERDE IS A boutique hotel and restaurant in Dominical, the quaint and quirky little beach town that Jake now called home. Aside from being popular accommodations for the seasonal tourists, it is a venerable and respected community establishment, owned and operated by Michael Witte. In addition to staging live music events, Witte's hotel hosts an annual benefit in support of the local lifeguards. Jake had come to know them, and him by extension, while running an adventure tour business out of Dominical quite a few years ago. Living here in the present, he could not think of a better place for this day than right here on this beach, surrounded by his friends and these people.

Except for what had almost happened…and except for what *did* happen.

As Jake emerged from the room set aside for him, freshly showered and wearing a change of clothes, cleaned up shoes, and his dress uniform jacket, he glanced over to the pool where most everyone seemed to be, sitting around umbrella-covered tables. The sun was shining and the lush palms were a vibrant green, a refreshing breeze riffling through their fronds. From what he could tell, no one seemed overtly stressed, most chatting and sipping soft drinks or juice smoothies, munching on snacks. He suspected Witte had kept them out of the restaurant so it would remain intact and pristine. When he got to the room where Callie was, he raised his knuckles to rap on the door and felt the knot in his stomach tighten.

He knocked lightly and a moment later the door opened, framing a lovely redhead, tall, svelte, and happy to see him, though her smile was subdued. Amelia Keogh was in her early forties but could have easily passed for much younger. Amelia and her husband, Cyrus, a multimillionaire philanthropist, had been at the center of Jake's recent mission which, in some ways seemed a lifetime ago and in others, as abjectly painful as yesterday, all they had been through still smoldering below the surface. She was smartly attired in a Teri John tea-length lavender cocktail dress with cap sleeves and a square collar that showcased her slender neck and the amethyst-jeweled necklace encircling it. Her russet hair was layered into a French knot with strands hanging loose by her face.

"Jake." Her Australian-accented voice exuded affection tinged with empathy. She embraced him and took a step back to study him. Whispering, she asked, "Is everything all right?"

Matching her lowered tone, his own voice naturally husky, he replied, "Yes, everything's fine," even though he was not sure it actually was.

"I'll just…step out," she said.

Jake gave her a nod as she left and closed the door. He could already feel his heart stuttering in his chest before he looked to the bed where Callie sat. His lips parted and, again, he could not catch his breath. And then he felt the waves of giddy elation colliding with sadness as he saw the anxiety in her beautiful face, the worry in those exotic brown eyes. In the exquisite long white dress, pale blond curls just brushing her bare shoulders, she was like a celestial creature not meant for this earth. He felt like his heart might explode.

And he was about to have one of the hardest conversations he'd ever had in his life. Weeks ago, there had been another one like it and, at the time, he'd thought that was the one that would gut him because then he was laying himself bare and knew it could change everything.

Today, all of it had become real.

Jake gingerly sat down beside Callie and his fingertips delicately touched her dress. For a moment, he was lost in the reverence of its detail and the intimacy of the flesh beneath. He took her small hands in his. The room was utterly quiet, sunlight filtering in through the drapes, dust particles drifting in the air. A tiny lizard waddled down a goldenrod-colored wall with a hand-painted mural of a palm tree. The air-conditioning cycled on with a hum. His head was down, he took a bracing breath, and then looked up at her. In a flash, it was just like the night he had first kissed her and she had been thrust into his world by the kind of berserk and brutal things that happened to him as regularly and routinely as clouds crossed the sun.

3

ON THAT NIGHT BACK in late spring, Jake had been standing on the upper balcony of what was not, as yet, his villa, his arms around a tremulous Callie Kane, telling her not to be afraid of him. They had just concluded a tour of the Costa Rican countryside after meeting by chance and misfortunate circumstance in San José during a short break from Jake's military contract in Colombia, where he was engaged in counternarcotics work.

The tender and precipitous moment had been disrupted by a violent intrusion downstairs, Jake securing Callie in a bedroom while he confronted the armed man. In retrospect, Jake realized that had been her first glimpse into what it would be like to be in his world. Seeing her now, sitting nervously on the bed, her pretty face drawn with anxiety, brought that initial revelation full circle as some kind of grim prophecy fulfilled.

But so much more had happened in between then and now, things even he could never have envisioned and, on the completion of the contract, he'd forced himself to take a hard look at whether a relationship with Callie would be good, or fair, for either of them. Because of him, she had endured unimaginable trauma, physically, mentally, and emotionally, all at the hands of the egregious cartel kingpin his ops had targeted.

Jake's feelings for Callie, which he'd been questioning, or maybe denying, not only put her life in jeopardy, but also made him inevitably vulnerable to his enemies.

But that night, he'd casually dismissed the incident. Later, in the weeks after Colombia, he could not bring himself to have the kind of serious discussion he knew should have taken place at the outset. In the harrowing aftermath of Colombia, the need for comfort and reassurance took precedence, and he'd thought there would be time. Then, the unexpected mission in Africa had come up, both of them still recovering and Callie suffering with extreme post-traumatic stress.

This time on return, it had been as if his life, his body, his heart and mind had undergone a seismic shift. Even before he'd entered the villa, gone up the stairs and into the bedroom, he knew. There was no more uncertainty or doubt or any question of the path forward. And Callie, who had been struggling to open herself up to him again, had also known.

Within days, Jake had been with her on the same balcony, and had the talk he both dreaded and knew was necessary.

JAKE AND CALLIE HAD sat in the cane-woven chairs outside their bedroom and gazed out over the expanse of rainforest, the ocean and sky exquisitely blue and seemingly endless. It was hard for Jake to look at her because he was afraid he'd lose his nerve and because, inside, he was engulfed in a fear that was entirely different and far more uncontrollable than what he was accustomed to in his line of work. He could be shot or knifed or tortured or left for dead anywhere in the world and manage to rebound, get back in the game, move on. But if, after this talk, Callie was lost to him, he knew he would be utterly destroyed. Still, she had to know. He did not want to scare her, certainly did not want to push her away, but she had to understand and accept who he was and what he did, what was always going to be at stake. Even so, he carefully skirted around the part about there always being people trying to hurt him. To kill him.

As the talk had gone on, becoming more and more serious, her face blanched of color, her eyes filling with some unknown emotion. It took every ounce of will for him to continue, but he had.

Finally, he said, "Callie, I love you more than I ever thought I could love anyone. But I need you to know what this is, what this will be. If it's too much, I will understand." He had swallowed and felt a sharp pain that was like a hot poker in his throat. "I promise it's okay."

When he was done, he'd tried to steel himself for a resurgence of doubt from her, maybe even tears. Because it was a *lot* to process and he was sure it was an agonizing ultimatum for her. But to his surprise and elation, Callie had simply replied, "I love you, Jake. It's…it's scary…but I can't imagine a life without you."

The next evening, they'd had a romantic dinner at La Parcela, a restaurant overlooking the ocean, afterward strolling the beach near the villa. As they walked, hand in hand, the moonlight glowing in a filament between dark ocean and sky and reflecting across the rolling waves, a semicircle of lanterns came into view, and Jake's face could barely contain the jubilation swelling inside him. He led Callie to a heart-shaped outline of red rose petals dappled on the sand and dropped to a knee before her.

He would not wait another hour, another minute, another second, all the darkness that locked on him like a heat-seeking missile vanquished from his thoughts.

Until now, seated beside Callie on the bed.

"YOU LOOK BEAUTIFUL, LOVE" he said softly, his face full of awe.

Callie looked back at him, her lashes flicking rapidly. Jake could see her chest rise and fall beneath the material of her dress. She was visibly shaking.

"First of all," he said in a calm, measured voice, "everything is okay." He caressed her hands to soothe the trembling. She averted her head and he waited. Saw her shudder. When she did not look up, he lifted her chin with a finger.

"Wh-what happened?" she stammered.

"Well," he began, and paused pensively. "That hard talk we had when I came back from Africa…what happened today is the kind of thing that talk was about."

He was struggling to compose a response that would be honest and forthright but also encouraging, finding it difficult to explain in a way that was not intimidating. Realizing there was really no way to mitigate the statement of facts, he said, "Someone took a shot at me, so Remy and I tried to find the guy."

She blinked, her eyes wide.

"He got away, but I don't think he made it. He was on a motorcycle and was going so fast that he went over the side of the highway and crashed. We left it to the police to handle."

"So he's...?"

"Probably dead, yes." He let that hang for a moment and then gave her hands a squeeze. "I know this is upsetting, so we will do whatever you want to do. Everyone is still here, everything is still ready, but if you want to take some time or postpone, even not go forward at all...even if you want to...rethink things..." He inhaled, held a breath, exhaled slowly. "I'll understand."

"You really think it's okay?" she asked.

"As much as we can tell."

Again, he waited, but she went quiet.

"Callie, it's okay."

After another minute, she asked, "We can go back to the beach?"

"Yes." He smiled hopefully, and stood. "Should I get Amelia?"

Another long hesitation and she said, "Okay," but did not stand.

Jake extended his hand, she took it, and rose. When she looked up at him, he leaned in, slid his hand around her neck, and tenderly kissed her.

JAKE WAS RIGHT, NOT a soul had left and now they were reassembled on the beach, sitting in wooden folding chairs. It was an hour from dusk, the sky beginning to blush its sunset colors. The music was playing once more, and Callie was walking toward the same place she'd been standing earlier when the bullet had ripped by Jake's head.

On hearing from Jake weeks before, Amelia Keogh had insisted on overseeing the wedding and launched into the planning and execution with an enthusiasm that Jake was pleased to see given the devastating loss she had so recently sustained. As much as Jake would have preferred something even smaller and more intimate—battling her PTSD, crowds overwhelmed Callie—in the end, he agreed to invitees that included a close circle of friends: Eddie Falcone and Curran Niles who were fairly new ones, and Nash Remington who he'd known since his early army days at Bragg, along with a few of Remington's guys that had been on their last op. Also present were Jake's villa staff, who he considered family, and many acquaintances from the community. Notably absent were any friends of Callie's or actual family for either of them; outside of Jake, Callie was virtually alone in the world with no siblings and deceased parents, and Jake, while having numerous comrades he considered friends the world over, never spoke of any family.

With the help of Michael Witte and Beth Sylver, another local Jake knew, Amelia Keogh had more than succeeded in creating a dream wedding for the couple. Even if it hadn't been for what had derailed the ceremony earlier, Jake was especially determined to embrace all the Cinderella magic, not only for Callie but, if he was being honest, for himself, as he never thought finding this kind of happily-ever-after would be possible for him.

Callie's procession to the driftwood threshold, entwined with the same flowers of her pink-and-white bouquet—roses, orchids, hydrangeas, peonies, eucalyptus, and lisianthus—was serenaded by the uncharacteristically light and melodically lilting Bon Jovi singing *Here Comes the Sun*, a choice suggested by Remington, to the surprise of no one who knew him. Jake winked at his friend sitting in the first row, Remington giving him a grin and a little salute in response.

The gown Amelia had brought for Callie was a mermaid-silhouette Stella York with a V-neck back and shoestring straps that clung to Callie's slim frame, almost as if it melted over her body, flaring at the bottom in a cascade of scrolling lace and scalloped trim. As clichéd as it was, Jake had never seen anything, or anyone, more beautiful in his life. He stood beside her in his dress uniform jacket, adorned with its full regalia of pins and patches and ribbons and metals, wondering how he came to deserve this.

Callie was trembling, her knees weak, and once, as a chair creaked with someone reaching to retrieve something at their feet, she flinched. But Jake held her eyes, smiling broadly.

When the minister who presided finished his recitations and Jake and Callie had exchanged their vows, he declared, "It is my pleasure to pronounce you husband and wife. Mr. and Mrs. Tyler, all of us gathered here wish you *pura vida!*"

To hearty applause, Jake embraced Callie with a long and passionate kiss.

While the officiant lawyer finalized the ceremony with the requisite paperwork, Eddie Falcone and Curran Niles, who had been filming, began preparing for the photo shoot. Although both came from a music industry background, the two had come to know Jake when they'd hired him as an advisor for a reality television project, but their tight friendship developed from the events they'd been unexpectedly drawn into while on location in Colombia. They had willingly risked their lives for Jake, not only there but also in the recent African mission when their call on him to help evolved into much more than any of them anticipated. Falcone was a dark-haired and -complected New Jerseyite, Niles, a fair-haired, gray-eyed Brit.

Directing Jake and Callie to places on the beach, Falcone filmed with a Canon video camera while Niles framed them in shots with a Nikon DSLR. Jake, with his trim and fit physique in the handsome uniform jacket, coal-black hair swept back from his forehead, and penetrating dark eyes, and Callie, swathed in the dazzling dress with her fair skin and champagne-colored curls, made for mesmerizing pictures.

Just as they had for the duration of the restaged wedding, Efron Kipnis observed from behind the scope of his own sniper rifle, a Barrett M82 wedged within a tall rock formation, while Remington's other men, Luther Baldur, Keanjaho Dmello, and Kent Sanborn, patrolled with binoculars and handguns. Fortunately, this time, all was quiet.

Packing up their video and photographic equipment, Falcone and Niles strode past Kipnis as he began to disassemble his weapon. "Dude," Falcone called out, "do you keep that thing in your back pocket?"

"Never leave home without it," Kipnis replied.

BY THE TIME BRIDE and groom and their guests had all moved into the Roca Verde restaurant for the reception, the sun had infused the sky with fire and descended beyond the ocean, leaving the rippled clouds coated in lilac, coral, and pink. Amelia Keogh and Beth Sylver had transformed the open-air venue to a level of enchantment that rivaled any

Disney prince-and-princess tableaux. The high, wood-beamed ceiling was hung with floral-laced tropical greenery and suspended teardrop lighting, twinkle lights strung throughout. The white-linen-clothed tables were accented with an abundance of flowers and candles and arranged with gleaming, gold-trimmed china, stemware, and settings. The look of awe on Callie's face as she made her entrance with Jake was captured on camera and, minutes later, projected with a slideshow of other images by Falcone and Niles onto the restaurant's inner wall.

Jake had removed his uniform jacket and was now wearing just the clean tropical-print shirt and slacks; Callie was in a white sundress which she had been wearing the first time Jake laid eyes on her in San José, but for this occasion, as with everything else, Amelia had made it over into something extra special by having it embellished with ribbons and lace and tiny pearls and sequins.

While the waitstaff served appetizers and salads, Michael Witte, eager to get their impressions, came by with a bottle of Dom Pérignon, popped the cork, and poured into Jake's glass. When Jake had taken a tasting sip and nodded, Witte proceeded to fill the other glasses at the table. Gregarious and animated, he had short brown hair with a trace of facial hair and wore an open-collar paisley-printed shirt.

"How'd we do?" he asked.

"Outstanding," Jake proclaimed. "Truly incredible."

Witte tipped his chin toward Amelia Keogh, who beamed. "This magnificent lady deserves the real credit. She had the vision."

"You are much too generous," Amelia said. "It was a team effort. I could not have done it without you and Beth."

When Witte had retreated, Remington raised his flute and toasted, "To Prince and Princess Charming!" After everyone at the table sipped from their champagne and began eating, Remington leaned over to Jake. "I could not be happier for you, bro...she's the sweetest thing and just right for you."

"Thanks, Remy," Jake said, his eyes on Callie. She sat quietly, her plate untouched, timidly scanning the large space, taking in the lights and the flowers and the movements around her. Gently nudging her, Jake said, "Eat, sweetie."

Glancing around the table, Jake caught Amelia gazing at him. "Cy would have loved this," she commented wistfully, her green eyes shining. "And this would have made him so happy." She paused to stifle the emotion, adding, "He was such a hopeless romantic."

"I wish he was here, too," Jake said dolefully. "I know this has got to be hard on you."

She dabbed her mouth with her napkin. "Honestly, this was such a pleasure and, in a way, therapeutic."

"Why didn't you bring Lula?" Niles asked from across the table, referring to the African child the Keoghs had adopted.

Before answering, Amelia nodded to Niles and Falcone beside him, remarking, "You boys look spiffy. I reckon we all look a lot more civilized out of the bush."

Niles, his collar-length hair pulled back with a clip in a style reminiscent of David Beckham, was wearing a Reyn Spooner shirt bursting with turquoise and teal flowers, cream-colored linen slacks, and Soludos espadrilles. Falcone, whose hair typically had a disheveled bent, was neatly groomed and dressed in a blue-on-blue Bonobos Madras button-up shirt, navy chinos, and Nike sneakers.

"I would have brought her," Amelia said brightly, "but my Lula-belle has a little bug or something, so I had to leave her behind. I already miss her terribly and have been FaceTiming every chance I get just so I can see her."

While they dined on grilled chicken and fish and a wide assortment of sides, plates being delivered and removed in succession and glasses refilled, people stopped by to personally congratulate the newlyweds. Jack Ewing and his wife, Diane, who were good friends of Jake's, embraced the couple and, before moving away, Ewing let Jake know he was now retired from Hacienda Barú, the wildlife refuge he had run for over forty-five years; Ewing was one of the first locals Jake had come to know while running his adventure tour company here.

Regarding the silver-haired bearded man, Jake declared, "Good for you! I know it's been your life's work, but it *is* work. Time to enjoy life a little more."

Ewing shrugged good-naturedly. "Hard to step away, but it's time. Truly happy for you and Callie." He gave her an affectionate smile.

There were quite a few of the Costa Ballena *Guardavidas* in attendance, including Alvaro Cedeño and Abraham Mendez Venegas, and while paying their respects to Jake and Callie, they also expressed kudos to Beth Sylver, one of their major supporters, for her role in the wedding arrangements. Standing with her husband, wearing a locally made floral dress, a pink plumeria bloom in her long ashen hair, she gushed, "This has been so much fun!"

She bent down and gave Callie a hug.

With the increasing amount of well-wishers, the comings and goings of the attentive waitstaff, and the rising volume of talk and music, the space, as expansive as it was, began to feel tight to Callie, and soon, she felt an all-too-familiar sensation begin to mount.

AS THE PLATES OF immaculately prepared food came and went, much of which Callie barely nibbled, as the deejay played a selection of songs that were a blend of slower romantic themes and more up-tempo numbers, as rainbow backlighting washed across vertical and horizontal surfaces, as china and glassware clinked and conversation hummed, even as familiar faces smiled and made happy talk, panic was starting to slide stealthily around her.

After getting past the big scare on the beach and then the even more frightening revelation about what had actually happened, Callie still had to push past a swell of nerves and anxiety to return to the beach, and walking between the rows of chairs filled with what seemed like so many more people than had been on the guest list had felt like an eternity. Her gait was unsteady, her arms and legs shaking, her head pulsing as if her brain was suddenly swollen inside her skull. But when she was finally standing next to Jake and he looked at her the way he did, she could feel the warmth and reassurance in his smile, the love in his eyes and, somehow, she got through it. Relief and exhilaration replaced the anxiety and she was feeling much better. Now, at the reception, she felt comfortable next to Jake, his hand or arm or leg almost always touching her.

But it wasn't long before the level of comfort began to evaporate. A steady stream of people pressed in, voices and music grew louder, and the images of her and Jake projected massively on the wall made her recoil self-consciously—not for him, he was the most handsome man she'd ever seen—but seeing herself in the images, especially so huge, made her want to disappear.

Once, Amelia Keogh caught her expression of mortification and chided, "My darling, these pictures are gorgeous! You are absolutely breathtaking."

But Callie felt the collective eyes of the room on her—and they were much of the time, but on Jake, too—and she tried to make herself small, felt outside of the close and easy camaraderie amongst Jake and Remington and Falcone and Niles and the others at their table.

She tried to tell Jake she needed to go to the ladies' room, but her voice stuck in the back of her throat. He was talking to Remington and did not notice as she stood unevenly and stepped onto the tile floor. All at once, the space was whirling and she felt dizzy and nauseated. Moving slowly toward the bathrooms, her feet did not seem to be touching the ground, everything in her field of vision blurred.

All of Roca Verde is imaginatively painted with vivid colors composing scenes of the rainforest and ocean; the restaurant's restrooms are bright turquoise and dark pink and swimming with black-and-white whales and whimsical bubble rings. To Callie, it all bled together, and she fumbled her way through the doors and to the sinks. She was panting and perspiring and her skin prickled with an electricity that reminded her of the ants in the jungle and the ants in her garden, ants that crawled all over her. Her pulse was racing, her heart was pounding. She slumped over the rim of the sink and tried to hold on.

4

A VOICE BEHIND HIM said insistently, "Jake, Camilla needs you."

Jake twisted in his chair to see Jesse Segura, the lifeguard who was living on-site as part of his security at the villa. The young man's forehead was lined with concern.

"Camilla? Where?" Jake turned to his other side, saw the empty chair, stood, and hurriedly left the table.

When he entered the ladies' room, he found their housekeeper dabbing Callie's face with a cloth. Camilla, a buxom middle-aged *Tica*, attractively outfitted in a navy and white dress with a printed scarf containing some of her thick, curly hair, said quietly, "Miss Callie… *marearse.*"

"Okay," Jake said evenly. "I've got her. Thank you, Camilla."

Camilla handed Jake the bottle of water she was holding and reluctantly departed.

Callie was seated in a chair, her skin almost as pale as the white of her dress, spots of color in her cheeks, quivering as if she'd been immersed in ice-cold water. Squatting down in front of her, Jake spoke gently. "You're okay, angel."

But *he* wasn't.

He was angry with himself for not noticing her escalating distress and catching the onset of the episode before it got out of control. The signs had been there—he knew them all too well. She was clearly overwhelmed, had been extremely nervous all day, especially after the shot fired on the beach. The amount of attention focused on her, though it was with the best of intentions, and the number of people clamoring to bestow it, had obviously been more than she could handle. He had kept a cautious eye on her and noted how minimally she ate and drank, but her appetite had only just begun improving in the past week or so since his return from Africa, so that had not overly concerned him.

But the PTSD was something he had been acutely aware of ever since Colombia, and it was always in the forefront of his mind. There were the frequent nightmares, the collateral fears and phobias, and even day to day life was often a real challenge. He had been encouraged in recent weeks and, after his proposal, they'd discussed what to expect with the wedding at length. He'd made it clear that it was her choice entirely, letting her know he was open to anything she wanted but, as with most things, he suspected she had based her choice on what she believed *he* wanted.

He felt a backdraft of sorrow, wanting this day and night to be special and memorable for her. He was still determined to make that happen, but first he had to dismantle the anxiety and panic and get her back to baseline at least.

Callie looked at him with tears pooling and then streaming down her face, her inhalations coming in gasps and wheezes. He continued to speak to her soothingly, repeating, "Slow, deep breaths," until she began to grow calm and breathe easier. He encouraged her to take sips of water, gently touching her face with the damp cloth to fix her makeup. Amelia had done such an expert job in the application that it mostly remained in place, just some smudges here and there.

Several minutes later, she said, "I'm sorry, Jake…I hope I didn't mess up everything." The fingers of one hand were moving over the lace on her dress, the others grasped the water bottle.

He smiled lightly. "You have nothing to be sorry about, baby, and you haven't messed anything up. The only important thing right now is *you*. Not me, not our friends—and they all understand—not anybody here. Just you." He paused, looking directly at her. "Do you want to go home? We can."

Her response was immediate, even desperate, and she almost spilled the bottled water. "No…no, no."

"Okay, hold on." He stroked her cheek, ran a finger through one of the swirls of her hair. "Just think about it for a minute. If it will be best, then—"

"No," she said again, almost pleading. "I really want this. I do. Please." The sincerity was lucid in her eyes, a tiny tremor in her bottom lip. She touched his arm.

"Okay, angel."

WHEN THEY WERE BACK at the table, the concerned eyes of everyone seated there looked the question, which Amelia Keogh voiced, asking, "Everything okay?"

Raising Callie's hand to his lips with a kiss and a smile, Jake said, "Yeah, just some nerves."

Following his lead, Remington remarked, "Well, you better get over that because, guess what? The bride-and-groom dance is about to happen."

Watching Callie's eyes go wide with new consternation, Jake glanced around, spotting Michael Witte hovering nearby. "Mike, can we have some gin and tonics?"

Remington grinned, drawling in his Tennessee twang, "Oh yes, let me square off with some Jack Daniel's, please, sir."

Falcone and Niles, noticing the lack of single women in the mix, asked Callie if she would save a dance for them. A little while later, between some light banter and the gin, Jake believed Callie's tension was easing, even if only slightly. But when the deejay made the announcement for their first dance, she looked at him as if a firing squad had suddenly appeared.

The chosen song was Don Henley's *For My Wedding,* and it had barely started when Jake began to regret having selected it for this dance, not because it was a bad choice, but because it was too *good* of a choice, the words resonating with him so personally that he found himself struggling with his own emotions even as he was doing what he could to handle Callie's. The song was a plea for prayer to make it in life, fortified by the strength of love, to put the darkness and all dark things in the past. Callie had brought the light into his life that he'd never had, and he knew beyond any doubt whatsoever that her light was his salvation. As for prayers, his most fervent one was that he would be everything to her that she needed and that he could always keep her safe.

She whispered, "Jake, I can't do this…I can't…" Her eyes were darting from side to side, watching all their guests watching them, watching her.

He led her to the center of the reception, his arm cradling the small of her back, pressed close and said, "Eyes on me, love…eyes just on me." He drew her even closer, could actually feel her heart thudding against his chest. Halfway through, with the gentle rhythm of the song and the sway of their movements together, she began to settle down, but both had tears in their eyes by the time the song was done.

In her ear, he said, "Callie, I love you more than anything in this world."

Their friends applauded, some also wiping their eyes, and the floor was opened up for everyone to dance as the deejay played records that ran the gamut of Van Morrison's *Brown Eyed Girl* and Keith Urban's *Memories of Us* and One Direction's *If I Could Fly* to the upbeat Black Eyed Peas' *I Gotta Feeling* and Walk the Moon's *Shut Up and Dance*. At Remington's urging, the spinmeister slipped in *Living on a Prayer*.

When Jake shot him a mocking look, he quipped, "What? It's a love song, too."

The mood had loosened considerably by now and Jake could finally relax himself as he observed Callie much more at ease. Michael Witte and some of his waitstaff wheeled out a cart with a multitiered wedding cake as smooth as white silk, spiraled with sugar roses and tasting of *tres leches* and *piña colada*.

Since Callie was too bashful to do it, Remington smashed a chunk of the spongy confection into the vicinity of Jake's mouth as Falcone and Niles laughed hysterically. They had been throwing back shots of Jack with their champagne and beer, trying to keep pace with Remington, which Jake warned them would be futile and get them mightily shitfaced.

Wiping cake from his mouth, Jake took a swallow of his drink and heard his name. Turning, he saw Jesse Segura again, this time with Jerry Hadley and Tara Tiedemann. Hadley and Tiedemann were also lifeguards, Hadley being a supervisor, both tanned and blond with athletic builds. Since the two of them had come around earlier with their felicitations, Jake's curiosity stirred.

Segura said, "Jake, can we talk to you?" He flicked his eyes pointedly in Callie's direction.

Jake stood and took a few steps from the table, glancing over his shoulder to make sure they were out of Callie's earshot. "What is it?" he asked, the curiosity bumping up to a more heightened state of guardedness.

"We were talking about what happened today," Hadley said, "and it reminded me of something I've been meaning to tell you. That day Callie was at the beach with Jesse, the episode she had…" He paused uncertainly.

"Yes, Jesse told me about that," Jake said.

Hadley continued, "We didn't make any kind of connection at the time, but I think Tara and I actually saw the guy."

Jake's eyebrows shot up. "What?"

Tara Tiedemann picked up the narrative. "There was a big storm coming and we were making a last pass, advising people to leave the beach, and this guy was just strolling along, totally oblivious. There was this…arrogance. From the description Jesse gave us of the man Callie said she saw…Jake, I think that was the guy. He totally fit the description…the slick dark hair, ponytail, tight shorts, gold chain."

Jake was speechless, his mind veering in all different directions. So there actually *was* a guy…who was he? *Dark hair, ponytail.* Could he have been the shooter doing advance scouting? Stalking Callie?

They were interrupted by Remington. "Jake, the police captain is here and wants to speak to you."

THE MAN WAITING IN the front of the restaurant was in a dark blue uniform, of medium height and build with short-cropped hair and a trimmed mustache. On seeing Jake's approach, Captain Daniel Picado Barrantes gave a nod and extended his hand with a restrained smile.

Jake shook the captain's hand and turned to formally introduce Remington. "Daniel, what can you tell me?"

"I apologize for coming here and intruding—congratulations, by the way—but I did try to call."

Jake absently touched the pocket of his pants holding his phone, head tipping back. "Oh, sorry…with everything going on…"

Barrantes flipped his hand dismissively, "No, of course, I would not expect you to be checking your phone right now. And I can certainly understand why you would not want to be detained for just having witnessed the accident."

"Did you find the wreckage?" Jake asked.

"Yes, well, we are required to turn accidents over to the *Policia de Transito,* but they were tied up at a big accident near Quepos. So I called Hacienda Barú and got Pedro Porras to come."

Porras, Jake knew, was Hacienda Barú's tree climbing guide and would have all the necessary gear with which to make a descent. "Okay, so what did Pedro find?"

"He brought a high-test rope and rappelled down the hill and found the motorcycle, but it was destroyed," the captain said, "so I do not think they will be able to get anything from it."

"And the guy?" Remington asked, and added, "I'm guessing it was a guy."

Barrantes looked from one to the other before replying, "Pedro did not find a body."

"Do you think the rider went into the water?" Jake asked.

"Jake, can I ask, why are you so interested? On your wedding day. Is there something else you need to tell me about this incident?"

"No, nothing else," Jake said quickly. "I just wanted to follow up, that's all."

The policeman stood wordlessly for a few moments and then said, "Again, congratulations to you and your new bride."

When Captain Barrantes had gone, Remington said, "Go, enjoy your wedding celebration with that sweet little thing for a little while longer. I am going to get my guys and head over to *tu casa* so we can have it and the property swept before you get there."

"I think Callie's probably ready to get home."

"Well, try to give me an hour at least."

"You okay to drive?"

Remington smirked and cut his eyes at Jake.

"Just making sure," Jake chuckled. "Amelia, Jesse, and Camilla want some time, too. They're going to do some things on the inside."

Remington smiled. "Yeah, I know about that." He hung one of his muscular arms over Jake's shoulders. "Just chill, bro. We got this."

WHEN JAKE PULLED HIS Jeep Rubicon up to the villa it was just after 10 PM. His eyes automatically scanned the illuminated frontage, even though he knew that Remington, Kipnis, Baladur, Sanborn, and Dmello were somewhere out there maintaining a perimeter patrol. He'd already received a text from Remington that everything was in the clear. Exterior lights swept upward from the ground and angled out from the corners of the roofline. Jake opened Callie's door and helped her from the vehicle, and they walked together to the villa.

With the money Jake had amassed from military contract work—high risk, high pay—some his and come by rightfully and some bequeathed to him from less than aboveboard means, he could have chosen to live most anywhere. And he had contemplated a fresh start somewhere else. He'd only actually lived here for as long as Callie had. But in the end, he chose to stay in Dominical. It was offbeat, wild, and rough around the edges, but primitive beauty was everywhere, the beach town populated by less than a thousand locals with a diverse mix of expats who came for the big surf or the creative energy or the ecological wonder and never left. Jake had moved around all of his life, living out of duffels and backpacks like a vagabond, his survival skills and adaptability making him well suited for such a lifestyle. But here, for the first time, he felt grounded, and it felt better than he ever believed it would. And even though he was living in a house that had belonged to his beloved and now deceased friend, with Callie, it finally felt like his; the fact that Haskell Delaney had willed the property to him did not make him want it or feel comfortable in it, but being with Callie did.

The villa was a thirty-five-hundred-square-foot two-story Spanish Colonial with a clay barrel-tiled roof, surrounded by well-maintained grounds that encompassed rainforest and tropical gardens. The rear sloped down across an expanse of immaculately coiffed grass and then to jungle and beach and ocean. The view, whether from the edge of the infinity pool which appeared to fall off into the Pacific, or the bedroom balcony, was breathtaking. Pure paradise.

Inside, the lighting had been selectively dimmed, and some of the slower tempo music from the wedding and reception was playing. They entered the foyer of the villa to another Don Henley song of significant meaning, *Taking You Home*, and he heard Callie sniffing back tears.

The floorplan was open and airy, with high ceilings and tall windows set across the back side, which looked onto the lanai and patio. Walls were taupe and beige, furnishings and décor were in earth and sea shades. Doors, windows, cabinets, and post beams were constructed of local hardwoods and the floors were tiled.

Jake led Callie through the living room, past the brick-arched kitchen and adjacent dining area and out to the large patio and semicircle pool, its surface wrinkling in the aqua luminescence of the underwater lighting. There, swim trunks for him and a bikini bathing suit for her were laid out on a table. Jake said, "I think, Mrs. Tyler, a dip in the pool is next."

When they were in the warm water, Jake drew Callie's arms and legs around him and they drifted in the weightlessness, dark sky overhead sparkling with stars that were like the heavens' chandelier. Jake gazed into her beautiful brown eyes, traced her face with his fingers, and kissed her. Softly, slowly, so gently. And then with growing hunger, longer, deeper, and he could feel his body wanting, craving, aching, hardening. Impossible as it was, he tried to keep his yearnings in check as much as he possibly could, knowing that he still had to go easy with her. But to-night, right now, he was past the point of constraint. Still, he would refrain, as he had before, if it was needed. He heard a voice inside his head pleading.

Finally, he moved to the pool's steps and guided her up to the stone patio. They donned fluffy terrycloth robes that had been placed by the bathing suits. Strode back through the villa and up the stairs to their bedroom, where candles had been arranged throughout, the rotating ceiling fan nudging their flames. The French doors to the balcony were open, a light breeze blowing in, the sound of waves breaking in the distance like a whispered promise.

Jake stood before Callie, who was now trembling in anticipation but also anxiety. Slowly and with great care, he peeled the robe off, kissing her neck and then her shoulders. He eased it down and let it drop to the floor, then unhooked her bikini top, slipping his hands over her small breasts. She stiffened and he waited, feeling her heart accelerate and, after a few minutes, slightly slow. He pushed the bikini bottom over her slim hips, felt the pelvic bones with his thumbs as she was still so skinny, and worked it off her feet. Knowing how self-conscious she was, he wasted no time stripping his trunks off, straightening and pulling her close.

"It's okay, angel. It's okay." He kissed her, felt their breath combine.

Sliding into the king-size bed with its upholstered headboard against a herringbone-panel wall and luxuriant sheets and nesting of plump pillows, he held her like the precious being that she was, talking softly into her ear, his hands and fingers caressing, his own heart hammering. As had been the way since she'd been finally able to open herself up to him again, there was an initial flare of fear, a tenseness that was a reflexive response built from everything that had been done to her. But he was patient and gentle and took his time.

She gradually unfolded in surrender and he eased inside, felt her open up to him in spite of the defenses, moved deeply inward and then began to lose himself in a way he never had before, not ever, the wetness, the warmth, the bliss that bloomed and expanded and exploded like the end of time and the beginning of everything.

From the sound system's speakers in the bedroom, the volume low, Eric Carmen's *Make Me Lose Control* was playing, the ecstasy of the song rising in its sensual and joyful crescendo. *Oh my God, Amelia, how did you do that?* Jake marveled, and let himself continue to be swept away, lost and found over and over again, and Callie was completely with him.

5

WHEN JAKE CAME DOWNSTAIRS the next morning, a blend of light sunshine and shadows was spreading across the living room, the smell of rich Costa Rican coffee wafting from the kitchen. He'd risen a little later than usual, around 7:30 AM, but, after all, it had been a long, adrenaline-charged day and night. Showered, shaved, and dressed in sand-colored G-Star RAW cargo shorts, a black Armani silk t-shirt, and OOFOS flip-flops, he stopped at the speckled granite bar and his housekeeper drifted over with a steaming mug of the fresh brew, which she placed in front of him.

"Buenos dias, Señor Jake. *Tuviste una buena noche?"* Camilla gave him a warm smile, inquisitively appraising his face for further clues. She wore a denim-blue dress with red paisley trim, her hair pulled back with a red bandana, twisted and knotted at the top, big gold loops dangling from her ears.

Camilla Orellana Márquez, like most of the villa's staff, had already been employed when Jake took residence—Jesse Segura being the one exception—and though he'd been acquainted with them from his prior visits, the relationship he had with all now was one of great appreciation and fondness, which only continued to build as he saw how much genuine affection they had for him and Callie and, most importantly, their protectiveness. They were a tight-knit group, personable and hard-working, and had demonstrated time and again that they would do anything for the couple.

Jake replied affably, *"Si, una buena noche, gracias,"* and, because he knew she would ask if he did not tell her, added, "and yes, Callie is fine."

Camilla's face beamed with happiness. *"Mija…*what a beautiful bride. *Muy, muy hermosa.* So happy for you."

"Thank you. Yes, yes." His eyes misted at the visual and emotional memory.

He took his coffee out to the patio, where he found Nash Remington seated at the round chocolate-colored table, mug in hand. Remington had been gazing toward the pool and grounds beyond, and turned his head at the sound of the French doors opening.

"Morning, Buttercup," he said, smiling crookedly.

"Damn," Jake said, "have you been up all night?" He pulled out a wicker-backed chair and sat.

"Nah, we rotated and each got some rack time. Jesse let us bunk in with him." Remington's smile broadened as he studied Jake's face. "So…a married man. I never would have believed it. Love looks good on you, brother," he mused.

Jake said nothing but grinned behind his coffee mug.

"How is the little missus this morning?"

"Sleeping, I'm glad to say. She still doesn't sleep much at all, so when she does, I let her."

"You know," Remington said thoughtfully, "I never would have pegged you with her until I saw you *with her.* She's a thousand percent not what your type is—correction, *was.*"

"That's true," Jake agreed.

"But she is, without a doubt, the right one for you. I can't really say why, but she is."

"Yes," Jake said simply.

"And this is a beautiful place," Remington remarked, panning the spectacular ocean view just over the tops of the trees from the hill sloping down. "How in the hell did Delaney afford it?"

Jake shrugged. "I don't even want to think about it. He told me he got it from an insurance settlement and some gambling winnings, but I think there was more to it than that. This place is worth a small fortune. All I know is the lawyers handling his estate said the title they gave me is clear."

"Guess we'll never know all the shit he was into."

Jake sighed, sipped his coffee. "He had his secrets, as I came to realize. But I don't want to know."

They sat in silence for several minutes, listening to the ocean waves breaking in the distance. Birds warbled and whistled as they moved about in the trees like audible sculptors whittling nuanced sounds into varying depths and heights of the foliage. The pair of gardeners and the pool man appeared, all greeting Jake and Remington as they dispensed with their work, Estabon Mina and Mauricio Leguizano heading into the lush gardens with landscaping tools and wheelbarrows full of fertilizer and other materials, Ramón Cárdenas speaking to Jesse Segura before rounding the side of the villa to get his equipment and supplies. The large storage space had been renovated to accommodate living quarters for Segura, who worked an eight-to-five shift five or six days a week as a *Guardavida*.

"Anything you need?" Segura called to Jake. He was suited up in his bright yellow shirt and red trunks, a duffel slung over his shoulder.

"Not at the moment," Jake responded. "Thanks, Jesse."

Remington chuckled. "You remember I said I hoped none of my guys would vacation here because I might never see them again? They are all obsessed with the beach, not to mention the whole chill vibe. Well, maybe except Kip…he could never be away from his ballistics and military techno bling for long."

"I'm glad I got to know and work with them and really glad you brought them." Again, they both took a moment to savor the tranquility of hushed surf and melodic birdsong, and then Jake asked, "How is Amelia doing?"

Remington set his coffee mug on the table, leaned back in his chair, and crossed his arms over the hard slab of chest, tattoos visible below the sleeves of his black t-shirt, a Special Forces arrow crest on one bicep and an elephant enclosed by the outline of Africa on the other. "There are good days and bad days, of course. But she's one tough lady and driven by new purpose. The place is taking shape and keeping her engaged, and that's a good thing. Lula is probably her real saving grace."

He was referring to the new IDP compound that Amelia Keogh had established in DRC Congo after the total destruction of the previous one, for which she and her husband had been hands-on benefactors. Remington and a few of his guys, along with Falcone and Niles, had stayed behind at the conclusion of their op with Jake to help her get everything up and running. That was the easy part; persevering after the personal loss was something else again.

Remington smirked, "Speaking of guys, those of yours are going to have some wicked hangovers."

Jake rolled his eyes. "I warned 'em."

"They are a handful, aren't they?"

Camilla had emerged, balancing a tray loaded down with plates of fruit and food and carafes of juice and coffee. Jake popped up from his chair and took the tray from her, setting it down as she arranged *gallo pinto*, eggs, *chorizo*, sliced avocados and tomatoes, sour cream, salsa, and tortillas.

Remington's gray-green eyes grew wide. "Good Lord, this will probably put me in a coma."

Camilla smiled and said, "If everything is good, I will take breakfast to your others." When both men nodded, she returned to the kitchen.

"God Almighty, that woman is a treasure," Remington said.

"More than you can even imagine," Jake replied.

Both began eating, but it wasn't long before conversation turned to the events from the day before. During the reception, and certainly afterward, Jake had managed to keep his mind singularly on Callie, but ever since waking this morning, he could not stop thinking about the shot fired at him and the shooter who had taken it.

"I guess that sniper was making a play on the contract that's out," he said bluntly.

"Unless you've pissed off somebody around here—and judging from the amount of adoration and admiration I saw last night, I would say that's doubtful—your assumption is probably correct."

"The Colombians?"

"Could be." Remington stuffed eggs, rice, and beans into his mouth, grunting approval. He chewed, swallowed, wiped salsa from his mouth and rust-colored whiskers, and gulped orange juice. "From the description the lifeguards gave of that guy on the beach, sure sounds like it could be a *Colombiano*. Would make sense that whoever is running that cartel now put the hit out and then sent a guy."

"Kip hasn't been able to find the source for the posting?"

"Not so far, but he's still working his intel."

"You really think the shooter didn't make it?"

"I think he's probably shark food."

Jake put his fork down, abruptly reached into the pocket of his cargo shorts, and took out his iPhone. Tapped a contact. "I can't believe it never occurred to me, but somebody who might know about the Colombians is the one person I wanted here for the wedding who couldn't make it."

Remington looked at him dimly.

Through his earpiece, Jake listened to dialing and, when the connection was made, smiled and said fondly, *"Mi hermano."*

On the other end of the call was Alberto Hernandez, one of Jake's oldest and dearest friends, a Special Forces vet from the Vietnam era. Despite having referred to him as "brother," Jake revered and loved him as a father figure. Hernandez had been responsible for recruiting Jake to Colombia and had worked alongside him for the duration of the contract.

Jake listened a moment as Hernandez spoke and, with unmistakable regret in his voice, responded, "Yeah, it absolutely crushed me that you could not be here, but I understood. It was very short notice." Another pause, listening, and then he said, "I need to ask you something. When I came home after my African op, I found out that a new contract has been issued on me. Have you heard anything?"

Several moments later, Jake sighed and said, "Okay, thank you, Alberto. Catch a big one."

Nodding in recognition, Remington said, "Hernandez. What's he doing instead of being here? Fishing?"

"He does these Amazon River group excursions from time to time, and had this one planned for a while, so he couldn't cancel it. And yeah, he always talks of landing 'the big catfish.' They can grow to three or four hundred pounds there."

"I take it he didn't know anything?"

"No, but he said he'd keep his ear to the ground, make some discreet inquiries."

"Well, just take into account that the price on this contract is *big*. It would entice a lot of bad guys looking for the score and not necessarily someone looking to score on you specifically."

"True. But you and Kip said yourselves that the shot was next level."

"It was."

"So, that doesn't sound like a just anyone kind of thing. I mean, come on…a fucking CheyTac. That's almost overkill." Jake stared at his plate sullenly as layers of thoughts wove tighter and tighter through his mind. He refilled his coffee, sipped, and brooded. "If it wasn't a Colombian, who the hell was it?"

"Okay, bro, I think you need to set this shit aside for the time being. Get your head where it needs to be."

Jake heaved a sigh, "I know. If it was just me, that would be one thing, but now there's Callie."

"Yeah, I get it."

Standing, Remington reached over, poured himself another mugful of coffee, slipped on his Oakleys, and said, "Okay, lover boy, I need to get on with it. I'm going to round up the guys and we'll be wheels up in a few hours. See you on the other side."

Jake got up and embraced his friend. "Thank you for everything, Remy. Love you, brother."

"Likewise. Take care." Remington thumped him heartily on the back.

They parted and Jake watched him stride across the grass and head around the side of the villa. He drank the last of his juice and rose from the table, went back inside the villa and up the stairs to the bedroom.

Callie was still asleep, curled up on her side facing the empty space where he had been. Her tousled hair lay in soft ringlets over her forehead and cheek and pillow. The sheet was drawn up to her chest, where her hands were folded as if in prayer. He stood for a minute looking at her, his heart in his throat, and then kicked off his flip-flops and climbed carefully onto the bed and propped himself up on an elbow next to her. Despite the desire that ignited the instant he thought of her or laid eyes on her, he tried not to move, did not want to wake her. She seemed so peaceful and, as was so rare, untroubled by bad dreams. So he just gazed longingly, but after only a few moments, he could not stop himself from brushing his fingers through her silky hair, tracing them down her cheek and to her neck and shoulder.

As he watched her, a stew of doubt was simmering in his mind, thinking about the threat that now hung over him and, by association, her. He was also thinking about her desperate struggle to cope with the all the PTSD triggers that flew around her like daggers all day and into the evening yesterday and wondering if he'd made the right decisions for what he had lined up in the coming weeks.

He knew with every cell of his being that he would do anything and everything to keep her safe, and if that meant dying, he would do that without hesitation. But in life and living, he also knew he wanted to find a way to strike the right balance between comforting her and making her happy and gently pushing her toward vitality. His fingers continued stroking her soft skin, but when she squirmed a little and murmured softly, he stopped. Inhaling, he lay back and concentrated on his breathing, trying to allay the ache in his loins, the throbbing between his legs.

She stirred, blinked open her espresso-colored eyes, and regarded him groggily. "Is it…morning?" she asked, even as sunlight had brightened the room, the windows filled with the greens of trees and the balcony's French doors spread wide to the blues of sky and ocean.

"Yes, my angel. Good morning, Mrs. Tyler." He slipped his arms around her small frame and drew her to him with a tender kiss. When she tried to pull the sheet to cover her nakedness, he chuckled softly. "Oh, my goodness, I think it's a little late for that."

A bashful smile played over her lips, her cheeks flushing with color.

He kissed her again and then said, "And I've got to stop or I won't be able to stop, and I have a lot to do today."

Her smile drooped and he could feel her tense in his arms.

"Hey, this is going to be wonderful, something we'll treasure for the rest of our lives."

She looked up at him, her expression docile and adoring, and he knew resistance was futile. Packing would have to wait. He pulled off his t-shirt, unbuttoned and unzipped his cargo shorts and pushed them down his legs and shoved the clothing off the bed. Rolled over and peeled the sheet away from the satiny skin, covering it with his body.

6

JUST AFTER NINE AM the next morning, Jake finished packing the trunk of his Jeep Rubicon, thumped the rear door shut, and watched as Camilla gave Callie a loving hug, the housekeeper clearly sniffling as she released her. Assembled nearby were Ramón Cárdenas, Estabon Mina, and Mauricio Leguizano, each of whom smiled and said a few words as Callie made her way to Jake. Jesse Segura opened the front passenger door of the Jeep for Callie, offering his hand as she climbed in. He slid into the back, and Jake got into the driver's seat.

Minutes later, they were driving north on the Costanera Sur, the day sunny and bright and already hot, cruising past the town, crossing the Barú River and the expanse of Hacienda Barú, tree-covered terrain on both sides of the highway. The green hills rose in elevation to the right and tumbled down to the ocean on the left, interspersed with lowland farms and scattered settlements mixed with housing and small businesses.

They were en route to the regional airport in Quepos, where Jake would turn the Jeep over to Segura. The previous afternoon, Jake had spent time with Segura and each of the other staff members, being straightforward about the attempted hit on him at the wedding and asking them to be honest with their concerns, letting them know he would understand if they were not comfortable staying on in his employ as their own safety was potentially at risk. Not a single one expressed a desire to leave; instead, they reaffirmed their commitment to Jake and to each other as a unit, assuring him they would be watchful and take every precaution. When pressed, each of them, in their own words, asserted they were not going anywhere.

As he drove, Jake cast several sidelong glances at Callie, sitting quietly with her hands in her lap. She was wearing a ballerina-pink Tommy Hilfiger sleeveless eyelet blouse with pearl-white Banana Republic linen capris that were gathered and tied at her waist, wedge sandals on her feet. Seeing the apprehension she was trying valiantly to conceal broke his heart, and again he wondered if he had made the right choice. What should be a joyful and exhilarating time was going to strain every thread-thin tendon of her courage until, he fervently hoped, she would settle in and slowly begin to allow herself to trust in him and the experience. But now, as she sat solemnly still and watched the scenery rolling by, Jake could see the tiny quivers along her cheekbones and jawline, the little shakes in her shoulders, like premonitory fault lines.

"Relax, baby doll," he said sweetly, and saw her body hitch in reaction. She inhaled and blew out a breath, but it did not stop the tremors.

Past Matapalo and across the Sevegre River, the forests gave way to vast stretches of oil palms and soon after that, over the Rio Naranjo, they approached Quepos.

La Managua is the second busiest domestic airport in Costa Rica but, by the look of it, one would never know. What is basically a hangar constructed of wood and metal, covered by a tin roof and plastered with travel signs, had been closed for much of the year in anticipation of a long-overdue renovation and improvement to its depreciated runway and then reopened after the contract was inexplicably canceled. Jake had been glad to find it accessible once more as it reduced what would have been at least a three-hour-drive to San José down to thirty minutes on the road and thirty minutes by commuter plane.

He turned off the highway onto the access road, the Jeep's tires bumping over cracked and pitted asphalt, and pulled up to the building. When he got out of the vehicle, before going to Callie's side, he did a furtive 360 survey, his eyes scanning the perimeter brush and trees. While he felt relatively confident there were no threats here, he'd also thought there were none on the beach at his wedding. *Sure as shit not going to drop my guard again*, he thought, and wondered if it was he that would have the harder time relaxing and enjoying this trip.

Once he was satisfied that all was secure, he opened Callie's door. Segura transferred their baggage to the Sansa Airlines trolley and bid goodbye to the couple, getting into the Jeep and heading back to the highway.

Jake checked in at the counter for their 10:15 flight and, after a short wait among a handful of passengers seated around square wooden tables or milling about—mostly tourists in shorts and sandals toting backpacks and absorbed in the screens of their cell phones—they were cleared to board the twelve-seat Cessna Grand Caravan waiting on the runway apron. Callie stopped at the plane's metal airstairs, glancing uncertainly at Jake, who gently nudged her to climb. He sat her by the window in the first twin seat behind the cockpit, his eyes once again roving to discreetly inventory the other passengers. Dressed in black, Ralph Lauren chinos and a Tommy Bahama pique polo open at the collar, he got a considerable amount of looks himself. Those checking him out did so in the normal, blatantly tactless way—until he returned their visual curiosity with a gaze that somehow managed to penetrate the blackness of his Outlaw Fugitive TAC sunglasses, causing them to hastily avert their eyes.

Even when he was not operational, Jake could not transition to that of a traditional civilian—he'd had too much military training and experience and far too many hostile adversaries—so he was not only always dialed in on situational awareness, he was tactically prepared in ways that were totally indiscernible to those around him. As a trade-off for boots, today he wore Hoka running shoes, comfortable and more leisurely appropriate, but ruggedly functional. The Garmin tactix Charlie watch on his wrist could tell him virtually anything he needed to know about geolocation and navigation, health and fitness and then some, loaded with sensors and map data and all manner of calculators, all of it working on land, in the air, and at sea, with or without night vision. He also had an array of meticulously selected EDC—everyday carry items— some universally recognized as such, like his Swiss Army knife, others more ambiguous but no less useful. He could blend seamlessly into his environment when he needed to, but now was not one of those times; his sole objective from the moment he'd left the villa this morning was to be present and sentient to his surroundings and to anything or anyone that affected Callie.

While the Sansa turboprop prepared for takeoff, the whine of its engine rising as the McCauley propeller spun, over the cabin noise Jake told her, "These small planes can be a little bumpy, but they are perfectly solid. I have flown in them more times than I can count—on the last mission, in fact."

He did not, of course, relate any of the turbulence, some of the extraordinary and death-defying kind, that he had experienced as recently as that last mission.

Eying Callie, blanched and rigid in her seat, he realized that this was only the second plane she'd ever been on, the first having brought her to Costa Rica from the States, and this one was nothing like the compressed comfort of a jumbo jet.

Abruptly, the Cessna taxied and barreled down the short runway, tall grass and scrub racing past and then dropping below as the craft nosed into the air. Soon, they were flying over endless fields of oil palms and sweeping green valleys and rolling mountains haloed in drifting clouds. But for several minutes, Callie saw none of it; her eyes were squeezed shut, her breath heaving from her lungs, her hand tightly clasping Jake's.

ON THE APPROACH TO San José, Jake noted a pensive expression on Callie's face as she peered through the window at the increasingly dense suburbia sprawled between the slopes. Ten or fifteen minutes into the flight, her nerves had eased and he'd caught a tentative smile or two when she glanced at him.

"What are thinking about, love?" he asked her.

She started to answer but had to swallow around a clot of emotion. "I was just thinking about coming into this airport…before…everything." She paused, ducked her head, looking down at her lap. "I can't believe I was…" She was unable to finish.

"I understand. You've been through a lot since then."

"The way I feel now, I just can't believe I was ever that person."

"Well, yes, you are a different person as a result of what you went through. Things that happen in our lives do change us, but the core of who you are is still there."

She looked at him with tears filming her eyes. "Does it change how you feel about me?"

He slipped his arm around her shoulders and pulled her into him, speaking softly in her ear. "No, angel. I fell in love with you then and that has never changed. I love you, Callie."

She lay her head against his arm and inhaled the scent of him that was both masculine and aromatically intoxicating, a scent that calmed her because of the associated intimacy.

Within minutes, the Sansa Cessna landed just short of its scheduled arrival time of 10:45 AM, taxiing from runway 7 to a 180-degree U taking it away from the main airport. Another series of turns brought it to the parking apron of the domestic flights terminal where it stopped. As Jake helped Callie down the steps from the plane, she commented, "This is different. The small planes come in here?"

Jake smiled to himself but said nothing.

A bearded man in a dark suit with a red-corded lanyard hanging from his neck strode to greet them, his hand extended to Jake. Behind him were a pair of young men wearing lime green safety vests. They nodded but kept going, continuing to the plane. The bearded man said, "Good morning, Mr. and Mrs. Tyler, welcome to San José. My name is Hector Umaña, and I am the operations manager with Universal Aviation. I will be taking care of you today." He gestured for them to accompany him, covering the short distance to a newer building next to the domestic terminal.

They were led briskly through a compact lounge, tastefully decorated in blue leather and cream suede seating over oatmeal-colored carpeting, stylistic paintings on the walls, not another passenger in view. The operations manager paused, indicating the refreshment station. "Your plane is ready, but if you would like something while we get you processed, please help yourselves."

Knowing the drill from his recent experience with the FBO, Jake said, "No, thank you, we're ready when you are."

Callie watched Jake with growing curiosity, her hand in his as he accompanied Umaña, continuing through the lounge to the check-in where, incredibly, their bags were already on the Orion screening conveyor. The security officer did his expeditious inspections while they stood at the immigration window. A young woman clad in a skirt and blazer spoke cheerfully to Jake, and he handed their passports to her. Watching the agent flip through the gold-embossed navy cardboard booklets, it occurred to Jake that these, as much as anything, were a profile of their stark differences; Callie's headshot was that of a wide-eyed first-time traveler, her fair complexion and hair saturated by the camera flash, while his displayed the military-stern mug of a well-seasoned globetrotter who had flown in every kind of plane imaginable and leaped out of many. Callie's passport was stiff with its newness, displaying only stamps from the U.S., Costa Rica, and Colombia; his was creased and stained and crowded with ink from more countries than he could count, many being among the most dangerous hot spots on the planet.

The woman handed the passports back to Jake, and Hector Umaña ushered them through a door that led to the outside where a car was waiting. They were driven a short distance, and Umaña stepped from the passenger seat of the car and opened the door on Callie's side while the driver let Jake out.

The whole plane-to-plane process had taken less than fifteen minutes.

As Jake went to get Callie, he felt a wave of déjà vu, the sun overhead blazing down on the tarmac and reflecting off the glossy white jet, detailed in strips of gray and blue. He turned to take in her reaction as she gaped at the spectacular Gulfstream G650ER, her mouth open in stupefaction. In an almost identical query as Jake's at the beginning of his African odyssey, she asked, "This is our plane?"

7

HALF OF THE UNIFORMED crew stood by the airstairs, beaming in hospitality as they welcomed the couple. The pilot, who introduced himself as Captain Lee Monty, had gold-blond hair with a thin stubble of beard to match and the ruddy complexion of one who probably spent the majority of his non-flying time in the outdoors. The flight attendant was an attractive brunette named Tabitha Radecki, her hair cut in a Cleopatra bob and a red scarf knotted loosely around her neck. Both Monty and Radecki were attired in black and white; black slacks and skirt, respectively, and tailored white shirts, the captain's displaying his gold-bar epaulets on the shoulders.

At the top of the stairs, the two pilots in the cockpit, captains Joel Silas and Alex Zamora, exchanged handshakes and introductions and resumed their preparation for taxi and takeoff.

Jake could not stop grinning as he watched Callie's face bloom with wonderment as her eyes explored the opulent interior of the stunning jet. The color palette of the carpet and upholstery was in shades of cream and taupe, the wood veneers polished to a high shine, every surface looking as if it had never been touched.

Callie looked at Jake, still stunned. "How…?"

"This is part of Amelia's wedding gift," he replied.

Behind them, in a distinctively southern cadence, Captain Monty remarked, "Mrs. Keogh is a most delightful lady. The arrangements were made by her assistant, but she spoke to me personally as the pilot in command, to tell us about you and to make sure everything was perfect. Which, I assure you, it will be."

The flight attendant began her orientation and was demonstrating the entertainment amenities, which included a large-screen HD TV and numerous other audio and video options, when Jake mused, "Would you look at this?" He pointed to a set of throw pillows on opposite ends of the Italian leather sofa. They were monogrammed with a big letter T, below which was scrolled: *Jake and Callie Tyler*. Nodding, Jake said again, "Amelia."

Since the seats in the forward cabin were singles on either side of the aisle, they chose a double pair in the aft section, Callie by the panoramic oval window. While the plane was taxiing to the runway, Tabitha Radecki brought them flutes of champagne, letting them know that she would get their lunch order after they were in the air.

Jake held his glass out to Callie, "To my beautiful wife and all the special moments of our honeymoon." He touched her glass with a soft clink, leaned in and kissed her, and they both sipped the frosty Dom Pé-rignon.

Ten minutes later, the Gulfstream's powerful Rolls-Royce engines were propelling it down runway 25 like a supersonic slingshot and lifting it smoothly into the air. Another five minutes and the nucleus of San José had diminished and then morphed into the whole of Costa Rican countryside, the jet cruising at Mach 0.85, forty thousand feet over the Atlantic, sunbathed clouds gathered below them with the billowy plump rolls of a goose down comforter spread over a drowsy world.

TABITHA RADECKI HAD MADE them a sumptuous lunch featuring artichoke and spinach quiche with salads, crusty baked bread, and a fruit tray, Callie beginning to feel her stomach settling down along with her nerves. When their meal was served, Jake had taken the seat opposite hers, and every time she looked up, he was smiling, his face radiating happiness. She, too, felt happy, her heart fluttering with giddiness from every one of those looks and, especially, every one of his touches.

But leaving their home this morning had launched an uprising of the distress that preceded anxiety and, often, full-blown panic. The villa, with Jake present, had become a cocoon of security and a wellspring of bliss she'd never known, but she had only just begun to be able to fully immerse herself in it. As much as she had been debilitated by the trauma of her ordeal in Colombia, something had happened during Jake's absence when he'd been on the Africa mission. Before he'd left, she was still hurting in every way it was possible to hurt, including physically, and as much as she loved him, she could not even give herself to that love. But when he had returned, after being gone for so many weeks, all she wanted was to feel him around her and inside her.

With him, she felt safe and loved and fully protected from anything bad.

The wedding had pushed her way out of the comfort zone she'd been nestling into, but the romantic soul in her yearned for it and the heart she'd given to Jake knew he wanted it for her, for them. So she had put up the bravest front she could manage, was almost across the threshold of forged confidence, and then Jake had almost been killed.

For the first time, the real word resonated in her mind. *Kill.* Jake said someone had taken a shot at him, but what he really meant was someone had tried to kill him. Ever since then, even as they'd left the villa hours ago, Jake assured her everything was okay, that there was nothing to worry about.

But *was* there?

Watching Jake, Callie sensed deep concern below the surface, something that had flared up in him after the shooting and never really left. She knew he was vigilant by nature and from his extensive military training and experience, knew that his astute senses became even more heightened when she was with him, but if he truly believed everything was okay, why was *he* on edge?

JAKE SAT ON THE sofa in the mid cabin, Callie snuggled next to him, Jimmy Buffett crooning *Uncle John's Band* through her iPhone earbuds. His MacBook was open on his lap, an action drama playing on the large-screen TV across from them. He'd suggested she listen to some music in the hope that it, along with the soporific sensation of the Gulfstream's flight, would lull her to relax, maybe even doze. For Callie, sleep was a perpetually elusive entity, and one which her mind and body desperately resisted. So intense and graphic were her nightmares—often paralytic to the point where she actually felt immobilized and suffocated—that she would will herself to stay awake until exhaustion defeated her. He'd found that resting during the daylight hours was easier for her, so he was pleased to see that her eyes had closed, her breathing slow and even. The fresh circulating air blew lightly through her curls, the dazzling three-carat cushion-cut diamond ring on her finger sparkling in the sunlight from the aircraft's windows.

Glancing back to the screen of his laptop, he resumed sifting through his email, which included some new information for his upcoming gig, and then reviewed confirmations for their itinerary. There were no updates from Remington or Kipnis, and he couldn't decide if he was disappointed or relieved. As his friend had advised, he needed to put all of that out of his mind—especially for now, on his honeymoon. Absently, he reached behind him to reposition the pillow wedged against his spine. Tugged it out and gazed at the monogram and their names embroidered in the material. A wash of emotion passed through him, churned with worry that he was not accustomed to feeling. He'd always only been responsible for himself, and anything he stirred up or fucked up came back only on him. Now he was responsible for another person, and she was his world. And in his world, there was constant peril and danger and retribution.

He could not stop wondering who the shooter had been, could not stop speculating about motive; was it purely bounty-driven, or was it payback or reprisal for someone or something from one of his ops? Did the shooter miraculously walk away from the highway accident and live to see another day when he could take another shot? Or would someone else take his place? Who had taken out the hit on him?

He closed the laptop, set it aside, and tried to focus on the television in an effort to stop the fatalistic thought train from gaining momentum. Minutes later, his eyelids drooped, his head lolled, and he was dozing, too.

A DISTINCTIVE THUMP JOLTED him from his haze, adrenaline

firing through his veins like electrical current. Lighting in the jet's cabin was dim, the windows black holes of night. He knew that sound, one as familiar to him as a pneumatic nail gun was to a framer—because certain suppressed firearms sounded just like that. He looked to his right on the sofa, panic sparking as he realized Callie was not there. He saw her iPhone and earbuds, the creases in the soft leather where her body had been.

He jumped up and swung his head in both directions, scanning the forward and aft cabins. Did not see her. He also did not see the flight attendant in the galley, but he could not tell if she was in the crew cabin as the door was closed.

Where had the sound come from? He didn't see anything out of place or anything that had fallen to the carpet.

Where was Callie?

He depressed the button that slid the door open to the VIP cabin and stepped inside, thinking she was probably in the bathroom, but when he put his ear to the lavatory door, he heard nothing. He rapped lightly and called her name, got no response. Opened the door, found the interior empty.

Now his pulse was racing, his mind whipping up frenzied scenarios as he strode back up the aisle to the galley. Crossing through, he came to the bulkhead for the crew cabin. He didn't bother knocking, but when he tried to enter, the door would not open.

And then he heard another sound, another muted thump, no doubt about it, coming from the aft end of the plane. He instinctively dropped down, twisting around on his heels to look behind him. The fact that he saw nothing, no one, was as confounding as it was horrifying…because he could not figure out where Callie was. Was she locked up with the crew?

Where the hell was the shooter? The shot had not come from the crew cabin or cockpit, but were they being held captive? How could that even be possible?

He was frantic to get to Callie, felt himself losing control of his defenses.

Another shot rang out from somewhere, this one strident and close.

And then his head seemed to blow up.

*   *   *   *   *

JAKE'S SHOULDERS HITCHED SLIGHTLY as his eyes blinked open. It took him a few moments to become oriented and realize that he had, in fact, been dreaming, the shots he'd heard courtesy of John Krasinski's Jack Ryan Jr. in pursuit of some bad guys on the television.

Turning his head, he saw Callie sitting up on the sofa, eying him with vague concern. He flexed his neck, feigning nonchalance, and said, "You should have woken me, love."

"I think you must have been tired," she replied, moving close to him.

"Maybe, but I would rather be awake when you're awake."

The deep blue light framed by the aircraft's windows told him they were coming into the nocturnal segment of the journey and were somewhere over the middle of the Atlantic. Tabitha Radecki appeared, inquiring about pre-dinner drinks.

"Definitely," Jake said, thinking he could use a couple to help scrub out the analysis of his dream. *God*, he thought wretchedly, *this is what Callie endures pretty much every single night*, but undoubtedly far worse in intensity and enactment. To the flight attendant, he said, "Gin and tonics. Got the good stuff?"

"Will Bombay Sapphire work?"

He smiled and gave her a thumbs-up.

After relaxing with their cocktails, they dined on roasted pork tenderloin with rosemary potatoes and grilled vegetables, and when the dishes had been cleared, Amelia Keogh's touch was once again in play as Radecki brought a single china plate, etched with their names in gold. Centered on it was a slice of their wedding cake with a scoop of imported vanilla bean ice cream drizzled with pineapple sauce.

They enjoyed the cake and ice cream and then Jake led Callie back to the VIP cabin. Tabitha Radecki had already converted the sofa in it to a bed, which was made up with fine Sferra linens, again, at the bequest of Amelia Keogh. Jake began undressing, toeing off his running shoes and pulling the polo shirt over his head. Unbuttoning the belt encircling the waist of his chinos, he looked up to see that Callie had not moved, her face full of confusion.

When he stepped out of his pants, she finally spoke. "Are we…?"

Jake felt a chuckle curling up his throat but managed to stifle it. "Sleeping in this bed? Yes."

"But…"

"But?"

She glanced uncertainly toward the closed cabin door.

"Sweetie, we have all the privacy in the world in here. I know it probably feels strange and uncomfortable to you, but trust me." He smiled sensually. "Are you going to get ready for bed or do you want some help?"

She blushed and bent down to her carry-on bag, now understanding why Jake had instructed her to pack overnight things in it. When she emerged from the bathroom several minutes later, she was wearing a white satin-and-lace cami set and very self-conscious in it, as if she expected one of the pilots or the flight attendant to burst into the cabin.

Seated on the edge of the bed in his underwear, Jake reached for her, brought her to his chest and slid his hands beneath the cami top. His fingertips moved from the small of her back to the elastic band of her short bottoms, nudging inside. His black Calvin Klein briefs came off about three seconds after that.

Once they were between the sheets, Jake held Callie for a long while, stroking her slowly and tenderly, letting her experience the ethereal feeling of being lighter than air. Through the cabin's oval windows, the night deepened and the miles passed, so swiftly that it seemed they were merely drifting. Making love to Callie here, so high in the sky, was like soaring and floating and diving into some kind of nirvana that was both celestial and subterranean. If there was a more rapturous feeling in this life, Jake could not imagine it, and it was one he never wanted to let go of; Callie quivered and shuddered and held onto him like she was about to fall off the edge of the world.

THEY WERE BOTH UP before dawn, Jake, because he was rested and feeling good and ready to get to their destination, and Callie, because of the ripples of unfamiliarity that drew her out of a sleep that had not been without dreams, but thankfully, minimally disquieting ones. Now they both sat in the double club chairs, sipping coffee after finishing a breakfast of omelets and croissants. Despite his cheerful attempts at conversation, Jake wasn't able to do much to steady Callie's nervousness as their arrival time neared. The flight attendant came by to clear and store their table, making sure they were buckled in. Jake was dressed almost identically to the day before in black shirt and pants, but Callie had traded her capris for a flowy wrap skirt patterned like Dresden china with a smocked white tank top.

Fifteen minutes to landing, the jet had drifted below the stratum of clouds into a light blue sky gilded with morning sun, boundless turquoise ocean below. Though her hands were clenched tensely in her lap, Callie was mesmerized by the sight through her window. She turned to Jake, her expression brightened with amazement, exclaiming, "It's so *blue!*"

"Oh, love, you have no idea," he said.

They continued to peer through the window, Jake taking in both the view and the profile of Callie's face as the Gulfstream coasted closer and closer to the magnificent azure water, then approaching and lowering over nutmeg-colored land dotted with chalk-white houses and buildings, and finally making contact with the tarmac of runway 34, almost imperceptibly. Twelve hours and seven thousand miles from its takeoff, the jet taxied in and came to a stop shortly after 8:30 AM local time.

Moments later, Captain Lee Monty met them as they prepared to deplane. Smiling broadly, he said, "Welcome to Mykonos."

CALLIE'S ENCHANTMENT DISSOLVED WITHIN minutes of leaving the tarmac. Although the newly renovated Mykonos airport has a dedicated fast-track for private flights, *Delos*, an upscale lounge where customs and immigration are conducted, it is always teeming with travelers. Though they were moved swiftly through, being exposed to such a crowd so abruptly was, for Callie, akin to being thrust into a bath of scalding water or the stream of an ice-cold shower.

Jake slipped his arm around her and held her close, assuring her that they would be on their way in just a few minutes, but the stunned look on her face told him his words were having very little, if any, calming effect.

In no more than ten minutes' time, they were escorted to a waiting rental car, a Jeep Renegade, and after making sure Callie was buckled in, Jake said, "That's the worst of it, love. You can relax now."

He drove the Jeep north along the Mikonou county road toward Mykonos Town. Since they were early for check-in at their hotel, he decided to take them on a stroll around the town, thinking it would be fairly quiet at this time of year in the waning weeks of summer.

Parking by the Kato Mili, five of the sixteen landmark windmills on the island, they took some pictures and stood gazing out at the postcard-blues of sea and sky, a warm breeze blowing through their hair, Callie's blue-and-white skirt swishing against her legs. There were only a handful of tourists wandering about, and Callie seemed to be just caught up enough by the picturesque setting to be too bothered by their presence. But as they descended the concrete steps to the stone-tiled promenade known as Little Venice, her earlier distress rekindled.

Like other warm-weather travel destinations, September is considered a shoulder season in Greece, but with the advancement of global climate change, tourists in increasing numbers have been extending their vacation calendars to avoid the infernal summer temperatures, and a lot more of them than Jake had expected to see were here today. Hopefully, he thought, that would not be the case everywhere, but with this insanely popular island, he was beginning to realize he might have miscalculated. When planning their trip, he'd purposefully left off places like Santorini and Ios, both renown as party meccas, but he'd chosen what was possibly the ultimate one, Mykonos, as their jumping off point because it made the most sense logistically for their itinerary.

Callie huddled up against him as they stepped along the stone walkway, and he could feel the tension in her body as she took notice of the growing flow of people. In an effort to distract her, Jake said, "These buildings have been here since the eighteenth century, built by rich merchants."

Clutching his hand, Callie hopped back as water splashed up against the narrowing promenade, laughing nervously as her ankles got a little wet.

Grinning, Jake said, "Get used to that."

They passed a series of tavernas, some with courtyards exposed to the sun, others tucked beneath the wooden overhangs of upper balconies and, before they reached the point where the remaining buildings jutted out over the water, Jake turned into one of the corridors leading into the town's commercial center.

The *hora* of Mykonos is perhaps best known for its complex labyrinth of whitewashed buildings, adjoined or packed tightly together with brightly lacquered doors and windows painted predominantly blue or red, balconies strung with twisting vines and massive awnings of tangerine and fuchsia bougainvillea. Except for the early mornings, it is filled with throngs of people, slow-moving tourists trying to get their bearings and fast-moving locals parrying around or through them. Shops selling every kind of souvenir and category of apparel vie with bars and eateries and even the occasional church. One narrow alley funnels off to another, and another, and another, and it is nearly impossible to avoid getting lost.

For the first hour or so, foot traffic came and went in clusters, some of the passages cramped and claustrophobic, others striped with empty shadows, and though Callie clung to Jake's side, her anxiety began to modulate. Jake maintained constant physical contact, holding her hand or putting his arm around her waist or shoulders. They stopped to browse the shop displays, and whenever he caught Callie focusing on something, he took the opportunity to take inventory of those around them. Along the way, they made a few purchases—a dress, necklace, and earrings for her, a couple of t-shirts for him—and he was reasonably satisfied they were only attracting the usual curious glances.

When they meandered to the port side of Little Venice, he spied a massive cruise ship disgorging a phalanx of passengers onto the shore and steered them back into the *hora's* maze. It was now approaching lunchtime, the stream of people building, women in big floppy hats and oversize Jackie O sunglasses jostling for the most Instagrammable selfie positions with their phones held high out in front of them while men canoodled and plied them with shiny trinkets, parents sparring over where to eat as they wrangled boisterous hordes of children.

Using the compass on his Garmin watch, Jake maneuvered south, Callie clamped onto his arm and breathing erratically. He paused to assess her and noticed they were next to the entrance of a restaurant courtyard swathed in bougainvillea. "We're almost to the car," he said evenly, "but let's get a bite to eat first."

She hesitated, but the restaurant's charming visage won her over.

Stopping at Mamalouka turned out to be a good decision, the enclosed courtyard sunny and bright and not yet full of the peak lunch crowd. They enjoyed salads with shrimp and avocado and artichokes, then shared some appetizers, and although Callie didn't eat much, the diversion succeeded in calming her.

It was a short walk from the restaurant back to the Little Venice promenade, the windmills, and the car. Glancing at his watch, Jake made a call on his iPhone, and programmed directions into the Jeep's GPS system.

*   *   *   *   *

FROM TOWN HE MERGED onto Ormou Agiou Ioanni-Agiou Stefa-
nou, driving east of the bay. The rural two-lane passed through a mix of
mostly commercial property spaced behind stone walls before coming
into more widespread low-rise structures scattered across the brown
hills. The road angled towards the sea, and a final 180-degree turn took
them up a steep rise with the water to their right and a rock escarpment
to their left. A reveal of stacked whitewashed cubes built into the hillside
and an ascending stone drive prompted the Jeep's voice navigation to
announce a left turn and destination arrival. Raised metal lettering on a
rock slab anchored at the foot of the entranceway confirmed it, the
eight-minute drive bringing them to their hotel.

Cavo Tagoo, a boutique five-star resort, is considered by many to be
not only the best in Mykonos, but the best in all of Greece, drawing
trendy celebrities and followed by millions on social media. Amelia
Keogh had most likely not taken the latter into account when booking
it, instead banking on their stellar reputation for service and luxury.
Upon entering, the impression is that of a minimalist modern art gallery,
the lobby furnished with an abundance of couches and chairs draped in
white or gray and squared off in sections over gleaming white marble
floors. The cavernous space is made subtly cozy with white columns and
beams and soft, recessed overhead lighting, accent tables and lamps in
abstract shapes. There are bold statements of bronze and gold, either
suspended from the ceiling, glazed in the tile, or hanging on the walls,
such as the rectangular metallic sunburst behind the bank of three marble podium counters, which are attended by white-clad hosts and
hostesses.

While Jake got them checked in, Callie stood in a kind of suspended
dimension, her mind not sure how to categorize the environment. On
the one hand, the overall effect of its aesthetics was somewhat soothing,
but she could not quite dispel the hint of bohemian grandness, watching
warily as patently attractive men and women seemed to glide through
the lobby wearing their confidence with the same coiffure of their designer threads. Her eyes followed them through glass doors that opened
to an outdoor space with enough movement of bodies to suggest a

sizable collection, and she felt her throat tighten.

Jake broke her trance, saying, "Let's go up to our room."

The "room" was actually a suite designated the Platinum Heart Villa and, as soon as they were ushered inside by a hostess in a flowing white dress, it was instantly obvious why; beyond the plush living area was a private, heart-shaped pool surrounded by rock walls on both sides and overlooking the spectacular Aegean Sea.

Callie's mouth dropped open speechlessly.

When the hostess had departed, Jake came up behind Callie, wrapped his arms around her waist and snugged his chin into her neck. "Does it seem like a fairytale?" he asked.

"Yes…yes, it does," she murmured, and turned to take in the interior of the suite with its golden-hued wood floors, white-cushioned furniture, natural wood slab tables, and contemporary art in more white and gold. A bowl of fresh fruit and an iced bottle of champagne with glasses were centered on the coffee table with a large porcelain vase overflowing with fresh flowers.

Jake felt her buckle against him and could now see the toll of jet lag and stress tugging at the corners of her eyes. He took her by the hand into the next room, which contained a king-size bed set against the wall and a bathroom suite that included a large hot tub and walk-in shower. Before she could think or say anything, he sat her down on the bed and knelt in front of her.

"You're exhausted, and I need to go out for a bit to take care of some things." Her expression went unnaturally bright with a flash of panic, her thoughts hazily disjointed but somehow making the dim connection that she was going to be left alone in an unfamiliar place. "You will be okay," he said steadily. "Just lay here and enjoy the view or, if you want, relax outside in the shade by the pool…maybe take a dip."

"Not without you," she implored. "Do you really have to go? Can I go with you?"

"Baby, you need *rest*," he emphasized. "Will you do that for me? I promise, I won't be long."

She exhaled shakily but nodded. "Okay, Jake."

*　　*　　*　　*　　*

AT THE WHEEL OF the silver Jeep Renegade, Jake took the cliff-hugging road and headed north, driving along the coast to the new port and then navigating onto an elevated single-lane road that turned inland. The surface was badly cracked, missing completely in places, and wound up into higher hills, short stone walls staggering along the edges of scrubland sparsely dabbed with white-cubed structures. The sun was high, clouds spread like gauze across the sky.

This was a side trip on which he'd had no intention of bringing Callie, even though it would take him to a scenic landmark with an incredible view.

A few minutes into the drive, his iPhone rang. He noted the caller ID and tapped his earpiece to accept the call, answering, "Really? This is my fucking honeymoon…I'll be seeing you soon enough." He chatted briefly, smiling, and disconnected.

As he drove, the landscape became increasingly rural, and he passed occasional small settlements of houses and farms. He'd gone about three miles when the shore came into view once more, the island of Tinos visible on the horizon in pale lavender smudges. Just a little farther down the road, at the end of a dirt track, sat the Armenistis Lighthouse, a maritime tower erected in 1891 atop the cliffs of the cape. He was sure there were tourists ambling around the grounds, but he could not see them from this vantage point. Though remote and surrounded by not much else, with people about it seemed too conspicuous a place to him, but he knew it had been selected merely as a waypoint. He made a right turn, drove a short distance, then a left turn and, when he had gone about 150 meters, pulled off the road. He got out of the Jeep and removed a duffel bag he'd left in the trunk. Slinging it over his shoulder, he checked the coordinates programmed into his watch, and began hiking to the northeast. This close to the sea and at this elevation, the wind was brisk, his shirt blowing flat against his skin, but with the afternoon temperature pushing ninety, it felt good.

After another 250 meters, he checked the coordinates again, made adjustments to his course, and continued. When he reached the precise spot, he dropped the duffel bag and did a complete 360 rotation. From the bag, he removed a pair of Steiners, pushed his sunglasses to the top of his head, and peered through the 10x50 binocular lenses, seeing nothing but vacuous land and sea. There were some rock formations in the distance that offered good concealment and he considered hiking over to check them out, but he did not want to be away from Callie any longer than he had to, so he let a five-minute visual monitoring suffice.

Seeing no movement but brush bending in the wind, he kneeled on the ground by the bag and took out a pair of MTP gloves and a tactical shovel tool. Next, he ran a gloved hand over the patch of low scrub until he found the gold coin embedded in the soil, a 10 euro cent. Jabbing the tip of the shovel into the ground, he began digging. The dirt was hard, but the way it gave with each pitch of the blade told him he had the right spot. Halfway through, he paused to swig from a bottle of water, and cast another cautious look toward the rocks. Just for a moment, he thought he picked up a slight shift of shadow, as if something—or someone—had changed position. But after waiting and watching the point for a few beats, he did not see anything more.

Twenty minutes of work and he had unearthed a metal box secured by a combination lock. Sitting back on his haunches, he took off his right-hand glove and thumbed in the series of numbers for his and Callie's wedding month, day, and year. The lock released and he lifted the lid.

Inside, sandwiched in foam, were three Glock pistols, a G17, G19, and a G43X, Trijicon night sights, several magazines and boxes of ammunition, as well as a couple of Spyderco Para Military 2 knives.

The gun laws in Greece are fairly stringent, particularly for handguns, so Nash Remington and Efron Kipnis had personally seen to the procurement and placement of the weapons cache. The potential consequences of getting caught would not have normally been a risk he was keen to take, but given the circumstances, there was no way he was going without protection. He figured if it became necessary to use any of the weapons, that would be more than enough justification.

He clamped the box shut, placed it in the duffel bag, and refilled the hole he'd dug. Standing, he brushed dirt from his bare arms and pants, took another quick look around, and carried the now heavier bag to the Jeep. He dropped it in the trunk, got into the SUV, and drove, this time taking a slightly different route.

He arrived at the Tourlos Marina twelve minutes later.

*   *   *   *   *

FROM BEHIND THE ROCKS, one of several groupings close to the cliffs, a man dressed in beige-and-green camouflage, wash-faded to better blend in with the landscape, watched as Jake departed. The camping gear he'd used over the course of the past forty-eight hours or so was stuffed in a backpack beside him. Once, when the subject of his surveillance had paused to drink some water and glanced again toward the rocks, the man had scraped an arm hunkering further down, drawing blood. He'd almost cursed out loud from the unexpected pain but managed to refrain. Still, for a moment, his subject seemed to sense movement, his gaze honed on the man's roost.

Now that his subject had left, the man pushed the talk button for his two-way radio and made the call.

The contact on the other end of the two-way acknowledged and waited. When he spotted the silver Jeep Renegade passing on the road by the Armenistis Lighthouse, he started his gray Toyota Tundra pickup, backed out of a line of parked vehicles, and pulled onto the road behind it.

CALLIE LAY ON THE comfortable bed for several minutes after Jake left, but as tired as she was, she did not want to fall asleep. Not alone, not in this unfamiliar, even if luxurious, place. She stood and took a few uneven steps, quickly realizing how dizzy she was, and reached to the wall for support. The whiteness of the room—walls, ceiling beams, bedding, and marble surfaces—did have a sedative effect, especially lightened by the sun that beamed through the glass of every window. But the effect was also dreamlike, and her dreaming world was a scary one.

She made her way into the living area where the L-shaped sofa faced a window wall of pool and ocean. It was almost too incredible to be real, and the longer she looked, the more she was certain it could not be.

Jake had been right, she admitted to herself, she *was* exhausted, her nerves frayed from the stress of being in the midst of so many people, the light-headedness now so pronounced that she had to lie back down.

She sat on the sofa and eased into the cushions, her eyelids heavy as she looked across the wood plank flooring that continued out to the deck of the pool, the gorgeous blues of pool and ocean and sky beyond.

Sometime later, her head felt lighter but not in the woozy way, and she sat up. Felt a prickle of wistfulness. She stood and, feeling steady on her feet, walked slowly to the glass slider and opened it, stepping onto the deck. The wood was warm beneath her bare feet, the breeze in her hair like the stroke of Jake's fingertips, the coolness on her face like the trickle of a melting ice cube. She lowered herself to sit on one of the daybeds, then reclined and turned on her side so she could gaze out to the water. Her eyes blinked open and closed as she tried to stay awake, tried and tried and soon, lost the fight.

The breeze was just too soothing.

A sudden, violent roll spun her from air to water, from dry to wet, from breathing to choking, and she realized in a typhoon of panic that she was actually in the water—no, *under* the water—and she could not get oxygen into her lungs. Had she fallen off the daybed? She didn't recall it being at the edge of the pool…no, it had been closer to the suite's window wall. As she struggled to pull herself to the surface, she felt arms clamp around her. Not Jake's arms, these were wrenching tighter and tighter and pulling her further down, away from the light at the top.

She could see the shadow of someone overhead, and an internal voice was pleading to be lifted up and out. She could not move a muscle, not even to breathe, the shadow right there but on the other side of this watery shroud.

Please…please…please…

"Callie. Sweetie, wake up."

Her eyes opened, the room came into slow focus, and she saw Jake's calm face directly over her. He put his arms around her, lifted her up to a sitting position. Her heart was throbbing. She glanced down, realizing she'd never left the bed.

BEFORE RETURNING TO THEIR suite, Jake had ventured into Cavo Tagoo's lounge, checked out the restaurant, and strolled onto the patio. Surprisingly, the 125-foot fresh water infinity pool was mostly empty, but that was not the case for the rows of floating sunbeds and deck loungers. Oiled-up cocktail-sipping guests occupied nearly every one of them, the area bustling with a nonstop parade of pretty people creating social media content with their soirées. He would have liked to bring Callie down here, for the view and the dining experience, but seeing the crowd made it a nonstarter. Then, when he'd found her in the throes of a bad dream, he knew he had made the right decision.

So instead, he ordered a room service dinner. As he finished placing the order, Callie looked at him with dawning dismay as she realized the concession he was obviously making for her sake. "You don't want to go downstairs?" she asked.

"Not really," he replied casually. "We've already had a pretty full day. Besides, we have everything we could possibly want right here."

She looked crestfallen, but also relieved. She watched as Jake dropped onto the settee in the living area, sagging with his own fatigue. "Can we call Amelia?" she asked.

They were close to the same time zone, so he leaned forward, tapped the contact, and put his iPhone on speaker.

Amelia Keogh answered, exclaiming, "What in the world are you doing calling me on your honeymoon?"

Jake chuckled. "Why not? Falcone and Niles have already called me."

"Those buggers! Well, how are things so far?"

"Everything is wonderful," Jake said.

Callie spoke up, gushing, "This is the most incredible place." Now knowing that Amelia Keogh had arranged and paid for the entire astronomical trip, she said, "I just can't believe everything you've done."

"Sweetheart, you have no idea the joy that Jake has given me. Listen…can you hear her?" When Amelia stopped speaking, gleeful gurgles and giggles could be heard in the background. Her voice cracked a little as she went on, "If you two have even a fraction of the special love that Cy and I had, and I just know that you do, you are in for a beautiful life."

Callie was wiping tears from her eyes.

"Okay, my darlings," Amelia said brightly, her Australian brogue pronouncing it 'ahh-kay my dahlings,' just enjoy and have fun. Jake, if you run into any issues, please call me or, better, Cam, since he handled all the bookings. And Callie, don't you worry about a thing. Jake will take good care and won't let anything happen to you."

From your lips to God's ear, Jake thought.

AFTER DINNER, THEY TOOK to the suite's private pool, with no small amount of coaxing from Jake. The disturbing dream made Callie reluctant to even go near it, but when Jake got in and encouraged her from the steps, she finally acquiesced.

Now, as he encircled her in the warm water of the neon-blue heart that overlooked the old port to the left, the new to the right, and the Aegean everywhere in between, any residual tension gave way to the romantic spell of the enchanted setting. To the sensual feel of skin on skin, hearts close, lips kissing as the breeze caressed through their hair.

His arms held her thighs around his hips and her hands were clasped behind his neck. Together, they gazed out to the sea where an orange-red line was the only trace of sun left in a sky turned the color of cobalt with stars winking on their night lights. In the distance, the illumination of a cruise ship's decks shimmered over the water like liquid gold.

Callie lay her head on Jake's shoulder, sighing deeply. He swayed her lightly against him, feeling a contentment for which there was just no words. He peered out to sea and thought about the days to come. Then he reached to a tray on the pool deck, his hand closing around an ice-cooled glass. He took a sip from the glass and held it to Callie's lips. Drew it back and kissed her.

Emotion and passion cascaded.

9

FOR BREAKFAST, THEY WERE able to enjoy the downstairs infinity pool view after all. With most of the previous evening's partygoers sleeping it off for another several hours, Jake and Callie found the Cavo Tagoo's dining room mostly empty and placidly subdued in the morning light when it began service at 8 AM. Callie stood gaping at the astounding array of food impeccably arranged in rows and columns and stacks on the white-linen tables, and while Jake had been told what to expect by one of the staff who recommended it, even he was a little overwhelmed by the spread. There were enough breads and pastries and cookies, pies and cakes and tarts, to stock a full-service bakery, along with meats and cheeses and fruits and nuts and seeds; granolas and yogurts and smoothies; jams and jellies and preserves and butters; fresh-squeezed juices and coffees and teas. Additionally, there was a long bar of silver chafing pans heaped with variations of eggs and other hot breakfast fare.

As Jake steered them to a corner table that looked directly over the infinity pool and glistening sea beyond it, Callie remarked, "I could consume a thousand calories with just a few bites of anything here!"

Smiling, Jake said, "It won't hurt you, love."

After filling plates with a variety of the offerings, they took their seats, Jake's eyes still cataloguing every person entering and moving about the area. He had started to feel his wariness abate, but the ever-present premonitory radar remained on point. Savoring a rich and flaky bite of pastry, something that was not normal breakfast fare for him, he turned his attention to Callie. Dressed in a blue-and-white-striped romper, her face had the soft flush of a newly budded pink rose, a much more rested composure than that of the day before. He was certain that would change as soon as they departed from the hotel and began the mainstream of their honeymoon. But for now, his gaze lingered on her, his mind and heart and body all remembering the sensuous night before.

Catching his look, the blush in Callie's cheeks deepened.

He put his hand over hers, the smile on his face radiating down to his core.

A THREE-MINUTE DRIVE brought them to Tourlos Marina. Jake dropped the Jeep Renegade off at the on-site rental agency and they were shuttled a short distance past fishing boats and motor yachts berthed within the interior, the big vessels of FAST FERRIES and HELLENIC SEA-WAYS extended anteriorly from the main dock. At this hour, outbound traffic was beginning to build, boats of every category and size maneuvering their way from the busy marina to the open sea.

They were deposited at the southern end of the marina, which hosted most of the sailboats, and the driver transferred their bags to the pier. Jake carted them the rest of the way to the stern of a forty-four-foot Jeanneau Sun Odyssey 440. Just as he had predicted, Callie's demeanor abruptly changed, all calm flittering away. Her widening eyes darted from the sailboat to the water chopping around its sides. The weather and winds were actually pretty ideal, but the conditions here were noticeably more robust than those they'd experienced in Costa Rica, the marina and its nautical activity of a much more voluminous scale.

Yesterday, on the way back from the lighthouse, Jake had spent almost two hours with the Sun Odyssey's owner, with whom the private charter had been arranged. Alex Nikolaidis was actually a business acquaintance within the Keoghs' immense global operations network and only too happy to avail one of his personal boats. All the necessary paperwork and license verifications had been handled prior to Jake's arrival, so the meeting was spent going over everything on board, from the layout and functionality to the requested supplies and provisions.

The boat, christened *Psamathe*—Greek goddess of the shores—was new and in pristine condition, and Jake was excited to get the wind behind her sails.

Callie seemed considerably less so.

When he had loaded the last bag onto the cockpit deck, he turned to look at her. "What's wrong, baby?" When she did not respond, he asked, "Nervous?"

She nodded slightly, glancing down at the water rocking the boat's hull.

He extended his hand to help her onto the swaying deck. "It will be okay," he assured. "You'll see."

When he'd still been contemplating destinations, the idea of honeymooning in the Bahamas held court in his mind; not only had he been many times, his own Beneteau sailboat—also bequeathed to him by Haskell Delaney—was docked there. But when Greece had come up as a potential gig, he'd ultimately decided that the Greek Isles would not only make for a quintessential romantic destination, they would be logistically accommodating. The decision had not come without some significant reluctance on his part, however; he had personal history here, mostly with the mainland, and was not keen to revisit it. Nevertheless, it made the most sense given the time window he had.

Jake had taken Callie sailing off the Pacific coast near their home on a few occasions, the initial time culminating in their physical intimacy and, therefore, special. But a day or overnight sail was one thing; multiple days in succession was quite another. So, in preparation for this trip, he'd taken her out a few more times before their wedding to convince himself that it was something with which she'd be comfortable. Now, as she fell into him coming on board the boat, her frame quaking, he felt a pang of doubt. Not for the first time, he pondered, *Maybe I'm pushing the envelope too far too quickly.*

While Callie glanced around the cockpit, Jake hauled one of his duffel bags to the bow, kneeling at the plexiglass panel for the sail locker and placing the entire duffel with the metal lockbox inside a nylon bag with a long rope, dropping it in the midst of other bags. He would have preferred to have it more accessible to the cockpit, but its invisibility was imperative—and he'd already lightened the box by one Glock, which was snugged inside the waistband of his navy cargo shorts, concealed by the white t-shirt he wore loose.

Returning to the cockpit, he transferred the rest of their bags to the master stateroom and then showed Callie around the boat. With a sleek design that was both performance- and ergonomically-driven, the craft had a side deck that sloped down from the bow and merged into the cockpit, providing ample space to walk around the twin helm stations without having to climb over anything. Jake was particularly pleased that the owner had opted for a Bimini splash and cover over the cockpit for some protection from the sun, knowing Callie's fair skin would need it.

As he conducted his tour, he was also discreetly rechecking everything Nikolaidis had shown him yesterday. He preferred to believe that he was simply being abundantly cautious and not overly paranoid, executing the same degree of thorough circumspection he would in any operation, especially those on foreign soil. But this wasn't an operation, it was his damn honeymoon. And yet, flashing on the feeling of his hand over Callie's at breakfast and the powerfully protective instinct it evoked, he thought maybe that *was* the reason to follow every security protocol…and then some.

So, as he moved from above deck to below, pointing things out to Callie along the way, his eyes, and sometimes his hands, roved over systems and components and storage and equipment, verifying levels and connections and capacity and power. Thankfully, everything seemed to be in order and exactly as it had appeared the day before. He led her through the open-plan cabin, and saw her take in the nav station with its table neatly ordered with a sheaf of charts, tide and current reports, weather forecasts and coastal guides. There was an abundance of natural light and wide sea views from deck hatches throughout, the interior spacious and practical. The U-shaped galley encompassed a dinette with seating and a countertop with stove and oven, microwave, refrigerator and freezer, storage compartments everywhere. Off the saloon was a stateroom fitted with a queen-size bed and walk-in shower bathroom.

Finishing his orientation with Callie—and confident he'd given everything on the inside a thorough check for tampering—Jake ascended the companionway steps to the top deck. But the problem with such security scans were just that; they were brief and could overlook something small or seemingly innocuous or even something more glaringly evident.

Maddeningly, he decided he needed to give the boat's exterior at least a cursory inspection, and that included the part that could not be seen. The underside. He reached around to his back and slipped the Glock from his waistband, furtively tucking it into a space down by one of the helms. Then he emptied the pockets of his cargo pants and stripped off his shirt, addressing Callie. "Why don't you go below and get us some cold bottles of water? I'm just going to check something under the boat real quick, shouldn't take more than a minute or two."

She looked at him with a mix of worry and confusion. "You're going to go in the water now?"

He shrugged, manifesting a casual air. "Yeah, no big thing."

Sitting on the open swim platform, he slid into the water, took a lungful of air, and pushed himself down below the hull. Even with the infusion of fuel and oil and other chemicals in the water, visibility was adequate enough for him to see the boat's underbelly and, knowing what to look for, he made quick work of running his hands around the keel, rudder, and propeller, also the inlets and outlets. Finally, he scanned the rest of the surface for anything suspicious, but mainly, he was looking for explosives. He was relieved to find nothing.

Emerging from the water, he hoisted himself back onto the boat, dripping water on the platform. Seeing Callie, he pointed to the seat bench on the left. "Can you toss me a towel, sweetie?"

She lifted the top, reached in for a towel, and handed it to him. As he dried off and put his shirt back on, she asked, "Did you think there was...something wrong?"

"No, no, not at all." He thought for a few seconds and added, "It's just like what pilots do before taking off, like a checklist."

Except his checklist included looking for sabotage.

Callie nervously took a seat on the lounge settee behind the helms and watched as Jake cast off, powering up the forty-five-horsepower Yammar engine, pulling away from the dock and motoring south and west. The sky was an intense blue with widely scattered tuffs of clouds, the water whipping in north winds of about sixteen knots.

Seeing the apprehension in her face, over the hum of the engine Jake said, "I know, this is more wind than we've had when we were sailing at home, but I can handle it. Don't worry."

A few minutes out, with the sailboat's bow pointing into the wind, he engaged autopilot and worked the winch to raise the mainsail. He turned off the power and hoisted the 125-percent genoa. When the main went up, the boat bucked as the wind took hold and Callie wobbled, grabbing her seat cushion, but when both sails were erected and Jake had them set, it sluiced smoothly forward and began to build speed. Standing at one of the helms, Jake turned the wheel, making adjustments until they were on course, the Jeanneau settling into a heady beam reach.

FOR THE FIRST HOUR, the wind and waves were boisterous as they passed through the Tinos-Mykonos channel, often pitching the boat up and down a bit like a surfboard cresting a big swell, the tall and billowing white sails pushing their speed to eight knots. Despite her initial apprehension, Callie did surprisingly well, Jake thought. At first he sensed she might be battling vertigo, with dizziness and a touch of nausea, but she'd not had any seasickness when they'd sailed at home, so if that was the case, he reasoned it was more from nerves than from the sea's undulations. He had to reassure her several times, but his skill and proficiency in handling the boat, coupled with the animations of enjoyment in his face, began to put her more at ease.

In truth, when reading up on sailing the Greek Isles, Jake had been a little concerned about encountering meltemi winds, which are legendary for their brute force strength and unpredictable eruptions. Typically, they are in play during the peak summer months of July and August, but have been known to break out in other months, most notably September. Lasting three to six days on average, they often reach 6 to 8 on the Beaufort scale, or from twenty-two to forty knots, the latter being gale force. They are northerly winds that follow the Greek and Turkish mainlands, diverging right through the middle of the Aegean, generating chaotic seas close to windward shores and strong katabatic downdrafts on mountainous leeward shores. While manageable by very experienced sailors, their powerful gusts and sustained speeds are definitely not suited for pleasure trips and can do extensive damage to boats. A major factor in his planning, the forecast for the duration of their trip was favorable, but he could not take that for granted, especially bareboating.

About a third of the way, as they sailed by the northern shores of Rineia, the current became calmer, though the wind had picked up a knot or two. Jake stood at the helm with his hands on the wheel, smiling into the brilliant sunlight that bounced around the edges of the Bimini shades, feeling the surge of exhilaration of being on the open sea, the movement of it thrusting and engulfing the boat and the boat responding, almost like the give and take of lovers. He caught glimpses of Callie, gazing out to the white-capped swells, occasionally closing her eyes and tilting her head back against the lounge seat, the wind tossing her curls up and around and into her face.

Rineia and Delos are a pair of mostly uninhabited islands known for their ancient ruins and frequented by archaeologists, Delos having been made a UNESCO World Heritage site. Considered to be among the most sacred places in Greece, there is evidence of habitation on Delos dating back to 3000 BCE. It is also considered to be the mythological birthplace of Apollo. Rineia, as a companion island, could be thought of as the siren sister with stunningly crystal-clear coves flowing around her shoreline like the skirt of an emerald-green ball gown, attracting affluent yacht owners and their harems of bikini-clad women.

Callie was mesmerized by those waters, sparkling in the sun as if millions of gems lay cut and floating on the surface. In contrast, the shores were golden, not a soul in sight. Jake knew from his guides that the coves could be quite crowded, especially to the south, but when he steered down the western coast, he found it wide open and devoid of any nautical traffic. Careful to navigate away from the reefs, he located a swath where he could come in close.

With the sails down, they drifted in the current just before the anchor was set, and Jake found himself equally captivated by the visage, thinking there was something magical about the approach to a coast that teased the beginnings of idyllic days and satiny sensual nights, of stories to be written and dreams to be sketched and brushed with vivid colors.

Not all of them were good or signed with the flourish of a happy ending, as he knew all too well, but looking at this particular coast in this particular moment in time, he could not imagine anything other than the elation that filled him to the bursting point.

Jake and Callie donned swimwear and reveled in the salty Aegean— refreshingly cool on entry and warm on acclimation—the glassy water simply surreal in its clarity and brightness. The sensory experience had a grandness about it that defied categorizing, so they were mostly silent, as if saying anything out loud might crack the magnificence.

JUST OVER TWO HOURS of sailing after their morning interlude, they passed the islet of Gaidaros, at which point Jake dropped the sails again and prepared the ropes and fenders for docking. He put the boat on power and radioed the marina of their approach. When he was about sixty meters from the dock, he turned the boat stern in, maneuvering toward his spot and using a remote control to lower the anchor. An employee of the marina was waiting to assist him in tying off.

Sixteen nautical miles had brought them to their second port of call and destination, Ermoupolis, Syros, with just over a dozen more to come in the days ahead.

10

ON ARRIVAL, THE HARBOR of Syros, traditionally known as Hermoupolis and named for Hermes, the Greek god of trade, rises to twin hilltops stacked with a hodgepodge of houses and buildings that tumble down from peaks crested with a pair of ancient churches, Agios Georgios and the Church of the Assumption. Nearby, the blue-domed Agios Nikolaos, with its terra-cotta roof and mustard-yellow exterior, is especially eye-catching and typifies the Cycladic style that blends Venetian and neoclassical architectural elements in an Easter basket pallet of colors.

Jake took some time securing the boat, which included making a quick video of the saloon and deck with the purpose of checking for discrepancies when they returned the next morning. Picking up their rental Jeep Cherokee, he drove along Iroon Politechniou, a road running from the marina to the commercial port north, cutting through the town center and turning east to their seaside hotel.

Ploes could not have been more different from Cavo Tagoo. Also a boutique five-star accommodation, its distinction of elegance is old-world traditional, housed in a 150-year-old two-wing mansion that gleams with marble tile and wood floors and ornate crystal chandeliers strung from high ceilings. The suites are a hybrid of the old and new, featuring four-poster beds and antique-style furnishings, classic drapes and handmade rugs, along with modern spa bath appointments and the paintings of contemporary locals.

Seeing the look of wistfulness on Callie's face as she took in the suite's composed luxury and recognizing her longing for recluse, Jake said, "Let's go do some exploring."

For a moment, it looked like the well of her anxiety was going to erupt, as it had numerous times since landing in Mykonos—often without any overt reason and, other times, triggered by something glaringly predictable—but she took his hand and they left the hotel.

Jake drove to Plateia Miaouli, the majestic town hall named after the naval admiral Andreas Miaoulis, whose statue is flanked by ceremonial cannons and a court of blue-and-white-striped Greek flags, preceding a steep, wide marble staircase fringed with palm trees. From there, they strolled the surrounding cobblestone streets, but as it was the peak time for lunch, the number of people quickly inundated Callie, so Jake ventured into the rural countryside, traveling north through the lovely settlement of Ano Syros, stopping briefly at Agios Georgios for the spectacular panoramic view over Ermoupolis and the sea. Resuming their drive, they traversed rolling valleys scattered with stone houses and vineyards awash in gilded sunlight. Navigating narrow, bending stretches of road, they wound up in the hamlet of San Michalis and Jake found the way to a family-run taverna called Plakostroto where they had a lunch of green bean salads and stuffed eggplants at a table tucked beneath a wood-beamed awning, overlooking the scalloped hills and Aegean farther below.

For the remainder of the day, they explored from the quiet sanctum of the Jeep Cherokee or from solitary walks off the back roads, Callie able to immerse herself in the experience without the press of people. As the sun began its decline, Jake took them back to the hotel and, after a short rest, they dressed for dinner and he drove to the western shore of Kini Beach to Allou Yialou.

From a corner table with the waves splashing right beside them, they watched the sun set in a darkening sky, festive Greek music playing and those around them enjoying their meals. It was pleasantly calm, the air cooled by a diminished breeze, the sound of surf buffeting the chatter from other tables. But Callie sat solemnly, her gaze and thoughts distant, and Jake could clearly see the cumulative fatigue in her eyes and face. He knew it had to be a lot for her to process, and it saddened him deeply to think of the struggle and inner turmoil she faced even in this mostly mellow place. He wished so fervently that she could somehow shed the bane of flinching at every shadow as if it were the looming wing of some demonic predator. Or the reincarnation of the one in human form, resurrected from the bowels of hell.

As they were finishing their dinner, the thump of bass from the amplifiers of a beach party began to ramp up, prompting Jake to settle their tab and let Callie know they'd be on their way momentarily. He was already thinking about a nightcap on the terrace of the Ploes, followed by a retreat to their suite and cuddling up in that exquisitely dreamy bed.

He briefly left their table for the restroom, his departure causing a spike of anxiety in Callie and, on return mere moments later, he was mortified to spot a young male leaning over her.

Goddammit it.

His defensive instincts combusted like the ignition of a blowtorch, and he hastened his steps toward their table, inwardly girding himself to exercise restraint. But that was going to be a real challenge as he heard the man making lewd remarks, speech thick with inebriation, lobbing lecherous phrases about the vitality of his manhood and what he'd like to do to Callie with it. Tall, slim, and wearing faded jeans that were threadbare by design, the guy had apparently wandered in from the beach party.

Callie had recoiled back against the short stucco wall and beam post that framed the sea, her face white with consternation.

When Jake was upon the young man who, at closer proximity appeared to be in his late twenties, he managed to bridle his fury. Black belt-certified in a variety of hand-to-hand disciplines, he could have executed any number of aggressive moves, but being subtle was a lot more difficult. He wanted neither the attention from patrons and staff nor the further distress it would cause Callie, so he put his right arm over the young man from behind, as if greeting a familiar acquaintance. At the same time, he thrust his left across the man's chest and pressed the index and middle fingers of his hand just beneath the clavicle. The man's knees buckled and his face contorted in pain, the veins in his neck popping. Maintaining the pressure, Jake spoke into the guy's ear, his voice low and steely.

"Man, I'd really rather not ruin your face or your evening, so I advise you to move the fuck along."

Without another word or gesture, the young man did just that, stumbling to get past another table and not daring to look back.

The whole incident had gone totally unnoticed, with the exception of a pair of men seated at the bar who had watched it all in avid fascination.

THOSE FIRST TWO DAYS in-country had proved more stressful for Callie than Jake had expected and, for the next few, the stench of the unsavory incident at Allou Yialou lingered. Prior to that, she had already been inordinately fearful of all unknown men, but the vulgar affront now caused her to cower into Jake every time a male got within a few feet of her. Added to the continual lack of good sleep, invaded by the usual nightmare themes as well as a few new ones, it made for a frail footing on honeymoon harmony. But the next island on the itinerary, Kythnos, began a transition to the kind of tranquility he'd envisioned, one that put Callie's tension on a slow fade.

Sailing into the southwestern Cyclades, they were moving away from the more populated and tourist-riddled islands, the ports and *horas* and rural settlements reflecting it. With the dramatic decrease in people and the smaller clusters of town colonies surrounded by ever-widening expanses of landscape, the quiet congeniality of the islands and their unique individuality opened up.

Over the next few days, from Kythnos to Serifos to Sifnos to Kimolos, propelled by brisk winds in vibrant waters, the sun shining in uninterrupted brilliance that warmed the air into the low- to mid-eighties, they fell into an easy groove of enjoying a leisurely breakfast, sailing an hour or so to the next destination, sightseeing, dining, and retiring to the opulent comforts of their hotels. They stayed in premiere resorts that ran the gamut of modern minimalist spa-like indulgence to old-fashioned elegance, all of them thoroughly romantic. The Jeanneau berthed in the picturesque ports of Loutra, Livadhi, Kamares, and Psathi—and, on arrival and departure of each destination, Jake performed his interior and exterior inspections of the boat, finding no apparent anomalies.

Everywhere they went, the splendiferous Cycladic palette reflected the ubiquitous Hellenic blue-and-white of the country's flag, from the sparkling blue sea and infinite sky to the whitewashed houses with painted blue windows and doors and the pristine white-walled, blue-domed churches. They walked through quaint villages whose archways and balconies dripped with cascades of bright pink bougainvillea and meandered cobblestone alleys and streets peppered with tiny shops and taverns and cafes; they drove the narrow roads that wound in hairpin curves and heart-stopping switchbacks that descended rolling hills and valleys dotted with grazing goats and sheep; trekked through forests of pine and cypress and groves of almonds and olives, meadows aromatic with wild-growing thyme and oregano and rosemary; marveled at the majesty of man- and nature-made artistry in cathedrals and archaeological ruins; strolled hand-in-hand along isolated stretches of golden sandy beaches, waded and swam in the jewel-toned water.

In Kythnos, they visited castles of Mazarakis and Oria and the church of Panagia Kanala, the red-tile-roofed hamlet of Dryopida, and the double-bay beaches of Kolona and Fykiada, considered by many to be the most beautiful in Greece. In Serifos, an island boasting seventy-two beaches, they explored several of them and also took in medieval and abandoned villages, ascending to the church of Agios Konstantinos where the astounding view of the horizon revealed the distant shapes of eight other islands. And in Sifnos, they rambled the burgs of Kastro to Apollonia to Artemonas to Faro and captured more breathtaking vistas from the precipices, such as that of the monastery of Prophet Elias on the highest peak and the Church of the Seven Martyrs, perched on top of a rocky islet surrounded by the startling agate-green sea.

On the sixth day, they sailed the short distance from the Sifnos port of Kamares to Kimolos, spending the early hours of it circumnavigating Polyaigos on the southeastern side. The largest uninhabited island in the Aegean, it is a stunning series of bays, coves, and seashores, attracting many sailing and diving enthusiasts, but they were happy to find it mostly deserted and took advantage of the serenity. Callie relaxed on the beach with a few tentative dips in the water while Jake swam and snorkeled close by.

After docking at the small marina in Psathi, Jake checked them into their hotel, The Windmill, an actual nineteenth-century windmill set atop a hill with 360-degree views of land and sea, comprising only five suites.

Kimolos is one of the least-visited islands and, populated by only about a thousand souls, it exudes the charm of simplicity. Ancient inhabitants referred to it as "Arzantiera," meaning "silvery," because of the proliferation of shiny gray-white rocks, its soil rich in layers of minerals and chalk. Exploring it is a leisurely and carefree affair and, after walking about the *hora*—here called *chorio* by the locals—Jake drove them south to the fishing village of Goupa to see the *syrmata*, a collection of boat garages with colorful doors carved into the craggy shoreline caves. Next, he traveled northwest along Route 5 where they hiked around the Sklavos and found Skiadi, the mushroom-shaped rock formation with its white stemlike base and reddish-brown cap, the terrain surrounding the barren land crossed with rambling stone walls and thickets of olive and juniper trees and scented with sage and lavender and honeysuckle. They watched the sun drain from the sky in a fiery melt of oranges and reds and, finally, purples that turned the horizon violet.

They had dinner at Postali near the port, sitting beneath the reed-roofed open-air section, where they watched a few boats come and go and could actually see the mast of the *Psamathe* in its marina berth.

The food, from their first stop to the current one, had been nothing short of a gastronome's fantasy. For Jake, who was not necessarily a foodie in the literal sense but, as one who had extensive and practiced knowledge of survival foraging, consuming the more eclectic staples of Greek cuisine came easily; for Callie, it was a little more ambitious. As with most new things, he'd teased her into sampling what was, to her, exotic and unappealing, and while she could never get past the appearance of the commonly served octopus, she admitted it tasted good. They'd dined in incredibly enchanting settings on panoramic overlooks or nestled within delightful town squares or, best of all, right on the sand with the sea lapping nearby and the stars glittering overhead. Their tables had been plated with the likes of *moussaka* and *papoutsakia* and *pastitsio* and *souvlaki* and *soutzoukakia*; all variations of the farm-to-table *horiatiki salata*; local garden-grown eggplant and zucchini and tomatoes and beans; the delectable pastries and pies and custards of *baklava* and *bougatsa* and *galaktoboureko* and *portokalopita* and *loukoumades*. And, of course, the bounty of seafood from fish to crab to crustacean, cooked in varying combinations of island spices, olive oil, lemon, and garlic.

Now, an hour after dinner, they were on the pebbled terrace of The Windmill, an outside space called Breezes which lived up to its name, the cool sea air blowing into their faces. They sat by the outer edge, the lanterns on the ground and candles on the tables glowing softly in the twilight. Below, they could see the marina, the islet of Agios Efstathios and Polyaigos across the water, a wedge of moon and smattering of stars bright in the evening sky. Traditional Greek music was playing faintly, a pair of tall, half-empty glasses at their fingertips. Though all five suites of the hotel were occupied, at this moment they were the only ones present, making for a relaxing and intimate ambience.

Callie's head was propped against Jake's shoulder, her arm looped through his, and he could smell the floral scent of her shampoo, salted by the sea breeze. There was heat in her skin and he reached to stroke her cheek, commenting, "You're getting a pretty good sunburn." She winced when he touched her neck. "Ouch," he empathized, saying, "I'll put something on it before bed."

The sun was every bit as hot at home in Costa Rica as it was here, probably even more so, but this was a drastic change in exposure time for Callie, so he was keeping a close eye on its effects; she'd been using sunscreen and had taken to wearing a stylish straw fedora he'd bought her, but the Grecian fireball was still having its way with her.

She lifted her head and looked away sheepishly. "I wish I could tan like you."

"Comes from years of the outdoors," he replied, adding, "and probably genetics."

He drew her face back toward his, her pale gold hair and sun-reddened complexion gleaming like satin in the moonlight's soft incandescence. Gazing at her, he felt the familiar rustle of butterflies in his stomach, the warm ache welling further below. Tonight Callie wore a peach-and-pink maxi-length dress with a ruffled high-low hem that she amusingly kept trying to rearrange to stop showing so much of her coltish legs. Given the split-front cut of the design and the will of the wind, her efforts were mostly futile and, at one point, Jake grinned and placed his hand over hers with a shake of his head, murmuring, "Let that sexy dress do its thing."

A server replaced their empty glasses with fresh gin and tonics and Jake took a sip from his, peering out to the horizon, island profiles in purple shadow. After a few moments, his expression seemed to grow distant, pensive.

Callie said, "It's so pretty here."

"It is," he replied absently, his eyes fixed on some undefined spot over the sea.

"Jake..." she began tentatively, "will you tell me..." Unsure of how to finish the sentence, she immediately realized he knew what she was trying to ask. He stiffened, almost imperceptibly, but she heard an audible intake of air.

It was as if he'd been standing in a gentle surf, water swirling around his ankles and calves, his eyes closed to a balmy breeze and then suddenly opening them to see and absorb the full-frontal slap of an oncoming wave that he'd instinctively known had been building from miles away. Callie was never intrusive in any discussions that hedged into his background—and, when it came to his own inquisitiveness of hers, he knew he could be, and often had been, inexorably incisive. Still, she had to be curious, and now that they were married, she was certainly entitled to know.

He recalled the conversation from the earliest days of their budding relationship, when he'd casually revealed to her that he was of Greek and American Indian descent. She'd astutely remarked that his name did not sound as if originating from either lineage, to which he'd replied, "That's a story for another time."

And that time had come.

He took a longer swallow of his drink, set the glass on the table, and sighed. "It's not really that I meant to be evasive about my ancestry," he began, "it's just not something I like talking about."

"Oh, I'm sorry...I didn't mean to—"

His face softened as he turned to look at her. "It's okay, sweetie. Always know that we can talk about anything." He paused, considering where and how to start, then said, "My mother was Greek and my father was Chiricahua Apache. My real father. But the man I grew up believing was my father was, first, a soldier in the army, and later, a gaming table dealer in Las Vegas. He was a pretty decent guy and I admired his dedication to the military, which ultimately was part of what motivated me to join up. My mom was a waitress and, between them, they were just barely making ends meet. So we wanted for a lot and it was a hard life. When times got especially bleak, I was shuttled around between friends and relatives, and as I got older I spent a lot of time living on the streets, scrounging for food and hustling for odd jobs."

Jake slumped back in his chair, his body language and expression reflecting the woe he was reliving.

As the significance of his words took hold, Callie's face grew solemn. "You lived on the streets…*outside?*"

He nodded.

"My mom was a good woman, proud, hard-working, and with the best intentions, but she was just not…" He was momentarily at a loss for words, finally continuing, "She just did not make good choices, I guess. With my dad deployed much of the time, he was not around, and she took jobs that would cause her to leave for long periods of time, sometimes even in another state, and I'd truly be on my own. My father finally had enough of that and they got divorced. She left me to live with him, which would have been okay were it not for the woman he married afterward. They'd met at the casino where he worked—I was never sure what she did there—and it became pretty clear that she was not down for the package deal with me in the mix. She was from Latin America and had a nasty temper, which she took out on me when my father wasn't around. I started spending more and more time away from home and finally left altogether.

"I think I always had a feeling something was off. I had some resemblance to my mother but looked absolutely nothing like my father. After I joined the army, I tracked my mom down during one of my leaves and went for a visit. By then, she had also remarried and was living in northern Nevada. It took a lot of persistence on my part, but she finally admitted that the man I'd known as my father and whose name was on my birth certificate, was not my biological father."

His eyes widened at the shock of the memory.

"She refused to tell me anything about him, insisting it was for the best. The only thing she did reveal, my only clue, was that he was Indian. I spent several years, when I had time, trying to find out anything I could. Turns out, there are relatively few Chiricahua Apache, most being from New Mexico, Arizona, or Oklahoma, but I had nothing to go on."

At this point, he emitted a wry laugh, but his face was mirthless. "During a visit with one of my mother's brothers, an uncle, I plied him with whiskey, got him good and drunk, and he let a few things slip, which gave me some places to start looking."

He stopped, downing the rest of his gin and tonic. When he didn't go on, Callie asked, "Did you find out who your biological father is?"

"No, I didn't. I never found him. I don't know if he was, or is, a good or bad man. I don't know if I look like him or if anything about me comes from him." His voice had become raspy with emotion.

Callie touched his hand, her eyes full of compassion. "Well, *you* are a good man, because or in spite of your background."

A warm smile tugged at his mouth, he held her gaze for a moment, and then kissed her tenderly.

"I guess, in a way, following the man who raised me into the military put me on a track to at least give me an alternate path from the bad one I was probably going to wind up taking. And, through the course of my army career, I met some great men who taught and counseled me and became father figures, something I now consider a greater good."

"Do you still have a relationship with your mother and the man you thought was your father?"

"No. Not long after my mother's confession to me, she also told him. To his credit, whether or not he ever suspected, he never let on to me, but once it was known, we became more or less estranged." He paused and sighed sadly. "My mom passed away a few years ago."

He stood and paced along the edge of the terrace, saying nothing for a while. Then he cleared his throat as if expunging the sordid film of his harsh upbringing, and said, "Which brings me to Greece."

He retook his seat next to her. "In the early years of my military service, I had spells where I would get angry at the world. I suppose it came from the atrocities I was exposed to, the biases that manifest from the bellicose mentality, the cruelties and inequities of humankind. When I was younger, until I learned how to channel my feelings, it would cause me to get into fights and I was constantly searching for answers that just didn't seem to be there.

"In between a couple of my first military contracts, I came here. One thing my mom did talk about was her Greek childhood, the people, the places, the culture. It was something I was curious about, so I decided to spend some time traveling the countryside to at least learn about one half of my ancestry. I looked up her relations, most of which were in Athens, Sparta, and the island of Corfu. I'm not sure what I expected, but I didn't expect the animosity I got. None of her people wanted anything to do with me and, at the time, I could not fathom the reason. Later, I realized it was probably because they knew I was a bastard child, the offspring of an affair, and for that reason did not consider me true family.

"For someone predisposed at the time to being mad at the world, that hostility and rejection set the fuse on a series of very bad experiences here. I'll just leave it at that."

Callie lay her head back on his shoulder. "Jake, I'm so sorry. Maybe we should not have come here for our honeymoon."

"No, love, on the contrary. I think this is good for me, really, because now it can be associated with the wonderful memories we are making."

He looked up at the moon and, for a moment, thought it looked a little like a deceptive wink in the sky. Because there were things he had not told her about his time here, and had no intention of doing so.

11

THE TALK OF JAKE'S background had swarmed unpleasant memories like a nest of hornets primed for agitation, but he tucked them away with the night and embraced the next day with what had become the prevailing beat of joyful anticipation for the ongoing journey and destination.

But Milos, the halfway point of their trip and the most southwestern island of the Cyclades, began an unsettling change of tone, one that stirred ingredients from the past, present, and future into a batter that bubbled with trouble and turmoil.

After docking at Adamas Marina and picking up their 4x4 Suzuki Jimny rental, Jake drove them around the port town and then navigated northwest to Plaka, the island's capital, which was set along a scenic escarpment overlooking the sea. They parked and hiked their way up through the village maze to the highest point of some 650 feet, a tourist mecca for sunset vistas, where the crumbling ruins of a Venetian castle and the churches of Panagia Thalassitra and Panagia Korfiatissa drew large crowds late in the day. For that reason, Jake had chosen to pursue a reverse strategy, with his ultimate objective—Sarakiniko—on the itinerary for later when its flock of visitors would be departing for the town pinnacle. They drove back to the south, bypassing the catacombs, which Jake would have liked to see but knew Callie would find frightfully claustrophobic, stopping instead at the ancient amphitheater built in the third century BC. From there, they continued on to another crayon-colored colony of *syrmata* lining the fishing village of Klima. Taking the Adama-Zephyria coastal road around the bay, they settled in for lunch at a popular tavern next to Papikinou Beach.

O! Hamos is a local treasure established and devotedly curated by the Psatha family, whose fare is homemade and self-sourced and served within the shade of a courtyard draped with thatches of greenery and embellished with overflowing earthen pots of geraniums. Creative and traditional touches are everywhere, from the poetic inscriptions etched into the wooden tables and chairs to the handwritten menu booklets, each unique with entries scrawled on notepaper in several languages and twine-bound in wallpapered cardboard.

Callie listened with admiration as Jake facilitated their young male server by ordering in Greek. He had already done so a few times, modestly explaining that in the course of learning multiple foreign languages, a prerequisite of his specialized military training, he'd developed an adaptive knack for others. While they waited on the food, his eyes roved the close quarters of the al fresco dining area, sunlight dappling through the leafy, flowering boughs and shadows partially concealing the faces of some diners. He was feeling relaxed, not expecting to see anything or anyone out of sync with the setting, just satisfying his routine radar check. But as he surveyed the occupants of each table, his gaze lingered on a pair of men seated in a corner near the entrance who fell in the one-of-these-things-is-not-like-the-other category. In a collection of people clad in shorts and polo shirts and stylish dresses, chatting animatedly and posing for pictures, the two men stood out to Jake in their nondescript manner and attire; they were riffling through the menus without really looking at them, both wearing jeans and long-sleeved button-up shirts and sunglasses. Even without being able to fully see their faces, Jake had a vague sense of recognition, though he could not place where he thought he'd seen them before.

When their meal came, a delectable assortment of *aginares milotikes*, *melitzana boulouka*, and *gourounopoulo metimezako*—salads with fried artichokes and eggs followed by stuffed eggplants and pork slow roasted in a molasses, mustard, and thyme marinade—it was served in glazed terracotta pottery dishes inscribed with *O! Xamos!* along the edges. While he dined, Jake's attention was divided between Callie and the pair of men, whose own focus never seemed to stray from their plates, and by the time he was paying the check, they had somehow managed to slip away unnoticed.

After lunch, Jake drove to their hotel, the boutique Milos Breeze resort in Pollonia, another quiet and charming fishing village. His eyes flicked to the Jimny's rearview mirror every few seconds along the way, looking for a vehicle mirroring their route, but observed none that stayed behind them for the duration.

They cooled off in the plunge pool of their honeymoon suite and lounged on the terrace. Laying against Jake on the sofa, Callie dozed as he brushed his fingers lightly through her hair, the day bright and beautiful and filled with all the elements of idyllic paradise. But as much as Jake would have relished a nap himself, his mind was restless, scanning the tributaries of his memory for a matching impression of the two men from the restaurant.

He failed to find a clear reference, but he could not dismiss his suspicion that there was one.

SARAKINIKO, OFTEN REFERRED TO as the "moon beach" is, to many, the most iconic landmark of Milos. Formed by volcanic rock millions of years ago and sculpt over time into abstract undulations from the salt and water and northerly winds, geologists might describe the phenomenon as light Neogene ash flows layered with darker quaternary lava and andesite, composing rocks of white diatomite and pumice tuffs in ribbons of gray and yellow; locals and visitors simply called it an otherworldly, dreamlike lunarscape.

It was late in the afternoon when Jake drove to the beach by way of the Triovasalou-Apollonion coastal road. As he had hoped, families and couples were making their way back to the parking lot, which he took as an indication his timing was just right. This was a special place and one best enjoyed minus the throngs of tourists, optimal windows being sunrise and sunset. The light and heat of the day were on the wane, the sun transitioning from its brilliant yellow to a softer molten butterscotch. Stepping along the path toward the beach, he watched Callie's expression slide from curiosity to wonder to amazement, taking in the swirls and dips and peaks of chalk-white rock that looked like both sand dunes and snow banks, stark in contrast to the still-vivid sky. Stunning ultra-white and bright blue.

Beside her, Jake remarked, "Incredible, isn't it? This is one of the places I've been most looking forward to seeing."

Speechless, Callie just nodded, but she was also noticing the dozens of people who had remained on the beach, holding out phones and cameras for selfies, laughing and calling back and forth as they cavorted across the tops of ledges and scampered along the bottoms of swells and around hollowed arches.

Jake slipped his free arm around Callie's shoulders, steering her to an elevated empty spot close to the azure water, the wind sending waves crashing into the base just below them. To lighten his load, he unfurled the beach blanket tucked beneath his other arm and planted a small cooler on it to keep it from blowing away. Then he took Callie's hand and they spent the next hour wandering, from a rust-corroded ship-wreck sticking out of the water to the other side of the beach where dramatic cliffs rose over cenotes and lagoons.

Returning to their spot, they sat on the blanket, Callie watching several groups of people clambering up and down a peak with an archway from which some of them were jumping. Jake took a bottle of Assyrtiko Santorini from the cooler, poured some into glasses he'd brought from the hotel and handed her one. They sipped the citrusy white wine and watched the sun lower, deepening from gold to bronze as it seemed to touch the water.

Jake's gaze was split between the stunning masterpiece being created across the horizon in fiery variations of late-day color and the stunning woman beside him, looking like a vision of heaven on earth. She wore a pale lavender-and-cream tie-dye slip dress, the pattern reminding him of spiral seashells, the brisk breeze dancing in the whorls of her hair. For the innumerable time, he was wondering with reverential awe how he'd come to be so blessed and, when she glanced up at him, he leaned over and kissed her, the soft warmth of her mouth sending a sensation coursing through his flesh and nerves and insides like an orchestral swell.

A chaotic eruption of shouts and screaming coming from the cliffs snapped him out of his romantic reverie, causing him to jump to his feet.

*   *   *   *   *

THE OUTBURSTS WERE FROM a group of about a dozen people, most in their late teens or early twenties, scuttling around the rock edge of the archway. Some crouched, looking down to the lagoon below, others paced aimlessly back and forth gesturing frantically, and at least one leaped into the water.

Instructing Callie to stay put, Jake snagged his backpack and sprinted toward the slope, scanning the rock pool for what he already suspected was a person in distress. While a number of possible injuries fanned through his mind, the immediate situation was quickly obvious to him as he saw a young man waist-diving in and out of the water, searching for or trying to retrieve someone submerged.

Turning to those gathered gaping at the edge, he said forcefully, "Call for emergency response." When the assemblage looked at him without reacting, he bellowed, "Now!"

Jake made a swift assessment of his options and, judging the steepness of the rock edge, picked his launch spot, unslung and cast his backpack over the side, and jumped into the lagoon. It would have taken him several minutes to make his way down to the water on foot, and that extra time might be critical. He was clad in Tommy Bahama black cargo shorts and a crisp gray-and-black IslandZone camp shirt labeled, ironically, *Pandemonium in Paradise*, the latter in particular chosen because of what he'd *not* planned on doing here—swimming. He was, however, glad to be wearing a pair of OluKai water shoes, which would provide him the protection and traction he'd need to make it back up the rock side.

But first he had to get to the victim.

He reached the young man attempting the rescue and took over, taking a lungful of air and plunging below. He saw the victim, suspended vertically beneath the surface, and swam to him, looping an arm around his torso and propelling them both upward. Blood swirled in the water and Jake speculated about what had happened…had the guy scraped the side of the rocks or, worse, somehow hit his head? There was sufficient diving depth here, but also rocky shelves that jutted out. In any event, the priority objective was to get him breathing.

Jake emerged with the lifeless man in tow and navigated to the low ledge where he'd tossed his backpack. The other young man helped him hoist the limp form up onto the rock, babbling, "Did he drown? We have been diving all day, nobody got hurt...*Oh mein Gott*...Dieter..." The man's accent and utterance with a name confirmed their German nationality, the pale coloring of their eyes and hair being a first clue. But there was a key difference between the two; the victim's skin was pasty white and his blue eyes dull and fixed, his lips looking as if he'd been sucking on a grape popsicle.

Checking for a carotid pulse, Jake said, "Hand me the first aid kit in my backpack."

The victim's friend, given a task, snapped out of his angst and did as asked, then watched with his hands clutched below his chin as Jake worked to revive the unconscious young man sprawled on the rock face.

With no detectable pulse or passage of air, Jake engaged in vigorous CPR, alternated with rescue breaths. It took him a few minutes before he got a response, the young man named Dieter seizing and gagging. Jake turned him as he vomited copious amounts of water, coughing and moaning. With the stethoscope from his kit, he listened to Dieter's lungs for a minute or so to make sure respirations continued, and then examined his head. There was a two-inch gash near the hairline, fairly deep and bleeding freely, which had been ignored in the urgency to get the young man breathing, and now Jake's concern shifted to blood loss and traumatic brain injury. He kept firm pressure on the wound but was careful not to apply too much in case there was a skull fracture. Directing Dieter's friend to stabilize his neck, Jake worked a bandage around the young man's head and spoke reassuringly to him in an effort to keep him calm but also to gauge his neurological condition, asking him his name, where he was, and what had happened.

Dieter could not tell him, murmuring unintelligibly. Jake grimaced inwardly, knowing this was not encouraging. He moved on to physical assessment, moving his hands down the young man's chest, arms, abdomen, pelvic ring, thighs, and lower legs, checking distal pulses and response to painful stimuli and evidence of fractures or breaks.

By now, the shrill pitch of sirens could be heard from the approach of emergency vehicles and a quick glance upward revealed a gallery of onlookers whose faces were rabid with a mix of horror and morbid fascination, most pointing their phones his way. Jake was torn between waiting to tag-team with the emergency responders and making a hasty exit; the last thing he needed was to appear in someone's social media feed. He checked Dieter's vitals again, found his pulse and breathing rallying, his color improving slightly.

Making his decision, he addressed Dieter's friend, who had identified himself as Rolf. "Keep bracing his neck and don't let him move, okay? That's crucial. Tell the responders what happened. Will you do that?" He paused, adding, "Also tell them he's a GCS of ten."

Rolf's mouth formed an O and he muttered, "A-a what? Is that bad?"

"Just tell them."

Rolf nodded. "Thank you…thank you so much. What is your name?"

Jake simply said, "Glad I could help," and gathered up his first aid kit, tucked it in his backpack, and climbed his way out of the lagoon. When he made it to the upper bank, he angled away from the crowd, medical personnel passing him with a stretcher.

He had no idea how much time had elapsed, but a sudden jab of worry about Callie quickened his step. The jab turned into a spearhead of anxiety when he crested the rise and found the spot where they'd been sitting.

Completely empty. No blanket, no cooler, no Callie.

12

CALLIE HAD WATCHED JAKE hurry off toward the cliff where the small crowd of people were growing in number and becoming more stridently vocal with the apparently dire nature of the situation. Being left alone always triggered an instant surge of anxiety in her, but most times she'd been able to stave off an escalation to panic because Jake was highly attuned to circumstances she could withstand. Most times it had been when they were in an isolated place with no one else around, or at a time and place where he could keep an eye on her as he stepped away. And most times, the brief separation did not result in any inordinate duress, the one glaring exception being the evening at the restaurant in Syros.

Now, gazing across the rolling slopes of Sarakiniko, losing sight of him as he disappeared over the rise, she could feel her pulse and heart rate spiking, breaths becoming shallower as her chest constricted.

Because instinctively, she knew he wasn't coming right back.

In the wash of heightening unease, she vaguely registered the peripheral movements of other people distantly passing, joining the crowd assembled by the cliff edge. Eyes riveted on the spot where she'd last seen Jake, Callie was not aware of the figure that had stopped just behind her, casting a shadow over the beach blanket in the diminishing light of dusk.

"I wonder what is happening?"

The male voice startled her so violently, it caused her already pounding heart to punctuate in a hammer blow, the stressed respirations momentarily stopping. Her head snapped to the source of the vocal, but she clambered backward away from it at the same time, clumsily crablike, almost knocking the cooler over.

The man seemed unaffected by her reaction, with an impassive smile and eyes obscured by sunglasses. Wearing a long-sleeved denim shirt unbuttoned over a white tee, he stood with his hands shoved in the pockets of relaxed fit jeans. He had the swarthy coloring of a local, hair worn in a medium length that flipped up in the breeze. Peering down at her, he asked, "What do you think is going on over there?"

Callie's throat was dry and tight, but after a few moments, barely audible, she rasped, "I don't know."

Surveying the area, the man canted his head sideways and asked, "Are you here by yourself?" His English was accented but in a generic way that made it undistinguishable.

This time, Callie spoke up immediately, gasping, "No…no, I'm not."

"Oh?" The man looked around again in a bemused, almost mocking fashion, as if he already knew the answer to his question.

Frenetic thoughts began to dart around in Callie's mind, the fight-or-flight impulse sparking. She'd only glanced at the man's face once, and in that instant she saw the face of another, the one that haunted her endlessly. She heard herself murmur, "No…no…my…my husband…"

"Is he in the crowd?" When Callie did not answer, he said, "Why don't we just walk over there and see what is happening." He leaned slightly toward her, offering his hand. He grinned, showing his teeth.

She recoiled further and stammered, "No, I…no, I need to go."

He waited, and when she did not make a move, commented, "I would be glad to accompany you."

With that, Callie was frantically gathering the beach blanket and cooler and stumbling away, glancing over her shoulder to make sure the man did not follow her. In the semigloom, she could not be sure but sensed motion and heard sound. Fight-or-fight sent her fleeing, her heart and mind tripping down the terror tunnel.

JAKE'S HEAD SWIVELED IN all directions, his head numb with the white noise of stunned disbelief. Stupefied, he stood staring at the spot where he and Callie had been sipping wine on the beach blanket, unable to make sense of the empty space. And then his heart imploded in a frenzied staccato of panic. Without thinking, he shouted her name once, loud and assertive, a second later silently berating himself for the outburst. He pivoted, his eyes boring into the twilight, the absence of sun giving more shadowed contour to the peaks and valleys of the ground surface and, in doing so, exposing its nakedness. There had been a few people widely scattered here when he'd left, and now there were none.

His heart pounded relentlessly as he spun around, scanning every direction, his brain firing off a mantra of *this can't be happening, this can't be happening…*

But it *was* happening—she was gone.

Oh God, where is she?

He began a grid search in all directions and, while he was laser-focused on the effort visually and physically, his mind was spinning into a furious cyclone of second-guessing the action he'd taken that had led to this outcome. With his years of military training and operational execution, he was uniquely wired to grind through tactical options and plays, to make critical lightning-speed decisions and on-the-fly maneuvers. But in this new realm of his personal life, he was navigating an altogether different battlefield that required a deeper level of insight and intuition, a sixth sense that transcended the normal range of thought and emotion and intellect. And in this field, the consequences of even the most minor misstep could be devastating.

Had been devastating. He had been there before, and he was not going there again.

But he knew he'd set himself up by putting the welfare of another— a total stranger—above that of the most precious one in the world to him. The distress call from the cliff had appealed to his default inclination to help others whenever he could, but in responding to that propensity, his mind had only presented him with the most basic of options—take her with him or leave her behind; in the flash of that moment it had not occurred to him to ignore the call. He'd committed to going but quickly rejected taking her with him, knowing that the crowd and the drama of the rescue would almost certainly unleash a deluge of anxiety, if not a panic attack. And now he was on the verge of having one himself.

He ran from one point to another, several times clutching his head, the reality he was facing looming larger and larger with each passing moment.

When Jake had canvassed the entire ledge and adjacent areas, even with stomach-clenching trepidation gazing down into the thrashing waves below, he returned to the cliff and wove through the crowd, which was beginning to disperse following the evacuation of the drowning victim. Though he'd been so prominent in the rescue mere minutes ago, most paid little if any attention to him now that the drama had come to a conclusion. His eyes roamed over each and every person, none of whom bore even the slightest resemblance to Callie.

Leaving the cliff from the opposite side, just to make sure he covered every square inch, he let out an anguished groan. Where could she be?

Running out of places to look, he chose one last possible course, retreating some three hundred yards down the path to the car park, where most of the vehicles had departed. Their forest green Suzuki Jimny rental was, in fact, the lone remaining automobile in the line in which it was parked. He paused at the rear, then walked around to the passenger side.

And found Callie huddled by the door.

Small and cocooned in the beach blanket, she sat with the cooler beside her, arms clutching her knees to her chest, head tucked. Shivering though it was warm. Heaving for breath.

At the sound of his footfalls, she gasped and shrunk even smaller.

"Callie!" he heard himself exclaim, his voice booming harshly in his ears. A heavy exhalation of breath left his lungs. He squatted down in front of her and said, "God, you scared the living hell out of me." Again, his tone was much more coarse than he would have ever intentionally used with her, but the adrenaline of the scare was still wreaking havoc in his nervous system.

She tilted her head up to look at him, her lips and chin trembling, brown eyes wide with both fear and relief. He helped her up and they embraced, his arms enclosing her tightly, one hand cradling the back of her head. She sobbed into his ear. His voice now soft and soothing, he said, "Okay, baby, I'm here. It's okay. Breathe…slow, slow, slow… breathe."

He held her, knowing something had happened, something was wrong, but just held her for a long time because all that he'd lost had been given back to him and he didn't want to let go. It took a while for her to grow calmer, drawing slower breaths, but she eventually did.

He loosened his embrace and looked at her, asking, "What happened, love?"

"I'm so sorry, Jake," she murmured, "I didn't mean to…I just didn't know what to do. Please don't be mad. Please?"

The despair in her plea made him physically ill and he felt tears stinging his own eyes as he drew her to him again. "Oh, sweetie, I'm not mad at you. I could never be. It's okay. Just tell me what happened."

She inhaled shakily and said, "There was a man who…who stopped and asked what was going on. I told him I didn't know."

"Okay, well, maybe he was just being friendly?" Jake suggested evenly, although he already suspected there was more to it.

Callie continued, "But he wanted me to go with him…"

Jake's expression hardened. "Go with him?"

"He asked if I was alone. I told him no, but then he said he could go with me to see…he reached his hand…I was afraid to stay there. I know you told me to stay, but—"

Weighing what to say, he replied, "Yes, I did. But in this situation, you did the right thing."

"I was going to look for you, but there were just too many people over there. I couldn't…" She started crying again.

"It's okay. I understand."

"I tried to call you…I couldn't get a signal."

"Okay, it's all okay." He thought for a moment. "What did this guy look like? Could you point him out for me if we go back, see if he's still there?"

Callie was shaking her head before he finished the sentence. "Please, Jake, can we go?"

As much as he wanted to pursue it, the need to alleviate her fear outweighed his inclination to push for more detail, so he nodded and helped her into the passenger seat of the Jimny. Walking around to the driver's side, he cast one last glance toward the darkened cliffs and wondered if the man who had tried to engage with Callie was a random passerby…or something else.

THE ORIGINAL PLAN FOR après sunset had been to have a romantic seaside dinner at the acclaimed Akrotiri Seafood Obsession near their hotel, but Jake knew Callie was too upset to eat and he didn't have much of an appetite, either, not to mention being wet and disheveled from the rescue. Instead, their evening consisted of a long, hot shower, room service, and an early bedtime. Neither of them got much sleep, Callie unable to stop the frightening encounter from replaying in her mind and Jake unable to dismiss the suspicious stirrings that began at O! Hamos and carried over in a dramatic way to Sarakiniko.

The next morning, his security sweep of the boat took those stirrings to a whole new place.

Though Jake had conducted an inspection prior to every departure, each one had been a little less intensive as, thus far, he'd not found a single thing amiss. His routine consisted of the same quick dive and examination of the *Psamathe*'s hull, check of its systems, and inventory of the layout and everything that remained on board during their overnight. After his initial explanation to Callie about it being akin to a pilot's preflight review, she had also become increasingly less concerned and accustomed to his checks. But this morning, curled up on the cockpit lounge, as she watched Jake poking around the deck, her face reflected the unease that lingered from the evening before.

He gave her a tight smile as he brushed by and descended the companionway to the cabin below. His hands and fingers probed around, over, and under trim and surfaces and fittings as he went, taking more time with the electronics and mechanics. Standing in the middle of the cabin's layout, he took out his iPhone and brought up the video he'd shot the day before, just prior to leaving the boat for their stay in Milos. Starting in the master suite, he compared the bed and surrounding storage compartments, confirming that the pillows and bedding were exactly as they appeared in the video. Luggage and personal effects left behind were all in place. Next, he panned the gallery and dining lounge, and also found everything as expected; since they had not been spending much time belowdecks, food and drink was neatly stored, kitchenware washed and put away.

But when he came to the nav station, even before consulting the video footage, he sensed something out of order. The last time he'd been seated at the chart table with his laptop, a sailing map of Milos—the one with depths and other nautical navigation information—had been spread over top of his spiral notebook log. Staring at the chart table, he paused the video and saw just what he remembered, then eyed the table again.

An electrical jolt ran from the base of his spine, his skin tingling with heat as all his hazy speculations clarified into something genuine.

The log book was on top of the map, open to the page of his latest entry where he'd penned notes about their next destination. On top, not below. Not as he had left it.

Someone had been on board the boat.

AFTER MAKING A QUICK check on Callie and telling her that he needed to do a couple of maintenance-related things before they departed from the marina, Jake returned to the cabin and retrieved a small case from one of his tactical bags. He'd used the contents just prior to their first sail but not since, primarily because using them could not be easily obfuscated, but also because he'd felt his other precautions would be adequate enough. Unless he was presented with a reason to believe differently, which he now was.

The REI case contained Mesa, Andre, Orion, and FLIR devices for TSCM—technical surveillance countermeasures—scanners and analyzers that would pick up Wi-Fi and Bluetooth signals, a broad spectrum of radio frequencies, electronics, and magnetic fields, all of which were present in various configurations and applications all over the boat. Which meant there would be a multitude of false positives to sort through, but it would be well worth the effort if, in the course of doing so, he uncovered what else might be emitting similar signals and frequencies, namely hidden audio and video capture.

He adjusted the settings on a device the size of a deck of cards and fanned its antenna around the interior shell of the boat, ceiling, sides, and floor, watching the animation of LED lights on the display and measuring the alert tones. As anticipated, there were plenty of detections as he swept over areas where he knew there were networks of the boat's own electronics and wireless transmitters and receivers, but it did not take him long to find a total of four sources that did not belong. They were in the form of quarter-size disks placed in the galley and the master suite, all well concealed. He removed each of the audio bugs and began a hunt for cameras with another device from his kit but did not find any. After a final sweep, using all of the analyzers and detectors and thermal imaging in his kit, he was fairly confident that the bugs were the only surveillance gadgets implanted in the cabin.

There was one more search to conduct, and for this he needed to find a way to keep Callie from watching him; even if she didn't understand what he was doing, he was sure she'd know it was not normal maintenance. Palming the device for the task, he was running various deceptions through his mind when he emerged topside to find her dozing. *Caught a break there*, he thought pensively, and began a deck canvass from stern to bow. He located and removed two more bugs, a stew of anger and worriment brewing with each discovery.

But it was the last finding that really sunk the hook in what was now a running fish. He had leaned over the stern, almost touching the water, and run the probe of this detector along the length from corner to corner. And got a hit.

What the hell?

He had been particularly thorough in his examination of the front and back of the Jeanneau, both visually and manually, before each and every departure. How could he have missed anything there? But sure enough, to his astonishment, just below the panel of the swim platform, he found something that was not flush with the hull, raised about a half inch from the surface. He was able to pluck it off and, when he was upright on the deck, studied it in his hand. It was magnetic and white—to blend in with the boat's hull—and no bigger than a thumb drive.

He immediately recognized what it was. A GPS tracker.

Staring down at the module as if it were some kind of vile parasite, his thoughts went into a tumultuous maelstrom of who, why, when, and how. Was this another bounty hunter in play for the Dark Web contract on him? It did not have that feel; any of those assassins would already know their target and not be inclined to take such extra measures. So if not…who and why?

He knew there were a multitude of possibilities. In his line of work he accumulated enemies like frequent-flyer miles, some known and many more unknown. Garnering a collection of adversaries with festering grudges or even standing vendettas was an occupational hazard, but one generally associated with areas of hot operation. It could be that this was a threat of unknown origin or agenda which, of the possibilities, was not necessarily better. The benefit of dealing with a known enemy was being able to at least strategize against a playbook you might be familiar with. It was much tougher to defend against what you could not define.

Which brought him to *how*.

Everything for their honeymoon had been booked through the Keoghs' organization and, as high-profile mega-wealthy philanthropists, he knew that arrangements for them were always well-cloaked in cutout identities and profiles, from the private jet and its flight plans to the destination hotels. Of course, someone good with the necessary technical means and mastery could broach even the most layered security protocols but, once again, that tended to point in another direction from a Dark Web bounty hunter, whose approach was typically more organic.

As for when, though he could not know for sure, his gut told him the bugs and GPS tracker had just been implanted. Right here in Milos, because this was the first time he'd observed anything out of place. Then again, since he hadn't swept the boat since their first departure from Mykonos, it could have happened in Syros or Kythnos or Serifos or Sifnos or Kimolos.

Fuck.

He thought about his under-hull inspections and how he'd somehow not seen or felt the GPS tracker. How long had it been there? No…all of this had to have been installed here, in Milos. He was sure he would have felt or seen it from his swims beneath the boat. Still, it made him realize that his state of alert had not been up to par.

Which offered the two men he'd pinged on at O! Hamos into the equation. And possibly the man who'd hit on Callie at Sarakiniko, who might be one of the two. They were being watched and tracked—at least until just now when he'd debugged the boat and removed the GPS. And those countermeasures would let the watchers know that *he* knew.

Fuck.

He glanced to the cockpit lounge where Callie was still lightly slumbering, thankfully unaware. Then he looked out to sea, the wind and water relatively calm, and prayed mightily that he would be able to draw from that serenity and maintain a steady demeanor for Callie's sake.

As if sensing his gaze on her, she stirred, squinting sleepily into the sun. Seeing the serious expression on Jake's face, she asked, "Is everything okay?"

He forced a smile. "All good, baby doll."

He went through the motions of casting off, starting the Jeanneau's engine and motoring into the bay, wondering again whose fixation he had drawn and for what purpose. But no matter who it was or what was going on, it begged the grim question of how he could keep them safe without being so guarded as to feed into Callie's anxieties, which were on a hair trigger as it was. And, on a more basic level…God in heaven, what else could happen to blow up their honeymoon?

13

FOLEGANDROS, AT THE SOUTHERNMOST edge of the Cyclades, with its wild and rugged beauty and sparsity of tourist traffic, was just what they both needed to restore at least a tentative bead on composure. As they had with the previous islands, their time was split between driving the winding, scenic roads and walking the *hora* and other villages. But while the breezy and mellow atmosphere put them both at ease on the surface, beneath the façade, Callie was still reeling from the incident at Sarakiniko and Jake's mind was fraught with the tension of the morning's revelation as they'd sailed out of Milos.

The first chance he got, when Callie had again succumbed to the fatigue of her restless night and napped as he navigated, Jake called Nash Remington and told him about the security breach on the boat. His friend listened, asked questions, and offered what they both knew was provisional reassurance because, in truth, there was every reason to suspect something malicious unfolding. More practically, Remington told him that Efron Kipnis would get a surveillance and monitoring package dispatched to his next port of call and, as promised, it had been there on arrival at the Karavostasis Marina. Jake was astounded at the speed with which Kipnis had managed to deliver the goods, in just a little over four hours after the phone call, dropped off by helicopter and delivered to the harbormaster.

The package consisted of a router-like hub that paired up with cameras and sensors, the entire setup installed in a matter of minutes. Jake downloaded the app on his iPhone and familiarized himself with the monitoring options that would provide the status of things such as the Jeanneau's bilge pumps, power, and battery; more importantly, it would let him know if security sensors had been triggered to indicate movement on the deck or if hatches had been opened. The system's GPS updated every fifteen minutes and would issue an alert if the boat itself was moved from the geo-fenced area. He could view images in real time from the cameras, and anything activating them would automatically be recorded. He was annoyed with himself for not having installed any kind of system in the first place, but then he supposed he could blame the dereliction on the fog of romantic bliss.

From the time they stepped off the deck of the *Psamathe* to the shore of Folegandros, Jake was constantly checking the app on his phone, but it showed no anomalies. This hardly surprised him; whoever had been tracking them would be more careful now that they'd been detected.

Jake was equally honed in on Callie, watching and reacting to any signs of anxiety and never leaving her side for a moment.

Thankfully, there seemed to be no sketchy characters hovering in the shadows, no incidents or encounters of high drama. Just refreshing breezes spiced with herbs and flowers, the bohemian character in the *hora* village squares of Dounavi, Kontarini, and Kritikos, and the rich colors of land and sea bracketed by sunrise and sunset. They enjoyed a sumptuous dinner at Papalagi Seafood, slept a little better in their plush suite at the Anemi Hotel, had a hearty breakfast, and set off for Antiparos.

The state of constant alert kept Jake's stress level elevated, which he had to manage internally to prevent Callie from drawing on it and, as disciplined as he was, given her skittish state, that was no easy feat. But the carefree time on Folegandros, followed by an even more laid-back day and night in Antiparos, the small, serene island wedged between the bigger, rowdy islands of Paros and Naxos, served to relax them both. A getaway haven for European royalty, Hollywood icons, and international rock stars, it is essentially a rustic and charming waterfront village that rambles out to open fields and pastoral countryside and quaint, mostly empty beaches. The privacy and anonymity it affords celebrities was more of the soothing elixir that emanated from the lesser-traveled and often more authentic Greek Isles and, from what he knew of their next destination, Jake expected the serenity to continue.

He could not have been more wrong, but what upended his dream honeymoon this time came from an entirely different and wholly unimagined source.

JAKE AND CALLIE SAT in white wooden chairs, a small round stoplight-red table between them. Beyond the stone edge at their feet was another blue-on-blue vista that here, if it was possible, was more intensely hued than anywhere they'd been so far. Amorgos is, in fact, known as the blue island, its shore outlined in a ribbon of turquoise and the deeper sea, a shade of neon royal that almost transcended the color spectrum. It was midafternoon, unremittingly sunny, a boisterous wind blowing in bursts that hummed in their ears and peppered the air with fine grains of sand and grit from Agia Anna below and the mountainside on which the taverna called Big Blue Café was perched.

In the hours since they'd arrived on Amorgos and checked into the Aegialis Hotel and Spa, a sprawling resort stacked into a hillside with a spectacular view of the Aegean, Jake had driven the length of the island, taking the Katapola-Thalarias road south through the *hora* and other port town of Katapola and then venturing farther west on Katapolon-Mavris Mitis, all the way to the tip between the beaches of Paradisia and Kalotaritissa. It was one of the loveliest drives thus far and took no more than an hour. The roads ascended steep hills and mountain slopes that scaled upwards of two thousand feet, twisting in serpentine switchbacks that had Callie squeezing her eyes shut and digging her fingertips into the seat leather. Jake smiled behind the wheel and gave her comforting touches, confident of his driving skills, which were put to the test several times along the way. Twice, he brought their rental jeep to a grinding halt just in time to avoid plowing into a logjam of bleating and bell-clanking goats and, in another defensive maneuver, was forced to swerve out of the path of an ATV buzzing them in the crook of a hairpin turn. The countryside was a desolate blend of tan and gray rock mottled with green and gold ground cover and, when they were not precipitously close to bluffs by the ocean, a pleasant ride. They stopped to see the shipwreck of Olympia in Liveros Bay, and Jake began telling Callie about the 1980s Luc Besson cult classic film, *Le Grand Bleu*, in which two friends form a rivalry in the extreme sport of free diving. The rusting bifurcated hulk of ship had been among the locations featured in the flick. In its final, fated resting place, the oxidized remains had the look of an abstract art exhibit in the glassy green shallows near the craggy shore.

Now, sipping iced coffees in the café on the opposite coast, they were looking down at the beach and the "big blue" waters made famous by the movie. Jake bent to pet a tabby cat snaking around his ankles, one of the feline multitudes ever-present throughout Greece, and explained, "Free diving is diving without any scuba equipment. I forget what was represented in the film, but I think the record is something like seven hundred feet, which is really deep, and that means the diver would have to hold his breath for about ten minutes."

Callie listened, her eyes wide with incredulity. "I can't even imagine that. It sounds really scary."

Jake said, "I've done it, but certainly not that kind of depth or time. It can be exhilarating, but taken to the extreme in sport is a challenge for even the most trained and conditioned diver." He paused, remembering. "It was a good flick."

Callie was looking at him in the way she did whenever a new layer of his hardcore entity or ideology was revealed, feeling both awed and a little detached, wondering, as she did so often, how he could believe she fit into his world—but abundantly thankful that he did.

"Just up the road from here is an amazing monastery built into the side of a mountain," he began, referring to the spectacular eleventh-century Panagia Hozoviotissa. "I'm thinking we…"

He caught the flash of consternation on her face and quickly finished, "We could see it from the base. It's obviously high and has hundreds of steps, which would be too much, but we're close enough we might as well see it." Even months after the brutalization Callie had endured, she still could not manage lengthy walking or strenuous climbing without discomfort, and the islands were nothing if not a hiker's Shangri-la, so Jake was always mindful of elevations and durations.

Callie nodded and peered out to sea, her expression becoming wistful. "This is really beautiful," she said, but there was a flatness in her voice.

Watching her closely, Jake asked, "But...?" He chuckled. "You're homesick? Really?"

She glanced at him, a demure smile erasing the pensive interlude. "Yes. This is a paradise, but so is home."

"Yeah, I know. Home is comfortable, and you're missing that."

They finished their drinks, stood, and strolled back to the jeep, gazing down the slope to Agia Anna where a group of people were arranging cameras on tripods, a man apparently in charge directing placement and production. "Looks like some kind of photoshoot," Jake remarked casually. Checking his watch, he said, "Let's pass on the monastery and head back to the hotel, maybe take a dip in the pool before dinner. Sound good?"

THE SMALL MARINA ACROSS the bay drizzled light into the dusk-darkened sea, shimmering like flickering candle flames, white block buildings glowing a trail up the mountainside. A semicircle of moon and a spray of stars were clearly defined in the equally darkened sky. This was the view from their linen-draped table on the terrace of the Ambrosia Gallery restaurant at the hotel. It was prime dinner time and the place was fairly full, but the tables were comfortably spaced, the atmosphere mellow and refined by the measured pace of the service and cheerful Greek music.

As they shared a dessert of crème brûlée, the finish for a dinner that comprised grilled shrimp and the hotel garden's vegetables nested in pasta, Jake was more mesmerized by the vision of his wife than that of the moonlit harbor below. Tonight she wore a white eyelet-detailed dress, strapped at the shoulders and tied at the waist and layered with a handkerchief hem. Her pale gold hair, sun-blushed ivory skin, and dark brown eyes, the feathery way her fingers touched the tablecloth, her napkin, and the material of her dress, all had a hypnotizing effect on him as he absently sipped his wine. Watching her, inhaling the air between them as if it were the oxygen of life's last existence.

Despite the harbinger of malfeasance that had loomed a few days before, a sense of calm now prevailed. Though still wary of trouble, his eyes constantly roving everywhere they went, nothing out of the ordinary had happened since Milos. Not in Folegandros, not in Antiparos, and not here in Amorgos. His surveillance had shown no breaches and he'd not picked up on any suspicious activity during their explorations and enjoyment of those islands. At this point, they were a few days from the conclusion of their honeymoon sail and he was increasingly optimistic that it might be all right the rest of the way. At least that's the way he felt tonight, in this moment, sitting across from this angel.

Huskily, he asked, "Ready to go, sweetie?"

She smiled, her face full of adoration and love, brimming with pure innocence swaddled around a latent sensuality known only to him. And now, he wanted nothing more than to lose himself in the nectar of that. He felt his heart kick up its pace, a thrum in his groin, heat in his skin.

He rose, took her hand, and they strolled from the terrace, back through the main dining room. Light beamed from domed ceiling insets, and glass panel windows overlooking the pool and bay were open to the mild evening air. Muted conversation and the clink of dinnerware drifted from the tables seated with diners savoring local culinary specialties. They paused near the restaurant's entrance as the owner's son, Stamatis, passed and stopped to serenade them with his violin. After a few fidgety minutes, Jake bowed to him with an appreciative smile and they moved on.

New dining patrons were entering, so Jake put his hands on Callie's waist, his body against her back, guiding her forward into a lounge area outside the restaurant's glass doors. He tucked her beside him and they continued past squared-off groupings of white sofas and chairs.

And then, from behind, he heard someone call his name and his flesh, from neck to scrotum, crawled with an icy voltage that chilled him like a blast of liquid nitrogen.

THE AIR IN THE common area just outside the restaurant was a sedate pool of trailing notes on the scale of dinner ambiance, the activity a normal flow of neutral energy emitted from the leisurely passage of those entering and exiting, their closer voices rising and falling in indistinct bubbles. But for Jake, it was as if a sudden and stupefying whiteout had isolated the sound of one voice, carrying it like an arrow from its point of origin to the aural receptors in his head where it pierced through the blizzard.

Oh God, it can't be. Don't let it be. No, no, no...of all things, no. Not here, not now. Oh fuck no...

"Jake Tyler."

Spoken again, the arrowhead dug into a bank of long-inhumed memory, ice cracking and crystals scattering like frozen embers.

At the vocalization of his name, Jake had instinctively moved to shield Callie, and now he turned stiffly, nudging her behind him. Turned and looked and felt the blood drain from his face.

The woman who had spoken said, "I knew it was you, *moro.*"

Jake flinched inwardly, the gratification of his dinner souring in his stomach, but said nothing.

A languid smile came and went as she studied him. She stood taller, stacked high into sandals that were all stilettos and straps, wearing a Beachside Bunny dress in a flesh tone monochromatic to her olive skin, the micro-sequined fabric snugly wrapping a voluptuous array of curves, her pubis wedged between wide hips only barely concealed and copious bosom perilously close to spilling out of the plunging cowl front. An elaborate Buccellati collar gleamed in diamonds and white gold from around her neck, but the abundance of cleavage on display below most likely rendered it unmemorable. Dark hair the burnt color of Italian roast coffee fell to the middle of her bare back, smooth and lustrous and swept from her forehead.

A full, interminable minute passed before she spoke again, her voice distinctively accented. "Do you say nothing?" she asked, her full lips, slick with clear gloss, forming a sultry scowl.

"Good to see you," he said thickly, though it was anything but good, and encountering her in Amorgos was just about the most far-fetched thing he could have imagined; she was from Athens and traveled the crown-jewel destinations of international hubs exclusively. But here she was, on this rustic island looking at him, but even more intently, looking at what she could see of Callie through her heavily lidded ice-blue eyes.

Peering shyly from behind Jake, ogling the imperially confident and stunningly gorgeous woman, Callie was overcome with a degree of vulnerability that made her wilt like a flower in the laser rays of a desert sun.

Stealing a furtive glimpse over his shoulder, Jake assessed not even a trace of jealousy in Callie, only wonder, but sadly he also saw complete intimidation, insecurity, and inferiority—worse, self-doubt.

Tensed as if sizing up the offensive front of an adversary, his tone dry and completely devoid of animation, Jake queried, "What brings you to Amorgos?"

"Photoshoot," she replied coolly, scrutinizing his face and seeing the same hard, chiseled features she'd known, the penetrating eyes, the licorice-black hair, but there was something very different about him she could not grasp. "What brings you here?" she countered. When he did not respond, her gaze slid lower, drawn like a Geiger counter to his hand, and discovered the answer to her question.

"*Gomena?*" Spying the gold band on Jake's left ring finger, her mouth parted then closed. "You are married." She flicked a glance at Callie. "*I gineka sou?*"

The words were enounced without emotion but the pupils in her eyes, constricting to black pinpoints, betrayed her true reaction. Just as quickly, the cryptic smile returned and she focused again on Callie, taking in the cowering waif all but obscured by Jake's body, polar opposite of herself in every perceivable way—fair and blond, impossibly skinny and diminutive and painfully demure, adorned in a lovely but what she considered chastely modest frock. The spectacular diamond dazzling from one small hand did not escape detection, its chunk of carats clicking the monetary calculator in her head well into five-digit territory.

"Yes," Jake replied, his hand closing around Callie's.

Looking at the meek little thing that Jake had put the ring on, the woman was thinking about the fiercely sexual animal she had been with and wondering what kind of perverse spell had been cast over him. But, if anything, absurdly, he appeared even more manly standing here with his flaxen-haired princess.

"Introduce us?" she asked, placing an expensively manicured hand on canted hip, nails long and lacquered. Before he could say anything—if he was going to say anything—the woman glowered, "What is wrong with her? What is she afraid of?" Her expression was full of acrimony and indignation. "What is wrong with *you*?"

Jake regarded her stonily, his face flat. Backing away, he said again, "Good to see you, Rina."

But before he could retreat further, the woman cut the gap between them and leaned in so close Jake could smell her piquant perfume and feel the heat of her breath on his face. Her voice projecting purposefully, blue eyes flashing from Jake to Callie then holding on Jake, she remarked, "Turns out, it was not yours after all, *gomenos*."

As she stepped back from him, there was a sharp look, some hidden emotion simmering in the icy eyes, but Jake did not care. Not even a little bit. But what he did care about, profoundly, was the look in Callie's...and she looked shattered.

DURING THE RETURN TO their suite, the pristine white honeymoon accommodations, Jake had plied some comforting words but they had little, if any, effect on Callie. Her pallor was ghostly, her expression one of glazed numbness, but the more telling thing was the involuntary tremor that quivered through her body every few seconds. Inside the suite, she'd moved to the bed and sat delicately, as if the contact might break her.

Watching her, Jake's anguish mounted. The run-in had been bad enough, but he knew he'd made it worse in the way he had reacted. Maybe if he'd not been so hostile it would have gone a little better, maybe she would not have said what she did—and Jesus Christ, what a thing to say. He stood for several moments, unsure of what to say or do, how to handle the unthinkable, before finally sitting beside Callie on the bed, putting an arm around her shoulders, and saying softly, "Sweetie, let's go relax in the Jacuzzi." She looked up at him plaintively, and he murmured, "Just come with me."

She rose slowly and dug a one-piece bathing suit from her bag, coyly slipping into the bathroom to change into it. When she emerged, wearing the pale pink ruffled-top garment, she reluctantly accompanied Jake to the outdoor veranda where a jetted marble tub the size of a small swimming pool overlooked the sea, enclosed by clear plexiglass panels and surrounded by candle lanterns. Through the panels was an almost identical view as that from dinner, the harbor lights twinkling, the half-moon glowing against a cobalt sky. At dinner, a magical vista in a serene, romantic setting, but now it was as if all the exquisite sensuality had leached from the tapestry and been absorbed by the dark sea.

Jake took a long look over the harbor, his chest aching with a mix of sadness and anger—sadness for the pain he knew was coming and anger that he was being forced to engage it. But as much as he did not want to tell Callie, he knew she deserved to understand what had transpired, and there was no way he could keep it from her now. Returning his gaze to Callie, the stricken expression on her face crushed his heart like ripe fruit bleeding pulp and skin and mangled core.

He sidled over to her in the warm, bubbling water, and slipped his arms gently around her. "I'm so sorry that happened, Callie," he began, grappling for the words to explain, as simply as possible, what she had witnessed. But the brutal truth was, there was nothing simple about it. So he just said, "She was a girlfriend from my time here."

The woman, Stavrina Papandreou, had been one of many over the years, but one of a few who had made deep imprints into his carnal DNA, and not in a good way; in short, their pairing was as volatile and combustible as nitroglycerin, hot and explosive and just as destructive. Like the other women who had come before Callie, she had aroused and fed his sexual appetite, which satisfied his wants, but it wasn't until Callie that the wellspring of need yawed open from a place inside he'd never known existed. That cavern was ravenous every second of every hour of every day and night, craving something that transcended anything he'd experienced before, actual love—something he didn't know how badly he wanted until he had it.

"She's very beautiful," Callie said. "Were you…together for a long time?"

"She's a model," Jake replied blandly, adding, "and the photoshoot must have been what we saw on the beach today." From the disconcerted look that passed over Callie's face, Jake guessed she was thinking that Papandreou's curves did not fit the typical parameters of the rail-thin fashion femmes strutting the couture runways. He did not further elucidate by qualifying Papandreou's profession as a lingerie-cum-swimsuit model.

Though he'd not responded directly to her question, Callie knew he'd had girlfriends, undoubtedly lots of them, but before now it had actually been easy to not think about that because of the way he was with her. Wherever they were, no matter how many attractive women she noticed in circulation near them, Jake's sole focus was always on her, the other women registering merely as a blur of background humanity. But there was no mistaking the kinetic effect of this particular woman, enough to know there was some kind of dramatic history.

"I was with her most of my time here," Jake continued, tilting his head skyward as if the moon might provide him some wisdom with which to harmlessly articulate the rudiments of that relationship. He sighed and looked down to his lap where he was holding Callie's hands. "Ultimately, it was just another part of the overall bad experience of that time."

They were both quiet for a while, Jake not wanting to say anything more, Callie uneasily processing what little he had said. He felt her quiver against him as she took in a deep breath. And then she asked what he had been dreading.

"What did she mean by what she said?"

Her sweet face upturned to his, the naiveté in her eyes made his chest tighten with a renewed twist of inner torment. Running his hands tenderly up and down her arms, he said, "I'm not sure…but she was referring to her pregnancy." He paused, pursing his lips, and exhaled heavily.

In his arms, Callie flinched.

"It was certainly not planned and came as a shock."

Remembering just what a tsunami of a shock it had been, Jake had later realized that he probably should have seen the probability of it. He had not always been sexually careful in his youth—hell, not always in his dalliances before Callie, either. And, as a young stud bursting with the bloodlust of war and the machismo of primal testosterone, it was too easy to forego protection when you were sloshing full of drink and libido was raging in your dick.

Callie blinked up at him, her eyes glistening with moisture.

He went on. "I told her I would support her. She immediately said she wasn't going to have it. I said it was her choice and I would abide by it. At one point, when the heat of the moment had settled, I asked her to talk me through her decision. I think I expected her to say that she wasn't ready, that she didn't want to have a child with me, something like that. Instead, she told me I was not a part of her reason for wanting to terminate, that it had everything to do with her career…which, again, I said I understood and would support. But there was something in the way she put it that got under my skin. She said: 'I will not allow a baby to alter my body, make me sick and fat and unattractive; my body is my money.'

"She had an abortion and we split. It wasn't because of the abortion per se, but what she said resonated in a toxic way. When I was with her, there were no other women. That is a principal I always upheld; if I was in an exclusive relationship, I honored that. There were times I suspected that she was with other men, though she always denied it. But when she told me she was pregnant, I was prepared to act responsibly. What she said tonight is unreliable and irrelevant as far as I'm concerned." Observing her as he pared out the reveal, which was significantly sanitized of detail, he could see how overwhelmed she was by it all, her mind and heart flailing for a soft landing where there was none.

Once again, they both lapsed into a short silence, the bath's jets lightly gurgling in the water, its surface frothing around them. And then Callie asked, "Do you think you would still be with her if…" She stopped, not knowing how to finish the thought.

There was no hesitation as Jake answered, "No. I've said this before, and I'll say it now. I believe everything happens for a reason, to lead us to where we're supposed to go, to what we're supposed to do, and to who we're supposed to be with." He cuddled her closer, placing his neck against hers, and whispered, "And for me, that's you, angel."

He tipped her chin to him with a finger and kissed her, feeling the love surge and wash over the rawness of his divulgence and hoping that he had repressed any further hurt—not from Papandreou's appearance and the groove of her in his timeline, but by the essence of what she represented.

BUT THE DAMAGE HAD been inflicted, whether directly or subliminally, as he discovered a few hours into sleep when he woke and sensed, rather than felt or heard, Callie's distress.

When he'd closed his eyes, physically tired and emotionally drained, Callie had been quietly snuggled in his arms. He had patiently waited until her body stilled and her breathing slowed and evened out before allowing himself to succumb. Now, inexplicably waking, he realized that she was no longer tucked in his embrace and, in the low illumination of the suite's night lighting, he saw her apart from him, curled in a fetal position. Both her face and pillowcase were wet, but the sound emanating from her was so faint he could not hear it until he slid closer; sobs were escaping her throat, but in what was clearly exhaustion from hours of crying, had been reduced to whispered sighs.

He gingerly stroked her damp cheek, trying not to startle her, but of course he did, eliciting a frightened gasp and recoil, her eyelids flicking open. Scooping her into his arms, he said, "Oh, baby…why didn't you wake me?"

She wheezed weakly and burrowed into him.

"Nightmare?" he asked, and then what had been just beyond his psychological grasp, slammed home like a wrecking ball hung up by a gale-force wind. Stavrina Papandreou's pregnancy. Never mind that it might or, according to Papandreou, might not be by him, or that it was terminated. It was the one thing that the entirety of Callie's love could not give him, and tonight that reality had been cruelly flaunted, made exceedingly worse by being something as yet unaddressed.

The brutal assaults Callie had suffered in Colombia left her unable to become pregnant or bear children, but Jake had never broached the subject because, for him, it was not a detracting factor—all he wanted or needed was Callie. But now he sorely regretted not having the discussion to evaluate *her* feelings.

Gently pulling back so he could look at her, Jake said, "Talk to me, love. Tell me what you're thinking about."

"I never really thought about having a baby with you," she sobbed, her words stuttering in hitches of labored breathing. "And then...and then I couldn't."

"I know," he said, rubbing her back. "So this ripped it all open."

She nodded. "Is it?"

"Is it what?"

"Something that—"

"No, sweetheart. No. I didn't marry you to have children. If that could have happened..." He paused, choosing his words carefully. "If it could have happened, that would be all right because it would be what was supposed to happen. Remember what I said before? But for it not to be possible does not change the way I feel about you, not in *any* way."

"Are you sure?" she asked, her eyes filling with a new eruption of tears.

He dabbed lightly at her cheeks and traced his fingers around her face and into her hair. "Yes, I am sure."

"But I'm not like her at all."

"No, no you're not. You're not like her or any other woman I've known." Confusion crept into her face, and he continued, "Which is why I never fell in love until you came along." Thinking about the insecurity he'd seen grip her in the presence of Papandreou, he said, "And you are the most beautiful woman I have ever seen. Do not ever think otherwise. If you could only truly know just how beautiful I think you are."

Color flushed her pale complexion.

He looked at her candidly. "Callie, you can tell me anything you feel, okay? Do you think you would have wanted to have a baby?"

She took a moment and then replied, "I really never thought about it, so I think I feel okay about being unable to. But if it's something you wanted, I..." She could not finish, choked with emotion.

"*You* are what I want and need. I love you, Callie, totally and unconditionally."

15

THERE WAS NO LINGERING over breakfast in the morning, both because Jake wanted an early launch into the forty-odd nautical miles to their next stop and, more compellingly, to avoid another encounter with Stavrina Papandreou. So the *Psamathe* had departed from the Aegiali Marina just as the first pink glow of dawn lined the horizon. There had been no more discussion about Papandreou or the despair her appearance had induced, but it hung over them like a stalled storm front, their demeanors solemn and drawn with fatigue. Now in the wane of the honeymoon sail, Jake really hoped Callie would be able to let the cataclysmic incident slip behind them and enjoy the remainder of their time.

And please, God, without further conflict or turmoil.

At least he could be encouraged by the lack of any perceived subterfuge involving the boat since he'd installed the surveillance and monitoring gadgetry, but that conjecture was tempered by the knowledge that whoever had been on board had seen their itinerary, thus minimizing the need for GPS tracking.

By the time they reached the shores of Patmos, the sun was high and hot, the sky brightly blue and feathered with clouds that looked as soft as goose down, painting the backdrop of a deceptively vibrant day. They were at the edge of the Dodecanese Islands, anchored by Karpathos and Rhodes to the south and here in Patmos to the north, skirting the Turkish coast.

In the winding hills above the marina village, the Porto Scoutari hotel, with its white stone façade and toothed battlement roofline, resembles a castle. Overlooking the beach of Meloi Bay, it is built around a lush garden landscaped with sculptures and pineapple palms and native plants. The hotel lobby is distinguished by a unique collection of antiques that include everything from elaborately carved wood furniture to ornate grandfather clocks to authentic nautical diving helmets and other seafaring memorabilia; the vintage maritime décor carries over to the dreamy, palatial suites.

After checking in and freshening up, Jake and Callie had lunch in the hotel's 12 Island Bistro, a white-draped terrace off the large heart-shaped pool, and then went for a drive.

Known as the "Island of the Apocalypse," where St. John penned the Book of Revelation, Patmos is steeped in theological history and is said to have the most monasteries per square meter than anywhere in the world. Navigating the roads through and beyond the southern side of Skala, then around the skein of the island's *hora*, Jake purposefully kept the drive unencumbered, making few stops and letting the terrain unfold naturally.

With Callie's innate shyness came a taciturnity that was normal for her, but where she would have remarked on how pretty the flowers in a courtyard were or the loveliness of a thistle-covered meadow, might have asked Jake to translate a sign or menu item or inquire about a particular landmark, she was even more withdrawn than usual during the ride. Her expression glazed, face turned into the Suzuki Jimny's open window with the breeze blowing back her hair, she watched the expanses of hills climb and dip, reverential pillars of ancient worship and jumbles of stacked houses going by in a blur of motion.

Jake could only guess at the disconsolate meander of her thoughts, and the sadness of the pall cast over what would have otherwise been another glorious day in love weighed heavily on him. Several times as he drove, he reached over and took her hand and got a scant smile. When they reached the southern end of the island, Jake asked Callie if she felt up to a hike, letting her know that there was a secluded beach at the end of a trail that stretched about three-quarters of a mile. About halfway along the path to Psili Ammos, which rambled narrowly down a slope of rocks and scrub, he was thinking he might have made a bad choice, but Callie clung to his arm and stepped carefully. He took it slowly, and in another fifteen minutes they made it past sweeping dunes to a tree-dotted cove with a rustic tavern and a crescent of golden sand.

Jake smiled and asked, "Worth it?"

Gazing at the near-empty beach and brilliant blue water, Callie smiled back, her face full of revived happiness. They spent the next hour or so strolling through the waves and lounging in the breezy shade of the tamarisk trees and, for a little while, the toxicity of the previous night dissipated.

On the drive back to the Porto Scoutari, Jake made the turn from the marina, continuing along a road that wound north before hooking east where the elevation rose to the hotel's grounds. A well-maintained regulation soccer field ahead on the right, Jake noticed there was some kind of airfield on the left, just barely in view from an open plateau downslope. The Greek flag whipped in the wind atop a pole sprouting from a white block structure wedged into the bank. His left arm propped on the open window frame, he glanced over casually and, at the same time, heard the familiar engine and rotor sounds of a helicopter on the approach. His foot unconsciously eased up on the Jimny's accelerator and he watched as a black twin-engine aircraft, a Leonardo A109C, hovered for landing and then disappeared below the hill. He felt his premonitory senses tingle.

Though tour companies commonly ran helos between the more popular islands and the presence of an airfield here offered a place to put one down, he could not imagine it was a regular stop in the circuit. On the other hand, like Antiparos, Patmos in recent years had become an off-the-beaten-track hideaway for the rich and famous. The view of the bird had been quick and he'd not seen a logo, which more than likely meant it was ferrying someone requiring discretion—perhaps of the same hierarchy as Richard Gere or Julia Roberts, both of whom were purported to have residences on the island.

If he'd been alone, Jake would have been inclined to appease his curiosity, if, for no other reason, to dispel any inkling of the arrival being connected to those who had been tracking him. But he was not about to give Callie anything else to spin a worry web in her mind. He turned beside the soccer field and pulled up to the hotel, a valet hustling over to intercept the Jimny. Jake and Callie strolled to their bungalow, a parrot's chatter—there was one named Aris they'd been told had been in residence for the past twenty years—and the distant sound of waves from the bay below striking a nostalgic note that Jake felt and also saw resonate with Callie.

HOURS LATER, AS NIGHT darkened the windows of their suite, Jake heard Callie sigh next to him. They were lying in the big, iron-scrolled canopy bed, sheer white linen swathed from the four posts. In this moment, he was fairly certain he knew what she was thinking, but asked anyway.

Earlier, they'd taken a drive north and had a wonderful dinner of freshly caught tuna at Nautilus, a seaside restaurant near Vagia Beach, savoring another cinematic sunset over the water. The essence of romantic quietude and without drama.

But before that, while dressing for the evening, Jake had received a FaceTime call he'd been expecting. It was one of several, spaced every couple of days at the same time—5 PM local time and 9 AM in Costa Rica—from his home crew. Conducted by Jesse Segura, there were always cameo appearances by the others, chiming in to say hello and ask about highlights from the trip. The purpose of the calls, of course, was to give Jake a domestic status report. Most of the time, he managed to converse privately in case there was anything serious or of a troublesome nature to address. Thankfully, so far all was well on the home front; according to Segura, there had been no suspicious activity or strangers lurking about the property.

Today, Camilla had squeezed in and demonstratively expressed her affections with an enthusiastic appraisal of Callie in a dress that fit and flowed in all the right places, the pattern a watercolor of blushing colors. The housekeeper bubbled, "Oh, *mija…muy hermosa!* You have good time? We miss you!" Not surprisingly, Callie had become tearfully emotional.

Now, in response to Jake's query, in a small voice, she said, "I want to go home."

Though he'd anticipated the sentiment and the ask, Jake could not formulate a reply for a few moments, pondering the best way to balance empathy and understanding with advocacy to persevere. He said, "I know you miss them and miss being home."

"I really do," she murmured, her voice breaking completely when she converted the statement to a question, imploring, "So…can we…go?"

He blew out a soft breath. "Sweetie, we've got one more island."

"But then…"

"Then we'll see."

She nestled into him, a hand on his chest, the silky chiffon of her short chemise brushing his skin.

His eyes closed and he lay listening to her breath sounds as they slowed and faded to faint, his thoughts unsettled and lingering on Callie's plea.

He had known from the outset that the honeymoon excursion was going to be a high hurdle for her, pushing her well beyond what she could handle psychologically, and he'd assessed where she was on the scale from moment to moment. And, in the harsh glare of reality reckoning, he knew she had been thrust over the top far too many times. From the occasional tourist swarms schooled with multiples more than she'd ever encountered in Dominical, to the targeted confrontations by individuals with intrusive, perhaps even malicious intent, he conceded it *had* been too much.

He'd also known the likelihood of the bad dreams continuing to plague her, especially away from the familiarity and comfort of home, was high, a dire prophecy that had, sadly, proven true. A full night's sleep had been a rare, if not impossible fulfillment prior to the trip and that did not change in the weeks to follow.

Add to that the misery wreaked by Stavrina Papandreou, he might as well destroy the scale.

But while he'd prepared himself for the possibility of catastrophic failure, had thought out contingencies and exit strategies, he could not bring himself to concede just yet. Setting aside the detrimental, there was so much more to rejoice in. The thrill of discovery in each place they ventured, the charm and hospitality of the locals, the uniqueness of each magnificent landscape and its venerable architectural treasures, the stunning views that defied adequate description. The precious and priceless looks of awe and joy reflected in Callie's eyes. The glorious sunrises and sunsets that began and ended their days, the rapturous evenings and sensual, silken nights in between. Like this…just like this.

He propped himself up on an elbow and gazed down at his beautiful sleeping angel, the moonlight filtering through the suite's windows glistening on her skin like fine porcelain dust.

They were so close, and what came next was going to be challenging in a different way, but in the end, he hoped it would get her farther along in the healing process.

He slid his fingers lightly through her curls, leaned over and touched his lips to her cheek. Then he lay back and fell asleep to the lullaby of Aegean waves rolling below, sinking inside his subconscious to relive the sex and love—and finding instead the hazy sight and sound of a black helicopter emerging from the rise.

16

IT WAS EARLY MORNING, earth and sky still veiled by plum-colored twilight, as Jake studied the forecast on the Windfinder and Navionics apps on his iPhone. His pre-sail integrity and security checks done, everything on the boat was ready for departure, Callie watching him sleepily from the settee. She sensed something of concern but was unable to read Jake's patent expression of stony composure, which gave no hint of emotion or thought or a shade toward something good or bad. The stoicism served him well in his trade, confounding friends and foes alike, but it simply worried Callie because she often saw the same dispassionate face in both favorable and adverse situations.

Swiping through screens on his phone Jake was, in fact, a little concerned. Today's sail would take them out of the sprightly waters of the south Aegean to the more tempestuous Icarian, and he'd been monitoring the development of big winds for the past forty-eight hours. The Icarian Sea was known for its capricious conditions, the north winds stronger and more disruptive to the straits between the islands, but the speeds of this system were trending higher than he was comfortable with. The forecast was indicating better conditions later in the day, but he didn't want to lose too much time as he'd already expended nearly all of the extra hours built into their itinerary, so his plan was to make it to the next island group before noon and reassess from there. If his analysis and timeline of the forecast conditions was on par, the final leg would still be plenty challenging but manageable and swift.

Motoring out from the port, the wind seemed no different than most other days they'd been at sea, but as he angled toward the northeast cape of Patmos, the choppy waves grew in height and force, wind blowing in heady gusts. Setting the sails, he configured two reefs on the main and unfurled a third of the genoa, adjusting the track and trimming the sheet. In the transition from power to sail, the *Psamathe* bucked and thudded heavily in the water, throwing him off balance several times, but he got his bearings and maneuvered the boat into a taut but smooth close haul at six to seven knots. He noticed Callie gazing out with trepidation, complexion blanched and hands tightly clutching the seat cushion, and spoke to her with reassurance, his own face breaking out a smile for reinforcement.

The sun emerged in grand fashion, setting fire to the sea's roiling surface and then ascending in a yellow dome that quickly heated the already warm air, salt from the sea spray stinging Jake's lips and cheeks. As they settled into the northwestern course past Patmos, Callie's tension gradually eased and she even stood at the railing to watch a cloud of gulls screeching and squawking overhead and a pod of dolphins stitching through the water alongside. Bigger waves bumping the hull of the boat, tossing it up and down, sent her clambering back to the cockpit and Jake saw that the forecast was indeed accurate. The anemometer displayed wind speeds approaching thirty knots and he'd already been noticing that the closer he got to the open waters of the west, the more massive the swells, cresting with tops that looked like crushed ice. So he steered the Jeanneau into short zigzagging tacks, navigating to the lee of the next cluster of islands. In the distance on either side, the mountain peaks of Ikaria and Samos rose into sweeping rolls of orographic clouds generated by the winds scaling their heights. But despite the environmental dynamics going on around him, Jake was unbothered as he drew closer to the sheltered channels south of Fournoi between the islets of Anthropofas and Makronisi, the former known as the "Man-eater" for its legacy of shipwrecks and drowned seamen.

Four hours since their departure, now fully in the lee of Fournoi's calmer waters, Jake rolled the genoa and switched to motor, looking for a place to set anchor. The island coast was rippled with protected coves, and he bypassed several southern-end beaches where other boats were moored either by choice or, sharing his intention, to kill some time while waiting out the improvement of the more severe weather ahead. The craft were all of the pleasure or sport variety, about the same size or smaller than the Jeanneau, some passengers sunning on the decks, others splashing around in the water. Peering off toward the north along the shores of the next island, Thymena, he spied more recreational and fishing boats and one large vessel of indeterminate type. Not quite midway of Fournoi's length, he found a deserted cove, its inland terrain rocky and steep. Plenty scenic, but without a beach not much of a draw for those cruising, which made it a perfect spot for him.

Fournoi, roughly ten nautical miles east of their final honeymoon stop, comprises some twenty islands, most of which are uninhabited. A hub for Greek, Algerian, and Tunisian pirates from the Byzantine era until well into the nineteenth century, its numerous bays and rugged topography have rendered it virtually untouched by tourism save for the settlement in the north. The lower part of this isle, also known as Fourni, was primarily desolate.

Dropping the mainsail, Jake motored to a depth of about thirty feet and lowered the anchor, extending and dragging a length of chain until he was sure it had set. He zipped the sail in its lazy bag and took a seat next to Callie in the cockpit lounge. Beneath the partial cover of the Bimini, she looked cooler than he was, the wind-swept heat radiating from his deeply tanned skin.

"Want to take a dip?" he asked, wiping sweat from his brow. When she hesitated, he noted the sags below her eyes and knew just how little sleep she must have had the night before. "How about this…why don't you rest, maybe even get a snooze, while I do a little diving? This island is a great locale for scuba and it will cool me off."

He caught the instant flash of separation anxiety in her reaction, saw her glance around, eyes scanning the surrounding water and nearby land. Though the sea here was mostly calm, the surface undulating in its jeweled splendor of greens and blues, the wind was still brisk, swaying the boat back and forth.

"Are you comfortable with that? It's okay if you're not. I can relax right here with you." He smiled and gave her hand a squeeze.

"No, it's okay," she said quickly. "You should." But her eyes flicked away to avoid his inquisitory gaze.

Jake kissed her on the forehead and stood, going belowdecks to gather his gear. When he emerged a few minutes later, he was wearing an Aqua Lung 3mm Quantum Stretch shorty wetsuit, hefting a Scubapro gear bag and an aluminum tank.

He set the bag and tank down and sat on the opposite bench of the settee to inspect and assemble his equipment; though everything had been checked and rechecked, redundancy was something Jake lived by. When it came to anything that could take your life as the result of an oversight or integrity breach—be it a parachute or rappelling rig or, in this case, scuba diving apparatus—you never wanted to later think *If only I had given it one final pass*. He had, in fact, closely examined every piece of his diving kit following the trespass of the boat, and while there had been no evidence of any tampering then or since, he was not taking any chances.

Although he had gone snorkeling several times during their trip, this would be his first scuba dive, something he'd not really considered because it would take him completely out of sight and sound of Callie, but if ever there was an ideal opportunity to do so, this was it. He removed the gear from his bag and spread it out for inspection and assembly.

When he was satisfied everything was in order, he attached his BCD to the tank, connected the regulator, turned on the air, tested the flow through the primary and octopus and checked the pressure gauge. He then checked his bottle of Spare Air, which was a small black mini tank, and attached it to his vest. He used two lights, one a Scubapro torch and the other, a SOLA spot and flood style, testing both for strength. Since there were no predatory sharks in these waters, he didn't think there was a need for his Ocean Guardian eSpear, which he'd put to good use warding off a shark in Africa, but he clipped it on next to his Aqua Lung Argonaut titanium dive knife. Finally, he slipped on his fins and examined his mask.

Glancing over to Callie, he saw that she was holding her iPhone and AirPod earbuds, staring blankly at the phone's screen. "Hey," he said lightly, causing her to look up. "I don't mind staying." Truthfully, he really wanted to go, wanted the time to relax and clear his mind. Handling the boat in the higher sustained winds had been invigorating but also a strenuous workout.

"No, I'm okay," she replied, but her voice was shallow.

He stood and made a full 360-degree turn, slowly surveying the shores of the cove, the waters within, and the distant sea. Saw not a single sole on the rugged terrain, not a single boat of any kind in the circumference of his view. They were completely alone—as an afterthought, maybe eerily so. But, in this instance, it made him feel better about leaving her, knowing there would be no one to cause any strife.

He knelt beside Callie and gave her a long, tender look. "We're by ourselves here, so you will be fine or I would not do it, okay?" He smiled, adding, "I'll basically be just below you."

She nodded mutely.

"I know you're tired. Try to get a little nap. I love you, baby."

They kissed and he padded out to the extended swim platform, pulling on his neoprene gloves. He tugged on his mask, mouthed his regulator, and dropped into the water. Overhead, the sky remained abundantly blue, a single Eleonora's falcon passing on a graceful glide of outstretched wings. Before deflating his vest, Jake took one final look around and slipped below the water's surface.

LEANING FORWARD ON THE settee, Callie watched Jake hop off the end of the platform, saw his head bob briefly and then heard the gulp of his submersion. One moment there, gone the next. She felt her throat tighten, a twinge in her chest, her hands become shaky and damp. Scooting across the cushion toward the helm, she peered out from under the Bimini and looked down to the spot where Jake had gone in, his descending figure distorted by the current and growing smaller in the depths until she could see nothing but a blur and miniscule bubbles in water as clear as bottle glass. Raising her head, she scanned the sea, wind blowing into her face and tossing her hair. The boat rocked at its will, causing Callie to brace herself, waves swishing and lapping against the hull. Seabirds flapped lazily above, sun bright and blazing. Turning toward the island, she saw steep mounds rising from the rocky shores, covered in thick greenery with splotches of yellow, purple, and gold.

She took a deep, queasy breath, and slid back beneath the canopy.

The acute anxiety she always felt when Jake ventured away, sometimes even the shortest distances, consumed her with guilt and shame. But as much as she inwardly berated herself or fought to overcome the syndrome, it seemed chronically ingrained. She constantly worried that Jake's understanding and compassion would eventually erode, that it would cause his love and attraction to deteriorate, that he would feel burdened by her dependency. But if he was feeling that way, he did not show it and, while he could bristle with impatience with some people or in some situations, he seemed to have an infinite capacity for understanding with her. In any case, because of who he was and what he did, she knew that their future would be one of transience; for every span of time they had together, there would be just as many, if not more, apart.

Those longer separations, like Africa, were much more consequential and something she dreaded but would have to learn to live with. But the immediacy of a brief stray always seemed to catch her off guard and snatch her breath as if she had been dropped over an unseen ledge. She had not wanted him to leave her alone on the boat, but would never have said so. Bad things tended to happen when he left her side. But she conceded that he needed some time for himself, and being in the water was something he relished.

She slumped against the seat cushion and thought about how much she missed being home with him. Catching snippets from the phone calls with Jesse Segura, hearing and seeing Camilla and the others, triggered pangs of wistfulness that were hard to dismiss no matter what beautiful place they were visiting. She missed their lovingly kept villa and impeccably maintained grounds, the lush gardens with the roses Jake had gone to great effort to procure for her, the exotic orchids and exquisitely fragrant lemon yellow ylang ylang. And while the beds in the luxury hotels on each island were amply comfortable and undeniably romantic, she yearned for their own bed—the touch and texture of the sheets and pillows as they cuddled together, the spin of the ceiling fan, the soft glow of the night-lights, the lightly salted breeze and faint whoosh of waves that flowed in through the terrace.

Admittedly, once she'd quelled her uneasiness about the prolonged sailing, she had enjoyed most of the trip. And knowing how much effort and expense Amelia Keogh had put into the arrangements, she was determined to appreciate every bit of it. She also sensed, even before they'd left home, the faith Jake was wagering for a successful milestone in her restorative path. But there had been times, particularly the unpleasant and unsettling encounters, when it had taken every ounce of will to keep going. What got her through was the profound desire to please Jake; just the thought of disappointing him in any way devastated her.

Then there was the appearance of the woman from Jake's past, Stavrina Papandreou. Callie's thoughts were a confused muddle of sadness, mystification, inadequacy, and dismay, the entire prototype of woman presenting like some kind of alien seductress from another world—one she'd never been a part of and could not possibly fit in. And yet, Jake had dwelled in that place, had been intimate with the woman there, possibly created an embryo of another life from their union. The two universes in which they existed were utterly antithetical. After the run-in with Papandreou, Callie had stood self-consciously in front of the bathroom mirror in their Amorgos suite and looked at herself, thinking of the curvaceous model with her long flowing hair and smoky-shadowed, kohl-lined eyes and sensuously swollen garnet lips, the glamorous designer dress and shoes and jewelry. In stark contrast, her own reflection was one of a slim frame that too often bordered on gaunt, petite breasts and hips; pale skin and small mouth; diminutive stature and unworldly essence. She was so in love with Jake…but what could he see of her that was beautiful or desirable when he had been with the gorgeous and bombastically sexy Papandreou and probably many more of the same caliber?

Without realizing it, tears had formed and rolled down her cheeks. She really wanted to go home, but she was pretty sure Jake was committed to going the whole way, had discussed at great length how beneficial the back end could be for her.

Brushing at her face, she peered out to the water, then back toward the island. Saw the unchanged landscape, the same irrationally calm sea that only rippled in the wind. It was plaintively quiet, but looking and listening, Callie felt an unnerving quiver, as if something in the atmosphere had changed. She peeked at the sky, but found it unwaveringly blue, clouds soft and white and as placid as a flock of sheep.

She sat for several minutes, looking back and forth between boat and water, fidgeting and unsure of what to do. She did not want to doze, did not feel comfortable enough to do that with him gone, so she fit the AirPods into her ears and tapped the music icon on her iPhone. Despite her unease, once again fatigue had the upper hand and it wasn't long before her eyelids drooped, the melodic harmonies of Coldplay resounding about bells ringing and choirs singing and sword and shield.

BELOW THE SURFACE OF the sea, Jake let himself sink naturally for the first ten feet or so, and then began turning in different directions to decide on a course of exploration. Right off, he could see that the fish and coral were not as plentiful and vibrant as those he'd seen in the Caribbean, but the clarity and warmth of the water was about the same, the immersion into the fluid prism of blues a blanket of tranquility. He submerged another twenty feet, which was close to the bottom depth here, and finned along the tops of reefs and volcanic rock formations and fields of green Neptune grass waving with the current. Shoals of fish small and large swirled together and broke apart like billiard balls, scattering to evade the presence of predators. Most seemed fairly indifferent to him.

Within minutes, Jake could already feel the balmy effect of the isolated undersea environment, and knew just how much he needed it. He was aware of how much tension had been building up inside him, especially since Milos; he'd been subconsciously stressed from the very start of their trip, concerned about Callie's level of comfort in all situations, but his stress had risen exponentially with the boat breach and personal encounters. The more recent one with Stavrina pushed him right to the edge. And now, at the end of the honeymoon excursion, he was about to enter into a whole new phase of potential stressors, the ones that he was conditioned for and singularly suited to deal with but for which Callie would bring an element of the unknowable.

Focusing on the scuba experience, he willed his mind to empty of everything else, enjoying the weightless sensation as he moved through the water, the rhythmic sound of his breathing and exhaust bubbles from his regulator augmented by the snaps and pops and grunts of aquatic life. Scissor-tailed damselfish fluttered about, joined by multicolored rainbow wrasse and combers and the occasional parrot-fish. He also saw silvery sea bream and mullet and, tucked in reef cavities, the big mottled-skin dusky grouper and numerous pockets of spiky black sea urchins. He spotted prehistoric-looking scorpion fish with their bulging eyes and poisonous spines and the bloated puffer fish. Near a bank of golden sponge coral, he was torpedoed by a school of barracuda, long and thick silver bullets packed with teeth. He went still, but the aggressive fish raced on past him. Other potentially dangerous species, eels and rays, slithered around and below but kept their distance. He saw dainty seahorses and undulating squids and unintentionally disrupted a massive octopus that had been so well camouflaged against the seabed that he only recognized it when the tentacled appendages began to flail; capable of changing their appearance in chameleon-like fashion hundreds of times an hour, they could be incredibly amorphous.

No longer able to see the hull of the boat, he kept track of his proximity by periodically checking the compass clipped to his BCD and his SUUNTO D6I computer dive watch, but a trail of pottery shards and other fragmented pieces of nautical relics captured his curiosity and lured him farther from his base. He'd read that there were numerous shipwrecks in the vicinity, and just ahead the remnants of a debris field from one of them came into view.

The Fournoi archipelago is geopositioned in a location with both northern and southern currents and is a convergence of two major sailing routes connecting the Aegean to the Black Sea. As such, the islands have seen a voluminous network of trade vessels dating back to the earliest BC centuries. Archaeological archives list the discoveries of over fifty shipwrecks in the corridor, the most in the world, taken down by abrupt changes in the winds and the rocky coastline.

Jake followed the barnacled pieces of amphorae, large jugs that had held everything from wine to fish sauce, pausing to examine some of the more interesting ones. He imagined anything of historical significance had been excavated and was now in the possession of experts in antiquities, but he knew weather and currents could uproot more over time. He came to a rock formation that had closed around a chunk of disintegrated cargo hold framework, creating a small cave. A rust-encrusted iron anchor as big as he was lay wedged near the opening, and he advanced to get a closer look. Paddling along the anchor chain and skeletonic timbers and drifting further into the shrouded hollow, he noticed a partially intact metal chest, variegated seaweed fingering from its top. He was picking through the outgrowth to see what might be secreted underneath when he sensed a change in the displacement of water behind him, heard a faint clink within the sound cloud of his inhalations and exhalations. Then, a distinct tug, a muffled wisp, and air stopped flowing to his regulator, water spurting into his mouth.

He twisted backward, the other end of the hose thrashing loose like a severed electrical wire, air bubbles exploding into the water. Before he could turn fully around, something slashed beside him and a thin string of red spiraled out, which he instantly realized was blood—*his* blood. His mind scrambled to assimilate some kind of reaction as adrenaline surged to put it into play. Backpedaling, he grabbed the regulator for his secondary air source, the octo from a pocket on the front of his BCD, and stuck it in his mouth, the yellow hose curling over his shoulder. He blew to clear it and air filled his lungs as he looked through the jets escaping the black hose of his primary, his eyes behind the mask widening in shock as he saw another diver positioned in front of him, knife in hand.

What the fuck?

The diver moved forward and lunged, knife thrust toward Jake's neck.

17

WHAT THE FUCK? JAKE'S brain demanded again, colliding with the next thought, which wondered where this guy could have possibly come from since there had been no other boats in the cove. But the urgent necessity for action flushed all of his shock and wonder for the onslaught of physical directives to defend himself. Jake pulled back and put space between himself and the other diver as he unsheathed his titanium Argonaut knife. A quick look over his shoulder reaffirmed what he already knew; the only way out of the cavern was the way he had come in, a way his attacker now blocked.

Son of a bitch...what the fucking hell.

The other diver was a hulking specimen, at least six feet in height with massive chunks of muscle straining the skin of his Cressi wetsuit, and he wasted no time taking further stock of Jake, advancing into the gap Jake had created between them.

Jake brought his knife up just in time to catch the guy's blade striking out again, and forcefully extended his arm to drive it back. They parried for a few minutes with their respective blades, strikes and blocks alternating with Jake holding his position—which wasn't saying much as he had nowhere to go but against the rock wall or through the attacker and, clearly, that was not happening without either a well-timed fake out or a supreme amount of clout.

While moving underwater might look graceful and fluidly balletic, and the combination of body weight and dive gear combines for neutral buoyancy, the weight of the water is double that of the surface, making even the simplest maneuvers feel like they are being executed in a wind tunnel. Add stress or exertion to the mix and it does not take long for fatigue to set in but, even as Jake was starting to slow and sag from the pressurizing effects, his breaths coming heavier and heavier, his opponent seemed superhumanly impervious.

In a determined foray to get out of the confined area, Jake launched an aggressive offensive, swinging his arm overhead and swiping down. His blade struck the attacker's upper arm, and a new stream of blood oozed into the blue. Taking advantage of the blow's disruption in the joisting, Jake shoved past the brute into the open water, kicking his legs to propel himself several yards away before he flipped around to get another look at the other diver.

It was a fleeting one, his opponent slamming into him like a battering linebacker, knife raised to strike again. Jake reached to his dive belt for the eSpear, jabbing it toward the man's chest and pressing the trigger. The spear's baton sprang out and emitted a charge that generated an electrical field effective only on a shark's sensitive ampullae, but when the tip came in contact with a human as it did now, a shock resulted. Though dispensing only a moderate jolt, it was enough to stun his opponent, affording Jake the opportunity he needed to give the guy a taste of his own tactics, slicing the air hose to his tank. He would have liked to cut the secondary while he was at it, but the man reacted quickly, connecting to his octo in the same way Jake had done.

Unsurprisingly, the move enraged his attacker, who converged with a renewed intent of deadly mission, stabbing at Jake as if he were the hapless victim in a slasher flick, some of the jabs cutting him. He felt the stings, saw the swirls of red drifting around him like incense, but was glad to see the consistency in strings rather than ropes, the color translucent. But he was tiring rapidly, shedding energy with every second, each breath seeming to take more from him than what it gave back. He had to end this.

Realizing that the fight had migrated over a shelf with a steep drop-off, he knew he would need to keep from being forced to a deeper depth, but within minutes that is exactly what his opponent managed to do, rising over top of him and then driving him down. As he swam in patterns to evade contact, the hulk blocking any path of ascent, it occurred to Jake that he'd already been about halfway into his dive time when the assault began, meaning he probably had less than half of his air left—actually, a good bit less than half. A standard six-and-a-half-pound tank held about eighty cubic feet of compressed air at 3000 PSI, which would last roughly an hour on a typical dive and in favorable conditions, favorable meaning at a depth of ten meters, or thirty feet, and without duress. Jake figured they were now at least forty feet and he was definitely under duress.

He took a quick look at his gauge and realized the hose connecting it to his tank had also been cut, but a minute later the remaining volume became irrelevant when his attacker descended on him in an impossibly locomotive burst and launched another round of knife sparring. Fatigue had become a secondary opponent for Jake, his offensive moves less and less effective, and it only took a few strikes for the hulk to knock Jake's knife from his hand.

Watching it slip toward the abyss, Jake debated going after it, but the decision was made when the hulk made a grab for him. Concentrating all of his energy on the guy's knife hand, Jake snatched his wrist and squeezed as hard as he could. As he did, he glared into his attacker's mask, hostility seething from the dark eyes staring back at him. And then the man's fist unclenched and the knife he'd been gripping also fell below.

They were now on an even battlefield again, brute-on-brute force, and Jake felt a resurgence of will. They wrestled for dominance, swapping arm holds and neck locks, looping legs and elbows. Until the hulk managed to get his hand on Jake's octo hose and yank it hard enough to wrench it free of the tank, leaving Jake with no primary or secondary air.

Having been subjected to innumerable dire situations, both militarily and in his so-called civilian life, Jake was predisposed not to panic, but the adrenaline infusion that had been fueling his fight momentarily threatened to trigger a rise until he remembered his Spare Air. Paddling backwards from his opponent, Jake removed the small black canister from the holster on his vest, put the regulator in his mouth, blew out, and resumed breathing. But with only three cubic feet of air in the miniature tank, or approximately fifty-seven breaths depending on the individual and the conditions, he knew he definitely had to end it now.

Fight or flight, this was it.

With a very imminent expiration on his last air supply, he chose flight, kicking to rise. Before he could gain much ascension, gloved fists as hard and heavy as lead weights grabbed him by the ankles and yanked him back down, farther down than he had been. For several seconds that seemed like minutes, he was held in abeyance as he fought with his arms winging ineffectually in the water mass, critically aware that each second was another breath squandered. He continued to fight, kicking and clawing, until his legs were finally released.

But he was given no time to make another break for the top.

The other diver was coming directly at him yet again, and this time, instead of facing off, Jake swam behind him and got one arm around his upper chest and the other crooked under his chin. He kept his own head turned to the side, knowing he ran the risk of having the Spare Air knocked away. With every bit of strength he could summon, Jake squeezed against the man's carotid, which also dislodged the octo regulator. Incredibly, he managed to break free of Jake's hold, replace his regulator, and swipe a gloved hand that looked to be the size of a baseball mitt, hitting the can of Spare Air and popping it free.

Jake watched in desperation as the black cylinder with the bright yellow logo rolled in the current, air bubbles streaming from the regulator like a whirlpool jet, propelling it farther and farther away. Even if he could have caught up to it, there would be little or no air left.

The reality of finality bit hard into his psyche.

His *only* choice now was to ascend as quickly and safely as he could—and hope he had enough air in his lungs to do so. But his opponent was just as determined to stop the escape, wrapping his arms around Jake's body, pinioning his arms. Jake's mind spun into a furious dual mode of calculating how much time he had holding his breath and what he could do to not only extricate himself from the brute but also take him out to put an end to the fight. His lungs were already starting to ache, his arms and legs turning rubbery. Despite his best resolution for bravado and endurance, the life force holding his core together was deteriorating.

Rather than expend more time and energy in countermoves, Jake's right arm strained for the eSpear that still hung from the clip on his belt, working the device up into his hand until he had the baton end in his fist, and plunged it backward. He heard a garbled grunt, the muscular vise around him released, and Jake saw that he'd succeeded in impaling the man's thigh. Arterial blood was seeping out in ruby-red geysers, each jet depleting heart and brain function like a running garden hose.

As his opponent realized what was happening, he executed one last vindictive deed in an effort to seal Jake's fate, yanking his own octo hose from the tank. His entire body drooped and he began to drift away like an inflatable car lot air dancer.

Quickly, Jake swam to him, grabbed and pinched the end of the loose hose and snatched the regulator still in the man's slackened mouth, put it into his own and received whatever air remained. It was not much. Then, glancing up, the more luminous water toward the surface seeming a long way away, he started the ascent.

In an emergency out-of-air situation, what would seem the most obvious thing to do, continue holding your breath, was actually the very thing *not* to do as it could cause collapsed or overexpanded lungs. What you did—and what Jake had trained for—was stay calm, above all, and after taking that last breath of air, swim slowly to the surface while making a kind of audible exclamation. Like a scream.

Rising through streams and swirls of fish, Jake blew out his breath.

EXCEEDINGLY FIT, JAKE WAS a strong and agile swimmer and diver with healthy and capacious lungs, but the intensity of the battle with a freakishly strong opponent at a depth well south of his intended range had taken a lot out of him. Whether he made it to the surface on his last breath or came up short was out of his control physically, his resolve to prevail the only leverage he had, but that survival instinct was an indomitable one and had not failed him—yet.

Ordinarily, such an ascent took perhaps a minute or two and was an easy feat for Jake on a single breath, but his lungs were burning and he was lightheaded with a fog of disorientation that had set in once the confrontation was over and adrenaline began to bleed off. For every foot he rose, the surface appeared to extend farther.

As he continued to rise through the water, even as he was able to mostly remain calm and believe that he was going to make it, a worm of doom gnawed through and, over the span of what seemed interminable, suggested he might not. And then he was injected with an impulse of horror that was so hot and bright and seizing that it felt as though he'd been zapped by a high-voltage current.

This guy was not alone…there had to be others. What was happening on his boat? What were they doing to Callie?

Oh fuck, oh fuck, oh fuck…oh God, please get me up. Get me up, get me up, get me up…

The pain in his lungs, in his chest, in his head, became almost unbearable in the last seconds, and a blaring white light blinded him as he felt the complete absence of air at once suffocate and ventilate him, burning and then bursting.

No, no, no…Callie…no! Not going to take me, not going to…

His head and shoulders broke the surface and he heaved, spitting sea water that he had ingested in the final seconds of his ascent, at first unable to take in any of the air. When he did, the initial inhalation was painful and he commanded his brain to slow down, control the greed of his breaths, at which point the stark purity of sweet relief came in a rush. Yanking his dive mask off and blinking in the sunlight, he frantically glanced around, looking for the Jeanneau. He was taken aback to find it quite a distance off and began to swim toward it, his mind swarming with escalating horror. As he stroked through the water, he looked for another boat, but saw none.

How could that be? The diver who had almost managed to kill him could not have just materialized out of nowhere…and yet, apparently, he had. But as Jake continued to swim for the *Psamathe*, as he closed the distance and it became bigger in his vision, the dread of certain tragedy consumed him.

When he reached the stern of the boat, he hoisted himself up onto the swim platform and immediately saw that the lounge was empty— no Callie. He wrestled out of his BCD, the drained air tank dropping and rolling across the wood floor with a hollow clank. In his haste, he forgot to unstrap his fins, stumbling at the cockpit table and fumbling to get them off his feet. Then he scrambled down the stairs to the saloon belowdecks.

He did not see her.

"Callie!" he called out, his initial vocal coming out in a hoarse croak. Louder and more full-throated, he bellowed, *"Callie!"* and tore his way past the galley, bare feet thumping on the teak panels. In the doorway of the master cabin, he found her seated on the floor at an end corner of the queen-size bed, tucked next to a storage cabinet, arms around her drawn up knees.

On hearing his voice, she had looked up, her eyes wide and face full of apprehension. For a moment, she did not move.

"Baby," Jake rasped, taking a knee and putting one hand on her shoulder, the other cupping her chin. Relief flooded through him in a lava of raw exhilaration as his brain began to recalibrate to the here-and-now, heart still pounding and amplified in his ears. "Hey, you okay? What's happened? What's wrong?"

She was staring open-mouthed at his face, words not coming.

"What happened?" he asked again, throttling the heavy breaths working up from his belabored lungs to his throat.

Though she was clearly traumatized by something—or someone— her first response was correlated to him. "Jake…Jake, you're hurt?"

He leaned back and touched his neck and face absently, hand coming away bloodied. Glanced down and saw the gashes on his arms, oozing and drizzling red. "Oh, no, love. I'm okay." Fumbling for something to tell her, he said, "I just scraped some coral." He reached for her hand and stood.

Coming to her feet, she continued to look at him in alarm, eyes shifting from his head to his torso and legs.

Before she could say anything, Jake turned the concern back on her. "What happened, angel?"

Fear rebloomed in her face. "He was here…he was here!"

"What? Who was here?"

Now she looked down uncertainly, her voice becoming small. "I don't know…I thought…I saw him. I was really tired. Maybe I fell asleep and had one of those bad dreams." She stopped and he waited patiently until she went on, saying, "It didn't feel like a dream."

"What do you mean?"

"Everything was dark, like it was nighttime, but that didn't make sense because I knew you would have been back. He…he was moving around, in the dark, and then…" She broke off, the remembrance crystallizing with inflating panic.

Jake was riveted, his reactive thoughts springing off in opposite directions—was what she was telling him a dream or something that had really happened while she was in a non-REM sleep state? Seeing her anxiety ticking up even more, he placed his hands on her arms and said, "Take a breath…you're all right," subliminally telling himself the same thing.

"He was coming for me and…"

She stopped again, and Jake's patience eroded but he kept his demeanor equable. "And what?"

"I don't know what happened. I don't remember. It's like everything went black and then I was down here. I wanted to go up and look for you, but I was afraid."

He took her in his arms, feeling the soreness in his muscles and tendons. In a soothing voice, he said, "Okay, everything is all right."

But he was far from sure of that and felt a pressing need to establish their security. He guided her to the bed.

"I want you to lay down and try to relax while I go up top and get out of my suit, tend to my gear. Then I'm going to get a shower and get cleaned up."

He bent over her, in that moment wanting badly to just hold her, kiss her, be inside her and connected to what fueled the core of his existence. To reestablish that he was alive, had survived yet another very close evasion from death, to feel the blood flowing and his heart and lungs pumping for the essence of life and not the battle for it. But instead, he brushed his lips lightly on her forehead and padded back through the saloon, up the stairs, and to the deck. He fetched his Steiner binoculars from the cockpit and put them to his eyes, panning in all directions. Seeing nothing but the desolate shore of Fournoi and the barren Icarian sea that stretched beyond.

WITH THE WATER FROM the spray nozzle of the starboard walk-in shower washing over him, Jake inspected the knife cuts on his body. He'd chosen to use this head over the one in the master cabin to prevent Callie from getting a closer look at his wounds, some of which were not insignificant, a few bleeding. Thankfully, none were serious enough to require more than basic treatment and bandaging, though one laceration had not only nicked a blood vessel but also cut into his collarbone and needed a Steri-Strip. Out of the shower, he dressed in cargo shorts and t-shirt and took a seat at the nav station to evaluate the weather. He was anxious to move on but had to make sure the wind speeds in the north had decreased.

His apps indicated that while the forecast had improved somewhat, the current conditions were still volatile. He gave it some thought and decided to venture out under power and judge for himself, knowing he could duck into another cove if need be. His real reason for being eager to resume sail had nothing to do with time; he wanted to survey the boats in the vicinity, see if he could find any that might be waiting for a diver who would not be returning to their craft. Enough time had passed for the guy's cohorts to probably be coming to that realization, maybe conduct a search and then depart.

Who the hell were they and what had prompted the ultimate aggression on him? With that escalation, which cast a glaring light on all of his prior suspicions, he had to find out—if he was under threat, so was Callie.

Motoring near the coast, Jake's focus was divided between navigation and looking for other boats. As before, he sighted some in the distance toward Thymena and approached a cluster in the northern coves where a string of beaches preceded the city center. He steered the *Psamathe* with one hand on the wheel and the other on his binoculars, aiming them from one vessel to the next, only seeing the normal activity of couples and families and tourists, captains and clientele, fishing and frolicking and placidly sunbathing. And because he was casing the boats he expected to see, he almost missed the one he should have actually been looking for.

He had set the binos down when something on the portside caught his eye, a shallow dark shape afloat that he instantly recognized because he'd operated in many of them—a Duratane tube FC-hull RIB, more formerly known as a rigid inflatable boat. Widely used in all amphibious branches of the military the world over, RIBs were versatile and lightweight but fast and durable. As much as he wanted and needed to maintain the calm that was just beginning to settle in after Callie's daysleep terror—if that's what it was—he needed to find out what he could about that RIB a lot more. Because he knew this was the apparatus that had brought his attacker, no doubt about it.

He steered the Jeanneau toward it, slowing and idling the engine when he was alongside. It sat bobbing in the water, tethered by an anchor, a black Zodiac about fourteen feet in length. Callie turned around on the settee to see what he was looking at and why he had stopped.

"It's okay," he said in a measured tone, "I just wanted to make sure nothing was wrong here. It looks abandoned, though."

It's abandoned, all right, he thought. From the cockpit, he could see down inside the inflatable, but spotted only a few bottles of water. If he boarded it, he might find a gun or radio stashed somewhere, but he knew that would be pushing his ostensible welfare check a bit too far.

He eased away and opened up his engine's throttle, surging forward.

Jake's mind spun up with an array of speculations, all of which seemed improbable to him, if not absurd or extreme. But an unknown assassin attacking him underwater off a desolate coast *was* pretty extreme.

Aware of Callie watching him uneasily, he inhaled deeply and tried to clear the tangle of troubling thoughts from his head, glancing over with a smile.

"You okay, sweetie?"

She told him she was and he returned his attention to the petulant Icarian Sea, which was still rough, pitching and heaving in the heavy winds. He maneuvered around the islet of Kisiria to the lee side of Thymena, went off power, and raised the mainsail. After handling the boat for ten minutes or so, he decided he would attempt to continue, the remaining stretch to Ikaria only about five nautical miles. He unrolled a third of the genoa and felt the wind take hold, pushing the Jeanneau's speed to a robust nine knots. As he steered west to the open channel, the big waves became wider, making passage over them smoother.

Just clear of the southern end of Kisiria, he began to pick up a familiar sound almost lost in the thrum of the wind in his ears. He glanced up, the sun filtered through his Outlaw shades but producing enough glare to prevent him from seeing what he knew was generating the sound.

A helicopter.

18

LISTENING TO THE DISTANT throp, Jake felt a prickly sensation that seemed to light up both muscle and mental memory, not only of what had just happened but also bringing more distinctive dimensions to what had been happening over the recent days. And even as he knew a random helicopter could be just that, random, and just like the guy on the beach who tried to engage with Callie in Milos could have actually been a random guy on the beach, part of him always outright rejected such a thing as coincidence; it was an inherent skepticism that encroached from his operator predilections.

As the boat bounced over the waves and sped along on the wind, Jake squinted into the sunlight and tried to get a visual on the helo but did not. At least not in the sky.

His thoughts looped back to his probe of the underwater assassin, adding the RIB into the analysis, which tended to imply a military background or training. Not to mention, a RIB could be deployed from a helo. Could his attacker have been a solitary European soldier of fortune pursuing the bounty on his head? Or someone and something else altogether? A helo in the mix suggested something else; to his mind, it upgraded the enterprise to likely that of a group. A killing squad?

Several minutes later, after clearing the northwest peninsula of Thymena, he spotted the large ship he'd seen earlier in the south that, even from a distance did not look anything like a fishing boat or pleasure cruiser. It was under sail, moving at a good clip to the northeast. He was too far away to see much detail, but he was able to identify by shape something on its deck—a helicopter.

Coincidence? He thought not.

Badly wishing he could take off in pursuit of the vessel for at least a closer look, he knew that would be a foolhardy gambit in these weather conditions, the big boat outpacing him only by a knot or two but much steadier in the water with its engines and build. So he took out his phone, grabbed a couple of images, and stayed on his western course. Remembering what Callie had said about seeing a man on board—in her mind, any intrusive man, real or imagined, would always be Valentín—Jake pulled up the app for the monitoring devices to see what had been recorded while he'd been underwater.

He was relieved to find that Callie's was the only human image present in the video, but it was hard for him to watch her in the throes of what he had witnessed many times before at their home—a panic attack occurring while she was still groggy from sleep, stumbling and almost falling on the steps from the deck to the saloon and then staggering to the master cabin and crawling into a ball by the foot of the bed. Regret bit deep, knowing that if he'd not gone on the dive, he would have averted the deadly encounter and been there for Callie, to prevent or mitigate her panic. That was followed by the harrowing thought that if he had not gone on the dive, the guy might have attacked him on the boat and gone after them both. Jake would have probably shot him, since he was always armed with his Glock when he wasn't in the water, but he might have been able to gain some intel from the body. On the other hand, there would have been a body, the violence that preceded death on full display for Callie to witness and carry over into future terror-filled dreams.

He looked at her, curled up on the cockpit settee, her gaze on the water sloshing by as the Jeanneau's bow cut through it like a speeding porpoise, vowing for the countless time that he would do anything to protect her—and feeling the sickening dagger of truth that it might not always be in his power.

THEY REACHED THE SHORES of Ikaria, their final honeymoon port of call, as the sun was in the midst of its slow dissolve across the sky, the white tumble of marina village fronted by the usual harbor esplanade and backed by a swell of mountainous landscape. The high winds had made Jake's approach to Agios Kirikos one of the more challenging he'd undertaken over the course of their entire trip, the northeast gusts pushing him out and requiring three attempts to get perpendicular to the pier and into his reserved slip at the marina. When he was finally successful and had tossed his lines to the dockhand, he set about to gather all of his gear topside while Callie collected some of the carry-ons and totes from below. Since this was their destination port and the owner of the *Psamathe* had made arrangements for it to be sailed back to Mykonos, Jake transported their luggage and gear to the Jeep Renegade rental parked by the end of the pier, loaded everything up, and set off to the south.

The ninety-minute drive to the hotel took them along the southern coastal road and then across the island through the Randi Forest, towering pines and oak trees hundreds of years old bordering the Sierra Atheras to the west. Reaching the northern coast at Evdilos, they continued on the Agiou Kirikou-Armenisti road to their hotel, the Toxotis Villas. Overall, it was a long, winding route bypassing numerous villages, verdant hills and steep slopes and stretches of shoreline below, and by the time Jake pulled onto the grounds of Toxotis, both were exhausted. As she'd done with every other resort, Amelia Keogh had ensured they were booked into the most luxurious and romantic accommodations which, in this case, turned out to be a self-contained stone-cobbled chalet with a spacious terrace and private saltwater pool, the vista overlooking sea affording horizon silhouettes of Samos, Mykonos, and Chios.

Even though Jake had managed to slip back into the lockstep of his typical equanimity, he could not rally much enthusiasm for an evening out, opting for a dinner the hotel appropriated for them. Afterward, they relaxed in the pool and reclined on the loungers by the balcony, watching the sun bleed out in a spill of reds and oranges over the water. A three-quarter moon now presided in the twilight sky, surface topography visible in its bright illumination. Waves crashed against the rocks below them, both lost in their own thoughts.

Jake had caught Callie peering pensively at him several times and while he knew his explanation for injury had been pretty flimsy, he doubted she disbelieved him. That did not mean she didn't wonder how he'd managed to get so cut up. Not being transparent with her wasn't something he intended—he was nothing if not brutally honest by nature—but being discretionary with what he shared or revealed about his work or the collateral consequences that infiltrated his personal life because of it was always going to be a judgment call to minimize her anxiety.

Casting a sidelong glance at Callie's face, soft and pale in the moonlight, Jake stood, held his hand out to her, and led the way back into the cottage.

The interior was a blend of modern and bucolic styles, the furnishings simple, the décor monochromatically earthy; walls and floors in stucco and stone, lamps and rugs in jute and rattan. Without words, Jake stripped down to his briefs and began undressing Callie, slowly and erotically, kissing her with a whisper-light touch of his lips on her skin as he worked his way down her body. His fingers slid under the straps of her white sundress and eased it off. The slow, gentle touching made both of them quiver.

But in bed, there was an almost guttural urgency in Jake's lovemaking that had been building from the emotions he had kaleidoscoped through in the aftermath of the murderous attack, when he'd been fighting to get his next breath and to make it to the boat to protect Callie. Life-and-death edges and precipices and free falls were always a hormonal cocktail of both ends of the experience, from the explosive and streaming currents of adrenaline to the wash of endorphins that brought mental and physical release and relief, and his passion this night was much the same. When the second wave came, it flowed with the initial tenderness but also a kind of intense desperation to hold on to the scale and peak until the last possible second, as if it were the last moment of life.

Deep inside, fire and silk, resistance and surrender and then, the mourning of separation.

As they lay together face to face, Jake traced a fingertip around her forehead and cheeks and slid it inside the coil of a curl. He looked into her eyes until she blinked down. "You have no idea how beautiful you are," he said.

He felt moisture on his hand, closed in and kissed her, tasting the salt of tears.

"What's wrong, sweetheart?"

She was touching his arms and, he realized, some of the lacerations he'd sustained in the attack. "I don't want anything to happen to you," she murmured. "You can't—"

He pulled her against him, cradling her head in the curve of his neck, careful to avoid the bandaged side, which was sore as hell. "Nothing is going to happen to me," he said, and even as the avowal left his mouth, he felt the monumental guilt of his lie.

THE FINAL DAY OF their honeymoon jaunt was everything newly married happiness should be, but above all, it was without any perceivable peril. They explored the widely untamed Ikarian countryside, put at ease by the placidity of a people known for an eccentric but mellow lifestyle that took a majority of them well toward three-digit birthdays. Known as one of the five "blue zones" in the world, a place where the life expectancy is at least ten years longer than typical, it shared the peaceful and healthy vibe of Costa Rica, making them both nostalgic for home. Callie did not repeat her yearning aloud, but Jake felt her emotional longing empathetically throughout the day, which did nothing to uproot the seeds of doubt beginning to germinate in his mind.

But both were able to embrace and savor the day for what it was, another romantic memory in the making, strolling the ruins of Artemis Temple, sampling the wines of Afianes in the terraced hills, wandering the village square of Christos Raches, and standing near the rock where, according to Greek mythology, Icarus flew too close to the sun, lost his wings and fell into the sea. They held hands on the stony overlook, the turquoise sea and sky brilliant in the late-day light, and Jake gazed at Callie beside him. The wind was making an enchanting mess of her curls and infusing her cheeks with rosy color, the skirt of her floral dress billowing around her legs, and he thought his heart might burst with joy. Forgotten in that moment were all the stressors of their trip, starting with the bullet that had whizzed by his head before they'd left home and almost ending him a second time yesterday beneath the waters of the Aegean. In thought instead were all the beautiful sights they had beheld, all the sweet moments they'd shared, all the spiritual and sensual depths and heights and intensities. He looked at her and could not imagine ever being more in love. She looked back at him, her pale golden hair lifting and swirling in the breeze, pink lips forming the diminutive smile that had smitten him in the beginning and ever since, and he knew she was feeling the same.

Leaving the landmark, Jake drove the south coast road to the northern tip of the island, crossing through rolling green terrain to the airport. There, they boarded a King Air 350 charter and waited for takeoff.

Peering nervously through the window, Callie seemed to be processing the fact that a significant transition was underway. The vacuum of the plane's engines filled the cabin, causing her to tense in her seat. Turning to Jake, she asked, "Are we going home now?" Her wide brown eyes were brimming with the guileless hope of a child asking to be excused from dinner though vegetables remained uneaten on the plate.

He paused before answering, then gave her a smile that reflected more optimism than he felt. Because he wasn't sure how he felt at this point. In a measured voice, he replied, "Not yet," and added, "we'll talk about it."

Her expression clouded with uncertainty. Jake squeezed her hand and she lay her head against his shoulder.

The turboprop rumbled and rolled forward and, with Callie tightly gripping Jake's hand, it gathered speed and abruptly ran out of runway, nosing up over the sea, flying toward the setting sun and the shores of Chios.

19

WHEN THEY TOUCHED DOWN at the Chios airport, Omiros, with its single runway that ran directly parallel to the coast and, surrounded by green turf looked a bit like a golf fairway, dusk had gilded the landscape in shades of copper and bronze. Again met by agents from the ground handler, Jake and Callie were standing by the trolley with their luggage in the FBO's lounge when a brazen voice called out, "Honeymoon Express!" The cadence and twang revealed its source before Jake turned to see Nash Remington striding toward them.

Clad in snug Wrangler bootcut jeans, a tobacco-colored t-shirt taut over the muscles of his biceps and chest, and a brown leather Stetson, Remington was flashing a mouthful of teeth as he grinned at the couple. He appraised them both, Callie in the high-low white-and-floral print dress and espadrilles, Jake in black Bonobo slim fit chinos and a black double-pocket button-up shirt, then gave Callie a delicate hug and embraced Jake more hardily with a slap on the back.

Stepping away, Remington studied him closer, locking eyes and nodding his approval. He did not have to comment, the curve of Jake's mouth and the essence he gave off telling him all he needed to know. But within seconds, much too soon, the expression and countenance of a contented man in love melded into one of cool inscrutability, and Remington intuitively knew something was up. He continued to eye his friend, not missing the bandage just inside the collar of his Armani shirt and also noting the small stripes of dried blood on both of his arms.

Looking a question to Jake, who shook his head imperceptibly, Remington addressed Callie, saying, "Darlin', you look absolutely radiant. Having a good time here?"

In truth, he thought she appeared drained, her face a little too pallid below the sunburn, raising his level of inquisitiveness to one of more concern.

Keanjaho Dmello was waiting for them outside the FBO in a gray Jeep Gladiator. He was beating a rhythm with his fingers on the steering wheel to local pop in the form of a song by Nikos Economopoulos on the radio, eyes shaded by sunglasses, his hair coiffed in intricate dreadlocks. At the sight of Remington with Jake and Callie, he swung his door open and jumped out to help the baggage agent load everything into the Gladiator's open cargo bed. He, too, greeted the couple with big smiles and hugs before retaking his position in the driver's seat, starting up the engine and pulling onto the airport's frontage road. Dmello drove like a local, effortlessly making all the navigational maneuvers and accelerating smoothly in sync with the work-time traffic, motoring south along a two-lane cordoned by stacked rock walls and eventually winding up next to a two-toned stone structure that looked like a cross between fortress and castle, the Greek and European Union flags flying from a battlement over the elevated entrance.

The Argentikon Luxury Suites, a palatial estate built in the sixteenth century, is a five-star treasure steeped in Genoese aristocracy, originally the summer residence for the Argenti family and restored throughout the decades as a prestigiously awarded historical monument that has accommodated royalty, diplomats, and world leaders. The estate is made up of a palazzo and two guest houses, whitewashed in plaster that is finished in what is known in architecture as the xysto technique, wherein geometric shapes are scraped from the façade. Outside, within its high stone walls, are pathways shaded by a variety of trees and arches, pebbled courtyards containing elaborate cisterns decorated with marble motifs and spouts, and spectacular Ligurian gardens that include citrus trees and roses. Massive entrance gates herald the coat-of-arms, and inside the grand reception rooms and hallways, suites and hospitality facilities, are appointed in rich, old-world craftsmanship, the furnishings and décor of which reflect the elegance of bygone eras.

The suite reserved for Jake and Callie was called the Kampos and encompassed a living room, bedroom, and Jacuzzi bath, the living room dominated by an engraved marble fireplace backed by a fieldstone column and a built-in wall of shelves and desk. The beam ceiling and floor were mahogany, area rugs, drapes, and bedding in empirical reds and golds; the bath gleamed in mottled marble.

After being personally and fastidiously attended by the manager, who went through the suite with them to make sure even the most minute detail was to their satisfaction, Jake and Callie freshened up and headed out to one of the courtyards. They had barely taken a few steps when Eddie Falcone and Curran Niles darted out, accosting them with a fusillade of affections and exaltations, mostly lavished on Callie. Both wore Bermuda-length shorts, Falcone in a red polo shirt, Niles in a Hellenic-patterned blue-and-white Kenny Flowers, their hair damp from showers taken after time in the hotel pool. Nash Remington strode around the corner behind them, Keanjaho Dmello joined by Efron Kipnis on his flank, all observing the feeding frenzy with amusement. A pair of Belgian Malinois dogs trotted placidly alongside, their heads on tilt toward Remington, ready for command.

"What do you think of this place?" Niles gushed breathlessly. "Wicked, yeah? So how was the boat? Was it really windy? Did you eat any octopus? What was your favorite island?"

Jake admonished, "Hey, go easy, okay?"

"Sorry, sorry," Niles muttered, "just want to hear about everything."

Jake knelt down to pet the two canines who wiggled and nuzzled and licked in happy remembrance. Introducing them to Callie, whose face lit up in delight, he said, "This is Luna and Solis."

"They're beautiful," she cooed, stroking their jowls and ears.

His arm around Callie, Jake strolled into the gardens, the others following. Even in the early-evening moonlight, color burst along every path from the multitude of rosebushes covered in flower. Callie halted and gaped, her mouth parted in wonder.

"Jake…"

He smiled knowingly. "I see, baby."

Tentatively, she ventured away from him to get a closer look, her hands reverently cupping blooms on the bushes. She glanced back, as if to implore him to make the same connection. Watching her, Jake got it, knew the emotions she was feeling.

Remington sidled up to Jake but said nothing. After a few moments of contemplative silence, he said, "She's missing home."

Jake sighed. "Oh yeah. She wants to *go* home."

"Having second thoughts?"

When Jake did not respond, Remington said, "Come on, let's get a drink…talk."

SEATED BENEATH A SHADED lattice supported by stone arches on one side and capital-topped columns on the other, the white-linen-draped table had been cleared of dinner plates, glasses refilled, linen-wrapped chairs askew. Falcone and Niles had peeled a reluctant Callie away with an invitation to resume touring the grounds. Jake had encouraged her to accompany them so he could speak more candidly with Remington, Dmello, and Kipnis.

Remington took a hefty swallow of whiskey and gave Jake a long, pained look. "Jesus," he huffed. "Sorry, brother, but I can see you've been through it. Yeah, you have that glow of love and satisfied swagger, but what the hell happened?" He fingered a place in the vicinity of his own collarbone to indicate the bandage on Jake's.

The trio listened with growing incredulity and shock as Jake chronicled the underwater attack. When he had finished the recitation, he slumped back against his chair, feeling frayed but relieved from the confession, and drained the last of his gin and tonic.

"Jesus Christ," Remington repeated.

"Who the fuck is this?" Jake looked from face to face but found no sign of enlightenment. He glanced pointedly at Kipnis, who shrugged, expression bland in his typical cryptic demeanor.

"If you're asking if it's the hit," he supplied, "I honestly don't know. Possible, yes…my guess, no."

"Why?"

"For me, doesn't track."

"Then who? What?" Jake asked.

Folding his cloth napkin in precise angles, Kipnis said, "I've been mining for intel on the shooter and assassination attempt since we left Costa Rica but—and it aggrieves me to admit this because there's almost no breadcrumb I can't find and analyze seventy thousand ways to Sunday—but it's been a dry hole."

Jake stared at him, dark eyes lasered with resolute inquisition.

Meeting his gaze with forbearing and honesty, Kipnis said, "I'm sorry, Jake. I am staying on it. What's happened here adds a new layer, to be sure. It might be connected, and if it is, that could provide the thread I need. If it's not, we'll expand the investigation."

He turned to Remington. "The linkup with my guy is all set."

"Linkup?" Jake asked.

"For arms," Remington answered.

Nodding, Jake went quiet, peering haplessly at the wedge of lime in his empty glass. A server magically appeared, replacing their drinks, and for several moments they sipped and mulled privately. Dmello was the first one to break the silence, saying, "I need to make some inquiries on that LZ." Excusing himself, he rose and left the table.

Remington and Kipnis scooted their chairs closer to Jake's, Remington filling him in on the state of execution for their endeavor. Jake's eyes drifted to the three figures in dim shadow moving about the gardens beyond them, his thoughts and emotions in conflict over what to do with Callie.

AT BREAKFAST, SPREADING SUNSHINE revealing the morning glory of the gardens they'd seen through the ghostly glow of moonlight, Jake addressed Falcone and Niles with the same austerity he would have manifest had he been reading them in on a mission plan. For their part, they took heed with as much, if not more earnestness than they would have given to the same.

Because he was entrusting them with what he held most dear in the world...Callie.

"You need to be aware of your surroundings at all times," Jake was instructing, his face rigid, voice deep and stern. "And just because you don't see a threat, does not mean one doesn't exist." He looked from one to the other. "You know that, right?"

They both nodded solemnly. It was early—as far as they were concerned, about three hours earlier than what they would have considered a civilized breakfast time—and their still-sleepy faces reflected the effort it took to fully concentrate, an observation not lost on Jake who was talking with the slow deliberation of an adult to children with attention-deficit disorder.

"Plan your movements, assess everyone around you. Stay away from crowds." He went on to explain Callie's fears and triggers, describing the signs to watch for that preceded an onset of anxiety or panic. Advising them on how to handle her in that situation made him want to call it off, but he could not take her on the excursion he would be making with Remington this morning; it was either a sightseeing outing with Falcone and Niles or leaving her alone at the hotel. He'd almost been inclined to choose the latter, but knowing there was just as much chance of her having some kind of episode here convinced him to put her in their care.

He continued, "Be mindful of anyone paying too much attention to you or who seems too friendly." He eyed them again, taking measure of their confidence.

Niles chuckled, a little too giddily. "Mate. We'll be fine, all right?"

Jake glared at him with an intensity that dissolved all attempts at levity, fraught from nervousness or not. "Okay," he said finally. Heaved a sigh laden with affliction, and stood, striding toward the gardens where Callie was once again admiring the roses.

Falcone scowled at Niles.

"What?"

"Don't be so flip. He's deadly serious."

"Don't you think I know that?" Niles retorted. "He'll crush our bollocks if we screw this up."

"That will be the least of our fates if we screw this up."

Falcone and Niles watched as Jake spoke with Callie, saw her glance uncertainly at them and then back at Jake, her sweet face full of pleading. After a few minutes, the two of them headed in their direction and they heard Jake say, "I'm sorry, baby, I need you to stay with Eddie and Curran for a little while. Remy and I have some business to take care of."

"I can't go with you?"

"No, love. But we shouldn't be gone long. Probably just a few hours."

He gave her a tender look that, at least for the moment, seemed to take the edge off impending anxiety but did little to abate worriment. They walked the rest of the way to Falcone and Niles, Jake handing her off with a tightness in his chest not unlike what he'd felt underwater just before he'd run out of air.

FROM THE PORT IN Chios Town, Jake and Remington took the thirty-minute Sunrise Lines ferry, crossing the twelve-mile channel to Turkey, where they deboarded in the resort town of Çeşme. From there, they walked past the majestic Ottoman castle that had dominated the harbor for five hundred years, continuing up the incline to the car rental agency where a Jeep Renegade was reserved for their pick up. While planning their singular objective, Jake had decided to add the side venture of acquiring new dive gear to replace what had been either damaged or lost during his assault, so their first foray was a short drive to the opposite coast. To get there, they navigated through the Turkish-flag-lined Atatürk corridor which segued into modern suburban retail and then to the Izmir-Çeşme motorway. Turning southeast, tidy, upscale residential neighborhoods shaded by cypress and palm trees led to the Setur Çeşme Marina, an oval basin on Ilica Bay annexed by the Grand Altın Yunus Hotel complex, a sprawling 465-room beach property with six swimming pools, tennis courts, restaurants, and shops.

While Jake and Remington had been patently vigilant from the moment they'd set foot on the ferry and throughout the drive, neither was alerted to a silver VW Tiguan lagging several lengths behind them. The SUV was moving at average speed for the zone, making no erratic or attention-arresting maneuvers, blending analogously with the automotive makes and models traversing the thoroughfares and streets. In fact, it did not follow them to the far end of the marina complex where they parked and left the Jeep to enter the dive shop there.

Inside, walls and shelves and glass-enclosed counters were full of every manner of scuba gear and equipment as well as surfboards and rigs for kite and windsurfing, the Izmir coasts pocked with surfing clubs and schools. They spent some time evaluating and purchasing and, after loading everything into the Jeep, got back on the motorway and drove east toward the burg of Alaçati, trees dotting the sides and medians with pleasant stretches of housing and businesses.

Remington turned off at the Alaçati exit onto Riza Ertan, which would take them into the core of town, and glanced at his watch. "We have some time to kill before the meet…want to grab a cup of joe?"

"Sounds good to me," Jake replied, his focus aimed out the passenger-side window, surveying the businesses and pedestrians spaced along the four-lane thick with traffic and commerce. He did not notice the Tiguan sandwiched in the mix of cars and trucks behind them.

Remington kept driving, turning down a narrow cobblestone street, vehicles beginning to give way to pedestrians.

Jake cut him a curious look. "Do you know where you're going?"

"I think so. I was here years ago." He began searching for a parking spot and, just when it appeared they were going to run out of real estate, found a gap along the curb that would accommodate the Jeep.

Some hundred or so yards back, a pair of automobile doors cranked open and closed with synchronized thunks.

Out of the Jeep, Jake and Remington stretched, and began strolling what became an alley bazaar of shops, eateries, and bars. Passing charming little boutiques and cafés with stone façades and trimmed in bright colors, soon Remington exclaimed, "Ah, there it is! I was hoping I had the right street."

Köşe Kahve, as one of the many such places in the Alaçati center, has a smattering of outdoor seating in the form of bistro-small tables and chairs, its vanilla-painted exterior turned antique by weather. Inside, is a rustic layout with more cozy dining, handcrafted accents and art distributed along the walls. Today, like most days, it was busy with a pre-lunch coffee crowd.

"Best java around," Remington remarked as he led the way.

Both having a penchant for rich, black brew, they ordered cups and took them to an outside table. Sipping the house blend, Jake mumbled his endorsement. Sunshine dappled through trees from the adjacent side street, the air warm and smelling faintly of sugary baked goods.

"That was a decent haul of scuba gear we got," Remington said. "I was really surprised to find the Hydros vest. Been wanting one."

"Yeah, the Hydros is a good get," Jake said absently, his gaze fixed on nothing in particular.

Peering narrowly over the edge of his coffee cup, Remington said, "Hey, brother. Where are you?" Leaning forward on his elbows, he looked at Jake and waited.

In response, Jake just exhaled heavily.

"Okay, I'd be damned freaked out if that had happened to me, so I get it." His gray-green eyes regarded Jake with stark sobriety.

"It's more than that, Remy. Most of my life there have been people trying to hurt me, something I accepted a long time ago. But this…this could have hurt Callie, could have cost her life. She was *right there*." He set his coffee cup in its saucer with a light clatter, jarred at the remembrance. "I'm beginning to think this was a bad idea. And, yes, Callie really wants to go home."

"I can see you're struggling with that, understandably so. But I think it could really be good for her."

"I don't know. With everything that's happened, I just don't know."

"We can, and will, keep her safe. I promise you that."

Jake almost said *Don't make promises you can't keep*, but caught himself, knowing Remington meant and believed what he said. That would have to be enough. Because, truth be told, he did not want Callie to be away from him…he was just not convinced she should be with him for this, either.

AFTER FINISHING THEIR COFFEE, they strolled farther down the lane beside the café, pausing here and there to browse shop displays. Planters brimming with flowers framed and lined windows, shutters, and doors painted in Easter-egg colors and vines of vivid bougainvillea fountained from overhead. More than once, Jake commented how much Callie would have enjoyed the pretty whimsy of the place, though certainly not the crowds; locals and tourists patrolled every alley and gathered around every doorway.

They had just passed the Pazaryeri Mosque, a nineteenth-century Greek church built of rubble stone, when Jake experienced the premonitory tingle he often got from an existential but unknown threat. He began to glance discreetly over his shoulder as they walked, detecting nothing unusual at first. Just guys on motor scooters, couples loitering to ogle souvenirs, young women holding up phones to capture themselves for Instagram, boys filming one another skateboarding for Tik Tok. A trio of stray dogs greeting each other with noses and tails. Upbeat music spilling from a tavern, a red country flag with white crescent and star flapping from a balcony.

And then he caught a glimpse of what had tripped the hair-trigger tensile wire of his animal instincts—a pair of men weaving in and out of the pedestrian flow, peering into windows without really looking, swiveling their heads back and forth but maintaining a straight-ahead focus that suggested their only true target of interest was moving at a measured distance in front of them.

Jake nudged Remington and said, "We've got a tail."

Remington did not look behind them, nor did he question Jake's observation. "How many?"

"Two."

"You recognize them?"

"No."

"Okay, let's do SDR to confirm, then we'll bag and tag."

"Yep, let's do it," Jake said tersely.

They turned onto another lane and walked the length, maintaining their same pace, but instead of going in a new direction, they circumnavigated back to Köşe Kahve and made their way down Kemalpaşa, its frontage corridor, which was bustling with foot traffic.

The two men followed.

Jake and Remington ducked into a shop, lingered for a few minutes, and resumed their surveillance detection route, mostly together but occasionally splitting up. When they parted, the pair of men also separated, one trailing Jake and the other, Remington. After fifteen minutes of crisscrossing a succession of alleys, corridors, and side streets, Jake paused in front of a merchandise table covered with jewelry and other trinkets. Picked up and pretended to examine a bracelet. Put it back on the table.

"Ready?" Remington asked him.

"Oh yeah. Let's get these bastards and find out what the hell is going on."

20

THE PAIR OF MEN tailing Jake and Remington had also stopped in front of a shop, and were going through an unconvincing pantomime of holding up sunglasses when they were already both wearing some. Physically, they were neither particularly brawny or lean, the same general age as them—translating as prime fighting age—with longish dark hair and beards. One man was clad in denim, tee and open shirt over jeans, the other wore gray joggers with a navy track-style jacket. At this distance, it was anybody's guess if they were carrying or not, but given that the temperature was hovering somewhere around eighty degrees, wearing the extra outer layer was a strong clue.

Jake and Remington were, Glocks tucked in their cargo pants and concealed by loose button-front shirts, but being armed was only a last-resort precaution. In this crowded commercial area, discharging weapons would mean things had really gone to shit. Even so, under the circumstances, both were glad they had taken the calculated risk of bringing them.

Heading east on Kemalpaşa, Jake and Remington stole furtive glances on their tails while looking for a viable side street to exit. Coming to a connecting alley with no pedestrians, they turned casually, but as soon as they were out of sight, took off in a trot. At the end of the alley was what appeared to be the back side of a residential or private business sector. Not ideal, but about as good as it was going to get here and it seemed to be deserted.

Ducking around the corner of a high stone wall, Remington asked, "What're you thinking? Ambush?"

Jake nodded, glancing ahead to assess their surroundings and options. He gestured to a heavily wooded area farther off that might have been some kind of park, but in closer range, a sea of headstones revealed it to be a cemetery.

"Shit," Remington muttered. "Kidding me?"

Jake scanned the grounds in view and the periphery. "You got a better takedown point?"

They could hear the scuffle of feet approaching. "Not really," Remington said, and they jogged toward the trees. Vehicles were parked along the curb of the cemetery knee wall but, as luck would have it, all appeared to be vacated. With their pursuers close, they did not have time to worry about the possibility that the drivers and passengers were attending a service or scattered about visiting interred relatives, but a quick survey found the premises desolate; the empty vehicles apparently belonged to employees of businesses and possibly overflow from local and tourist traffic.

As they made their way into the cemetery, Remington remarked, "This might be a good spot after all." He pointed to a copse of pines shading a corner where a backhoe sat next to an open metal gate. Across the cobblestone street was a short alley lined with the oversize metal and wooden doors of storage spaces. No pedestrians, no vehicles, and most importantly, no exit, which meant no through traffic.

They took cover in the trees, staggered rows of stones and monuments engraved with lengthy names full of consonants and accent marks all around them. It was not long before the pair of men that had been following them appeared on the same path they'd walked, sure that Jake and Remington were just ahead. When the men moved past their position, Jake and Remington rose and swiftly came up from behind, locking them in choke holds until they sagged and then dropped them to the ground. With knees pressed into the men's backs, they were able to quickly search and find handguns—Turkish SAR 9s—which they put to practical use. After checking to make sure the 9mm mags were loaded, they jerked the men to their feet and prodded them out through the gate, across the street, and into the alley, the SAR 9s jabbed into their backs. Momentarily weakened from the oxygen deprivation of the chokes, the men stumbled like drunks, but by the time they were in the alley, began to regain vitality and appeared ready to put up a fight.

While crossing to the alley, Jake and Remington had secured their captives with rear arm-and-wrist locks, but with each having one free hand and unencumbered feet and legs, they were not about to await interrogation or, worse, execution with their own guns. In nearly perfect synchronization, the two men twisted backwards toward Jake and Remington, grimacing and grunting from the pain it caused them in the holds, but going for face strikes nevertheless. At the same time, they brought their legs up in attempts to jab knees into groins.

With conditioned reflexes for such countermoves, Jake and Remington engaged the safeties of the confiscated pistols and shoved them into their waistbands and, while pivoting away from the men's leg hikes, brought their hands up to palm-plant solar plexuses. Close-quarter fighting is exponentially more difficult as there is less area with which to generate energy and force, so it was easier for Jake and Remington to regain control than it was for their captives to take it away.

They kicked the men to the ground and stood in front of them. Catching his breath from the skirmish, Jake leaned over and plucked the sunglasses that had managed to remain on their faces and tossed them aside.

Looking directly into the eyes of each man, Jake asked, "English?"

Neither responded.

An edge of frustration creeping into his voice, he demanded, "Who are you? What are you doing?"

Again, there was no response, but their expressions had turned surly.

Though he was fluent in Russian, Jake only knew a modicum of Turkish and was sifting through his language repository when Remington came up with the equivalent query, asking, *"Kimsin? Ne oluyor?"*

After a brief hesitation, the pair exchanging petulant looks, the one in denim spitting out, *"Amina koyayim."*

Jake knew that phrase, and replied, "Fuck you, too."

The guy wearing the joggers and track jacket snarled, "What is this?"

Jake put his hands on his hips and took a step toward them. "You're the ones who need to answer that. Why are you tailing us?"

Denim guy muttered, *"Yarrağımı ye,"* followed by, *"bok kafali."*

Jake frowned at vulgarities he also recognized and knew they were not getting anything from these guys. He took another step forward, Remington right beside him, and glared.

In that instant, he saw a subtle shift in both men that was as if an invisible switch had flicked and knew they were about to try something. Before he could gauge what that might be, the two men, their asses on the ground, somehow got their feet under them and sprang up, launching into the air and scissoring both of their legs into a flying kick like some kind of Baryshnikov *grand jeté*. Instinctively, Jake and Remington ducked and avoided getting boots to the head, but in the process, the two men vaulted over top of them and landed on the open side of the alley.

There were three things that could have happened at this point: the men could have simply fled; Jake and Remington could have drawn either the men's guns or their own Glocks and shot them; or another hand-to-hand battle could ensue.

One of those things did occur, but not right away.

Instead, the sudden cacophony of a gang of barking dogs racing after a trio of kids on bicycles hijacked the moment, freezing all four combatants as their collective attention was diverted to the activity stream that flashed by on the adjacent street.

Jake and Remington were the first to react, charging directly for the lower bodies of their captives to enact a quick throwdown, but both were thwarted. These guys, clearly endowed with some advanced skills, responded with a round of jabs and punches and kicks in what quickly became a brutal bout.

Thinking he was on the verge of turning-point domination and ultimate submission, Jake had denim guy in a tight clinch hold and was preparing to enact a twisting neck lock that could potentially tear the spinal column, when he was distracted by the realization that one of the handguns in his waistband was no longer there. An instant later, the barrel of the gun was stabbed into his side. Altering his position to free up one arm, he swung down and struck the gun, dislodging it from his side and out of his opponent's grip. He heard it hit the cobblestones and redoubled his efforts to finish the fight. So focused on that objective, it wouldn't be until much later that the realization he'd almost been shot occurred to him.

After a few minutes of grappling, Jake and Remington were finally able to put them down for good, successfully making the moves that rendered the two men unconscious—possibly permanently.

Looking hard at each other, Jake wheezed, "You okay?"

Remington sucked blood between his teeth, answering, "Yeah, you?"

Jake nodded, and they each bent over the man they'd fought, pillaging pockets.

"Anything?" Jake asked.

"Naw, just a burner phone."

Jake held up a duplicate. "Same." He shoved it into a pocket of his cargo pants.

"Maybe Kip can get something off them."

Jake slid out his iPhone and snapped photos of the two men's faces. He straightened up and exhaled agitatedly.

Remington wiped some blood oozing from a cheek gash, noticing blood spatters and rips in his shirt.

Jake stomped off to retrieve the SAR 9 he'd knocked to the ground and stuck it back in his pants next to his Glock. Looked again at the two lifeless bodies on the cobblestones and glanced around to see if they had any witnesses. Fortunately, there were none.

They headed back to the main drag, teeming with lunch traffic and filled with the sounds of chatter and laughter and competing blasts of music from every direction, the smell of pine and jasmine now mixed with the aromas of grilled meat.

Jake and Remington hobbled back to the Jeep, inwardly wincing and watching their path, front and back.

NEITHER GAVE ANY THOUGHT to grabbing a bite to eat on the way out, both eager to put the now-sullied charm of Alaçati quickly in the rearview. Remington drove south on the Riza Ertan road which became the 12500 artery, passing through well-to-do suburbs and businesses and, on the other side of the Izmir-Çeşme Otoyolu overpass, entering a mostly flat expanse of rural landscape of low brush and scrub. There was no talk for several minutes until Remington finally blew out a breath and said, "Goddamn."

He waited for Jake to comment but got nothing.

"Have to say, I'm thinking this might not be just about you, brother."

"I'm inclined to agree with you after that back there. But what the hell *is* it?" Jake asked. "You think it's connected to what we're doing here?"

"Have no idea," Remington replied, "but I know one thing. I'm glad I insisted on getting us some hardware."

"Were we ever not?"

"Not on my watch, no, but weapons are prohibited on his projects."

Jake turned in his seat, looking at Remington with astonishment. *"What?"* A trickle of blood escaped from his nose, which he quickly swiped.

"Yep. Same reason as the moratorium on booze on the project. Potential triggers, pardon the pun. The protocols are to prevent any kind of Wild West environment."

Jake's expression turned to confusion.

"On paper, we're logistical support," Remington explained. "Practically speaking, we *are* security, but it is kind of a new concept for them. They've been doing these things in the States and England, with no real problems or need, but after doing a few in Italy, he decided it might be necessary. He was further convinced when it provided him an insurance deduction. So yeah, security and medical. And, as far as Caspian goes, you might say it's need-to-know." He winked. "He doesn't need to know that we'll have more than a couple of Glocks."

"Well, you know how I feel," Jake said. "Better to have arms and not need 'em than to need them and not have 'em."

"Damn straight." Remington glanced at him and smirked.

Jake was trying to clean himself up with a cravat he always carried, swabbing his face and neck and checking the cloth for blood which, unsurprisingly, he found. He grimaced and kept wiping, running fingers through his disheveled hair to comb it somewhat into place.

Still grinning, Remington said, "Give it up, stud. Not gonna be able to pretty that mug up enough to hide the battle wounds."

"Shit." Dropping the cravat in his lap, Jake asked, "Have you noticed anything suspicious since you've been here?"

Remington gave it some thought and shook his head. "Not that comes to mind. But when I think about everything you've encountered—the tracking of the boat and especially the underwater attack—what happened today definitely makes me think that it's not tied to the Dark Web contract on you. Don't know what it is, but I'm with Kip, I think it's something else."

"Do you think we've been compromised enough to put the gig in jeopardy?"

The muscles of Remington's face tightened, and even behind the sunglasses he wore, his determination was evident. "No," he said. "Not going to let it be."

Tidal pools had begun to crop up amidst the grasslands, a roadside billboard illustrated with a big white egret identifying the stretch as Iaçati Sulak Alani, the Alaçati Wetlands. Around the bend from that was another sign, this one in the shape of a surfboard, advertising the Çağla Kubat Windsurfing Academy, though there was no indication such a place was anywhere nearby. The flat terrain was barren, broken only by the shallows and occasional low hills, the sky high and wide and cloudless. The two-lane before and after them was empty of other vehicles, the air blowing through their open windows smelling of the decomposing marsh silt. A few more miles and the ponds to their right expanded into a stream and then a sea inlet with residential and commercial development on the far side, the Alaçati Marina coming into view. Here, the route turned inland, the drab scrub greening up in sporadic rolls of bushes and groupings of trees. With the northeastern bent, the elevation rose, the shoulders rising and falling away in jagged shelves and craggy strips.

They drove on for another mile, at which point the road turned back to the south and once again paralleled the water, passing the aforementioned windsurf academy compound. Jake had begun to notice Remington's frequent glances in the Jeep's side and rearview mirrors and twisted around to see what he was looking at.

"How long has that pickup been on our six?" He was referring to a bronze-colored Toyota Tacoma several lengths behind them.

"Since just before the windsurf place," Remington replied.

"Goddammit," Jake sputtered in exasperation, "we should have checked for a tracker before we left."

"Yeah, we should have, but all I was thinking about was getting the hell out of there in case those guys miraculously regenerated brain activity."

"I'd say we're probably being paranoid, but I've only seen one or two vehicles total since we cleared the city."

"Yep. Thinking the same thing. And with the few side roads and all this rural terrain, turning off might put us in a field or dirt track that goes to nowhere."

Increasing their speed, Remington and Jake watched as the Toyota pickup kept pace, a blur of boundless land on one side, a bay of the Aegean on the other. The road edged closer to the shore as the flatter grade narrowed below an expanding upswell of sparse earth. Behind them, the pickup closed the gap and barreled toward their rear bumper.

"Oh fuck," Jake said, "are they going to do what I think?"

Pressing his foot down on the accelerator, pushing the Jeep past eighty-five miles an hour, Remington said, "Hold on, bud."

They surged ahead but could not maintain the distance separating them from the pickup as it put on a burst of speed that brought it back to their tail. After a brief interval of holding position, the Toyota began to drift into the left-hand lane. Remington who, like Jake, had been extensively schooled in tactical driving as part of his Special Forces training, ran through possibilities in the split seconds he had before the vehicle made its initial move. Of the various scenarios he imagined occurring, the two he believed were in play involved either impact or shooting and, while both could be evaded with skills and maneuvers he had successfully executed before in various environments and conditions, he knew on any given day the other driver could out-maneuver or overpower or simply have fate rule in his favor.

"Can you see any weapons?" Remington asked, easing up on his speed and cutting in front of the pickup to prevent it from coming up alongside them. In response, the pickup slid back over to the right lane and accelerated. Remington stomped the gas pedal and shot forward to overtake and block them again.

"I can't tell," Jake said, and already had his Glock in hand.

The zigzag from lane to lane went on for a minute or so with Remington looking for a section of road with enough shoulder room to perhaps execute a reverse 180-turn to force the pickup to make an evasive move and disrupt the pursuit, put the driver on the defensive. But, if anything, the ground on either side narrowed even more, the water now so close the outline of rocks below the rippling waves of the bay could be seen.

"I see two guys," Jake reported.

"Surely not the fuckers we took out?"

"No." Jake saw the driver yank the wheel and lean forward in the driver's seat of the Toyota, his head in shadow but aimed toward their rear bumper. "Oh shit. Remy, they're going to PIT us."

"I've been expecting that. Hold on." Remington floored the accelerator, but the Toyota caught up before he could move to block it, and while the Gladiator and Tacoma are basically of the same class and performance, inches and seconds was what it came down to here—inches of advancement in milliseconds, the front right bumper of the pickup angling into the Jeep's left rear quarter panel.

The PIT maneuver, or pursuit intervention technique, is used to great effect by law enforcement and, when expertly done, usually immobilizes a fleeing vehicle. But while it typically causes a spinout and loss of control that stops the target, it can also cause a more dramatic outcome.

As it did now.

The Toyota pickup's first attempt was a graze that offset the Jeep's course and speed, sending it swerving erratically back and forth between the road's two lanes, Remington wrestling with the steering wheel to regain control. But the second time, a solid clip just behind the rear wheel well, nailed it, grinding metal and spraying sparks. The Jeep wound into a furious spin, spiraling toward the inland bank at an angle, the impact launching it high and backward across the road. It flipped and rolled multiple times midair and flew out over the shore side to the water.

21

JAKE AND REMINGTON WERE partial to Jeeps for many reasons, not the least of which was their overall ruggedness and ability to navigate almost anywhere but, as most off-road four-wheeler enthusiasts know, one of their major drawbacks is the likelihood of rollover in a side collision due in part to a high center of gravity and narrow base. That said, the Jeep's bulky body and frame is impressively durable, and in most safety tests the structure around simulated driver and passenger retained integrity and theoretically kept all safe. Theoretically.

In the real world, all bets were off when actual humans and locational terrain and encompassing geography were part of the equation. Not to mention malicious intent.

The rental Jeep Gladiator containing Remington and Jake spun and vaulted and flipped and rolled, crashing into the rocky shelf lining the bay shore, making one final somersault before it landed on its top in the water—shallow, but high enough to sluice inside the open windows and cover the ceiling and the tops of their heads. Strapped in by their seatbelts, Remington and Jake hung upside down, scalps pressed against the Jeep's crushed roof, dazed but conscious, the world thrumming and blaring in a wail of white noise. The shock and pain of impact was instant and detached and then hammeringly close. Airbags had reliably deployed, undoubtedly cushioning blows to the dashboard, but there were plenty of other detriments to contend with. Remington's left arm was torqued behind his neck at an awkward angle, Jake's arms were still clutching the frame of the door and windshield which, with its Mopar Corning Gorilla Glass, had not shattered.

As more seawater sloshed across the ceiling-turned-floor of the cabin, Remington brought his arm slowly out from his neck with a painful grimace and let it hang free, and looked at Jake.

Before he could ask, Jake said, "I think I'm okay. You?"

"My arm...but I don't think it's broken."

"Did you hit your head? Anything else hurt?"

Remington actually laughed. "Fuck, Jake. What do you think?" Gritting his teeth, he asked, "Can you get free?"

"Can you?"

"Feels like I'm stuck."

Trying to unfasten his seatbelt and finding it jammed, Jake dug for his Swiss Army knife, the extraction from a pocket in his cargo pants a task made considerably difficult by gravity and restriction of movement by the compression of space. He flicked out the blade cut his belt, bracing himself against the seat as he did and manipulating his limbs and torso until he was upright. He did a quick but limited assessment of Remington as he cut him out of his harness and remarked, "You probably know this, but pretty sure you've got a dislocated shoulder."

"Yeah, thought so. Hurts like a mother." He drew in a hissing breath.

Jake poked around for his Glock and the SAR 9 he'd confiscated, found both and shook the water off, sticking them back in the waistband of his wet pants.

The Jeep's doors were somewhat intact, but with the compaction they were not budging. Jake pulled himself through his window, thankful to discover that his own arms and legs were functional. Still, everything hurt. He'd already been hurting after the fight, so it was hard to tell what was a new hurt, what might be something potentially serious. But before he could let his medical knowledge base propagate a thorough triage on either of them, he recognized a more immediate problem that had resulted from his exit—the force it had taken to climb out and the sea's currents were moving the Jeep, six thousand pounds of metal being lifted like a shell in the tide, dislodged from the landing spot and shifting ever so gradually into the wash of waves coming in...and going out, a fifteen-knot wind factoring significantly.

"Whoa," Jake muttered, half to himself. "Remy, we need to get you out *right now.*"

"Well, good luck with that," Remington called out to him. "I've been trying to move, trying to open the fucking door, and it's not happening. But yeah, I can feel the movement." Water covered his scalp, lapping at his brow line.

Gazing past their landing spot, Jake could see that the darker blues of deeper waters were just beyond them. Much farther out, the horizon was dotted with the colorful sails of windsurfers, obliviously enjoying this perfect day for the sport, bouncing along in bright sunshine against the vivid blue sky. Glancing back to the coast road, Jake saw nothing— no passing cars, no people.

Where was the Toyota truck?

Splashing around to the driver's side of the Jeep, Jake gave Remington's door a yank but, like his, it would not open. He leaned down and stuck his head inside the window, looked up to where Remington's legs were and saw that the dashboard and steering column had become mangled just enough to obstruct exit. He instantly dismissed the idea of trying to remove the door; for all of a Jeep's removable parts—doors, windows, roof—the process could be as infuriating as trying to disassemble made-for-assembly furniture, which was to say a pain in the ass, and would take way more time than he had now.

As he stood by Remington's door trying to come up with an expedient extrication strategy, he felt the Jeep's chassis move again, this time tilting and pulling away in the water. He grabbed a part of the frame in a futile effort to stop it, but was tugged along with it, his boots scuttling across the rocky sea floor. The air smelled of gasoline and oil and burnt engine parts, smoke puffing from the Jeep's undercarriage. Despite being in and surrounded by water, much of the vehicle wet, he knew a fire erupting could not be ruled out.

Getting a better grip of the frame and digging in his heels, Jake asked, "Can you *feel* your legs? Your feet?"

"Yeah, yeah," Remington muttered. "Just not sure if you get the door open that I'll be able to get out. The dash or the steering column is pushing down on me."

Glancing at the bottom of the Jeep, which was on top, Jake said,

"There's an indentation behind the front wheels that probably caused that." A sudden thought sent him scrambling around to the rear of the vehicle. He unlatched the tailgate and, seawater rushing in as he held it up, leaned into the space between cargo bed and upside-down Tonneau cover. Getting his hands on one of the just-purchased scuba tanks, he dragged it out and carried it to Remington's side, using the bottom to strike the edge of the door frame. Two hard strikes and the impact broke the seal, yawning it open. Next, he hammered upward on the steering wheel as Remington twisted and turned and pushed with his feet.

As Remington continued to struggle to free himself, the Jeep was suddenly swept several yards away by the wind-driven current.

Jake watched helplessly as water filled the cabin and Remington's head and shoulders were submerged. He was charging after the drifting and sinking chassis, pushing through water now past his waist, when the sound of gunfire split the air, rounds plunking into the sea around him, another few pinging the vanishing surface of frame and undercarriage of the Jeep.

Jake turned to see two men at the top of the bank, both in shooting stances with guns aimed in his direction, firing in rapid succession. Dropping the scuba tank in the water, he pulled his Glock and sent several rounds their way, but his more urgent attention was on getting back to the Jeep and Remington, knowing the window for rescue was quickly closing.

He squeezed off a few more shots, then dove underwater. When he got to the driver's side door he'd just smashed open, the space where Remington had been wedged was empty. Relief coursed through him but was almost immediately replaced with alarm as he surfaced and did not see his friend.

He waited, expecting to see Remington's head and shoulders appear at any moment, but that did not happen.

"Remy!" he called out, looking in every direction and still not seeing him. "Remy!" He heard nothing in the water around him, only the blasts of gunfire from shore, rounds landing closer with each volley.

Jake was pivoting furiously to keep a bead on the men and on the water, desperately watching for Remington to emerge. He was about to go under again to search when the sound of gunfire became jarringly louder, exploding right by his ear. Jerking around, he discovered Remington coming up behind him, shooting with his own Glock.

"Thank God," Jake muttered breathlessly. "What—?"

"I wasn't going to let that heap sink with our Hydros and other shit," Remington replied, and Jake noticed their packages from the dive shop tucked awkwardly under Remington's injured arm.

Jake shook his head in disbelief and reached over. "Give me that stuff."

Side by side, they trudged through the water toward the shore, firing on the pair of men who, either because they were out of ammunition or because they did not want a more direct engagement, made a run for the Tacoma, jumped in, and sped off in a rumble of engine noise and a spray of grit and dust.

"Goddamn," Remington said, groaning as the pain in his shoulder bit down like the jaws of a spring trap had just snapped shut.

They waded through the shallows and stepped into the scrub of the short bank, crossing the road to the other side where more brush covered the slightly elevated expanse of uncultivated countryside. Finding a bare spot, Jake dropped the scuba gear and let out a long breath. Looked haggardly at Remington.

"Want to do it yourself or want me to do it?" he asked.

Prodding the distended bones of his shoulder joint, Remington grunted. "Son of a bitch. Go ahead, you do it."

Jake took Remington's arm, gripping his wrist, and pulled firmly out until he felt and heard the telltale pop. Remington moaned and then sighed as he flexed his arm up and down. But Jake's gaze had moved downward to Remington's legs, the cargo pants covering them torn and bloody in several places. He knelt for a look and found a long gouge on one calf that was actively bleeding. Ripping strips from Remington's pants, he wrapped and tied the wound and stood.

"Need to keep an eye on that," he remarked, and glanced at his Garmin tactix watch, navigating to the map screen. "We're about three klicks out from the LZ. What do you want to do?"

"Well, we can't call an Uber, can we?" Remington sneered.

He reached into a pocket and took out his phone. It was wet but still worked. There was a text message from Dmello, thirty minutes old, saying he was waiting for their linkup. He tried to make a call, the signal too weak for it to go through. "Looks like we're hoofing it, bud."

Gathering up the gear, they headed south on the coastal road. Across the bay, the Port Alaçati Marina and adjacent Biblos beach resort were a posh study in contrast from the nondescript inland shore they hiked, more of the jaunty windsurfers and a sailboat scooting through the sparkling water in the distance.

THEY MADE IT TO the rendezvous, a trek of not quite two miles, in just over thirty minutes, the hot sun without the shade of trees or clouds sapping what remained of their stamina. When they approached from the southern end of what was, by all appearances, an abandoned and minimally maintained paved strip about six thousand feet in length, they spotted Keanjaho Dmello standing with another man beside a Pilatus turboprop plane. A black Ford Ranger pickup with a covered bed was parked just off the airstrip.

Dmello jogged over to them and then halted abruptly, his face reflecting shock at their appearance. With his bloodied pants leg, Remington arguably looked the worst, but both had tears in their clothing, greasy spots from leaked oil, dried dust and mud, lacerations and the beginnings of bruises from both the fight and the wreck.

"Oh God," Dmello exclaimed, "what happened?"

"We'll fill you in," Remington replied, "but first, water, please."

"And the first aid kit," Jake added.

While they waited for Dmello to climb the airstairs to the plane's cockpit, Jake eyed the other man standing on the strip. He was tall and thin with a wiry physique that suggested underlying fitness, precisely barbered dark hair and a thick but trimmed beard. He wore sunglasses and was dressed in belted tan chinos and a cream-colored collared shirt.

Stepping up to the man, Remington extended his hand and said, "Good to meet you personally, Neval." He nodded to Jake. "Jake Tyler, this is Neval Tashkiran. He and Kip have worked together in the past, go back some years." Jake had already been briefed on that relationship, as well as the Turk's military background which, as part of the *Özel Kuvvetler Komutanlığı* or OKK, the country's special forces, was impressive.

Tashkiran shook their hands and returned the greeting. He was cool and mildly inquisitive but socially at ease, and Jake got a credible read from him. Which was a good thing at this point because his nerves and threshold for sketchy people and unfortunate events were worn pretty raw.

By now, Dmello had returned and handed out bottles of water. Jake and Remington promptly emptied theirs, Jake opening and sifting through the contents of the first aid kit while Remington gave Dmello and Tashkiran a rundown of their morning in the city center of Alaçati. Jake dressed and bandaged Remington's leg, offering him a sling for his arm, which he rejected.

Tashkiran's eyebrows hitched as he listened to the mind-boggling recount, but if he was stunned or in any way disconcerted, his expression did not manifest it. When Remington finished speaking, he said, "I will take care of the car rental agency for you. There will be no need for a police report." He offered a faint smile, implying there was also no need to ask why or how that would be handled.

"Thank you," Remington said. "I'm sure Kip will follow up with you on all that later."

"Of course."

Tashkiran led them to the back of his Ford Ranger, opened the tailgate, and flipped up a panel of the Tonneau cover. Inside the truck bed were several heavy-duty Pelican-style cases. He slid one out and unsnapped the latches. Secured in slots and protected by foam were a half dozen M4 carbine rifles. Tashkiran proceeded to open the rest of the cases, showing them a supply of AKs, additional Glocks, a couple of Barrett sniper rifles, optics, and a generous stock of ammunition and other equipment.

Jake and Remington could not restrain their satisfaction, grinning at the Turk. Nodding and patting him on the shoulder, Remington remarked, "You did good, man."

"Efron gave me his list and I filled it," Tashkiran answered simply.

Jake's smile faded and he looked alternately at Remington and Dmello. "We have a plan in place to get all this through the Chios airport?"

"Kip assured me he had that covered."

"Okay then," Jake said. "Let's get it."

Another round of handshakes and the arsenal was loaded into the Pilatus, a PC-12. Dmello settled into the cockpit and began working the avionics, Jake and Remington relaxing in leather seats in the cabin. They strapped in and, within minutes, Dmello had the plane rolling down the strip. Takeoff was blessedly uneventful, no men storming the runway pelting them with a hail of bullets. Wind turbines and low hills sped by their windows and then they were in the air, climbing to a thousand feet and the short cruise at 230 knots that would get them to Chios in less than ten minutes.

As the plane flew west over the Izmir peninsula in the bright blue afternoon sky, Remington turned to Jake, taking in his battered appearance. He had a gash across his forehead, cuts and swelling in his face, a split lip, and bruising around his eyes. "Jesus Christ…you look like shit."

"So do you," Jake replied dully.

"God, I need a drink."

"No fucking kidding."

They lapsed into silence and then Jake said, "If I was on the fence before, I'm not anymore. After everything that's happened, it's pretty damn clear that something's going on."

Remington sighed, rubbing his sore arm. "Can't say I disagree, brother. What do you want to do?"

"I think I have to get Callie home, Remy. She already wants to go, and now I think it's best. Thing is, she wants *us* to go home. Together." The plane's engine hummed, the sound and sensation it created making him suddenly woozy, the strain of high-octane reacting and executing catching up.

"You want to pull out?"

Jake thought about it for a moment, his face betraying the conflict he was feeling; the other side of this trip was something he'd been really looking forward to, a mission he embraced and believed in and wanted to give his full support. Finally, he said, "No. I want to do it."

Remington said, "We can send one of my guys back with her, if that would ease your mind a bit. Fly with her and then stay on overwatch until you return."

"Yeah, that would be good." He lay his head back against the seat and gazed somberly through his window, his heart laden with sadness and worry. Closed his eyes and sank into a gray place.

His earpiece beeped. He dug his iPhone out of his pants pocket and glanced at the screen, eyes widening at the name displayed. Sitting forward, he tapped the Bluetooth device. "Hey. Everything okay?" He listened to the response and felt his jaw tingle, the muscles in his face go slack. He did not immediately speak and, when he did, his voice was low and thick, his mouth dry. "I'm in a plane about to land. I'll call you back in a few minutes."

He ended the call and stared straight ahead, his eyes still wide but glazed.

Remington had been watching him with concern and asked, "What is it?" He waited.

Jake swallowed, ran a hand through his hair, and said nothing.

"Jake?"

Turning back to Remington, the pallor of his skin as gray as his thoughts, Jake said, "Callie going home now is not an option."

PART TWO

DIGGING IN THE DIRT

22

FOR THE STAFF OF the Tyler villa, the day had begun in the same general way as each of the other days since Jake and Callie's departure for Greece; the Dominical sun began its rise from behind the hills about halfway between five and six AM, ascending to its kingdom in the vast Pacific sky where it would roast the coast until an afternoon drama of gray and black clouds built and burst overhead for an hour or so before clearing the stage for the reliably stunning 5:45 PM sunset. During these daylight hours—sometimes a little before and often a bit after—the entire staff worked in comfortable congruity in each of their established roles and routines. As Jesse Segura emerged from his living quarters, joining Ramón Cárdenas, Estabon Mina, and Mauricio Leguizano arriving and congregating around the patio lanai, Camilla Orellana Márquez would be dispensing coffee and preparing breakfast. Though Segura enjoyed the morning and midday offerings from area eateries that were donated and delivered to the lifeguards throughout the week, he never passed up anything that came from a plate presented by Camilla.

The passage of days was different without Jake and Callie in residence, activity more inclined toward maintenance than management, but the disposition of the staff and the dedication to their work was the same.

Jesse Segura dressed, walked the perimeter of the property and combed the interior grounds, looking for anything out of the ordinary. After breakfast, Segura would head down to the beach for his shift and the others would commence their daily tasks and particular projects, some in solitary administration and others in a joint effort of group participation and support. They shared refreshments and lunch and snacks; did their work inside and outside of the villa; Segura returned from the beach at the conclusion of his eight-to-five shift; the group exchanged conversation; and Cárdenas, Mina, and Leguizano departed. Segura and Márquez would have dinner, usually on the patio, and then retire, Segura to his quarters and the housekeeper to the guest bedroom appointed for her.

But on this particular day, their comfortable synergy was seismically rocked, the reverberations of which would be felt long afterward.

JESSE SEGURA'S SHIFT THIS day was about as stressful as it got. From the moment he had set out the status flags which, for the entirety of his nine hours had been mostly yellow ones that read: *Bañarse con Precaución* or, Swim with Caution, to his final patrol of the strip of beach in his purview, he'd been fighting the conditions, fighting the crowds, fighting the stubbornness, the carelessness, and even stupidity of the people. *Turistas* he could give a pass, but the noncompliance of locals was another thing; for the most part, they knew better. And the conditions today were not to be taken lightly; they could, and tragically did, kill.

His shift partner was his boss, Captain Alvaro Cedeño, who he loved working with, not only because of Cedeño's professionalism and skills, but for his ability to be a combination of team leader, goodwill ambassador, and enforcer when necessary. And while he was a strict adherent to the rules of the road—or beach and ocean as was the case—he was also a friend with a limitless supply of wit, humor, and compassion.

Over the course of the morning and into the early afternoon, the volatile conditions kept them in constant motion up and down the sand and in and out of the water, staging preventions, issuing strenuous warnings, diplomatically admonishing and, occasionally, reprimanding. They spent a great amount of time explaining the deceptively dangerous rip currents, Cedeño even bringing out his phone to show video taken by drone, enhanced with arrows and highlighting to show the patterns they identified by directional changes, differential breaks or lack of, white or yellow foam returning to the wave lines, and brown spots in the sea where sand and sediment were disrupted and billowing in the currents.

They were also beset with a series of medical situations, including the usual scrapes and cuts from rocks and surfboard injuries, as well as heat-related distress and sting wounds from the numerous *rayas* that got stepped on in the tide.

Segura and Cedeño were seated in the bright red *Guardavidas* tower taking a rare break in the action, munching on Jerk Chicken Tacos courtesy of La Junta, when Segura saw something through their Vortex Optics spotting scope. At the same time, Cedeño's Motorola radio crackled with the urgent voice of Jerry Hadley, confirming what Segura had seen—a man drifting from a "safe" zone into a channel marked from the beach with red flags designating it as *Prohibido* due to a wide stream of rip currents, Hadley's transmission reporting that the man had gone under and not reemerged.

The two lifeguards climbed from the tower and hopped onto a royal blue Yamaha Wolverine ATV, rumbling off down the beach. Up on the ledge behind Segura's empty chair, his phone rang and went unanswered.

AS CAMILLA CLEANED UP after lunch, rinsing the melamine dishware on which she'd served *casados*, the catchy tune and Latin beat of Cocofunka's *Suele Suceder* was looping continuously through her head. It had been playing from Cárdenas' Bluetooth speaker, and the fact that it was no longer playing did not stop her hips from swaying to the ghost of its rhythm. And then she thought about the latent meaning of the song's lyrics, literally: Often happens that God be around the corner...what life has given and taken away. Inexplicably, she felt a shudder slide across her shoulders.

The windows that ran the back length of the granite countertop looked out to the lanai, the sky over the distant Pacific beginning to fill with the clouds that would soon bring an afternoon downpour. Filling the dishwasher beside the sink, her thoughts floated to Jake and Callie. It had only been two weeks, but it seemed like so much longer; she missed the magical aura of their love in the house. From everything she'd heard, they were having a wonderful time on their honeymoon, and she could not have been more delighted. It was something both of them needed and deserved. But while the gleaned snippets of their trip seemed, on the surface, to be everything a romantic excursion should be, full of inspired sightseeing and heavenly interludes and delectable cuisine, she could not dismiss the feeling that something was off.

Peeking over Segura's shoulder during his scheduled calls to check in with Jake, she'd picked up on an underlying tension—not so much from Jake, who was a master at keeping his emotions and thoughts well hidden—but from Callie who could not. From the couple of glimpses she'd caught of Callie in the background of a FaceTime session between Segura and Jake, Camilla could not help but notice the pallor and etched fatigue of stress in her complexion.

The housekeeper was drying her hands on a dish towel when she heard a sound so rare and unexpected that it took a few moments to register and process.

The front doorbell.

Reflexively, she peered through the kitchen windows, looking for the gardeners or pool man, and then remembered they were gone. The villa was quiet, and she was alone. There had been a discussion during lunch about the three of them driving to Uvita, just over twelve miles south of Dominical. Known for its Marino Ballena National Park with a peninsula shaped like a whale's tail, the town was a go-to for provisions unavailable locally—in this case, some PVC and couplings from Colono Construcción for irrigation system repairs, and Pacific Pools for filter cartridges and light bulbs. The gardeners, Mina and Leguizano, had also mentioned swinging by Blooms and Vivero Siempre Verde to check out the current selection of plants. Camilla had given them a short list of items to pick up from the BM supermarket.

The doorbell tolled a second time and the housekeeper stepped toward the open dining area just off the kitchen and glanced in the direction of the double front doors. Across a wide, tiled foyer with lighted glass shelves opposite the staircase, globe chandelier suspended from the vaulted, bricked ceiling, the entry was made of hand-carved wood panels arched at the tops. Through the inset glass strips she could see the shadowy shift of a male figure standing in the middle, placement that blocked most of his body.

Camilla reached into the pocket of culottes printed with big green jungle leaves and vines, and took out her phone, navigating to the security camera app. The video stream showed a man in a white polo shirt, a logo near his collar that she could not identify. A navy ball cap was on his head, the bill tilted down just enough to conceal his face.

She hesitated indecisively, her instincts telling her to dismiss the caller, and she was about to retreat back to the kitchen when the man rapped on the door's wood, the bark of his knock startling her almost more than the chime of the bell.

Tapping an icon on her phone screen, she asked, *"Hola, quién eres?"*

From beneath the cap, a masculine voice with the mellifluous intonation of a stranger willing ingratiation responded, *"Buenas tardes, Señorita."* Here, he paused, flashing slick white teeth below the cap brim, then continued, saying, *"Soy de los servicios de seguridad."*

"Servicios de seguridad?" Camilla echoed quizzically.

Now he held a laminated lanyard badge in front of the camera lens of the video doorbell. It read: SEGURIDAD PACIFICA. Below the company name was smaller print, which the man narrated himself. "Javier Villalobos, *consultor técnico.*"

Staring hard at the image of the man standing on the other side of the doors, Camilla heard herself ask, *"Por qué?"*

Continuing in Spanish, the man who had identified himself as Javier Villalobos, technical consultant for Pacifica Security, stated, "I am here to investigate an error alert from your system."

Again, Camilla's instincts were throwing up defensive flags. *"Qué?"*

"I am sure it is of no concern," the man replied evenly, "but it warrants a check to be sure nothing is amiss, and probably a reset of the system."

"Un minuto, por favor," Camilla said, and tapped her contact screen for Jesse Segura. Putting the phone to her ear, she listened. Heard a few dial tones, followed by: *"Este es Jesse, deja un mensaje."* Segura's voicemail.

The housekeeper looked at the front doors and pondered what to do. Warily, she crossed to the entrance and reached for the handle.

* * * * *

THE MAN WAS TALL, with the stocky build of a weight trainer, his neck thick, chest pushing out against his shirt, arms brawny and corded with veins. He was, however, neatly dressed and groomed, the polo shirt and chinos free of wrinkles and tucked into a leather belt, dark hair on the longish side but styled with product. The now-visible logo imprinted over his left pectoral, was that of Pacifica Security, a curling blue wave graphic above the name, replicated in an embroidered patch on the side of a black messenger bag slung from a big, bladed shoulder. The only elements of his appearance that got a sharper look from Camilla were his shoes, which resembled the tactical kind Jake often wore, and his tattoos; the tail of a snake coiled below the sleeve of one arm, an unrecognizable design with a density of intricate detail extended from the sleeve of the other, and a script-laced barbed collar circled his neck.

Camilla was trying not to stare as she attempted to decipher the gothic lettering inked in his skin when the man grinned with a shrug and said, "My youthful defiance."

Reaching inside the canvas bag at his side, the man withdrew a computer tablet and swiped his way to a screen, briefly reviewing the information it held. He looked up and queried, "*Señor* Tyler…*está aquí?*"

"No," said Camilla, quickly adding, "he is not available."

The man consulted his tablet again. "Oh, yes, yes. He is on his honeymoon." He glanced up, his dark eyes filled with false light.

The housekeeper's brows hiked at the statement, wondering with alarm how he could possibly know that, prompting the man to say, "It is noted in my dispatch report." He went on, "I see here that I have an emergency contact number for a…Jesse Segura?"

Still dumbfounded by information she was sure Jake would not have disclosed, Camilla stiffened, crossing her arms. "Yes, I spoke to him just now," she lied. "Let him know you are here."

"Very good." He began walking toward the living area, eyes roving the space.

Camilla was on his heels, her voice rising. "*Adónde vas?*"

He stopped and turned to her with a solicitous smile meant to disarm, but she was having none of it. Though older than him by a handful of years, she knew she was an attractive *Tica* woman, and it was not uncommon for men to flirt with her. But this man's attempt at charm reeked of inauthenticity.

Aware of her mounting distrust, the man became more perfunctory and said, "If you will show me to the control hub, I will do a reset, then I will check all of the sensors and cameras and be on my way."

Camilla bit her lip, weighing the consequences of overriding her skepticism of this man's presence and the alternative of potentially leaving the villa insecure and vulnerable. As if he could read her thoughts, he crooked a finger and led her back to the foyer, up the two wide steps trimmed in decorative tile, to the keypad mounted just outside the archway covering the entrance.

His hand was in a pocket of his pants and, as they approached the wall, a shrill beep sounded. He said, "Look at the display, *Señorita*. You hear the alert. See the error symbol with the exclamation mark? That means something is not right."

Camilla saw the symbol with the exclamation mark, and realized several things at once. She realized she could not recall having ever seen it on the display before, she realized she was going to have to take a chance and go against her judgment…and she realized she agreed with the man about one thing—something was not right. She just could not decide what it was.

DESPITE HER RESERVATIONS AND skepticism, Camilla took the Pacifica Security technical consultant through the villa, showing him the other keypads for the security system. He paused at each one but made only a cursory inspection. What he was paying more attention to as they walked were the doors and windows and cameras and, while she supposed that was a logical point of focus for a security tech, she found herself once again feeling a sense of wariness. When she could do so discreetly, she made a few more attempts to call Segura, each time getting his voicemail.

Upstairs, she led the man to a storage closet where the system's master control hub was located and watched from the hallway as he studied it, tapped the keypad, and made some entries on his tablet. His back to Camilla, he whistled under his breath and, still dabbling, asked, "*A donde fue el jefe?*"

"*Cómo?*"

"So where did the boss go?" he repeated, his tone casual. "On his honeymoon."

Camilla was flabbergasted at the brazenness of his inquiry and did not respond at first. Recovering her aplomb, she said, "That is not for me to say."

"Ah, of course," the man replied. "Good practice, *Señorita*."

She did not reply at all to that and found she was disturbed by his references to her as *Señorita* instead of *Señora*, the former address meant for a younger woman. In another situation, from a different person, it might have been complimentary, as he probably intended, but now, from him, it sounded smarmy.

After a few minutes, he stepped back and announced, "Okay, the system is reset." He paused quizzically. "There is one room we did not go in that I would like to check."

Camilla knew the room to which he referred but said nothing.

The man walked down the hall and stopped outside a closed door. The entry hardware was different from any of the other interior doors, with a latch and an electronic lock. "This is a bedroom?" he asked.

There was a fractional hesitation, and then Camilla replied, "Yes."

"Can we get ins—"

"No," she cut him off bluntly. "And there is no need."

The man's facial features were frozen in his spurious geniality, but an involuntary tick in his cheek betrayed a flash of anger. He seemed to withdraw inside himself for a moment, as if winding a spool of wire to its tautest tension. Slipping back into an air of restrained professionality, he said, "I just want to be thorough, *Señorita*, and I would not be doing my job if I did not make sure everything is functioning correctly before I leave."

Camilla drew herself up and looked directly into his face with dauntless authority. "I understand. But we will not be going in this room." Before he could say anything else, she turned and strode toward the stairs.

The man stared at the door for several moments, as if trying to mentalist himself to the space on the other side, and then followed the housekeeper.

Back on the first floor, the glass doors and windows had filled with the gloom of the coming storm, droplets of rain beginning to patter. Expecting the man to be departing, Camilla was further vexed to see him head into the living area and cross through the bricked archway of the kitchen. She watched as he inspected the windows along the countertop, moving to the dining area where he stretched up and bent down around all of the French doors, opening and closing them and running his fingers along the edges.

Hands on her hips, Camilla asked, *"Qué haces?"*

"Just checking the sensors," he said, again with the unctuous smile. "And I am done."

The housekeeper trailed him to the front entrance, bid him farewell, and closed the doors with a solid thud. Outside, the rain began to pound, drumming the tiled roof over the porch. Camilla peered through the doors' glass insets, looking toward the driveway. Oddly, she did not see any kind of car or truck or van.

Shuddering with delayed revulsion, she retreated to the kitchen to make some coffee, glad the service call was over.

23

BY THE TIME JESSE Segura left the beach and headed for the villa, the storm had come and gone, and the sky was awash with streaks that were the colors of crushed berries, sun departed. He had stayed well after his shift ended, as one of a multitude of people amassed to search for the man lost in the ocean and now assumed to have drowned. When word had spread of the incident, the beach quickly filled with onlookers who were a mix of the morbid and the concerned, and also with a contingent of experienced local surfers and area officials from law enforcement; among them were police and coast guard and, likely soon, the OIJ.

After an hour of searching, which included combing the beach to the south where the current often pulled, the rescue transitioned to recovery. When the storm blew in, all but the lifeguards and officials retreated to the cover of their vehicles or town restaurants and shops. Segura, Alvaro Cedeño, Jerry Hadley, Tara Tiedemann, and a handful of other off-duty lifeguards remained in and around the lifeguard tower, giving their accounts while they waited for the conditions to allow a resumption of canvassing. Of course, at that point, tragically, it was more a matter for the police and coast guard.

Trudging up the slope of rainforest, Segura was laden with a dismal sense of defeat and utterly wrung out from the challenges of his entire shift, let alone the rigors of their failed rescue. He knew everyone could not be saved, but the loss of even one life was one too many and something they all took personally. Making his way through the rain-soaked vegetation, all he wanted was a shower, some dinner, and a beer. He had trekked about halfway to the villa when he stopped to dig a bottle of water from his duffel bag, a sheen of perspiration coating his skin and keeping his new-issue blue *Guardavidas* shirt damp. Rummaging in the duffel, his hand touched his phone, bringing up the lock screen, and he saw the missed calls from Camilla for the first time.

He felt a spike of urgency—she would not have called multiple times unless something was wrong—and sprinted the rest of the way to the villa. When he reached the edge of the property, he could see the figures of his three compadres seated by the pool but, as he got closer, none of them appeared to be in a state of distress. Camilla was not with them.

"*Qué es la vara?*" he puffed, slightly out of breath.

"Just waiting on you, man," said Cárdenas, smiling faintly. "You get him?"

"What?"

"The man…you make the rescue?"

"We hear about it," Estabon Mina supplied.

"Oh." Segura glanced away. "No."

"*Lo siento.*"

"Hey, where is Camilla?" Segura asked. "She tried to call me."

"Inside," Cárdenas told him. He paused, exchanging glances with the two gardeners. "Will let her tell you. Since you are here, *nosotros vamos.* Okay?"

Segura nodded. "Yeah, yeah, *buenas. Mañana.*"

The threesome stood and shuffled from the patio.

The housekeeper was waiting for Segura in the kitchen, perched on an upholstered bar chair, a mug of coffee in her hand. She swung her head toward him, a strained look on her face. He stood close, waited for her to speak. And then she told him.

THE SHOWER, DINNER, AND beer later, Segura had rejoined Camilla and now sat with her in the living room. After she'd gone over the entirety of the security service call, Segura's first response was that of calm reassurance, to ease her feelings of guilt and irresponsibility. Truthfully, he was more than a little disturbed—certainly not with her, but with the circumstances of the call. The security company had his number and he'd not received a notification or message. He had also checked the monitoring app on his phone and found no indication of any kind of an error or malfunction. Next, he went through the house, room by room, and inspected every component of the system, finding nothing to make him particularly suspicious. He then placed a call to the company's after-hours number. They were only able to confirm that, from their end, everything appeared to be fine, telling Segura that he should contact the business office in the morning to inquire further about the nature of the on-site visit.

He was also told that there was, in fact, a technical consultant on their roster named Javier Villalobos but they did not have access to his job logs.

Seated opposite each other in a corner of the sectional sofa, Segura and Camilla sipped from frosty bottles of Imperial, her first, his second. Earlier, she had fixed them a dinner of *arroz con camarones* with fresh shrimp the guys had picked up at the market on their run into Uvita. Segura wore gray drawstring pants and a faded blue Nike t-shirt, his close-cropped hair damp from the shower.

Legs folded up on the mocha-colored sofa, Camilla was gazing with vacant fixation at the black eagle logo on the red-and-yellow label of her beer bottle. With an abrupt inhale, as if she'd just remembered to breathe, she looked up, and caught Segura watching her.

Speaking in Spanish, she repeated what she had said numerous times during her recount of the service call. "I should not have let him in."

"Hey, stop beating up on yourself," Segura said. "You did nothing wrong. I just wish I had been able to answer your call."

"What would you have told me?"

He hesitated for the briefest moment, but it was enough to cast renewed self-doubt in Camilla. She was shaking her head woefully as he remarked, "I would have come if I could have, of course." He sought a response that would lessen her angst, settling on, "I cannot say that I would have done anything differently."

She frowned, not quite believing it. "I do not like the way he was questioning about Jake."

"Well, I think you handled it the right way. Is all okay." He downed the last of his beer, putting a fist to his mouth to stifle a burp that turned into a yawn. "*Ay, ay, ay,*" he bemoaned. "*Tan cansado.*"

They both rose from the sofa, embracing companionably. "Get some rest, Jesse," Camilla murmured.

"I can stay up here tonight if it will make you feel better."

"I am okay," she said, and took their empty bottles to the kitchen.

He followed, exiting through the French doors to the patio.

Before retiring for the night, Segura did a full walk-around of the entire property. He tested the perimeter motion sensors, purposefully setting off and then resetting the alarm. With Camilla on the phone, he passed by every camera and had her verify that she could see him in the feeds. Lastly, he checked the door locks, again purposefully tripping the alarm to ensure they were all fully functional.

Though he was satisfied that all was in order, the property safe and secure, he was still troubled about the service call. But there was nothing more he could do until the morning when he planned to follow up with their account contact at Pacifica Security. He stood by the pool for several minutes, villa lights dimmed behind him, the semicircle of water a shimmer of turquoise at his feet.

Jesse Segura stepped around the edge and down to the grounds beyond it, heading for his living quarters, the night bright in the illumination of a nearly full moon. A low breeze rustled through the tree leaves and palm fronds of the rainforest periphery, the sound of distant surf a sorrowful reminder of a life lost on his watch.

CAMILLA CAME AWAKE WITH a start, a muffled thumping prompting her to spring up in bed. For hours, she'd been unable to fall asleep, her mind overwrought with a preponderance of paranoia stemming from the unexpected security service call. She kept telling herself that she was probably blowing it all out of proportion, that her worries were unfounded and being fed by her distaste and distrust of the technician. But she had also sensed that Segura harbored some doubts. Despite his reassurances, which she suspected were dispensed to assuage her feelings of ineptitude, his thorough inspection and testing of the system led her to believe he had not ruled out something less than aboveboard.

Sometime past midnight, the housekeeper had finally slid into slumber, but not for long.

Now, sitting on the side of the bed, she listened to the thumping and felt her heart jump in her chest. Something…or someone…was in the hallway.

With the moonlight beaming through her windows, she could see well enough to move about without turning a lamp on, so she padded to the door, took a steadying breath, and turned the knob. Opening the door a crack, she peered through the gap in the direction of the sound.

Unlike the interior of her bedroom, the hallway was murkily dark, and she waited for her eyes to adjust, squinting into the gloom. There was a switch for the sconce lighting spaced along the walls and, when her vision failed to bring the corridor into enough focus to see more than a few feet, she reached out and flipped it, a bloom of dread sprouting in her chest.

Nothing happened. She flipped it again, to no avail.

While she was still processing the worrying significance of the lights not working, a sequence of things happened so quickly she had no time to react; the thumping ceased, heavy footfalls scuffled hurriedly toward her, and she was grabbed around the midsection with a hand clamped over her mouth.

Her fight instinct kicked in immediately as she tried to break free, arms coming up and hands latching onto the attacker's bicep. She bucked backward and twisted to the left and right as he cinched his grip tighter, pressed his hand harder into her face, preventing her from trying to bite and greatly obstructing her breathing in the process.

She heard a ripping sound and seconds later the hand over her mouth was replaced by a thick swath of duct tape. Exclamations pushed up and out from her chest and throat but died in the sticky fabric and polythene binding, and while she was ineffectively exerting herself vocally, her attacker had zipped her wrists up in flex-cuffs.

Camilla still could not see the man—and now he was shoving her from behind—but he was big and strong and she had little doubt it was the same man who had been in the villa earlier. She was thrust back into her bedroom and slung down to the floor by the bed, the impact with the ceramic tile sending pain shooting from her pelvis up her backbone.

The moonlight shining in the room exposed her attacker, and she saw a man of the same size and build as the one who had introduced himself as Javier Villalobos, but she could not be completely sure because this figure was clad entirely in black, including a balaclava over his head and face.

He leaned down, the black beads of his eyes encircled by the holes of the mask, the knit covering his mouth inflating and deflating with his breath.

She glared up at him, bug-eyed with fear but defiant, waiting. He glared back, and said nothing. Producing the ring of duct tape he'd ripped from, he pulled the end free and began wrapping her ankles.

And then he stood up, gave her another look, and left the room.

THE MAN RETURNED TO the task he had been engaged in when the housekeeper had opened the door to her bedroom, working on the entry hardware for the locked room to which he'd been denied access.

When he had been on the premises that afternoon, he'd not procured much in the way of actionable information, but he was successful in staging the means for his nighttime intrusion. He'd always intended to return but had thought it would merely be to take more time in rooms already cased and identified as probable repositories of the kind of documents he sought. But not being able to get into this room earlier meant more effort to do so now.

The man who was not, in fact, Javier Villalobos of Pacifica Security, had spent some days observing company field personnel, watching them go out on their calls, even closely shadowing them when they were at residences. Nosing around near them was easy enough; wearing a shirt with the *Instituto Costarricense de Electricidad* logo and carrying a metal clipboard case, no one gave him a second look. Then, armed with enough general knowledge of the systems installed, he was able to acquire a signal jammer he was reasonably sure would work.

As for the real Javier Villalobos, he would wake in the morning with a nasty headache, wondering why he'd gone to sleep in his work van and what had happened to his shirt, lanyard, and ID badge.

While the man found the security system at the Tyler villa vastly more comprehensive and sophisticated and multilayered, it was not impenetrable. Every system had its vulnerabilities or work-arounds or exploitable backdoors, but even the more challenging ones could be breached with the right approach, tools, and skills. He was no black hat hacker or break-in artist, but he could pick most locks and had honed enough other penetration skills to get the job done. Sometimes there was a human lapse—though not with this bunch who were as suspicious and prudent and protective as hell—or an opportunity, whether by chance or design. For him, it was the latter, and when he'd seen the pool man and gardeners drive off the property, leaving the housekeeper alone, he could not believe his good luck.

To her credit, the woman had not been a pushover and, for a minute, he thought she was not going to let him inside voluntarily, but she did. From there, it was a matter of finding the door or window he could rig, which turned out to be the French doors to the patio. All of them were fitted with Cremone bolts, hardware that was particularly difficult to defeat from the outside. But in anticipation of encountering such an obstacle, he'd come equipped with a block of minicell foam, which he'd stuffed into the bolt holes while "inspecting" the sensors. Step two was the application of thin rare-earth magnets the size of a dime, stuck with a dot of Gaffer tape over the sensors of his chosen door.

As a result, after using the jammer to interrupt the alarm's detection frequencies, in timed bursts that would be perceived as dropouts attributed to background noise, the man had made it past the perimeter motion detectors. He forced open the French doors, the rare-earth magnets effectively masking the alarm sensors, and now he was upstairs working on the door handle to what he believed would give him what he needed.

With a penlight clamped between his teeth, he resumed rapping on the door handle with a rubber hammer he'd brought with him, and after a minute or so the handle broke hold and the deadbolt retracted. Not the most elegant way to force entry or—as proven here—the most stealthy, but quick and dirty got the job done. For a residence with such solid security installed, the man was a bit surprised at the choice of hardware; this type of lock was known to be susceptible to the very kind of brute-force penetration he'd just performed.

The man picked up the duffel bag at his feet, dropped the hammer inside, and slipped into the room, which was filled with the candescence of moonlight. He immediately saw that, as he'd guessed, it was not a bedroom. It had been converted to an office.

Jackpot.

With a spike of exhilaration, he took in the layout. The room was every bit as large as a master suite, with a wall of hand-carved wood-panel windows and French doors that matched those downstairs. The curtains were drawn back, revealing the glowing silhouettes of trees tucked amidst thick foliage, the globe of moon suspended in the night sky over the distant ocean, its light coating the water with a pale gold sheen. On one adjacent wall, a big trestle-style desk made of indigenous hardwood faced the interior of the room, a credenza and executive chair behind it. The opposite wall contained built-in bookcases populated with a wide-ranging assortment of books and reference materials, also curios from every part of the world. Scattered around open wall space were framed posters of fish, maps, and military decorations and awards, which he found himself compelled to step over and peruse.

But as he moved about the room, the initial glee he'd felt on accomplishing a successful breach quickly evaporated. Beyond the interesting décor and regimented order of the space, he realized there was nothing of any probative value. The desk and credenza tops, save for things like a small antique globe or a pair of bronze soldier bookends or a wood-and-brass clock, were utterly empty and pristine. No paper stacks, no folders, no notebooks, no calendar, nothing at all for him to riffle through—and no computers or electronics of any kind.

Next, he looked at the drawers and cabinet doors of the credenza, discovering that access to all was secured by smart locks. He thought he could probably hack them given some time, but that was something he did not have. Yes, he had restrained the housekeeper, but in a few hours the lifeguard would be up and he intended to be gone by then.

Frustrated now, for the first time since making entrance to the room he noticed what could be a holy grail of discovery. In an interior corner was a wide door that undoubtedly opened to a closet, probably a big walk-in. What made his pulse prickle with anticipation was the lock hardware, which tended to confirm his speculation; above the handle on this door was a sturdy-looking cylinder combination lock. What he did not know was that the lock, which was electronic and mounted on a deadbolt base plate, was a DoD-approved high-security Kaba Mas CDX.

He was betting this vault would contain exactly what he had set out to find—the treasure trove of computers and electronics and storage drives, the documents and data and records that could compromise and render vulnerability of its source. Not to mention, as a bonus, it probably held an embarrassment of tactical riches that would include all manner of weapons and ammunition and gear. His objective was to come away with Tyler's whereabouts, personal information, and known associates, but this…this could potentially give him a lot more.

First, he had to figure out a way to breach, because attempting to crack this kind of lock was a nonstarter. Weighing the risk and reward, he decided it was worth a gamble and dropped his duffel on the floor in front of the door, extracting cordless DeWalt power tools—an angle grinder and reciprocating saw—a demolition screwdriver, and his standard array of lock picks and bump keys.

Glancing at his watch, he saw that it was approaching 2 AM, so he wasted no time with analysis and got right to work. He quickly decided his best approach was the most roughshod, and even though he had unarmed the master security system after entry, there was a good possibility of triggering a separate alert, particularly a remote one. Picking his spot, he powered up the saw and began his attempted penetration.

Nearly forty-five minutes later, soaked in sweat and sapped of patience, he stepped back and shook his head in defeat. He had managed to get through a layer of plywood, at the cost of one of his angle grinder's discs, but that had not been what stopped him. Below the exterior drywall and plywood were sheets of metal, including iron and copper, shavings of which now littered the floor—all that was necessary to cease his operation because, even with a thermic lance, chances were he would never have succeeded.

"*Mierda,*" he muttered.

He was so disgusted that if he'd had an axe he would probably have demolished the room with the rabid ferocity of an HGTV fixer-upper, leaving a rubble of splintered and shattered framed material, pulverized sheetrock, and wood lopped into chunks of lumber. Even with all that destruction, he thought, this fortified security vault might well have remained mostly intact. From what he had encountered in its construction, there was no telling what other measures had been implemented.

He had one last point of leverage.

Gathering up the tools and tossing them into his bag, he let out a shrill growl, scooped up a cast-iron pineapple grenade paperweight and hurled it toward a framed photo on one of the bookcase shelves, appreciating the irony of the target it took down. In his exasperation, he had not aimed at anything specifically, but his toss had struck and cracked and sent flying an image of a younger Jake Tyler clad in battle dress, an AK-47 clutched over his chest.

In the picture, Tyler was standing in front of a location the man knew very well.

ENTERING THE HOUSEKEEPER'S BEDROOM, the man saw that she had tried to move around, but without much success. She sat on the floor in a spot no more than a foot or so from where he'd put her, legs folded to the side, duct tape intact over her mouth and ankles, zip-tied wrists behind her back.

She glared up at him, but her eyes widened with apprehension.

He dropped his duffel bag, stooped down in front of her, and drew out a knife. After working without it, he'd pulled the balaclava back over his head, leaving his mouth exposed, and now he leaned close to her face, the knife point touching her chin.

"I am going to take the tape off so we can have a talk...but if you raise your voice, it will be the last sound you make, *Señora.*"

The change of personal prefix was hardly lost on her, his diction crisp and menacing. He ripped the tape from her mouth, causing her to wince and gasp for air at the same time. When she could circulate enough saliva, she spat, *"Vete al diablo!"*

"I did not say you could speak, *puta*," he hissed, and pressed the blade of the knife against her neck, not quite drawing blood but with enough pressure to sting like a wire garotte.

She glowered at him, her nutmeg-colored eyes brimming with tears of anger and fear. "I tell you nothing," she said fiercely.

The knife edge bit into the flesh of her neck and she felt blood ooze from the cut. She prayed silently, her eyes closed. As she did, the poignant lyric from the song she'd heard earlier replayed in her mind: *Often happens that God be around the corner…what life has given and taken away.*

The man snarled, "Tyler, *dónde está?*"

She did respond, did not look at him.

"Dónde está, puta?" Holding the blade in his mouth, he took her by the shoulders and shook roughly, got nothing, and grasped the knife again. "I give you one last chance. Where the fuck is Tyler? Right now…where did he go? Tell me!" he screamed. "You know! You tell me right now!"

When the housekeeper refused to answer, he emitted a low howl of rage, and stood. Over his shoulder, through the windows, he noticed that the lunar light in the sky had flattened and changed hue as the solar ambers of dawn began to infuse.

He whipped back toward Camilla Márquez, the knife lashing viciously across her body.

JESSE SEGURA WOKE TO the musical alarm set on his phone, unusual for him as he was nearly always up before it went off. But last night he had slept like a comatose man, dead tired from yesterday's activity. He was sitting on the bed, stretching sluggishly, when he felt a sudden impetus rush through him in a hot jolt, as if raw caffeine had been injected directly into his bloodstream.

And then his mind brought the sense of urgency into clarity as he remembered the way the previous evening had ended. Upset with himself for sleeping so solidly—he had intended to make a couple of patrols in and outside the villa during the night—he rushed through a shower and hurriedly pulled on a fresh uniform of red swim trunks and blue shirt. Jabbing his feet into flip-flops, he sprinted through his door, strode briskly around the side of the villa, up the hill to the pool and patio, and headed for the lanai. The sky was barely blue, a stratus of cloud cover giving it the texture of cotton candy, the first flush of sunlight edging up from behind the eastern hills and casting a low glimmer over the Pacific to the west.

Segura tried the French doors by the kitchen, expecting them to be unlocked, Camilla in the kitchen preparing for breakfast; they were, and he stepped inside. But the kitchen was dark and empty, no coffee brewing. He glanced at his watch. It was 5:45 AM. She would be up.

"Camilla?" he called out, striding into the living area, which was also dark and still. A sourness spread in his stomach, a fluttering in his chest, and he padded to the stairs, climbing to the top, the sound of his flip-flops thwapping on the tiles.

"Camilla?"

He continued to call her name, his voice deepening in pitch, knowing now that something was wrong. Dreadfully wrong. He turned down the hallway and hurried to her door, which was ajar, and lurched inside the room.

And found her.

Jesse Segura sank to the floor, his knees in her blood, his throat collapsing in horror.

24

ON LANDING AT OMIROS, for all the lack of attention given them by airport personnel, they could have been a ghost plane, thanks to the advance machinations of Kipnis who had an established alliance with a local fixer. Moments after the Pilatus taxied in and came to a stop, an agent from the ground handler drove right up to the turboprop in their Jeep Gladiator, which Keanjaho Dmello had parked at the airport that morning. Without the scrutiny they might have otherwise received, they were able to quickly load the cases of procured arms into the SUV's cargo bed and exit.

Heading out along Leof. Enoseos, which traced the eastern coast, Remington and Dmello were tensely silent as Jake returned Jesse Segura's call. Jake had known something was wrong just by the timing; it was midafternoon here but barely past sunrise in Dominical.

When Segura answered, Jake listened for a minute and then asked, "So you're with her at the hospital in Cortés? What's her condition? I can be there—are you sure? Have the doctor call me, okay? Jesse…Jesse…no, it is *not* your fault. Okay, yeah, go be with her. Let me know anything you need or if anything changes." He ended the call and rubbed his temple, a dull ache spreading through his head as he tried to absorb what he had heard.

Beside him in the Gladiator's back seat, Remington asked, "What's her status?"

"Lost a good bit of blood and she's weak, but they got her stabilized."

"You want to go?"

With a weighty sigh, Jake replied, "I do, but it sounds like he's handling it. He says they don't think she'll be in the hospital more than a day or two."

Remington said, "We'll get Kip on this. He can scrub through the security feeds, maybe get something we can pursue. Also, how about I send a guy, maybe Sanborn?"

"That would be great."

Dmello spoke up. "Are we going straight back to the hotel?"

Jake and Remington exchanged bedraggled looks, Remington answering, "We look like a couple of dudes on the rough end of a roundup. I think we better find us some new clothes and get as cleaned up as we can, we're scary looking enough as it is. What do you think, partner?"

After doing a Google Maps search, they found a sports clothing store to the north, a six-minute drive to the seaport. Unlike the airport, their shopping stint in Cosmos drew quite a few stares and, while their appearances were vastly improved by the change of attire—a Lee shirt and Timberland cargo pants in khaki colors for Remington, black Columbia shirt and Gabba Rufo cargos for Jake—there was not much they could do to disguise the wounds of battle.

Back at Argentikon, they found Falcone and Niles with Callie lounging on chaises by the pool, all in swim attire and sunbaked. At the sight of Jake and Remington, all three sat up in astonishment, Callie's hand going to her mouth to cover a gasp.

"We're okay," Jake said peremptorily, his eyes honing in on Callie's.

Falcone blurted, "Jesus, you two look like—"

Before he could finish, Remington said, "Nothing a hot shower, some ibuprofen, and a stiff drink or three won't address. We broke up a fight."

"Bloody hell, mate," said Niles. "What do the other blokes look like?" He snickered, but watching Jake's face, went quiet.

Forcing a lighthearted smile and a tone that was full of false levity, Jake asked, "Where did you guys go today? Did you have fun?" He glanced hopefully at Callie, who ducked her head to hide culpability.

Falcone said, "Uh…we decided to just hang out here at the pool."

Jake's shoulders sagged, but after the day he'd had he was more relieved than disappointed, knowing that at least there had not been any stressors or traumas for Callie from what would have been innumerable launch points in a sightseeing jaunt around the city. "Okay." He held out his hand to her. "Let's go inside, love. I really do need that shower."

AFTER A LONG SHOWER and a short nap—which was not so much a nap as some reassurance intimacy that only involved gentle cuddling to let Callie know he was really all right, even if he was sore all over—Jake carefully rolled out of the ornate wooden bed in their suite, wincing with each movement. The punches and chops, the knee jabs and kicks to the kidneys and gut and chest, the impact of being tossed and slammed inside the Jeep, had all settled deep into his muscles and joints, the hot water and anti-inflammatory medication only helping so much.

As he had lay with Callie nestled in his arms, kissing her with swollen lips, he knew there would be a lifetime of duplicity on his part; *I'm all right, baby, I'm fine...no need to worry about me.* He felt bad about lying to her although, technically, this time it had been Remington who had lied, but he realized it was going to be a compulsory element of his safeguarding her emotional security.

He heard her stir in the bed and turned, smiling and trying his best to mask the discomfort he was feeling on all fronts.

"Hungry?" he asked her. "I know I am."

JAKE JOINED THE OTHERS in the courtyard restaurant realizing that, in the chaos of the day, there had been no lunch and, with the excessive amount of energy expended, he was struck with a sudden onset of hunger. Callie was clinging to his side, her hand tightly clasping his, sensing he was about to nudge her away, which he did, asking her to take another walk around the grounds with Falcone and Niles. Once he'd convinced her to go, he dropped into a chair at a table where Remington already sat, a tumbler of whiskey in hand.

When the server had brought Jake a gin and tonic, he took a generous gulp and groaned softly. "God, what a day."

"Hell of way to wrap up your honeymoon," Remington commented drably.

The sky had paled with the departure of sun, early stars dotting the cornflower blue like tiny dabs of white paint. The stone pavers were dark, the foliage of encircling trees illuminated by the flames of the table candles flickering in the breeze.

Remington asked, "Heard anything else about Camilla?"

"Jesse called back and put her doctor on. He said she had a pretty major wound across her front requiring a lot of stitches, but she's responding well. He also said there was a less serious knife wound on her neck."

He paused, took another draw from his drink. "Jesse said she hasn't been able to talk much, what with the drugs they've got her on, but he did say she told him something to the effect that she didn't tell."

Remington stroked the copper whiskers on his chin, thinking. "The guy must have been interrogating her about you. But he didn't kill her. He could have, but he didn't."

Jake let that sink in, his forehead furrowed with anguish. "I consider them to be family." He met Remington's eyes. "Like you."

"I know, bud." He leaned close. "But she's alive. She's going to be okay."

Neither spoke for a few minutes, simply sat in the gathering shadows of evening, two men adrift in their own thoughts but as connected as two birds on a wire. Both looked up with the appearance of Efron Kipnis. He took a seat between Jake and Remington, a computer tablet in his hands.

"I wish I had something," he said solemnly.

"Shit. You don't? Nothing at all?" Jake tipped his head back, squeezed his eyes shut, visibly frustrated.

"This guy knew what he was doing. It's obvious that a lot of planning went into his invasion. Not only by being able to breach, but also taking the cameras out."

Kipnis flattened his tablet so they could both see the screen, swiping through images. The first few showed Camilla responding to the doorbell, hesitating and then reluctantly letting the technician who was not a technician inside, his face completely obscured by a downward tilt of his head and the ball cap on top of it. Soon afterward, the feeds went black.

"There's no visual of the guy after his entrance?"

Kipnis shook his head.

"Fuck," Jake bristled.

"I'm going to keep working on this," Kipnis told him, and turned to Remington. "And I'll be guiding Sanborn through upgrading the property security even more as soon as he's on-site. I also spoke with your police captain in Dominical, to see what they were able to determine from the scene. Unfortunately, they didn't turn up much, either, other than the guy drugged a real Pacifica technician and used his creds."

"How did he get in?"

"Well, parsing the metadata, he used a high-quality jammer…initially to trigger an error and later in timed bursts that allowed him to outwit the alarm. I made sure your system was damn near impossible to jam, but apparently he was able to capture the frequencies and knew exactly how long to shoot the pulses without triggering. As far as entry, he got in through the rear patio doors."

Knowing what had been done to reinforce each and every door and window in the villa, Jake asked, "How in the hell?"

Kipnis shook his head. "Like I said, the guy knew what he was doing. At least the storage room we fortified held up. He attempted to cut his way in, but didn't get very far."

"Then he went after Camilla," Jake said, his expression gaunt with gloom. He sighed heavily. "It seems like shit's coming from every direction. Here, there…what next? And is any of it connected?"

No one had an answer.

"I just worry that whatever is going on will put our gig and everyone involved in jeopardy. I don't want that. I can't have that."

Unexpectedly, it was Kipnis who continued speaking, a steeliness surfacing from behind his studious and composed façade. "We won't let that happen," he said evenly.

Remington nodded with affirmation in Jake's direction and raised his nearly empty glass. He upended it into his mouth and set the tumbler on the table. "Brother, we've got you and we've got this."

But all Jake could think about was his beloved housekeeper, slashed and bleeding in his home, refusing to divulge anything and almost losing her life in the process. He felt responsible and helpless and out of control.

The muted sound of a buzzing phone drew his attention back to Remington.

After a short exchange with the caller, Remington said, "That was Caspian. Everything is on schedule, so they'll be here in the morning. Going to be a busy evening." He looked a question to Jake with a mix of compassion and conviction.

Jake said, "All right, let's get on it."

25

THE BACK END OF Jake's honeymoon trip commenced at 8:20 AM the next morning with the touchdown of a forty-eight-seat Olympic Air ATR out of Athens, nearly half of which was occupied by the contingent of MVAA staff and military veterans. They filed down the airstairs and spilled onto the tarmac, mostly men and some women, mostly young to middle age but some older, walking in an almost synchronized cadence without being consciously aware of it. Collectively, they wore jeans and t-shirts and ball caps, backpacks and duffels slung over their shoulders, their expressions guardedly inquisitive.

MVAA stood for Military Veterans Archaeology Alliance, and they were Jake and Remington's contract gig.

Preceding the group down the stairs was a woman in her early thirties with an athletic build and assertive demeanor, toffee-colored hair worn long and loose past her shoulders, khaki chinos and a navy blue t-shirt imprinted with the org's American flag-backed logo. Bookending was an equally fit-looking but lankier man in similar attire—with the exception of Western-style Double H work boots—wearing Ray-Ban shades. His hair was light brown, short and wisping in the breeze, a hand brushing it back in an ineffectual attempt to keep it tidy. He flashed a winsome smile as he approached, his freckled face translucent in the sun.

Remington strode to greet him, returning the smile and extending his hand. "Caspian, hey. Good to see you, man."

"Likewise!"

In the way of explanation for his and Jake's facial cuts and discolorations, Remington offered, "Minor vehicle accident." Then, turning to his friend, he said, "Jake, this is Caspian Bachman."

Handshakes were exchanged, and Bachman introduced the woman from the front of the pack as Shelby Hoskins, his operations manager, and gestured to another woman of about the same age with bob-cut dark blond hair, in jeans and MVAA t-shirt, who had been patrolling along the line, her gaze trained on the faces and movements of all. She was presented as the group's mental health clinician, Gwen Maddigan.

Most, if not all of the veterans she was so keenly observing were suffering from some degree of PTSD, a few from TBI, several from other combat-related disabilities.

Already, the travelers were beginning to fidget and shuffle, so Bachman said, "Let's get everyone on the bus. We need to keep things moving."

Remington nodded knowingly. "Regiment. Gotcha. We're parked over by the bus, so as soon as everyone is on board, we'll lead the way."

Caspian Bachman, a former staff sergeant in the U.S. Air Force, had come to contract Remington's *Habari* by way of Kipnis, who had met Bachman during a previous MVAA joint archaeological expedition with a group in Beth She'arim, Israel. While attending a defense expo in Tel Aviv, Kipnis had taken a side trip to visit their site to catch up with a comrade running the Israeli effort. The acquaintance, who had served with Kipnis in the Israel Defense Force, introduced him to Bachman and, subsequently, when Bachman had sought a logistics recommendation for this Greek venture, he'd thought of *Habari*.

With the shared military background, Remington and Bachman hit it off, both, like Jake, also passionate about supporting other veterans.

After his military service, Bachman had earned a Ph.D. in archaeology from the University of Cambridge and, while volunteering with an organization for traumatized vets, came up with the idea for MVAA. His was not the first of its kind—Bachman had become familiar with a British initiative built around assisting in the recovery of service personnel injured in conflict—but he decided to shape the clay of their base model into something even more impactful and sustainable and one which put more focus on mental health. In the initial years, his projects had been tweaked and refined to the point where, for the most part, they were now a fairly smooth and structured operation. But there were always challenges and complications that threatened to disrupt the harmonious congruity critical to the mental and emotional stability of the vets in his care, especially with projects on foreign soil.

Walking to the bus parked on the airfield, Bachman said, "I definitely made the right decision in contracting you guys. Normally, I am already stressed at this point, juggling the details on both ends. Having you handling things here has really lightened my workload significantly."

Remington smiled. "I'm glad. That's the whole point."

Jake said, "We're honored to be involved because we really believe in the objectives. And I'm intrigued to see how it all works."

Bachman beamed with pride. "Pretty sure you'll be impressed."

A SHORT DRIVE TOOK them to the Chios Chandris, a five-floor oyster-colored hotel lapped on two sides by the Aegean. The coach-style bus pulled up beside the building next to the seawall, and its passengers began to disembark, stopping to gaze out over the sparkling azure water. Several snapped pictures, some were simply entranced.

Bachman sidled up to Jake and Remington. "We don't normally do four-star luxury accommodations," he remarked, but his expression held no disapproval. He added, "Given the more primitive setup for the rest of the duration, I'm sure it will be appreciated. Unfortunately, we'll probably also hear some grumbles about not having something equally as cushy the rest of the way."

"No worries," Remington remarked. "We'll deal."

Jake had only been half listening as he looked for any sign of Falcone and Niles who, with Kipnis, were supposed to be bringing Callie from Argentikon. He was about to make a call to check on them when a gleaming silver-gray Mercedes GLS drew up beside him. The driver's window slid down, framing the head and shoulder of Kipnis, Falcone riding shotgun.

Jake whistled. "Nice ride." He bent down, trying to get a glimpse into the back seat.

Kipnis gave him an indulgent smile. "Relax. We've got her."

The SUV's passenger doors swung open, Falcone and Niles popping out from opposite sides and converging on the right rear door, which they held for Callie's exit.

She stepped out uncertainly, looking nervously around for Jake and, on seeing him, smiled with relief. The looks she got from the vets assembled nearby, ogling the pretty blond wrapped in a blue-and-white floral silhouette sheath, spiked instant insecurity. Her hands fretted with the spaghetti straps and ruffles of the frock's front slit.

As she stood in the morning sunshine, pale hair lifting and falling in the blowing air, slim legs outlined by the thin fabric of her dress pressed against her in the breeze, Jake felt his heart convulse with a joy that—at least for the moment—washed over and rinsed away all griefs and gravities like the warm, rejuvenating rush of an ocean wave.

He went to her, slipped an arm around her shoulders, and kissed her lightly. Feeling his touch, his closeness, his breath on her skin, her pulse raced but anxiety eased. In her ear, he said, "You look beautiful, love."

The group was settled into their rooms with instructions to reassemble at eleven o'clock in the hotel's Elinda restaurant, where a buffet lunch with salads and appetizers, meats and seafood and pastas, fruits and desserts were arranged. On convening there, they found their pre-assigned seats at white-linen-covered tables with a palm tree-lined view of the harbor, mountains rising in the near distance.

Bachman had explained that, for these vets, precision and routine and explicit direction was key in everything, from travel arrangements to housing assignments to itinerary and program objectives. With that in mind, Remington had followed his requirements to the letter, making sure every aspect was set with nothing left to be determined. Logistics being a significant part of Remington's *Habari* operations, he was accustomed to managing on multiple fronts simultaneously and, to that end, had delegated and deployed members of his team to their next destinations. Earlier that morning, he had checked in with each to ensure that everything was fluid and totally prepared.

With Jake making the arrangements for a private jet charter to expedite the travel of Kent Sanborn to Costa Rica, Remington had also reached out to and subsequently contracted another associate to be picked up in Morocco.

The number of the MVAA group doubled in the restaurant as they were joined by locals that included archaeology experts and undergrad students who had been arriving since the day before.

At noon, they gathered in a conference room, which was every bit as elegantly appointed as the restaurant, bright with the daylight from floor-to-ceiling windows, round red columns interspersed with white cascading chandeliers. Rows of gold-trimmed chairs were labeled with each participant's name and stacked with org t-shirts, caps, and information packets. A long banner with the MVAA logo hung above the speaking dais, which was where Caspian Bachman now stood. Behind him in a line of chairs were Shelby Hoskins and Gwen Maddigan, and a scholarly looking bearded man in his thirties with prematurely graying hair wearing a sunburst-patterned Dickies shirt open over a tee which read *I DIG DIRT*. Jake and Remington sat on the other side of Bachman with Kipnis, Dmello, and Falcone and Niles seated in the first row of conference chairs.

Callie sat between Falcone and Niles, her legs crossed at the ankles, hands clasped in her lap, and eyes wide with wonder as she stole looks around the big room, avoiding contact with the assortment of strange faces gaping at her from their seats.

Tapping the microphone to test the volume and get heads looking in his direction, Bachman announced, "Welcome, everyone! Some of you have been on other projects and know the drill, but for many this is the first time, and we also have the company of local students and a few area archaeologists. In this orientation, I'll be going over expectations and objectives, our rules of the road, and answer any questions you may have."

Next, he introduced everyone behind him, identifying the scholarly man as Kostas Demetriadi, the project's lead archaeologist. Pointing out Falcone and Niles, Bachman said, "And these two are with Nash Remington's outfit and will be our documentarians."

He sipped from a glass of water on the lectern and continued. "Let me begin by saying that this is not a vacation or a field trip or any kind of junket. We take this work seriously with the full intent of meaningful results, and make no mistake, it will be hard and physically demanding work. Eight-hour days beginning at dawn.

"You have probably read about this project's mission objective, but for those who might not be completely familiar…we will be conducting our dig in the hope of recovering the remains of U.S. airmen and the wreckage of their B-24. This venture is being executed in conjunction with the DPAA—Defense POW/MIA Accounting Agency—from a newly declassified top-secret OSS mission from World War II, in which a squadron of Greek American airmen were en route from San Pancrazio, Italy to overfly Rhodes. The aircraft was thought to have crashed or been shot down over the north Aegean, but newly uncovered archives, along with some recent debris recovery, suggest a possible terminus on Antipsara. There's a detailed account in your information packets."

After summarizing past MVAA projects, Bachman turned the podium over to Shelby Hoskins for an overview of the daily work schedule, meals and breaks, and rotation of assignments for routine responsibilities, such as cooking and cleaning. She also discussed his principles for personal comportment and the protocol for reporting any problems or issues with the work or individuals in the group.

When she began going over rules and regulations in more specificity, Niles leaned back behind Callie until he caught Falcone's attention and whispered, "Bloody hell…Jake never said anything about no boozing!"

Falcone frowned and shushed him but wasn't thrilled with the revelation, either.

In coming to the close of the orientation, Bachman said, "We will hold you to the highest standard, not only to elevate you personally but to also reflect our military professionalism while casting the best possible light on archaeology. That, to me, is as essential as anything.

"All that said, enjoy the experience, learn things, become immersed and invested in discovery. As I said, the work will test you, so pace yourself. You know the saying…it's a marathon not a sprint."

BACHMAN HAD LET THEM know that he only allowed a limited amount of activity outside of their projects, primarily because of the need to keep his charges in a controlled environment and under his supervision, but for this day he had set aside time for an afternoon of attractions within close proximity to the hotel. These included the

Castle of Chios and the Byzantine, Maritime, and Archaeological museums. Jake and Remington spent the time in the sitting area of Jake's suite while Callie rested in the bedroom.

Her anxiety level had been rising ever since arriving at the Chandris, and though Jake had tried his best to allay her qualms, he could see that it was all just too much. The departure from Argentikon without him, being thrust into the midst of so many people that were strangers, albeit invited ones, and most of all, realizing that his focus was being pulled away from her, had pushed her toward a panic state. He'd sat beside her on the bed as long as he could, finally telling her gently that he needed to work with Remington.

Now, slouched back on the sofa, he raked a hand through his black hair and heaved a forlorn sigh.

Finishing a call with Luther Baladur, who was overseeing things on the other end, Remington asked, "Any better?"

Jake shook his head disconsolately. After a long silence, he said, "And I doubt it's going to be. This was a bad idea for her…but I can't change course with what's happened."

"What's the latest?"

"I called Jesse early this morning to get him in the evening there, and he actually put Camilla on the phone. She was more upset about being deceived and the damage done to my office than she was about what happened to her. I told her not to even think about going back to our villa, but she would not hear it. She's a damn force of nature."

"That she is," Remington agreed. He then said, "We will make it work. Give it a chance."

Jake blew out a breath. "Well, I have to." In an effort to balance his emotions, he sat forward and affirmed, "Bachman's impressive, and so is this initiative."

"I knew you'd think so." Remington edged up in his chair and leaned over the coffee table where notepads and folders were strewn along with schematics for what would be their basecamp. "Okay, let me catch you up with where we are with everything."

AS THE SUN BEGAN to lower in the sky, its blue fading as that of the sea below it deepened in the waning light, Jake sat with Callie on the balcony of their suite. He had been trying to draw her into a light dialogue, but so far she had been pensively reticent, her gaze on the sailboats creasing the water.

Scooting his chair over and pulling hers toward him, his legs straddling the sides, Jake reached for her neck and cupped it in his hand, his fingers caressing and threading the curls of her hair. She looked as lovely as ever, fair skin suffused with the rubicund pinks of the sun's heat, but the sags and shadows around her eyes exposed the bane of extensive restlessness.

"Sweetie, I know you're feeling anxious about everything now, but it will be all right. I'm going to be busy, yes, but I will be with you and make sure you're as comfortable as possible." With his other hand, he lifted her chin so that their eyes met and said, "I'm sure it will be a little unnerving at first, but I think it will get easier as we settle into the day to day."

She blinked, the last touching a strident chord. "Day to day?" she questioned.

Realizing his unfortunate choice of words, which implied what was the reality of a longer rather than shorter term, he attempted to ameliorate his reassurance, adding, "I mean, when the initial adjustment of settling into a new scenario…"

But there was no pulling it back, and Callie seemed to understand exactly what he'd meant, even if she did not really know the full scope. She knew they were not going home anytime soon. She tucked her head, not wanting Jake to see the tears beading in her eyes.

STANDING IN THE EXPANDING shadows of the stone-paved promenade at the sea edge that ran along the side of the Chandris, a lone man dressed in tan slacks and a mint-green shirt was looking up, head tilted back, cigarette dangling from his mouth. He was peering through dark sunglasses at the balcony where Jake and Callie sat, not really seeing them but knowing they were there. Knowing, because he had been watching from one point or another since earlier in the day when they had arrived at the hotel in various vehicles, along with a big coach bus filled with a group of stalwart, no-nonsense-looking men and women. Perhaps a little cagey, some with slightly less fluidity of movement, but venerable.

He had observed the arrival with growing curiosity and a considerable amount of tension as the intelligence was bearing out, even if intent and motive were not at all clear. But one thing was clear—the presence of all these people was a major complication.

He smoked his cigarette and turned to survey the harbor, watching a Fairline Phantom motor yacht coasting into the marina, watched as it maneuvered to reverse into an open slot farther down the promenade. Finishing his smoke, he dropped the butt on the stone pavers and ground it out with his shoe.

Then he took out his phone, tapped the screen, and held it to his ear. A second later, he said, *"Evet, buradalar."*

26

THEIR CARAVAN ROLLED OUT before the first kiss of daylight had touched the ground, something to which the internal time clocks of the vets and even the few archaeologists were well accustomed. The students in the group were less adapted, but their excitement—and the bountiful breakfast buffet—made the early rise a little more tolerable.

Driving in front with Dmello and Kipnis in the Jeep Gladiator were a droopy Falcone and Niles; Remington drove with Jake and Callie in the more comfortable Mercedes SUV, the Malinois dogs enjoying the windows on either side of Callie. Trailing the bus, Remington toggled through radio stations on the sleek infotainment screen, micro blitzes of music spritzing the air as he searched for something he wanted to hear. Amidst a crazy-quilt mix of traditional Greek and globally popular tunes, he landed on an oldies station playing White Snake's anthemic *Here I Go Again*, and lingered, robustly singing along.

Jake give him a look from the passenger seat. "Remy."

"What?"

"Brother…not this early in the morning."

"Oh, come on. Well, I'm not playing Ed fricking Sheeran…I'll be nodding off at the wheel." He continued his search, finally settling on a channel streaming the mellow but baroque strains of Fleet Foxes.

Glancing into the back seat, Jake saw that Callie was hypnotically watching the landscape roll by, the music seemingly calming her jitters. He gave Remington an approving nod and they both went quiet and concentrated on the drive, Jake surveying the road in their wake as much as that unspooling before them. Except for the few locals entering and exiting from town side roads, they were the only traffic.

The hour-long trip north across the island took them through barren, mountainous terrain ribboned with steep and acutely twisting switchbacks. Dawn broke over the lunarlike peaks to the east behind them, painting an apricot and saffron canvas for the flame of sun that followed. The Chiou-Keramou road carved its way to the western coast, skirting the town of Volissos, the legendary birthplace of Homer, and winding up at the port of Limniá.

The small marina, bracketed by the pebbled-beach coves of Lefkathia and Magemena, held a dozen or so modest boats within its scooped anchorage, most tethered to a square dock. A couple of taverns along the frontage were lifeless at this hour of the morning save for a smattering of older men having coffee outside one of them, their curiosity piqued by the large group disembarking from the bus that had turned in from the road. It parked on a large concrete pad on the other side of the dock, the Gladiator and Mercedes pulling in next to it.

Anchored just off the pad was a boat that stood out from the others, more for its size than appearance, some seventy-five feet in length with an awning-covered upper deck. It had clearly seen a few decades but was well-maintained, freshened by new coats of white paint trimmed in wide blue stripes and christened *Blue Zone.* Its captain, leathery-skinned and silver-haired, looked to have aged right along with it but had also withstood the years in similar fashion, muscular and energetic. He moved along the vessel's deck, issuing brisk instructions to a pair of young crewmen. Parallel to the dock, a boarding ramp had been extended, another pair of men ferrying the group's luggage from the bus.

The captain strode across the ramp to the dock and went straight to Remington, with whom he was obviously already familiar, letting him know that everything was in order and they could depart as soon as all were boarded. Remington introduced him to Jake and Caspian Bachman as George Salivara, and then captain and crew resumed preparations for departure.

Bachman was just preoccupied enough with the sorting and settlement of his group that he paid no heed to Dmello and Kipnis transporting the cases of arms, which were stowed in a secure cargo hold the captain had cleared for them.

Falcone and Niles had cameras out and were circulating through the crowd but not finding anyone particularly enthusiastic about being filmed.

After noting some recessive, even surly rebuffs from the prospective subjects, Jake sidled over to Falcone and Niles as they fumbled disconcertingly with their equipment, most of which was new since the previous ensemble had been pretty thoroughly ravaged in Africa. Once again, the limitless generosity of Amelia Keogh had seen to it that they got the best, including a high-end Sony Venice cinematography camera, a Canon EOS Mark III, and an upgraded GoPro Hero.

"Ease into it, guys," Jake advised evenly. "You've got to remember who you're dealing with. You're going to have to gain their trust, build a rapport." He paused, then candidly added, "You can be…a lot."

Falcone was instantly defensive. "What?"

Niles echoed his response, though his expression was one of whimsical impertinence. "What'dya mean by that, mate?"

Jake said, "I think you know what I mean by that. Just take it easy on them, okay?"

"Yeah, okay," Falcone replied.

Watching the two of them gather their gear and board the boat, Jake turned his attention to Callie, pressed close to him. Her face was a rising flood of resistance churning against submission, desperation meeting in the vortex. Her widened eyes darted from the milling vets and academia and archaeologists to the vessel they were boarding. Jake had come to know the look and the feelings coalescing behind it.

Calmly, he said, "Come on, baby doll, let's find us a good seat."

THE PASSENGER BOAT NAVIGATED the choppy waters of the Chios crossing with surprising speed and stability. Most enjoyed the commute, some from seats inside the cabin, others from the rows of benches on the top deck, and a few from the side railings and bow. There were, however, a handful whose stomachs did not take well to the constantly fluctuating equilibrium, keeping Jake busy checking vitals, hydrating, and dispensing meclizine for motion sickness.

Like Jake, Bachman and his staff kept up a continual rotation to monitor the comfort and countenance of all, Bachman already honing in on a few individuals he would be watching the most closely for one reason or another. With each project, MVAA saw a number of returnees, some vets becoming so hooked on the work and experience and team dynamic that it became an ongoing commitment. But there were always newcomers and, no matter how much vetting was done—and Bachman was meticulously thorough—what was revealed in pre-screening interviews and DD-214s or archived in files, paper or digital, did not always expose potential problems.

As it would turn out, the one he should have been watching did not initially throw up any red flags, did not stand out in a good or bad way, did not really blend in but managed to be achromatic enough to stay outside the margins of early extra diligence.

At the marina, this member of the group had been furtively scoping out land and sea, his eyes sweeping the taverns and businesses of the port's frontage and the boats lining the dock. He had looked out to the watery horizon, to the small and larger vessels staggered at various distances, and then back to the craft they were about to board. Panned the group as a whole and individually, as he had done from the first gathering. And began to analyze and assess those running the show.

THE PASSAGE OF SEVENTEEN nautical miles took just over an hour, the *Blue Zone* sailing northwest to what would be their base of operations for the days ahead.

With its quaint fisherman's port encircled by white block buildings and houses roofed in terra-cotta ceramic, Psara is a diminutive and, on the surface, homogenous kind of island. But what it lacks in a visually dazzling harbor front chock-full of estates cascading down from the hills or majestic castles and chapels rising into the sky, it makes up for in a natural, bare-bones beauty that has withstood centuries of tragic history, notably the thousands of lives lost at the hands of the Ottomans during the Greek War of Independence.

In one of the most infamous confrontations, invading Turks stormed the fort of Palaiokastro—contemporarily known as Mavri Rachi or Black Ridge—where the island's citizens had taken refuge, and rather than surrender, they made a final stand, throwing out a white flag with the words *FREEDOM OR DEATH*. A valiant Psariot by the name of Antonios Vratsanos lit the fuse to a stock of gunpowder and blew up the marauders, killing them but also taking their own lives. The destruction of Psara was memorialized in the verse of poets Andreas Kalvos and Dionysios Solomos who penned: *Glory walks by herself taking in the bright young men on the war field…the crown of her hair wound from the last few grasses left on the desolate earth.*

The seven small islands of the North Aegean chain include Antispara, Ai-Nikolaki, Prasonisi, Daskalio, Kato Nisi, and Nisiopoula, all uninhabited except Psara, which claims a mere three to five hundred full-time residents.

After docking, luggage and gear was distributed between a fleet of SUVs that had been appropriated and transported by ferry from Chios; with very few vehicles on the island and no buses, this had been one of the more essential arrangements. Bachman, Remington, and lead archaeologist Kostas Demetriadi spent some time entertaining the pleasantries of a local welcoming committee that included the mayor and a few members of the city council. News of their presence had also drawn a throng of inquisitive and enthusiastic town locals which, apparently, was something MVAA frequent-flyers were used to but an unnerving spectacle for some of the newcomers.

Also in the mix were a group of correspondents from various media outlets, most by prior coordination and with whom Bachman would be granting limited access and interviews. Articulate and engaging, he took advantage of all the positive press he could get, advocating for both the field of archaeology and his organization. On hand today were reporters from the *Greek City Times*, *Greek Reporter*, and *Hellenic News*, as well as *Archeology* and *Smithsonian* magazines. Bachman greeted all, gave some remarks about their endeavor, and then fielded questions. Pictures were taken and arrangements made for additional press coverage on-site.

The late morning was bright and hot, and while Jake and Remington would have preferred to proceed directly to the restaurant on the beach side of the port, it was suggested they first take the short hike along a stepped stone path going uphill toward the southernmost peninsula of the island. At the summit was the small church of Aghia Anna and Aghios Ioannis and, nearby, the Mavri Rachi war memorial, where they took in the panoramic view overlooking the town settlement below and the sea all around, Antipsara looming just across to the west.

THE RESTAURANT KNOWN AS Spitalia is an eighteenth-century structure that extends over the edge of Katsouni Beach, its roof scalloped atop cobbled stone walls and a series of turquoise doors opening into five rooms with five fireplaces. The word *spitalia* translates as hospital, which is what it once was, a quarantine facility for returning sailors. Converted in 1976, it has been a family-run fish house serving freshly caught seafood and local meats and vegetables ever since.

Like everything else, lunch for the group had been planned in advance and, while there was ample room for their number inside the restaurant, Remington had chosen al fresco dining on the terrace surround. White wood tables, seated with chairs painted in pastels and shaded by wide aqua umbrellas, accommodated the vets and others in fours while Jake and Callie sat with Falcone and Niles, Kipnis and Dmello, at the end side of the building, water from the bay lapping close below. Remington shared a table with Bachman in the MVAA mix, taking advantage of the time to discuss rollout of the afternoon.

Restaurant staff and members of the family began setting out Greek and house salads, the former composed with the traditional fresh garden vegetables and feta, the latter also locally sourced with figs and green apples and cashews, followed by *bourekakia*, an appetizer that everyone was scarfing down with unbidden enthusiasm. The fried phyllo-wrapped ham and cheese rolls quickly disappeared and were replaced by shrimp and lobster pasta and grilled goat with rice. The festive music of Chios-born Mikis Theodorakis, known for *Zorba the Greek*, played from speakers, a hum of casual conversation hovering just below its volume.

The setting had the chill feel of a backyard pool hangout, the temperament of the group accordingly amenable, all enjoying the sunshine and sea breeze and port scenery. All consuming healthy amounts of food in a manner that suggested it might be their last of such quality and quantity for a while.

All except for one.

In the chair beside him, Callie's leg touched Jake's and he could feel spontaneous tremors. He had been watching her steadily, had seen the light sheen develop on her face and neck, the vacant glaze in her eyes. And, despite his occasional nudges and coaxing endearments, she had done little more than poke at her salad and swirl pasta around her fork. While he'd been hoping she would settle, this was a state he knew so well, one that more often than not was unstoppable once it initiated. He could sometimes sense the onset before the first harbingers manifested, but it could spring up as suddenly and unexpectedly as a storm without a foreboding front.

Such was the nature of PTSD, whether borne of a military battlefield or of something else. Her something else was, in his mind, every bit as traumatic if not much worse.

Jake finished chewing a chunk of lobster and wiped his mouth on his napkin. Leaning close to Callie, he put his arm around her shoulders, which hitched involuntarily. "What's the matter, sweetheart?" he asked, though of course he knew.

She looked up at him, her expression empty of explanation, eyes blinking with helplessness.

They sat at a table next to the low stone wall encompassing the terrace, and as Jake was gazing into her face, trying to transmit calming telepathy, he saw the pupils of her eyes dilate, her breath catch. He turned, glancing toward the sea, and spotted what had arrested her attention—a pair of white swans, paddling and floating and flexing their long necks.

Smiling, he said, "Well, look at that." Seizing the opportunity for deflection, he took her hand and stood up from the table. She rose on wobbly legs and went with him to the stone wall but hung back. He sat on the ledge and gestured for her to join him.

She edged over cautiously and he drew her into his torso, easing her onto his thigh and reassuring, "I've got you. Look...aren't they beautiful?"

The two of them peered down at the elegant birds coasting back and forth in the water, their feathers as white as arctic snow in the sunlight, pointed orange bills and foreheads outlined in black that looked like the work of a felt-tipped pen. He watched her watching the swans and briefly thought he might have pulled her out of it. She was captivated by their synchronized gliding, side by side, the tips of their bills dipping into the water, creating spirals in the glassy surface, the sand underneath gleaming like molten gold.

And then, inexplicably, something broke the blessed gift of their tranquility. The pair of birds erupted in a frantic fit of flaring and flapping wings, feathers fluffed, necks extended, hissing and honking and squawking, thrashing wildly in water that, moments ago, had been undisturbed enough to reflect delicate ripples.

Jake could see no reason for the uproar, but his bafflement jumped track immediately as he felt Callie begin to convulsively shake in his arms.

SHE WAS BLINDED BY the white and thrust into a purgatory of blackness that had snared and drug her down into the infernal abyss all too many times. The clamor of the swans with the outstretched capes of their wings and the fluster of their feathers had blurred into a whiteout that morphed into something else.

A cloud of white powder.

And in that abyss, she was slouched on a sofa, paralyzed, the room with the sofa going in and out of focus. Even in the state of incapacitation and mental fogginess she'd been in, terror had consumed her. The white powder had come from a decorative china tureen in the middle of a round, glass-topped mahogany table, upended by one of two men in the throes of a heated interchange. The crock had shot up and then dropped, hit the tile floor, and shattered into shards scrolled with little flowers, the cloud of white caking the air and atomizing as it drifted and thinned into smoke and coated surfaces like sifted flour.

The two men—both dark-haired and swarthy and utterly horrifying—screamed at each other, their faces contorted with fury, but their shared intent had not been compromised and, at some point afterward, she had been snatched from the sofa and deposited in a locked, dank room.

Not long after that, the invasive and relentless brutalization had begun, leaving her violated and broken in ways that defied all elucidation.

The depth and darkness was closing up around her, her heart and lungs flailing in her chest.

"CALLIE."

Jake's low, husky voice, close and soothing.

"Sweetie."

She heard him and then she felt him, his cheek against hers, arms snug around her.

"You're all right…I've got you. I'm right here." His fingers on her wrist, he was still counting close to two hundred beats. He pulled his head back and said, "Look at me, love." When she did, gasping and not really drawing any air, he said, "Slow, deep breaths…in, out…slow, slow…that's it."

He continued for several minutes, his demeanor firm but gentle, and gradually got the desired outcome as her pulse slowed and breathing regulated.

When she spoke, it was two single words in pleading desperation. "There…he…" And a shuddering exhale that was like the liberation of something tortured and trapped.

Enfolding her completely, he stroked her hair and murmured comfortingly. "I know, I know. It's okay, you're okay."

The calmness he projected concealed the pain he actually felt, reliving some of his own hell with each and every time she was stricken.

Kipnis and Dmello, Falcone and Niles, stood nearby, their faces mirroring concern, but Kipnis wisely advised them to give Jake his space.

Bachman's mental health clinician, Gwen Maddigan, had somehow gotten wind of the episode and appeared from the side terrace, starting toward them.

Jake wordlessly held out a hand to stop her advancement, giving a light nod to let her know he had everything under control.

Maddigan stood for a moment, observing thoughtfully, but a commotion from back around the corner diverted her attention and she turned to see what was happening.

Bachman and Remington were positioned between two male vets, both in their thirties and, by their aggressive posturing, clearly alpha types. One was more physically imposing, with gym-maintained musculature, toned arms and thick thighs, somewhat longish, sun-lightened hair and beard; the other was wiry and runner-fit, with a razor cut, bronzed skin, and an angular face.

The stocky bearded guy, a former U.S. Marines master sergeant named Kirk Perry, had participated in multiple MVAA projects and held a squad leader position as a result; the leaner guy, Daniel Rodriguez, a former senior airman, was a first-timer and probationary candidate.

Both were talking over each other and jostling shoves, buffeted by Bachman and Remington.

Perry was red-faced with outrage. "Dude, you don't know what the fuck you're talking about, but you need to shut your fucking mouth right now."

"If I don't know what I'm talking about," Rodriguez asserted, "why is it out there? More to the point, how the hell did you get on here with that in your fucking jacket?"

"Out there?" Perry yelled. "What the fuck, man?" His arm shot past Bachman and would have reached Rodriguez, but another squad leader stepped in to provide additional support.

In response, Rodriguez lunged toward Perry, but Remington held him back. "Hey, hey, bud. Stop it. Stop it right now."

Bachman asked, "Kirk, what's this about?"

Perry blew out a frustrated breath, grabbed the top of his head, and looked away in despondence, realizing for the first time the dilemma he'd become a part of. "Shit. Caspian, I'm sorry. Christ."

"What's this about?" Bachman repeated, his voice brittle.

"Dude's talking shit about my service."

Bachman cast a hard glance at Rodriguez, who was now also looking away, gazing over the water beyond the wall surround. "Is that true, Danny?"

Rodriguez sniffed and drew himself upright, but his certitude was wavering. "Yeah."

"And?"

"The sergeant…" The volume and rancor in his voice drained like a battery running out of charge. He cleared his throat and started again. "Sergeant—"

"Master Sergeant Perry," Bachman corrected him.

"Sorry. Master Sergeant Perry abandoned his team in Raqqa."

At the pronouncement, Perry's eyes bugged out, nostrils flaring, but before he could react further, Bachman said, "One hundred percent wrong. Where did that bullshit come from? Did somebody tell you that?"

The operation to which Rodriguez referred was Inherent Resolve and, in truth, Master Sergeant Kirk Perry had led a team of marine Raiders in a coalition with other special forces on a hunt for an ISIL deputy leader in Syria, who was ultimately tracked down and killed. Perry had, in fact, sustained shrapnel wounds in an arm and a leg that pained him to this day—not to mention the mental trauma that had followed him out.

Rodriguez opened his mouth, as if about to defend himself with a substantiation, and then, unaccountably, realized he could not—not because he intended to protect anyone, but because suddenly he could not clearly remember how he had come by the claim.

He stammered, "I…uh, I don't know."

Bachman glanced from one to the other, his expression morose. "Well, you know I have a zero tolerance for fighting."

His statement had an instant and identical effect on both antagonists; they were mortified to the core, Perry, for all his brawny machismo, looking like he was on the verge of tears. Rodriguez grabbed his own biceps and choked back a whine.

"Please, Caspian," Perry begged. "I'm really sorry. You know me…I would never do anything to jeopardize this. Never. Please, I need this."

"Kirk, I expect so much more from you," Bachman snipped bitterly.

"But he—" Perry began.

"Look, I understand defending your honor, and you absolutely should. But there's a way to do it with dignity.

"And Daniel, you certainly should know better than to make an accusation against a brother in arms without having anything to back it up. This is hardly the way to establish your bona fides with us. Shit like this pisses me off."

"Caspian, please," Perry beseeched, his bottom lip actually quavering.

Bachman gave it some more thought and sighed ponderously. "Okay, here's what's going to happen. Both of you are going to ride together from here. You're going to apologize to each other and Danny, you're going to listen to Kirk tell you what really happened on his mission. If he chooses to tell you."

He looked again from one to the other. "Are we in agreement?"

Both nodded readily and vigorously and conciliatory handshakes were exchanged. As they retook their seats on the terrace, Daniel Rodriguez was still puzzling over how he'd come by what had turned out to be egregiously erroneous information.

THIRTY YARDS FROM THE restaurant, the provocateur of that information retrieved a package from a drop spot on the beach at the base of a tamarisk tree. A master manipulator, he was constantly amazed at the relative ease with which he was able to play individuals against each other; in this case, he had accomplished his objective by executing a variation of the old telephone game, casually sowing seeds of the real story to multiple people. When he began to pick up snippets being relayed, he made subtle edits that he knew were ripe for misinterpretation and exaggeration and, ultimately, denigration.

The ensuing skirmish had provided him the time and cover to slip away unnoticed. Brushing sand from his pants, he stuck the cloth-wrapped bundle in his waistband, the hem of his untucked shirt concealing its bulk, and made his way across the beach back to the restaurant.

At the water's edge, the pair of swans were paddling in tandem toward the port, skimming along like white clouds on glass.

27

THE ROUTE TO THE western coast took their caravan of SUVs north through hillsides stubbed with low, spiny brush and not much more, the ten-minute excursion occasionally interrupted by lazy herds of wild goats loitering in the roadway. Driving along the bay of Agios Dimitrios, they passed a wind farm on a ridge above pebbled beaches and a couple of modest white block churches. The afternoon sky was light blue and seamless, the sea pooled with agate-like floes of blue and green that were almost fluorescent in luminosity.

The road took them higher inland, past another tiny church before making a final sweep down toward the bay and the location of their basecamp.

Archontiki is the site of a Mycenaean settlement dating back to the twelfth century BC, first excavated in the early 1960s when hundreds of tombs were discovered and surveyed late into the 90s. An organized necropolis built on a north-south grid, it yielded an impressive collection of artifacts that include decorated ceramics, bronze swords and daggers, metal and glass and gold jewelry, clay pottery, and vessels in many sizes and forms. It is now a protected archaeological park, mesh-fenced with access granted for tourists who may marvel at the ruins but, for the most part, do not grasp the significance of its discovery and revelations.

The local expert guiding them around the grounds was full of fascinating details and lore that ignited the passion of their cause. With the sea rolling out from the rocky edge of the bygone colony, its short stone-stacked walls mapping the neighborhood of ancient life, there was an air of the past beckoning and beseeching recognition.

And reclamation.

Peering over to the nearby islets of Daskalio and Agio Nikolaki and, a little farther out, the island of Antipsara, many were wondering if their work here would fulfill that mission for the MIAs they were tasked to find.

THE BASECAMP WAS IN an open field set back from the ruins and about a hundred yards from the beach, where the *Blue Zone* was now anchored offshore, having continued around the southern peninsula and up the western coast. The group's personal baggage was unloaded from the fleet of SUVs, while the bulk of equipment and tools had been retained on the boat.

Again taking advantage of the jumbled activity as the vets and academics and staff checked out the camp setup, Jake and Remington met with Luther Baladur who let them know the arms had already been offloaded.

Baladur said, "They are all secure at the cottage."

"Good man," Jake remarked.

With Callie clinging to his arm, he surveyed the site and nodded favorably. "You guys have done an incredible job here."

In the days following Jake and Callie's wedding, Remington and Kipnis, in coordination with Bachman, had finalized the permissions and permits process for their presence and mission. This involved government agencies and officials, archaeological authorities, and locals in Athens, Chios, and Psara. During the past week, prior to reuniting with Jake, Remington's team had procured and staged what made up the infrastructure of the camp. Two large security tents flanked a covered cooking and dining area with seating, a stoned grill station, and food storage; a row of single tents for Bachman and his senior staff separated sides for men and women, each of those with tents sharing four; on the other end were portable latrines and shower stalls. All of it had somehow been tied into the island's power supply which, given the remoteness of their location, seemed a tall order, but one of many the municipality willingly fulfilled at the behest of a mayor thrilled to be hosting the group.

Jake turned to study Callie, saw the glassiness of her eyes as she took everything in, her throat working as she dry-swallowed. He gave her hand a squeeze.

"Remy, I'm going to get us settled at the cottage."

"All right, brother. Take your time."

WHILE EVERYONE ELSE WOULD be living at the basecamp, Remington had managed to find a cottage for Jake and Callie, one of the only houses—or structures, for that matter—in the barren countryside, and now, for Callie's sake, Jake was extremely grateful for the privacy.

During the ride from the restaurant, she had been nearly catatonic, which was a common aftermath of such episodes, and what would usually come next was the trifecta of total physical, mental, and emotional collapse.

Within hiking distance, the cottage was also accessible via the Archontiki road, which Jake drove, taking the turn by the church and then, a short distance past, finding a dirt lane that went south back toward the coast. He pulled up to a single-story rectangular rock building, enclosed by a matching wall with a wood-and-iron gate. The courtyard surround was shallow, but there was an attractive patio in the rear, shaded by fig trees and affording a view of the sea some two hundred yards away.

The house had been restored and modernized, but overall it had the look and ambience of its nineteenth-century origin. The walls were textured stucco, the ceilings high and framed in dark wood beams and hung with ornate chandeliers. Furnishings were sparse and simple, old woods refinished and gleaming with polish, seating neutrally upholstered, décor tasteful but minimal.

Jake urged Callie to lay down on the antique brass bed and rest and, as he'd anticipated and in spite of her heightened anxiety and the unfamiliar setting, he was pleased to see her succumb to a doze by the time he'd made his third trip transporting their bags from the rental Jeep. He could use the time to unpack, locate the stored arms, and review the security system Kipnis had set up inside and outside the cottage. It was too early in Costa Rica to call Jesse Segura for an update on Camilla, but he planned on doing so in the next few hours.

Jake finished bringing everything inside, checking and finding the kitchen fully stocked and, after making sure Callie was still asleep, stepped back outside to take a walk around the property. The cases of arms and ammunition and other gear were neatly packed into an attached outbuilding, secured by an electronic lock that Kipnis had masterfully wired and concealed in the stone. Continuing his inspection, Jake located each of the perimeter sensors, lights, and cameras, selected the app on his phone and went through the settings. Satisfied with the security setup, he strode to the gate and was opening it when the soft sound of tires rolling over dirt and rock caused him to turn.

A light-colored pickup truck was ambling down the road, its speed decreasing as it neared. When it was within fifty yards or so, it stopped, engine idling. Jake squinted into the late afternoon sunshine, trying to make out who was inside, but from his vantage all he could tell was that there were two people in the cab. He did not recall seeing a truck in the mix of SUVs in their caravan, but he supposed it could be one in use by Luther Baladur or another person in the team that had already been on-site. Unlikely, he decided, as any of them would have phoned. It appeared to be an older model pickup, maybe a Toyota, so possibly a pair of curious locals.

He waited and watched, thought he saw the passenger raise binoculars. A gust of wind blew a bale of loose scrub and a cloud of dust across the road. The two heads visible above the truck's dashboard moved as if in conversation with one another.

Jake reached behind his back, hand closing around the grip of his Glock, but before he had slipped the gun from his waistband, the truck backed up and continued in reverse until it was no longer in sight. He stared down the road for several minutes, wondering if his suspicion was manipulating an incident without reason. But given everything that had happened leading up to the start of the gig with MVAA, he was inclined to think otherwise.

WHEN JAKE RETURNED TO the site by Archontiki, the earlier

disorder had scattered and reassembled into the feel and structure of a military base, tents functionally arranged with clothing and personal belongings, occupants settled in. Individuals were relaxing with reading material or phones or music playing from headphones and earbuds; groupings of two or more were casually meandering about or engaged in communal activity. A volleyball pit was hosting a lively game, the dining area bustling with prep and grilling. Some had gone back to survey the ruins, others had spent time sunbathing and swimming at the beach and were now returning for the evening meal.

The sun was flaming out over the horizon in a beacon of tangerine strobing across the purple profile of Antipsara, its land looking like the lumpy back of a semi-submerged sea creature. The sizzle and smoke of fish and meat roasting in the heat of charcoal and wood drifted on a breeze spiced by salt and wild-growing herbs. Men and women on cooking detail poked and prodded about the grill platform while others rhythmically chopped onions and peppers on a wood plank shelf. All seemed to be at ease in each other's company and enjoying the repartee.

Jake led Callie through the camp, finding Remington in conversation with Bachman and Shelby Hoskins, nodding to them and continuing on toward the beach. There, he spotted Falcone and Niles in shorts and t-shirts, chatting in canvas folding chairs, Kipnis with Baladur and Dmello just beyond. They were standing off from a cluster of vets lined up to watch the movement of a ship in the distance, Kipnis peering through a pair of Steiner binoculars.

When Jake came up beside him, he said, "Hellenic Navy warship, Elli-class frigate." He passed the Steiners for Jake to have a look and, as he did, Jake reached into a pocket of his cargo pants and fished out a folded piece of paper. When he returned the binos to Kipnis, the paper was passed along with them.

Kipnis waited a few moments, then gave the note a quick read. On it, Jake had jotted the general description of the truck and the words: *2 pax, recon?* The Israeli's expression remained impassive, but he met Jake's eyes in tacit cognizance.

Jake and Callie strolled the length of the beach, pebbles crunching beneath their feet, gazing over the shimmering water as the glow of sunset slowly dissolved and the wash of color in the sky was replaced by a ceiling of deepening blue speckled with early stars.

Turning, he drew Callie into him and kissed her, feeling and tasting the sun's warmth in her lips, smelling the faint floral scent from her hair. Lovingly caressed her face. She looked at him with wistful resignation, her complexion both pale and flushed in the waning light.

"It's going to be all right, angel," he said, and smiled.

His dark, rugged handsomeness, the strength and confidence he exuded, made her always want to believe it. She tried to return his smile, the pit of her stomach aching with despondency, and only managed a shallow sigh.

She tucked her head against his chest and he held her, wishing he could better allay her unease, could somehow recapture and maintain the enchantment and joys of their honeymoon, but knowing a threshold had been crossed and this realm on the other side was going to be lean on that kind of bliss.

Jake heard the scrape of boots on rock and looked up to see Remington coming their way, the Malinois in step by his side. As Remington passed the group watching the water, the dogs halted, their postures stiffening. The hackles of their necks bristled and growls vibrated from their throats. They started toward the brush behind the beach and Remington stopped them, commanding, *"Blijf."*

The dogs' growling mixed with a higher pitched whine as their focus split between owner and desire to investigate the source of their agitation, which was soon revealed with the emergence of a lone male vet. He was dressed in camo pants and an olive t-shirt with a grunged motorcycle graphic, lean but toned. His dark brown hair was side-parted, long on top and trimmed around the neck, where a silver skull necklace hung at the front. Shading his face were contoured Wiley X sunglasses and a coarse stubble.

"Whoa there, guys," the man said, beginning to stoop down to the canines.

Their response was a unified lunge and throaty snarl, which Remington curtailed, repeating, *"Blijf."*

Remington stepped over to speak to the man but, without another word, he'd retreated, taking another path through the scrub.

The Malinois continued to watch with overt belligerency, something unknown setting off their instinctual defenses. Remington said, *"Hier,"* and the two dogs followed him as he made his way toward Jake and the others. As they got closer, the fierce demeanor of the Malinois abruptly flipped to one of effusive happiness, and they looked to Remington in avid appeal.

"Okay, *voruit.*"

The release sent them scampering to Jake and Callie, Callie kneeling to respond with copious affection.

Standing next to Jake, Remington glanced over his shoulder, scratching the whiskers on his chin. "Odd," he muttered.

"What?" Jake asked.

Remington shook his head dismissively.

They edged over to Kipnis, whose binoculars were still aimed at the water. Only now, there had been a new development. "This is about to get interesting," he remarked.

Jake and Remington followed his line of sight, beyond the far side of Antipsara some four to five miles out, and saw what had caught his attention. Another ship.

Kipnis said, "Barbados-class frigate." Pausing for emphasis, he added, "Turkish Navy."

"Oh shit," Remington said in hushed foreboding.

As the distance between the two warships narrowed, the muted rumble of a helicopter amplified into the recognizable resonance of some variant of a Bell, coming into view in the swath of sky over the opposing vessels.

"Oh *shit,*" Remington said again, this time with more gravity.

Kipnis pointed the Steiners upward. "Looks like an AH-1 Super Cobra...and"—he made a focal adjustment and through the 8x magnification could see enough to make out the red-and-white flag emblem—"it's also Turkish."

The sound of the helicopter had drawn quite a few more vets and some of the others to the shore, all captivated in a kind of thriller movie impending-crash-scene way, expecting a bad outcome but not able to look away. Even so, what happened next stunned nearly everyone observing.

The Hellenic naval ship fired into the airspace above the Turkish frigate, an Oto Melara 76mm deck gun booming multiple rounds in rapid succession, thick gray smoke curdling over the water, macabre in the semigloom. If the intent was to annihilate the Turkish warship or vice versa, with the powerful array of armament on board—which included Harpoon and Sea Sparrow missiles and MK-46 torpedoes—that could have quickly been accomplished.

The raucous blasting continued for about a minute before the Turkish warship made a slow turn and, along with its aerial escort, headed back to the north.

But while what might have been a catastrophic and possibly retaliatory incident had been averted, there were repercussions on shore that would not be so straightforward to resolve.

Speaking to Jake, Remington said, "We've got our work cut out for us."

Before he could respond, Jake realized the vets were not the only ones in need of attention. Callie was shaking violently in his arms, her senses in complete overload.

28

THOUGH BUFFERED SOMEWHAT OVER the distance separating the ships and Archontiki shoreline, the concussive blasts were still plenty loud, and while the effect on the assembled vets was combat-familiar and, in many cases, intensely harrowing, for Callie it was even more personally visceral.

In her mind, where the toxic cauldron of her traumas were so readily stirred and stoked, she was right back in the Colombian jungles.

The night Jake had found her in the cartel kingpin's hacienda, extricating her in the midst of yet another brutal assault, the surrounding territory had been under a massive bombardment by the U.S. and Colombian militaries. To this day, most of what had happened during the rescue was obscured in a fugue-like fog, but the onslaught of deafening explosions and the fires and smoke were sensorially memorable and, by association, horrifying.

As the warship's deck cannon boomed from the sea, Callie's head swelled and pounded, her heartbeat and chest hammering, heat scorching her skin, the claws and talons of jungle brush grabbing and digging in. And then, the sudden sensation of falling over a vast, black void…falling, falling, falling. All the while, the sky was exploding.

She held onto Jake as if his body was about to crumble like sand, a weak keening sound coming from her lungs.

Holding her tightly, Jake glanced around, taking a quick assessment of the vets, momentarily conflicted; his overriding care and focus was always going to be Callie, but here he also had the responsibility of his commitment with Remington to MVAA.

By now, Caspian Bachman and Gwen Maddigan had joined the mix. Like Jake and Remington, they were taking inventory of those gathered, noting body language, facial expressions, mannerisms, and dialogue, and saw enough to warrant concern.

"What do we think is going on?" Bachman asked. "Territorial thing?"

As part of their intelligence assessment prior to arrival, Remington had briefed Bachman on the geopolitics of the region, a large part of which involved the longtime and ongoing dispute and brinksmanship over maritime sovereignty. Though Greece and Turkey are both NATO allies, they are locked in a bitter rivalry for undersea resources and access to research and mapping. Also in contention are the division of Aegean islands in close proximity to the Turkish mainland with Chios and Psara among the contested. In recent years, as tensions have increased, so have the number of military incidents.

Kipnis replied, "It would appear so." He had been studying one of the many encrypted intel apps on his phone. "The Turkish warship and helo are actually part of an advance front for one of their survey vessels that is charting territory for possible oil and gas drilling. The Greeks have been tracking it, and when it encroached, they issued several warnings that went ignored."

Bachman's eyes flicked between Kipnis, Remington, and Jake. "I know you told me about all the possible issues, but I never really expected to have this kind of clash right on our doorstep. If this is going to be a regular—"

"Let's not get ahead of ourselves," Remington interrupted evenly. He cast a trenchant look to Kipnis and said, "We'll stay on top of all activity in our AO. That's part of our job. Right now, let's round up the troops and get some chow in them."

With the air clear of gunfire and sea visibility increasingly limited by the darkening skies, calm began to restore and spread from one individual to the next as the pack was shepherded back to camp. Those more resistant to moderated behavior or whose dialogue was trending toward obsessive or incitement levels were discreetly engaged by Maddigan, others encouraged to channel their energies into dinner consumption and carefully mediated group discussion.

Jake hung back from the rest and took his time giving comfort and reassurance to Callie and, once they were in camp, fetched plates of grilled mackerel and vegetables, which he set on one of the tables. Falcone and Niles took seats at the next, the Malinois eagerly following with their noses honed on their beef kabobs. But not even the happy presence of the canines was able to bring Callie out of the crisis state she was in, so Jake sent Remington a text to let him know he was leaving and returned to the cottage.

WHEN THE SUN ROSE the next morning in widening bands of peach and pink and, finally, a butterball burst of yellow, the sea was empty of nautical traffic with the exception of a container ship well off in the expanse. A light breeze rippled the near water, the sky overhead peppered with cawing seabirds.

Much of the group had brought their coffee onto the beach to experience the sunrise, Jake and Remington set apart in private discussion. The rest of the *Habari* team listened, Falcone and Niles puttering with their camera equipment. Callie huddled solemnly next to Jake, the Malinois vying for attention. They nosed her hands, licked, and took turns laying their heads in her lap, sensing the need for emotional security, but she stroked them absently, her gaze fastened on Jake as he drank his coffee while reviewing data on a computer tablet.

On Jake's departure from the basecamp the previous evening, Remington had sent one of his guys to patrol the cottage overnight while the others worked in rotational security shifts on-site. Kipnis took point on communication with the navy and local coast guard and monitored intel, reporting that the two sides were effectively back in their respective territorial corners but exchanging some bellicose barbs and accusations. There was some talk from the Greek military of redeploying or augmenting groups already staged for a large-scale joint training event, a frequent go-to strategy to send an implicit message.

Looking up from the tablet, Jake reached over and pet both dogs, smiling on the outside but deeply sad on the inside. After the tough day, in many ways, it had been an even tougher night, Callie all but inconsolable. Though fatigued and in need of a good sleep to recharge before this first day of the dig, he had stayed awake with her until very late, trying to soothe her by dreamily recapping all the magical highlights of their honeymoon days and nights, perhaps as much to put him back in a good head space as to reassure her. Now, as he thought about how he was going to balance his work with MVAA and his devotion to Callie, he was once again seriously questioning the logic he'd conjured to overlap the two.

He called over to summon Falcone and Niles. To Callie, he asked, "Sweetie, will you hang with Eddie and Curran for a little while so I can do some work?" He appealed to the canines. "You guys want to go for a walk?"

The Malinois sprang to their feet, rear ends and tails wagging in enthusiastic anticipation.

Before she could attempt any kind of demurral, Niles took Callie by the hand, his face full of boyish glee. "Come on, love, let's take the hounds for a stroll!" He wore patterned khaki shorts and a button-up shirt swimming with brightly colored abstract fish, blond hair pulled into a knobby, bedraggled ponytail.

Jake gave her a kiss, smiling encouragement, and watched her grudgingly go with them, glancing over her shoulder as they parted. He felt an undertow in his heart that was like a lead anchor sinking to the seabed.

He took a focusing breath and swiped through screens on the tablet, which included each veteran's records and a snapshot of military service, any injuries or conditions, psychological profile, and medications. Then he began his pre-launch rounds to not only check on general health and well-being, the quality of prior sleep, and required prescriptions, but also their state of mind following last night's incident. He strode toward Gwen Maddigan who was sitting cross-legged in a circle of vets and made his first stop.

SHORTLY AFTER EIGHT O'clock, Captain Salivara docked the boat at a temporary floating wharf that had been constructed, with permission, just for their project in the deepest point north of the eastern side crescent beach. Overall, the island of Antipsara, not quite two nautical miles from Psara and less than two square miles in area, is encompassed by waters so shallow that the rolling ripples of pale sand can be seen through the sparkling prism of aquamarine color.

In the minutes it took to make the crossing, Jake had been heartened by Callie's calmer demeanor—mostly, he attributed, to the lethargy of sleep deficit—and from the call he'd made earlier, speaking to Jesse Segura and Camilla. While Jake much preferred and had suggested Camilla not return to their villa for the time being, the housekeeper would hear none of it and was already fussing at Segura to allow her to resume her regular household routine. Jake had also spoken to Kent Sanborn who, with the other *Habari* associate picked up in Morocco, had arrived in Dominical and was working on property repairs and security enhancements. They would remain in place for protection until Jake's return home.

It was another gloriously beautiful Aegean day, the sky over land and sea vast and profoundly blue and meringued with fluffy clouds, the temperature comfortable in the upper seventies.

Stepping onto the starkly barren shore and beach had the feel of alighting on virgin ground, devoid of human imprint or essence, low scrub and rock swelling upward in the backdrop, the rest of the civilized world seeming far away and unimportant. The stillness was unsettling and pacifying and intriguing all at once, the natural quiet almost spiritual in its reign.

But the stillness was dispelled as soon as feet began moving across ground, a buzz of excitement and anticipation beginning to build and intensify. Shelby Hoskins handily harnessed that ardor into the unloading and transporting of gear and equipment from the boat to their site, which was nestled within a valley between two primordial little churches, accessed by a brief hike across low hills. The group members were dressed in either short or long utility pants, tees and loose button-front shirts, bandanas and headbands, caps and hats, boots and sneakers, and strapped with loaded backpacks. Wheelbarrows and crates full of buckets and tools, tarps and supplies, thumped and rattled over the craggy terrain.

Bachman, accompanied by Kostas Demetriadi and a few of the more experienced local archaeologists, set off ahead of the rest to reestablish the virtual grid that the survey team had laid over the site, which extended from the valley basin up to the northeasternmost ridge of the island. The location was determined in part by information from the World War II archives, the DPAA surveyors who had found bits of corroded aluminum, and LiDAR mapping, the latter being a laser technology using light detection and ranging from the air. The compilation of data was not an absolute confirmation of the presence of wreckage and remains, but was enough to justify an archaeological excavation.

For the grid, established by layering the LiDAR over topographical maps with a computer program called ArcGIS, they used handheld GPS to locate the exact corners in the ground and then meticulously measured out squares with rebar and wooden stakes and string. Even working efficiently together, the task took up a good two hours, during which time Shelby Hoskins directed the distribution of tools and equipment and started the all-important introductory training session.

For veterans, direction and instruction was not only wholly acceptable, but expected as something line-stitched into all military assignments, duties, jobs, and missions. With the basics and parameters setting realistic expectations and objectives, morale got a sturdy and level foothold, and anxieties were minimized.

Using the seasoned squad leaders and most senior archaeology academics as demonstrators, Hoskins went through each step with the careful articulation and patience of a grade-school teacher, the inspired dynamics of a collegiate coach, and the blunt candor of a drill sergeant. As with all things in her operations management role, she commanded and got the collective attention and respect of all, even those who had participated in other MVAA projects and knew enough to watch and listen as if it were their first experience, because doing so promoted harmony in the pack.

As Hoskins wound up her overview and moved on to the more categorical and specific instruction, Bachman and Demetriadi—both soiled and sweating and breathing heavily from their efforts defining the grid—joined the session, all three demonstrating the proper way to dig a unit. This included techniques, the handling, recording, and storage of finds, and the responsible usage of tools; Hoskins was precise in her stipulations for the order and placement, and adamant in her safety protocols.

"Always make sure your shovels, trowels, spades, and the like are face down," she cautioned. "I don't want to see anyone getting popped in the face."

Jake added, "Nor do I. Trust me when I say it does not feel good and can cause a serious injury. It's also not a good look for the mug."

There were a few snickers, and Hoskins used his comments to parse out a segment of time for him to go over some health and medical basics and recommendations, discussing hydration, sunscreen, and monitoring physical limitations and stress levels.

Although it was nearing lunchtime, vets and academics and archaeologists alike were all eager to get started, so squads dispersed to their assigned units and the work began.

THE COMMENCEMENT OF A dig, on the first day, in the first hours, in a new environment and on a new mission, with a newly integrated group, was inevitably hectic and often a little bit like a runaway horse lathered and pent up with copious energy to expend. Enthusiasm and excitement, coupled with the veterans' innate determination to achieve and accomplish, drove a relentless pace that Bachman and his staff often found challenging to regulate until the initial adrenaline jettison occurred.

Today was no different, and the scene very quickly transitioned into a canvas of purposeful activity; lumber A-frames with mesh screens were erected, tarps were draped overhead for shade and spread on the ground with tools and brushes of every kind, black plastic buckets distributed around every section of the grid. The chink and scrape of mattocks and shovels breaking into soil punctuated an animated mosaic of voices, layered with problem-solving discourses and jests of laughter and grunts of exertion as the first stages of the project got underway.

Early excavation was especially labor-intensive, the island soil dry from minimal rain in recent days and salt-battered by the summer meltemi winds, untouched by cultivation and dense with loam and rock. Vets from prior MVAA projects had encountered similarly challenging soil conditions and dispensed tips to the newcomers toiling in the pits they were forming. Eventually, murmurs of success could be heard as perseverance paid off and progress became measurable.

As part of their defined roles in the capacity of logistical support and security, Remington and his team's engagement was mostly limited to operational facilitation and observation, but Jake, in his primary duty as medic, had more flexibility and took advantage by getting some dirt time himself. Not only would it allow him to bond with the vets, he hoped it would inspire Callie to take part because he believed it might benefit her in the same way it did them. Given her enjoyment of gardening at home, he was optimistic that she'd join in, but he also knew it had triggered some flashbacks to her time in the jungle.

With that in mind, Jake did not push her, and was pleased to see curiosity slowly develop into interest as she watched him work his spot and listened to Falcone and Niles interviewing some of the veterans close to them.

Glancing back as he prodded dirt with a four-inch pointed trowel, a man in dark brown pants and matching tee peered uneasily at the Sony Venice camera propped on Niles' shoulder. He paused his digging, brushing soil from the front of his shirt, which was imprinted with a vintage-look American flag. He wore wire-frame sunglasses and a floppy boonie hat, his face in shadow and etched with the stencil of razor-resistant hair growth. What none of those covers could conceal was the pitted, oatmeal-like texture of half his face and neck.

"So," Niles was saying, "this is a bit like Indiana Jones, innit?"

The former army infantryman, whose name was Jayce Ruda, replied, "I thought so at first. But no, it's not like that, really. Archaeology in movies is all thrills and monumental finds, but you don't get the true sense of the hard work or even the personal reward."

"Tell me about that," Niles said. "What does this do for you?"

Ruda did not respond for several moments and appeared to be debating whether he wanted to share anything further. He cut a sideways look to Jake, as if to seek affirmation. Then he said, "This is my third dig with MVAA, and it's changed my life."

He pointed a gloved finger at his face. "This came from shrapnel. Roadside ambush in Kunar Province, Afghanistan." He paused again, swallowed.

Jake said, "Thank you for your service, man."

Ruda regarded him with perceptible reverence. "Thank you for *yours*. From what I understand, you've got some wicked pedigree and background."

Jake said nothing, his lips pressed into a thin line, aware of looks from Falcone and Niles and also Callie.

The vet continued, "My unit was 2nd Battalion, 12th Infantry. We were part of the force in the Pech River valley, which was under constant onslaught at the time from every kind of arms, including RPGs and IEDs. When this happened, we were doing a sweep, visiting villages, making some headway with locals and elders. That particular day was about as peaceful as it got and, in retrospect, I think we let our guard down a little."

He looked off, his thoughts seeming to slip away like an untethered balloon. "You can guess the rest of the story." He glanced back at Jake. "You served in the Sandbox…you know."

"Yeah," Jake said quietly. "I do."

"All that gunfire last night took me right back there. But then, it doesn't take much with my PTSD."

Jake felt Callie shift uncomfortably beside him, heard a quick intake of breath. He squeezed her hand.

Ruda returned his narrative to Niles' question. "So yeah, what this has done for me…is help me reconnect to a more stable place within myself, give me a new purpose. Lots of veterans' organizations do good in that regard, but typically it's more like doing arts and crafts at day camp, you know? This is a real vocation, and you're in the trenches with others that have been through similar things, all working toward a common goal and with a work ethic we're all used to…the defined responsibilities and command structure, the camaraderie, the culture that's mostly lacking in the world outside of the military. It's really helped to put the past in perspective. You don't forget, but somehow it re-channels a lot of emotion."

Falcone said, "Thank you for sharing that."

Work resumed with minimal talk and, as Jake concentrated on the space in front of him, he watched the nuances of Callie's expression as she seemed to be processing the vet's somber vignette and knew it had stirred a confusing mist of familiarity.

It took a little while longer, but she finally slipped on the gloves Jake had brought for her, and began moving her hands in the soil.

THE LUNCH BREAK WAS called at 1 PM, Shelby Hoskins assembling the group beneath a tarp that had been set up away from the excavation grid, tablecloths spread on the ground and anchored by several big yellow coolers. In addition to lunches, each person had carried their own bottled water, but a surplus was always on hand and would be replenished every day.

Jake slipped on his backpack and extended his hand to Callie. "Let's take a little walk," he said.

Her eyes were drawn to Remington and the Malinois, who were slurping water from a plastic bowl. "Can we take Luna and Solis?" she asked.

Jake smiled. "Let's see."

Overhearing, Remington replied, "Sure you can." He then addressed the dogs, wagging an admonishing finger. "No digging."

Like a pair of children in guilty remorse, the two looked away from him, the dust ringing their dark snouts now muddied from drinking.

"*No* digging," he repeated with emphasis.

Jake let out a hearty guffaw. "Highly trained canines or not, I think that's a tall order here, bud."

With the Malinois leading the way, Jake took Callie up to the ridge and found a smooth place on a rock slab overlooking the sea. They sat and took in the spectacular view of sky and water spanning the horizon, the swirls of current frothing around outcroppings below, the sage-colored ground cover rolling out behind them.

Jake dug into his pack and took out gyros, grapes, and bottled water. He had hungrily consumed one sandwich before Callie even bit into hers. She was gazing pensively over the blue beyond, her face clouded with the complexities of past and present.

"What are you thinking?" Jake asked, at the same time pointing to her lunch.

She took a tiny bite of her gyro, chewed and swallowed. "The veterans here have been through so much—*you've* been through so much."

He waited for her to continue, half-formed questions dissipating before she could piece them together. When he could see that she was unable to express her thoughts, he said, "We're all wired differently, and our minds and bodies respond differently."

"But I have what they have?" When he did not reply right away, she asked, "It won't ever stop?" Her bottom lip trembled.

"The best answer to that is what I keep saying," he said gently. "We take it moment by moment. And, again, it's only been a few months. It takes time, love."

"But for some of them, it's been *years*…"

He had no immediate counter and tears were already moistening her eyes, but just as he was moving to give comfort, the two Malinois caught his attention. They were pacing and poking at something in the brush past their picnic spot.

Jake rose, saying, "Let me see what they're into over there," and stepped through the low vegetation. When he reached the dogs, they backed up, glanced pointedly at him and then to something flopping on the ground.

He knelt down and saw a large bird, long-winged and -tailed at over a foot in length, plumage mostly a sooty brown. He recognized it as an Eleonora's falcon, and it was lying on its side, floundering weakly in an effort to get upright.

Callie had come over and now, from behind him, gasped. "Is it hurt?"

"Not sure," he said, but he could already tell there would probably not be a good outcome. He'd seen birds stunned and in shock, had in fact on one occasion spent an hour rejuvenating an egret that had flown into his windshield, but this bird was more than dazed; the lack of focus in its normally keen eyes told the story. "Will you get my pack?" he asked Callie.

When she retrieved his backpack and placed it beside him, Jake took out a pair of nitrile gloves and put them on. "Okay, big guy, I'm just gonna take a look," he said, and carefully rolled the falcon back and forth to examine it. When he was able to see under the wings and chest, the source of incapacitation became evident in a sticky, crimson blotch the size of a half-dollar. Uncapping a bottle of water, he trickled enough to reveal the wound and found not only exposed tissue, but bone.

"Shit," he muttered under his breath, and wondered what could have caused this kind of injury as there were no trees or structures and certainly no predators, unless it had been attacked in the air, which he thought highly improbable given the falcon's position atop the food chain.

Jake repressed the disappointment he felt, knowing Callie was watching him for any sign of optimism. Stroking the distressed falcon's head and neck with his finger, he noted the labored breathing and knew what he had to do.

Without looking at Callie, he said, "Sweetie, take Luna and Solis back to where we were having lunch, okay?" To the dogs, he issued a command he'd heard Remington use. "*Voruit.*" They eyed him ponderously for a moment but obeyed, accompanying Callie as she retreated.

Scooping the falcon off the ground, Jake cradled it in his arms and murmured a brief prayer. "I'm so sorry," he said dismally, and then grasped the bird's neck and twisted, quick and forceful, feeling the snap of spinal cord. He knew it would not be instantaneous, but fifteen to twenty seconds to unconsciousness and death was certainly better than what might have otherwise stretched to minutes or even longer had he left the bird to perish naturally.

Next, he got his compact shovel and began digging a hole for burial. It was when he had finished and was thumping dirt from the tool's blade that he discovered what had taken the bird down. He stared at the bloodied object incredulously and then stood, frowning.

Returning to Callie, he leaned over and gave each dog a commendatory pat, cheerlessly remarking, "Good job."

Reading his face, Callie sniffled. "Did it…did you…"

"I ended it humanely," Jake said lightly, and enfolded her with a hug. He added, "It did not suffer."

Not by my hand, he thought. But it *had* suffered by the hand of someone on the island. *That rock did not throw itself.*

29

THEY WERE HEADED BACK down the ridge when Jake realized the dogs had disappeared. Even when they were allowed to move about freely, they always stayed within close range as their discipline dictated. Turning, he scanned the open countryside and, still not seeing them, whistled sharply. When there was no response, he called them by name. That got several distant barks.

Going in the direction of the barks, which was on the far side of the ridge, Jake spotted the Malinois standing together in a field mottled with grass. He whistled again and commanded, *"Hier!"*

But the dogs did not move.

He felt a jab of dread, and thought: *God, I hope they haven't found another bird.* Callie was beside him and he considered instructing her to wait while he investigated but did not want to alarm her unnecessarily; she was already upset enough, and maybe this was nothing more than the dogs being dogs. But as he closed the gap and recognized the rigidity of their postures and concentration of their gazes, he knew that was not the case.

When he reached the canines, they both sat, as regal and motionless as Egyptian Anubis statues, and the next and conclusive tell was their silence.

Jake took out his iPhone and called Remington.

"You need to come up the ridge. And bring Caspian."

*   *   *   *   *

WHEN REMINGTON, BACHMAN, AND archaeologist Demetriadi appeared on the ridge, Remington saw his dogs and immediately said, "Oh yeah, they've alerted on something." The Malinois hopped up and came to him, awaiting praise and direction. He provided both with instruction to remain at his side.

Belgian Malinois, originating in the 1800s and used for herding livestock, have become one of the top breeds sought by law enforcement, trained in protection, tracking, apprehension, and the detection of everything from drugs to explosives. And while most were groomed in a specific category, Remington's duo could detect and distinguish within a whole gamut of sources, synthetic and organic. He had acquired Luna and Solis as adolescents from a comrade who had served with Keanjaho Dmello in the Kenya's KDF. Dmello's friend, on departure from the military, had applied his experience working with their elite Rapid Response Unit to the founding of what came to be a world-renowned canine training center in Nairobi.

Dogs, in general, with over two hundred million scent cells, have an eminently superior olfactory system that is up to ten million times more powerful than that of humans and capable of detecting at an astonishing parts-per-trillion level; with the comprehensive training Remington's dogs had undergone, which encompassed land, air, and sea in a multitude of climates and conditions, his canines performed with exceptional range and accuracy.

Bachman consulted the screen of an iPad he'd brought with him. "This spot is not in our survey parameters." Using his fingers, he swiped and zoomed in on the imagery, adding, "But it is close."

"How far down can your dogs detect?" Demetriadi wanted to know.

"Deeper than you'd think," Remington replied. "Overland, they can do miles. Underground, I've had them hit on thirty to forty feet."

"Any idea what they've picked up?" Bachman asked.

"The way I know them and their behavior, I'm going to say that it's most likely remains."

Bachman eyed him narrowly. "Are you saying this could be the

MIAs?"

"Or even something much more ancient."

A smile cracked Bachman's face. "Amazing." He looked at the archaeologist. "Kostas, I guess we're extending our grid."

WHERE THE ONSET OF physical labor had begun to tamp down initial excitement, word of the possible discovery reignited and reenergized the group like a wilderness fire jumping a containment line. It took considerable effort on the part of Shelby Hoskins to keep everyone focused on their assigned units and tasks while Bachman and Demetriadi worked up on the ridge. By day's end, they had it ready for excavation.

The tired but excited group packed up and boarded the boat, which returned them to the Psara basecamp. Dinner crackled with speculation about the big find and talk of other, more typical ones; some of the pits had already yielded shards of clay pottery and fragmented beads and stones.

It had taken all afternoon, but Jake had seen Callie's despondency over the bird incident yield to the buoyancy of spirit and industrious work going on around her. By the end of the day, she was digging in the dirt with a level of contentment that came close to what he'd seen from her gardening at home. He hoped the physical exertion would result in a solid night's sleep, which they both needed. Now, as he stabbed a fork into a plate piled high with salad greens and vegetables and cheese, he smiled at the sight of Callie doing the same.

At this second evening of communal dining in camp, as social circles were beginning to form with a pecking order of seasoned MVAA members presiding, a more casual but inquisitorial process of vets vetting vets was underway, and Jake observed and listened with interest. The you-show-me-yours I'll-show-you-mine game was a frequent parlay, comparing careers and deployments and testing the six degrees of separation theory by swapping the names of comrades and commanding officers. In his experience, military personnel on the whole tended to be above average BS detectors, and anyone who exaggerated or gratuitously embroidered on their background or similarly embellished tales from the trenches was quickly singled out. In a kind of ass-sniffing and territorial marking equivalent, interrogatory questions were making the rounds.

Jake heard snatches of:

When did you rotate through Benning?

You were at Leatherneck when the Taliban hit Bastion?

You re-upped and deployed to Djibouti?

Which carrier? Oh yeah? I had a buddy on the Fitzgerald…when were you stationed?

You ever make it to the Haunted Head when you were at Pendleton?

Did you have Lanciano in Airborne?

Oh yeah…Sir Lancelot, that was one mother ballbuster!

You met your husband in Kabul?

You worked on FA 18 Super Hornets?

Most of the men and women vets in his proximity were either contributing to the back-and-forth or paying some degree of attention. But as Jake's eyes wandered over the mix, he noticed one member who was adroitly managing to evade most inquiries directed his way by stuffing food in his mouth and chewing thoughtfully, sometimes smirking or shrugging. He saw that a couple of the others seemed to be regarding the man with either detachment or creeping disdain, but there was something off about him that made Jake give him a second, more scrutinizing study. At one point, their eyes met and, as was usually the case, Jake's hawkish visual penetration caused the man to quickly look away and Jake made a mental note to keep him under further observation.

He watched as the man hastily collected his plate, utensils, and cup, rose, and retreated from the dining area, passing Nash Remington with his dogs, both of which reacted with a low growl, causing the man to give them a wide berth and Remington to curb them closer to his side.

From their respective positions and views, neither Jake nor Remington noticed the gray-brown feather tucked in the pocket of the man's shirt.

Stopping at Jake's table, Remington asked, "Can you break away for a ride through town with Kip and I?"

"Okay…" Jake said slowly, his gaze sliding to Callie, who had glanced up from her plate, which was still mostly covered with salad. The clue as to the reason for the ask came from the inclusion of Kipnis.

"Darlin'," Remington said, voice softened by his southern drawl, "would you mind keeping Luna and Solis company? We won't be gone long."

"You want to stay here until we get back or go to the cottage?" Jake asked.

Callie's expression reflected the panicked quandary that had descended on her, eyes darting between Jake, Remington, and the dogs, so Jake made the decision for her.

AFTER GETTING CALLIE SETTLED at the cottage, Jake armed the security system and joined Remington and Kipnis in the Mercedes GLS brought over from Chios. He was a little uneasy leaving her alone, particularly since the guy Remington had stationed there the previous night was back at the Archontiki camp, but with the exterior lighting on and his rental Jeep prominently parked in front of the property, it would appear that he was in residence. And, of course, there were the dogs who, arguably, were the best deterrent and defense.

Piloting the svelte SUV south along the road toward town, Kipnis explained, "That pickup truck you saw by your cottage…I saw it today."

Jake leaned forward from his back seat. "You saw it where?"

"On the camp access road."

"You're sure?"

"Oh yeah. It was exactly as you described, including two guys in it. Obviously, there has been a steady stream of the curious, some parking cars and walking over to ogle the camp. I spoke to a few of them. These guys did not get out of the truck."

"Did you get a look at them?" Jake asked.

"No, I didn't have binos on me at the time, and when I started toward them, they took off."

"So we're going to search for it in town?"

Seated next to Kipnis in front, Remington said, "I thought we should try. Village this small with so few people and only a handful of vehicles, I like our chances."

"Well," Jake mused, "there was a point when I might have dismissed some of these incidents as coincidental, but the sum of them says differently. We're being watched and, more extremely, attacked, and I'd sure like to find out why…to know whether I'm the target and the rest of you by affiliation or if it's something else altogether."

For the next few minutes, they drove in silence, countryside bathed in the lavender filter of twilight. Entering the modest settlement around the Prophet Elias Church by Lakka Beach, Kipnis ventured down the tentacles of side roads, finding them utterly empty, and resumed their travel south. On the outskirts of the tiny village hub, he took a turn off toward the sea, pulling into a red-and-white EKO gas station. After unproductive inquiries inside, they continued on the harborside road into town and spent a little over an hour winding in and out of the narrow warren of streets splintered with cobblestone alleys of red-roofed stone structures. They drove slowly, passing rows of houses interspersed with courtyards and scattered small businesses, stopping wherever people were gathered to ask if any knew of the Toyota truck. The question garnered nothing but blank or puzzled looks, and while it became increasingly odd that not one person acknowledged having seen it or knowing who it was associated with, there was no hint of deception; it had apparently just managed to elude attention.

As the early evening haze deepened, filling the neighborhood nooks and niches with shadow, there was no sign of the Toyota pickup, and it was becoming harder to see much except what was in the path of the vehicle's headlights.

They had traveled through the core of town and circumnavigated the outer boundaries when Jake and Kipnis simultaneously got alerts on their phones. The notification was not yet familiar to Jake, but Kipnis immediately recognized it and turned the SUV back onto the road to Archontiki, stomping the Mercedes' accelerator and speeding north.

CALLIE SAT ON THE edge of the bed, petting the heads of the Malinois at her feet as she valiantly tried to grapple with the acute anxiety that had arisen with Jake's departure. Her throbbing heart was starting to slow in pace, the presence of the dogs having a calming effect, as did the steady splash of water coming from the adjoining bathroom, a faucet filling the big clawfoot tub.

Before he'd left, Jake had offered the bath suggestion and, though resistant, she soon relented; she'd only rinsed the dirt from her arms and legs and face, and her muscles were sore from hours of digging. She still struggled with showering, especially alone—and certainly in a strange place—a fear associated with having been abducted those months ago as she'd stepped from the shower at home, but she thought she could manage a bath without duress.

She stood up from the bed and stripped to her undergarments, glancing around self-consciously and padding into the bathroom, where she dropped her shorts and top into a laundry basket. She gave a skittish start as one of the dogs brushed up against her leg. Catching her breath and exhaling in relief, she saw that the tub was full, turned the faucet off, and removed her bra and panties.

She climbed into the tub, eased down into the warm, fragrant and bubbly water, and sighed as the liquid and heat enveloped her in comfort, the frothy suds and delicate floral scent like a sensory feather stroke.

The Malinois stationed themselves close by, one lying on the tiled floor, the other slouched against the tub, muzzle propped on the edge. But despite the physical comfort, Callie could not fully relax; she never could when Jake was absent. Anything could happen. Things *did* happen. So, as she reclined in the bath and washed off the soil of the day, her frame and the lean muscles on it remained tense, her eyes warily watching the doorway, ears straining for the slightest sound.

Perceptive of her unease, the Malinois were attentive in their repose but did not seem to share her apprehension.

Reflecting on the hours before, in which she had begun to understand the nature of the archaeological operation and Jake's role and commitment, she was also starting to realize why he'd thought it would be beneficial to her. But instead of being reassured or validated by being in the company of others who were similarly impacted by trauma, she felt a crushing sorrow and hopelessness on recognizing in them something she could not overcome—the brokenness that was embedded within her like fragments of glass.

A slow drizzle of tears mixed with the moisture on her face, her chest aching with a forlorn sense of yearning to be the woman who could be whole and vibrant and fully confident for Jake. And fully sensual. Like Stavrina Papandreou. And, for now, here, at the very least, be stable and not give him something to worry about and distract him from his work.

Callie had finished her bath and was pulling on a terry cloth romper when the Malinois scampered to the cottage's patio door, their tails extended and rigid, the hair on their necks and backs stiff. She felt her spine tingle, a thump of dread in her stomach.

"What is it?" she asked shakily.

The dogs' heads swiveled to look at her, both issuing a short but shrill yip in response.

"Do you need to go out? Can you wait until they get back?"

This time she got sharp and decisive barks.

Callie reluctantly went to the arched door and turned to study the security system panel, remembering that she would need to enter a code to disarm it. And saw a flashing red light. A spike of panic bit at the back of her throat and, for a moment, she could not breathe. Then she gulped and eyed the dogs, torn with indecision. Was the flashing light signaling something amiss or a false alert? She knew those had happened on occasion with their security system at home, but Jake or one of their staff was always there to handle it.

The system had not emitted any kind of sounds—no beeps or ear-piercing notes—so what was the light indicating? Jake had not covered that or shown her how to reset it. But what if it had been tripped for a valid reason?

Now the Malinois were whining and scuffling at the door and Callie asked again, redundantly but in an effort to compel action on her part, "Do you need to go out?"

Unsurprisingly, the inquiry was met with even more insistent barks.

She tapped in the numeric code Jake had given her and reached for the doorknob. Turned it and tried to slowly open the door—tried but was pushed aside by the dogs bursting into the small courtyard. She stepped out onto the patio, a cushioned stone bench and wood plank table highlighted by the amber glow of a single lantern mounted next to the doorway. The rest of the yard was illuminated by a full moon as gold as bullion, so big in the evening sky that it seemed mere miles away.

But Callie did not notice the moon. She was looking on in horror as the dogs launched and leapt over the rock wall with the effortless grace of a pair of gazelles.

30

AS THE MERCEDES SUV carrying Jake, Remington, and Kipnis sped along the rural route, Jake was repeatedly trying to call Callie. His voice thick with anguish and frustration, he snapped, "Kip, can you go any faster?"

"He's going as fast as he can on this road, Jake," Remington said. "We're almost to the cottage road. Hang on."

At the turnoff, Kipnis cut the steering wheel and the vehicle swerved onto the narrow lane in a sharp spin, which the Israeli expertly corrected and then mashed the accelerator. They had driven about three hundred yards when the cones of light from the Mercedes' high beams washed over a rolling commotion of forms in flight.

"God Almighty!" Remington exclaimed. "That's Luna and Solis!"

"They're pursuing someone," Kipnis said, and slowed as they approached.

Remington did not wait for him to come to a stop, flinging his door open and bolting from the vehicle, running down the road. Kipnis put the SUV in park, reached for his handgun, and took off after him.

Jake followed until he got to the cottage, not bothering with the gated entrance, hoisting himself over the rock wall and plunging through the front door. Glock G43X aimed in front of him, finger poised by the trigger guard, he advanced through the interior of the cottage, pivoting to clear all directions. When he had swept the living area, bedroom, and bath, he crossed the kitchen and dining area and saw the open patio door. He distractedly noticed the flashing red light on the security panel, the motion sensor alarms set to silent but dispatching the alert on his and Kipnis' phones to indicate having been triggered.

He stepped through the door, immediately saw Callie, saw no one else, and lowered his gun. Dispelling a breath charged with adrenaline, he went to her, engaging the Glock's safety and tucking it in the back of his pants.

She stood, visibly shaking, small and pale in the moonlight. Startled by Jake, she turned and cringed.

He crossed the patio and took her in his arms.

"It's okay, baby," he said as unemotionally as he could manage. "Didn't mean to scare you, but I was worried when you didn't answer your phone."

He loosened his embrace to look at her.

Callie's expression cycled through relief to befuddlement to contrition. "Oh no…I'm sorry! I must have left it in the bedroom when I was in the bath…but Jake, Luna and Solis—"

"I know. We saw them in the road. Remy and Kip will get them."

He was wondering how to frame the inquiry about the security breach and fleeing suspect or suspects when Callie said, "They really wanted to go out, and I thought…I just…when I opened the door, they took off. I don't know why, but the light on the panel was red and—"

"Probably tripped by an animal," Jake interjected. "They probably got a whiff of cat. You know they're everywhere here."

Of course he knew it was not a cat the dogs were after and wondered if Remington and Kipnis had apprehended the culprit or culprits. Maybe, he speculated, it was one or both of the guys in the pickup truck. Maybe the reason they'd not found it in town was because it was tucked away in a hidden spot near here.

His earpiece beeped and he tapped to answer, hearing Remington say, "Got the hounds, but no joy on the quarry. Sitrep on your end?"

Glancing at Callie, who was anxiously watching him, Jake said simply, "All up. See you in the morning."

WHILE JAKE AND REMINGTON began the next day preoccupied

with the previous night's happenings, their focus was abruptly preempted a few hours in. As it turned out, the Malinois extraordinary detection abilities had been spot on; they had, indeed, discovered a burial site for human remains—but not the ossified ones from some eighty years ago.

As the team assigned to the appended grid began their excavation, it became clear fairly soon that they were dealing with something much more recent, the soil more pliant and giving off an odor like spoiled cheese mixed with fermenting fruit, causing the gagging members to don face masks and take breaks for fresh air with increasing frequency. At a depth of about three feet down, they came to the spongy top layer of decomposition, the local archaeologist included in their group calling a halt to their work.

A lean woman in her fifties with close-cropped graying brown hair, she stood, stepped back from the trough and turned to address Caspian Bachman and Kostas Demetriadi, both of whom had been observing from a short distance. Like her, they were wearing N95 masks over their mouths and noses, which they now peeled off.

The archaeologist, whose name was Mariza Skiadaresis, held a PhD from the Aristotle University of Thessaloniki with postgraduate studies in the U.K. for forensic anthropology. Nearly a foot shorter than Bachman, she peered up at him, her expression dour. "You will need to contact the local police in Psara right away of course, but as you know, also the Ministry of Culture." Glancing over her shoulder at the trough, she added, "As much as I would like to continue to at least get a better idea of what, or rather who, we might have here, this now comes under the jurisdiction of the local authorities."

She paused, a troubled expression creasing her forehead. "Most likely, this will be declared a crime scene."

Bachman thought about that and remarked, "Yeah, you don't just bury someone on an uninhabited island in an unmarked grave. You have any kind of guess as to timeline for death?"

"Well, I can see only partial skeletonization and, with the insect activity and organics, I would say perhaps just over a month. Maybe two."

Bachman blew out an exasperated breath and announced, "Pack everything up and rejoin the rest of the group." He watched for a few moments as the unit of four gathered their tools and gear, then trudged down the ridge to confer with Jake and Remington and make the series of calls that would probably result in at least a temporary suspension of their work.

MUCH TO THE FRUSTRATION of Caspian Bachman, but as expected, the required notifications effectively shut down the dig as local and regional authorities descended, assessed and declared the crime scene, and set up shop. While Bachman and Demetriadi were sidelined for questioning by the Hellenic police and involved in protracted discussions with officiants from the antiquities and archaeology side, Shelby Hoskins organized downtime activities for the group. Some chose to spend the day at the Psara campsite beach; others went out to sea on the boat for a fishing excursion with Captain Salivara.

Falcone and Niles had been entrusted with Callie, opting for sun and sand and the crystalline waters extending from the Archontiki shore, allowing Jake to work with Remington on Antipsara in securing the integrity of their primary dig site.

As they strolled along the perimeter, Remington remarked, "Caspian seems to be keeping his shit together, but I think he's buzzing close to tirade tower."

"You can hardly blame him. Look at what's happened in just the past forty-eight hours…the hostilities between the warships and now a buried body. And that's not even the half of it. If he knew about everything else that's been going on with me, with us, he'd probably be pulling up anchor."

They walked on in silence for a while, eyes scanning the upturned and displaced dirt cordoned off in four-by-four-meter squares, mentally inventorying the equipment that had been left in place and checking for any disturbances. Finding all as it should be, they hiked up to the ridge where the burial site was now crawling with investigative personnel that included the first respondent warrant officer and lieutenant sergeant from Psara, a captain from the jurisdictional Police Directorate of Chios, a couple of forensic experts, and the coroner. They watched for several minutes and then continued further up the slope, stopping at the crest.

An unbothered sea and sky stretched out below and above and to a horizon speckled with the faint and faraway blips of fishing vessels and cargo and container ships. Both men stood and took in the vista, eyes panning the vast span of blues, gulls and other seabirds looping overhead. At one point, Jake identified another falcon, idly wondering if it was the mate of the one he'd put out of misery. Following its flight path, he saw it circle and then drop down to the parcel of land where the stoned bird had been discovered.

His somber reflection shifted with the sound of an approaching helicopter, coming in at moderate speed from the northeast. Beside him, Remington commented, "Wonder how many more law authorities they can accommodate on this rock? Or maybe it's media."

But as the helicopter came into a range where they could make out some detail, Jake knew it carried neither—he was just not sure who it did contain, or what their mission was. Knew, because it was a black Leonardo A109C, like the one he'd first spied nine days ago in Patmos and then possibly again in Fournoi, where he had been lethally attacked underwater.

He said, "Remy, I've seen that bird."

Remington's head swiveled to him and he reached to the radio clipped to his belt, selected the channel for his network only, and spoke through his Invisio X5 comm. "Eyes to the sky due north, black helo on approach. Any with binos, track and report. Copy?"

Receiving a round of affirmative responses, Jake and Remington tilted their heads back, watching the helicopter as it passed overhead, its speed decreasing to a rate conducive to surveillance. Watched it bank and circle back, then fly off in the direction from which it came, the rhythmic sound of its rotors fading as the visual diminished with distance. Moments later, Kipnis reported, "Got the tail number. No surprise, it's Turkish. Appears to be private, maybe mil convert. I'll dig deeper."

Jake and Remington turned to find Caspian Bachman striding toward them, an expression of weary resilience on his sun-flushed face. When he reached them, he said, "Good news. Looks like they'll be releasing the site by tomorrow and allowing us to resume our dig."

"Wonderful," Jake remarked. "Have they shared any findings with you?"

"Not much, but Kostas got a bit of intel from one of the local archaeologists which led to tentative identification of the deceased. Apparently, in the months preceding our arrival, this guy, a scientist, was doing some work on the island. No team, just him. He was surveying and cataloging biological samples…soil, rock, vegetation, organic material, and whatnot."

Bachman was interrupted by a relay on his own radio channel. Listening to the transmission in his ear, his eyes widened and his mouth went slack. He replied, "Okay, I'll be right there." To Jake and Remington, he said, "I'm beginning to think we're under some kind of hex. Word from forensics is our dead guy died from a knife wound to the throat." He paused, shaking his head in astoundment. "Not only that…there are signs of torture."

"No shit?" Remington rolled his eyes to Jake.

"I need to get back," Bachman said, "but I'll keep you updated."

In the quiet that followed Bachman's retreat, Jake gazed upward, deep in thought, sunlight glinting off the dark surface of his Outlaw shades. Hands on his hips, he finally looked down and paced, questions compiling in a campaign for conjecture but landing like randomly tumbled dice.

"What are you thinking?" Remington asked him.

"I'm thinking I'd like Mellie to take us up for some recon, see if we can find that helo. And, I'm wondering if the target that's been on our asses is in any way connected to the dead guy."

"I'm wondering the same. He didn't get tortured and have his throat slit over rocks and moss."

31

THEY WERE IN THE air before lunch, first flying north over sea, the sky mostly clear with feathered strips of cirrus clouds. Where their inaugural Chios to Psara journey via passenger boat had taken over an hour, a bracing, high-speed expedition in a Technohull RIB with speeds averaging fifty knots cut that transport by more than half. At the Chios airport, there had been a brief debate over the choice between taking the Pilatus parked there and leasing a helicopter. Aside from the extra time it would take to make arrangements for the latter, the plane had several advantages, such as range and less conspicuity, but the most significant factor was the superior surveillance equipment installed on this particular model of the Pilatus, an NGX Spectre.

When planning logistics for the contract with MVAA, Kipnis and Dmello had procured the Spectre for the same reasons their team had provisioned the inflatables and, more extremely, undertaken the risk of acquiring a secret arsenal of weaponry—Jake's and Remington's standards of operation embracing the philosophy that being prepared for the worst-case scenario, whatever the impracticality or liability or cost, was far preferred over being in need when options could be limited or totally lacking and the necessity might be urgent. In the case of today's spontaneous outing, their all-encompassing preparedness was delivering in spades.

They flew west past Psara toward Skiros, then northeast toward Limnos, and finally back to the south where they circled Lesvos and edged into Turkish airspace. Normally, permission for such was required forty-eight hours prior to departure, not to mention exponentially more complicated but, with the facilitation of Kipnis' contact, Neval Tashkiran, it had been obtained without delay. Now, as they cruised along the coast, they passed the provinces of Çanakkale and Balikesir on the approach to Izmir where there were a handful of public and private airstrips and heliports. While they did not necessarily expect to find the Leonardo at a logical installation, checking these was a starting point.

From leather seats on opposite sides of the cabin, Jake and Remington scanned the land below through the plane's porthole windows. Though their vantage was not as ideal as what a helicopter would have afforded, the more intensive search was being orchestrated by Kipnis, who sat in a compartment behind the cockpit that was configured with the surveillance suite. It included multiple displays, audio and video recording components, and controls for the key piece of equipment, a deployable electro-optical and infrared sensor located in the plane's tail cone. With a 360-degree view and 120x magnification optics, the FLIR Star Safire EO/IR was providing remarkably detailed images in high definition. After going through an initial sequence of calibrations and adjustments, Kipnis handed off a pair of computer tablets with streamed video feeds that allowed Jake and Remington to see everything he was seeing.

Dmello had settled into a moderate cruise of two hundred knots at altitudes under five thousand feet, the landscape below becoming more barren and then rolling and green as they bypassed the coast where Jake and Remington had been run off the road and the airstrip where they'd linked up with Tashkiran. They were two hours into the flight, coasting over the urban sprawl along the E87 corridor southeast of Izmir when Kipnis said, "Mellie, let's go another hundred miles or so."

"Where are you thinking?" Remington asked.

"Down to Muğla province. Just a hunch."

In thirty minutes they were approaching the prime real estate of what is known as the Turkish Riviera or turquoise coast, six hundred miles of golden beaches stretching from Çeşme to Alanya. Dating back to the time of Antony and Cleopatra, it has drawn a stream of royalty and movie moguls and rock stars and, more recently, the superyachts of the ingloriously powerful in search of sanction asylum. It was the latter that had piqued Kipnis' stellar intuition. With the Greek islands of Samos, Leros, Kalymnos, and Kos of the Dodecanese some twenty miles offshore, they overflew the resort strip from Kuşadasi to Güzelcamli then banked eastward over the evergreen forest and mountains of the Dilek Peninsula and a swath of verdant farmland in the alluvial plain of the Büyük Menderes River. Nearing the core of Didim, another popular holiday destination, Kipnis directed Dmello to head out to sea and over the small islands of Agathonisi and Farmakonisi , both of which had heliports. Looping back to land, they passed over a pad at the D Marin, a marina with over five hundred berths, more than a few of which housed sizable yachts.

Studying the screen of his tablet intently, Jake sighed and said, "Guess this wasn't the best use of our time. That bird could be anywhere from Istanbul to Athens to Crete."

Kipnis did not reply but glanced briefly over his shoulder with a typically cryptic smile.

They crossed the bay and flew over a heliport in Bozbük, then beyond another span of forested mountains. On the Güllük side, Dmello circled the Milas-Bodrum airport, engaging with the tower for clearance to come within range to get a sufficient view of its helipad adjacent to the runways. While they had yet to sight a helicopter at any of the private and commercial pads they'd surveyed, there had been a few at the military ones and various airports. None of the images captured in their video feeds were of a black Leonardo.

Kipnis instructed Dmello to head to the next heliport, south in the town of Kumköy. They were now in the airspace of one of the most prominent coastal resorts, described by Homer in the *Odyssey* as "the land of eternal blue." Located at the entrance to the Gulf of Gokova, Bodrum is also referred to as the pearl of the Aegean Riviera with its towering fifteenth-century Castle of St. Peter and fourth-century Tomb of Mausolus, one of the original Seven Wonders of the Ancient World. Its more contemporary draw was that of international tourism, more particularly those of the uber-wealthy echelon.

There are three luxury marinas on the peninsula, all of which have helipads, but the most prominent of the group, the Yalikavak, is considered by many to be the best superyacht marina in the world and, as such, offers berthing to vessels up to 140 meters, or 460 feet, in length. As soon as they approached, crossing the bay of Tilkicik Koyu, Jake felt his own intuition prickle with anticipation, now tracking along with Kipnis.

And, as was almost always the case, the Israeli intelligence savant had nailed it.

"Holy shit, there it is," Jake proclaimed incredulously, his eyes riveted to the video stream on his tablet.

But the black Leonardo was not parked on the marina's helipad, a green circle with a yellow bullseye on the rooftop of the Asian Novikov restaurant lounge; instead, much to everyone's amazement—except that of Kipnis—the aircraft sat on the top deck of a yacht parked stern-to just past the tip of the teardrop-shaped rocky promontory that extended out from the interior of the marina. And, among the nearly full to capacity six-hundred-plus berths, the host ship was easily the largest vessel there, dwarfing its closest in class by more than half, at least fifty meters longer.

From his seat at the surveillance console, Kipnis whistled softly. "That boat's about a hundred and thirty meters. Bill Gates has berthed here, and his is a little over a hundred."

Jake was reminded of the superyacht in Colombia belonging to the Valentín cartel, a third the size of this one, which he had similarly discovered hiding in plain sight.

For the next several minutes, Dmello flew lower and slower, making passes overhead long and wide and irregular enough to avoid undue attention. The other three scrutinized the images in their screens, probing for revelatory details. But despite the powerful capabilities of the Spectre's surveillance technology and varied approaches and altitudes, there was not much they could extract other than the positive identification of the Leonardo A109C and the ship's flag, which was red and emblemed with the Union Jack and a coat of arms.

Glancing at his watch, Jake said, "I know we should start heading back, but I think we need to get down there while we have it within our reach."

Remington did not hesitate. "Roger that. Mellie, are there any strips close?"

Dmello, who not only routinely mapped out the geography of his planned flight paths but also a vast expanse in all directions, factoring in every conceivable contingency as well as any inconceivable ones he could think of, replied, "Unfortunately, no."

"Okay, put down at the airport and I'll get us a vehicle."

Dmello flew them back across the bay toward Güllük, the azure water below glistening in the late afternoon sun, stitched by the movements of a variety of sailing and motor vessels populated with tourists and dignitaries and executives and fishermen and maritime laborers. But the only seafaring passengers that held any interest to those in the seats of the Pilatus above were the ones associated with the massive boat flying a Cayman Islands flag.

THE FLIGHT TO THE Bodrum airport took only minutes, customs clearance expedited and hassle free with a call-ahead channeled through Neval Tashkiran and processed by one of the FBOs. The ride in a rented Peugeot 4x4, however, with their collective anticipation on edge, seemed interminable. Even in light traffic motoring at maximum speed along the D330 highway, the route took almost an hour, bypassing several city centers before hugging the coastline and then crossing into the density of the Bodrum peninsula. On the other side of the mountainous terrain of Dağbelen, the Peugeot's navigation took them to several winding two-lanes through the streets of Yalikavak and, eventually, onto Çökertme street, which fronted the marina.

More than a waypoint for yachts and other pleasure craft, Yalikavak Marina is a luxury destination in itself, a complex comprising world-class restaurants and nightclubs and hotels, fitness centers and spas, and a shopping plaza resplendent with high-end designer icons; among these are the likes of Louis Vuitton and Chanel, Dior and Gucci, Valentino and Prada, Audemars Piguet and Rolex. One of an exclusive handful designated the British Yacht Harbor Association's 5 Gold Anchor Platinum rating, in addition to Bill Gates, it has seen the boats of rocker Mick Jagger and politician magnate Roman Abramovich and a coterie of the similarly rich and prestigious.

They were stopped at the street entrance security gate, checked in by a uniformed guard, and then continued to the parking lot. From there, they strode briskly toward the commercial concourse, a layout of geometric structures of varied heights and angles skinned in sand-colored travertine stone. Colonnaded promenades were lined with shallow reflective pools, rows of palm trees, and islands of architecturally landscaped trees and shrubbery and flowering bushes. Storefronts gleamed with full plate glass, over which were the iconic names etched in their identifiable script or bold block letters. Taking in the sequence of shops, Remington remarked, "Well, this is the swankiest marina I've ever seen."

"No kidding," Jake replied.

They had merged into the throng of people, most strolling at a leisurely pace while sipping Starbucks or other beverages, lapping ice cream cones, taking photos and videos with their phones, chatting and texting, pushing strollers or dragging suitcases on wheels or interacting animatedly in pairs and clusters—locals and tourists, businesspeople, families with young children, teenagers, and the rest bridging the alphabet gens. More the typical crowd of a megamall than that of an affluent yacht basin.

Stepping from the pedestrian pavement, they crossed the limited-access cobblestone street to the waterside and immediately realized the impediment they had; the walkway directly encircling the harbor was not only lowered but also fenced off by cable railing and an imposing bank of palm trees set in big stone bases. Moreover, access to the berthing docks and pontoons was restricted by electronic card-controlled gates with manned guard stations at primary junctures.

"Shit," Jake muttered.

"Let's just get as close as we can," Remington said, and they picked up their pace, heading for the farthermost appendage of the marina.

They strode alongside the Charlie quay, boat sterns of tall and wide and glamorously appointed yachts tightly slotted and abutting the dock with uniformed crew polishing surfaces or passengers lounging on various decks. Imprinted names and flags tagged a diversified international field from all parts of the Mediterranean and beyond. Reaching the Bravo quay, they passed the Italian Novikov restaurant, a cylindrical structure vertically beamed in dark brown wood, and could now see where the walkway stopped, by Zuma, a Japanese restaurant with a swimming pool.

Beyond the row of sailboats and yachts moored the length of Bravo, there was a single vessel backed up to the Alpha quay, and there was no helicopter on its top deck. Because it was not the boat they were looking for.

The four of them stood staring wordlessly for several moments before Jake broke the dumb silence.

"Goddammit," Jake exclaimed. "It's gone?"

"Even with an hour lead time if it departed right after we spotted it, it is probably only about twenty or so miles out," Dmello said.

Gazing up at the sky, which had taken on the shadow cast of a declining sun, Jake said, "We don't really have time to launch another search." He didn't say it, but everyone knew his need to get back to Callie.

"We could try to get some general intel from the marina office, maybe the boat name," Remington suggested.

Kipnis shook his head skeptically. "Place like this, all the security…"

Jake had been scanning the people shuffling about nearby, honing in on one in particular, a young man who did not have the look of a tourist, clad in white shorts and a red t-shirt, ball cap worn backwards over a minimalist haircut. And he was pointing a phone at the boats lined up beyond the railing.

"These yachts are mind-blowing," Jake remarked, approaching the young man with the insouciance of a random passerby killing time.

The casual demeanor was rewarded with a friendly smile and an affable response. In a faintly accented voice, the man laughed and replied, "Some of them are bigger than the building I live in."

"Did you happen to see that massive one that was here earlier, berthed at the end?"

"Oh yeah. Seen it several times."

"You come here often then?"

"Most every day, in fact." The man gestured with his phone. "This is my favorite photography spot."

"Got any shots of that boat?"

That inquiry elicited a more guarded expression. "I do…why?"

Not wanting to prolong the premise, Jake got right to his agenda. Indicating Remington, Kipnis, and Dmello, he said, "My friends and I have been looking for that boat—actually saw it from the air a little while ago—and were really hoping to catch it here. Obviously, you can't see much of the detail from above."

The young man seemed to be vacillating between suspicion and intrigue, eying Jake and those with him. Finally, he shrugged and showed Jake the screen of his phone, tapping and swiping to an album with hundreds of photos. Of the marina, of people and places in it, but mostly of boats. A lot of *the* boat.

Trying to check his excitement, Jake asked, "Have you got air drop on your phone?"

IN THE BACK SEAT of the Peugeot SUV, Jake and Remington scrutinized the dozens of photos that had been sent to Jake's iPhone; next to Dmello in front, Kipnis was reviewing the same from his tablet. The young man at the marina had been a little hesitant to share but had done so without added persuasion. For his cooperation, Jake had compensated him with a handful of hundred lira notes in the equivalent of just over forty dollars, framing the offering as "dinner or drinks on us."

Now, as they went through the images, what they were seeing in shots that were not only composed with a better-than-decent photographic ability but also from the advanced lens of the latest model phone camera, was astonishing and, at the same time, perplexing. In spite of the several hundred feet between the end of the publicly accessible pedestrian walk and the anchorage of the yacht, the level of clarity was quite good.

After a spell of stunned silence, Remington said, "That is one big-ass boat."

"A hundred forty meters, beam of sixty-five, fifteen to sixteen thousand tons, and probably five hundred million dollars' worth," Kipnis surmised matter-of-factly.

The yacht was an all-white steel-and-aluminum behemoth stacked with sensuously curved decks, one of which exposed part of a large swimming pool. The Leonardo helicopter was also captured in some of the images, in the process of takeoff and landing and parked on the top deck; as it turned out, the vessel had a second helipad on the bow of the primary deck. While some of the images included people on board, even a few guys standing by the helicopter, there was nothing particularly distinguishable about any of them. Just figures—passengers or crew or principals—partially visible at various points about the tiered decks.

Kipnis was zooming in on key shots and running enhancement filters, minimizing and navigating to a number of resources, including several that tracked marine traffic in real time.

Remington asked, "Get anything with the name, Kip?"

Gold block lettering on the side of the yacht spelled out the suitably grandiose moniker GALA.

"Some general stats, but nothing of substance. I got the size and value about right. Built by Lürssen of Germany, a company that's produced half of the top fifty superyachts in the world."

"I can't fathom how that bird is connected to a luxury boat of this magnitude," Jake commented.

"I have my thoughts," Kipnis said, but did not elaborate. He continued, "If you'll look at the image that has the best view of the upper bridge, the configuration of the radomes tells me it's got air defenses. And in another image, one with a tender garage shell door open, pretty sure I see a minisub."

Still studying information on his tablet, he said, "I was hoping we could pick it up on traffic, but apparently it's got the AIS turned off or cloaked."

He was referring to the Automatic Identification System, transponders installed and required on all ships of three hundred gross tons or more to signal their GPS location as a navigational aid to avoid collisions and as a beacon in the event of distress. It was, however, not uncommon for boats—especially those of the luxury class—to disable their AIS to conceal movements and locations.

"Can we get some sat images?" Jake asked.

"Yes, and I'll see if I can dig deep enough to trace ownership, but so far all I can tell is that it's layered behind multiple shell companies."

Their conversation was interrupted by Remington answering his phone. After a brief discourse, he ended the call and announced, "That was Caspian. The police have released the scene and given us clearance to continue the dig. They passed on some information that might be behind the homicide…and maybe even have something to do with whatever else is going on with us. As we suspected, their investigation into the scientist revealed that what he was working on involved more than a mundane survey."

"Well, yeah," Jake said. "Being tortured and having his throat slashed would suggest as much."

"Caspian said he would give us the full sitrep when we get back."

They drove on in silence for a few minutes and then Jake spoke up. "Kip, you said you had thoughts about the yacht?"

"I do. I believe we'll find it tied to a Russian oligarch."

32

AS EAGER AS JAKE was to hear what had been uncovered in the homicide investigation, after their long day all he wanted in the immediacy
was to turn his full attention to Callie and rejuvenate in a hot shower,
ideally both at the same time. The reverse leg of their recon excursion—
from the marina to the Bodrum airport, followed by the flight back to
Chios and finally the jaunt by RIB to the basecamp in Psara—took them
into the early evening, a lot longer than Jake had intended to be gone,
and now, at the cottage with Callie, he was dealing with the effect of his
extended absence.

Even though he'd been determined to not let her out of his sight after
the very first upsetting incident during their honeymoon, he'd known
the nature and scope of his responsibilities here might necessitate some
more extended separations; he just never anticipated the reason being
for an off-mission pursuit.

Callie clung to him in the shower, leaned against him as he wolfed
down a slice of pizza from the camp's dinner leftovers.

"Did you eat, baby doll?" he asked lightly, chewing a mouthful of
salad. She nodded, drawing a doubtful glance from him. Reaching for
another slice of the pizza, oozing with fresh tomato sauce, local cheeses,
and vegetables, he prompted, "Have some of this, it's really good." In
answer, she nudged even closer, and he chose not to push.

Afterward, snuggling her to him in bed, he tried but could not elicit
more than a few vague and dispirited sentences about her time at the

beach with Falcone and Niles. She burrowed into his side, tensely tremulous, and he realized she'd had a long, stressful day, too.

Ultimately, her heart and mind's desperate need for reassurance through trusted intimacy surrendered to his primal need to provide it and recalibrate his own strained emotions and snarled mental mesh. Sleep followed swiftly and deeply in the cooldown from sexual heat to the sensual glow that fades and clings at the same time, like the blurred line of light between darkness and dawn.

THE NEXT MORNING, JAKE spent his time on the boat ride to Antipsara and the first hour at the dig site primarily with Callie, occupying himself with the excavation work that had resumed and making light conversation with her and the others around them. When he saw that Callie had become relatively comfortable and was beginning to commit to the activity again, he excused himself to make a medical wellness sweep, which was essentially to meet up with Remington and Kipnis.

They strolled a short distance away from the grid, Jake keeping Callie in view. The morning was warm and bright, bees and dragonflies buzzing over field grass swishing in the breeze, the faint bleating of goats drifting from beyond slopes to their west.

The Malinois canines trotted just ahead, happily sniffing the organics of air and ground as the three men found a grouping of rocks and sat, Jake immediately asking, "What do we know?"

"Our dead guy is, or was, Panos Korkizoglou," Remington announced. "Had quite the CV. PhD, multiple masters, lots of postgrad work…biology, chemistry, physics, geology."

Kipnis elaborated, "National and Kapodistrian University of Athens, which is considered one of the top global universities, particularly for science, the University of Patras, and the University of Crete. Also put in some time with FORTH, the Foundation for Research and Technology and TPCI, the Theoretical and Physical Chemistry Institute."

Remington added, "Prestigious awards, some published work, some teaching."

Jake could not see Remington's eyes behind the sunglasses, but the corners of his mouth had ticked up as if he was teasing something tantalizingly revelatory.

"All the academic background is well documented…but what the homicide investigation exposed was another side of Korkizoglou. On the surface, he was the proverbial loner research scholar, eccentric even. Didn't circulate much and tended to shun the usual events in the scientific community. In his mid-fifties, divorced, no kids, no social media."

Jake waited for the curveball, which Remington now served up.

"But…it seems ol' Korki had a secret side hustle. It might not have come to light, especially not so quickly, were it not for one social indulgence he did partake in. He had a regular watering hole in Chios and, after a few rounds, apparently became a little more outgoing."

"And?"

"And he made some pretty provocative statements. But I'll get to that." Remington deferred to Kipnis with a nod.

"The secret side hustle was consulting for Pallas." He paused to gauge recognition from Jake and, not seeing any, said, "They are one of the major defense technology companies in the Mediterranean region."

"Okay, well, that *is* interesting," Jake said, "but I don't see how—"

Remington interrupted, "Which is where Korki's loose tongue comes in. When the homicide investigators were doing their background canvass to come up with any kind of working theories or persons of interest, they interviewed staff and regulars at this bar, an off-the-beaten-track hole in the wall in Chios Town called *Yamas*. The last time any recall seeing him there, which falls within the timeline right before his death, he was blabbering about a discovery he'd made while he was collecting those biological and geological samples."

"What kind of discovery?" Jake asked.

"He said he'd found something that would upend the defense industry."

Jake looked at him blankly. He stood and rotated slowly, panning the barren landscape, trying to imagine what was thoroughly unimaginable. Finally, he asked, "What the hell could he have possibly found like that *here?*"

"He didn't get more specific, and those interviewed by the investigators seemed to think it was the booze talking. But a scientist of his caliber, the under-the-radar work he was doing—and who he was doing it with—you have to wonder…"

"Well, as far-fetched as all this seems, his find must be pretty fucking radical to not only get him killed, but maybe be the reason we've been targeted," Jake stated. "What is Pallas' profile?"

Kipnis replied, "Testing, development, design and, purportedly, some manufacturing, of advanced weapon and missile systems, surveillance and reconnaissance tech, naval and aerospace innovations, and that's just scraping the surface."

Jake's mental gears were turning, cogs seeking grooves of connection but not quite aligning enough to interlock. He was mentally rewinding through all the incidents that had occurred since he'd first landed in Greece, some of which had seemed totally random and innocuous and others, wholly intentional and pernicious.

"If this guy really did find something…I mean something really and truly game-changing in defense…and the wrong person or organization got wind of it—"

Remington picked up that thread. "It could explain the surveillance, on you during your honeymoon and on all of us now. We were here before you, setting up everything for the dig, which would have effectively stopped any other presence or activity on Antipsara. And with us doing all this excavating, if whatever Korkizoglou found is still here, they'd be wanting to keep a close eye on us and our work."

Jake thought again about the men he'd believed were shadowing him and Callie in Milos, followed by the breach of the sailboat to implant monitoring, about the multiple Leonardo helicopter sightings. About the underwater fight to the death that was intended for him, the men tailing him and Remington in Izmir that had culminated in the brutal ambush and the nearly fatal road incident not long afterward. About the men in the truck outside the cottage and, later, the dogs chasing one or more who had been lurking outside with the possible intention of intruding, or worse. He'd been pondering on all of this already, but now he was thinking from a new perspective.

"We're definitely on somebody's radar. My gut says it's connected."

Remington and Kipnis both nodded in agreement, Remington saying, "Our dig is a big problem for them."

"Anything on the boat or the helo?" Jake asked.

Kipnis replied, "The boat is managed by Lorenzi, a yacht brokerage in Monaco, but getting around those shell companies to determine core ownership was like bouncing around a constellation of proxy IPs. Caymans, British Virgin Islands, Cyprus. I did get enough intel to draw my own conclusion, however. I believe it belongs to a Russian billionaire energy mogul, Taras Ignatkovich."

"An oligarch, just as you guessed," Jake said.

"Yes. Worth somewhere around ten billion, owns Titaneft."

"Okay, I'm familiar with that. Wow." Russia being among the top three oil and gas producing countries, Titaneft, he knew, was one of the largest syndicates. It also incorporated other enterprises, some of which included finance, iron and steel, and mining.

"Another juicy detail," Remington quipped, "Ignatkovich is former GRU."

Jake's eyes widened but he did not know what to say to that, so he asked, "Any more intel on the helo? What about sat images?"

"I think the bird is also his," Kipnis replied. "I've got some sats, but no, I have not located the yacht yet. I'm waiting on more and will keep you updated."

They all fell silent, ruminating on the astonishing pieces of information and the potential fallout on their gig with MVAA going forward. Jake's gaze drifted to Remington's hounds several yards away, chasing each other and rolling in the grass, playfully biting necks and rumps, and felt a pang of envy for their blithe oblivion. He peered across the span to check on Callie and saw that she was watching him. When she caught him looking at her, she quickly turned back to the work at hand.

She was trying, he thought, really trying to repress or at least conceal her anxiety, to manifest ease and easiness when, for her, nothing was.

Observing his friend, Remington said, "I've been speaking to Kent regularly since he arrived at *tu casa* and all is quiet, nothing suspicious."

"I've spoken to him a few times, too," Jake said. "I still don't know what to think about all that, but it seems a stretch to connect it to this."

Remington whistled to get his dogs' attention, calling, *"Hier!"*

The Malinois disengaged from their wrestling and sprinted to him, tongues dangling from their romp.

Jake reached down, patting both on the head. Straightening up, he glanced from Remington to Kipnis. "I'd sure like to find out what the fuck is going on. But, for now, we should get back to the job…do some digging in the dirt and see what we can find."

33

IN THE DAYS FOLLOWING, while their collective priorities turned to fulfilling the contracted responsibilities with MVAA, Jake found his own focus fragmented between keeping Callie secure and comfortable, tending to the mostly minor medical issues that came up, and wondering about a possibly volatile secret hidden by earth or sea. Because they were so certain the scientist's death was linked to the sequence of importunate events involving them, Jake and Remington wanted to pursue what the man had discovered. Caspian Bachman wanted to know, too, but was not inclined to cede any more of his time from the dig mission, indicating that he was okay with their tandem quest as long as they were able to maintain team coverage.

To aid in their inquisition, Bachman and lead archaeologist Demetriadi had reviewed the site survey maps and imagery, concentrating on the area extending out from where the body of the scientist had been found, and suggested parcels to explore. With the dogs, Falcone and Niles tagging along, and Callie with Jake, they hiked within the circumference, carefully troweling through any depressions in the ground or soil that appeared to have been recently disturbed.

Remington had begun by having the Malinois refresh their scent reference from the burial site, now staked and cordoned by crime scene tape, which yielded numerous hits but nothing of material value.

On the second day, Remington brought his R80D SkyRaider drone from Teledyne FLIR to cover a larger area. The versatile and rugged military-grade UAS was his workhorse model and had been used in Africa with Jake to great success. On accepting the archaeology gig with MVAA, Remington had acquired a new Teledyne LiDAR payload which he'd be trying out today, along with the StormCaster dual EO/IE imager.

Watching as Remington set up the spiderlike device, attaching the four legs, Niles reached into the customized hard case and passed over the battery packs.

Seeing the boyish enthusiasm brimming in his face, Falcone told his friend, "He's not going to let you fly it."

"We've got to get us one of these, mate!"

"Yeah, would be cool to do aerial work," Falcone agreed, and handed him their Sony Venice. Niles adjusted the Sony's settings and began filming; Falcone did the same with the GoPro.

For the next hour, which was the charged flight time allocated on one run, Remington sent the drone in widening circles over the rolling terrain, maneuvering the SkyRaider over hills and down into valleys. The imagery in view on the controller was a fairly monotonous quilt of scrub in drab browns and yellows and greens when seen in regular daylight and, alternately, neon-colored through LiDAR or infrared.

"Without having any idea what we're looking for, this is probably a waste of time," he eventually remarked. "Not to mention, whatever 'it' is could have been taken off the island by Korkizoglou and stashed somewhere or taken by whoever killed him."

Jake ruminated on that and posed, "If the killer or killers have it, why would they be all over us in such an aggressive manner and risk exposure?"

"Good point."

Later in the afternoon, after more hiking and without uncovering anything even remotely promising, Jake sighed wearily and said, "I think it's time to put our efforts back on the boat and bird."

THAT EVENING AT THE basecamp, they sat with Kipnis who had been working his intelligence sources, most of whom were current or former Mossad like himself. He had news.

Showing them an image on his tablet, he said, "I have the yacht."

Jake and Remington leaned in and looked, recognizing the vessel they had spotted in flight. Seen from above, its randome globes looked like silver pinballs against the ultrabright white shell, lower decks stacked and graduated like Russian Matryoshka dolls, the open extensions of each outfitted for lounging, sunning, soaking, swimming, and dining. The upper deck helipad, designated by an encircled letter H, was empty; the main deck helipad's symbol was obscured by the black Leonardo helicopter parked on top of it.

The resolution was remarkably clear, Jake commenting, "This sat is amazing. Got to be well under thirty."

He was referring to the level of detail in centimeters of very robust satellite imagery, the top range for the best commercial grade generally being around thirty centimeters, meaning objects of that size could be seen in detail. Military satellites—of which this was—were exponentially more graphic.

Kipnis smiled, and said, "Actually, it's less than half that and not even our highest res."

"With the AIS turned off, how did you find it?" Jake asked.

"HawkEye 360, which has an emergent technology for dark ship tracking using RF analytics in conjunction with satellites." He further explained, "That yacht, like most other things in motion over land, in the air and at sea, have all kinds of radio frequencies…as you know. VHF marine radios, two-way radios, L-band satellite devices, X- and S-band maritime radar systems. HawkEye 360 uses a satellite constellation to triangulate all that. They can cloak or turn off the AIS, but they can't do it for all the RF—at least not all the time. "

He swiped the screen to an overlay with geolocational data and reversed the zoom. Now they could see that the yacht was positioned approximately fifty nautical miles north of them and about twenty to the northwest of Lesvos.

Remington asked, "Do we know its bearing?"

Kipnis tapped the speed and directional data on the screen and said, "North, between three fifty and five degrees at seventeen knots. It has been recently tracked to Çanakkale and other ports of call around the Sea of Marmara, including Istanbul, so that's a possibility. Going further back, it has been all over the Med, but has spent most of the time here in the east."

"So are you able to track it now?" Jake asked.

With another sly smile, he added, "Working on that."

"How old is this sat?"

"A few hours."

"Any more intel on the Russian?"

"Taras Ignatkovich," Kipnis mused, "is intriguing. He was high in Putin's inner circle, but a couple of years ago had a pretty vicious falling out when Putin swung a massive energy contract to a young rival on the rise. I get the impression there was more to it than that, and Ignat subsequently broke from Putin's cabal, pulled out of Moscow altogether. He has property in Turkey, Greece, Cyprus, and Cap d'Antibes, but not sure which is considered the primary residence."

He paused, his face going flat in the dead-calm state that was his default. Nudged the tinted wire-frame glasses up his nose. "This is where it gets much more interesting. There is some intel, though not yet verified, that he recruited a significant number of mercs from Wagner as well as SADAT."

This revelation caused both Jake and Remington to sit upright, their eyes boring into Kipnis.

The two organizations, from Russia and Turkey respectively, were high-profile PMCs—private military groups—battalions of proxy warriors or, put more bluntly, nefarious guns for hire at play on the global battlefield. And, in the case of Wagner, following the demise of its commander, many from that group would have been looking for a new gig.

Aghast, Jake asked, "For what purpose?"

Kipnis gave a small shrug and quipped, "This part of the world, who does not have an army?"

"SADAT," Remington repeated. Looking at Jake, he said, "That could explain the Turkish guys that you, and now we, keep encountering."

"Maybe the Turkish helo as well. But this intel prompts more questions than answers." Jake mulled the new information for a moment, then said, "I think we need to try to catch up to the boat again and recon."

"Roger that," Remington said.

A few yards from where they sat, Falcone and Niles had obliged Jake in keeping Callie busy playing with the Malinois but, as he glanced over, he could see she was growing weary and restless. Standing, he announced, "Thanks, Kip, good work. Remy, see you tomorrow at o dark thirty."

THE BLACK RIB WAS virtually invisible as it sped forth in the predawn darkness, sleek thirty-six-foot frame zipping through the water. Jake and Remington spoke sparingly at first, concentrating on their trajectory as the miles rapidly passed. But knowing him as well as he did, Remington began to sense a bead of preoccupation in Jake.

"You okay, brother?" he asked, his voice raised over the thrum of the craft's powerful engines and the thrash of sea spray.

Extracted from his thoughts, Jake responded defensively, "What? Of course. Mind on the mission."

In truth, while his mind was always on the mission, lately his heart had a weighty sway. As was the case now. He was having a hard time dismissing, or at least compartmentalizing, the moments preceding his departure.

When he had awakened, Callie was tightly curled into him, raspy sobs trapped in her throat which, he could tell were the diminishing efforts of drawn out crying. Immediately feeling guilty for not having roused to comfort and coax her to sleep, he tried his best to instill calm and reassure her about the nature of his agenda, but she remained distraught. Once again, he was starkly reminded of the short timeline, a few mere months, between the horror she'd suffered in South America and what he'd hoped would be glorious recovery and renewal here in Greece. There had been a good bit of that, but it was unrealistic not to expect frequent and debilitating relapses, and these times away from her had done nothing but further stoke abiding separation anxiety.

On the drive over to the basecamp, he'd continued to normalize the rationale for the excursion he would be making, telling her, "It's all part of our responsibilities and scope of work with MVAA, which sometimes means investigating things. In this case, Remy and I are going to check on a ship. Just routine."

But of course it was not routine and he was fairly sure Callie suspected as much. He didn't know how much longer he could keep her in the dark about what was truly going on. She trusted in him completely, but his hypervigilance and numerous security measures had prompted her to ask him several times if anything was wrong or if he was in danger. He tried to mitigate the whole truth by simply saying his demeanor and actions were requisite precautions for travel, especially for someone with his military background. But he knew she was undoubtedly thinking back to the attempt on his life at their wedding, about the hard talk in the days preceding and the even harder one following the incident.

When they arrived at camp, a sleep-disheveled Falcone and Niles greeting them in their tent, Callie had looked imploringly at Jake and pleaded, "Do you really have to go?" And: "Can you bring me? Please?"

He'd struggled to deflect the molten vulnerability in her eyes and the soft quaver of her voice that could completely dismantle him. With a long embrace and loving kiss, he'd said, "I will get back as quickly as I can." Guiding her to an empty cot, he'd eased her down and tenderly brushed at the curls touching her neck. "Be good for me, sweetie, and try to get some sleep, okay?"

Her eyes were glistening in the dim lantern light as he had released her and slowly retreated, exhaling pensively and exiting the tent to join Remington on the beach.

Now, as Jake steered the boat along their northerly course, he took the mental wheel on his thoughts and steered them as well, putting his errant heart in check.

The waning gibbous moon was fading in the ceiling of sky, its blackness ebbing to an inky blue and stars all but gone. Pinpoints of light in the far distance mapped the presence of tankers and cargo ships, the peaks of Lesvos faintly visible to the east.

They were navigating on updated intel that Kipnis had passed along prior to their leave. In the hours since reviewing the satellite, the yacht could have easily sailed over a hundred nautical miles but had apparently set anchor or docked somewhere for an increment and was just beginning to resume sail. Its current coordinates, which Kipnis had extrapolated from HawkEye 360, set it sixty-five north and about midway between Limnos to the west and the Turkish coast. From there, the yacht could be headed farther into Greek territory, to a Turkish port, or perhaps the Dardanelles Strait toward Istanbul.

The locally produced Technohull Sea DNA 999G5 they were operating, while categorically a RIB by virtue of its rigid inflatable hull, is a fairly dynamic variation in most every other way and more reminiscent of a flashy sport craft with its teak wood decking, shock-absorbing helm seats, ergonomic carbon console, and multi-display control and information touchscreens. And if they had enjoyed the smooth ride to and from Chios at the boat's cruising speeds, they were even more thankful for the stability it afforded at the higher knots generated by the combined nine-hundred-horsepower twin V8 outboards.

They were an hour in, starting to bounce and bump a little more as the speed displayed on the digital dash climbed toward the seventy-knot range. Toggling between the satellite imagery and intel loaded into his Toughbook tablet and the various charts from the boat's Raymarine nav screen, including its Quantum radar, Remington said, "I'm seeing several big ships in the general vicinity, any of which could be our boat."

He paused, scrutinizing the images and data in relation to the colorful moving shapes scattered around the radar field like blobs of paint. Compared them to the screen populated by boats and ships identified by AIS and saw the one shape, bigger than most, that was missing. Because its transponder was still turned off.

"Jackpot," he announced. "And it's just about exactly where Kip projected." Remington glanced up, noted the readout of their speed and remarked, "Okay, start easing up, cowboy." Referring to the distance from which their silhouette could, with the right light and/or optical device, be observed, he said, "If I'm right, we're about to hit our horizon threshold. We're coming up on an area of shallows that extend several miles out from Limnos, and to get us in comfortable range we should drop anchor about three miles to target, which"—he consulted the screens again, watching as their position advanced—"is *now*."

Jake drew the RIB's throttle back and maneuvered to a spot over the shoal that put them exactly where they needed to be. He slowed to an idle and, while he deployed the anchor and worked to get it set in the sand, Remington left his seat and clambered to the stern where their gear was organized. They were about eight miles off Limnos, and even though he had not seen any local fishing boats, Jake did a scan of the island coastline through his FLIR MilSight night vision monocular. Not seeing marine traffic in that direction, he turned and surveyed the open water, finding nothing close and only a few big ships visible by profile in the distance.

Satisfied they were alone, he waited as Remington got his drone ready for launch.

SUNRISE WAS EDGING CLOSER, nautical twilight forming a thin filament of electric blue slowly bleeding between sea and sky. The muted sound of current sloshing against the RIB's Orca tubes was momentarily augmented by that of the whirring SkyRaider as it lifted into the air and then quickly disappeared.

Back in his seat next to Jake, Remington held the tablet controller and directed the drone to the current coordinates of the ship he had pegged as the superyacht. The two of them were glued to the controller's screen and, in a matter of minutes, the massive vessel materialized, illuminated in bright oranges and reds and yellows and purples through the Boson infrared thermal. The *Gala* logo confirmed identity, but size and architectural structure would have also done so. Riveted, they both watched as Remington lowered the drone to five hundred feet and flew it the length of the yacht.

The first thing they noticed was the security presence, in the form of several manned tenders hugging its sides like suckerfish on a shark, as well as figures whose heat signatures randomly appeared on the exposed areas of decks and along the railings. Switching from infrared to the normal EO view, though dim in the low light, the 13MP camera with its 4X digital zoom was able to provide a surprising amount of detail, so Remington alternated between the two modes as he dropped the drone even lower to do a complete circuit around the yacht at horizontal level. He was running the drone with its red and green flight beacons off and far enough away not to be heard, but if any of the security detail were equipped with night vision devices, he knew there was a chance they'd spot it.

Even so, after an initial orbit, Remington pushed his luck and flew the SkyRaider closer.

In the controller screen, they saw what they had viewed before in the digital images acquired from the photography buff at Yalikavak, but now actually alongside the moving vessel, it all came into much more expository focus. An exotic fish out of the tank and into the wild.

Through the lens of the drone's camera, they were seeing the Leonardo helicopter, the gem-shaped swimming pool, the Jacuzzis, the immaculately arranged and set dining and lounge areas, a fitness and yoga platform, a fire pit, and a sun deck outfitted like an exclusive beach club—complete with bikini boutique, pool inflatables, and cocktail bar. Also seeing the onboard security detail up close, they were able to discern the unmistakable outlines of long guns. The tenders schooled around the yacht numbered six, each helmed by a pair of similarly armed men. By their shapes and configurations, it appeared that the tenders were also made by Technohull, possibly Omegas, and no doubt at least as fast as the model they piloted.

"...the fuck is with all that security," Jake muttered.

Remington ventured, "Well, I'd say if nothing else, it corroborates Kip's intel about the yacht belonging to Taras Ignatkovich…billionaire, guy on the outs with the Russian regime, good reason for protection…"

"Yeah, but if Kip is also right about the mercs in his employ and these are some of them, it brings me back to what the fuck are they up to and why are they on our asses?"

There was still some charge left on the SkyRaider, but Remington needed to allow enough time for the drone's return, so he was inputting the commands when Jake honed in on one of the security men who had just put a pair of binoculars up to his face.

"Oh shit. Remy, one of the guns—"

"Yep, I see him, too, and if it's a NOD," he said, which was an acronym for night observation device, "I think he might have spied it. Get ready to blast off."

Jake weighed anchor and restarted the RIB's engines.

Remington sent the drone high above the yacht to get it out of viewable range for the man with the binos. In the few minutes it took for the drone's return, a pair of the yacht's tenders had peeled off from the mothership, one steering beyond it, the other in their direction. With the SkyRaider's air speed clocking about thirty miles an hour, they were forced to wait, but once Remington had the device back in his hands, Jake pushed the boat's throttle forward, swerved into a wide turn that tilted them sideways, and raced off. The Technohull hurtled through the water barely scoring the surface on its nearly airborne ride, wind roaring in their ears and churned sea curdled and white in their wake.

With Jake running the RIB at maximum speed, the dash's digital readout ticking between the upper eighties and ninety, it was all Remington could do to keep himself in the boat much less get the SkyRaider securely stowed. But he somehow managed to fit it and the controller into the case and stumble back to his seat.

Looking at the nav screen, he called out, "One of them is on our tail—like us, probably tracking by radar. About two klicks behind but closing." He reached into the glove box where Jake had stashed the monocular, put it to his eye, and twisted around. Through the lens, bouncing water and horizon went from deep blues to emerald greens and soon, the superyacht tender came into view, entering the fluorescent glow.

Jake said, "I think I'm going to divert to the east, toward the Turkish coast."

"That's what I was going to suggest," Remington replied. "There is a good bit of marine traffic that way, hopefully enough to throw them off." He peered through the monocular again, and this time caught a sequence of flashes, followed by another, and another.

"Jesus Christ," he sputtered.

"What?"

"The fuckers are shooting at us. They're not in range—yet—but they're gaining and will be."

"Hang on," Jake shouted, and spun the RIB's steering wheel, making a steep forty-five-degree turn, heading for the island of Bozcaada. Even at this early hour, the surrounding waters were cluttered with big bulk carriers, tankers, and container ships navigating to and from the busy trade channel connecting the Aegean and Black seas via the Dardanelles and Bosporus straits on either end of the Sea of Marmara.

Approaching the density of maritime commerce, Jake gradually eased up on their speed and began a series of maneuvers, slipping around a number of ships until they were well into the midst. He slid in between a pair of crude oil tankers and slowed to an idle.

Beside him, Remington wiped sea spray and perspiration from his face and handed a towel to Jake, who did the same. They both studied the radar screen and, after several minutes had passed, saw the tender reverse course and head back to the yacht.

Taking a rough swipe at his wind-blown and sea-dampened hair, Jake asked, "What do you think?"

Grinning, Remington said, "I say let's forego the croissants and coffee and get rolling. How we doing on fuel?" The Technohull's tank held 570 liters which, under most conditions, would easily cover a distance of two hundred nautical miles, perhaps more, but they had pushed the RIB pretty hard. For that reason, they had brought a container of extra gas.

Checking the dash gauges, Jake replied, "We're good," and added, "this is some sexy hot number of a boat. I want one."

Remington chuckled. "Put it on your Christmas list and if you're good maybe Santa will drop one off in CR for you."

Jake wove their way out of the shipping flotilla and into the open water, bearing southwest. Passing Lesvos, dawn crept over the mountains in a pink haze and then spilled down into the valley of Skala Eressos in a cloud of rose gold. Ahead, the sea toward Psara was clear and glimmering like polished pewter in the morning light.

34

THE DAY'S DIG ROUTINE was already underway when they returned, Caspian Bachman, his staff, academics, archaeologists, and vets entrenched in the work. Remington's team members were in their designated placements, some at the basecamp, some with the MVAA group on Antipsara, and one or more patrolling the cottage and access road. Before making the sea crossing to rejoin the dig group, Jake and Remington sat down to brief Kipnis and give him the drone footage for in-depth analysis.

Falcone and Niles, at Jake's prior instruction, had taken Callie and gone over to Antipsara, photographing, filming, and interviewing. To keep an eye on Callie, they let her begin organizing the growing array of media, entries and notes for which were recorded in their pen and pencil hieroglyphics in several spiral notebooks.

She strolled with them as they continued documentation of the site activity and participants, jittery as her eyes flicked between their subjects, others all around, the notes she was reviewing, and the trail that led back to the shore where she hoped Jake would be arriving any minute. The beach and floating wharf were out of view, so her gaze kept going to the closest point across the swale, willing his handsome physique to appear.

"Darling," Niles said, "mind your steps."

Snapping out of her misdirected attention, Callie glanced down, saw that she was about to put her foot into a divot big enough to turn an ankle, and wobbled unsteadily to plant it on solid ground. In the process, the notebooks she clutched slipped apart and dropped in a flutter of bound pages and loose papers that were tucked within.

"Oh no," she gasped and bent down, scrambling to collect the assortment, unfastened material quickly scattering in the breeze. "No, no, no…"

Falcone and Niles simultaneously stopped in their tracks and pivoted to her aid, Falcone saying, "Hey, it's okay…it's okay, Callie. We've got it."

The two of them scuttled after the sheets that were flitting over the vegetation with the carefree whim of butterflies, and had gone a considerable length downrange from her when Callie heard a voice she did not recognize. From directly behind her, a man said, "Here ya go, sweet thing."

Startled, Callie jumped and turned, finding one of the vets holding out several pieces of paper. He was slender but clearly sinewy by the way his jeans and t-shirt form fit legs and biceps, swarthy skin and brown hair made to look even darker by the curved sunglasses concealing his eyes.

Rocking on his booted feet, his mouth broke into a sneer and he emitted a haughty laugh. "What's wrong, princess? I'm not the boogeyman." He gesticulated with his extended arm, cocking his head to one side when she did not reach to accept the papers he'd picked up.

Falcone and Niles were on either side of her now, both openly glaring at the man. Taking the papers from him, Falcone said, "Thanks."

The vet continued his brash assessment of Callie and, even with his eyes covered, she felt the intensity of his scrutiny. Falcone and Niles sensed it, too, Niles slipping a protective arm around her.

Addressing them for the first time, the vet asked, "Did the police find out what happened with the dead guy?"

Falcone eyed him narrowly. "It's nothing for you to be concerned with."

The man shrugged. "Just wondering. A shocking thing, yes?"

When his statement got no response, his focus shifted back to Callie.

"Pretty little babe…what are you doing out here in all this dirt, hmm?" He smirked again, licking a corner of his lips.

Falcone stepped into the man's personal space, inches from his face, and under his breath bristled, "Stop that shit. She is totally off limits."

The vet held out his arms in mock surrender and said, "No doubt. I know she's married to the Special Forces dude, but I can look and appreciate." Still grinning.

"That Special Forces *dude* will fuck you up if he catches you 'appreciating.'" Falcone snipped. "Get me?"

As if a satirical mask had been suddenly stripped away, the man standing in front of them seemed to transform into another personality altogether, his jaw dropping and taking all hints of lascivious scorn with it. He moved several feet back, his posture becoming almost elastic.

Stuttering, he said, "L-l-look, I'm sorry...I didn't mean to...I was just..." He waved his arms in front of himself like a baseball umpire ruling a runner safe.

"Okay, bud," Falcone said. "We'll call it a misunderstanding. Thanks for your help." Flustered, he cut a quick glance at Niles, whose expression was equally baffled.

And in that few seconds, as both were looking at each other and not at him, the man dipped his head, allowing his shades to partially slide from his eyes. Gave Callie a wink, and walked off, his initial stride one of insolent swagger which, just as abruptly, transitioned into a sheepish skulk.

"Maybe we overreacted," Niles suggested. "I'm thinking about what Jake told us, how these vets can have quirky behavior."

Falcone squinted warily, unconvinced. He said nothing for a few minutes and then asked Niles, "Who is that asshole?"

Niles opened a notebook he had picked up from the ground and fingered through a section with names and photographs, replying, "Logan Hays...1st Recon Marine."

Falcone shook his head, scowling. "You sure? Doesn't look like a Logan Hays. Just seems...I don't know."

Niles handed the notebook to him and, after reviewing the information associated with Hays' name and picture, Falcone remarked, "He's one of the few on the DND list."

He was referring to a form everyone on the dig was required to sign, accepting or declining the release of their images or comments for all media platforms, the DND standing for "do not disclose." Some vets were guarded with their privacy, even emphatically so, but while Caspian Bachman encouraged compliance for the vital part publicity played in the success of his organization, he maintained a nonjudgmental stance. He made it known that participation in press events or social media posts or anything else—including the documentation Falcone and Niles were undertaking—was entirely voluntary. Additionally, all material would be thoroughly screened to ensure that any individuals on the DND list were not included, or at least not visibly identifiable in whatever was published or broadcast.

"Well," Niles said, "definitely need to keep an eye on the bloke. Something's not right with him."

"Tell you something else," Falcone said, "the dogs don't like him. And dogs know."

WHEN THE MAN KNOWN as Logan Hays rejoined the others, he walked on past his unit, bending his knees and wanding his arms as if stretching to loosen cramped muscles. Absorbed in work and conversation, his team members paid him no heed, and he continued moving up the slope toward the location of the crime scene. Stopping at the edge, he dropped to one knee and gazed over the earthen pit where the remains of the scientist had been excavated. The red-and-white barrier tape and miniature marker flags flapped in the breeze, the stench of decomposition still discernible but lessening with exposure to the air.

Glancing over his shoulder every few moments to make sure his absence from the dig group remained unnoticed, he was mentally chastising himself for the reckless interaction with Falcone and Niles and Tyler's woman. Taking target practice on birds was one thing, but allowing his libidinous predilections to break out of the gate was an unacceptable lapse. Up to this point, he'd managed to skim along obscurely below the surface of the mix and, as far as he could tell, not register inordinately on anyone's radar. But frustration with a lack of results and festering boredom were beginning to loosen the reserve he was normally able to maintain.

He had recognized the challenge for what it was, having to conduct his objective in the midst of others who, like himself, were by nature and training especially observant and innately suspicious. And although he had been well briefed on Bachman and the MVAA staff, he'd not anticipated the level of discipline by which Bachman ran his operations. And, he had definitely not counted on the extra layer of logistics command and control that Remington's team added to the equation.

That additional element had, in fact, totally derailed his plan to make solo excursions to Antipsara at night when everyone was asleep. Straying from the group was prohibited and strictly enforced—even bathroom breaks were exercised in the company of others and with supervision—and the members of Remington's team kept overwatch 24-7. He'd been assessing them from the outset, individually and as a whole, looking for deficiencies or potential opportunities to exploit, but thus far—to his surprise and vexation—had found absolutely none.

He stood, let out an irritable groan, and went back to the grid area. Retaking his dig spot, he pulled on gloves, picked up a trowel, and chunked it into soil. *Fucking dirt*, he thought dourly.

Then he noticed that, while he'd been AWOL, his unit had begun to accumulate some actual findings from their pit. Eyeballing the spoils—consisting of ceramics and various metals in bits and pieces and whole articles—he felt his interest tick up.

JAKE TOOK ADVANTAGE OF the lunch break to spend a little quality alone time with Callie. He led her to a familiar spot where they watched gulls and terns, shearwaters and cormorants, and the occasional falcon circle and glide in the abundance of blue sky, some of them looping in intricate patterns as if scrolling an invisible banner. When they finished their sandwiches, Jake took Callie's hand and they began walking across the meadow, green and gold grasses that gave way to a fading purple haze of wild thyme, the distinctive aroma layered in the air. But as Jake nuzzled close to Callie, he was inhaling the natural fresh scent of her skin and hair, curls softly tousled by the breeze, wondering how she could possibly manage to smell so fresh and lovely after hours in sun and soil.

She smiled and he kissed her neck and squeezed her hand, which got him a sweet smile in return.

Venturing a little farther than they'd gone in the vicinity, a sliver of bright color in the distance caught Jake's eye. Given the mostly drab hues of the island's topography, he was immediately curious, and headed toward it. As they advanced, more flashes of color came into view—yellows and blues and greens and reds—and then, the muted sound of buzzing.

Jake halted in his tracks, looked and listened, and commenced walking in another direction, toward the sea. At the island's western edge, he came up on what appeared to be a trail sloping down to a secluded cove. He could not recall seeing this particular inlet during their aerial surveys and wanted to see if there was anything worth exploring.

Explaining to Callie, he said, "Stay right here. I'll just be a few minutes." She glanced anxiously around, seeing nothing but the scrub-covered landscape they'd traversed. Placing his hands on her shoulders, he assured, "It will be fine. I won't be more than a dozen or so yards away, and I'll be right back. Okay?"

She nodded limply and watched as Jake headed down the path.

It became apparent by the breadth, tamped down vegetation, and bare dirt that this was a man-made trail, used at least several times and recently. He descended the length of it, half upright and half scooting, grabbing handfuls of brush and strands of vines, which also showed signs of previous use. The slope was not particularly steep, the decline gradual, so Jake was easily able to get to the bottom. Standing on a narrow strip of shore, he spotted a grouping of rocks with an opening and treaded toward it. Now in front of the rocks, he saw that they formed an entrance to a cave.

Ducking inside, he could feel the moisture from the earth and hear the hollowed sounds of sea water dripping from the rocky surfaces, his sinuses filling with the salted loam. He slipped off his backpack and dug out a Nitecore flashlight, illuminating the dim confines with 4000 lumens. Hundreds of thousands of years had defined and deepened the cavern, water smoothing the circular walls and floor, the strong beam of his light pointing into a maw that extended much farther than he would have guessed. He'd only gone a short distance into the tunnel when his flashlight beam washed over a cavity carved out from one sidewall. It was waist-high, about four feet square, and draped on the inside by a plastic tarp.

Jake lifted an edge of the covering and found a mound of dirt, loose from being dug out but damp and dense from the humidity. He poked around and extracted fragments and chunks of ceramic.

On the one hand, he thought, this could be the site of a random island visitor's discovery or that of one or more archaeologists. But it was not too much of a leap to believe that Panos Korkizoglou had been in this cave and, very possibly, made the discovery he'd postulated would revolutionize the defense industry.

But if that was the case, what could have been entombed here…and where was it now?

Jake wanted to continue his exploration but, out of sight and earshot of Callie, he needed to get back. He took a handful of soil, sealed it in a Ziploc bag, and exited the cave.

He was halfway to the top of the slope when he heard Callie cry out, and knew in an instant what had happened. He tore up the remaining length of hillside, already unslinging his backpack and digging into the contents.

IN THE TIME JAKE was gone, Callie's gaze had been mostly fixed on the point of the trail that disappeared over the hill, watching for him to reappear. She'd checked behind herself a few times, uneasy to be alone, but felt her guard lessening as she peered out to the open sea and up to the boundless sky, finding tranquility in their vastitude and balance. And, in spite of her uneasiness with Jake's absence, she was so much more comfortable away from the group and reveled in any time they had together, just the two of them.

She knew there was something going on of great concern to Jake and Remington and his team, knew that it seemed to be continually evolving, maybe even escalating, but she had no idea what it was. It worried her considerably, but she also knew she had to trust Jake's capacity to deal with any situation and keep them safe.

Imagining him coming over the ridge, seeing his jet-black hair blowing in the wind, his stoic, tanned face breaking into a smile at the sight of her, his trim, fit body, she felt the familiar butterflies fluttering riotously in her stomach, warmth flooding all her most intimate places. Inhaling and blowing out a breath, she looked upward, her eyes following the flight path of a falcon, one just like the poor creature the dogs had found on the first day of the dig. Watched it glide across the sky with seemingly no effort, wide wings outstretched, majestic and graceful. Even its name, Eleanora, personified elegance.

She was so caught up in the avian splendor that she did not detect the subtle sensation by her neck, only making out the low buzz, as indistinct and brief as a hummingbird's pass, at the last second.

And then every one of her senses was overcome with a shrillness of pain she'd known before, her skin on fire, neurons in her brain screaming in agony. She heard herself cry out, a disembodied wail that seemed to come from elsewhere.

Jake came pounding over the slope, sprinting to her, his eyes honed on her face, which was deeply flushed and beginning to swell. He wasted no time with further assessment as there was no need, his right hand working the cap off an EpiPen, one from a supply he always had on hand. The moment he'd heard Callie's cry, a sensory wave of scent and sight and sound—her sweet smell, the snippets of color nearby, the buzzing—told him what had happened.

She'd been stung by a bee.

"It will be okay," he said, the tone of his voice a balance of authority and calmness though his mind was ramped up with the more frenzied reaction that emotion infused. "I need you to stand totally still for me, okay?"

She looked at him, panic stark in her eyes and face, gasping for breath.

He could see the hysteria and dominance of the pain had not only overtaken her physically but also blocked the capacity to respond to his direction, so he clamped a leg firmly in his free hand with enough force to immobilize and jabbed the injector into her outer thigh. She let out a strangled yelp as the needle impaled her leg, which Jake left in place for several seconds. Withdrawing it, he kneaded flesh and muscles through the material of her pants.

She continued to struggle for air, and he said, "Takes a few seconds. Try to relax."

"Hurts," she rasped, tears streaming. "Hurts so much."

"I know, baby."

He sat her down and began monitoring vitals while watching for any exacerbation of the anaphylaxis that had set in. Epinephrine was included in any of his medical kits, but after learning of the severe allergic response Callie had experienced from ant bites while he'd been in Africa, he now kept an EpiPen on him at all times. He'd shown her how to inject herself in case he wasn't around and insisted she carry the application but, to his dismay, fear of having to use it stopped her from doing so. As worrisome as that was, it was a concession he'd had to live with, making sure that their home staff and anyone else accompanying her was equipped and capable.

Callie sat panting and shaking, the spot on her neck as glaring as a bullseye, an angry red blister amidst skin mottled with hives. Issuing a steady mantra of gentle commands to regulate her breathing, Jake swabbed delicately to free the barbed stinger, applied antiseptic and hydrocortisone cream, and activated a cold pack. His diagnostic questions confirmed that she was dizzy and nauseated and extremely uncomfortable with the pain, her respiration labored but starting to flow more freely. He gave her some Advil and Benadryl and watched her intently for several minutes, also keeping an eye out for other bees.

While Jake had been tending to her, a flyaway strand of thought was flicking in his head. He stood and helped Callie to her feet, mentally trying to grasp the thread while concentrating on what was now the paramount objective—getting her out of the sun and, as soon as she was a little more stable, taking leave of the island for their cottage in Psara. With his arm around her, he walked slowly, steadying her teetering steps.

Crossing the meadow, once again Jake picked up the bits of color, and the errant thought came to him.

Bee boxes.

35

"THEY SHOULD NOT BE here," Kostas Demetriadi told him the next day.

Jake looked at the project's lead archaeologist, waiting for some kind of clarification and, getting none, asked, "What do you mean? They shouldn't be here because of our dig or they shouldn't be here at all?"

"They should not be here at all," Demetriadi replied. "I am sure you know by now, there are beekeepers in Psara and, in fact, many throughout the mainland and islands."

Jake did know this, and nodded. Not only had the dig group been supplied with a large stockpile of local honey, he and Callie had already sampled a good bit over the course of their honeymoon as it was a common staple with breakfast fare.

It is believed that beekeeping originated in Greece as early as 1500 BCE, mythology's first keeper, the demigod Aristaeus, said to have been taught by the Nymphs. With the greatest density of colonies in Europe, the Greeks consume more than double the honey of Americans and, thus far, have not suffered the mysterious losses of catastrophic hive collapse. The country's dry summer heat with minimal rainfall creates optimal conditions for the organics that make indigenous wild herbs especially intense which, in turn, provide powerful nectar for bees. The honey that is produced is widely considered the most unique and flavorful in the world.

Demetriadi went on, "Antipsara was recently included in the

European Natura 2000 Award, which is a recognition for conservation success. From that point, ongoing human activities, such as beekeeping and goat herding, were prohibited." He paused, scratching his beard. "I want to see these bee boxes."

Well, I do, too, Jake thought, but his reasons were not the same as Demetriadi's.

Callie, who'd had a miserable and sleepless night, despite several doses of Benadryl, was not with him today. Of course, she had wanted Jake to stay with her at the cottage, but yielded with little resistance—a testament to how badly she felt—and he let her know that Remington would have a couple of guys on the grounds. He'd texted and FaceTimed her frequently since his departure, satisfied with her welfare from a security standpoint even if not from one of comfort.

"We should not go without the proper protective gear," the archaeologist advised.

"I don't think we need to get that close," Jake said. "Not for what I'm thinking."

Demetriadi regarded him quizzically but replied, "Okay, let us go."

As they hiked from the dig site to the meadow, Jake revisited a theory that had occurred to him—absurdly illogical, but if it bore out, kind of ingenious.

When the splashes of color came into view across the field, Demetriadi said, "We should not get more than three or four meters from them."

They advanced, taking slow and deliberate steps, stopping a half dozen yards from a clearing in the vegetation. There, a row of wooden boxes, painted in the primary colors Jake had glimpsed the day before, were evenly spaced and stacked two high. Secured with metal hasps, each box was compartmentalized, single sections known as broods for the queen bee, and others called supers for the honey production of the worker bees. The double-boxed stacks were set in bases, each individual unit topped with inner and outer covers and bottoms, the supers fit inside with vertically hanging frames.

Studying the boxes from their distance, Demetriadi commented, "I do not believe these have been here long. They appear to be newly constructed and painted."

Jake did not reply, but the observation tended to support his hunch.

His gaze shifted away from the boxes to the ground surrounding them, most of it spread with maquis scrub. Though by no means obvious, he soon found what he'd been looking for and moved carefully toward a thatch of growth that was thicker and taller than the rest of the vegetation in the clearing. It was closer to the boxes by a few yards, so he kept an eye on them as he went. Downwind of the colonies, the faint buzzing became more audible, coalescing into a dull drone, bees soaring and circling and hovering in the air, which was now pungent with the feral smell of beeswax and pheromones and pollen and wood.

Kneeling in front of the brush, he pushed apart sprays of grasses and probed through clumps of sage and mounds of thyme. A couple of bees whizzed randomly by but were non-threatening as he did not swat at them or emit any fearful stimuli. He was immersed in groundcover up to his elbows when his gloved hands encountered a patch of loosened soil. Digging in the dirt, he scooped by the fistful until he touched something solid, then dredged around the object until he could get a grip.

What he dislodged was a clay jug the size of a flowerpot. It was rounded with a neck only slightly smaller than the body, a cover flush inside the top. Copper-toned in color, it was elaborately decorated with a blend of floral and geometric designs. Holding the piece of pottery in both hands, Jake gave it a slight shake, felt the muffled rattle of loose contents inside. He was trying to pry the lid with his fingers when he realized Demetriadi had come over to see what he'd found.

"Wait!" the archaeologist called.

Jake blew out the breath he'd been holding in his eagerness. "Yeah, I'm getting ahead of myself. Need to do this the right way." Pointing to the ground he'd dug up, he said, "I think there are more of these buried here."

"I will get someone to come with a wheelbarrow," Demetriadi said, and got on his radio.

Minutes later, Remington appeared with Caspian Bachman. Addressing Bachman, Jake asserted, "I want to open this." He gave both men a cogent look to impart his sense of conviction.

Bachman replied, "Since this is undoubtedly not associated with our recovery mission and not in our defined grid, it will have to be turned over to antiquities." He paused, registering Jake's determination. "But as long as you're careful…what is it you suspect?"

Remington knew the answer. "You think this is Korki's find."

Jake nodded and told them about the cave, saying, "I think maybe he was there, probably collecting his biological samples, and found the cache of whatever these are. And, I'm thinking his big find is whatever's inside these jugs. He had the cleverness to remove them from the cave and hide them in a place"—he waved an arm in the direction of the bee boxes—"that would provide a natural deterrent. Hell, he might have even paid the beekeeper to set up here. Based on what Kostas told me about the restrictions in place, I would assume locals know it's off-limits."

"But why wouldn't he have taken what he found off the island?" Bachman asked.

Remington said, "He might have been waiting for a window when he could move without being observed, and whoever tortured and killed him—whoever *was* watching him—knew our dig was imminent and took action."

Jake set the piece of pottery on a square of plastic tarp in the basin of the wheelbarrow, the other three men drawing nearer around it. Bachman took pictures of the jug with his phone, remarking, "The elements are consistent with the Mycenaean period, which is the Bronze Age, so at the very least, it's a significant artifact." He moved aside for Jake, who had taken out his Leatherman multi-tool.

Removing his gloves, Jake used the small screwdriver with a delicate touch, taking a few minutes on a seal that was surprisingly snug. When he was finally able to loosen and lift the jug's lid, he squinted inside. And saw a handful of rocks in various sizes.

Tipping the jug, he dumped one of them into the palm of his hand. A silvery gray, it had the look and texture of schist, rough-edged with tiny veins of blue-green. One side, which appeared to be a break, was as smooth and pristine as a royal tea service, gleaming like liquid silver in the light.

His forehead creased with a mix of puzzlement and disappointment. "Rocks? This can't be what he was killed for." He cast a glance at Deme-triadi. "Kostas, what am I missing?"

It took the archaeologist a moment before he replied, "Maybe you are not." He reached over and took the rock from Jake's hand, scrutinizing it closely. "I have spent some time in geological studies and have participated in field work all over the country. I have never seen this particular rock."

Bachman spoke up. "Why don't we excavate whatever else is in that cache?"

The four men each took a section of the swath and, for the next hour, dug through the soil and extracted additional ceramic vessels, all of which were roughly the same size, identically colored and embellished and tightly sealed with fitted lids. When the area had been completely cleared out, they had accumulated ten pieces.

Expecting to find more of the same rocks, the first one Jake picked up to examine felt different. It did not have the same muted rattle, but something shifted inside, suggesting perhaps a pulverized form of the stone. He worked to remove the lid and peered into the rounded chamber.

And saw nothing.

Baffled, he gave the vessel a shake from side to side and, again, felt the shift of contents—contents that seemed to be invisible. He tucked the piece under his arm and tilted it toward his hand. As the substance sifted and slid, he could see movement without actually being able to define outlines or dimensions. When the first of it made contact with his skin and was exposed to the daylight, miniscule fractals glinted but did not reveal their source. Instead, he now saw the ground below—his hand had all but disappeared, as if it had been partially obliterated by some imaging software's eraser.

For a rapt moment of stunned incredulity, the four men just gaped at what their minds could not comprehend. And then Remington blurted, "What is this shit?"

Massaging the substance with his fingers, Jake muttered, "I can feel it. It's...it's like a liquid but solid, soft but hard. How can that be?" He watched as Remington ran his own hand back and forth underneath, watched as it, too, seemed to blend or merge into the ground below.

Remington began, "Could this be..." But before he finished his conjecture, the substance in Jake's hand began to subtly change—not fully materializing but becoming more distinguishable, its properties possibly altered by air or light or atmospheric elements.

Jake said, "I'm no scientist or archaeologist, but from what we're seeing here, I wonder if the composition of the jug is actually part of the formula to create this transparency."

Looking from Demetriadi to Bachman, Remington's expression animated with a sudden jolt of perspicacity. "Are there any rare-earth minerals in the Aegean?"

Demetriadi nodded. "Yes, some have been found here, but not much. The Greek scientific community has always believed that there are undiscovered fields in Rhodope, Thessaloniki, Kilkis, Strymonikos Bay…" He paused, smiling. "And Chios." Excited now, he continued, "Most are thought to be underwater. If these vessels did, in fact, come from that cave, they could have been excavated from parts of the seabed that were once exposed or accessible to the ancient civilizations of the Bronze Age."

He went on, "I do not know enough about the subject, but it is conceivable that the rock was put through some form of process they created by experimentation, reducing it to"—he rubbed a thumb and forefinger together—"like a powder…and, over time, being sealed up in the ceramics and possibly mixed with something indigenous to the region…"

The other three listened, enthralled, waiting for him to continue his speculative spin, fantastical as it was. After a few moments of thought, the archaeologist pressed his hands together. "You know what it could be? Masthiha."

"And what is that?" Jake asked.

"The mastic tree. The bees brought it to mind as they feed on the tree sap, which makes a specific kind of honey. The trees only grow in the southern part of Chios, but I do remember from my studies that the resin has been linked to a naturally occurring polymer of monoterpene."

Further enlightening them, Demetriadi said, "The resin has been called the miracle tear, from the legend of an Egyptian Christian sailor who was martyred in the third century during the reign of the Roman emperor, Decius, dragged by horses through Chios. As the legend goes, when the lentisc trees saw his suffering, they cried tears of Masthiha. The mastic sap contains some eighty identified components. Besides the honey, it has been used in everything from foods and beverages to cosmetics and pharmaceuticals but, as you may know, in Chios it is also integral to the unique process of coating houses that are then elaborately engraved."

He went on, "I seem to recall a strange story about one house that had been finished this way, and when the engraving was completed, the unetched painted parts were said to be translucent. The house was eventually recoated for more complete coverage."

They all went silent for several moments, gazing in wonderment at the substance in Jake's hand while trying to wrap their minds around the hypothetical implications. And then Remington voiced what Jake, and possibly Bachman, were already thinking.

"Every military on the planet—most particularly us, the Israelis, the Russians, and the Chinese—have been working on some variation of invisibility cloaking. Kip will tell you the Israelis are damn near close, if not there. But no application has been a hundred percent solid. If these rocks turn out to be rare-earth, anything like neodymium for one, it would definitely be the game-changer Korki thought. With his defense work and scientific acumen, he would know."

Bachman said, "Let's not get too far ahead of ourselves. We should get a more expert opinion on the substance. One of our local archaeologists, Giannis Magheras, is credentialed in biology and chemistry."

"Can he be discreet?" Jake asked.

"Yes," Bachman replied, Demetriadi nodding in agreement.

Jake carefully tapped his hand over the jug's opening, returning the contents to the interior and replacing the top. "Okay then," he said. "Let's load it all up and see if we can get it back to camp without arousing any curiosity."

For the first time during the interchange, Bachman cracked a smile. "In a group of archaeologists? That's a tall order."

"Well, we need to find a way," Jake said. He gave each a serious look. "This has to be just between us—and Kip—for now."

FROM HIS SIDE ON the parcel of his unit, the vet's head turned synchronously with the other three assigned there, watching with interest as Caspian Bachman, Kostas Demetriadi, Nash Remington, and Jake Tyler made their way back to the dig site. On seeing the two wheelbarrows Tyler and Remington pushed, both transporting some kind of cargo covered by plastic tarps, the vet's attention jumped ship from that of languid curiosity to a call for action. He watched as the foursome circumnavigated the parameters of the grid, bypassing the designated staging area where all excavated items were evaluated, classified, and recorded. A significant amount of time and emphasis had been devoted to expounding on this part of the process, so for them to deviate from Bachman's ironclad regulations meant something beyond the ordinary was going on.

He resumed his site work but kept an eye on the four as they steered the wheelbarrows toward the path leading to shore. He thought about making an excuse to leave, but his group had just taken their scheduled bathroom break, so he'd need to come up with another credible ploy. When the other three were all looking down and focusing on their efforts, he slipped a hand up to his head and scooped off the camo cap he wore, stuffing it into a pocket of his cargo pants.

Then, the pantomime began. He gulped down the last half of his water bottle, huffed and puffed, blew out an exaggerated breath, and announced, "I must have left my hat on the boat when we took a piss." He shook his empty bottle for added effect. "Need more water, too, or I'm going to heat"—he caught himself, amending—"overheat."

He paused for some reaction or acknowledgment but got no more than an upturned head or two, a negligible shrug, impassive expressions all around. So he stood, snagged his backpack, and trotted off in the direction of the beach.

Reaching the sand just in time to see Bachman and Demetriadi standing alone on the floating wharf, he took out a pair of binoculars and peered through the lenses. Saw them unloading what looked to be pottery from the pair of wheelbarrows.

Jugs? *What the fuck?*

The *Blue Zone* was moored alongside the dock, but the captain and crew were not in sight; having been on board to use the facilities earlier, the vet suspected they were all probably lounging below.

But Bachman and Demetriadi were making handoffs to Tyler and

Remington on the opposite side of the platform, the men's upper torsos and outstretched arms moving up and down with each transfer. When all of the jugs had been passed over, words were exchanged and, moments later, motors growled to life. The vet knew the passenger boat had several skiffs but was a little surprised to see a high-powered RIB shoot from the wharf, twin engines jettisoning it out across the sparkling sea.

Before Bachman or Demetriadi could spy him, the vet scurried off, running close to the bank until he got to an inlet about fifty yards away. Here he had stashed his own inflatable. Nothing like the fast and sleek water bullet he'd just seen, his was of the same category but much smaller and lighter—if you could call eighty pounds lightweight—and folded up inside a thirty-five by thirty-five-inch bag. Unlike the package he'd retrieved from outside the Psara restaurant, this bundle had been strategically placed near the basecamp in such a way that, had it been found, the assumption would be that the inflatable belonged to a local. When the *Blue Zone* had been loaded up for its initial crossing to Antipsara, he'd had no trouble fitting it into the considerable mix of equipment and then hauling it out. He'd paused to catch his breath, waited until no one was looking his way, and slipped off to hide it along the bank. The second trip to and from the boat to retrieve and stash the Mercury outboard motor had been a little trickier, but he'd managed with some minor subterfuge involving a crate pilfered from the *Blue Zone*'s food storage and layered over with bananas.

Now, his contingency preparation was paying off by providing him the means to quickly take off and return, hopefully without anyone noticing his prolonged absence. He glanced at his watch, calculated the time needed, and decided he could just make the window to get back for end-of-day wrap-up, during which all group members would be accounted for as they boarded the passenger boat.

It took him no more than five minutes to open the bag, unfold and inflate the F-RIB, set and fire up the outboard motor, and take off in the wake of white foam churned by the Technohull Sea DNA.

CASPIAN BACHMAN HAD JUST begun conducting his last round of

the day, inspecting each unit's excavation progress and examining the fragmented pieces and parts and whole items extracted from the pits, which were now quite deep. He crouched by the side of one, marveling over a small pile of gold coins unearthed by a female vet on her first dig. The gloss of enthusiasm in the eyes of Aisha Cole, a former chief petty officer, made him beam with pride and happiness.

Comprehensively knowledgeable on each of his vets' backgrounds and unique challenges, Bachman knew that in Cole's case, as part of the U.S. Navy's Sixth Fleet deployment for Operation Odyssey Dawn in Libya, she had been responsible for leading and mentoring junior sailors. Throughout her military career and during that particular stint, Cole had performed her duties proficiently and professionally. But years later, after reintegrating with civilian life, she found herself battling increasingly extreme depression stemming, in large part, from the suicide of one of her sailors—on mission, on her ship. Post-traumatic stress takes many forms, not all of which are caused or manifested by physical factors.

"Well, look at you," he remarked brightly as the attractive African American woman wiped the grime of sweat and soil from her face, lips forming a wide grin.

"This is so amazing," she sputtered breathlessly.

Bachman conversed with Cole and her group for a minute or so and then moved on to the next unit. His thoughts were drifting back to the bizarre and potentially consequential discovery from the bee meadow, but while the revelation was certainly provocative and intriguing on a number of levels, he was concerned it would only add to the growing distractions that had been occurring on an almost daily basis. And no matter the significance of the preternatural substance discovered today, his focus had to remain honed on the experience and well-being of his vets and the mission to recover American remains from the World War II plane. He simply could not let himself get caught up in any dramatics outside that objective.

He heard a sharp whistle and exclamation from the other side of the grid and quickly crossed to see why he was being summoned, thinking, *please, just let it be something related to the project.* To his relief, it was something even better, what he sometimes called an "X marks the spot" moment. In the little over a week since the dig had begun, the group had exhumed all manner of typical objects, some more neoteric and mundane, many more of archaeological origin and distinction. Much of the latter consisted of pottery vessels and figurines, but what he saw spread out on the tarp by Kirk Perry's unit gave him reason to be optimistic if not somewhat jubilant.

Mixed in with dirt-encrusted ceramic and stone and wood were objects that reflected in the late-day sunlight—dull and corroded, but unmistakably metallic and textured with turquoise- and rust-colored grunge.

Although he could not be completely sure without further analysis, he believed he was looking at fragments of the B-24 plane. But as encouraging as this was, his excitement would be tempered until, or unless, they also found bones—old ones. Finding the plane's wreckage would be a victory but, without remains, an incomplete and unsatisfying one.

Bachman knelt on the ground with Perry's team members and pawed and poked through the slivers and chunks and gnarled configurations, not finding anything of exceptional interest. But as he stood and thumped soil from his gloved hands, a larger piece caught his eye. It had been moved aside from the metal, grouped with a collection of stone lumps ranging in size from a few inches to over a foot. What grabbed his attention was an edge protruding from the soil packed around the piece, something vaguely reminiscent of a design partially visible. Close up, he saw that it was not rock but a combination of wood and metal.

With his gloves and a coarse brush, he worked to expose enough of the surface to reveal an amazing arrangement of gears. That alone gave his heart a charge, but it was the fancy geometric patterns that made his jaw unhinge.

Because the design replicated what they had seen on the jugs from the bee meadow. He took out his phone, scrolling to the images he'd taken earlier just to be sure. And then, on the just-discovered item, he also noticed strings of tiny symbols.

Every archaeologist knew about the Antikythera mechanism, an artifact discovered in 1901 amidst the wreckage from a ship off the coast of that island. Found as a hunk the size of a large jewelry box, it had broken apart to reveal a layout almost exactly like what he was looking at—bronze gearwheels—the eventual analysis characterizing it as something of an analogue computer. Covered with intricate inscriptions, the Antikythera mechanism is thought to have been created by Greek scientists circa between 87 and 205 BC to track the movements of the sun and moon and make astronomical calculations. To this day, the device is considered one of the most technically complex discoveries from ancient times.

Had he not seen the jugs and witnessed the mind-boggling phenomenon of the substance they contained, Bachman would have been inclined to believe what he held in his hands was another such wonder. But gazing at the design and etchings on this piece, he believed it represented something more. And Panos Korkizoglou, on finding the jugs, had known it, too.

36

AFTER RETURNING TO BASECAMP with the group, Caspian Bach-man reconvened with Jake and Remington in Remington's tent, Kostas Demetriadi bringing Giannis Magheras into the fold. Efron Kipnis had also joined them and was studying the artifacts on display with even more interest and intensity than the archaeologists, taking a series of pictures with his phone. As Remington had implied, the former Mossad operative made the instant correlation and conceptualization of elements and device, but took it one step further.

Eying Demetriadi and Magheras in a way that acknowledged their categorical expertise, Kipnis said, "I see what the scientist saw here and, in my opinion, this find could absolutely be the game-changer in military technology, even in this most rudimentary form." Pointing to the piece Bachman had likened to the Antikythera mechanism, he added, "And seeing these symbols and the patterns that link it to the vessels, I have to think the ancient civilization that created this substance might have been in the process of mathematically refining the formula."

Giannis Magheras, a clean-cut, dark-haired man in his mid-forties, had been listening keenly and was now nodding at Kipnis' assessment. "I know almost nothing about the military or its technology," he stated, "but I concur…at least with the hypotheticals."

Like most of the local archaeologists, Magheras' degrees were issued from among the most prominent Greek universities, but he had also attended and received such honors from the MIT School of Science, which is where his curriculum had been more attuned to biology and chemistry. Picking up one of the rock samples, he continued, "I completed some courses in earth sciences and am familiar with rare-earth minerals, of which there are seventeen recognized as such. They are not, as the characterization would suggest, rare in the broad sense as they are actually abundant in the earth, but unlike the more common metallic elements, such as iron, aluminum, and silicon, they are generally found in lower concentrations and therefore cannot be mined in the usual way."

Turning the rock over in his hand, Magheras said, "This has very similar properties to neodymium."

"Which is used extensively in the defense industry, particularly for missile tech," Kipnis said distractedly, monitoring something on his phone.

Magheras went on, "As to the substance in the jugs, I would need to analyze and test it in a proper lab to know if it was derived from this rock, but given the properties we are observing, I think it is a reasonable assumption." He continued thoughtfully, "When you mentioned the mastic and polymers, this is an interesting theory because, while the first synthetic polymer was discovered in the nineteenth century, polymers in nature have probably been around since the beginning of time. With neodymium specifically—"

Kipnis finished for him. "It has not been fully established but is being developed as a catalyst for high-performance polymers with superior properties of lightweight composition, thermal and radiation resistance, durability and flexibility."

Demetriadi and Magheras both seemed astounded by the Israeli's scientific acumen, but Remington was not, a self-indulgent smirk dimpling his face.

Kipnis returned his attention to the symbols etched around the metal device and remarked, "As I said, this could be some kind of mathematical formula, but some of these numerical sequences resemble GPS coordinate combinations. Global positioning, as we know it today, was developed in a joint civil-military technical program back in the early seventies, but primitive variations—which is what this very well could be—have been in existence as long as humans have navigated."

"So…maybe locations for rock deposits?" Jake suggested.

"Lots of possibilities," Remington mused. Looking to Bachman, he asked, "What do we do with this? Given the potential military implications, I'm thinking we should reach out to command, and I have a trusted contact in mind."

Kipnis glanced up pointedly from the screen of his phone but said nothing.

Bachman's face clouded over with uncertainty. "This presents me with quite the conundrum because our permits are strictly for aircraft recovery. We're required to turn over anything else that is excavated by us to the Greek Ministry of Culture. Not to do so is a cardinal sin in archaeology."

Self-aware of his propensity for straight, if not blunt talk, Jake tried to moderate his reply, but in truth he was feeling some strong pangs of portent. Carefully, he said, "Caspian, with all due respect to the mission and your absolutely honorable code of conduct…" He paused to choose the right words, then continued, unable to be anything but direct. "At the risk of sounding melodramatic or out of line, in the wrong hands, this could be, at the very minimum, a massive fiasco."

Normally reticent with his emotions, Kipnis punctuated Jake's statement with an emphatic but enigmatic, "Yep."

Noting a twitch and sharp inhale from Demetriadi, Jake quickly added, "And I don't mean to imply that the Greek authorities or government would, in any way, be incompetent in their chain of custody or subsequent handling"—he turned back to Bachman—"but you have to know that this is simply beyond the scope of a typical archaeological find."

"No doubt," Bachman said, his expression still reflective of his conflict.

"Maybe we follow the proper protocol but delay long enough to make some inquiries on our side," Jake proposed. "Once you notify antiquities, what happens?"

"Find like this? I imagine they'd have somebody here tomorrow and it would be out of our hands, literally, within hours of their arrival." Bachman mulled his dilemma some more, then made his decision. "Okay, actually, I am in full agreement with you. This one hundred percent needs to be turned over to our military channels."

To Demetriadi, he said, "For sure we need to get all this secured like Fort Knox."

"Let's keep the pieces here in my tent," Remington said. "We'll have them guarded all hours, and I will personally take overnight watch."

Bachman left with the two Greek archaeologists, heading off to select appropriate storage cases for the ten vessels and metal-geared device.

Remington reached into a cooler, extracted and tossed bottles of water to Jake and Kipnis. They all settled into plastic chairs, taking a moment to quench their thirst and collect their thoughts.

After a few minutes had passed, Jake said, "You know a lot about this, Kip."

Kipnis did not immediately respond, reading a message from his phone. When he looked up, his expression was one of onerous calculation, as if deciding how much information to divulge. Speaking in a low voice, he said, "I sent images of the rock to a contact and just got a preliminary confirmation of the mineral I believe it is. The only reason I recognized it is because I have seen it before, in defense development. There are actually two ways this rock and substance could be potentially impactful. Obviously, in stealth and invisibility, but also in hypersonic technology. As for the former, I'm sure you are familiar with Quantum Stealth, the patented prototype developed by Canada's Hyperstealth Biotechnology, primarily for the military."

Jake nodded. "I know they're conducting trials on uniforms, vehicles, and aircraft. I've seen some demonstrations."

"Yes. In simple terms, that technology is based on material that bends light waves around the target, removing visual, infrared, and thermal signatures in addition to the target's shadow. Pretty amazing stuff, but not perfected to a practical level yet. But there is some newer tech involving the manipulation of magnetics and metamaterials. Without getting into too much detail, neodymium has been used there, but again, inconclusively."

He paused, glancing around to make sure no one was loitering outside the tent's openings.

"As to the latter, there is a top-secret project, initiated by my government with joint U.S. involvement, seeking to take hypersonic tech to another level. They are experimenting with a new mineral that is like a super version of neodymium."

Jake and Remington's faces were slack with confusion.

To clarify, Kipnis said, "The mineral is a synthetic of neodymium, but I believe—and so does my contact—that this is an organic form, which would be monumental. It could provide what they are trying to create to fulfill both applications of invisibility and superior hypersonics."

Remington muttered, "Well, color me mind-fucked."

"I've still got connects at SOCOM," Jake said. "Let me make some calls."

Remington shook his head. "Too far removed for the timeline we've got. Guy I have in mind is right here, right now, for military exercises with the Greeks—Greece, U.S., Israel, and Cyprus. Kip?"

Kipnis pondered briefly, then said, "My guy is ready to jump on a plane, but I told him to give us forty-eight hours." He sighed and added, "I am a patriot to the country of my birth, but my first allegiance now is to you, Remy."

In response, Remington thumped him lightly on the shoulder.

The three went silent again, all trying to process the credible and incredible and what to do with it all.

Eventually, Jake asked, "So, where are we with intel on the ship?"

Kipnis leveled his tablet between them, tapping to bring up the photos they'd collected with the drone's camera. He had visually enhanced the images to lighten the darkness and better define details, particularly those of the men on board and in the patrol tenders. Jake and Remington studied as Kipnis flicked through the selections, not saying much at first, and then Jake stabbed a finger at the tablet.

"*That* fucker. Remy, wasn't he one of the bastards we ambushed in Izmir?" He stared, toggled to another image, toggled back. "Yeah…yeah, that's him, and here's the other asshole."

They looked at Kipnis, who said, "Both with SADAT affiliations. I was not able to ID or get backgrounds on all in these images, but those that I did are mostly tied to PMCs, including that one and Wagner, a couple of others."

"Are we thinking everything is connected to Korki's discovery?" Jake asked. "His torture and murder, the surveillance and attacks on us?"

"Maybe not everything," Kipnis replied.

"What makes you say that?"

"I have been doing more in-depth tracking of the ship, and its presence in the area—around Psara and Antipsara specifically—predates our arrival and also Korki's time and work here."

Remington said, "So there's something else going on."

Now Kipnis swiped to a series of satellite images. These showed the *Gala* and also another ship, a 350-foot vessel laden with a large communications dish and tower, a helipad, A-frames for remote operated vehicles otherwise known as ROVs, hangars and side-launch davits for submersibles, and twin bow thrusters. There were also a number of unclassified frames of unknown purpose, suggesting special or specific operations, and several big blue shipping containers.

"That is *Zorya*. Technically, it is operated by the Russian Navy's GUGI, the Main Directorate of Underwater Research, but it's widely known as a spy ship. These are commonly referred to as special purpose or oceanographic research vessels, which are, of course, euphemisms for espionage."

Jake's dark eyes filled with enlightenment. "Oh, yes. I am familiar with *Zorya*. It's been all over the place…from Greenland to Guantánamo Bay to South America and the Med. It was even spotted off the U.S. Atlantic coast. And it's connected to the *Gala*?"

Kipnis nodded. "It certainly appears so. I am working with multiple sources to see what I can find out, but in intelligence circles it is believed to be engaged in ongoing surveillance of undersea cables. I have a theory or two about Taras Ignatkovich's connection, but I need to work my sources further before extrapolating."

"Whatever those two ships are involved in must be goddamn critical for them to make us such a hot target," Remington asserted. "We disrupted their activity and are posing a threat, not only by our proximity but because of who we are."

"That would be my guess," Kipnis agreed.

Remington said, "Could be, in the course of their op—whatever it is—they got wind of Korki's careless dissemination and it became an added objective, maybe even a priority."

"Well, one thing is for sure," Jake said sternly, "we need to find out what they're doing and expose them or, better, stop them—show them the head of the hammer and pound them out. Because until we do, not only do we continue to be at risk, but so is the entire group we're here to protect."

All three turned at the sound of an entrance to the tent, expecting Bachman or Demetriadi with storage containers but instead finding Falcone and Niles with Callie. The Malinois trailed behind, tongues lolling from a high-energy session of ball play.

On arrival earlier, after transporting the jugs and device to Remington's tent, Jake had gone to the cottage, bringing Callie to camp. She was still experiencing discomfort from the bee sting, the point of impalement only slightly less red and swollen, but she had not wanted to spend another moment at the cottage alone. By the time they got to camp, the *Blue Zone* had returned with the dig group and dinner prep was underway. Jake had enlisted Falcone and Niles to take Callie and the canines to the beach while he, Remington, and Kipnis met with Bachman and the archaeologists.

Now, with dusk darkening the tent and infusing the sky outside with swaths of pink and purple, he was ready to get some food and then take Callie and turn in for the evening. Despite resting all day, she looked tired and worn down, he thought, in a kind of cumulative way, and he wished again that he felt confident enough to send her back to Costa Rica. Check-ins with Jesse Segura through the week since the Dominical home invasion had been benign, Remington's security team reporting no signs of further trouble and Camilla fully recovered. But he could not convince himself that it was soundly, 100 percent safe—not until he could investigate the motive behind the violation himself and be on the premises with Callie.

He gave her an affectionate smile, opening an arm, and she came over, folding into his embrace.

Falcone and Niles stood looking at him, their faces flush from the beach activity, their attire change to shorts and tees wet from stomping through the waves.

"What?" Jake eyed them crookedly, already sniffing out an ask in the making.

"We've got a bit of a shambles," Niles said.

When neither was more forthcoming, Jake prompted, "Which is?"

"The bloody Sony cam has gone a bit wonky…s'been putting up error messages all day. Some sensor malfunctioning."

Falcone said, "We did some checking, and there's a camera place in Chios that can look at it, maybe repair."

"So, what are you saying? That you want to go to Chios?"

The duo nodded, awaiting his consent. Requests from them were often much like a child's beguiling appeal for the sugar-loaded candy—with charm that softened resistance even as underlying hints of mischief were always just below the surface or, sometimes, more patently apparent.

"A sensor sounds expensive and probably not a quick fix."

"Dunno," Niles admitted, "but we need to see about it."

Jake held Niles' eyes, looking for any trace of a ruse. He knew the two were growing restless and this struck him as an ideal excuse to concoct a getaway from the dig.

Reading his skepticism, Niles quickly added, "We're pretty much bugger-all without that camera working properly."

Jake mulled it a few more moments, then relented with a tolerant smile. "Okay, well, you guys have been working hard, and I also really appreciate all the time you've spent with Callie. I think you deserve a little break, chill a bit."

"Great, thanks," Falcone said, for his part managing to keep his tone free of enthusiasm to push the sell.

Jake's expression flattened again. "Just be sure to stay in touch with me. I want to know when you get there, your itinerary and timeline for the repair, your return time. Everything. Got it?"

"That's affirmative, mate," Niles gurgled happily. "And I promise we will stay out of trouble."

Jake completely doubted that, but he was unbothered by the notion of them having a little fun.

IN THE TENT HE shared with three other guys, the vet listened to his cell phone through a pair of wired earbuds. With it being dinnertime, he was fortunate to have the space to himself but kept his eyes on the adjacent cooking and eating area in case any of his tent mates wandered in. Not that it mattered, he thought; most of them listened to music or audibles on their phones.

Earlier, after arriving in his F-RIB on the tail of Tyler and Remington, he'd stashed the inflatable behind some bushes and followed the two men as they transported their cargo to Remington's tent. At that point, he'd been playing it loose, not sure what he was going to accomplish but, at the very least, wanting to know what they had. Quickly realizing by the vigilance they were maintaining that he was probably not going to be able to see much, he'd decided to fall back on listening.

While the vet had watched Tyler head for the nearby road and get in the vehicle he was using, a Mercedes GLS, he saw Remington take a precautionary look around and then duck into one of the portable toilet units. Knowing he would have minutes, if that, the vet made a run for his tent and ducked inside, taking out a different cell phone he kept in one of his duffel bags. He tapped to connect to the device he'd implanted on their very first day in camp, and set the phone to record. He slid it under the pillow on his cot and then dashed back to retrieve and launch his inflatable.

He had managed to reintegrate with the rest of the dig group on Antipsara just as the day's work was wrapping up and, in doing so, was included in the head count as they all boarded the boat to return to basecamp.

Now, he sat on his cot and listened to the playback of what had been recorded by the GSM device in Remington's tent. On the broader spectrum, Global System for Mobile is the digital cellular technology for the transmission of mobile voice and data services, but in this case, it was the means by which the vet was able to eavesdrop, simply and discreetly and without any fancy tech. GSM devices generally consist of a transmitter, a microphone, a battery, and a SIM card. The one he used was smaller than a matchbox, which had been affixed to the underside of Remington's cot. Dialing the number assigned to the SIM, the vet could have listened in real time, but the range was limited to about fifty feet, and since he'd needed to return to the dig, he recorded the session.

As the conversation between Remington, Tyler, and the others present replayed in his ears, the vet felt his chest expand with excitement, his mind racing like an electric slot car on a twisting track.

And he knew, in that moment, he needed to formulate a new plan.

His excited mental reverie was abruptly broken by the phone vibrating in his hand. Looking at the screen, he read the single-word text message transmitted via the encrypted Signal app.

Status?

Without the slightest hesitation, he typed: *Nothing to report.*

37

EDDIE FALCONE AND CURRAN Niles stood at the harbor front, glancing up and down the seaside road of shops and eateries and small businesses, Chios Town stacked against mottled green mountains swelling into the blue morning sky. They were outside the electronics store whose name, spelled out in Greek lettering, they could not interpret or pronounce. With some reluctance, they had just dropped off the Sony Venice, leaving it in the hands of a service technician who seemed to be knowledgeable despite a lack of specific familiarity with the sophisticated and expensive piece of equipment. The tech had been cheerfully optimistic but, while his assessment of the malfunction downplayed the degree of severity and associated cost of repair, he'd admitted he could not quantify the time it would take, especially since one of the parts would have to be overnighted from Athens.

Niles slipped his phone into a pants pocket, strands of his longish jute-colored hair loosened from the knot at the back of his head by the breeze coming off the water.

"Now what?" Falcone asked, his brow furrowed above a pair of gray-tinted Versace sunglasses.

They both looked the part of tourists, clad in Bermuda shorts and casual shirts and shoes. Niles, as usual, was the fashion bohemian, royal blue Tommy Bahamas covering his thighs brightly flowered like an exploding Hawaiian party; fortunately, he had foregone the matching shirt and chosen a solid IslandZone button-front in a color called pink confetti. He wore canvas Columbia slip-on shoes, blue Maui Jim shades over his eyes, a choker chain with a silver padlock around his neck, and a zipper pull dangling from one ear. Falcone, whose perpetually disheveled dark hair was even more displaced by the air, was clad in the relatively more conservative attire of Puma Bermudas in navy with a lighter Ralph Lauren Polo, and Nike sneakers.

The call Niles had just been on was with Jake, fulfilling their promise to check in, informing him of the verdict on the camera. A little over two hours earlier, not long after the sun had broken over camp, Falcone and Niles had been dropped off at Psara's port, Jake imparting his standard precautionary precepts and reiterating to them the importance of being ever mindful of situational awareness. Falcone and Niles, in turn, had then given him their standard assurances that they would be careful and vigilant, and boarded the ferry for Chios. They had been joined by a handful of others, all but two of whom were locals.

"What did Jake say?" Falcone asked. "Do we leave and come back when the camera's been repaired?"

"Don't be daft, mate," Niles squawked. "He said we could have some fun, so that's what we're going to do." He glanced up and down the road again. "For starters, I say we find a nice pub around here and get us a couple of pints. It's been too bloody long."

"I'm with you on that, but it's not even ten o'clock, Curran."

Eying a sign a few yards from where they were standing, Niles said, "Fine. A coffee then."

They strolled into a wood-framed, brick-walled establishment identified by carved wood and etched glass signage with the number 44 and the designation of bar and coffee shop. At this hour, midway between breakfast and lunch, it was surprisingly crowded and they quickly realized why.

44 Bar Coffee Shop, appropriately named for its numbered address on Aigaiou Avenue, is a chic and popular tavern serving AM and PM fare until four in the morning, seven days a week. Seconds after entering, the rich aroma of freshly ground and brewed roasts, mixed with the wholesome sweetness of grilled batters, had Niles dismissing any thoughts of an early tipple and both of their stomachs rumbling with cravings.

Taking a seat at the long, dark wood bar, handsomely constructed and inventoried with rows of bottled liquors and gleaming glasses, they were given a tablet and began tapping through the digital menu. As they were trying to make a near-impossible choice from a plethora of options, the bartender, a bearded young man in black sporting a tan logo-branded apron, asked, "Are those guys with you?"

Falcone and Niles looked up in unison, their heads swiveling. Near the tavern's entrance, a pair of men quickly turned as if they were on the way out, but remained in place.

"Um, no," Niles said dismissively, and returned his focus to the tablet.

Falcone's gaze held on the men for another few moments, unable to tell much about them from behind, only that they were generally fit by body weight and proportion, dark hair closely cut, and similarly dressed in dark brown or black chinos and collared shirts. Without turning around, the pair exchanged words and stepped outside.

The bartender said, "Sorry, my mistake. The way they were looking, I thought they might be with you." He smiled. "Have you decided?"

When their orders arrived, they spent several minutes plowing into mounds of scratch-made waffles and pancakes layered with bacon and tomatoes and topped with eggs, plucking French fries from wire mesh baskets and slurping cups of savory coffee; sweet cappuccino for Niles, strong espresso for Falcone.

Around a mouthful of pancakes, Falcone asked, "You think those guys were following us?"

Wiping foam from his upper lip, Niles said, "Dunno…maybe. But if they were, weren't very good at it."

"So, what do you want to do today?"

"F-U-N, mate."

Reflecting on the castles and museums and monasteries they'd seen during their initial time on the island, Falcone said, "Well, in case you hadn't noticed, this is not exactly a party island. Not like Mykonos or Santorini."

Mischief glinted in Niles' gray eyes, cheeks blooming with color. "Oi! Let's go there then!"

"No," Falcone said resolutely. "We'll have to find our fun right here somewhere."

Niles thought about that for a minute and said, "Right, then. Let's get us a car and find some."

BY LUNCHTIME THEY WERE cruising north along the harbor road in a rented Hyundai i20, Falcone at the wheel and Niles syncing his iPhone to the vehicle's infotainment system. They laughed and bickered lightheartedly as Niles shuffled through various playlists, randomly blasting out snippets of his musical repertoire, which ran the gamut of classic pop and rock and punk to almost anything indie and alternative.

Raising his voice over the driving, anthemic sound of The Killers, Falcone bemoaned, "Did you really have to get a freaking orange car?"

Singing along with Brandon Flowers, Niles retorted, "It was all they had, this size…or we'd have wound up with a midget car or a bloody van."

"It looks like a pumpkin! How do Jake and Remy always get the good shit, Jeeps and Mercedes?"

"Because it's Jake," Niles said. "Nothing wrong with this one…it's roomy enough and a fun color. It's called sunburn sway."

"It's *orange.*"

Niles bumped the music volume up, rhythmically thumping his hands on the inside of his door, wailing, *"When you were yo-uuuung…"*

Falcone shook his head, but he was grinning. "God, you are such a loon." And then he joined in the singalong.

After finishing their brunch, they had rented the car and driven to the Chandris Hotel, booking a pair of rooms for their overnight stay. Now, as they merged onto the national road, they skirted the harbor and passed a diminishing number of businesses, some residential neighborhoods, and a smattering of churches. The sea, rippled and lightly capped, was just over a low rock wall. There were small marinas and town settlements of mixed housing and commercial establishments, restaurants and boutique hotels and rentals. They stopped at a few beaches, none really stirring much interest, so they continued.

At Daskalopetra, a landmark where Homer is said to have sat upon a stone narrating his poems, the route turned briefly inland and the elevation became steeper, the road twisting sharply as it wound around rock-and-scrub slopes, the water slipping farther below. Working the

Hyundai's gears, Falcone's grip tightened on the wheel as they climbed. The grade dropped again and they were back beside the sea, a slab of barren mountainside rising high on the inland side in a wash of grays and browns with only the occasional stubble of green. By all appearances, they were in a remote outpost removed from humanity and yet, to their amazement, they came to a line of vehicles parked end to end along the road shoulder, the caravan leading into a sand-covered pit packed with more cars.

Falcone had pulled over and heard Niles exclaim, "Hey, there's a beach down there…in the middle of all those rocks! Like at the bottom of a quarry. How cool! We should check this one out, Eddie."

Before Falcone could respond, Niles had grabbed his backpack and was hopping out of the car. Getting his own pack, Falcone followed Niles to the top of a wood-railed path, colorfully painted plank signs reading: GLAROI BEACH BAR, COCKTAILS, CANOE & KAYAK, and BEACH LIFE.

"Some of my favorite words!" Niles gurgled gleefully, and scampered down the spiraling trail, adding, "And it's all knees up, mate!" Which Falcone knew was his friend's Brit-speak to indicate there was alcohol and music in play.

At the bottom, they stepped off to a concave wedge of beach that flattened out of the landslide tumble of rocks like a pale tongue dissolving into the most glorious gradients of turquoise and green and blue. But that was where the unusually striking vista stopped, as nearly every square foot of the compact allotment of sand was occupied. There were rows of blue chaise lounges and round straw umbrellas, all of which were in use. Tucked in the shade of bushy olive trees was a small bar and a concession stand, surrounded by people with food or beverages in hand. The as-advertised kayaks and canoes were lined up near the water or afloat in it, singles and couples and families with kids bobbing or splashing about in the crystal-clear depths.

There was, in fact, music, but it was less beach party and more traditional Greek folk.

They stood taking in the scene, the abundance of sweaty middle-aged flesh and tourist clusters and rowdy children giving even Niles second thoughts about lingering. His enthusiasm withering, he said, "Why don't we get us some beer, yeah?"

"We can get us some beer at a bar. Let's go, bud. This place is packed and not the party scene I think you were expecting. Come on." Falcone started back toward the path they'd descended.

From behind them a female voice said, "It would be a shame if you left."

The tone was deep and velvety and distinctively accented, though it was hard to tell if it was one of local origin. They turned to see a pair of tall, long-legged brunettes, clad in Day-Glo-bright bikinis that were generously filled out in all the right places. Their skin was oiled and tan, hair past their shoulders, straight and glossy. Each carried an oversize straw tote, stuffed with a rolled up towel and probably a whole sundry of beachy accessories.

A little dumbfounded, Falcone appraised the women's assets and felt his clothing get tight—more specifically, his Bermuda shorts. Niles was also enthralled, but as usual, he was expressing his thoughts out loud and in his charmingly loquacious fashion.

"Well, hello, lovely ladies! Are you from 'round here? Up for a day at the beach, are you? So you recommend that we stay for a bit? And what are your names?"

The woman who had spoken said, "I am Katarina and this is Selene. We are not from here but have been staying for the summer." She flicked sand from her cheek with an elongated fingernail, lacquered in the same retina-scorching fuchsia as her bathing suit.

"Oh, so you're from…?" Niles baited, his face full of flirtatious aspiration.

Her friend promptly replied, "We are from Greece, just not here." Her skimpy beach attire was the color of tangerine, crevices and curves spilling from the seams. Batting thick black lashes that swept over piercing blue eyes, she said, "This beach will be different in a little while."

Still skeptical, Falcone cocked his head inquisitively. "Yeah? How so?"

The woman named Katarina smiled slyly and said, "Well, you would have to stay to find out."

Niles glanced to Falcone, catching a lusty grin of endorsement. "In that case, we're in. What say we buy you lovelies some beverages?"

As they strolled to the concession area, Falcone found himself scanning the trail from the road for no perceivable reason other than a hazy sense of something not quite in symmetry. Realizing he was automatically implementing the situational scrutiny Jake had ingrained in them, he saw nothing of probable concern and felt his initial wariness start to melt away.

Bracketing the alluring pair of females, Falcone and Niles bought a round of drinks—bottles of Mythos lager for themselves and, for the women, vodka-and-grapefruit cocktails spiked with Campari that the barman called *Santorini Sunrises*—and set off to find an unoccupied patch of sand amidst the crowded covey.

Poking Falcone in the ribs, Niles leaned into him and muttered giddily, "Dog's bollocks, innit, mate? Can you believe our bloody luck?"

KEEPING HIS EYE ON Callie, who was assisting with a unit a few yards from him, Jake listened as Remington informed him on the call made to his military contact in the region. While Jake was more attentive to Callie, acknowledging her frequent over-the-shoulder glances toward him with encouraging nods and smiles, he could not help but also notice his friend's fatigue from the previous night watch of their sensitive cargo.

Hoarse speech interrupted by sporadic yawns, Remington was saying, "Lieutenant Colonel Merriweather—Atticus Merriweather—is running the show on the U.S. side."

He was referencing the joint multinational military operations currently underway in the Mediterranean, dubbed Aegean Forge. As part of the Defender Europe Large Scale Global Exercise, conducted by the United States Army Europe and Africa forces—USAREUR-AF—Aegean Forge was one of the largest NATO exercises and involved some ten thousand troops from the U.S. alone. Encompassing air, land, and sea, the mission was one of rapid and cohesive deployment with allied forces in response to any and all global threats. Leading the contingent from the U.S. was the 173rd Airborne Brigade, of which Lieutenant Colonel Merriweather was the deputy in command.

Merriweather, a West Point and Army War College graduate with a master's degree in military arts and sciences and a bachelor's of science in civil engineering, had made his way through the requisite courses and specialties of Ranger School, which is where he and Remington first became acquainted. From there, on a career military trajectory, Merriweather navigated his way through leadership programs and various assignments with Ranger and Infantry regiments and deployments to the Middle East and Africa. The lieutenant colonel and Remington had crossed paths again when Merriweather was attached to the U.S. Army Special Operations Command, but after landing on the conventional forces side, Merriweather rapidly rose through the ranks until achieving the elevated position he held today, as commander of the 1st Battalion, 503rd Infantry Regiment, 173rd Airborne Combat Team out of its base in Vicenza, Italy.

Stifling another yawn and giving his head a rousing shake, Remington said, "They're in Thessaloniki right now, but he told me he could break away from ops sometime tomorrow, fly over by helo."

"What was his reaction?" Jake asked.

"Oh, he was pretty motivated and cognizant of the same implications we expressed."

"Think he'll take possession?"

"Most likely." Remington grinned. "And I thought this gig was going to be on the boring side, like playing in a sandbox without all the fireworks. But we've had plenty of those."

"We sure have," Jake agreed. "Okay, well, nothing else for us to do on that front for now, so you go get some rack time."

"Since I'll have at least one more night watch, I think I'm going to do just that," Remington said, and strode off toward the trail leading to the wharf.

Jake had just settled in beside Callie when his radio crackled. Responding, he listened through his comms and quickly got back to his feet, reaching for Callie's hand. Grabbing all of his gear, which included his backpack and another larger, heftier pack, he set off across the grid where he could see a group assembled and gesturing his way.

EVER SINCE HIS AUDIO surveillance the evening before, the vet had been running scenarios in his mind but repeatedly came to the conclusion that the multiple layers of vigilance and security in place presented him with an almost insurmountable challenge. He would have liked to simply use the weapon he'd extracted from the drop point near the restaurant where they'd had their first meal in Psara. But he dismissed that option, knowing the odds of a clean getaway were not in his favor. Too many bodies and in close quarters.

And the damn dogs.

He had laid awake in his bunk for hours that night, his ploys becoming increasingly far-fetched as he connived well outside the box, but he finally came up with a scheme he thought could work. It was somewhat complicated, convoluted really, and would only succeed if every aspect fell precisely into place, but he knew his window to act was shrinking.

Refining and reviewing each part of his plan and troubleshooting possible glitches, he had decided it would work. While his bunkmates slumbered, he'd sat on the side of his cot and reached into one of his bags, taking out a compact knife-sharpening tool that fit in the palm of his hand. Studied it thoughtfully. He was determined to make his idea work, one way or another; the fate of his future rode on the outcome of the gambit.

Now, as the midmorning sun shone brightly over the dig site, baking into the soil and the skin and clothing of those moving and working about it, the vet watched and waited for his moment. His gaze was fixed on the individual he had singled out as the unwitting participant, a man wearing wire-frame glasses and a boonie hat, portions of his face and neck pocked and scarred by shrapnel. Jayce Ruda.

The vet prepared for his first play, saw the opening—Ruda and the others in Ruda's unit completely absorbed in a new find they'd unearthed from their pit—and strolled ever so casually to their space in the grid. Bending to ostensibly tie the lace of his boot, the vet wedged a trowel sideways into a groove he'd made in a solid patch of dirt directly behind Ruda. Then, the vet stood, reversed, and walked several yards in the direction from which he'd come. Watched and waited for the next moment, the crucial one that would make or break his scheme. Seeing Ruda lean back from the pit, the vet smiled triumphantly and again strolled toward the unit, only this time, as he came within an arm's length, he lunged into and over Ruda as if he'd lost his balance.

And, just like the perfect accordion topple of dominoes, one into another in synchronized succession, the next part of his plan fell right into place. Literally.

Ruda twisted sideways and backwards, one arm pinned beneath his torso as he was bowled over to the ground. He bellowed in pain.

The members of Ruda's unit and others close by descended on him to see what had happened as Ruda continued to howl, rolling on the ground and clutching his forearm, which was now bleeding profusely.

The vet joined the expanding group of onlookers, willing his expression to display some semblance of concern as his eyes now sought, and sighted on, the hustling figure of Jake Tyler on the approach. Right on cue. His crazy, complicated plan was working. The vet surveyed the flock converging, a bubble of glee in his chest as he realized who was missing from the mix: the troublesome pair of documentarians and, more importantly, Remington and his fucking dogs. He could not believe his luck.

Almost there, the vet told himself, and watched Tyler kneel beside Ruda, placing his voluminous medical bag on the ground. Riveted, the man observed as Tyler unzipped the kit and laid it open, exposing its cornucopia of contents.

AS JAKE SET HIS medical bag down and opened it up, he was already making rapid visual assessments of his patient, Ruda, noting the amount and color of blood, the placement of Ruda's hand over the wound, the pallor of his skin, and his breathing.

Easing him into a prone position, Jake saw that Ruda's black MVAA t-shirt and dark khaki pants were splattered, the towel wrapped around his arm saturated.

With a reassuring smile, Jake snapped on nitrile gloves and said, "Okay, bud, let me see what we've got. The good news is, your arm is still attached."

Ruda hissed out a strained chuckle and slowly unclamped his hand. When Jake removed the towel, blood as slick and bright as ripe cherries bloomed from a laceration about three inches in length. He heard a startled intake of breath from behind and, without having to look, said, "Sweetie, stay close but don't watch. Okay?" When Callie did not answer, he repeated, "Okay?"

"O-Okay, Jake," she replied shakily, averting her eyes.

Shelby Hoskins had crouched down to assist him, cleaning Ruda's wound with a bottle of water. "How did this happen?" she wanted to know.

There were blank expressions all around, and Ruda replied, "Somebody tripped over me and I fell on something sharp."

Another woman, an Asian veteran named Alice Fujimura who was a former air force captain, joined them, telling Jake, "I can assist, if you like. I have some first aid training." When Fujimura took over for Hoskins, the operations manager pivoted to search for the source of injury, finding it still embedded in the ground—the trowel, blade side up.

"Damn it," she muttered, giving her long hair an angry flip. "This is why I preach about the safety protocols for these tools."

"Well, accidents are going to happen, despite the best intentions and efforts," Jake told her. Addressing Ruda, he said, "Jayce, this requires a pretty good stitch up. Can you handle that?"

Ruda bit his lip and nodded stoically but did not say anything.

"Don't worry, I'm good, and I'll numb you up."

Jake selected a suture kit and then unfolded the medical bag to a separate section, spinning the numbered wheels on a small combination lock securing a zippered compartment. When the padlock released, he peeled back the cover and extracted a hypodermic and vial of lidocaine. With this kind of injury and mindful of the extra vulnerability integral to PTSD and the associated challenges of these vets, Jake was watching for signs of shock, so his gaze lingered on Ruda as he set up. In those moments of concentrated observation and arrangement of items on a sterile cloth, another's hand hovered over the medical bag and dove into the organized rows of vials and ampoules and syrettes and needles.

Before he began the procedure on Ruda, Jake resealed and relocked the compartment in his bag, unaware of the sleight of hand that had taken place behind his back.

Now, he took his time with Ruda, injecting the lidocaine around the laceration and then beginning the series of sutures, fingers working deftly with the honed skill of one who was well familiar with the instruments and curved needles and closure techniques. When he was done with the stitchwork, Jake dressed the wound and checked Ruda's vitals.

The mental health clinician, Gwen Maddigan, took his place to follow up with a psychological evaluation, and Jake joined Shelby Hoskins and Caspian Bachman who were in serious discussion.

"Do we need to get him to the hospital in Chios?" Bachman asked.

"No," Jake replied. "He'll be fine. From my study of the group's medical records, I know that you require updated tetanus as part of the required inoculations. That would have been the only consideration. I'll keep a close check on him for wound management, watch for infection. He'll be on oral antibiotics."

He looked at Hoskins. "What did you say was the cause? His cut was pretty severe to have come from the tools we're using. More like that of a knife."

She held out the trowel, one edge caked with dirt, the other sticky with Ruda's blood.

Jake whistled. "That's awfully sharp." He took the tool from her, holding it by the handle, and examined it more closely. He poured some water from a bottle in his hand, cleaning the blade.

Watching him, Bachman asked, "What do you see, Jake?"

"This has been sharpened. See the difference between the two sides?

Bachman studied the tool. "Son of a bitch. Why the hell would anybody do that?"

Obviously to cause exactly what had happened, Jake thought. But was it just for some perverse thrill or for something much more premeditated and purposed? Glad to feel Callie pressed against him, he encircled her waist with his free arm, and glanced around those gathered and scattered about the area, a renewed sense of foreboding stirring.

Somebody in their midst was a very depraved person, a sociopath at the least, possibly even a psychopath. Most military people he'd come to know or know of were thoroughly decent human beings, but there had certainly been a few who were offensive or immoral or abhorrent or pure evil. One he'd known and operated with who fell into the latter category, Aris Xavier, had found his way back across Jake's path in Africa. Karma usually had a way of balancing the scales on these wretches, but not always; fortunately, justice had prevailed in X's case.

Jake thought of the stoned falcon and a hard frown creased his face.

Somebody here had managed to defy Caspian Bachman's austere background diligence, and he needed to find out who it was before something more catastrophic happened. As soon as their discovery was dealt with, he would get Kipnis to go full rectal on every single person in their camp.

38

HOURS AFTER FALCONE AND Niles had happened upon Glaroi Beach, the atmosphere was, indeed, quite different. As a retreating sun spilled a glaze of caramel and gold over a sea darkened to cobalt, the spread of travelers languidly broiling on loungers or standing like doughy bowling pegs in the water had departed, taking their noisy hordes of children with them. In rather dramatic fashion, as if the banal day crowd had been switched off and an electric signboard had been switched on in scrolling liquid neon, the small cove underwent an astonishing transformation. Replacing the young families, middle-aged tourists, and septuagenarian pensioners was an ebullient throng comprised of primarily twenty-somethings whose energy levels were set somewhere within the range of Cancún spring breakers and Rio de Janeiro Carnival celebrants. Which was to say, explosively wild.

Because gone, too, were the quaint, acoustical string- and wind-instrument melodies of musical heritage that had floated through the air like coasting seabirds landing with random whimsy. That was replaced by a deejay-driven agglomeration of contemporary European pop and techno fusion, and it was *loud*. Eardrum-pulverizing loud. Though the music wasn't their style, the Brit and Jerseyite were both just buzzed enough to not really care.

They were still swigging bottles of Mythos beer but, as the evening progressed, had also begun downing shots of Plomari ouzo. Most locals of course know that the pungent anise-flavored liquor is meant to be sipped and savored and enjoyed with *mezethes*, or tapas, that might include feta and hummus and kabobs and *souvlaki* and falafel chips. The rationale for such temperance would become apparent later, but for the time being its punch helped dull the deafening volcano of sound. As an added bonus, it also seemed to spike inspiration for the men's libido, not that they needed any reinforcement there.

The pair of women were in full party mode, staying well-quenched with vodka, wiggling and bouncing to the music. Earlier, time had been spent relaxing on the beach or playing in the water, carefree fun without much meaningful conversation, and now, of course, that was impossible. The rocky slopes enveloping the cove vibrated with bass and percussion and twanging electronics that could have drowned out the engines of a jumbo jet passing directly overhead.

While the women had not been coy in telegraphing their motives during the day, teasing and tantalizing on an upwardly sliding scale, by evening their lustiness was totally unfettered, arms and legs and lips all over the two men, their dancing becoming increasingly body-on-body. Head spinning and loins throbbing, Falcone wriggled his way to Niles and shouted in his ear, "Hey, this is crazy."

"Fucking mad, innit, mate?" Niles shouted, his face flushed with intoxication, eyes lit with lascivious fervor.

"Oh yeah, but Curran, we need to get out of here before we're too drunk to drive or fuck."

Laughing bawdily, Niles shouted back, "Pretty sure we're there on the drive part, mate, but yeah let's go."

The duo, with the women readily trailing along, wove through the raucous party crowd, being jostled from all directions by males and females who seemed to be athletically engaged in some kind of sport that did not require a ball or net or playing field with boundaries; they were sprinting and leaping and diving and whooping just the same. When they got to a spot where they could stand without being knocked around, Falcone asked, "Would you gals like to leave with us? We're heading to our hotel."

Katarina puffed her full lips, squinting her eyes as if she was giving the question some serious debate. Then she laughed. "But of course!" She cast a conspiratorial look to her companion, Selene. "I will be right back."

Falcone watched her sashay past the concession and bar area, where she approached a bearded man in slim fit black jeans and a button-up black shirt worn loose and open to mid-chest, exposing multiple gold chains. He was an easy fit in the youthful mix, perhaps a little older than the median age, but his physique matched that of many males in the crowd whose gym and weightlifting regiments were evident in bulked pecs and biceps. Even so, there was something discrepant about his vibe, made even more pronounced by the shades covering his eyes. And, as his gaze lingered on the man, Falcone had a vague sense of recognition but could not decide how or from where.

Katarina carried on a short, mostly one-sided conversation with the man, who did not look their way. When she returned, Falcone asked, "Who's the dude? And who the fuck wears sunglasses at night?"

Niles chortled, "Oi, that eighties bloke, Corey Hart...remember him?" He began singing the song's signature line, but Falcone cut him off.

"He isn't your pimp or something?"

Katarina stared at Falcone, icy blue eyes boring into his for several charged seconds, and then her hand whipped out and slapped him solidly across the face.

Falcone's mouth went slack with shock, his skin prickling as color rose in his cheek. He could find no words of response and, most uncommonly, neither could Niles.

The two women looked at each other, their expressions mirroring hostility, and then they both broke out in uproarious laughter, clutching their bare midriffs and bending their heads back, long hair swinging. Falcone was petulantly confused, but Niles joined in the hilarity, grinning even though he was equally befuddled.

Katarina blurted, "Got you!"

Falcone still said nothing, but felt anger threatening to move in like a sudden storm front invading a sunny day.

Punching him lightly in the ribs, she said, "That was our ride. I told him we had made other arrangements. You idiot."

Flustered, Falcone murmured, "Oh...okay. Sorry." Recovering from the affront, he now became more acutely aware of his level of inebriation and had significant doubts about his ability to drive their rental car. But, evaluating Niles, whose glibness and unrepressed behavior had expanded exponentially, he decided that, of the two, he was in better shape—if only marginally.

As if reading his mind, Selene spoke up, asking, "Do you want one of us to drive?"

Not for the first time, Falcone wondered how the two women, who had easily drank as much, if not more than they had, did not appear to be as intoxicated. He started to voice his notion, but no longer trusting his social graces, kept silent.

Before taking their leave, Falcone cast another glance across the clam pit of revelers. The bearded guy Katarina had been talking to was no longer in view.

With the two brunettes in front, Falcone and Niles ascended the path leading up to the road, leering at the women's practically naked asses, curvaceous flesh rolling and hips swaying. Leaning into Falcone and almost toppling over in the process, Niles muttered, "God, I'm horny as hell."

"Same," Falcone laughed.

When they reached the orange Hyundai, in the dark looking even more like a pumpkin on Halloween night, Falcone dropped the keys twice before managing to unlock the vehicle.

"Shit," Niles muttered, "you're bloody pissed, mate. Let me drive."

"No freaking way," Falcone replied haughtily. "I've driven the Jersey turnpike drunker than this."

What he did not disclose was that he'd been a lot younger at the time.

FROM HIS BUNK AT the dig basecamp, the vet consulted his phone to check the time, something he had been doing all night. He was eager to get on with the final part of his plan, but he knew his best bet was to wait until the wee hours when he'd be least likely to run into someone making a trip to the latrines. These vets were a restless, dysfunctional bunch, and many had sleep disorders or did not sleep soundly, so to minimize the risk of crossing paths with any of them, he would wait a little bit longer.

He was still amazed that he'd been able to pull off his improbable gambit. From his observations, he knew that Jake Tyler always kept the medical bag in reach and in sight or securely stored, so targeting it as he had was a huge risk. But, as the saying went, with huge risk came huge reward…and he was on the verge of reaping the huge reward. The next part of the plan was also risky, but would be easier to enact.

He let another twenty or thirty minutes elapse, and glanced at his phone again. Three thirty AM. Go time.

The vet got up from his cot, visually confirming that the other three occupants of his tent were asleep. Satisfied, he stepped outside and strolled quietly toward the camp's dining area. While the cooking facilities were not supposed to be used after the nightly curfew, he was pretty sure one or more of the restless had bent that rule, as he was about to do.

Some fifteen minutes later, he was stealthily crossing the compound, a duffel bag slung over his shoulder, a bottle of water and a covered cardboard cup in one hand. He also had two wrapped sandwiches in one of his pockets—and his weapon, a Zigana semiautomatic pistol, tucked in his back waistband, just in case. Passing a trash receptacle, he reached down inside it with his other hand, which was gloved, and pushed something beneath scraps of food and paper and other waste. He used the lip of the bin to nudge and roll the plastic glove off his hand, burying it in the trash with a stick.

He caught himself whistling lightly as he walked on, went quiet, and continued toward the other side of the compound. It was comfortably cool, the sky still inky dark with stars overhead diminished to fine points, a faint breeze peppered with the intermittent trilling of crickets. He was almost to his destination when he heard another sound, that of low growling.

IN HIS TENT, NASH Remington was propped up on his cot, awake and relatively alert but beginning to feel the leaden cloak of fatigue as his eyes blearily focused on the screen of the Toughbook in his lap. To pass the hours of his night watch, he had been catching up on emails associated with upcoming jobs and also analyzing all the intel Kipnis had sent him to this point. He was currently studying the latest sea traffic, particularly the movements of the *Gala*.

His pair of Belgian Malinois lay by the cot, both dozing, Solis lightly snoring. Glancing at them in peaceful repose, he envied their ability to rest and still be able to suddenly waken and detect and react to things before he was able to see or hear them himself.

Which is what they did now.

Remington's gaze was back on the Toughbook when he heard the two dogs stir. Looking down, he saw that they had lifted their heads, ears erect. A moment later, the fawn-colored hair on their necks and backs went as stiff as the tines of a metal brush and they rose to all fours, growls rumbling from their throats.

Without a word, Remington set his laptop aside, reached a hand behind his back, and withdrew the Glock snugged there. He swung off his cot and a male voice, just above a whisper, asked from outside, "Permission to enter?"

The growling from the Malinois became more guttural and rose in volume.

"*Bewaken*," Remington told his dogs, and they stood rigidly still, eyes on the tent's opening, which was zippered shut. Their growls persisted in lower resonance. With authority, directing his voice to the inquisitor, Remington asked, "Who is it?"

"Logan Hays."

The name gave Remington pause, but in his weary state and caught somewhat off guard, he could not grasp why. "Something wrong, Hays?"

With a shuffling and slight hesitation, the vet standing outside the tent replied, "Uh…no, not really. I was just…I couldn't sleep and was taking a walk." He paused again, adding, "I knew you were on guard"—he corrected himself—"on watch…so I brought you something."

Before responding, a fuzzy, half-formed thought came close to the surface and then evaporated, dimly related to the mention of his being on watch. Remington remained in place, his inclination to send the vet away but, as if sensing the dismissal, his visitor began unzipping the opening. The canines resumed growling in sustained idling.

When the entrance flap was peeled back, light from the tent's lanterns cast a glow over the vet standing in the opening, one hand holding a cardboard cup and the other a bottle of water. He was dressed in Multicam black camo cargo pants, black tee and tactical overshirt, his hair neatly combed and face freshly shaven—a grooming detail that, under the circumstance, Remington found peculiar. The vet's eyes were on the dogs but he seemed unafraid of them, a composed smile on his face. He started to take a step, his arm extending to offer the cup to Remington, but the Malinois stopped him with a pronounced elevation in gravelly vocalization.

For Remington, the move here would be to either let his dogs take the lead—which could mean a more aggressive escalation based on their perception of threat—or command them to hold their status or stand down. He made none of these moves because, in truth, he was not sure what his reaction should be. Throughout the course of their presence on the dig with MVAA, Remington and his entire team had operated with care and sensitivity toward the vets but, like his dogs, he was picking up a disconcerting note. He was also remembering the Malinois' assessment of Hays early on when they had actually lunged at him, and Remington trusted the instincts of his dogs absolutely.

Reaching to accept the cup, he said, "Thank you, Hays, very thoughtful. But now I have to ask you to return to your bunk. Can't be out wandering after curfew."

The vet handed him the coffee and smiled apologetically. "Oh, yeah, sure." He half turned and, remembering something, bent to stick his hand inside a pocket of his cargo pants, extracting a paper-wrapped item.

As soon as he did, the canines' noses became more noticeably engaged, quivering as a new smell invaded their space. It was customary behavior, but what they did next was more unusual.

They sat.

This, Remington knew, indicated recognition of something they'd been trained to detect and alert on...but what? He could not imagine any kind of contraband attainable here, in their strictly controlled premises, so possibilities eluded him. He would later—much later—recall the moment with grievous mortification.

Handing the wrapped item to Remington, Hays said, "I made myself a sandwich, so brought you one, too."

"Okay," Remington replied simply, and held it together with the cup of coffee, keeping one hand free.

The vet took slow backward steps, glancing quickly down once, and muttered, "Oh…sorry…my boot hit your dogs' water bowl." Unscrewing the cap of the plastic bottle he'd also been carrying, he bent over and dumped the contents into the tin container on the ground. Before straightening up, he dug into the same pocket of his cargo pants, removing something that Remington did not see.

Ducking through the tent's opening, Hays said, "See you later."

Remington went to the threshold and watched the vet retreat into the darkness, staring after him with a troubled sense of perplexity. He zipped the flap shut, waited a few moments, and returned to sit on his cot. He kept the Glock beside him. Oddly, the Malinois remained in position, but now their heads were twisted to look back at him. Luna let out a low whine.

"All good. *Braaf, vrij.*"

The Malinois pair stood but padded to the tent's entrance, sniffing the area previously occupied by the vet, winding up near the tin he had refilled from his water bottle, the ground wet from spillage. They both sighted on what Hays had dropped and, again, sat. Looked pointedly at their master.

But Remington's eyes were, at that instant, averted, lids closed as he took a sip of coffee from the cup Hays had given him.

39

EDDIE FALCONE AWOKE TO a climactic implosion; an avalanche thundering through his head, a percolating volcano threatening to erupt in his stomach. Eyelids flickering against the assault of ambient morning light, he moaned, "Oh God," and tried to remember where he was and what had taken place in the prior hours to induce such misery. At first, his mind was an unnavigable field of smoke and mirrors, but after painstakingly forcing himself out of a luxurious bed that looked like the aftermath of a frat party—pillows and sheets and covers tossed and twisted and sprawled about the floor—some of the mental corridors began to clear, dialing into his location at the Chios Chandris.

Naked, he stumbled to the bathroom, wincing at the grotesque image of himself in the mirror, thick dark hair in bouffant Einsteinian disarray, face puffy and coarse with stubble, eyes bloodshot and swollen. Stepping into the sleek, marble-walled shower, he turned on the water and stood in the steamy stream, fighting the nausea grumbling in his gut and the sledgehammer pounding his brains.

Then it hit him.

"Oh shit," he blurted, lunging and almost falling out of the stall, water still running, grabbing for a towel and staggering back to the bedroom, dripping on the wood floor. He looked for the woman whose company he just remembered he'd shared the night before. Drawing the towel around himself, he padded into the living area and found it as unoccupied as the bed, no sign of a female presence; no clothing, no purse, no toiletries. There was, however, ample evidence of previous companionship in the glassware scattered about the various tables, including empty bottles of Mythos, Stolichnaya, and Plomari. Seeing the latter made Falcone retch with gustatory repulsion. Jesus Christ, how much of that stuff had he consumed?

Too goddamn much, that was for sure. It was nothing short of a miracle that he'd not been pulled and arrested for drunk driving.

He made his way back to the bathroom and finished his shower, disjointed thoughts floating in the hangover haze. Although he was all but certain there had been sex during the night, he was having a hard time conjuring images and sensations associated with any such carnal activity. As he worked to sequence the hours that followed their time at the beach, he vaguely recalled a stop for burgers and another at some kind of nightclub with more pulsating music. And, of course, more drinking. He was missing pieces of the remaining nocturnal span, but when he pushed the membranes of his memory, visions of the woman whose name was Katarina washed into the ethers. Dimly, he could see her on top of him bucking and grinding, could hear her shrill utterances in the throes.

Shaking his head as if doing so might clear the cognitive cobwebs, he got out of the shower and dug into his backpack, glad to find he'd had the foresight to bring a change of clothes since those worn yesterday reeked of sweat, sand, sea, beer, and God knew what else. As he took out the fresh set of shorts, shirt, and underwear, a vaguely unsettling feeling came over him, the reason for which he could not grasp.

Anxious to reunite with Niles, Falcone got dressed and groomed and left the suite.

BUT IF FALCONE WAS hoping his friend could fill in missing chunks of their night, his optimism was woefully awry. As they sat sipping coffee at the 44 bar, Niles was recounting his version of events, which included similarly fuzzy vignettes of sexual frolic with Selene but not a whole lot more.

Blond hair pulled back from his forehead and clipped, Niles also wore clean clothing—a matching J. Crew set of gold shorts and shirt covered with palm trees. His normally flushed cheeks were splotchy, fair complexion pasty, and the gray of his eyes had the hue of dull nickels.

"Not sure if the shag was worth it," he bemoaned. "Bloody hangover from hell, innit."

Setting second cups in front of the two, the barman gave them a sympathetic smile. "You guys look like a donkey trampled over you."

"And took a good shit while doing it," Falcone added.

"Hit the party scene?" the server asked. "Let me guess…consumed quite a few ouzos."

Both men nodded morosely.

Knowingly, he said, "Too late for the advice, but those are supposed to be enjoyed in leisurely fashion…like fewer and slowly."

"Would have been nice if our lady friends had warned us."

"Locals?" the barman asked.

Falcone and Niles looked at each other, the first shared wavelength of skepticism about their foray registering. Falcone said, "Not really sure. They said they were Greek and they did have accents."

The bartender moved off to serve other patrons, Falcone and Niles wading uneasily into a new hedge of doubts. They sat in gloomy silence for a while, lost in thought as they drank their coffee.

Falcone was replaying the admonitory speech Jake had dispensed prior to their departure for Chios. Having heard versions of it innumerable times before, he had only been half listening as Jake instructed: "Have fun, gents, but be vigilant of everyone and everything all the while. Do not give your full trust to anyone or any situation, ever. Keep a healthy amount of wariness as a cautionary filter. Be mindful not to talk about yourselves, about us, about who we are, what we do, where we come from, what our agenda is. Because, bottom line, you never know who you're dealing with when you're in unfamiliar territory and with limited time to make assessments."

Niles had piped up, blustering, "Mate, what *can* we talk about then?"

Jake had shot him a mildly reproachful look and both men knew not to press for further elucidation.

Now Falcone was more fully appreciative of the weight and measure of those wise words from one who knew volumes about the wiles of the world and its denizens. Turning to Niles, he asked, "Did you notice anything missing from your stuff this morning?"

Niles eyed him crookedly. "What'dya mean, mate? Coin, cards, and the like?" He fished his wallet from a pocket in his shorts, opened it, and inspected the contents. "Seems to be all here, from what I remember having left. Got my cards." He reached into his pack slung over the back of his barstool, fumbled around, and said, "Passport's here. What else?"

"I don't know…I just have some strange feelings. I mean, them being gone when we got up isn't all that surprising. It's not like anybody expected more than a one-night-stand deal. But when I was getting my gear together, I had the distinct feeling that it had all been rummaged through."

"How would you know if nothing is missing?"

"Well, given our state of brain fog, I guess we wouldn't."

Niles took out his phone, brought up the home screen, and toggled to photos he'd taken the day before, remarking, "Oi!"

"What?"

"All the snaps from yesterday and last night—ussies with the birds—are gone!"

"Gone? As in deleted?"

"Yeah."

Falcone took out his own phone and checked the images, also not finding any with the two women. "What the fuck?" he muttered.

"Why would they do that?" Niles asked incredibly. "How could they get into our mobiles?"

"Well, again, given how drunk we were, it probably wasn't too difficult. I know I had my phone out several times…maybe during a trip to the bathroom."

"But why?" Niles asked again.

Falcone shrugged. But now he was thinking back to Jake's warning dictum and wondering how much they had revealed to the women as the alcohol lessened their inhibitions and loosened their tongues. Niles had, of course, been especially garrulous. The more Falcone ruminated on the conversations by day and what he could remember of the night, the more he realized just how little substantive information they'd gleaned from the females who had so conveniently shown up just as he and Niles were about to leave. Running the segments he could piece together in his mind, snippets from day to night of frivolous chit chat about music and fashion and pop culture, flirtatious interactions and frivolous play, and all the drinking, one frame came into more lucid focus.

Katarina astride him.

In his mind, he saw her head thrown back, grapefruit-size breasts bouncing as she hopped up and down, a hand clawing at her long, straight hair. And then he remembered her vocalization at the peak of the ride, a string of words he did not recognize and which he was now pretty sure were not from the Greek language.

Falcone hung his still-throbbing head, clutching it in both hands as if it might roll off his neck and land with a heavy thud like a boulder. "Jesus," he moaned. "Oh my fucking God."

AFTER COPIOUS AMOUNTS OF the savory coffee, some extra-strength Tylenol, and the squeamish consumption of English muffins stuffed with eggs and ham, they stood at the service counter of the electronics store, the technician having just informed them that the Sony part was not expected to arrive until sometime that afternoon.

"Well, what do you want to do, mate?" Niles asked his friend.

"For sure not have any more *fun*," Falcone replied dourly.

"Right," Niles said. "I think we could use a peaceful day."

"You going to call Jake?"

Niles scowled. "Um, not at the moment. *You* want to call him?"

"Not really. Why don't we just wait a while."

The duo were almost out of the store when Niles grabbed Falcone by the arm, his eyes as wide with excitement as a child at a Christmas parade. "Eddie, look!" He was pointing to a locked, glass-enclosed case where several rows of drones were on display, price tags ranging from under a hundred euros to well into the thousands.

Seeing what had caught his zeal, Falcone said, "No, Curran…just no. That's another disaster in the making."

Niles hugged him by the shoulders, his face full of newfound enterprise and energy. "Please, Eddie…it would be brilliant! You know you want one, too. Please, please, please."

There was almost no deterring or dissuading Niles once his aspirations were set on something, so Falcone looked over the selection, comparing the specs listed on each information card. Niles, however, had already become infatuated with one in particular and, of course, it was the most expensive of the offerings.

DJI's Mavic 3 Pro Cine is a triple-camera, four-armed model featuring a 4/3 CMOS Hasselblad primary with two telephotos; 70 to 166 millimeters, 7X optical and 28X hybrid zoom, capable of producing 12MP photos and 4K video. Its transmission provides a 1080P/60FP HD live feed at a distance of just over nine miles with a flight time of up to forty-six minutes on a single battery.

Niles was salaciously gawking the array of accessories, which included filter packs, additional lenses, extra batteries, a shoulder bag and, of course, the DJI RC controller, and Falcone could hear the *cha-ching* of charges amassing on their credit cards. He briefly considered making a pitch for a less exhorbitant model but, seeing the glazed and fixed focus of Niles' eyes, he knew that would be a wasted effort.

Twenty minutes later, after a short operational overview from a sales clerk, they were in the orange Hyundai i20, Falcone again at the wheel, Niles viewing a YouTube instructional video on flying the DJI drone. Before leaving the electronics store, they had also been supplied documents outlining the legalities and restrictions for drone operation in Greece, the clerk helpfully loading the Drone Aware Greece app on their phones. Niles had given the paperwork a cursory inspection, his broad takeaway being that, as long as they flew in restriction-free zones and kept the drone within line of sight and below a 120 meters, they would be good.

Now, motoring north along the coastal road, passing the same landmarks as the prior day, Falcone took them farther. When they drove by Glaroi Beach, neither said anything, but both gave it a lingering, regretful look. Glad to put it behind them, Falcone followed the sprawling EO Chiou Kardamilon route through sparse, rolling countryside that skirted the sea, dipping in and out of valleys and worming steeply into the higher, forested slopes inland. Thirty minutes out, they made a hairpin turn and drove east through more evergreen-covered terrain, winding their way back toward the coast.

It was a splendiferous day, the drive scenic and serene. Overhead, the sun-infused cerulean sky stretched endlessly, occasionally amended by massive dollops of clouds as light and white and plump as pure whipped cream. And when the elevation rose and their direction gravitated eastward, the stunning vista of the Aegean below was like something from the canvas of a Renaissance master.

Falcone had loaded the destination into the Hyundai's navigation and, miraculously, it got them to the last offshoot, another twisting road that led down to a desolate seaside spot north of Paralia Pirgia, a small obscure beach seldom patronized.

Earlier, studying a map of the island, Falcone had chosen the place because it was within the allowed territory, as outlined in the Drone Aware app, but also isolated which, he felt would make them less likely to get into trouble. His supposition worked out well for the most part.

Until the boat.

STANDING ON THE SHORE in the radiance of late-morning sunshine, a moderate breeze boosted by occasional heartier gusts, Eddie Falcone watched as Curran Niles launched their new drone into the air and directed it out over the turquoise sea. In that moment, seeing the rapturous glee on Niles' face, boyish excitement gushing as he worked the controller and directed the DJI Mavic high above them, it was impossible not to share his joy; one of the qualities that had bonded them early on was Niles' contagious spirit and zest for life. He could be maddening—exasperating, nerve-racking, impertinent, rash, and a hundred other patience-trying adjectives—but being his friend was the best, and never without passion or limitless generosity and loyalty.

And it was always an adventure, sometimes to their detriment or debacle or even disaster, of course, but also, on occasions such as this, priceless and wholly treasured.

Cackling giddily as he thumbed the control switches and monitored the video feed, Niles exclaimed, "Eddie, look at this, wouldya? Oh my God, it's bloody amazing!"

The imagery spooling slowly within the five-and-a-half-inch screen was remarkably vibrant coastal landscape and stunning seascape, the translucent shallows of which revealed a pod of dolphins streamlining in tight formation. What they were capturing with the impressive technology of the Mavic had all the full dynamics of a Nat Geo epic with a touch of Disney magic.

Smiling broadly, Falcone replied, "Sure is, man. I'm glad we got it."

Niles returned his smile, the rosy blush back in his cheeks, eyes sparkling like crystal prisms.

Falcone took in their surroundings, barren scrub that rose behind them, a thin strip of sand at the waterline before them. For the first time, he noticed that they were not entirely alone, a slate-colored Toyota Grand Highlander parked about two hundred yards to the south at the end of another road descending from the slopes. Nearby in the water, perhaps a half mile from the shore there, was a modest twenty-foot skiff, a man fishing from its stern. Dressed in shorts and t-shirt, he sported a wide-brimmed straw hat and held a rod in one hand, a bottle of some beverage in the other. Absorbed in his activity, he showed no interest in their presence whatsoever.

They were halfway through the battery charge when Falcone said, "Hey, I can't see it anymore. We have to keep that thing in our line of sight, remember?"

"Right," Niles said. "But who's going to know? I was just thinking…"

"Shit," Falcone murmured. *Here we go.*

"No, no, nothing dodgy, mate. That island across from us…what's it called?"

"Oinousses," Falcone supplied.

"Yeah. It's just over there," he said, indicating the island's pale gray silhouette visible at the horizon. "Maybe we can even reach Turkey, that would be cool! This thing can go nine miles."

"Ohhh-kay, reel it in, buddy. You're going to deplete the battery, and with this being the first use, we can't know one hundred percent it will even go the full time its rated for. We'll need to have some trial and error."

Niles let out a disappointed sigh but began to change the drone's course for return. It was a few miles over sea and still out of their sight when the RC controller screen framed the top of a patrol-style boat, coasting at a leisurely pace. Mildly curious, Niles brought the Mavic lower and put it in a hover as he tried to make out more detail. The boat was white and, though he could not tell, forty feet in length, a wide red stripe on either side of the bow and a red flag flying atop its bridge.

Falcone caught a glimpse over Niles' shoulder and said, "Okay, let's bring it in now. We can swap the battery, maybe drive somewhere else and send it out again."

"Right."

Niles put the drone back in flight formation and, as he did, the patrol boat suddenly made a sharp turn and accelerated. Aimed like a torpedo, it was coming toward the coast—coming, it now seemed, toward *them*.

"Hey!" Falcone exclaimed. "I think that boat might be police or military…or something…and it's headed for us!"

Staring at the controller screen, they saw the craft jetting through the water, bow bumping the surface, a flume of white foam in its wake. Moments later, the boat came into their actual view, no mistake as to its target, the rumble of its powerful engine now audible.

At the speed it was maintaining, the boat would reach the shore—and them—in minutes, probably less.

"Hurry up, Curran!" Falcone shouted frantically, grabbing their backpacks and the drone's shoulder bag.

"I am hurrying! Why are they coming after us? We didn't do anything wrong!"

"I don't know, but I sure as hell don't want to stick around and ask them. Come on, we gotta go!"

In their haste to evacuate, Falcone dropped the keys to the Hyundai, Niles scooping them from the sand and sprinting to the car's driver's side. Unlocking the door, he slid behind the wheel and started the engine.

"Curran, what the fuck?" Falcone blustered, for an instant frozen with a mix of outrage and consternation. A quick look over his shoulder found that the boat, a 122-ARES 35 FPB which now presented as the stalwart, intimidating patrol vessel that it was, had made a beach landing with several men climbing over the sides. And they were armed with long guns.

40

"JESUS!"

"Get in, get in, get in!" Niles yelled, and wrenched the Hyundai's steering wheel, stomping his foot on the gas pedal, engine revving and tires spinning in the sand.

"I should be driving!" Falcone barked, but he wasted no more time, jumping into the passenger seat, slamming his door, and harnessing himself in. He shoved everything he was carrying into the rear seats, twisted around to see where the armed men were in relation to them, and put both hands on the dashboard, bracing as Niles crudely put the car in gear and shot forward.

Niles took them up the incline and back through the densely forested terrain, Falcone still grumbling about his takeover of helmsmanship. Falcone's eyes darted between the car's rear and side mirrors, but so far they appeared to be in the clear. Since the men from the boat were on foot, he was reasonably sure they had made a clean, if haphazard, getaway. By the time they got to the first acute switchback on the route a few minutes later, his tension had started to abate and his confidence rebounded.

They had not quite driven a mile through the rolling woodlands, the road taking them almost to the north coast before turning to the south, when that confidence totally evaporated. Peering into the side mirror, Falcone was flabbergasted to find the gray-blue Toyota Grand Highlander he'd spotted earlier barreling up the road behind them. Focusing hard on the vehicle's windshield, squinting to penetrate the sunlight's glare, he could not tell specifically who was driving or riding shotgun or if there were any other passengers. But what he could tell was who the driver was *not*—the man who was presumedly the owner or renter, last seen fishing offshore.

"Shit," Falcone muttered. "Curran, those guys from the boat are on our ass. You're going to have to—" He lost the rest of his words as they got stuck in a chokehold in his throat, Niles changing gears and propelling the Hyundai to speeds that, on this road, were not likely to be death-defying. "Christ, I should be driving," he repeated pointlessly, one fist pressed into the dash, the other clutching his seat.

"Why are they bloody chasing us?" Niles asked again, catching a glimpse of the follow vehicle in the rearview mirror.

"Just concentrate on your driving," Falcone pleaded.

For the next few minutes, which seemed interminably drawn out, they hurtled along the single-lane road as it wound through thick, overgrown brush and dense swatches of pine, cedar, and cypress trees. Every hairpin turn, superfluously marked with yellow-and-red caution signs, caused Falcone's heart to seize in his chest. They were traveling in mostly elevated stretches with steep embankments, not all of which were hemmed by guardrails. The anemic horsepower of the Hyundai was no match for that of the Toyota, so Niles was unable to put much, if any, distance between them.

They were just coming out of a suicidally looping curve, tires barely clinging to the pavement, when Falcone screamed, "Goats!"

Niles' head jerked reflexively toward Falcone. "What?"

Louder and with more force, Falcone bellowed, "*Goats!* There's fucking goats in the road!"

Niles' eyes came back to the front just in time to see the herd of animals—longhaired black, brown, gray, and tan—not only in the road but taking up residence; a couple dozen standing or lying down and not moving at all.

"Bloody bollocks!" Niles exclaimed, and pounded on the Hyundai's horn. He was already pumping the brakes, but the momentum of the car's speed was carrying them inexorably forward, less than fifty yards from the animals. Neither the blare of the horn or the impending impact of the vehicle it was associated with had any effect on the goats and, to add to the jeopardy, the Toyota had also cleared the turn and was directly behind them.

To their right, the land rose precipitously without so much as a shoulder abutting the rocky base; to their left, scrub graduated down to a forested ravine.

"Oh God…oh God," Falcone was saying, bracing himself with both hands as the Hyundai kept moving forward, closing in on the goats. And then he felt the car swerve erratically and actually increase in speed. "Curran! What the hell are you doing?"

Niles had done the only thing he could given the obstacle and circumstance, which was to consider the two inevitabilities, either crash into the goats and be caught by whoever was pursuing them or plunge down the slope and hope for the best. He chose to act on the one that he felt gave them the best chance at a hopeful outcome.

With Falcone cursing and yelling and bumping roughly around in his seat, Niles fought against the harsh grade and angle of decline, which was pulling the weight of the vehicle down. As he yanked the steering wheel and grappled with gravity, pressing the gas pedal to the floorboard, the Hyundai's carriage wobbled and tilted toward the ravine, tires sliding in the brush. For a moment, it seemed they were about to flip sideways and tumble to the bottom of the slope, but he kept his foot on the accelerator and the tires' tread caught enough traction for him to regain control.

Niles got them up the hill and back on the road on the other side of the goats, worked the gears and sped forth, once again careening around the bends and twists and racing precariously along the straightaways, few that there were. In the middle of the mountainous terrain they were traversing, some new options emerged at a three-way junction: head north, following the ridge to coastal settlements; head south through a route which, though desolate, would take them back to Chios Town; or continue westward and into what signage indicated was the hamlet of Kardamyla. The close proximity of the latter made their choice.

The Toyota Grand Highlander, presumably with its cabin of boatmen had, incredibly, also managed to circumnavigate the bunch of goats in the road and was, once more, right on their tail. Soon, the two vehicles were driving the irregular, unevenly paved streets of a village divided into two sections, one by the sea and one spread about the eastern slopes of Mount Kranos, where they now found themselves.

The small burg of Kardamyla, known as Ano or Upper Kardamyla, is built on the ruins of ancient history that includes the Greek Revolution of the 1800s. A wedge of fertile plains separating it from Marmaro, the seaside colony, provides a wellspring of agricultural sustenance and livelihood with fields of citrus, pomegranates, grapes, figs, olives, nuts, grains, and vegetables. The town's structure and architecture is a blend of aged, crumbling stone dwellings and restored versions of the old. Like most of the islands, its town nucleus is a cobweb of narrow, intersecting alleys and cobblestone streets.

Forced to slow down as they entered the mix of houses and shops and tavernas, Niles said, "Maybe we can lose them in here."

"Oh, right," Falcone said sarcastically, "because this orange piece of shit car just blends right in." But he had actually been thinking the same thing, peering through the windshield and their windows in search of such opportunities.

"I just don't know what we could have possibly done for them to nick that bloke's auto and chase us across the countryside," Niles said.

"Must have been something to do with the drone," Falcone replied. "You didn't spend a whole lot of time going over those regulations."

"I read enough to know the essential stuff," he retorted.

"Maybe so, but we apparently set off something."

"Yeah, but to come after us with guns?" Niles paused ponderously. "Maybe we should surrender to them, just say we're wanker tourists that didn't know any better. I mean, that's true, innit? Since we don't know what we did…"

"No. Just keep driving."

They passed townspeople ambling along the street sides, a few on bicycles, scattered children at play. Maneuvering around the occasional parked car, Niles tried to increase their speed to stay far enough ahead of the Toyota while looking for roads to turn down. Passing through residential sections, where the modest houses were surrounded by iron fencing or stone walls and spruced up with flowers and fruit trees, they drew bewildered stares from the locals who were going about their everyday business. The day had edged into afternoon now, sun high and blanching the blue from the sky. As the Hyundai's horsepower struggled to deliver what was being demanded of it, so did the air-conditioning against the outside heat, and it did little to dissipate the stench of perspiration stagnating inside.

After winding their way in and out of a dozen or so corridors, Falcone said, "They're still right on us. I think their strategy here is going to be pinning us down somewhere. Try to pick up the speed a little, find a way to get some separation."

"Right," Niles replied, mashed the accelerator, and cut through an alleyway, tearing across the pavement like a weekend drag racer. He kept it up, steering in and out of the hodgepodge of streets, eventually coming to what appeared to be a small town square, the center of which was surfaced with geometrically aligned pavers. It was mostly empty, but there was through traffic, so Niles drove across and turned onto another street and continued making turns, going as fast as he dared, watching for errant kids or animals; there was the usual abundance of cats, a random dog or two, and he'd even seen some chickens. So far, thankfully, no goats.

Niles had just driven past a small parking lot when he came to a covered alley. Just before that, the streets ahead had seemed to be more open and with less concealment so, at the last moment, he whipped the steering wheel and plunged into the corridor, which was tight and shrouded in shadow. There was a scant amount of daylight at the other end of the passage, which was a relief because he'd not been sure if it was a throughway or a dead-end. But very quickly he had a problem his seat-of-the-pants driving had not anticipated.

They were barely a couple of car lengths in when their movement came to an abrupt—and grinding—halt, the sound and impact of metal scraping against concrete like a heavy shovel thrust into a pile of rocks.

"Oh my God," Niles said, his voice soft with dread.

"Damn it, Curran, this isn't a street!" Falcone declared. "Back up!"

Panicking, Niles put the car in reverse gear and depressed the gas pedal, engine responding but the Hyundai not budging. Beneath them, they faintly heard the whine of rubber, pressure on tires that could not even spin. Niles tried again and again to move the car either forward or backward, but it moved not an inch.

They were stuck.

Falcone and Niles had also been attempting to open their doors which was, of course, completely futile. They pounded the panels, shook and jiggled the handles, shoved their bodies against the frame, all to no avail.

"Oh God," Niles wailed forlornly, grabbing his neck and squeezing his eyes shut. His pale face had gone feverishly red. "We're going to suffocate in here!"

"Open the windows."

Niles pushed the buttons that automatically lowered the driver and passenger windows, the result of which actually made their air quality worse as it mixed dust and humidity with the controlled interior climate, infusing trapped heat from the alley into what minimal coolness had been circulating.

They both coughed, Falcone reaching to his footwell where a plastic bottle of water had rolled. He unscrewed the cap, took a long swig, and passed the bottle to Niles.

Falcone said, "Well, one good thing…I think maybe we've actually managed to lose those guys." He twisted in his seat to look through the hatchback window. And got an idea. "Hey, see if the back will open."

Niles popped the latch and they heard a muted thump, but in the dim light could not tell if the hatch had released.

"Okay," Falcone said, trying to reclaim his composure. "Let's get these rear seats down."

From inside the vehicle, from the cramped confines of the front, with the two of them frantically working together, this proved more difficult than what would have been the standard way by outside access. It took them several minutes of maneuvering, but they finally got the seats flattened, Falcone crawling over to the hatch. He nudged, then pushed and tugged, but for whatever reason—maybe in solidarity with the rest of the jammed car—it refused to open.

Sweating and breathing heavily, his frustration mounting again, Falcone sputtered, "Goddamn it."

"What are we going to do, Eddie? Oh God…I'm sorry. I'm sorry, I'm sorry, I'm sorry! You're right. You should have been driving. I'm a shit driver and I'm such a bloody idiot."

"No. No, Curran, you're not. We'll get out of this."

"How?"

Clambering back to his seat up front, Falcone heaved a defeated sigh and conceded, "Hell if I know. We'll never be able to break the windshield. If we were freaking runway models, we might be skinny enough to slip through these windows."

There was a beat of silence and they exchanged deadpan looks.

And then they were shoving their backpacks and the shoulder bag with the drone and accessories out of their opened windows and up onto the Hyundai's roof. In doing so, they realized that the car's front end contour allowed them enough room to stick their heads through as well, if they bent a certain way. The gap between the sills and side walls was impossibly tight, but it appeared to be their only way out.

After minutes of torturous effort and preposterously contorted positioning, Falcone squeezed his body through the window opening, painfully compressing his chest, stomach, and hips. He pulled himself up onto the roof of the car and scooted to the other side to help Niles. The more svelte of the two, the Brit was not as physically fit and was struggling. Falcone grasped him by the arms to provide more leverage.

The sound of a motor caused them to look toward the entrance of the alley, both seeing a vehicle slowly pass, reverse, and then stop. Heard doors clank open. It was the Toyota Grand Highlander, its passengers getting out.

Falcone strained to pull his friend up and got him onto the Hyundai's roof just as footsteps hastily shuffled into the alley. The dank air filled with an influx of body odor and the cloying density of human forms in close quarters.

In a harsh whisper, Falcone hissed, "Grab your gear and fucking go!"

They slid from the roof to the hood and hit the ground running for the opposite end of the alley, desperately hoping none of their pursuers had split off to intercept them.

When they burst from the shadowy tunnel into the sunlight, their hope collapsed.

JAKE TYLER'S DAY HAD begun before daylight and in a chaotic barrage.

Years of elite Special Forces military operations in every kind of austere environment and high-risk situation, coupled with extensive, exhaustive, and comprehensive training at the top-tier level, kicked in instantly, automatically, from deep core and backed up with mental and muscle memory. So when Jake was suddenly jarred from what was, for him, a relatively sound sleep, his reaction was typical and on par with that baked-in conditioning; he immediately came fully awake and alert and ready for whatever action was required.

Next to his head on the pillow, his iPhone Bluetooth device beeped and earbud radio comms came alive with vocal noise and, from the front of the cottage, someone was pounding loudly and incessantly on the door. His eyes flashed open, he sat bolt upright and swung his feet to the floor, snatching his Glock from the nightstand, instinctually checking it though he kept it loaded. His head swiveled back to Callie. She had been jolted awake with him and was recoiling in fear.

He reached for the iPhone, glancing at the screen, and put the Bluetooth earpiece and Invisio X5 buds in place. Responding to phone and radio at the same time, his voice commanded, "What's going on?" As he spoke, the pounding on the cottage door became even louder, wood rattling against wood.

He reached over, gave Callie's arm a squeeze, and stood, pulling on the t-shirt and cargo pants set out on a chair next to the bed, jabbed his feet into his boots. With the Glock in hand, he went to the door. Swung it open, ready for whoever, whatever, was on the other side.

But by now, familiar voices stridently clamoring in each ear, he was already assimilating the who and what, his expression stony. Standing breathlessly in the amber spray of lamp light at the door was the normally jovial figure of Keanjaho Dmello, looking gaunt and grimly spectral.

Jake said, "Okay, Kean…let me just speak to Callie."

His voice strained, Dmello urged, "Hurry, please."

Instants later, after notifying the man on cottage patrol, Jake was in the passenger seat of the Jeep Gladiator of their rental fleet, Dmello tensely silent as he steered the vehicle down the dirt road and across the field to their basecamp. Jake felt awful leaving Callie in the state she'd been in—terrified from the trauma of the harsh awakening—and he'd had no time to comfort her or offer much of an explanation for his urgent departure. But he could not allow himself to think about that now.

The predawn sky was just beginning to lighten, a pale sickle moon winking over the sea. When they came to a stop, Jake jumped out and bounded toward Remington's tent. Several people were gathered outside the entrance and, as he approached, they parted to allow his passage.

The moment he saw his friend sprawled on the ground, unmoving, Luther Baladur and Caspian Bachman on their knees on either side of him, Jake felt a gut punch of visceral emotion but pushed past it, knowing he'd need to insulate himself from all personal feelings in order to do what was needed. Baladur and Bachman, trying to rouse Remington, looked up at Jake, their faces drawn with dread. Jake thought that Baladur, as solid and seasoned a professional as he'd ever worked with, was fighting back tears.

It was he who said, "Jake, I came to relieve him, and found him like this. I think he stopped breathing, but I did some CPR. I do not know…what…" He stopped, at a total loss of words.

From a front corner of the tent near the entrance, Kipnis called out, "I have the dogs, Jake. They are down, too, barely breathing."

"What?" Jake asked unbelievably. "Do you see any wounds?"

"No," Kipnis replied. "I have checked them over thoroughly."

Marshalling his fortitude, Jake knelt by Remington and opened his medical kit, taking out a stethoscope, which he put to immediate use, handing a BP cuff to Baladur. As he listened to Remington's heart and lungs, which were in grave decline, Jake assessed other signs that were pointing to an unthinkable diagnosis; the pupils in his friend's eyes—the green of which had turned as drab as worn khaki—were constricted, his tanned skin sallow, cool, and clammy, his lips and fingernails bluish. Jake felt for a pulse, first on Remington's wrist, then on the carotid in his neck, finding it faint.

"Blood pressure is very low, Jake," Baladur reported. "Seventy over forty-five."

Jake rubbed his knuckles hard into Remington's sternum, saying, "Come on, brother…come on. You're not doing this to me."

But Nash Remington was fading, his mouth slack, his body limp, and now, as Jake leaned close, he heard a faint gurgling sound coming from Remington's throat and saw the subtle rise and fall of his chest cease. Listening at his nose and mouth, he heard and felt no air moving. Pinching Remington's nose, he administered rescue breaths and, after several rounds, got him back into a shallow respiratory rhythm, kneading his chest again but still unable to get a response.

To Baladur, he said, "Take over for a minute, make sure he keeps breathing."

Baladur did as asked and Jake opened the combination lock on the drug compartment of his medical bag. A quick look confirmed what he had begun to suspect, as inconceivable as it was.

Under his breath, he muttered, "*Fuck*." Then, to everyone: "It's opioid overdose. Poisoning."

Bachman, who looked uncharacteristically shell-shocked, asked, "How could this happen?"

"Some of my fentanyl is missing."

"Your…?"

Though this came as a surprise to Bachman, the fact that Jake's kit was stocked with a number of controlled substances for his exclusive and legal medical application, was not unusual nor improper. These substances ranged from schedule II to V and included the fentanyl in several forms which, though he seldom needed to use it, was a go-to in certain specific situations. As a synthetic opioid similar to morphine, which he also carried, fentanyl is typically fifty to a hundred times more potent, with a dose of only 100 micrograms being the equivalent analgesic to 10 mg of morphine. In the competent hands of medical professionals, properly accounted for, securely stored, and responsibly administered, it has solid, legitimate benefits.

But in the hands of someone with abusive or nefarious intent, it was very often deadly and now, as Jake extracted what he needed from the controlled substances section of his bag, he worried that Remington might already be beyond the threshold of recovery, especially given he had no idea of the dosage amount or how much time had elapsed. This worry was amplified by Baladur's recitation of Remington's blood pressure numbers. They were tanking.

Jake did not waste any time with explanations for Bachman, his entire attention laser-focused on what had to be done, and critically. Extracting packages of Narcan, the naloxone reversal agent he stocked, Jake opened several and said, "Kip, if the dogs are still out but breathing, give each one a dose." He handed a pair of the nasal sprays to Dmello who had been hovering helplessly. To him, he added, "You do one, Kip the other, and both of you be prepared for erratic behavior when it takes effect, maybe biting. If they stop breathing, you'll need to do rescue breaths. Call out your actions and updates."

Eager to be able to do something, the Kenyan took the sprays and went to join Kipnis.

Supporting Remington's neck with one hand, Jake tilted his head back and shot the spray in his nose. He set the counter on his watch to two minutes, the minimum recommended wait time, and said a silent, fervent prayer. The two minutes seemed like ten, and he thought of all the close calls they'd experienced in Africa, big, bombastic moments on the precipice of life and death that they'd blown through together and come out on the other side. And here, in these more intimate and fragile moments, he felt so impotent, so unable to manipulate fate. He flashed back to the freeze-frame of devastating loss in South America, losing Haskell Delaney, seeing him standing in the hatch of that plane, grinning and full of all the life he possessed in the boldest way—just like

Remington—and in the next instant, gone, so totally gone.

No, no, no…that can't happen again, I won't let it.

He reached for, and clasped Remington's hand, holding it tightly. Watched his eyelids and lips for the slightest movement, a twitch. Something. Felt a jab in his chest, a chasm in his gut. He looked at his watch, saw the digital display still counting down.

Before the time was up, he heard commotion from the Malinois, Kipnis calling over, "They are both responding, and yeah, Luna bit me and Soleil is fighting Mellie."

"Just reassure them, they don't know what's happening. They'll calm down. Make sure they stabilize and don't regress. Keep them awake."

Jake's timer sounded to indicate the two minutes had ended, but Remington remained unresponsive. He reached for a second dose, again trying the painful stimuli to Remington's chest, grinding his knuckles with pressure.

"Come on, you son of a bitch…don't be such a drama queen." More softly, he implored, "Come on, brother. Please. Come on." His inner reserve of emotion threatened to erupt as his mind again tipped into a morbid territory where Remington's outcome was the bad one, but he willed himself to concentrate on what he could do in the present moment.

He administered a second dose of Narcan and, before he had withdrawn the spray nozzle, Remington shuddered and groaned and rose up into a full sitting position like a resurrected Frankenstein, eyes absurdly wide, half growling and half grunting, arms thrashing in fight.

Jake put his arms around his friend and struggled to maintain a firm lock until the combat instinct began to abate. "Hey, brother…you're okay. I got you. Settle down."

For several moments, Remington seemed to be trapped in a panicked trance, clearly reactive but unable to put thought or speech together. Then, glancing around the tent, eyes wild with a confused mix of alarm and hostility, he exclaimed, "What the fuck is happening? Where are Luna and Soleil?"

At the mention of the dogs, the energy of his resistance resurged and he broke free of Jake's embrace, but when he tried to stand up, his muscles betrayed him and he dropped back to the ground.

"Goddamn," he murmured. "What's going on?"

Jake said evenly, "Well, you gave us one hell of a scare, my man, and I need you to calm down and cooperate with me, okay? Luther came to relieve you and found you and the dogs all unconscious."

"What?" Remington tried to stand again, this time getting to his feet. He staggered unevenly to the front of the tent where Dmello and Kipnis were tending to the Malinois, stroking them with a repetition of good-girl, good-boy reassurances.

Following him, Jake made Remington sit down and let him get settled with his dogs, then resumed monitoring his pulse, blood pressure, heart, and lungs. He said, "Your vitals are improving, so I think you're going to be fine. Might not be a bad idea to have you checked out at the hospital in Chios, take the dogs to a vet."

"Hell no," Remington said adamantly. Considering the Malinois, both nuzzling and licking his hands, he amended, "Maybe a vet. Let's just see."

Jake spent a few minutes examining the canines who, if anything, seemed to have rebounded with more resilience than Remington. Eying him attentively, he asked, "How are you feeling?"

Remington actually laughed. "How do you think I feel? I feel like shit."

"No doubt. But specifically, if you don't mind. Headache? Nausea? Dizziness?"

"All of the above. Let's just say, I won't be doing any salsa dancing anytime soon."

"Well, that's a shame," Jake chided. "How's your breathing?"

"Still working. Look, I'll be fine."

"Okay. In any case, I need to keep a close check on you and the dogs most, if not all day. Got that?"

Remington gave him a pointed look. "So you still aren't telling me what happened."

"Hopefully your short-term memory will return and you can tell us, but the essential answer is, someone stole fentanyl from my kit…guessing it was when I handled the medical this afternoon. I had to get into the narcotics to stitch up one of the guys."

As soon as he completed the sentence, he glanced over at Bachman, whose face reflected that he'd strung the same thoughts together. Bachman said sourly, "The accident that wasn't an accident."

"Yep."

For the first time, with the exigent circumstances under control, those in the tent all seemed to be pondering the bigger picture. Kipnis spoke up before the rest had a chance to speculate further, saying, "When I got here, of course I went straight into response mode, but you know my observational skills…there is spilled coffee and, by the dogs' dishes, pieces of some kind of sandwich." He looked at Remington.

"I just don't fucking remember," he said disgustedly.

Kipnis continued, "I also saw the cabinet. It has been broken into."

"Everything's gone?" Bachman asked, his head swiveling to the storage container that had secured the jugs and Antikythera mechanism-like device.

Kipnis nodded gravely, "Afraid so."

"Damn it," Bachman blustered. He fumed silently for several moments, then said, "Make no mistake, I am beyond pissed about that. But I'm losing my mind over what almost happened to you, Remy…and your dogs. I am going to turn this camp inside-out until I find out who did this."

Remington's face turned dark with fury. "Almost killing Luna and Soleil? Whoever that is better hope *you* find them and not me."

BUT LOGAN HAYS WAS long gone, already miles out to sea as the deep blue glow of twilight began its languid ebb, a thin hint of dawn seeping up from the horizon.

After leaving Remington's tent, he had only needed to wait about fifteen minutes. He'd circled back and reapproached, creeping up until he was close enough to hear movement inside and soon, he had heard what he'd hoped he would hear—the muted thump of Remington's body dropping to the ground—and did not hear anything else; most notably, he did not hear growling. Slowly unzipping the tent flap, he had peeked inside, seen Remington and both dogs down, and entered. He then went to the rear of the tent where, earlier, he'd spotted the storage cabinet. Took out a pair of bolt cutters from his duffel, broke off the padlock, and emptied the contents. The jugs and geared device made for heavy, bulky cargo, but all fit into the bag.

With the cumbersome loaded duffel and the rest of his gear, Hays had made his way to the beach where his F-RIB was stashed, inflated it, loaded up, and quietly pushed off. As he'd powered the outboard and steered to the north, he dug all of the cell phones out of his pack and tossed them into the sea.

Now, with the islands of Psara and Antipsara receding behind him, he cackled out loud, smacking the side of the inflatable. He had done it. His crazy, half-assed plan had gone off without a hitch, and he was on his way to making it pay; this unexpected stroke of serendipity was going to make him a very, very wealthy—not to mention powerful—man.

LESS THAN THIRTY MINUTES after watching in horrified shock as Jake had worked to revive Remington, Bachman reappeared in the tent, where he found the two of them with Kipnis. Remington was on his cot, Jake in a folding chair opposite, taking another blood pressure reading.

"How you doing?" he asked Remington.

He got a dismal nod but no verbal response.

Jake reported, "He's doing much better. You find out anything?"

"Oh yeah." He paused, looking directly at Remington. "It was Logan Hays."

During the time away, Bachman, accompanied by Shelby Hoskins, had gone to the opposite side of camp where the living quarters housing male personnel were situated. In the last of those four tents he found three puzzled-looking vets in various stages of dress, their cots neatly made up with backpacks being readied for the day. When questioned about the missing fourth bunkmate, the others said they had just assumed he was in the latrine or shower, but a search of Hays' section revealed that all of his belongings were gone.

Asked about their impressions and observations of Hays, one vet said, "Something seemed off about him, but I mean, most of us are a little off, aren't we?"

A second one chimed in, "Well, I thought the dude was creepy."

Now, watching Remington's face for signs of recognition or

recollection, Bachman asked, "Anything coming back to you about what happened?"

Remington cocked his head, repeating, "Logan Hays…" And then, as if a door had flung open in his mind, exposing a chamber bursting with light, his eyes filled with clarity. "Jesus Christ," he muttered, and bounced from his cot, lunging for his dogs. They sprang to their feet and moved apart, eying him with confusion. Remington grabbed the tin container with the dogs' water, pushed past Bachman, and hurled it through the open tent flap, issuing a scream of pent up wrath and frustration.

He retook his seat on the cot, glowering. "I remember now." Through gritted teeth, he snarled, "*Him*. That motherfucker came into my tent. Said he was out walking and knew I was on watch…he couldn't have known I was on watch or even what for, we were keeping all this just between us, right?" He was speaking rapidly now, his thoughts coming in a furious jumble. "He gave me coffee, and I—" He broke off, glancing around his quarters.

From his chair in a corner on the other side of the tent, Kipnis looked up from his tablet computer. "Yes. It was spilled." He pointed to a drying spot on the floorboard, the top of the platform built for each tent in their camp. "I believe that is how you got dosed, but there were also the sandwiches."

"Sandwiches?" Remington asked blankly. He glanced around again.

"I threw them out," Kipnis told him. "You had not touched the one on your nightstand, but there was another one on the floor by the dogs' dishes. It looked like they might have licked or nibbled it."

"God Almighty," Remington groaned. "They are trained *not* to touch food or water unless I—"

Jake spoke up, calmly reminding him, "Luna and Soleil are incredible and absolute machines, but like all of us, they are fallible, Remy."

"The bastard also kicked their water dish and refilled it from his water bottle."

Kipnis nodded. "They could have been dosed by that, too. With the coffee and water and sandwiches, he was implementing redundancy. Making sure."

"Motherfucker," Remington said again, his voice laden with hatred. Remembering something else, he turned woeful. "They were alerting me." He cast a glance to the corner where the two dogs had laid back down and were watching him anxiously. "They're trained to detect drugs, all kinds, and they got a hit of the stuff from the sandwich. I remember them signaling me, but I could not fathom what they were picking up."

He put his head in his hands and, for several minutes, no one spoke.

Then Kipnis got everyone's attention. "The guy is not Logan Hays."

They waited for him to continue, riveted as his fingers tapped and swiped and scrolled on the tablet. Then he said, "He is probably not even a vet."

Bachman's hostility flared up, the freckles on his face standing out like spots of burnt cinnamon. "That son of a bitch. How could his creds have been bulletproof enough to pass the vetting? Kip, do you know who he is?"

"Not yet. But I assure you, I will find out."

Bachman heaved a morose sigh, ran a hand over his short brown hair. "All right. I'm going to meet with my staff and we'll decide how to best deal with what's happened from our side. This is really bad, a big blow on so many levels, but I guess it's a good thing I had not already involved antiquities on the finds or it would be an even bigger mess."

Jake said, "My suggestion would be business as usual. The less attention drawn, the better and the easier path forward. Let us do what we're here to do, which is handle problems."

Remington gave Bachman a nod. "What he said." As further assurance, he added, "I'm okay. No worse than a bad hangover." He offered a weak smile; in truth, he'd never had a morning-after that felt anything like the disorienting debility he was experiencing now, but he was not going to let on and invite even more coddling and encumbrances.

After Bachman departed, Kipnis also left to join the rest of the *Habari* team in the security station, a larger tent nearby. When they were alone, the air went out of Remington's bluster, his posture deflating. "What a clusterfuck."

Jake put his hands on Remington's shoulders. "We'll get through it." He paused, gazing into his friend's eyes, the vibrancy restored but the skin around them still dull and heavily creased and droopy with fatigue. "Brother, I'm not gonna lie. There was a moment or two I thought I'd lost you, that you weren't coming back."

Remington smiled wanly. "Pretty sure I passed my expiration date a long time ago, but I'm not going out unless it's in a hail of bullets or something even more incendiary."

"I hear you."

He blinked, his voice cracking as he said, "Thank you, Jake. God, I'm glad you were here."

Pressing his hands together as if in prayer, Jake smiled and gave him a bow. Then he said, "Let's just not do this again, okay?"

"Not planning on it," Remington replied, his mouth working around a yawn. "I'm really, really tired…but…guessing you're not going to let me snooze for a while."

"Nope. Sorry, bud. I need for you and the pooches to stay awake for a couple of hours, and even after that, only short, monitored naps."

That got a groan from Remington.

"Fortunately, there's plenty to keep us busy. Let's head over to the cottage so I can get back to Callie."

Jake knelt down, straightened and packed up his medical bag, the near-emptied compartments for the fentanyl and naloxone causing him to shudder with both revulsion and relief.

42

SEATED AT THE WOOD plank table in the courtyard of the cottage, Jake and Remington drank from glasses of fresh lemonade, sunlight dappling the patio through the leaves of overhanging fig trees. They watched as Callie played with the Malinois, tossing rubber balls for them to catch or chase and retrieve and alternately brandishing thick, knotted rope toys which they eagerly implemented in games of tag and tug-of-war.

As much as Jake had wanted to spare Callie from the utterly horrific incident to which he'd responded—in much the same way he'd been able to conceal almost all of the other ominous or perilous occurrences—he realized this was one she would have to be read in on; there would be no getting around his regular medical monitoring of Remington and the dogs. Even if he could have kept the reason vague, it would have been tough to come up with an explanation for depriving them of the sleep they so sorely wanted and needed. So he'd told her what had happened in the most low-key, minimal way possible, but the revelation still upset her.

Remington had done his best to reassure, flashing the big, charismatic grin that could have charmed the ducks off Walden Pond, quipping, "Darlin', your hubby and I must have some kryptonite in our blood. And it just wasn't my time to kick it."

While Remington made contact with Lieutenant Colonel Merriweather to let him know about the latest development, effectively changing the officer's travel plans to meet with them, Jake checked back in with Bachman and was glad to hear that the MVAA leader had decided to keep the project on track. Next, Remington spoke with Baladur to go over the day's assignments and ensure his team was operationally status quo.

Jake made perfunctory calls to both the port and town police, mostly just for the purpose of making a report as he did not expect much in the way of results. The police departments' resources and personnel were limited, both staffed by two officers, but checking in with them established a spirit of cooperation and alliance in case their assistance or support was needed at some point. He kept the details of the crime generic, characterizing it as a theft and providing the physical description of the man calling himself Logan Hays, nothing about the compelling nature of the artifacts or the overdose executed in the act. Predictably, the port police had not observed any unusual activity within the small harbor but said they would conduct a canvass amongst the boats and their operators. The lieutenant sergeant from the town police, a young man with whom they had become acquainted during the investigation of the murdered scientist, also opened a case and pledged that he and his warrant officer would make inquiries of the locals.

When Jake and Remington had finished their calls, Callie came over and sat next to Jake, the dogs slurping water from a pan and then laying down in the shade. "Is that okay?" she asked, her face solemn with worry. Earlier, Jake had asked her to keep the canines busy to dissuade them from sleeping.

"Yes, love," Jake replied. "They've been active enough to earn a little respite. If they do doze, we'll keep an eye on them, maybe wake them after fifteen or twenty minutes."

"What about me, doc?" Remington asked, his voice tinged with sarcasm, already knowing the answer he was going to get. "Have I earned a little respite?"

"Not yet. Let's give you a little longer." Jake cracked a snide grin. "You haven't been running around the yard."

"If I have to do that, all bets are off." Gazing at the Malinois, Remington smiled with abiding affection. "I swear, poisoning episode aside, between being pampered and spoiled by this little angel and your two hooligans, those pups are going to need rehabilitative training when we get home."

Jake glanced at his watch with a scowl of annoyance. "Speaking of my two hooligans, I just realized that they haven't checked in since yesterday morning." He took out his phone and scanned the logs, commenting, "No missed calls, no texts."

He tapped the contact for Falcone, listening through his Bluetooth earpiece, but the call went straight to voicemail; he got the same result for Niles. He said, "I guess I shouldn't be surprised. They probably had some kind of big night and are sleeping in late."

Remington stood, stretching his arms out and springing up and down on his toes. "Well, I'm getting mighty stir-crazy, partner. If you're not gonna let me sleep, I need to go somewhere, do something."

Jake pondered that for a few minutes as his friend paced the circumference of the patio, then said, "I have an idea. Why don't we pack up some lunch and go over to Antipsara…go to the cliffside where I found the cave I believe had the jugs initially."

"I thought you said there wasn't anything there, just a hole in the wall."

"I'm not thinking of the cave, I'm thinking about the sea below it."

Remington looked at him blankly, not tracking. He ran his fingers over the light pelt of whiskers on his chin, auburn hair like polished copper in the sunlight. "Forgive me, but I guess my bean is still mush. What are you proposing?"

"A dive…I want to do a dive."

JAKE PEERED OUT OVER the shimmering blue water, from this side of the island nothing visible beyond the cove but sea. The sun was high in a cloudless sky, small waves brushing the narrow lip of sand. Behind him was the cave he had explored and where he'd discovered the excavated sidewall. Standing beside him on the sliver of beach was a tall, husky man with Nordic features, intelligent blue eyes and light blond hair, crew-cut almost to the scalp. His broad chest and thick thighs were sheathed in a short-sleeved and -legged wetsuit, exposed forearms showing the outer edges of tattoo ink.

Virgil Oleski, from Remington's team, was a former navy SEAL out of Little Creek, Virginia, recruited during a mission *Habari* had undertaken in conjunction with several special forces units to train Kenyan troops. On completion of the assignment, Oleski had planned to rotate out of active service and was looking for work compatible with his background. Since coming into the employ of Remington, he'd been thoroughly content and robustly challenged but did not get many opportunities to utilize the aquatic-related training and skills acquired in his military ops. So to be suited up for a dive in the Aegean sent his happy meter high up the scale.

When Jake had brought up the idea of the dive to Remington, he'd been contemplating the possibility, though remote, of finding more jugs in the waters by the cave. During initial discussions about rare-earth minerals, Kipnis had informed them that undersea mineral beds, if they existed here, would be thousands of meters below and well beneath the floor, so there was no chance of finding any—unless they could get their hands on more of the sealed vessels. Jake had further speculated that the cave had probably been underwater at some point in time; therefore, it was conceivable that the vessels had been, too. Admittedly, it was a stretch but, as he had told Remington, without having anything to show or turn over to Merriweather and the military, no one would take the potential repercussions seriously. After all, without seeing the phenomenon with his own eyes, he would never have believed something like it was conceivable outside of a science fiction movie. And now that the substance was in the hands of an unknown actor with possible malicious intent, he thought they should at least make an effort to look.

Remington had been enthused about the dive until Jake let him know in no uncertain terms that he could not partake so soon after his deadly episode. This gave rise to a spirited but losing argument from Remington, who then enlisted Oleski to buddy up with Jake for the venture.

To make the crossing to Antipsara, it would have made more sense to take the Technohull RIB and sail directly to the western side of the island, but with Callie and the Malinois coming along, they opted to have Captain Salivara pick them up in the *Blue Zone*. After docking, they had stopped by the dig site, been joined by Oleski, and hiked to the field above the cliffside. There, Remington and Callie settled into canvas chairs beneath shade umbrellas spiked into the ground. Though Callie was nervous with the implied responsibility of making sure Remington and the dogs stayed awake, she was glad for the company, thinking of the bee meadow nearby and what had happened the last time she was here with Jake.

Now, after hauling air tanks and gear bags down the incline, Jake and Oleski went through their equipment inspections, checked all the connections and gauges, tested regulators and octopuses. Secured tanks and BCDs, adjusted weights and masks, synchronized their dive watches.

Turning to Oleski, Jake asked, "Ready?"

"Hooyah…let's do it," the big SEAL said, and the two waded into the sea.

The water was comfortably cool with remarkable clarity of some seventy-five to a hundred feet, the shallows hugging the coastline less than twenty feet deep. As they descended, the sun prismed through the shimmering surface overhead, rivulets of light rippling across the velvety, pearl-colored sand below. Swaths of pebbles and rocks glittered like loose gemstones.

Jake had outlined the dive plan to commence with a sweep of the area closest to the onshore cave, followed by a drop into the next depth level of thirty to forty feet about a hundred yards out. It was here the underwater environs began to come alive.

Much more colorful and dynamic than the waters he'd explored during his near-fatal dive in Fournoi, Jake marveled at coral reefs blooming in fiery reds, oranges, and yellows, spiny fingers and undulating clusters and willowy sprays swarming with fish and other sea life. There were the schools of brightly striped wrasses and silvery sea breams and arresting orange parrotfish that he'd seen before, but also packs of corpulent-bodied tuna and long, spear-nosed swordfish. He even spied several sea turtles finning across their path.

Oleski kept close and followed Jake's hand signals as they swam aside a brick red rock colony, looking for any kind of apertures to probe for pottery. Twenty minutes into the forty he had allotted, Jake was beginning to think the dive had been a frivolous and unrealistic bid, enjoying the relaxation of the activity but not finding what he'd hoped for or even a promising repository structure. Consulting his SUUNTO dive watch, he felt a slight pang of uncertainty and thought he should probably wrap it up. With almost a half-day elapsed, he was fairly confident that Remington and the dogs had turned the corner and were not at much risk of medical complications, but he knew Callie had been stressed about being left alone to watch over them.

He had just given Oleski the signal to return when something caught his eye. Holding up his hand in a stop gesture, he pointed two gloved fingers at his eyes, then directed the SEAL's attention to what appeared to be the opening of a cave. They both swam over and into the entrance, finding a surprisingly tall and wide corridor with another opening about fifty yards on the other side. They advanced, poking and prodding about the rock walls, gliding slowly along the length.

The interior of the cave passage did not yield anything but, several minutes later, the outside did; not at all what Jake had been looking for or imagined finding, but it made the dive entirely worthwhile and incredibly significant.

Kneeling on the seafloor, Jake found a cable with a diameter slightly larger than a garden hose. It was black and thick and extended in each direction as far as he could see. Jake followed the line and, at the opposite end of the cave near the egress was a clear plastic cylindrical enclosure encasing a portion of the cable, watertight protection for some type of device that was attached; Jake could not tell much as the device—about the size of a miniature Hershey bar—was also black, rectangular, and itself apparently housing something. The plastic cylinder was locked on and, as Jake ran his hand over it, he located a minute slot for an access key.

Reaching to his vest, Jake unclipped the Olympus Tough camera he'd purchased when he had replaced his damaged dive gear, and took several pictures. Checking his watch again, he knew it was time to resurface, so he signaled Oleski and they ascended. Returning to shore, they removed masks and regulators but left the rest of their equipment and gear on for an easier climb up the cliffside.

At the top of the slope, Jake saw Callie fluttering over Remington in visible distress and hurriedly shrugged out of his BCD. Setting it down, he rushed to her, calling, "What's wrong?"

"Oh Jake…I can't wake him up," she said, her voice dredged in desperation.

When she moved aside, Jake saw Remington reclined in his canvas folding chair, arms and legs hanging off the sides, eyes closed and mouth agape. The Malinois lay upright on the ground beside him, mostly still, their gazes shifting from Remington and Callie to Jake.

Bending close, his face directly above, Jake bellowed, "Remy!"

His friend's eyes came wide open and he sprung up, almost bumping heads with Jake and nearly collapsing the chair. "JEE-sus!" he exclaimed.

Straightening, Jake gave Callie a coy smile and said, "Just takes more of an outside voice."

Seeing the despair in Callie's face, Remington looked somewhat remorseful, drawling, "Sorry, sweetness, didn't mean to scare you. I was just napping. You all know I'm tired, and the sun felt so good, the sea, the breeze..."

"Yeah, yeah," Jake scoffed.

"So, did you find any jugs?"

"No, but I do have something to show you and Kip."

GATHERED IN THE LIVING room of the cottage early that evening, Jake and Remington were waiting for Kipnis to update them with his intel and analysis. On return to basecamp following the dive, they had reconvened with Bachman over dinner before making their retreat. The MVAA leader was still enraged over the egregious turn of events but determined to keep the mission on track and moving forward and, after a normal day of archaeological activity not fraught with chaos or calamity or catastrophe, and a conciliatory discussion and strategy session, reasonable order had been reestablished. When all was said and done, Bachman wasn't as upset about the loss of artifacts that, after all, were not relevant to his project, but he remained infuriated about the infiltration, treachery, and atrocity of the man who had perpetrated the act.

Now, with the shadows of sunset beginning to darken the bright white stucco walls of the cozy cottage, the three men were positioned around a mahogany coffee on which Jake's and Remington's Toughbooks, Kipnis' tablet, the Olympus camera, folders, and printed images were arranged.

Remington, in stonewashed Wrangler jeans and a navy paisley-patterned snap-front shirt, was relaxing on the comfortable couch, throw pillows wedged behind his neck and arms, the Malinois stretched out on the floor beside him. Kipnis, who somehow almost always managed to look as chill and collected and fastidiously groomed as a collegiate on yearbook picture day, sat in an adjacent chair, crisply dressed in tan chinos and a beige striped button-up shirt. Sitting next to him, Jake was freshly showered and wearing black Under Armour shorts and t-shirt, having just left Callie resting in the bedroom. Her disrupted night, while not an uncommon occurrence, added to the tension of the day and was drawing her into a doze, for which Jake was thankful as he did not want her to hear all the dark and sordid details of their conversation.

Kipnis reached for his tablet, and while he navigated through various files and shared items to the Toughbooks for them to view, Jake studied Remington in repose, his face haggard, eyelids sporadically closing.

He asked, "You okay, bud?"

"Still feel like I've got some dust in the attic and could probably sleep for twenty-four hours straight, but yeah, I'm okay." He sat up and rubbed his eyes. "So, did you find out who that asshole really is, Kip?"

"I did. I just sent the intel to your laptops." Jake and Remington leaned forward to view their screens. Kipnis told them, "That is Kirill Vasić. Russian."

Staring at an image of the man who had been passing himself off as Logan Hays, neither Jake nor Remington said anything for a moment, absorbing the revelation, and then Remington muttered, "Fucking Russian?"

Kipnis continued, "I have not gotten much on him yet, but the vet jacket as Logan Hays is one of the best backstopped files I have ever run across. Believe it or not, it is actually built from a real vet's record, a Logan Hays out of California."

Jake was flabbergasted. "How is that possible, Kip? Stolen valor is one thing, but this is a complete co-opted military record?"

Kipnis nodded soberly. "In talking with Caspian, he told me every piece of paper, every digital file, all checked out—as, being attached to an authentic vet, would be the case—but the images and physical aspects were somehow replaced and incorporated."

"But how the hell?" Jake persisted.

"The only way I can see this being pulled off is with some pretty damn next-level hacking. It took some doing, but I finally made the real identification through facial rec. Took me multiple databases before I got him. Everything kept coming back to the actual Hays. Like I said…next level."

"I'll need to make the notifications to DoD," Remington said.

"Already done," Kipnis told him.

"I'm still trying to figure out how he got into the MVAA program…and why," Jake said.

"Let me answer the second part first," Kipnis said, and reached into a pocket of his chinos. He produced the GSM device that had been implanted in Remington's tent and placed it on the coffee table. "After what happened, I did a sweep this morning. That is how Vasić found out about the vessels and device and knew where we were storing them, Remy. It was attached to the table by your cot."

Remington slapped his thigh and groaned. "And *that's* how he knew I was on guard. Son of a bitch."

Kipnis continued, "As to the why, or really, who…I have connected Vasić to Taras Ignatkovich."

Jake said, "So Vasić was what…a plant?"

Remington picked up the thread. "With all the weeks that went into the logistics for setting up the dig—we were working on this long before Africa—Ignat could have known we were coming in plenty of time to get Vasić in play."

"Exactly," Kipnis said. "Caspian said he had a first-timer who canceled late, which created a slot. I am making inquiries on that front, to find out if anything…unfortunate…happened to that guy."

"Christ Almighty," Remington murmured.

"As to what and why…Jake, what you found today might be at the root of all that." Now Kipnis reached for the memory card from the Olympus camera and inserted it into his tablet. When the image files loaded, he also shared them to the Toughbooks.

Jake said, "From earlier conversations, I knew what this was, but wasn't sure how, or if, it's relevant."

What they were all looking at was a segment of one of the more than one and a half million submarine fiber optic cables spooled across the bottoms of the world's oceans. The vast network began some 150 years ago with the installation of a commercial line extending between England and France and, with at least one million kilometers active today, has become a crucial communication nexus for connectivity and data transfer in business and commerce, government and the military. More broadly, global access to information and financial transactions are dependent on this cable infrastructure, which transacts the overwhelming majority of all voice and Internet traffic around the world. And, with dependance, comes vulnerability and exploitation, which has made these undersea cables a source of espionage and tampering, particularly to intercept financial, government, and military data.

Kipnis navigated to a site on his tablet and held it out for Jake and Remington to see. He said, "The world's commercial cables are publicly mapped. You can see them all here on TeleGeography."

They peered at the chart with a spaghetti of colored lines running to and from and around every continent, noticing a lime green one that crossed the Mediterranean, west to east from Italy to Israel and up the Aegean to Turkey. It also connected to Greece and extended north to the Black Sea; on the way, it ran right by Antipsara.

"Is that the cable I found?" Jake asked.

"Actually, no." Kipnis replied. "The one mapped here is MedNautilus, which is owned by Telecom Italia Sparkle, and though you can't really tell by this, it is farther out from us. The cable you found is not mapped."

Mulling the response, Jake remarked, "It's a military cable."

"I think so. I am looking into it…obviously, these are classified." Kipnis pointed to one of the camera images on the screens of Jake and Remington's Toughbooks, indicating the plastic cylindrical container cupped around the cable in the undersea cave. "*That* is a tap."

Jake said, "So, you think this is what Ignatkovich is doing, why he's threatened by our presence."

Kipnis nodded.

"What about Korki's discovery?"

"My guess is that was just coincidental," Kipnis said. "When Vasić heard about us finding what we did, realizing what it could mean, he turned from spy to opportunist."

"What he is," Jake asserted, "is a fucking psychopath. But I don't know how we'd ever find him now."

Remington massaged his temple and blew out a breath, saying, "All of this is giving me a headache."

"No shit," Jake agreed, glancing toward the corridor that led to the cottage's master suite. "Why don't we take a break? I need to check on Callie."

Remington got up, flexing his arms, and strolled into the kitchen. When he returned with bottles of water for the three of them, he said, "This sounds like some kind of spy movie shit."

Kipnis cracked a wry smile. "It does. But the undersea cable spying is very real, and the Russians in particular have been doing it for a long time. This is all making a lot more sense, Ignatkovich's yacht and the so-called research vessel, *Zorya*." He paused, reflecting intently. "Whatever intel he is after—and maybe is in the process of attaining—is apparently worth killing for."

Jake came back to them, touching the Bluetooth earpiece for his iPhone as he ended a call, his expression grim. He said, "We've got another issue."

Right away, Remington asked, "Is Callie all right?"

Jake nodded. "Yeah, she's asleep, believe it or not. No, it's Eddie and Curran. I think something might have happened to them."

43

BY EIGHT AM THE next morning, Jake and Remington were flying from Psara to Chios by way of a chartered helicopter. They were in an Airbus H135 on a flight that would get them there in just under fifteen minutes. Remington exuded more vigor and a resurgence of healthy color after finally getting a good night's sleep. He'd brought the dogs, who had flown in all manner of aircraft and were unperturbed by the flight itself but frisky with excitement for the opportunity to work.

In contrast, Jake's mood was becoming increasingly bleak.

The previous night, when he'd gone to check on Callie, he had tried again to contact Falcone and Niles. He had not kept track of how many times he'd texted and called during the afternoon and evening, but there had been no response to any of his attempts. It had then occurred to him to call the Chandris Hotel, and when he was told the duo had departed that morning, checkout time being noon, he felt his threshold of concern go up several notches. At that point, he still wasn't ready to suspect anything ominous, but when he had again failed to make contact on waking this morning, his concern edged into worry territory. As much as Falcone and Niles had a tendency to wreak havoc, frequently pushed his buttons and, on occasion went fully off the reservation, Jake knew they had a deference for him that precluded deliberate disregard of his directives.

Which inclined him to believe his gut feeling—something was not right.

In light of everything that had been happening, he was also uneasy about leaving Callie behind. Prior to their departure, she had pled with him to let her come but, unsure of what was going on with Falcone and Niles, he'd decided it was best that she stay either with the group or secured at the cottage; she had cheerlessly opted for the latter.

When they set down on the helipad at the Chios airport, Jake took a call from Kipnis while Remington led the dogs to their rental Jeep Renegade parked a short walk away. Conversing as he followed them, Jake checked the screen of his iPhone, reviewing the information being sent.

Climbing into the passenger seat of the Jeep, Jake said, "Kip got their credit card charges. I haven't gone through all of it yet, but the electronics store where they left the camera for repair is right by the marina." Studying the email Kipnis had sent, he added, "He's already spoken with the car rental place they used and says their ride has not been turned in, so he got the GPS tracking and is working on that."

He paused, sorting through the rest of the listed transactions. "I don't know what to make of the charge from the electronics store…I can't believe a part and repair would cost this much. While we wait on Kip to get back to us on the GPS, let's head there."

A quick drive along the coastal road took them to the marina, passing restaurants and bars and businesses on the left and a busy harbor on the right, boats abutted to the other side of a promenade lined with palm trees. About halfway down, now with only a span of brick pavers separating them from open water, Jake announced, "We're coming up on it…thirty yards."

At this hour, with eateries wheeling at the peak of their breakfast service, finding a parking spot was a challenge but, after passing the electronics store, they got lucky and slid into a just-vacated slot by the curb. Cracking windows for the dogs, Remington and Jake exited the Jeep and walked to the establishment, which was deceptively modest by its storefront profile but surprisingly comprehensive on the inside. They shuffled past rows of computers and printers and peripherals, video consoles and gaming paraphernalia, phones and tablets and cameras, audio and video components, and found the service counter manned by the technician who had assisted Falcone and Niles.

Explaining who they were, Jake asked when the duo had picked up the video camera, which prompted a bewildered look from the technician.

He said, "Oh, but they haven't. I called and left a message yesterday and was surprised they did not come right away. They were eager to get it back."

"You mean it's still here?" Jake asked. "They haven't come back in?"

"Not since yesterday morning when they stopped by for an update. I let them know the part would be in later in the day, told them I would jump on the repair and call them as soon as it was done. Which I did."

"And you left a voicemail?"

"I did. Is something wrong?" For the first time, the young man whose store badge identified him as Yiannis, sensed something amiss, his affable disposition fading.

Jake pressed his lips together, hands on his hips. Sighing, he said, "Well, we'll go ahead and get the camera."

The technician retreated to a back room, returning a moment later with the Sony Venice, encased in plastic and tagged. Setting it on the counter, he detached part of the tag and presented it to Jake. It was an invoice for the camera part ordered, other in-stock parts, and the repair that had been done.

Glancing at the figures, Jake's forehead creased in confusion. "This amount hasn't been run on their card?"

Before the technician could answer, Jake took out his phone and navigated to the list of credit card charges, using his fingers to enlarge the exhorbitant euro amount debited by the electronics store.

Looking at the charge on the phone's screen, the technician chuckled nervously. "Oh no, no…that is for the drone."

Now Remington chimed in. "The drone?"

"Yes." The technician came out from behind the counter and led them to the front of the store, pointing to a glass case full of drones and accessories. Indicating the DJI Mavic 3 Pro Cine on display, he said, "This one."

Remington shook his head, smirking, but held the retort on the tip of his tongue.

Jake did not seem surprised nor amused, but his expression registered a shift in thought. "Okay," he remarked abruptly. "Let's finalize payment for the camera and get going."

Remington said, "We'll check with Kip, see how he's faring on the GPS tracking." Back in the Jeep, he chided, "Drone…we should have seen that coming. It could explain the radio silence. Those two with a new toy…except it's not. We've got some DJIs, and while they're not as advanced as what I typically use, they are great drones and would take some time and effort to master. They're probably out in the countryside somewhere, maybe where cell service is nil, all caught up in learning how to operate the thing."

He started the Jeep's engine and pulled out into the flow of traffic. The end of the marina was just ahead. He cut a sideways glance at Jake, who had gone quiet in reflection.

Jake's iPhone displayed an incoming call from Kipnis, so he answered by putting him on speaker.

They heard Kipnis say, "I am sending you a pin for the car. It's in a place called Kardamyla, about eighteen kilometers to the north of where you are…all the way north to the coast."

Remington grinned winningly. "See? Told ya."

There was a beat of silence and then Kipnis said, "The car has not moved since yesterday afternoon."

DRIVING THE SAME ROUTE taken by Falcone and Niles the previous day, they cleared the environs of Chios Town and hugged the coastal road as it climbed along the upslope. They were passing Glaroi Beach when Jake commented, "There's a hell of a lot of charges from the beach bar there on the night of their arrival. A shitload of drinking for just the two of them."

"You know they had company," Remington remarked.

"Yeah, I'd say so, judging from what I'm seeing here." Jake continued reviewing the line items of expenditures, mentally assimilating a time-line to correspond with their travel. Switching back to the GPS tracking log, he said, "From the electronics store yesterday, they came this way again but ventured farther. Their car was stationary for a while north of here, at the coast, in the middle of nowhere."

"Probably where they were flying the drone," Remington suggested.

They drove inland through rolling hills and forested swaths that cut across the amphitheatrical valley of Lagada township before turning westward into the barren, higher elevations. More sweeping peaks and valleys through Marmaron, and they were navigating the twisting, often treacherous, switchbacks leading into the burg of Kardamyla, Gria Mountain rising to the south, the coastal village of Marmaro sprawled to the north.

Observing the somber expression that had set in on Jake's face, Remington said, "Hey, I'm sure there's an explanation. They could be holed up with whoever they were partying the night away with."

Jake said nothing.

They turned left, leaving the Chiou Kardamilon national road for the narrow, single-lane city streets lined with their modest iron-railed and stone-walled houses, mountain slopes swelling into the swirling clouds of what was becoming an overcast day, the sun shrouded like a cataractous eye.

Peering through the windshield and windows, up and down the tight village lanes, Jake said, "Okay, here, for some reason, they were driving all over the place. Not sure if they were looking for something or just being random."

"I would say let's just go to the endpoint," Remington proposed, "but to save time backtracking and cover all ground, we'll take their exact route."

"Yep," Jake agreed, and recited the turn-by-turn directions.

Soon, they were crossing a village square, its bricked courtyard shaded by big, spreading trees and encircled with quaint shops and bistros. There were a few parked vehicles off to the sides, a couple of vendors out sweeping or wiping down tables and chairs.

"They drove through here?" Remington asked.

"Yeah," Jake said, and pointed down a side alley next to a parking lot. "The car's last position should be just past it."

"You said it's an orange Hyundai?"

They slowed, and came to the covered corridor.

And spotted the car.

*   *   *   *   *

STANDING AT THE REAR bumper, Remington said, "Goddamn."

Jake just shook his head in disbelief, unsure of what else to say. Instead, he observed the Malinois prancing around, noses at work.

"How in the hell did they get out?" Remington wanted to know, hoisting himself up onto the car's roof, balancing on his chest, and looking down both sides, which were wedged—crushed, actually—against the corridor's stone walls.

"I have no idea," Jake said. "There's not a millimeter of space." He stuck his fingers in the trunk access notch and, though the hatch had been released, the panel only opened about an inch. "Not from the rear."

Remington crawled toward the front of the vehicle, noting, "Windshield's intact, but the front windows are down. I guess that's how they got out. That would have taken some crazy contortionist shit."

"Can you see any of their belongings inside?"

"Can't see much, but no, don't see anything."

Below him, Remington heard both canines whining, looked, and saw that they had found their way around to the other opening of the alleyway and were standing directly in front of the car's hood.

"*Blijf*," he commanded them, and slid down from the Hyundai's roof.

Jake had brought an unwashed t-shirt of Falcone's and tossed it over the top of the car to Remington. Then, because he could see no obvious direct way to the opposite side of the corridor from the outside, he climbed over the Hyundai in the same manner as Remington.

When the Malinois were offered the t-shirt for an enhanced scent reference, they both gave a bark but remained in place.

To that, Jake remarked, "Well, we know they were here."

Remington said, "Yeah, but they're telling us this is where their scent stops, too."

"Meaning?"

"Meaning they didn't leave this spot on foot." Thinking about that, he added, "Maybe they got a ride from a local."

"Maybe," Jake said, "but that doesn't explain why they haven't been reachable by phone and haven't contacted me any other way."

Remington did not reply.

Jake and Remington searched the ground, which was made up of cracked and broken asphalt, but did not find anything significant; there were no visible tire treads, no foot or shoe prints in the dust, not even any cigarette butts. Nothing at all. They walked the narrow lane that extended beyond the corridor, the length of it lined with rock walls, scrub, and trees. There were no houses or businesses for about a hundred yards or so, no humans or animals in sight. As they strolled, the dogs were at heel, but their interest level had returned to one of a baseline state of alert and inquisitiveness, seeking stimuli but not capturing.

Stopping at the end of the lane where it bisected another nondescript street, Remington peered in all directions and asked, "What do you want to do? Contact the local police?"

Jake mulled that and said, "No, I don't want to get tied up with them. One of Kip's texts had their info, and the station is in the port part of the township. I'll get him to report the car and deal with the rental agency. Honestly, I don't know what else to do here except maybe drive around the vicinity some more, but even that seems a bit pointless. Something has clearly happened beyond the car getting stuck. I keep going back to their phones."

With that statement, Jake called Kipnis, giving him an update and asking if there was any new information. Kipnis reported that he had repeatedly attempted to ping the two phones without success.

When Jake had ended the call, Remington suggested, "Maybe their phones fell into the water while they were flying the drone."

Jake knew that Remington, who was usually as pragmatic as he was, was trying to play the part of hopeful optimist; in reality, he suspected his friend was equally doubtful.

"Don't think so. If they lost them or if they were mugged—which I think is unlikely around this place—they would have found another phone to use and call me. They would have bought burners. No, it's all got something to do with the car."

"Okay," Remington conceded, "so they got into some kind of collateral trouble. I'm still betting they show up on our doorstep like a couple of stray mutts."

But Jake did not think that was going to happen. Every wire in his cerebral and sensory network was twanging. Loudly.

Remington said, "Why don't we go back to Chios Town and talk to the police there. The colonel we met during the scientist's murder investigation seemed like a pretty astute guy."

Jake nodded. "Yeah, that was my take as well. Let's do that."

DRIVING SOUTH TO THE Chios hub took them twice as long as the trip north, encountering heavier afternoon traffic within the city limits as they wove their way from the coastal route into the maze of urban commercial roads. They navigated to the headquarters of the Chios Police Directorate on Polemidi street, a yellow stucco building with a modern geographical grid spanning the entryway. Too warm at this time of the day to leave the Malinois in the vehicle, Remington asked at the guard station and was granted permission to bring them inside.

Directed to the security department, which was located at the rear of the ground floor, they were shown into a small, uncluttered office with a black leather couch, a floor fan moving air around. Bookcases held thick binders, a desktop computer and monitor were arranged on a sideboard with little else, framed certificates on the wall. At the desk was a man in his forties clad in a pressed pale blue shirt and gray slacks, buzz-cut dark hair. The spartan order of the space and clean lines of his attire suggested a respect of decorum with utility and forthrightness. Standing next to him was a slightly younger man with a similar haircut and the shadow of a faint beard, wearing tan slacks and a short-sleeve plaid shirt. The nameplate on the desk read: COLONEL ARISTIDIS KYRGIAKOS.

The colonel stood to greet them, extending his hand. The other officer followed suit, introducing himself as Lieutenant Lambros Skiadaresis. Jake and Remington took a seat on the couch, the Malinois sitting at their feet.

The lieutenant gestured to Remington as a way of inquiring if he could pet the dogs and, getting a nod, squatted down to them.

Colonel Kyrgiakos smiled, but his eyes were giving his visitors a shrewd assessment. "So, we meet again, in my jurisdiction. I am guessing this is not to follow up on the homicide investigation?"

"No," Jake said. "Unfortunately, it's something else." He proceeded to tell the two officers about Falcone and Niles, providing the primary details without offering any backstory or speculation while sharing what they had done so far

"Those two I remember," Colonel Kyrgiakos mused. "Quite the characters. Has this kind of thing occurred with them before?"

Jake felt Remington shift beside him with a little clearing of his throat, but no remarks were made. Jake replied tightly, "Not really," and, even as the words left his mouth, wondered if the colonel was astute enough to see through his obfuscation.

"Well, you have done a lot of what we would do initially, tracking and locating the rental car, trying to locate their phones. Did you contact or make a report with the police in Kardamyla?"

"An associate did," Remington said.

"And he spoke with the rental agency? Kampas, was it?" he asked, referring to the outfit a few doors down from the 44 Bar Coffee Shop.

Jake nodded.

The colonel was writing in a notebook, the lieutenant now standing and looking over his shoulder. "All right, we will coordinate with Kardamyla and check with all of the other stations around the island, also the hospitals and clinics."

Jake was sure Kipnis had already done so but did not let on. He asked, "Do you think this had anything to do with the drone? Could they have gotten into trouble with regulations?"

Lieutenant Skiadaresis spoke up. "I doubt it. Especially not in a remote place like where you say they were. We have lots of recreational drone activity here, especially a lot of video." He smiled lightly. "As for the car incident, I will tell you, getting stuck is not as unbelievable as you might think. It almost happened to me the first time I visited the place."

He paused, considering something. "Has it occurred to you that this might be some kind of road rage thing? Maybe they were being harassed?"

On a subconscious level, Jake had actually wondered the same thing but not voiced it, and now, hearing it from the police officer, prompted him to take it a step further—what if they had been pursued in the same way he had been, in the same subsequent way as he and Remington?

Distracted by this disturbing line of thought, he heard Colonel Kyrgiakos ask, "Can you text me photos of them?"

"Yes." Jake took out his phone. "And I'll also send you images of their passports, which I keep."

"Very good. I assure you, we will do everything we can to locate your friends and keep you apprised of our process."

"Thank you, much appreciated," Jake said.

They stood, hands were shaken again, and the colonel said, "Mr. Tyler…Mr. Remington…I am sorry for your troubles. You seem to be encountering a lot in such a short time and in such a usually peaceful place."

Jake almost said, *Trouble seems to find us everywhere*, but thought better of it. Instead, he commented, "Hopefully this is just some kind of minor mishap."

As they walked back to the Jeep Renegade, the dread that had been creeping into his gut was taking root. Though his instincts, good or bad, were seldom off the mark, he reminded himself that when he'd had these same feelings about Falcone and Niles in Africa, he had been wrong—thankfully, triumphantly wrong. Maybe that would prove to be the case this time, too. For now, he had to lean into that, but he was finding it more and more difficult with each hour that passed.

Waiting as Remington opened the Jeep's rear hatch, the pair of Malinois jumping into the extended space, Jake gazed skyward, ashen clouds drifting and colliding overhead as the breeze kicked up. To himself, he muttered, "Fuck," and then he placed his hands at his temples, feeling a band of pressure building in his head.

44

THEY HAD NO CLEAR concept of the amount of time that had passed since being ambushed on the other side of the alleyway in Kardamyla. This was due to several factors, one being what had been an interminably long, fragmented journey over land, then sea, then land again, and another being that they'd been blindfolded the whole time. But the primary reason for their disorientation was the place where they now found themselves—a dim, iron-barred, concrete-lined cell not much bigger than a garden shed—and the hours that had elapsed without contact from a single person since being impounded.

Eddie Falcone and Curran Niles were seated on a dilapidated wooden bench, wobbly and riddled with splinters, each of their hands tightly cinched together, their ankles bound by rope.

After using the walls to leverage themselves into standing positions and hobbling over to the narrow gateway, they had spent their initial moments shouting and banging against the bars, but the ruckus seemed to go nowhere except into the musty airspace around them, their futile outcries stirring up dust that invoked bouts of coughing.

However many hours earlier, when they had managed to extricate themselves from the stuck Hyundai and come out on the other side of the covered alleyway, four decidedly bellicose-looking men, all armed with assault rifles, stood in their path. They wore mostly identical but ambiguous militaristic garb in a color that fell in between gray and black, matching caps without emblems, tactical vests, kneepads, and gloves;

they also donned balaclavas that obscured most of their faces. Two of the four had immediately stepped forward, barking something in an indeterminate language, and roughly grabbed Falcone and Niles by the arms. The remaining two men locked onto them and the duo was forcibly propelled by means of stumble-walking, dragging, and shoving, to the gray Toyota Grand Highlander. All resistance and protestation on their part was quickly quashed by jabs from the assault guns, gloved fingers threatening trigger action. Their backpacks and duffels were confiscated, pockets of their shorts emptied, hands zip-tied and heads hooded, and then they were pushed into the third-row seating compartment of the vehicle.

Not more than a minute later, the Toyota wobbled as the men climbed into the front and middle sections, their weight hitting the seats, doors thunking heavily shut. Falcone and Niles swayed into each other as the vehicle made a 180-degree turn, straightened, and sped off.

Falcone had mustered his bravado and demanded, "What the hell is this? Who are you?" When he got no response, he asked, "Police? Are you police? What have we done? Are we under arrest?"

At that point, the two men in the middle section had raised up, bent over seatbacks, lifted the hoods of their detainees, and plastered duct tape over their mouths. For the remainder of the twenty-minute drive to the eastern coast, Falcone and Niles heard little more than the drone of the vehicle's engine as it modulated in adjustment to the undulating topography, the other men limiting their exchanges to indiscernible one- or two-word utterances.

When the SUV came to a halt, doors cranked open and there was a shuffle of movement as the four men exited, two of whom grabbed Falcone and Niles and marched them haphazardly over uneven ground, followed by sand. Staggering as their feet scuffed bumps and holes and then sunk into silt, the duo had to be yanked upright several times along the way until being hoisted over the side of the patrol boat like sacks of grain. They were dropped on their haunches, the bottoms of their shorts soaking up water from the deck, and lashed together with a thick strap. Within minutes, they heard and felt the propulsion of the vessel as it buzzed out to sea.

The patrol boat's passage over water was swift at a speed of thirty-five knots and, in fifteen minutes' time, during which their backsides were continually pummeled by the deck, they were docking. Their captors hauled them off the boat, shoved them along a concrete walkway, and then loaded them into the empty cargo hold of some kind of van or truck. Here, they were not strapped in and, for the duration of the overland journey, rolled from side to side and slid front to back across the metal floorboard—which made for a very long and punishing trip to somewhere.

When the transport vehicle finally came to a stop, Falcone and Niles were pulled out and trudged inside a facility, a determination they made from the change in what little light filtered through their head coverings and the more level surface beneath their shoes. Thinking they would at last be enlightened of the reason for their apprehension, they were stupefied to instead be taken directly to the cell. Though their hands and feet remained in restraints, the hoods and duct tape were removed. The man who had done so, his face still cloaked by a balaclava, had turned on heel and departed without saying a word, despite assertive protests from Falcone and Niles.

Now, as they sat in the dirty and cramped confines of the concrete enclosure, the grim reality of their predicament was as vividly frightful as the slow approach of a rollercoaster car to the apex of its erratic course—nowhere to get off the ride and the track about to plunge steeply into nothingness.

Niles said, "We have to get hold of Jake."

Falcone looked at him, almost too dumbstruck for words. "And how do you think we're going to do that, Curran? Do you think we're going to get our phone call? They haven't even told us what we're in here for or, for that matter, *who* they fucking are."

Sheepishly, Niles murmured, "Right."

Falcone continued, "I didn't see any kind of insignias anywhere on them. Did you?"

Niles shook his head. Glancing around, he began to squirm. "Um…how are we supposed to take a piss? I have to go."

Falcone followed his gaze, noting a crooked pipe topped with a rust-encrusted spigot that looked like it had been dry since the Stone Age and, next to it, a hole chipped out of the floor. With a tip of his head, he said, "That would be my guess."

"Okay, well, how are we…?"

They exchanged a look of resignation and took the next fifteen minutes or so going about the awkward and effortful task of helping each other off the bench and into position over the hole, struggling to work the fly-fronts of their respective shorts with the limited dexterity of plasticuffed hands, not to mention the inability to strike an optimal pose with their equally constrained feet. Both eventually managed to relieve themselves, but not without considerable splatter.

When they had made it back to the bench, Niles stated what was now a mostly foregone conclusion. "Don't think this is for a breach of drone regulations, mate."

"No shit."

They fell morosely quiet, and it did not take long in the close, non-ventilated space for the steeped-in grunge and sour odors and stifling heat to permeate. The stone walls and floor reeked of urine and feces and vomit, their own sweat mixing with the stench. Several times, Niles gagged but fought back the growing urge to regurgitate what little sustenance was in his stomach, which was percolating like cooking oatmeal. His pale face was suffused and wet, cheeks blowing.

In an attempt to distract his friend from the queasiness, Falcone said, "Maybe they just stuck us in here until the dude in charge arrives. Then we'll be told what they're holding us for, maybe charge and book us. Ask who they can contact on our behalf."

Niles blew out a breath, winced, and scoffed, "Now who's being daft? You really think that's going to happen?"

Falcone did not reply.

After another passage of silence, Niles asked, "Where do you think we are?"

"Not being able to see anything, I have no idea. Could be another part of Chios, but I doubt it. That was a pretty long way. Could be another island." He paused, pondering. "You know, that patrol boat looked like some kind of official craft…like coast guard or navy."

"Well, that could be encouraging," Niles said, but his expression was void of reciprocal hope. "Blimey, I'm thirsty."

"Me, too, bud, but I don't think we're gonna get any water—or any drinkable water—from that pipe in the ground."

"Probably just puke it up anyway," Niles remarked woefully.

Both leaned their heads back against the dingy wall behind the bench, and seemed to notice the one window in the cell for the first time, not much bigger than a cinder block and set too high to see through. The paltry light it allowed was waning, the dimness inside losing translucency.

"Where *are* we?" Niles asked again.

And then they heard something that at once brought back the electrifying fear that had gripped them with their earlier reality reckoning—a long, melodious vocalization, distant but resonating.

Their heads snapped forward and they looked at each other, eyes bugging in the gloom. Neither spoke for a moment, thoughts and emotions colliding in an onslaught of consternation.

Niles finally blubbered, "Bloody hell, Eddie."

Staring back at him, Falcone said, "Oh my God."

In the expanding darkness of their cell, they listened in stunned silence to the plaintive and distinctive incantation known the world over.

The Call to Prayer.

PART THREE

BRINGING HOME THE BRAVE

45

A BARROOM SETTE SURROUNDED by a crush of people, conversation all but lost in a tsunami of sound, would seem an odd choice for a clandestine rendezvous, yet it was just that for the four seated around it.

A little over forty-eight hours before, after finding the trail to Falcone and Niles essentially cold, Jake and Remington had returned to the dig basecamp, where they met with Caspian Bachman and Shelby Hoskins and then strategized with the *Habari* team; priorities for Jake had profoundly shifted, with Remington's intention to fully support him, so assignments were adjusted accordingly to allow for the potential reallocation of one or more guys in search operations. Networking calls were made to contacts in and associated with the region and, as expected, it was Efron Kipnis whose efforts got results.

Arrangements were made to meet up with one of his sources the following evening in Mykonos, which aligned with Jake's plans to send Callie home, coordinating the flight with their Gulfstream pilot for the next day. There was no longer any equivocation now that his full attention was needed for Falcone and Niles, with the near certainty of quick mobilization that would likely require extended time away. Jake had been in regular touch with Kent Sanborn since Remington had dispatched him to oversee security at their Dominical residence, and he was assured all was well in hand; while he was still wary after the breach, he knew Callie would be more secure there than here from this point on.

That morning, Keanjaho Dmello had flown them back to Chios in the chartered Airbus helicopter and then in the Pilatus PC-12 to the FBO at Mykonos International Airport. They had checked into the neoclassical mansion housing the Semeli Hotel near the hora center, five-star luxury that was a welcome indulgence after the rustic accommodations of the past few weeks in Psara though, under the circumstances, less than enthusiastically so with the collective mood being somber. While Dmello stayed at the airport with the plane, the others had spent the afternoon availing themselves to some rest while they had the opportunity, Remington and Kipnis relaxing in the hotel's lounge bar, then taking a dip in the beautifully designed and landscaped pool.

For Jake and Callie, however, the respite had not been so easy and, while Jake had been mentally preparing himself, the emotions were predictably tougher. As he had cuddled with her on the bed in the hotel's premiere Semeli suite, as lovely as any they'd stayed in over the course of their honeymoon, a serene wash of minimalist white with sunlight streaming through the French doors, he could feel the tremors of an imminent breakdown.

Gently brushing the tears rolling over her cheeks, he said softly, "Talk to me." When she did not say anything, he prompted, "You know it's time for you to go home. I know you want to."

She still said nothing, her eyes overflowing.

"It's been a truly magical time, but it's been a little hard on you, too," he said, thinking of all the bouts of anxiety and panic attacks as she continued to struggle with and suffer from her PTSD, the anaphylactic shock and excruciating pain from the bee sting, the upsetting incidents incurred between unknown males and one especially vindictive female from his past. The trauma of Remington's brush with death and now, Falcone and Niles, potentially the greatest tragedy of all.

"It's time for home, sweetie."

She nodded imperceptibly, her voice barely a whisper as she replied brokenly, "But not without you."

Jake swallowed around the knot forming in his throat, his fingers lightly sifting through the swirls of her hair. "I know, angel. But I would never leave without trying to find Eddie and Curran. And with my focus there, I can't keep you with me or fully ensure your safety. You are always my first priority and then everybody, everything else."

"What do you think has happened with them?"

He sighed glumly. "I don't know, love."

He had held her quietly for several minutes, comforting her with his touch and hoping she'd expend the emotion, surrender to fatigue and allow them a small interval of preservation; neither had slept much since the disappearance and, like her, he'd not been able to rest his worried mind long enough to grab even a catnap. Because he was sure there was a world of trouble ahead.

Ultimately, he'd experienced more of the release he needed, making love to Callie with the breeze blowing in from the veranda, giving his brain at least a short reprieve from the obstacle course of harrowing premises and postulations and transcending them both to the sensual and spiritual and bodily realm that provided a sanctuary of calm. His mouth on hers, he tasted the salt of tears and sweetness of her essence and felt her small hands in his as he moved inside her, wishing the world and all of its impossible problems and indelible nightmares could be reduced to the visceral purity and simplicity in that moment.

Later, they'd shared a subdued meal with Remington and Kipnis in Krama, one of the hotel's two exquisite gourmet restaurants overlooking the pool, dining on the gastronomy of chef Ioannis Parikos, trying to mitigate their stress with artistically plated black angus steak and twelve-hour lamb and seafood in decadent configurations, followed by the confections of *baklava* and sour cherry *mille-feuille* and ice cream. The fine food and elegant atmosphere had helped to atone the underlying tensions of the group, but with each of the men excusing themselves to take calls throughout dinner, the grim pall of the situation ticked up as relentlessly and deliberately as the measure of a doomsday clock.

As they had dined, Jake did his best to conceal his deepening worry for Falcone and Niles, casting loving glances at Callie and giving her hand a squeeze each time she looked at him uneasily. She was also clearly feeling out of place in her frilly white dress, an off-the-shoulder-sleeved eyelet frock that flared from the waist, surrounded by the three sober-faced men uniformly clad in black cargo pants, tees, and button-up overshirts.

Afterward, Jake had taken Callie back to their suite, gotten her as settled as he reasonably could, and rejoined Remington and Kipnis. Then, under the cover of an indigo sky, the three of them had done a thorough canvass of the hotel property and set off on foot, downhill on a cobblestone path from the Semeli along the pedestrian streets weaving into the maze of Little Venice.

The night air was slightly cooler, a stirring wind and the moving shadows of clouds overhead suggesting an impending rainstorm. Making their way past the open-air Theater Lakkas, a stone pit that hosts movies, concerts, and live cultural events, they had traversed the street of Panachrantou, through a collection of other hotels and joining streams of locals and tourists strolling to and from shops and taverns and restaurants. In their black attire, they blended well with the dark, but they maintained a heightened state of alert and situational awareness, watching for suspect individuals or anyone who seemed to replicate their movements. To that end, they had conducted a lengthy SDR—surveillance detection route—splitting off at junctures and maneuvering side alleys and parallel streets, communicating by comms and reconvening as they turned onto Kalogera, a boutique-lined corridor heading west toward the waterfront neighborhood. From there, they had wound their way down Delou to Agiou Dimitriou, which had eventually led them to the establishment where they now congregated.

BAOS COCKTAIL BAR IS among the most popular night hangouts in Mykonos, located right on the waterfront promenade of Little Venice. By day, it is a charming bistro-like lunch spot, with small round tables fancified by white macramé umbrellas and wicker chairs lined up along the outside stone walk and, inside, more tables and lavishly decorated and geometrically arranged sectional seating. But on any given night during the season, every inch of the interior and exterior is packed to capacity.

The place was certainly at or beyond capacity tonight, throngs of exuberant imbibers as tightly gathered as a Mardis Gras blowout.

Lanterns hung from the beamed ceiling, bathing the interior in an amber glow, glasses and bottles highlighted by LED light strips and sparkling across the bar shelves. Energetic music reverberated throughout, loud enough to hinder talking but also providing an ideal deterrent against eavesdropping in the same way the volume of people provided a barrier against interlopers. Which was why this busy, crowded night-spot had been chosen for the linkup; cloak-and-dagger back-alley exchanges were more the stuff of fiction and, in practicality, much riskier for exposure.

When Kipnis had first announced the meet with his source, he'd inferred that he would make the trip solo. Jake and Remington's stated plans to accompany him were met with an unusually demonstrative objection, followed by brooding displeasure. For a man whose expressions were consistently inscrutable and whose emotions rarely surfaced, he'd been visibly sulking up until they had stepped off the plane. Now, looking across the table, Jake understood why.

Kipnis' source was an agent with the *Direction Générale de la Sécurité Extérieure*, or DGSE, the French equivalent of the CIA and Mossad, which was to say, like Kipnis had been, she was a spy. And, observing the body language and chemistry between the two, it was not hard to deduce that they were—or had been—acquainted on more than just a professional level.

Jake cast a stealthy sideways glance to Remington, who smirked and gave a little nod in confirmation of his presumption.

The woman, whose name was Sabine Brisepierre, was tall and alluringly attractive, her neck-length hair cut in a bob style that contoured her jawline. It was pinned on the sides with rhinestone-studded clips, and the café au lait color, in the dim lighting of the bar, was the satiny matte gold of a Christmas ornament and matched the irises of her eyes. Her attire was a fusion of fashion model-chic and tactical badass, making her look as though she'd stepped straight from the screen of a James Bond movie. Like the men, she was clad in black, leather pants stretched taut over long legs, zippered and tucked into knee-high Christian Louboutin boots. Her silky halter tank top was worn loose; if she was carrying, and Jake was fairly certain she was, that would be where her weapon was stashed.

Introductions had been made, with Brisepierre telling them that she and Kipnis had worked a few joint DGSE-Mossad operations together. When she spoke, words rolled off her tongue in the distinctive French way that made even the most banal expressions sound like soft porn, the undertone husky and consonants flowing into vowels. Kipnis' gaze was locked onto her eyes and lips with the hypnotic fix of a cheetah frozen in predatory anticipation.

"Little Venice is full of crowded places for meeting, but I absolutely love Baos," Brisepierre was saying. "It is just too bad we cannot enjoy it properly." She flicked her eyes at Kipnis and reached for the martini in front of her, stirring it with skewered olives and then taking a sip.

Their server brought over another round of drinks and, while the bar's beverage menu was quite extensive, not to mention inventive, featuring cocktails with colorful names like *Mango Dazzle* and *Call Me Doctor* and *Rehab,* they stuck to the more traditional fare each favored—a Tanqueray gin and tonic for Jake, Jack Daniel's for Remington, and Grey Goose martinis for Kipnis and Brisepierre.

"I take it you've been here before?" Jake asked.

"Mykonos, yes, many times," she replied, adding, "and here."

While using the cover of plain sight in a crowded, popular public place was, arguably, a strategic advantage, the packed house could present a significant hurdle in the event a rapid exit became necessary. With that in mind, on arrival, Jake had explored the entire layout and located all the ways in and out; there were almost always private-access doors, particularly in establishments where celebrities and VIPs were prone to make an appearance, and he found those, too. Mostly, it came down to two primary sides—the doorways opening to the village and, opposite, those opening to the sea.

Kipnis bent over the table, signaling a shift from the pleasantries to the critical reason for their huddle. The others did the same, and he said, "I had already been in touch with Sabine for much of the intel pertaining to Ignatkovich."

Brisepierre said, "I am sure you understand that I am limited as to what I can share, even though I have full confidence from your affiliation with Efron."

When she enunciated his name, there was a subtle change of tonal inflection that brought a flush to the Israeli's face, which he tried to hide by taking a swig from his martini and adjusting the position of his wire-frame glasses.

She continued, "I am part of a top-secret op in Cyprus, which involves Syria and Turkey, also a few other countries. When Efron made inquiries about Ignatkovich and let me know what has been going on with you, I told him what I could. Now, given the circumstances, I will tell you a bit more as it might have some bearing on your missing friends."

Jake leaned in closer to make sure he heard every word, the noise from the room making it difficult. The groupings around them were chattering loudly, laughing, some singing along with the music.

"Hearing about the cable tap you discovered confirmed what we have been suspecting. We had reason to believe that he was going to make some kind of power play and, in tracking his yacht and the special purpose vessel associated with it, the theory all along was that he was gathering intelligence."

Jake gripped his arms impatiently, wanting her to get to the point.

"Do you know what for?" Remington asked.

She nodded but did not respond directly. "Ignatkovich has built a legion of Russian dissidents in the region, most notably from Turkey, and has assembled quite the paramilitary force."

"So…he is considered an enemy of the state?" Jake conjectured.

To this, Kipnis nodded. "Yes, but just so it is clear, not in any kind of 'an enemy of my enemy is my friend' kind of way. He is even more extreme than Putin on his worst day."

Brisepierre went on, "Your presence—as Efron indicated to me—has made him feel threatened. Before your arrival, his operation had been mostly unencumbered…except, of course, we were aware and watching."

"Yeah, the last thing he would want is a bunch of American military guys smack in the middle of his AO," Jake said.

"*Exactement*," she said. "So he has been—how do you say it?"

"Fucking with us," Remington supplied.

Brisepierre gave a throaty laugh, again causing spots of color to bloom in Kipnis' complexion. "Yes. Which brings me to some very bad news about your friends, or at least I believe so. You will have to tell me what you think."

Now Jake's eyes fired with an intensity that was almost hostile, an edge to his voice when he said, "Maybe you should have led with that."

Across from him, Brisepierre sucked in a breath and Kipnis downed the rest of his drink, setting his glass on the table with a thud.

If she had been intimidated or taken offense to Jake's statement and tone, it did not show, but her demeanor became more grave as she said, "There was a report, confirmed just before this meeting, that two men have been detained...a Brit and an American."

Jake put a hand to his head and groaned. "Oh God. Where?"

"In Turkey." Before he could ask, she said quickly, "We do not know who or why, and we do not have names."

"A Brit and American," Remington said, "has to be them."

Jake still looked infuriated, so Kipnis explained, "The reason Sabine led with Ignat is because he has deep connections within the ranks of Turkish police, military, and intelligence...he could very well be behind this. It would track."

Jake heaved a sigh. "Okay, well, what are our options here?"

"Not good ones," Kipnis said. "I am sure I don't have to tell you that dealing with the government or consulate, any official channel, is a waste of time."

Thinking of all the exasperating red tape that had thwarted him at every turn while he'd been conducting his search and rescue of Callie in Colombia, Jake muttered, "No shit." He raked a hand agitatedly through his hair. "What can we do?"

Kipnis said, "I will contact Neval," referring to their Turkish fixer. "He can get us a list of detainment centers, prisons, and the like, but working sources and back channels is our best bet. There are hundreds of those places spread all over a massive area, and that does not even take into account the black sites."

Brisepierre pursed her lips, shook her head bleakly. "Turkish detainment and imprisonment of foreign nationals is notorious. As we speak, they have several Americans and dozens of other Westerners, some of whom have been in their custody for many years. More often than not, they are not allowed contact with lawyers or their consulates."

Jake sat back, laboriously thinking, the loud music thumping dully in his head. Leaning forward again, he said, "If this is Ignat, maybe we'll have a better shot at finding them...as in, the devil we know."

"Not as much as we need to, but yeah," Remington agreed.

They all worked on finishing their drinks, Jake addressing Brisepierre. "I'm sorry for snapping at you."

"*De rien*," she replied casually. "It is a stressful situation."

"Yes, but it's more than that. These are my guys, and they mean a great deal to me."

The Frenchwomen caught the sentiment in his voice and said, "I understand." She rolled onto a hip, removing her phone from a pocket and glancing at the screen.

Eying her as she evaluated what he recognized as a text message via the encryption of Signal, Jake saw her expression change. "What is it?"

"There is more intel now. Still no identification and still no confirmed source…but they are being held for espionage."

"Spying?" Jake sputtered.

"The goddamn drone," Remington said.

"This is not good," Kipnis said.

"No, it is not," Brisepierre echoed. "This development brings us back to what I was speaking of. These detainees who have been captured and held for espionage are handled in the same manner as terrorists."

"Does it give us any clue as to who might have them?" Jake asked.

Kipnis shook his head. "Until we find out more, no. It could be any of those mentioned, even special forces, and there is a good chance they will be moved around."

Jake could not hide his anguish. "Fuck."

No one said anything for a few minutes, the festive atmosphere around them only amplifying as the night grew late, but during a fractional break in the music mix, a clatter nearby got Jake's attention.

"Is that thunder?" He took out his iPhone, saying, "I need to check on Callie."

Before he had a chance to clear the lock screen, Remington clutched his arm and said, "Jake." He was looking toward the bar's entrance closest to them, one of the doors on the village side.

Following Remington's gaze, Jake looked up and, in that instant, his head imploded.

46

CURLED UP ON A sofa in their suite, Callie gazed through the adjacent window, which framed a panoramic view now darkened by nightfall, the twinkling lights of town and boats at sea blurred by heavy cloud cover. Glancing around the beautiful accommodation—one of the largest they had occupied to date—the whites and neutral colors of the floors and ceilings and walls and modern furnishings were effective in promoting tranquility, but she was finding it hard to embrace. As the time since Jake's departure lengthened, her recurrent separation anxiety set in and began to heighten.

She got up and paced about the space, feeling the quivers spreading like vibrating wires through her neck and shoulders, her arms and hands, her hips and knees, her ankles and feet, felt the claustrophobic tightness enveloping. In an attempt to slow the escalation and minimize the severity, she did what Jake always told her to do, taking slow, measured breaths, trying to hear his voice in her head. Next, she thought about what she could do to relax. Before leaving, he had suggested she have some wine, maybe listen to some music. Stepping over to the mini fridge, she bent down, opened the door, and scanned the assortment of bottles from the Seméli Estate collection, contemplated one labeled *Oreinos Helios,* a strawberry-colored rosé. Unable to sell herself on the notion, she closed the cooler door and returned to the sofa.

Knowing that she would be on a plane tomorrow, without Jake, brought forth a renewed flow of tears, but she knew being away from him was something she'd have to endure many times in the future—it was part of who he was and the work he did. They'd already had variations of the conversation several times, but it was still hard to accept in the present. Even as she was immersed in the distress of the impending separation, she was also feeling a compensatory sense of relief because, truth be told, she was acutely homesick.

Jake was right, she thought; the honeymoon, though exquisite and enchanting and romantic in all the expected ways, had exceeded anything she could have ever dreamed…but there had also been plenty of unpleasant, even traumatic and painful episodes and incidents throughout, stressful and utterly exhausting to her tenuous defense system. Arranging and plumping the pillows on the sofa, she lay her head back and closed her tearful eyes, trying to reflect on all the wonderful places they'd been, the incredible scenery and delicious food…all the love they'd shared in the luxurious bedrooms from one gorgeous island to the next, with a sparkling sea surrounding in shades of otherworldly blues and greens that could only have come from God's own heavenly reservoir.

But right now, all she could think of, all she yearned for, were the comforts of home in Dominical. The sand on its beaches was not as fine or as pale, the waters not as crystalline, the scenery not so epic. But it was *home*. It was where *her* bed was, the love with Jake in it no less intense or sensual or blissful. She found herself missing Camilla and Jesse and the rest of their household, because they had quickly become family.

Her thoughts turned to Falcone and Niles, who she also cherished dearly and could not bring herself to conjure what might have happened to them. She was really worried and knew Jake was, too; as usual, he'd managed to uphold his stoic disposition for the most part, but as the hours had passed and one day rolled into another, and then another, his inner turmoil became more perceptible.

Deciding to undress for bed, Callie rose shakily and went to the bathroom, to the double vanity where she stood at one of the bowl sinks, avoiding her image in the big mirror and instead reaching beneath the countertop for a washcloth. Feeling lightheaded and queasy, she turned the faucet on. She was looking over the selection of Chopard toiletries and had picked up the cream soap, when she was startled by a robust knocking on one of the suite's exterior doors.

Callie froze, her heart lurching and then pounding in her chest, her joints elasticizing so completely that she needed to lean on the vanity to keep from slipping to the floor. Several moments passed, but the knock was not repeated. Turning gingerly, she attempted to regain control of her mobility and took tentative steps from the bathroom into the sitting area, gazing with consternation toward the pair of doors, one of which let out to an interior hallway, the other to an outside staircase.

Opening either door was not even a consideration; prior to leaving, Jake had adamantly instructed her to, of course, stay inside and, in the unexpected case of someone knocking, to not respond. But as she came within a few feet of the doors, she saw something on the tile floor, a manilla envelope that had been pushed most of the way through the minute gap at the sill. She stood staring, reluctant to touch it, but she finally bent down and picked it up, teetering and almost losing her balance.

She made her way to the sofa, using the backs of chairs and the top of a desk for support, and sat, placing the envelope on a small round coffee table. She lifted her head, closed her eyes, inhaled and exhaled in an attempt to steady her nerves. Then, leaning forward, she looked at the envelope. The first thing she noticed was a folded piece of white paper taped to the outside, on which was computer-generated san serif print that said: URGENT—IMMEDIATE ACTION REQUIRED.

Callie's heart tripped again, her pulse racing, the impact of the words *urgent* and *action* punctuating like staple barbs. Reaching for the note, the palms of her hands damp with perspiration, she removed it from the envelope and, with trembling fingers, unfolded it.

Inside, typed in the same font was: CRITICAL TIME-SENSITIVE INFORMATION ENCLOSED FOR JAKE TYLER, EYES-ONLY. HAND DELIVER IMMEDIATELY.

Callie blinked rapidly, her eyes going to what was printed at the bottom—a warning that served to answer the obvious, peremptory questions that might arise: DO NOT BREAK THE SEAL, DO NOT PASS OFF TO A THIRD PARTY, DO NOT MAKE ANY CONTACT (PERSON-TO-PERSON OR BY ANY ELECTRONIC OR OTHER MEANS OF COMMUNICATION AS DOING SO COULD COMPROMISE THE CONTENTS).

And, finally, in case the critical nature of the envelope's contents or sense of urgency was in doubt, repeated was: HAND DELIVER IMMEDI-ATELY. The words seemed to clot inside her brain. *Hand deliver. Immediately.*

Callie set the piece of paper on top of the envelope with the feather-light touch of an explosive ordinance tech, as though its weight might shift and cause it to disintegrate. Once more, she froze.

And then she spiraled into full-blown panic.

IN THE MINUTES THAT followed, Callie's mind burst into cascading mushrooms of hysteria, each cavalcade blowing up brighter, hotter, and more all-encompassing. Her whole body was racked with shivering, her heart pounding so hard it seemed to be pummeling her rib cage. She was so dizzy she felt as though her head might come off, bringing an erup-tion of nausea. But the worst was the hyperventilating because, of all the acutely physical distress she was experiencing, this was the one thing she found nearly impossible to get under control without Jake's interven-tion. And Jake was not here.

As her lungs labored and the breaths fought for clear, clean flow, des-peration swelled and the whole world tightened, siphoning all the oxygen, blotting everything to black. Just when she was on the brink of going under, from somewhere in a disjointed universe, miraculously, she heard Jake's calm but authoritative voice: *Breathe, Callie...slow, deep breaths. Breathe.*

Her brain and body began to obey by rote and, though her respira-tion was still rapid and forced, she was able to put thoughts together.

The first determination came in the form of an instant denial; the message was directing her to leave the hotel and take the envelope to Jake. She could not do that—not only because he had instructed her not to leave, but because she just could not do it. Jake would get it when he returned. But...

Hand deliver. Immediately.

The next thought was one of transgression, as she debated calling him, which would go against the directive explicitly spelled out. *Do not make any contact.* She pondered what that could possibly jeopardize, and how the source of the information would know if she made a call. But in the unconventional and technologically advanced environment in which Jake operated, she suspected anything was possible and most, if not all of it, well beyond her scope of knowledge.

She sat shivering, as if the room's air-conditioning was on Arctic-blast, her panic level threatening to resurge. Now, as emotions gushed forth, anguished tears formed and streamed, and she thought: *What do I do?* And: *I can't...I can't...I can't.*

Breathing strained again, she drew herself up, rocking on the sofa and softly wailing. *I can't...I can't.*

Time-sensitive. Deliver immediately.

Then, a random thought crash-landed in the muddle—what if the information pertained to the whereabouts of Falcone and Niles? *Oh God, oh God...what do I do?* The tears were coming in torrents, her mind tormented and her motor functions incapacitated. But, in that moment, the answer overrode every physical and mental obstruction with the emotional impetus compelling the decision.

On the chance that the envelope contained something as truly critical as it purported, something possibly of life-or-death consequence to Jake or, perhaps, Falcone and Niles, Callie knew she had to act.

Wiping her tears, she reached to the coffee table for a Post-it note with Jake's handwriting. She picked up her iPhone and navigated to Google Maps.

MINUTES LATER, DESCENDING THE stairs outside the suite, Callie peered out over the illuminated entrance and stone pavers, wondering if the person who had delivered the envelope was somewhere in the shadows, waiting and watching to see if she complied. This made her stop, brace against the stucco wall and gulp, for a few moments fighting the overwhelming urge to quickly retreat to the safety of the suite.

But she took several stabilizing breaths and continued down to ground level, passing the arched hotel entrance, luminous white light and ambient music spilling from the open doorway of the reception area. The lovely young woman at the Krama hostess stand gave her a smile as she stepped from the curb and crossed to the metal railing, beyond which was the pedestrian route into town. Prior to making her exit from the suite, Callie had loaded the directions into her phone; though Jake had instructed her to stay inside, he'd provided the name and number of the place for the meeting…in case of emergency. She supposed this constituted such a case.

For a second time, she debated calling Jake and, for that second time, declined out of the uncertainty of consequence.

Glancing around nervously as she walked, the depth of darkness told her it was later than she'd realized and, checking her phone, she saw that it was after eleven o'clock. She was gripped with another wave of nausea and dizziness, her heart thumping. The streets were well-lit with plenty of people still out, mostly couples casually meandering, none of whom seemed even remotely threatening. Even so, every time she passed a lone man, she kept her distance and hurried on.

Much of the way was on one continuous stretch lined with white-washed buildings and trees, their branches and crowns moving in a stiff breeze with intermittent gusts of wind that swept the skirt of Callie's white dress around her legs. It became increasingly difficult to keep locks of her hair from blowing in front of her eyes, and she moved closer to the exterior walls of the buildings for better shelter. By the time she reached the edge of what was a maze of small hotels and restaurants and shops, minute specs of rain were dotting her face and arms.

All at once, the atmosphere changed as she encountered a convergence of locals and tourists, crisscrossing from intersecting streets and merging onto this primary artery. Now she was surrounded on all sides by bodies, some lingering in front of storefronts or cafés and taverns, some shuffling lackadaisically along, others more aggressively jostling their way through the throngs. The mishmash of dialogue multiplied in volume, music coming and going in random blasts from the bars and restaurants, the spices of late-night Mediterranean cuisine mixing with the grassy smell of rain in the trees. All of which was probably pleasant to most of those around her, but for Callie, it was triggering renewed anxiety and then, panic—particularly when she reached the point where she needed to turn onto another street.

The crowd grew even thicker and she soon found herself in the midst of a confusing labyrinth of feeder corridors. It did not take long before she became disoriented and displaced from the route mapped out on her phone. The rain had also transitioned from a faint drizzle to a more persistent shower, prompting umbrellas to pop open and impede her range of view. Legs like rubber, Callie staggered and stumbled, heart galloping. Her dress was plastered to her torso, hair hanging wetly with rain trailing down her face. Here and there, she stepped into puddles on the cobblestones, splashing her already waterlogged espadrilles.

Blinking in the rain, looking in every direction and not seeing any street signs, Callie realized in horror that she had no idea if she was still on track for her destination. This caused her panic to expand into paralyzing hopelessness and, for several minutes, she fought the overpowering duress to shut down. Finally, convincing herself that not moving at all wasn't going to help her find the way, she resumed walking, pausing frequently to lean against building walls. Her wobbly gait over the slick stone made for slow progress, and she felt close to the point of collapse with each few steps as she traversed one passage after another only to find herself in endless lanes of commerce.

The crowd seemed largely undeterred by the storm as they sauntered along, perusing merchandise displayed in vivid windows and arranged on racks and shelves—hats and shoes and belts, t-shirts and jeans and dresses, postcards and posters and art prints, sunglasses and jewelry and souvenirs, perfumes and candles and cosmetics—bright lights, bold colors, wall-to-wall people and products. The corridors contained doors and windows and stairs, balconies and overhangs, their breadth narrow, sometimes barely wide enough for two-way traffic, and Callie was hemmed in by elbows and shoulders and bumped by inattentive pedestrians.

And, once again, she felt the onset of hyperventilation as the claustrophobic passages closed up around her.

Wedged against a stucco sidewall, she dropped weakly to the wet ground, arms coming up over her head. *I can't do this...I can't...do...it. Got to go back.*

But she could not go back, she knew that. She was totally lost, and visions of her horrific time in the Colombian jungle swam into the margins of her delirium. The sound of her heartbeat was deafening in her ears, the thrum of wilderness buzzing like a hive of bees. *Bees...oh God, bees…*

A cat emerged from the shadows, rubbing its wet fur against her thigh, and she jumped, sending the feline skittering away with a sour yowl. The jolt got her back on her feet, and she took a shaky step. Then another. But each one seemed to go nowhere.

She was on the verge of total breakdown, her mind drowning in cyclonic hysteria, when she took a turn and caught a glimpse of something that gave her reason to keep going—the waterfront. It was some distance away with more masses of people to plow through, but she knew if she could get to the promenade, she would eventually find the bar. Or, at least, it was her best chance.

With every bit of determination and courage she could summon, wheezing and reeling, she staggered forward in the rain, tottering as she was jabbed and joggled by passersby, who probably thought her unsteadiness was due to intoxication.

She had just spotted the sign, the O graphically rendered as the top of a cocktail glass with an olive spear, when the black sky flashed, followed by a deafening boom of thunder that shook the ground. Callie cried out and lurched for one of the open blue doors, pitching forward inside.

47

JAKE LOOKED TOWARD THE bar's town-side entrance, and was beyond blindsided. He was utterly gobsmacked. For an instant he was aberrantly unreactive, his eyes seeing what his brain could not process. And then he bolted from his seat and shoved his way through the gaggles of bar patrons blocking his path.

Callie hung onto the doorframe, the sights and sounds of jaunty people packed tight in a swirling blur of motion in the lantern light, a wave of babel cresting and falling below the bigger tidal sweep of music, blindly seeking the one and only body in the multitude that could pull her up from the sucking pit that felt like quicksand. Whatever weak stream of adrenaline had allowed her to complete the footslog through the stormy night, lost and overwhelmed in an interlocking puzzle of streets, was now completely depleted.

Jake got to Callie just as her legs folded, catching and supporting her with an arm.

His voice unintentionally harsh and strained, he gasped, "Callie?"

She shivered in his arms and he leaned back to study her. Ghostly pale, blond hair hanging in dripping tendrils, her pretty white dress was soaked through and clung to her skin like wet tissue. "Oh, baby," he said softly, brushing hair away from her glazed eyes. When she did not respond, he pulled her close to him, felt her throbbing heart against his chest and, for the first time, took a pointed look around in search of threats. Slowly, he steered her to the group, who were watching in their own wide-eyed astonishment.

Easing her down on the settee, Jake daubed her with some towels provided by their server, and saw the manilla envelope Callie still clutched in one shaky hand. "What is that, love? Is that why you're here?"

Her head quivered in response, and he took it from her, still honed on her face, concerned about the stupor she was in. He put the envelope on his legs momentarily and continued to focus on her, rubbing her arms as he spoke soothingly to regulate her breathing. When some color began to develop and she was more visually conscious, he held the envelope up, asking, "How did you get this, Callie?"

Teeth chattering, she replied, "U-under the d-door."

"Okay."

Callie had reattached the taped note, but the ink was smeared considerably by the rain, making it difficult to read. Though most of the printed letters had bled together, after a minute or two of deciphering the probable words, Jake glanced up and, for the benefit of the others, summarized, "It's an eyes-only, deliver-by-hand"—he stopped in mid-characterization, like a car about to roll through a traffic sign—"wait…it instructs no commo, by phone or otherwise." He glanced at Callie, a cryptic and ill-boding notion forming.

He reached into a pocket of his cargo pants and dug out his Swiss Army knife, flipped the blade open, and slid it along the seam of the damp manilla envelope. Peeled the front and back apart, and saw a single piece of folded white paper, also damp, adhering to the inside. With the tip of his blade and a thumb, he carefully extracted the paper and placed it on the round cocktail table. Used the blade to separate and unfold the two halves.

The others seated opposite him leaned close, all gaping in bewilderment at the exposed sheet. Which was blank.

JAKE'S HEAD SNAPPED TOWARD the entrance where he'd found Callie as she and the others stared at the wet, empty sheet of paper. Her semi-catatonic state broken, Callie stammered, "I don't understand…"

Remington, Kipnis, and his former lover, Sabine Brisepierre, did understand and, even as Jake was making the declaration, they were all scrambling to their feet.

Jake said, "We've been burned," and drew Callie up next to him.

Just as he uttered the words, his statement was confirmed by the appearance of several male figures in not one, but both doorways from the street. The profiles were indistinguishable in the low light, but their rigid postures and stances and the panning swivel of their heads told Jake everything he needed to know—which was they had not come to Baos for drinks and socializing.

"All right," he commanded, "let's go. Back exit." Taking Callie's face in his hands, he said hurriedly, "Baby, I need you to stay right with me, right in front of me. Okay?"

He could not wait for any kind of response, taking her by the hand.

Pushing through the patrons packed between the bar walls, they exited to the waterfront promenade which, despite the rain, was also jammed with people, many at the tables or huddled beneath the shallow overhang. The line of seating left a width of only a few feet to maneuver along the walkway, so Jake kept his hands on Callie, guiding her ahead of him, the others bringing up the rear.

Remington reported over comms, "They're on our six and closing."

Jake reached for the Glock 43 in the back of his waistband and held it at low-ready as he hustled forward.

"How many?" he asked.

Glancing over his shoulder, Remington said, "Four, maybe more. Not sure."

It was still raining, but the storm appeared to be moving out to sea, thunder rumbling more distantly and veins of lightning rippling on the horizon. Wind sloshed waves of water into and sometimes over the cobblestones, making the surface slippery in the darkness, splitting Jake's attention between Callie's movements in front of him and the men somewhere behind them. Twice she lost her footing and almost fell, once flailing toward the sea, Jake grabbing her just in time. The glow of outdoor lighting from tavern cafés helped illuminate the path ahead, but it was a challenge to advance swiftly with couples and larger parties having late snacks and dinners and drinks, many blocking their way taking selfies and bunching for group pictures. No one seemed to notice the pursuit underway or, if they did, pay it much heed.

That all changed when they reached the busy bistro restaurant toward the end of the promenade.

Nice N Easy is a covered, open-air eatery with rows of white tables and chairs that can accommodate up to three hundred and, like Baos, on most days and nights, all of its space is taken up with diners seated, standing, and milling about—as it was tonight. So when the buoyant music broadcasting from speakers was interpolated by the sound of muted pops, not unlike a string of firecrackers, there was a delayed but chain reaction of heads turning toward the noises, at first not sure what they were hearing. But once a few astute individuals guessed correctly, there was a chorus of exclamations and confused utterances, and soon, the crowd became a bedlam of furniture scraping and tumbling over, people running and shouting and screaming.

Remington declared, "The motherfuckers are shooting at us! Son of a bitch!"

Jake replied, "I don't want us returning fire amidst all these civilians, but I also don't want us to get"—he clipped off the rest of his sentence, unsure of how much Callie was grasping—"we've got to lead them away. Head for the windmills."

Just beyond the restaurant was the parking lot surrounding the five iconic landmarks Jake and Callie had seen on the first day of their honeymoon. They were lit up against the dark sky, the site and lot crawling with people, even at the late hour.

When they got to the path leading up to the windmills, Jake turned down the adjacent fork, going southeast past them. As he hurried on, tactical thoughts were racing through his head, tantamount among them how to get Callie to safety. Without their stamina and fitness, she was struggling to keep up and had already expended a lot of mostly adrenaline-fueled energy going from the Semeli to Baos.

Channeling his quandary and deliberation, Remington said, "Jake, get her somewhere out of this. Let Kip, Sabine, and I deal with these goddamn fuckers."

"That's my intention, but you might be outgunned here."

Jake had no sooner spoken the words when shooting began again, this time without the bottleneck of people, the spit of suppressed semiautomatics closer and resonating more distinctly in the vacuity of the street.

Jake twisted around, Glock aimed in front of him, now telling Callie, "Get behind me!"

She was gasping breathlessly, clutching her midriff as running stitches bit, her face stark with terror.

Remington, Kipnis, and ostensibly Brisepierre had already begun returning fire, the reports from their weapons—which were not fitted with suppressors—raucous. Out of the corner of his eye, Jake saw Callie's hands go to her ears.

They were venturing into a less commercialized neighborhood with a few small hotels and businesses that were either closed or closing, passing a deli, a scooter rental place, a hair salon, and a laundromat, their windows dark. If there had been any pedestrians loitering or walking nearby, the racket of the gunfire had sent them fleeing, and Jake realized it might not be long before someone summoned the police. Knowing the shooters would make the same assumption and probably intensify their efforts, he got off a couple of shots and backpedaled, making sure Callie was still behind him. From the opposition's muzzle flashes and the green glow of his Glock's Trijicon night sights, he estimated the shooters were thirty to forty yards away, which was within marginally effective range for ideal conditions. At night, with rain and humidity, targets on the move, that efficacy was reduced but no less potentially lethal, especially if the shooters were pros; from the trajectory and proximity of the shots being fired, Jake had no doubt they were just that.

The three men and Frenchwoman continued retreating, dodging around the corners of buildings where they could, taking defensive shots and zigzagging to make themselves tougher targets. Whenever the others fired, Jake grabbed Callie, shielding her with his body, and took strides to increase their distance. But it was becoming clear they were losing ground, bullets smashing into stucco and stone and, in a few cases, the metal of parked cars. More than one bullet sailed directly over his head or within inches on either side of him, crumbles of concrete and chips of rock spraying the air. The goon squad's aim was improving.

As Jake was pulling Callie into a cutout between two buildings, she fell into him and he lifted her by the waist to help her up.

She looked stunned, her eyes wide, and he asked, "You okay?"

At that moment, Remington, Kipnis, and Brisepierre rushed in behind them. Kipnis said, "We're all about black on ammo and these assholes have apparently reloaded and are still going hot."

Remington said, "Time to lose 'em."

They ducked off the street into another maze of pedestrian passages, maneuvering around buildings and heading back in the direction of Little Venice. After a succession of random turns, Jake spotted the tower of a church up ahead and led them toward it. In front of him, Callie was stumbling weakly, barely remaining upright, so he held out his hand to halt the others. As he did, he heard Remington say from behind, "Jake, you're bleeding. Were you hit?"

Jake looked at his hand, saw smears of blood on his palm, knuckles, and wrist. It was a significant amount, and fresh. He was unsurprised to have not felt anything—he'd been shot before and not immediately felt the impact, only the excruciating pain soon afterward—but, as he took visual inventory of his limbs and torso, he failed to find a telltale wound.

Then he saw Callie, blood welling through a ragged tear inside the off-the-shoulder sleeve of her white dress, trickling down her left arm. Parts of the dress's bodice and skirt were stained in dribbles and big splotches. He could see the glassy fear in her eyes, though totally uncomprehending what had happened.

She was the one who'd been shot.

Oh God…no, no, no.

He fought to keep his spontaneous reaction internalized, but Remington could not contain his own, muttering, "Jesus," under his breath.

In the darkness, Jake could not tell the exact color of the blood which would, to a degree, be a preliminary indication of the wound severity, but he thought it looked somewhat like spilled red wine; that was generally better than bright red, which could mean arterial. He willed himself to believe this was venous but, in any case, it needed to be controlled.

Remington said, "Let's get to that church. We haven't covered much ground since we lost them and I haven't heard any sirens, so they could still be on the hunt." Referencing Callie, he pointlessly added, "And you need to deal with that, see how serious it is."

Jake was already removing the button-up shirt he wore over his tee, wrapping Callie's upper arm and tying it tight. Now, she cried out in pain, and he said, "I'm sorry, baby," pressing his fingers into the location of her brachial artery in an effort to staunch the blood flow.

"Okay, let's go," he said, and they began moving again.

THE DIMINUATIVE CHURCH WAS a Greek orthodox chapel at the back end of a short cobblestone corridor, other whitewashed stucco buildings on one side, a high, stacked rock wall on the other. Below the simple bell tower was a narrow pair of doors painted the color of brick which, luckily for them, were unlocked.

Inside, aged bronze wall sconces lit an empty one-room chamber with two rows of ancient, dark wood pews, polished to a high sheen. The stone floor was dull from wear but spotless, the ceiling high and inset with a round stained-glass panel featuring an archetypical depiction of a sunburst-radiant dove in flight. Other framed panels evenly spaced on parallel walls had similar religious-themed designs of praying hands and crosses and shepherds and floral flourishes. At the rear of the space was a platform with a pulpit and little else.

This chapel, as one of the over twelve hundred places of worship on the island, had been built during the Byzantine era representing familial clans, honoring the Virgin Mary and to celebrate the annual religious festivals known as *panigiri*. Tonight it was as silent and somber as a mausoleum.

Remington bolted the lock on the doors and made a cursory circuit, looking for anything of medical use. He found nothing—no water source, no first aid kit, not even any kind of cloth—and reported the lack thereof to Jake, who was in the process of laying Callie down on one of the pews while maintaining his tight grip on her arm.

Sighing in dismay, he said, "Okay, well, without any medical supplies, I can't do much right now except, hopefully, get the bleeding under control."

Callie had gone limp, fading fast now that they were no longer moving and the distraction of amped-up flight had been eliminated. Speaking to her in soothing tones, Jake decided not to let her know what would have been, at least at this point, obvious to any of them, telling her instead, "We're going to get back to the hotel."

To that end, Remington said, "Yeah, I'm going to call them, see if they'll send a car—not our rental, obviously—to the closest point on the next trafficked street over from here. I certainly don't want us to bring our trouble to their doors, but I can't think of another good option."

Seeing the blood expanding into the fabric of Callie's sleeve around his grip, Jake said, "Agree. Make it happen fast."

Kipnis said, "Even if we lost them or if they bailed on their op, there is a good chance they will be staking out the hotel, possibly have an ambush set up." He sniffed with an air of conquest. "I hit at least one of the bastards."

Making the call to the Semeli, Remington remarked, "Casualties or not, I doubt they'll be giving up."

Unwrapping the blood-soaked shirt from Callie's arm, Jake delicately picked at the tear in her dress and found the source of bleeding—two, as it turned out—an entrance and exit wound, which was actually good news; she had taken a bullet through-and-through. Even better was the incredibly miraculous location. As he tenderly positioned her arm to make the assessment, he observed a dime-size hole and, on the other side, one slightly larger. Both were in what was the only fleshy part of a tiny arm—the underside of her triceps—and, on a petite figure with virtually zero body fat, it was an astoundingly fortuitous best-case scenario. Even so, she'd lost a good amount of blood and he needed to determine the extent of injury. His medical attention was required very quickly, and he had absolutely nothing to work with here.

If Jake had needed to make a concerted effort to tamp down his emotions while resuscitating Remington from the narcotic overdose, with Callie he had to force them into a vault of isolation. Rewrapping his shirt around her arm, making it as tight as he could, he looked up to check his friend's progress on the call to the hotel and registered something or, rather, something that had changed.

"Kip…where's Sabine?" he asked, glancing around the meager chamber and no longer seeing Brisepierre.

The Israeli met his gaze, then looked away evasively, casually replying, "This was a good time to send her off."

"Send her off? Off where?"

"To get her in the clear."

Jake frowned, inwardly chafed. He strongly suspected Brisepierre had been withholding information that could have a bearing on Falcone and Niles, and he'd intended to press her on it at the first opportunity.

Recognizing Jake's grievance, Remington mediated, gesturing with his phone. "The manager is sending a car. I have a pin for the coordinates, and there is one helpful thing in this church…a rear door that leads to the alley, which connects to the street."

WITHIN MINUTES, A MEMBER of the Semeli staff had picked them up from the street just behind the chapel and whisked them back to the hotel. Their luck held; no individual or group was spied as they got into the vehicle and no one appeared to be following as they rode.

Having been apprised of their need for covert entry, the driver turned down a restricted-access alley near the hotel and led them in through a private entrance. In Callie's condition, this was not ideal as there was more walking involved, Jake carrying her in his arms—and there was the possibility that their predators had the passage under surveillance— but entering the hotel at the front would have been considerably riskier. During the short drive from the chapel, Remington had selectively briefed the Semeli manager over the phone, omitting the more egregious details of their ordeal, most notably the shooting. For his part, the manager was instantly and unequivocally committed to tackling the situation.

On arrival, Kipnis took up the task of patrolling the interior of the property while keeping an eye on the exterior wherever he could do so furtively. Remington, with the assistance of staff, gathered their belongings from the suites and packed everything onto a luggage trolley.

Impervious of the late hour, the Semeli manager had been waiting on them in person.

Alessandro Lattanzio was a dapper and naturally genial man whose flecks of gray peppered neatly cut dark hair and a closely trimmed beard and mustache. His youthful energy, engaging deportment, and enthusiasm for his work made a lasting impression on guests, many of whom returned year after year. And tonight, now actually the next morning, he was demonstrating his appeal in spades, not only by being hands-on in the situation without question or judgment, but in going well above and beyond in proffering a solution. Jake knew Lattanzio was well-acquainted with the Keoghs, but he suspected the man was just characteristically gracious and capable.

Escorting Jake to the hotel's on-site medical suite, Lattanzio said, "Please, make full use of the facilities and let me know if there is anything else you need." Referring to the medical bag slung over Jake's shoulder, he added, "I imagine you are quite competent but, again, if you would like me to have our on-call doctor—"

"No, that won't be necessary," Jake replied hastily, setting Callie on an examination table. Taking a quick look around at the impeccably designed and ordered suite, his eyes landed on a glass cabinet. "Actually, if you can access the IVs—fluids and antibiotics—that would be great. But if not—"

Before he could finish the sentence, Lattanzio strode to the cabinet and used a key card to open it. "There you go," he said.

While Jake selected items from his medical kit, he told the manager, "We won't be able to use our rental car…would it be possible to get another?"

"No worries, Mr. Tyler. I have one you can drive to our other property as soon as you are ready. In fact, I will provide a driver if you would like."

"No, we'll drive. That's great." He managed a scant smile. "Thank you for everything. You have been incredible."

The manager gave a courteous bow and took his leave to ensure everything else was being handled.

Turning his full attention to Callie, Jake wasted no time in assessing her pain, preparing a ketamine injection. Having experienced being shot himself, he knew firsthand how it felt, which was like being impaled with a red-hot branding iron, only far worse. And he had a fairly high tolerance for pain—she did not. If the bee sting had been agonizing to her, he could not imagine the threshold this hit. He tried to keep his face expressionless or, at the minimum, compassionate, but seeing her sobbing and shaking uncontrollably, tears flowing freely, made it hard for him to keep his emotions in isolation—so he felt, but did not externalize them.

Injecting the ketamine into the shoulder of her wounded arm, he said, "I know how much it hurts, baby. This will help."

He spent the next ten minutes or so cleaning and thoroughly examining the wound, which was still bleeding. She was recoiling and crying with every touch and, when he probed, as lightly as he possibly could, she writhed in agony. Her vitals were not good but at least mostly stable and, from what he could tell, the loss of blood was probably no more than a few pints—again, not good, but if her condition did not get any worse, he might be able to forego a transfusion, though that would remain to be determined. He was type O and, as a universal donor could do a direct donation, but only when they were secure and had the hours it would take. After conducting an anatomical and neurological check, he was relatively sure she had not sustained bone or nerve damage, which was nothing short of amazing. But when he slipped off the top of her bloodied dress, he found divots for a couple of fragments embedded in her side below the armpit, apparently from the bullet ricocheting off the building they'd been next to. Those would have to come out, but for now his objective was to slow and stop the wound bleeding with a sterile pressure dressing.

He was sorting through his bandages when Remington entered the suite. "We're ready to roll," he said, coming up beside Jake and looking down over Callie, who had begun to drift in and out of consciousness. "She gonna need blood?"

"Don't know," Jake replied.

"Can you do the minimum now and finish the rest on the drive? I don't want to see this fine place and people turn into the OK Corral."

"Yeah, we need to get out of here. I'll just do a temporary wrap."

"Poor little darlin'…I know it hurts like a son of a bitch. How the hell did she get hit? You were all over her."

"Fuck if I know," Jake said, his face betraying the anguish he'd been trying to suppress.

Green eyes fluid with empathy, Remington asked him, "How are *you*, brother?"

A dark frown and shake of the head was the only answer he got. But Remington had a pretty good idea.

48

WITH MORE TIME TO time to process the emotions he'd kept on lockdown, Jake was feeling a *lot*, not the least of which was murderous rage for the man, whoever he was, that had fired the gun with the bullet that had penetrated Callie. He was collaterally eaten up with the frustration of knowing he would probably never get the shooter's identity and therefore never be able to specifically target him and retaliate. But more than all that, he was consummately distraught at having failed the sacred vow he held in the highest order of his being, which was to protect and keep her from harm. Somewhere in that heroic creed, embedded like a splinter in the flesh or a crack in the armor, was the wild card of reality, of things that cannot be controlled. Even conceding this, he had believed in his convictions…and his belief had let him down.

Now, as he lay next to Callie in the bed of their new suite, he was awash in a waterfall of angst and anger, grief and sorrow, and of the same feelings he'd experienced after finding and bringing her home from South America. After she had been viciously violated and he'd realized how close he had come to losing her, as he had hours ago. From a bullet, like the one on the beach in Dominical, that had been meant for him. If it had struck even a millimeter off in almost any location—or, worse, a few inches off—she would have most likely been critically wounded with severe, possibly debilitating injuries…or dead.

He closed his eyes, strangling on the emotions evoked by these thoughts but, again, pushed them down.

Earlier, on departure from the hotel in a late-model, luxury-class Land Rover Defender belonging to the Semeli manager, they had made the twenty-minute drive to the northeast coast of the island. Alessandro Lattanzio had personally seen them off, thoughtfully providing fresh coffee for the men, a blanket and pillows for Callie, and giving his steadfast assurance that they would be completely secure at the Semeli property at Merchia Beach.

A remote and secluded location on a small bay in a stunningly beautiful setting, it had very little in the way of commercial development, only a handful of other resort accommodations nestled around the cove, along with the inevitable church, this one Saint Nicholas, perched atop a rocky protrusion. The Semeli Coast, while designed and built from the same sleek and stylish template, loaded with every luxury and amenity conceivable, is an even more organic and cutting-edge conception; where the town property is light and bright and artistically modern, the coast reimaging is textured with even more natural woods and stone and layered, architectural accents.

During the drive to the property, with Callie in his lap, Jake had hung and initiated the IV fluids, monitoring her vitals, checking the wounds, and rebandaging. Head and arm propped on the pillows, cold pack on her arm, the ketamine had started to produce the palliative effect he'd anticipated, and she'd become calmer.

There had not been much talk, Kipnis making a call and speaking in a tone too low for Jake to hear the conversation—though he was pretty certain it was with Sabine Brisepierre—and Remington checking in with Keanjaho Dmello and Luther Baladur. Dmello, at the airport FBO, reported that he'd not observed any suspect personnel or suspicious activity anywhere near the plane but said he would be extra vigilant and make more meticulous inspections of the Pilatus, inside and out, up until and immediately prior to their return flight to Chios; one of the reasons he had stayed with the plane was to safeguard against sabotage. Baladur, at the Psara basecamp, conveyed that all was status quo with Bachman and MVAA.

Arriving at the other hotel in the predawn hour, they were greeted by a responsive team of staff who had been instructed by Lattanzio to ensure every need was anticipated and every hospitality extended.

Entering their suite, Jake had carried Callie to the big bed and made her as comfortable as possible, stripping off her dress and slipping on a loose-fitting shorty chemise. He'd hung the IV, adding the antibiotics and another small dose of ketamine to the fluids.

Sitting next to her, he had leaned down and lightly kissed her forehead, then straightened up and lifted her nightie, more closely inspecting the punctured skin of her upper side lats muscle. Like her arm, it was an angry red, as if scorched by a blowtorch. Thankfully, by then she'd become sedated enough to remain unaware of what had happened and what was about to. Even so, he said, "Angel, I need you to lay very still for me, okay?"

She'd blinked blearily at him and closed her eyes.

He had reached for a hypodermic with lidocaine, injecting it around the entry wounds. She'd squirmed and whined softly with the sting and burn of the local anesthesia but went quiet as the numbing set in. Next was the painstaking procedure of extracting what turned out to be two fragments. To accomplish this, he'd had to make cuts with a scalpel, poke and pluck with pointed forceps, and close with sutures, all the while carefully monitoring and evaluating the potential need for a transfusion from him. In the end, he decided she was okay without it.

Then, he had poured himself a stiff drink, slumped into a chair, and heaved a breath of relief. The hand gripping the glass of gin shook as he put it to his lips, and he realized just how tense he'd been—not from tending to the gunshot wounds and the extraction procedure, both of which he had plenty of experience with, but because it had been *her*.

Now, as he lay holding her, stroking her skin and feeling every inhale and exhale she made, he felt tears burning behind the lids of his own eyes. She moaned faintly and stirred against him.

"I'm right here, sweetheart," he cooed. "Just rest."

Cradling her close, he could feel the last bastion of his defenses collapsing like a demolished building, thinking about what he'd just had to do…removing pieces of a bullet from the flesh of the one he loved more than anything in the world. In his years on Earth, he'd been hurt in just about every kind of manner—beaten, choked, cut, stabbed, shot, drowned, crushed—and then some. But seeing her hurt was more torturous than anything a human or the universe could do to him.

He closed his eyes again, and this time, did not even try to stop his own tears or the convulsing of his chest, the conjuring of Callie being taken from him just too much.

AS STRESSFUL AND MISERABLE as the night hours had been, in many ways the daylight following was worse. Though Jake kept Callie's physical pain medically controlled, the psychological and emotional was a wholly different challenge. But now, she was beginning to reconstruct the events of the previous evening, which started when she awoke from a predictably terrifying nightmare and dull throbbing in her arm and adjacent side.

He helped her get dressed and led her out to the terrace by the suite's private pool where they reclined on one of the double loungers, the pale aqua water shimmering in the sunlight. Handing her a glass of orange juice, he sipped coffee and watched her as she twisted her head, looking at the bandages with budding distress, then gazing over at him, her face a heartbreaking picture of despair.

He gave her hand a squeeze and said, "It will be all right, love."

"Is it…is it bad?"

Despite his outward composure, he felt his stomach knot and he was sad and angry all over again. A gunshot wound was a bad and ugly thing, but it would eventually heal, this kind much better than others—though none were good. And there would still be scarring, and he knew she would be upset about it, which he hated because she was self-conscious and insecure enough as it was. Then there was the trauma from the event that would be added to the catalogue of existing ones that plagued her.

Talking over the catch in his throat, he replied, "You caught a bullet, but it went through and didn't hit anything vital, like an artery or a bone. A few small pieces from it went into your side, but I got them all out. So, it's not as bad as it could have been, and it should all heal nicely."

She looked at him in wide-eyed horror. "A bullet? Shot?" Her lip began to quiver.

He swallowed thickly. "Yes, love."

Shame seeped into her expression. "Was it…did I…do wrong? I'm sorry…I…"

"No. No, baby. You didn't do anything wrong. It was a trick."

He thought of all she'd had to battle through and overcome to do what she'd done, the trials and fear she had braved to get to him, putting that presumption of unknown consequence above everything, all because of the perception it could impact him in some way.

"So…so I shouldn't have—"

"Well, no," he said slowly, "but you really were incredibly brave."

"Why did it happen?"

Of course, he knew the answer but said, "Nothing for you to worry on." He mustered a thin smile. "We've got some time to rest before we need to leave, so let's just relax."

She looked at him blankly. "Leave?" And then, remembered, her eyes registering more dejection.

"For the airport, sweetie. For you…home."

They were the golden words Callie had been longing to hear for a while now, but appended with *us*. Jake wanted that, too, more than ever, because sending her back to Costa Rica alone meant ceding her aftercare to others, even though they had his complete trust. It was something he would normally have never done after she'd sustained such an injury—he would have preferred to keep her here with him for at least a few more days—but it was just too dangerous. And he had a new mission, and with each hour that passed, it elevated to a greater level of crisis with a higher probability of a disastrous result.

LATE THAT AFTERNOON, WHILE Remington and Kipnis waited with Dmello on the tarmac outside the Mykonos FBO, the Pilatus ready to go, Jake accompanied Callie onto the Gulfstream. They were greeted by the same pilot and crew, all of whom took a few moments to socially reconnect. After getting Callie settled in one of the seats, Jake strode to the forward cabin to speak with the pilot and copilots.

From his seat in the cockpit, Captain Lee Monty said, "Jake, I'm so sorry about what happened to Callie. I can assure you she will be well taken care of. You know she will be treated like a princess anyway, but we'll pay extra close attention with all the care that's needed." He added,

"We have every kind of medical gear and abundant supplies on board."

One of the copilots, Captain Alex Zamora, added, "We're all first aid certified."

"Great, thank you," Jake said, and handed Zamora a pack that he'd been carrying. "Actually, I put this together from my kit. I've got all the bandages and dressings, antibiotics, and pain meds here, along with instructions." He went on to explain the wounds Callie had sustained and outlined the care plan. Each of the three pilots nodded their understanding and Jake left them to prepare for takeoff, returning to Callie.

Looking small in the oversize cream-colored leather seat, she was twisted around to look down the aisle in his direction, her face full of anxiety.

When he got to her, he propped a leg on the polished wood sideboard by the oval window, giving her a reassuring smile. She was wearing a blush-pink spaghetti-strapped midi dress, wrap-tied at the waist and, like so many of hers, floral-printed and enchanting. But this had a different look by way of the necessary accessorizing; the top of her side bandaging could be seen at the V-cut bodice, her arm wrapped in layers of gauze between shoulder and elbow. Gazing at her, his heart swelled with love, but there was also the gulf of sorrow for everything she'd endured on a trip that was supposed to be all romance and happy times. He could only hope she would take away some essence of that.

Leaning down, he took both of her hands in his and looked into eyes glistening with tears she was trying to hold back, sadness deepening. "I wish you were..." She turned her head away.

"I know, sweetie...I know. I wish I was, too." He reached up, nudging her chin toward him. "You will be okay. Just try to relax and enjoy the flight. It will be as nice as the one over." Seeing her unwavering disconsolation, he tried waxing poetic, saying, "Savor some of the sumptuous food and sleep just below the stars..." But his cajolements were lost on her, as there was nothing that could mitigate his impending absence.

Dispensing with the attempted lightness, he asked, "Does anything hurt?"

She seemed to hesitate but shook her head.

"They have everything to take care of you and will make sure you're comfortable, okay?"

She did not respond, her expression changing. He waited patiently and, after a few moments, she asked, "You're going to find Eddie and Curran?"

Solemnly, he said, "I'm going to do my best."

"And then you'll come home?"

"And then I'll come home."

Her eyes held his, desperate to believe the promise that, in brutal honesty, was not one he could ever truly make.

He stood and she glanced up, her voice a whisper as she pleaded, "Please don't go, Jake."

Bending down again, he held her head in his hands and kissed her tenderly, feeling the heartache to the marrow of his bones. "I love you, precious," he said.

"I love you."

With that, he cupped her cheek, smiled cheerlessly, and stepped back for one last look at her. Then he walked slowly through the cabin, his gait stiff and, moments later, exited the aircraft.

TWO HOURS EARLIER, THE drive to the airport had consisted of an elaborate and lengthy SDR, navigating in and out of Mykonos Town, southwest to the settlements of Ornos and Agios Ioannis Diakoftis, then to Psarrou and, finally, to the international airport. At no time did they observe any evidence of a tail, so Kipnis drove Alessandro Lattanzio's Land Rover to the Universal FBO and parked, Jake taking Callie to the Gulfstream, Remington and Kipnis reuniting with Dmello.

Now, as Jake stood watching the G650ER taxi into position on the runway, his heart and mind were wrestling with the turmoil of resignation and letting go. The previous evening's storm had washed the sky clear, the late afternoon blue empty of clouds except for widely scattered airbrushed feather trails. A faint breeze riffled his black hair, dark eyes pensive behind the lenses of his sunglasses.

He felt the presence of Remington come up beside him, neither of them speaking for a few minutes as they watched the jet, engines powering up to a shrill whine and then thrusting forward as it began to gather speed. They continued watching as it raced toward the end of the runway, nose tilting upward, wheels leaving the ground.

All too soon, the Gulfstream with his sweet wife on board was higher in the sky and rapidly shrinking with distance, evaporating into the horizon extending over and beyond the mountains to the north.

Jake did not budge from his spot or look away until Remington placed a hand on his shoulder. "She's going to be safe now, brother."

"Yeah, I know," Jake said wearily, but he was not altogether convinced. It was just his only and best option.

The two of them strode a short distance across the tarmac to the Pilatus PC-12, where Kipnis had already boarded and Dmello was in the cockpit going through his preflight. Jake and Remington climbed the airstairs and took their seats, Remington next to Kipnis and Jake opposite. As Dmello got the plane rolling, Jake removed his Outlaw shades and leveled a flinty gaze at Kipnis.

The Israeli did not avert his eyes, his expression as flat as a glass pane but in no way transparent, though Jake was sure Kipnis knew what was coming.

Arms crossed over his chest, Jake asked bluntly, "What was Sabine not telling us?"

Kipnis cut a look of vexation toward Remington but got no outward support. He clamped his jaw, retreating somewhere within himself and a dilemma mired in accord or duty or, perhaps more of a carnal connective; at the crux of his identity was the unimpeachable ability to keep secrets and to uphold confidences. But he'd come to realize that his professional affiliation and friendship with Remington, when tested as it was now, would need to prevail. Further complicating this particular dilemma was the implied entrustment of historical intimacy that was, if he was being truthful, on an ambiguous tether at best.

When he remained tight-lipped, Jake pressed, "Whatever it is, it fucking nearly got Callie killed, not to mention us. And if it's something possibly connected to Falcone and Niles, I need to know."

Kipnis visibly deflated, blowing out a breath laden with remorse.

Next to him, Remington turned and cocked his head. "Kip?"

Kipnis eyed them both in a way that asserted his integrity while also affirming and fortifying their alliance. He said, "Everything...all of this…is about a massive arms deal between Russia and Turkey."

The significance failed to elicit much reaction from Jake or Remington, Jake querying, "Arms? As in weapons?"

"Weapons, yes," Kipnis replied. "But not what you might be thinking." He glanced back and forth between them again. "Missiles. Hypersonic missiles." When neither Jake or Remington immediately responded, he continued, "Her…the intel supports the premise that Ignatkovich's operation of cable tapping was with the objective to intercept specifics, including location, of the deal. It has been long rumored but without much verifiable intelligence, and of great concern to NATO, which has been adamant in its stance opposing any kind of deal."

Now, both Jake and Remington were nodding, acknowledging their familiarity with the political discord.

Kipnis went on. "Ignat could be the fuse on the powder keg, because his coalition with the Turkish regime is hazy, but his intent to avenge Putin is thought to be of epic proportions. So you can see why this pursuit would be deeply troublesome." He paused, inhaled heavily. "And why he would be hellbent on taking out anything or anybody standing in his way of not only becoming a global baron of power but also bringing humiliation and defeat to Putin."

49

THREE DAYS EARLIER, AS JAKE and Remington were conducting their fruitless search in Chios, Falcone and Niles had watched haggardly from the confines of their chamber as the first finger of light stole through the small square gap at the top of the concrete wall behind them. After hearing the first Call to Prayer late the previous afternoon, there had been four more instances, the most recent finishing moments ago. With the dissipation of darkness came the scuttling of cockroaches and a couple of rats, the former nearly the size of the latter. Neither man had slept, soreness from the rough transport of the day before entrenched in muscle and bone. Their mouths and throats were parched from dehydration, stomachs griping from hunger, though neither felt a hankering for food.

They did thirst mightily for water, but a few more hours of daylight passed before a single drop hit their tongues.

Groaning against Falcone's shoulder, Niles croaked, "Well, this establishment won't be getting a favorable Yelp review from me."

There was no response from Falcone, but soon after the remark, the sounds of shuffling could be heard and a pair of burly men appeared at the cell bars. They were dressed head to toe in the same mostly black clothing as the others, including balaclavas, their eyes as flat and hard as hockey pucks; they were also similarly equipped with assault weapons.

The iron gate was opened, Falcone and Niles yanked from the wooden bench and frog-walked down a narrow, unlit corridor. They were pushed into a chamber not much larger than the cell and shoved to metal chairs on one side of a table made of rough-hewn lumber. A chair on the opposite side remained unoccupied for perhaps fifteen or twenty minutes, but during that time one of the guardsmen deposited bottles of water, which they immediately grabbed and fumbled with their zip-tied hands to uncap and guzzle.

The rapid consumption was almost regurgitated by both but, after fighting their gag reflexes, they managed to quell the uprising.

The next man who had entered the space was clearly, as Falcone had prognosticated, the "dude in charge," a heavyset figure aged somewhere in the north fifties or older as the fleshy creases in his face and ash gray hair and mustache suggested. His attire more closely resembled a uni-form, fitted slacks and shirt in a truer shade of black, head uncovered, an indecipherable emblem patch over a pocket. Taking his seat across from Falcone and Niles, he placed a file folder, spiral notebook, and a ballpoint pen on the table. Leveled a deadpan look at the two of them and said nothing.

"Right then," Niles blurted, drawing a sharp head pivot and wild-eyed glare from Falcone. "This is some kind of misunderstanding, mate, and I'm sure we can get it all sorted, but something here's a bit wonky. We just—"

With his ankles constrained, Falcone was unable to kick him, so he leaned as far sideways as possible and hissed under his breath, "Curran, shut up!"

Niles closed his mouth with an abrupt snap, spots of color rising in his pale cheeks, eyelashes blinking rapidly and, for a moment, Falcone thought his friend might throw up. But Niles recovered, manifesting an expression of penitence.

The man seated on the other side of the table continued to stare wordlessly at them with overt hostility, provoking another injudicious outburst from Niles, which was probably the intent.

"What are we doing here?" Niles demanded. "Where are we?"

Beside him, Falcone muttered, "Curran, for the love of God, shut the fuck up."

Again, Niles went quiet, nervously clenching and unclenching his empty water bottle, the crackling sound it made loud in the void.

Several minutes of tension-filled silence passed, and then the man finally spoke, his voice guttural and heavily accented. "Who are you?"

"Why the bloody hell would you ask that?" Niles snorted. "You have our passports."

Falcone let out a noise that resembled a growl, again berating, "Shut up, Curran."

The man's inimical expression and tone did not change. "I ask again…who are you? What is your objective?"

This time, Niles bit back his impulse to respond, casting Falcone a frustrated and confused glance. But now, it was Falcone who spoke up, trying to project aplomb. "Are we under arrest? What are the charges?"

The man retorted, "I am the one asking the questions, and I asked who are you."

Falcone's attempt at civility cracked apart, anger furrowing in his face. "We were snatched and brought…wherever the hell this is…without any explanation. We're not telling you shit until you tell us why."

This got no response, just the sustained glower. A moment later, the man slid his notebook and file from the table top, rose from his chair with a grunt, and exited.

Falcone and Niles looked at each other incredulously, Niles blustering, "What the bloody fuck?"

The two armed thugs, who had been standing at guard rest behind the uniformed man, marched them back to the cell where, thankfully, the restraints were cut off their hands and feet. A bucket was plopped on the floor and they were given another bottle of water each and a crumpled brown bag containing two bread rounds that were as dense and dry as blocks of wood.

Niles took one of the pieces of bread, fingered it suspiciously, scowling at the tough texture, sniffed, then returned it to the bag. He looked at Falcone. "Why'd you tell me to shut it, when you—"

"Yeah, yeah, I shouldn't have said anything, either, but he pissed me off. Look. Something is obviously not on the level here, no doubt about that. This is not a police station and those dudes are not cops. I mean, the guy in there had a patch on his uniform that I couldn't make out, but definitely not cops…at least not traditional ones. And you were right about the passports. Asking us who we are is not a good sign—makes me think our identities don't mean shit to them."

Rubbing the indentations from the zip ties that had been cinched around his wrists, Niles asked, "So why do you think they're holding us?"

"Spying, probably. The drone."

"Lots of people fly drones!"

"That's all I can think of."

"Oh bloody hell," Niles bemoaned. "Can't we just tell them we—"

"No," Falcone snapped. "Seriously, Curran. Remember what Jake has told us. We say nothing. You hear me? Nothing."

"Right," Niles said sullenly.

"They aren't going to believe us, anyway."

"D'ya think Jake's looking for us by now?"

Falcone gave Niles' leg a pat. "I'm sure he is."

They sat quietly for a few minutes, nursing sips of water. A glimmer of insight came into Niles' eyes. In the dank chamber, they were the washed-out color of putty. He asked, "Do you think those birds had something to do with this?"

"That thought has crossed my mind more than once," Falcone replied disdainfully. "Even if they had nothing to do with this, they were up to more than fucking."

Niles stood up from the bench, paced around, and retook his seat. "So, what now, mate?"

Falcone shrugged with a ragged sigh. "Don't know, bud." He glanced over to the bucket in the corner by the rusted pipe. "But doesn't look like we're going anywhere anytime soon."

AS IT TURNED OUT, Falcone was wrong on that assumption, but before leaving what they would find out was an exceedingly hospitable circumstance by comparison, their local hosts held a number of additional question-and-answer sessions. Initially, they were again restrained and marched from the cell to the barren chamber, seated together, and confronted by the uniformed man presumably in charge. His line of inquiry did not change much as he continued to demand who they were and what their intention was. At one point, he modified his approach slightly, asking, "What are your real names?"

Falcone and Niles held fast to their conviction, and said nothing.

Likewise, they were told nothing, and the sessions ended abruptly.

The fourth time they were taken for questioning, after another long and virtually sleepless night, they immediately knew the inquisition was about to take a turn in a less than pleasant direction when they were bound to their chairs with rope. The wood table had been removed and, instead of the older superior, they found themselves only in the company of the guardsmen—one who repeated the same questions and two others who attempted to incentivize answers.

After the opening round went nowhere, in accented and broken English, the masked questioner said, "I ask one more time, polite. You will want to give answer."

Falcone cut a glance at Niles, who had turned as pale as candle wax, his arms and legs twitching nervously. When he caught his friend's eye, Falcone gave him a look that he hoped conveyed strength. Since their association with Jake, the duo had been through a lot of austerity and adversity together—which had included a number of perilous predicaments, many resulting in injury—but Falcone now suspected they were about to be tested at another level.

Much to Falcone's horror, Niles became the first subject of the shift to physical provocation. Niles was by no means unmanly, but Falcone knew that the Brit's more refined features, hair, and fashion sense, coupled with the jittery demeanor, had made him the easy choice for an opening round.

One of the thugs grabbed Niles' chair, dragged it over the concrete floor, and slung it and Niles into a wall. It slammed against the stone and teetered forward, almost tipping over from the force. On impact, Niles emitted a heaving gasp, breath trapped in his lungs, his head lolling forward and back as if on a coiled spring.

Pitching in his own chair, Falcone shouted, "Hey! Asshole! Cut me loose and we'll have a real fucking fight."

That caused the two designated enforcers to turn their attention from Niles to Falcone, which was what Falcone wanted.

Niles shook his head frantically, wheezing, "No!"

The first guy swung around with a leg kick and sent Niles' chair toppling sideways to the ground, stomping an arm and shoulder with a booted foot. Niles cried out in pain, wailing again, "No!"

But now the two guardsmen were focused on Falcone, one holding his chair while the other smacked him from both sides of the face. Red welts appeared almost instantly. Through the material of his balaclava, the attacker sneered, "This you want? Yeah? This you want?" And smacked him again, and again.

The blows hurt but were nothing like being hit with a fist, which followed—square, solid shots to the jaws. Without being able to maneuver, these had a more stunning effect, but Falcone gritted his teeth and kept up an indomitable front. His unwillingness to show concession or subsidence incited them to escalate to elbow strikes and kicks.

But, at least for this installment, there seemed to be some kind of set limit to the punishment, so the assault was halted after a few minutes, the questioner telling the other two guardsmen, *"Onları geri götür."*

Falcone was fairly certain the language was not Greek, thinking maybe Turkish, and had a spontaneous new thought. He repeated what Niles had said the day before, "You have our passports," but also added, "you have our phones."

From the chair that had been righted next to him, Niles' head bobbed up, his eyes widening in bafflement.

If there was any reaction from the thugs visible in their eyes—the only facial feature not obscured by their head covers—it was indiscernible. The guardsmen who had brought them into the chamber removed the ropes, yanked them up, and marched them out. Wrist and ankle flexicuffs were cut, bottles of water tossed, and they were left alone in the cell.

When the guardsmen had retreated, both took some time to run hands over their faces, limbs, and torsos, assessing the degree of battery. Niles slurped from his water bottle, hand shaking as he held it up. He coughed, and a spittle of blood expelled from his mouth. "Why did you say that about our mobiles?" he wanted to know. "They will see our contacts and pictures and—"

Falcone was wiping dribbles of blood from around his own mouth. "I just had an idea, but if they're smart, they'll see through it."

Niles looked at him, uncomprehending. "See through what?"

"Think about it. If they switch the phones on..."

It took Niles a moment, but enlightenment dawned. "Jake, or rather Kip, could track them, get this location."

Falcone touched a finger to the tip of his nose, smiled lightly, and winced at the sting. Turning to appraise Niles, who had some lacerations on his face, scrapes on the exposed skin of his arms and legs, and the discoloration of bruises already forming all over, Falcone asked, "Anything broken?"

Niles rolled the shoulder and arm that had taken the boot, and shook his head.

"How bad?"

Niles shrugged but inhaled unevenly, his eyes moistening with emotion. "I'd say a tad better than you."

THEIR CAPTORS HAD APPARENTLY not taken the bait Falcone teased with the phone mention. Since both of their devices were secured by face ID, he'd been expecting a guardsman to appear with the phones and brandish them for unlocking, but that did not happen. He concluded that either they recognized the risk of revealing their GPS location or, possibly, the devices or SIM cards had already been destroyed. Ultimately, his ruse would have been only marginally helpful for tracking purposes because, on the third day, Falcone and Niles were moved.

Shortly after hearing the Call to Prayer occurring before dawn, they were restrained, this time with their mouths duct-taped and their heads hooded. They were pushed along the empty corridor in silence and then were surprised to feel the slightly cooler fresh air of the outside. They were then shoved into the empty cargo space of what seemed to be the same transport vehicle that had brought them to the outpost.

After the battering they had sustained the day before, the rough-and-tumble trip was even more miserable, taking about two hours along a route with the consistency of surface and speed that suggested a major highway. When the vehicle came to a stop, they were unloaded, the rear doors slammed shut with a heavy clunk.

Almost instantly, they knew where they were by the sounds of rumbling engines, whistling and hissing, and deafening roars.

They had been brought to an airport.

Sight and speech occluded, Falcone wobbled in his steps until he bumped into Niles, who acknowledged a shared alarm with a strangled murmur from behind the tape over his mouth.

They were walked a short distance over asphalt and marched up a ramp, their footfalls clanking on metal. Next, they were dropped into pouches of webbing strung to a sidewall and further restrained by straps. The space around them had the cavernous sound and sensation of a wind tunnel, the noise of which quickly began to rise to a thunderous clamor, accompanied by a piercing whistle and sonorous vibration that resonated in their bones. Very soon afterward came the rocket rush of powerful speed and the disorienting displacement of gravity.

As the high-winged gunmetal-gray CASA CN-235 took flight, Çiğli Air Base and the surrounding parcels of land and townships shrinking below, Falcone and Niles were gripped with a magnified sense of doom.

The real nightmare was about to begin.

50

A FEW THOUSAND MILES over the Atlantic, not quite the halfway point of the flight, Callie was in the familiar throes of a sleeping nightmare.

It had taken the better part of the first hour or so on the plane for her to achieve any degree of composure, her body tense and stomach queasy. The crew had gone out of their way in showering her with attention, inquiring about her state of well-being, frequently offering her food and drink—which she had mostly declined, sipping the water and juice the flight attendant continually brought to keep her hydrated. Even more constantly, they checked on the status of her pain. Jake had been emphatic in making that stipulation to the pilots and flight attendant and equally so in his plea to Callie to be totally forthcoming and not wait to be asked, urging her to let them know if she experienced anything more than mild discomfort. He had transitioned her to heavy-strength acetaminophen and NSAIDs but told her the supplies he'd provided included the narcotics if needed. Truthfully, she was hurting, her arm and side throbbing dully, but the more potent pain medication made her feel woozy in a way that was somewhat disorienting.

Despite her attempts to keep the unease and soreness to herself, the astute observations of flight attendant, Tabitha Radecki, had resulted in a gentle query and Callie's reluctant acceptance of a codeine tablet. Not long afterward, with the opiate sinuously curling its way through her system, she'd drifted off to sleep, and demons from the crucible of terrors that seemed to always lay in wait within the recesses of her mind resurrected in vividly hallucinatory fashion—now, with more than a few new ones.

Perhaps subconsciously triggered by the weightlessness of the jet's smooth ride or the soft, somnolent hush of its engines, a deeply repressed memory had unfurled to open the horror show.

When she'd been abducted and taken from Costa Rica to South America, she had been on a plane not unlike this one, but it was something she'd not remembered as she was similarly adrift in a sedative haze, trapped beneath a fog through which every sight and sound was as blurred and colorless as rain streaming on glass. Now, sinking into her frightening dream state, the power of the narcotic luring her to a much deeper dimension than her sleep typically allowed her to go, Callie was seeing fuzzy outlines of the men, fractals of faces swimming in and out of focus…dark hair, dark eyes, swarthy complexions…hearing echoes of incoherent gibberish and laughter…feeling and not feeling hands on her, hands and fingers crawling over her skin like spiders. And she was completely paralyzed, panicked cries lodged in her throat like wads of cotton.

And then she was violently spun from the suffocation of that aberration into a stark black void filled with an unrelenting barrage of gunfire that came from every direction, fire bursts of orange exploding in the darkness like Roman candles. She was in Jake's arms and he was running through the jungle like his life—their lives—depended on it. He carried her and ran…far through endless blackness broken up by the deafening noise and flashes of fire, thrashing through tall grass and low-hanging vines and outstretched limbs, over stumps and grounded trees…and then hurtling over the edge of the world into a bottomless cavern.

The gunfire rattled into the attack of the night before, a staccato hailstorm of bullets pelleting from behind…and then the hot ember that soldered into her with a pain so searing it took her breath away. Next, in a disconnected sequence, she was lurching and staggering from one alleyway to the next, each becoming darker and narrower and all leading into crowds of people that shuffled aimlessly like packs of the Walking Dead. Blood as red as ripe cherries gushed and soaked into the fabric of her dress until it was no longer white…blood dripping from the hem and mingling with the rain, pooling in crimson puddles. The shooting was ongoing, seemingly closer and getting louder but, oddly, of no matter to those surrounding her. After clawing her way through the sluggish morass of bodies, she ducked into the doorway of a bar, its interior strobing waves of colored lights, dancing patrons writhing and bouncing to music that blared over the gunfire.

She was swept into the masses and the room spun, her feet leaving the floor, and she was gazing up into a dizzying swirl of red and pink and purple and blue…and into the face of the ravishing woman from Amorgos, her olive skin glistening in the rainbow lights, long, lustrous hair flowing like a fountain of dark chocolate. A sneer formed around lips so plump they appeared to be swollen, the tip of her tongue poking between them in derision.

And then, the woman was taunting, speaking in Greek, inches from Callie…her breath as heated as a flame, her perfume permeating the air…and from somewhere in the vertigo periphery, another face appeared next to the woman's. A man's face…a face she'd seen before.

Callie cried out—or, at least, in her mind she did.

"MRS. TYLER…CALLIE…"

A concerned but polite voice, a woman's, but not that of the woman from Amorgos. Distant and then close.

Callie gasped and flailed, breathing rapidly, grimacing as her injured arm brushed against the back of the cream-colored sofa. It took her several moments to become oriented, recalling the lovely flight attendant plumping pillows and draping a blanket over her. Now, Tabitha Radecki was bent down, her expression full of compassion. "Bad dream?" she asked.

Easing herself up, Callie exhaled and said, "I think maybe I shouldn't have taken that…"

Radecki offered her a reassuring smile. "Oh, sweetheart, you were in pain, so yes. Your husband was quite adamant in his instructions about pain management. But you haven't had anything to eat, and it would probably be better with food…what would you like?"

Callie shook her head glumly. "No…thank you. I'm not hungry."

"I bet you ate a *lot* of seafood in Greece," Radecki said. "Why don't I get you some good old-fashioned chicken soup? Honestly, we have some of the best I've had, the kind with the fat egg noodles and chunks of carrots and celery."

She caught a glimmer of wavering in Callie's eyes and said, "I'll bring that for you." And she was off to the galley, her tailored uniform skirt moving against long, toned thighs.

Callie returned to the seat she'd occupied earlier, where Radecki had already set the table with china and cutlery and linens, an arrangement of fresh flowers in a Waterford crystal vase. Peering through the big oval window next to her, Callie gazed out over the roll of clouds, tinted tangerine by late-day sun. Checking the screen of her iPhone, she saw that the updated time was approaching 5 PM, hence the threshold of dusk, but in the Greek Islands it would be almost nine o'clock in the evening. Flying back across the time zones, their arrival in Costa Rica would be a whopping nine hours behind Greece.

The calculations were confusing and she was not entirely sure she had it right, but one thing she did know; there were roughly seven more hours of flying time and, even with the brief—and disturbing—nap, she was growing more fatigued by the minute. The thought of falling asleep again and returning to that horrorscape filled her with dread.

She looked up as Tabitha Radecki set a silver serving tray on the table in front of her and placed a steaming bowl of soup on the china dinner plate, along with salad and a basket of rolls. The flight attendant poured Perrier into a glass and smiled pleasantly, asking, "What do you think? Am I missing anything?"

Callie thought, *Jake…Jake is missing*, and felt another ache that, in some ways, was more painful than the ones caused by her wounds. But she said, "No, this is really nice. Thank you."

When Radecki had retreated, Callie contemplated the soup, which truly did look and smell wonderful, picked up her spoon and slowly wove it around the noodles and vegetables. Removed it and set it delicately on the plate, a tear drizzling from her eye.

Once again glancing through the window, she watched the clouds glide like floes of foam, interspersed with apertures showing the deep blue Atlantic forty-five thousand feet below. She was so very tired, and it was such a long way yet; staying awake was going to be a monumental struggle. Her thoughts turned to the events leading up to the departure. She still did not understand what had happened the previous night or why, or who the men were, but she'd figured out that by taking the envelope to Jake, she had led them to him, and even though he insisted she'd done nothing wrong, she knew her action could have gotten him killed. Now, a wellspring of tears were threatening to stream, her heart hot with that different kind of hurt that no pain medication could relieve.

The episode in Mykonos, along with the near-miss shooting in Dominical on the day of their wedding, had also directly exposed her to the harsh reality of the dangers inherent to him and the work he did. While he had discussed it with her, before and especially after the shot on the beach, being hit herself put a whole new and glaring light on what was possible. But while it was terrifying to think of what other jeopardy the future with him might hold, being without him was more terrifying.

Gazing over the dreamy drift of clouds, Callie tried to clear her mind of distress and dread, visualizing home and the time when they'd be there, safely together.

IT WAS EIGHT PM local time when the Gulfstream landed in San José, the new moon faintly visible in the evening sky. After the customs and immigration process was completed onboard, Captain Lee Monty escorted Callie down the airstairs, walking with her to Jake's Jeep Rubicon, which was parked on the tarmac nearby. Standing beside the SUV were Jesse Segura and Camilla Márquez, both smiling as the two approached. When they were within a few yards, the housekeeper bounded over and scooped Callie into an effusive hug, causing Callie to emit a soft wail.

Mortified, Camilla murmured, *"Dios mío, mija!* Your injury…I hurt you!" Her face filled with concern as she loosened her embrace to assess Callie, who was trying to assure the housekeeper that she was fine, despite the pain radiating from arm to side.

But the smile Callie gave Camilla and Segura came freely with the elation she felt on seeing them, tears that spontaneously sprang from the inflamed soreness turning to those of joyful emotion. "I'm so glad to be home," she said.

"We are also glad," Segura said, beaming.

Like Camilla, he was attired and groomed in much the same way as he had been for the wedding, wearing pressed slacks and collared shirt in lieu of his usual jeans or chinos and tees or polos. The housekeeper had on a fashionable dress, belted at the waist and brightly colored, a flowered comb tucked in her thick curls. They had both clearly dressed up in a reflection of their enthusiasm for the occasion.

Segura stepped aside with Captain Monty, the two conferring while Callie's bags were loaded into the Jeep. Then he slid in behind the wheel of the SUV, gave a final wave to the pilot, and followed the Universal van to the exit.

ON ENTERING THE GAT for Juan Santamaría, the general aviation terminal which housed the Universal FBO, Captain Lee Monty strode into the private lounge to wait for his crew, who were finishing their post-flight on the aircraft. Though the flying time had been shared with the two copilots, the trip had been a long one and he was looking forward to a bit of downtime in San José.

He went to the refreshment station and made himself a cup of hot tea, then took a seat in a leather chair, reaching into an outer pocket of his Briggs & Riley rolling bag for a printout of travel accommodations. As always, the Keoghs'—Amelia Keogh's—travel coordinator had booked them into a five-star hotel, the InterContinental at the Multiplaza Mall, located in the heart of Escazú. He had stayed there before and was looking forward to visiting some of the high-end shops but, in the short term, a great meal, a luxurious night's sleep, and possibly some spa time. He was also anticipating a few days of sightseeing, something he took advantage of whenever he could and, with the wide diversity of world destinations that made up the business and leisure travel of the Keoghs, it was a perk he'd enjoyed with great frequency.

Absorbed in his thoughts, he had barely noted the presence of another pilot in the crew lounge, seated across the room from him. Rubbing his tired eyes, Monty slipped the paperwork back into his bag and took a sip of his tea.

"Good flight?"

Monty looked over to acknowledge the other pilot who, by the inflection of his voice and dark features, appeared to be a local or, at least of Latin descent. He wore a standard pilot's uniform comprised of white, epaulette-shouldered shirt, black necktie, and creased black slacks, jacket draped over the arm of his chair. His eyes were shaded by sunglasses, which Monty found odd given the time of evening and interior setting, and that was not the only thing that struck him as somewhat off-kilter. Though not necessarily taboo, the man's hair was on the longish side, slicked with gel and pulled into a twist behind his head, and Monty could see tattoo ink partially visible below the bottoms of his shirt's short sleeves. Most airlines, commercial and private, actually allowed their personnel to have tattoos, provided they were covered; by those standards, a long-sleeved uniform shirt would have been in order.

Lee Monty, as an individual, was naturally warm and engaging, congenial even with most strangers; Lee Monty, in his professional capacity as captain, was more cautiously circumspect. As he was here, something about this pilot just not sitting well for a reason he could not yet pinpoint.

Nodding to the man, Monty replied, "Yes…you?"

Showing a set of gleaming white teeth, the man said, "I am waiting on my plane."

Plane, thought Monty, *not aircraft*. "What are you flying?" he asked.

"Cessna Citation."

Again, Monty nodded but said nothing, sipping his tea. He nudged strands of blond hair back from his forehead and peered down the hallway toward the access doors, looking for his crew.

"Not a Gulfstream, but a nice ride," the man commented.

This remark immediately jangled an admonitory nerve. It was dark, and much of the ramp was not visible from the interior of the FBO. And, access was restricted, even to those authorized. *So how the hell did he know I came in with a Gulfstream?* Pondering that, Monty supposed it was possible the man overheard one of the handlers mention it, but now his suspicions were mounting.

It was not good form for pilots—particularly those who flew in the private sector—to discuss specifics about their aircraft, certainly not about their itineraries and, no matter who or what enterprise they worked for, all flight personnel were under strict non-disclosure agreements. But Lee Monty decided to push the envelope in the way of a test, asking, "You like those turbojets?"

The man cocked his head, as if sensing the challenge, possibly reviewing stored data in his head, then replied, "I think you mean turbo*fans*, yes?"

"Right, that's right…the Citations have turbofans." Lee Monty stood, dropped his cardboard cup into a trash cannister, and reached for the handle of his rolling bag. He could see his two copilots and flight attendant coming through the glass doors.

"So, where did you fly in from? Just the one passenger on that big plane? Must be some kind of special VIP," the man remarked. Still displaying the toothy, disingenuous grin.

Captain Lee Monty crossed to within a few feet, regarding him with reproach but refraining from saying anything—because it wouldn't be so nice. As he continued past to meet his colleagues, he heard the man mumble, "*Buenas noches, amigo.*"

At the reception desk, Monty let the Universal attendant know they were ready for their transport. Then he said, "That pilot in the lounge…do you happen to know who he's with?"

The young woman got up from her seat, came around the desk and strolled down the short hallway. When she returned, she responded, "There's no one in there at the moment."

EARLIER THAT EVENING, THE man in the pilot's uniform had casually sauntered into the Universal FBO and, looking every bit the part he had assumed, was unbothered by anyone. It had been busier then, staff engaged with passengers and other airport personnel, so he'd had plenty of time and opportunity to observe. They ran a tight operation, security protocols in place and followed consistently, but there was always a loophole or a vulnerability or, more often, a corruptible human. And thus, it had been that human—one of the younger and probably less experienced ground handlers, a baggage attendant—who had become his liaison. It hadn't even cost him that much.

While he'd cooled his heels in the comfort of the crew lounge, the handler had sent him texts with the arrival of the jet, which he then learned was a Gulfstream, along with images of the pilot and lone passenger. He already knew that she would be greeted and picked up by the lifeguard property manager and housekeeper in Jake Tyler's Jeep Rubicon. What he had not known was if Jake Tyler would also be on that plane.

And now he knew.

The men Tyler had put in place at his property about two weeks ago were something of a setback, their security assessment and subsequent fortification subverting most of his prior efforts. However, for all their cutting-edge gadgets and equipment and capabilities, they had missed one of the devices he'd implanted and, luckily for him, it happened to be in a spot that picked up a smattering of household conversation, just enough to tip him off to the incoming flight and window of time.

He had hoped to glean some additional information from the pilot, and being shut down by the principled bastard was a disappointment but, going forward, he would bide his time and get what he could. He was patient and he was persistent. And he was nothing if not resourceful. For all the high-tech security and surveillance and strongholds Tyler's men had implemented, sometimes all it took to circumvent was the low-tech, old-school approach.

THE THREE-HOUR DRIVE from San José brought them to the Dominical villa around eleven o'clock, all of them weary, but Callie most of all; her petite frame was shrunken, her complexion drawn and pale, the skin around her eyes both swollen and sagging.

On entering the home's foyer, Camilla encircled Callie with her arms, this time with great care not to disturb her injured side, and said, "Oh *mija*, you are tired…did you not sleep on the plane?" Looking her up and down, she added, "And so skinny. Too much."

Segura touched the housekeeper's shoulder, nodding toward the kitchen and telling her, "It is late, and we need to take care of Callie's wounds."

"*Sí, lo sé.*" Camilla said, and steered Callie to one of the bar stools.

When Segura set the medical bag Jake had sent on the counter, Callie realized what was in store and pleaded, "Please, no..." Glancing back and forth between Segura and Camilla, she asked, "Tomorrow? Wait until tomorrow?"

But Segura shook his head and was already unpacking items from the bag. "Sorry, sweet girl," he said sympathetically. "I promised Jake." He brightened for her benefit. "But we get to call him, right now."

The prospect of talking to Jake worked as intended, momentarily distracting Callie as Camilla assisted Segura in delicately removing the outer layers of bandages on Callie's arm and upper side while Callie dug into her purse for her iPhone.

When Segura got to the final layer of bandaging, Callie cried out in pain, causing Segura and Camilla both to flinch and, with wounds exposed, the two inhaled sharply at the sight. The housekeeper reached for the edge of the counter to steady herself, feeling lightheaded and nauseous; Segura, who had encountered some fairly nasty injuries in his work as a lifeguard, such as those from shark bites and jet ski accidents, was himself caught off guard. He had never seen a gunshot wound, hers looking all inflamed and shredded and encrusted around the edges where the bullet had scorched, reminding him of a bloodred rare steak charcoal-seared on the sides.

Quivering now, Callie began to sob, breathing through her teeth with the rawness of new pain.

Recovering her equanimity, the housekeeper put an arm around Callie, holding her still and murmuring reassurances. Callie was dimly aware of Segura taking her phone and then speaking with Jake. They were FaceTiming, with Segura holding the phone so Jake could see the wounds. Then, Segura stepped away and conversed in private for a few moments before returning and passing the phone back to Callie.

Gazing at Jake's face in the phone's screen, Callie said tearfully, "I wish you were here."

"I know. I do, too, baby. Everything looks pretty good. Just understand, it will get better, but it's going to look rough and hurt for a while. It's important that Jesse keeps a regular check to watch out for bleeding and infection, and he'll be changing those dressings. Okay?"

"Okay." She sniffled and tried to smile, but her mouth would not cooperate.

"Now get some rest if you can." His dark eyes filled with emotion. "I love you, angel."

He let her know he'd be in touch whenever he could, explaining that there would likely be days at a time when he would be unable to call or be reached.

Segura finished redressing Callie's wounds and Camilla accompanied her upstairs to help her get ready for bed. It was after midnight when Callie finally settled down, alone, propped up by pillows and bathed in the low glow of the bedroom's LED nightlights. A vase brimming with her roses, gathered by the gardeners and lovingly arranged by Camilla, sat on the nightstand, their scent and colors soft. The French doors were open, the night sky blue-black and too dark to see ocean, but the waves could be heard in the distance and a refreshing breeze was blowing in. It was cool and soothing on her feverish skin and, closing her eyes, she heard Jake…*I love you, angel*…tears forming once again, and she wondered how there could possibly be any left to cry.

She lay trying her best to ignore the pain, and how much she missed Jake, failing at both.

Wincing, she struggled to roll to the nightstand, opening the drawer and reaching inside for a tissue. Her hand brushed something she couldn't readily identify but which, for some reason, caused her heartbeat to spike. Scooping what felt like tiny loose things, she drew her hand back and looked at what was in her palm.

And, in utter astonishment, found the lovely seashell necklace Jake had given her on returning from the Bahamas after they'd first met. It had been lost sometime after that, but she'd never known when or how. Maybe Camilla had found it while cleaning. She fingered the little shells, remembering Jake putting the necklace on her and, not long afterward, they had made love for the first time. She flushed and shuddered with the remembrance and wanted more than anything to be in his arms right now. Looking at the necklace more closely, she realized that the opal heart was missing. Deep, at the far end of a long, black tunnel in her mind, a micro-second of memory flashed like a spark of fire on flint, flashing hot and then going quickly out. But in that pop of light…a hand snatching at her throat, the necklace breaking.

*　　*　　*　　*　　*

EARLY THE NEXT MORNING, as Callie finally slept after resisting for hours, Camilla assembled the components for breakfast while Jesse Segura and pool man, Ramón Cárdenas, drank coffee on the patio and watched Estabon Mina and Mauricio Leguizano working in the landscape on one side of the villa.

They all wanted to make Callie's return home as special as possible, Camilla preparing everything she knew Callie liked, the men decorating the patio with flowers and even some balloons, Cárdenas streaming some of her favorite music. Upstairs, Callie slept, but the usual demons were holding court.

Joining the others on the patio, Camilla set out a platter arranged with sliced fresh fruit, commenting, "Callie needs to eat, but she also needs to sleep."

"The food will keep," Segura said.

Nearby, the pair of gardeners were surveying branches and limbs and palm fronds that were scattered about the ground. "What happened here?" Leguizano asked quizzically. "We had no storm."

Looking upward at the canopy of trees closest to the master bedroom balcony, Mina grinned and replied, *"Monos."* Monkeys.

51

AFTER ENDING THE FACETIME call with Callie, Jake slipped his phone into the pocket of his cargo pants and remained seated on the bed of the Psara cottage, taking a few minutes to process his thoughts.

He was relieved to know that Callie was safely home and knew she was in good hands, but it pained him not to be there comforting and caring for her himself. Segura and Camilla had both seemed visibly shaken by the extent of Callie's injuries—he could see it in their eyes—but he was confident that the lifeguard's first aid skills afforded him the necessary level of competence for the aftercare, provided there were no complications. In truth, that worried him, as her wounds were a lot more serious than he'd let on to them and, certainly, to Callie. And what he'd observed through the phone had, in fact, looked somewhat worse than his last examination. Disturbed by that, he felt an onslaught of doubt in his decision to stay behind, but he quickly shut down the judgment as he knew it was what he'd had to do. He would just have to defer to faith and trust and stay in close contact as much as possible so he could monitor visually and advise accordingly.

He was also thinking about how dramatically rundown Callie appeared since he'd seen her just prior to departure. It was obvious she'd had little, if any, sleep. But he knew Camilla, with her protective and affectionate solicitude, would be tenacious in her pampering and ministrations.

Checking his watch, he saw that it was just after seven thirty, and knew Remington and Kipnis were waiting on him, so he heaved a sigh, put on his game face, and walked from the bedroom to the sitting room, exiting to the outside.

On the other side of the gate, Remington was standing by their leased Mercedes GLS, arms crossed over his chest. Kipnis was in the driver's seat, immersed in his phone.

"All okay?" Remington asked.

"Yep," Jake said tersely, getting into the SUV's rear seat. "Let's roll."

Remington took his place in front, and they were quickly en route across the island to the heliport, where Dmello was waiting with the Airbus H135.

On the return from Mykonos the previous evening, they had hit the ground with a frenzy of activity; Jake had packed up his gear at the cottage, including the arms and ammunition stored there, Remington had spent time with his team, making sure all aspects of their MVAA responsibilities were thoroughly covered, then met with Caspian Bachman and his staff to coordinate; Dmello had seen to all the arrangements for the helicopter and Pilatus plane; and Kipnis had been working his intelligence on all fronts, reconnecting with Sabine Brisepierre, who continued to provide him with the latest leads she had.

Jake was surprised to learn that Remington had thought to reach out to Amelia Keogh; he knew that, with their wealth and global business empire, the Keoghs had been well-connected in a multitude of realms, but what he had not realized was the extent to which they—and now, she—was connected in diplomatic circles. Even so, not much was prompting reason to be hopeful and, in the unlikely event they got some inroads there, initiatives would not be fast.

By 8 AM, they were in the air, making the hop to Chios, followed by another quick flight aboard the Pilatus to the FBO at Izmir's Adnan Menderes Airport. There, they were met by the Turkish fixer, Neval Tashkiran, who had procured private hangar space and the discretionary indifference of a few ground handlers, allowing them to depart with ease but, more importantly, all with weapons. The Turk had also leased a black Mercedes Vito van, the larger capacity being needed to not only add Tashkiran, but also to make room for the Malinois and, hopefully, Falcone and Niles on the return.

Remington did a comms check with Dmello, who was again, remaining with the plane, and the rest piled into the Mercedes, which turned out to be unexpectedly posh and comfortable for a van. While everyone got settled inside, Remington giving his dogs some water, Tashkiran and Kipnis went through a list they had compiled from all the intel, entering locations into the vehicle's navigation system. The number of entries was daunting, hundreds spread across over three hundred thousand square miles and, for each black site that had been identified, there were many, many more they did not know. Their initial list had been whittled down to the most likely places and sorted geographically, starting with Izmir.

Turkey is sixth in the world for the greatest number of imprisoned, ranked just below Russia, many of the detainees migration-related, others in the mix being those accused of crimes, dissidents of all stripes, and individuals perceived to be terrorists or spies. Since the government coup attempt in 2016, a colossal building spree of more than a hundred new incarceration facilities, many designed to hold thousands, has sounded alarms throughout the world's human rights watch organizations. Particularly since the majority of the facilities are of the infamous high-security prisons categorized as F-type and known the world over for their harsh conditions and brutality. In the most recent years, more ominously, two newer types have been developed, dubbed S and Y, respectively, described as high-security closed penal institutions.

As they took the highway north from the airport, heading to the first location on the list, Tashkiran said, "I do not believe your guys are in a police station or removal center, but it is possible they were moved through one, which is why we will start there with the most likely one." He was referring to a facility close to the coast, a thirty-minute drive through the dense morning traffic of the Yeşillik corridor, a multilane thoroughfare known for its proliferation of furniture manufacturers and stores. They traveled across the districts of Gaziemir and Karabağlar, making up some time on the way to Konak, until they approached the port where traffic congestion built once again.

Tashkiran, who was driving, appeared to know the way, steering around vehicle bottlenecks and paying attention to the route without the aid of the van's navigation system. Turning down a road parallel to the port, he drove past a series of decrepit industrial buildings, most of which were well on the way to ruin, and drew up to one that stood out from the rest. Three stories of crumbling concrete the color of yellowing teeth, it was surrounded by a high, chained metal fence fringed with concertina wire, a Turkish flag at the electronic gated entrance. A uniformed guard emerged from a detached booth, gesturing for Tashkiran to lower his window. They had a brief exchange, and the guard retreated to his station to relay their request to come inside.

A few minutes later, the guard reappeared, this time walking around the van, checking out each occupant through the windows. When he spotted the Malinois in the rear, he halted in his tracks and stared. This got him a chorus of menacing growls, prompting him to take a step back. Remington lowered his window and said, "Don't worry, they will stay in the vehicle."

Tashkiran repeated what he'd said in Turkish and, in turn, the guard let him know that one or two of them could enter. The fixer countered that it would be himself plus two, Kipnis remaining behind with the dogs. The guard hesitated but nodded and opened the gate with a keypad.

As they approached the front of the building, Jake looked up and saw faces crowding the steel-barred windows, their features indistinguishable but quite a few hands visible against the glass. Once inside, the squalor of the interior was immediately evident, plaster peeling from walls layered with decades of stains, floors cracked and grouted with grime, the stench of bodily odors and stale cigarette smoke hanging in the air like rancid cooking oil.

Jake had seen plenty of these kinds of hellholes and was somewhat desensitized, but the thought of Falcone and Niles being held in such a place made him sick to his stomach.

There were no metal detectors or screening machines, but the three of them were manually wanded by a squat and hefty man in a uniform two sizes too small with more hair sprouting from the collar of his shirt than the thinning nest on his head. When he had completed his sweep, they were led further inside to a counter manned by an official who looked the complete opposite of his cohort, tall and lanky with enough hair for a reasonably even crew cut. His uniform was loose on his frame, a lanyard identifying him as operations manager. One thing he did have in common with the other staff they had so far encountered was a dour and leery demeanor. Jake surmised that it was probably a prerequisite for working in this environment.

The officer did not speak English and no associate was offered up as translator, so Tashkiran let Jake present their inquiry and then dictated in Turkish. Almost from the first sentence, the facility manager was shaking his head, and by the time Tashkiran had finished, the man had become even more insistent in his disavowals.

Turning to Jake and Remington, Tashkiran explained, "He says there is not an American or British person here, of that he is quite certain as it would make a…I think your term would be commotion. Those detained here are mostly migrants from Syria, Iraq, Iran, Afghanistan, and some Ukrainians. He did mention something of interest. There was a big roundup at sea on the day your guys disappeared, and because this facility is overfull most of that group were diverted to Harmandali. It is on our list."

"Okay," Jake said. "Ask him if we can do a walk-through before we leave."

The request was quickly rejected and Tashkiran said, "A waste of time, really. I believe him. Let us check Harmandali."

LOCATED FIFTEEN MILES NORTH of the port, the next removal center was much like the first, only more upscale, which was to say less dilapidated and more institutionalized in appearance; were it not for the security obstructions, it might have been a borderline-seedy motel. Another thirty-minute drive along the D550 highway took them into the district of Çiğli. Here, they turned eastward onto a curving road that led to an unpaved stretch that traversed rolling, rural landscape comprised of grass and trees and nothing else until they came to the center.

Jake found himself thinking there was something not quite right about packing up people and hauling them off to a stockade in the middle of nowhere. The thought also reminded him that Falcone and Niles could be absolutely anywhere and, at the same time, utterly nowhere.

Harmandali, whether called a removal or repatriation center is, like the rest, at its very fundamental, a place of detention for migrants; by the standards of innumerable human rights advocates, foreign government officials, lawyers, and detainee families, there is not much daylight between it and a prison, ripe with abuse violations and vastly subpar conditions. It is always full beyond its capacity of 750.

As they approached the facility, a red-and-cream stucco building, five stories and barricaded by high razor wire fencing, it was immediately evident that this visit would not be so cut-and-dried. For one thing, the driveway up the incline was lined with a few other vehicles and protestors, one group holding an oversize sign emblazoned with Bar Association logos.

Translating the bold black print, Tashkiran told them it read, "Immediately put an end to your arbitrary practices and unlawfulness that hinder law enforcement." He parked the Mercedes van and added, "Needless to say, if these lawyers are not getting inside, our chances are not good."

"Well, let's see if we can at least make an inquiry," Jake said. "This place looks like it has more of an administrative structure to it." He was eying the half-dozen uniformed men assembled outside the guard station behind the green metal fencing, one of whom seemed to be some kind of supervisor, addressing the squad and occasionally waving an arm toward those assembled on the outside.

Kipnis, who had been mostly quiet during the ride as he'd continued to monitor and study intel, spoke up. "My recommendation is just tell them we simply want to have their names run, to see if they have been passed through. Frankly, I am doubtful."

"Have you picked up anything new?" Remington asked him.

"Nothing revelatory, but as I am analyzing everything we have and seeing these centers for what they are, I just do not think an American and a Brit would be held here. So, yes, inquire, but then I think we move on."

The implication that they were wasting time caused Jake to frown, especially since Kipnis had been the one to compile and vet their list, but he knew the feasibility of leads was always subject to change based on real-time developments.

He exited the van with Remington and accompanied Tashkiran to the gate, stopped on the way by a distinguished-looking gentleman in a suit, undoubtedly one of the attorneys. Speaking English, the man asked, "Do you have someone in here?"

"We don't know," Jake replied. "That's what we need to find out."

"Good luck, my friend," the man said cheerlessly. "I am one of several lawyers here, representing families of detainees, and we are not being allowed inside, which is our right. They give no explanations and no information."

Jake did not know what to say to that, just shook his head to convey sympathetic futility. And then he proceeded to the gate, determined to find out something, even if it was inconclusive. To get to the guard standing on the other side, he had to bypass at least a dozen men and women lining the fence, many shouting in various foreign languages. For his part, the center's employee was unmoved, his expression one of callous detachment, thumbs hitched in his belt.

Tashkiran managed to get the guard's attention by opening a leather card case, flashing a military ID he used for just such situations. The man was obviously familiar with it because his posture and level of regard distinctly changed.

"*Selam*," he said by way of greeting.

Tashkiran went through their request and, when he was done, the guard seemed to think it over, gave him a brief reply, and walked off. Turning to Jake and Remington, the fixer shrugged and told them, "He said he will check the intake records. Whether or not he actually does, who knows…but it is all we will get here." His eyes rolled to reference the protestors around them.

While they waited, another man, younger than the suited one and, as it became clear, not a lawyer, addressed them. He spoke in broken English, his voice plaintive. "They have my brother, long time."

"Yeah?" Remington replied, asking, "From where and for how long?"

"We come by"—he paused to land on the correct word—"arrangement, but he get…" He struggled again to complete the sentence, so Tashkiran helped him out, speaking Arabic, which both Jake and Remington knew. The young man listened, vigorously nodding his head. "Yes, yes, Syria." He finished by holding up eight fingers. "Month…*thamanya*."

"Your brother has been in here for eight months?" Jake asked, astounded.

"Goddamn," Remington muttered, glancing somberly at Jake.

Minutes later, the guard returned to the fence, shaking his head. He said something to Tashkiran and reverted to his impassive stance.

Once they were back in the van and headed away from the center, Tashkiran explained, "He said their names are not in the system, which he says is linked to a bigger database. I have my doubts, but I tend to agree with Efron. I believe our next line of investigation should be the intelligence agencies. Not sure they will be any more cooperative, but there I should have some influence."

THEY SPENT THE REST of the day stopping by the specialized gendarmerie units in and around Izmir. While these come under the country's national force and are the armed general law enforcement organization, the commands differ by branch, some judicial, some civil, and some military. And some are attached to the penitentiary system, which they hoped might bring some results, or at least new leads. But, as had been the case with the removal centers, none were helpful or forthcoming and, in a few instances, leaned toward the antagonistic. The next tier, that of special operations police, were, in fact, more respectful and responsive due to Tashkiran's status and connections but, in the end, yielded nothing of merit.

Feeling defeated, the mood was dismal as they made the drive back to the airport to rejoin Dmello. They were pulling into the hangar when Tashkiran's phone rang. He listened, said a few words, and ended the conversation with, "*Teşekkür ederim.*"

"Got something?" Jake asked.

"Perhaps. Let us not get our hopes up, but that was something of an anonymous tip from one of the stations we visited. I say anonymous because he did not reveal himself, but I know who it was. He obviously did not feel like he could or should speak freely when we were there. He says there was some talk of a high-value apprehension and, from what he could put together, the subjects were not processed in the standard way."

"In other words, off the books," Jake said.

"Yes."

Jake looked to Remington, seated beside him. "That's got to be them. Neval, are they being held there now?"

"No, he said they have been moved and he says he does not know where."

"So…what? Prison? Black site?" Jake asked.

From the front passenger seat, Kipnis said, "Black site. That is what we target next."

WITH THE SHIFT IN game plan, for their search the following day, Jake and Remington switched places with Tashkiran and Kipnis, Remington at the wheel of the Mercedes Vito, Jake riding shotgun, the Turk and Israeli is the seat row behind them. Spread across the laps of the two native Middle Easterners were regional and satellite maps, marked up and tagged with Post-it arrows and notes; Kipnis also had his tablet, and both were working with their phones.

They spent the morning hours driving to the south, the afternoon to the north, extending their range farther out from the Izmir center.

While black sites are, as such, unacknowledged locations and facilities, they exist all over the world, some operated in conjunction with local and state governments or police or military, some by the less defined deep state entities, and some by those of extreme and shadowy agendas. Most of them are tucked away in remote and obscure places, but a few are within a stone's throw of municipal infrastructure—as was the case of the one they found in the day's dying light. Up until that point, the locations they had scouted were all, more or less, in the former category and, at least this day, by all appearances, unmanned and nonoperational.

On the return from their exploration to the north, Tashkiran and Kipnis were reviewing the search grid on the map, consulting their data, and comparing it to the list that had been compiled. Abruptly, Tashkiran said, "Up ahead, the 300 junction, merge west."

"What?" Remington asked. "I thought we were wrapping up for the day."

"There is one I know of, and it is not on our list."

Following Tashkiran's instructions, Remington drove through Bornova, Izmir's third largest metropolitan district, passing the nine-hundred-acre complex of Ege University and medical center. At this hour, early-evening traffic was building, the sun setting behind them in a fiery blaze, vehicle headlights coming on, the highway ahead growing dim and the mountains beyond the urban density shrouded in gloom. They continued toward the sector of Kavaklidere, a neighborhood nestled in a heavily forested valley known as Belkahve Mesire Yeri, the peaks of which are some of the highest in Izmir. Tashkiran told Remington where to turn off, directing him to a primary road and then onto a secondary one that passed a small mosque at the edge of town, winding up amidst an industrial complex with rows of metal buildings and shipping containers. To the south was a span of wooded land, a narrow unpaved access trail leading to a clearing where a pair of concrete structures sat in isolation a few hundred yards ahead.

Remington pulled the van beneath a copse of trees and they all exited, taking out their handguns and making a visual survey. As Remington opened the rear doors and let the dogs out, he asked, "This is the site? Right here with all this commerce so close?"

Tashkiran nodded, and cautiously led the way. As with the sites they'd previous investigated, the property here appeared to be unoccupied but, as they got closer, its secret purpose became evident in the security measures in place. At a hundred yards, a driveway had been lift-gated, meaning some kind of invisible perimeter fencing or motion detection probably surrounded it as well. Kipnis was aiming a handheld electronic device as they approached and, when they came within range, he gave a thumbs-up to indicate they could continue.

The Malinois were prancing along in front of them, noses sweeping the ground and air, both harnessed in their K9 Storm tactical vests and in full work mode. Several times that day, Remington had given them Falcone's soiled t-shirt to refresh the reference, as he did now, though he knew they didn't really need it; their sensory memories were phenomenal. Also, after so many dry holes on their search, his expectations were low. But, to his surprise, almost as soon as the group got past the gate, the dogs' interest spiked and they began to make the whining sounds that indicated a scent hit.

With that, Jake held up a fist, signaling everyone to halt. Then, fanning out around the two buildings, Jake and Remington went one direction, Kipnis and Tashkiran, the other, each pair with one of the dogs. The structures were high-sided and set close together, having only one entrance and a couple of small window openings just below the roofline. After completing the circuit around the two buildings, their focus settled on one—where the Malinois sat and were looking pointedly at Remington.

Kipnis stepped forward, unzipping a leather tool kit and selecting a hooked pick. The building's door, made of weathered wood planks, was secured by a hasp and heavy-duty padlock, which Kipnis defeated in seconds; his skill made it look simple, inserting the pick, finding and fitting it in the precise place, applying the push and movement, and freeing the bolt.

Tashkiran and Kipnis stood guard outside while Jake, Remington, and the dogs went inside.

With Glocks raised in front of them, Remington illuminated the darkened enclosure with a Nitecore flashlight. The space was a stagnant chamber of bad smells that only canines could get excited about and, as soon as they entered the first room, the Malinois immediately trotted toward the wall, glancing back at Remington. They were on the far side of a table with one chair upright and two strewn sideways on the concrete floor.

Jake and Remington knelt, Remington pointing his Nitecore over the floor, and both saw trails and spots of dried blood. Neither had the need to say anything, standing and following the dogs down a short corridor, and found the crude cell, railed front gate ajar.

On stepping into the cell, Jake felt his jaws clench, his stomach go sour from the stench. Falcone and Niles had been here and, judging by the look of the dried blood—more of which was on the floor and a wooden bench against the back wall—not all that long ago.

Remington came up beside him, placed a hand on his shoulder. "Come on, brother," he said quietly. "Nothing else to see here."

Jake still said nothing, stood a few more moments, gazing fixedly at the bench, at the rusted pipe and bucket in the corner. Then, he turned and retreated with Remington and the dogs. He remained speechless until they were all back in the Mercedes van, and Remington knew to let him be, watching his friend silently ruminate.

Distantly, the Call to Prayer began, drifting over from the nearby mosque. The sun had fully set, the roads and land structures losing their shape and color in the deepening dusk, traffic a stream of red and white lights. Several minutes into the return drive, Jake asked Tashkiran, "What made you think of that site?"

"Because the highway we are on, which runs east-west, goes to An-kara." He paused, and said, "That, my friends, is where I am thinking our trail now leads."

Jake frowned, his thoughts steeped in grim reckoning; if Falcone and Niles were in Ankara, they were already slipping farther into the bowels of hell, and he feared that the longer it took to get a bead on their loca-tion, the greater likelihood that they would not be found until it was too late…or maybe not at all.

52

SOME 360 MILES EAST, Falcone and Niles had been hauled from the big transport plane, loaded into the back of another van, and driven a short distance through a heavily trafficked stretch, after which the noise diminished and died out with a turn down a surface road. The destination spot was a contradictory mix of clandestine and conspicuous, isolated in the midst of well over six hundred acres of open land, but wedged between two major boulevards and no more than two miles from the country's capital core and presidential palace.

They were marched across the grounds to a building densely encased by tall, mature trees and, once inside, had their hoods removed, finding themselves in a bare, compact room. Off-white walls, tile floor, dim fluorescent lighting, and no furniture. A negligible trace of bleach only managed to tamp down the mosaic of malodor and stink of cigarette smoke permeating the space. Two men, identically clad in black tactical wear, sidearms tucked into leg holsters and slung with assault rifles, left them there but stood just outside the door to the room. Within minutes, another pair of men entered, these in black tees and cargo pants, arm and chest muscles bulging and machine metal-hard. Their weapons were not visible, but they clearly had no need as their hands looked like they could crush bones into grit.

This second pair of men wore nothing to obscure their faces, which were squared, strong-jawed, and pelted with dark, thick beards.

Falcone and Niles exchanged nervous glances and flinched as the duct tape was ripped from their mouths. They cringed inwardly as knives flashed in the hands of their custodians, slashing the plastic restraints free from wrists and ankles.

What happened next made their bowels curdle.

The two men snapped on latex gloves.

In a commanding, accented voice amplified by the empty room, one of the two barked, "Clothes off!"

"Wh-what?" Niles stuttered, his bottom lip quivering.

"Clothes off!" the man repeated, yelling, "Now!"

Falcone and Niles had been thoroughly searched at the point of abduction and, while they'd been groped in all the vulnerable places, had not been made to divest.

Both began to slowly remove their clothing, Falcone pulling his polo shirt over his head, Niles fumbling with the buttons on his palm tree-patterned shirt.

The man who had given the order made a winding motion with his arm and spat, "Fast, fast!"

When their shirts and shorts were off, piled on the floor, they stood with hands clasped protectively over their crotches, prompting the second man to point to their feet and underwear and shout, "All of it! Off!"

Under his breath, Niles whined, "Oh God," and stepped out of his canvas shoes, then tugged off his underpants as Falcone did the same beside him. Now totally naked, the pair eyed the two intimidating men who stood before them, trying without much success to put on an intrepid front; both were lathered with perspiration and could feel their pulses throbbing in their eardrums.

The first indignity came in the form of a cruel move that immediately changed the dynamic in the room, as the second man reached to Niles' throat and snatched the choker chain, breaking it off his neck. Niles barely had time to exclaim in surprise and pain when the man shot his arm out again, pinching the zipper pull earring between two chunky fingers and ripping it from his earlobe.

Yowling, Niles clutched his ear, which streamed blood down the side of his face and neck to his shoulder, and hunched forward.

Without a single thought of consequence, Falcone lunged for the thug, an infusion of fury fueling the punch he landed in the guy's stomach. In response, the two men standing guard outside rushed in, grabbing Falcone by the arms, holding him while the guy Falcone had punched put his weight behind an open-handed smack across Falcone's face that had the impact of a cast-iron kettlebell and burnt like coarse sandpaper afterward.

Falcone glared at both men with undisguised vitriol but, mindful of the guards restraining him, fought back the urge to verbally lash out. Moments later, one released his hold and stepped over to Niles, latching onto his arm.

Now the two men in t-shirts moved in closer, and clamped gloved hands under their chins. The lead man ordered, "Open mouth."

Each did as they were told and endured an unpleasant oral probe, fat fingers poking under their tongues, around their cheeks, and down their throats, causing them to gag. Noses and ears were inspected, their hair raked like a pitchfork digging through hay bales.

And then they were subjected to what both had been dreading from the moment they'd seen the gloves come out. Their arms were pulled behind them and restrained by the guards while the men in t-shirts roughly clutched their genitals, squeezing as if it were physically possible to conceal contraband in penises and scrotums. Falcone and Niles grimaced and grunted and recoiled from the intense discomfort. The two men inflicting the distress shared perverted smirks, taking extra time in the vulgarity.

Falcone bit his lip and closed his eyes; beside him, Niles was breathing raggedly, tears streaking the blood smeared on the side of his face. They had both guessed what was coming next.

The guards changed positions, restraining them from the front while the men in tees kicked Falcone and Niles' legs apart from behind and shoved them down by their heads. Falcone braced himself, gritting his teeth, but Niles began to jerk spastically and make guttural noises as if he were having a seizure.

In a low voice, Falcone said, "Hey…it's gonna be okay. It'll be over in a minute."

Falcone's attempt at reassurance did little to calm his friend, but the guard holding Niles put a knee on his neck, suppressing much of his movements and muffling his vocals. Until they were harshly reamed with the gloved fingers.

Falcone stiffened, his sphincter clenching, inciting his abuser to prod with more force. He groaned audibly, suffering through it. Niles was louder, and he bucked on contact, provoking a hard smack to the head from the guard pinning him down.

When the men in t-shirts had completed the body search, Falcone and Niles were left alone in the room, the guards back in place outside the door. They collected their clothing and redressed, neither speaking for a few minutes. Eying Niles with compassion, Falcone asked, "You okay?"

Niles did not immediately respond and would not look directly at Falcone. His face was flushed, the dried blood nearly washed away from tears and sweat.

Falcone stood close but left Niles alone, giving him the privacy to work through the humiliation they had sustained. He was having a hard time himself, but he'd been a little bit shaken by Niles' reaction, which had seemed almost feral.

Finally, Niles turned to him and blustered, "Bloody arseholes. That was one of my favorite earrings…neck chain, too."

THE GUARDS CAME IN after a short while, grabbed their arms and took them from the room, down a plain hallway and into another similarly sized room. This one, much like the one in the previous place of detainment, had a table and some chairs. The interrogation room.

As they were shoved into the chairs on one side of the table, which was metal, they exchanged knowing looks and nodded imperceptibly to each other in a mutual pact of silence.

The man who entered the room and sat in the chair opposite them was unlike any of the others they had encountered since their abduction, clad in a pressed black business suit, a spread-collared white shirt, and a micro-patterned red tie. He was tall, broad-shouldered, and neatly groomed, silvered dark hair precision-cut short with matching facial growth that covered his chin and jaws, combed mustache and thick eyebrows mostly black. His eyes had the sheen of licorice, making them shiny and dull at the same time, and were devoid of expression; he did not look at them when he spoke which, in some ways, had the effect of making him more menacing.

The man took a few moments, shuffling through some paperwork in a folder he'd placed on the table in front of him. He glanced up briefly in a perfunctory way of acknowledging them, then looked back at his papers and said, *"Merhaba."* In near-perfect English enunciation, he remarked, "You will state your full actual names."

They did not respond but, below the table, Niles' knees immediately began to jitter. Falcone slipped a hand over and touched Niles' leg, which momentarily stopped the bouncing.

The next question was another that had been repeatedly asked in various ways: "Who are you operating for?"

Niles rolled his eyes toward Falcone, who gave him a subtle head shake.

"This does not have to be so unpleasant," the man said.

Niles' leg bouncing resumed.

The man said nothing for a few minutes, checking his watch and penning some notes on a sheet in his folder. Then, he stood and said, "Well, if this is the way, so be it." This time, he gave them both a direct look before turning in retreat.

THE CELL IN WHICH they were incarcerated at this site was something of an upgrade, in that it had an actual toilet and sink—though characterizing them as such was a gross overstatement—and the amenities ended there. A pair of worn mattresses lined opposite walls, soiled with stains that left little to the imagination and not much thicker than a kitchen sponge. The walls were painted concrete and windowless with an iron-barred square at the front; the floors were the same tile as the interrogation room, apparently mopped with bleach as they caught a similar whiff, but years-old grime was lacquered to the surface. Several plastic bottles of water had been provided, but no food.

There was also no light and, without a window to the outside, it was not long before the space darkened significantly.

Pacing back and forth, Falcone said, "God, I don't know which is worse…sitting on the floor or these nasty bedrolls." He looked at Niles, who was standing in the middle of the cell, motionless and shut down. Going to him, Falcone touched his arm, handed him a bottle of water.

Niles uncapped it, took a swig, and lowered himself to sit on one of the mattresses, grimacing in discomfort as he did. Falcone sat down beside him. Neither spoke for a while and, for Niles to be so quiet was disturbing; Falcone suspected there was some inner turmoil that went well beyond the blatant humiliation they'd just undergone.

Finally, Niles asked, "Why d'ya think they're so convinced we're some kind of bloody spies? You really think it's just the drone?"

"Don't know," Falcone replied. "I've been wondering that myself. They've been through all of our stuff."

"It's got to be the cameras," Niles said. "The Canon and the GoPro."

They both thought about that, mentally reviewing the media stored on the 256GB memory cards, which could hold a lot—over two hundred thousand photos or a thousand-plus minutes of video—or, in their case, some combination thereof. Both cameras had cards in them and there were other cards full of media in their packs, so plenty of material to evaluate, much of it probably of little interest to their captors, just a group of people digging. Except the people were military veterans. Could that be the incitement?

Suddenly, Falcone muttered, "Oh shit…I think I know what it is." He ran the scene through the lens of his mind and said again, "Shit, that's probably it."

Niles regarded him cluelessly. "What's it, mate?"

"I'm thinking of that one heated discussion we filmed during one dinner."

"Well, there were a lot of those."

"Yeah, but this one…this particular one involved an operation in Syria, and—"

Niles' expression changed, remembering. "And Turkey…also Turkey."

"Oh God."

They took a few minutes to mull the idea, then Niles seemed to brighten, asking, "Why don't we explain it to them? Tell them the truth, that we're just filmmakers documenting—"

"We can't do that, Curran, we really can't. For one thing, they won't believe us. These situations, these kind of fuckers, they only believe what they want to believe or what they need to believe to suit their purposes. And we have to protect the vets, no matter what."

"Right," Niles said, and exhaled a deflated breath.

He slouched lightly against Falcone's shoulder, peering harrowingly into the darkness, desperately trying to suppress the dreadful thoughts twisting through his head. Sometime later, Falcone felt Niles shaking, heard garbled sobs coming from his throat.

"Hey," he said lightly. "Hey, bud, we'll be okay."

Hoarsely, Niles said, "No…no, we won't. Eddie, they're going to torture us."

Falcone put an arm around his friend and said, "They'll probably just keep smacking us around." The words hollow and insincere.

"They're going to hurt us," Niles insisted tearfully.

"They're just gonna keep bullying us to see what they can get."

But Falcone did not believe that, and neither did Niles, Falcone thinking grimly to himself, *It's going to be bad*.

He had no idea just how bad it was going to get.

53

THEY HAD PASSED AN interminable and miserable night in the cell undisturbed by any of the men but visited by a number of the usual crawling, flying, and skittering critters. No food had been brought and their paltry supply of water had quickly been depleted, the deep muscle and bone soreness distributed over their bodies well beyond the efficacy of aspirin or ibuprofen, if they'd had any. Sleep came and went in accidental spurts when fatigue overcame the determination to remain awake and on guard; deprivation, along with the hunger and minimal hydration was already taking a toll on their mental clarity and acuity.

With the advent of day, though they had no way of judging time without the reference of outside light, the same pair of guards that had deposited them in the cell took them to an equally dark, windowless room and, immediately on entrance, it was all too evident what was about to happen in here.

The walls and ceiling were bolted with heavy metal chains and shackles and hooks; a number of grated drains were embedded in the floor; an industrial tackle box was open atop a rolling metal cabinet, beside which was a carton that appeared to be filled with rolls of cables and wires and leather, another with plastic jugs and glass bottles and metal cans. There was also an unrolled pallet displaying a terrifying assortment of hammers and mallets and blades, not to mention tools that were both familiar and totally inconceivable.

Another pair of men had joined the guards and now each one stepped in, forcibly removing Falcone and Niles' shirts, snapping iron shackles on their wrists, which were raised by a connective chain. Next, their shorts were pulled off, ankles put in shackles and anchored wide apart. The four men withdrew, standing near the door, conversing inaudibly.

"Sweet bloody Jesus," Niles whispered, already shaking and perspiring profusely, his face and hair damp.

"Listen," Falcone said tightly, "we're important to them, so that probably means there's a limit to what they will do." Nervously eying the assortment of sinister apparatus, he was not at all convinced of his prediction but needed to project strength for Niles' sake. He added, "Knowledge is power, so the more we hold onto, the more leverage we have."

The men by the door abruptly parted, like a school of fish clearing the path of a shark, a man entering who was a full head taller than all of them and built with body proportions that were almost cartoonish in physiognomy, Jason Momoa-jacked, emanating the combustible force of a rocket ship idling on a launchpad. His head was shaved, with the shine and hardness of a bowling ball, lead-colored eyes as opaque of expression as vapor. He wore gray-and-black camo pants, his tumid chest and abdominal muscles bulging against a gray tank top, exposed arms wickedly inked with skulls and daggers and serpents, a spider tattoo spread across the back of his neck.

At the sight of him, Falcone and Niles gulped and felt their insides liquifying. "Oh my God," Niles rasped. "We are so fucked."

The man stalked across the room, which was walled and floored in concrete and framed with big wood beams, and stopped a few feet in front of them, looking from one to the other in a way that seemed to suggest that he was reviewing his blueprint for interrogation. But he turned away without speaking, going directly to the apparatus, scanning the choices available. Surprisingly, when he returned to Falcone and Niles, his hands were empty, his mouth crooked into a cruel grin.

And then the assault began, the man alternating between the two of them, pounding his massive fists into their torsos as if they were heavyweight punching bags, at first eliciting groans and grunts and a few exclamations. But after a few minutes of the unremitting beatdowns, Falcone and Niles could no longer summon the breath for such exhalations; by the time his knuckles began to strike their faces, they hung limply from their shackles, heads flopping with each blow, spittle and blood spraying from their mouths, blood and mucus from their nostrils, and just blood from everywhere else.

The man had broken a light sweat, tank top adhering to his skin and defining the carved contours of pecs and abs, but he was breathing as evenly as if he'd just completed a leisurely stroll around the block. Struggling to remain conscious, Falcone peered at him through the hair hanging over his eyes and thought, *Motherfucker can do this all day long*.

Stepping back to appraise his work, the brute smiled with satisfaction, strolled to the metal cabinet, and again surveyed his selection of tools. He came back to them brandishing a wooden mallet, smacking the head against his hand.

Niles had lost consciousness intermittently, but now the new thwapping sound made by the mallet to the man's palm, stirred something in his primitive mind and his head jerked up.

"Fucking bollocks," he muttered. "Why aren't you asking us any questions?"

Panting beside him, Falcone huffed weakly, "Shhhh."

The man apparently found the question amusing, the cruel smirk reappearing briefly, but did not respond. Instead, he swung the mallet sideways and struck Niles at the side of his hip, causing him to bellow in pain. He followed this with a similar strike to Falcone, then inflicted hits to the side of their knees, targeting and connecting with force and location calculated to dispense just enough injury for maximum agony without complete ruination.

After a series of whacks, the man exchanged the mallet for a length of braided leather, wrapping one end around his hand. With this, he struck Falcone and Niles across their bare chests, which were already lacerated and abraded, both of them screaming. When the man stopped, he returned to the cart and reached into one of the cartons beside it, extracting a pair of plastic jugs. Standing in front of them, he uncapped one of the jugs and splashed the liquid it held onto their torsos, causing them to writhe and scream even more shrilly, the harsh sting of vinegar burning like liquid fire in their open wounds.

The second jug, which he lifted, uncapped, and pitched forward, contained salt.

THEY WERE LEFT TO hang for hours, dripping sweat and blood—until it clotted—and smelling sourly of the perspiration and their own urine. Drifting in and out, they moaned but neither spoke; there was just no energy or acumen to conjure and string together words and thoughts. By the time guards returned to free them from the shackles, their limbs were numb and dysfunctional, their muscles strained and atrophied, so they were dragged back to the cell.

Both lay motionless on the bedrolls in their soiled underwear for some time before attempting to speak, wheezing and murmuring. Niles rolled on his side, grimacing with the explosion of pain from all over his body, reaching for one of the bottles of water the guards had left. Lifting his head, he swilled, swallowed, and then retched violently, throwing it all up. He continued to heave until there was nothing left in his system to regurgitate.

With a great deal of effort and agony, Falcone managed to sit up. "Curran, are you okay?"

There was a breathless inhalation from his friend, followed by more gagging. Weakly, Niles replied, "Brilliant."

He dropped his head and passed out.

Much later, in darkness, Falcone was drawn out of the torpor he'd lapsed into by the sound of Niles sobbing. "Hey…hey, Curran," he said.

"What?"

"Can you tell if anything's broken?"

"Like bones?" he asked feebly. "Yeah, mate, I'm bloody well broken all over."

"I know…I know. But yeah, bones."

"Dunno."

It took him almost fifteen minutes, but Falcone clambered across the cell on his hands and knees, gritting his teeth and pausing every few inches to suck in breaths that felt like gravel scraping his lungs. When he reached Niles, he crawled onto the mattress beside him, feeling something sizable scuttle alongside his leg. Brushing it away, he winced and exhaled in exhaustion.

Close enough to see Niles more distinctly, he was horrified to take in the garish injuries that had been inflicted, dimly realizing he looked much the same. Niles' hair was loose and matted with dried blood, eyes swollen to slits and pouched in purple and black; his nose and mouth were cut and disfigured; his limbs were covered with bruises and lacerations; his pale chest was crisscrossed with welts.

"Oh God, Curran," Falcone said softly.

"What're we going to do, Eddie?" Niles whined.

Falcone placed a hand on Niles' leg, stroking it with an affection and care he'd not even shown a woman. "I don't know, bud…I don't know. But we'll hold on and take it until we can't."

Niles made a small sound, like that of a bird's tentative plea in the isolation of an unfamiliar forest. A tear seeped from beneath one fused eyelid, trailing down a battered cheek. "Right," he whispered.

But as Falcone lay awake that night thinking about their horrific situation, he was seriously worried about what was to come, knowing things would not get any better. His mettle and temperament—not to mention fighting skills—had been put to the test many times over his formative years, growing up in the infamously gladiatorial streets of Jersey and later in the ruthless concrete jungle that was New York. Eddie Falcone was, at least several layers thick, a tough contender—not Jake Tyler-tough, but tough enough for the usual kinds of conflict; there was nothing usual about this.

He had seen Curran Niles put up a pretty impressive front in many of the adversities they'd braved together, but Falcone knew Niles would never survive this.

Knew it, because tough as he considered himself to be, Falcone doubted that he, himself, could.

THE FOLLOWING MORNING, SOMETIME in the wee hours, Niles groaned miserably, cold and shuddering, Falcone huddled next to him on the filthy bedroll.

Stirring slowly, Falcone inhaled sharply and muttered, "Jesus Christ, I feel like I've been crushed by a trash compactor." He squinted at Niles. "You with me, bud?"

"Yeah."

Niles said nothing more for a long time, but Falcone could tell his friend's mind was ruminating. Finally, Niles asked, "Why can't we just tell them something? Anything…just bloody make something up."

Falcone sighed morosely. "We can't do that, Curran."

"Why? Better than having the shit beat out of us, innit?"

"It would be, of course," Falcone replied. "But that's just not the way it works. As soon as we say anything, whether it's true or not, we will be forced to sign a confession. And, before that, we'd probably be interrogated and tortured even more aggressively."

"How do you know that? Maybe they would accept it and stop."

Falcone shook his head. "No, Curran. I've heard about this stuff, and I remember some of what Jake's said. Their whole objective is to get something from us, like for the record, only it won't matter because they will generate their own statement of confession…which we won't even know because it will all be in their language. And, once we sign it—hell, even if we don't sign it—they'll cart our asses off to prison. So, no…please try your best not to say anything to them."

He gazed at Niles with profound compassion. "Okay?"

Niles looked away without answering.

They spent the better part of an hour in the laborious effort of toilet routines, which were anything but routine, both urinating blood and discharging runny excrement—although how there was enough sustenance in them to generate any was a mystery.

They were once again taken to the interrogation room. And, once again, the man presumably of some elevated stature entered and took a seat across from them. Wearing another refined suit, pressed shirt and tie, he was freshly groomed and displayed no sense of botheration whatsoever. He placed his hands on the table atop his file folder, fingertips touching, and gave them a deadpan look, waiting.

Falcone and Niles, who had been pressure-hosed down prior to entry and allowed to put their shirts and shorts back on, sat slumped in the chairs, shivering and dripping water on the floor. They remained silent, and the man asked no questions.

After about ten minutes of the standoff, the man rose without a word and exited the room. Falcone thought he sensed relief from Niles, but he did not share it and, sure enough, when the guards extracted them from the chairs, what Falcone had been dreading all along happened.

They were separated.

While Falcone was hauled back to the cell, he could hear Niles protesting in shock and alarm and then panic as he was taken the other way—to the torture chamber. Slung toward one of the mattresses by his guard escort, Falcone slid down to the ground, put his head in his hands, and prayed. Despite his desperate entreaties, it was not long before he heard Niles screaming.

HE WAS SHACKLED AND hung from the same spot as the previous day. The wall behind him was painted in wild, abstract patterns with their dried blood. Again stripped to his underwear, Niles immediately began to shake, from the chill in the chamber and from his abject fear. There was no use in trying to control or disguise it; the monster administering the brutality was well aware of the terror he induced. Thinking of Falcone's counsel, the only objective Niles had was to somehow just get through it.

When the tormentor entered the room, looking exactly the same in appearance and countenance as yesterday, he stood for a moment to size up the state of his victim and, without any discernible reaction, went to the collection of tools and materials. He took his time in contemplation, then reached for the handle of a dolly that held a box somewhat resembling a receiver or controller. With a number of dials, switches, and gauges, it was plugged into a receptacle in the floor and connected to a thick coil of cable. Stopping a few feet from Niles, the man leveled a probing gaze and spoke for the first time.

In a voice that was almost robotic in its lack of modulation but accented to match the native language of the others here, he asked, "What have you to tell me?"

Niles felt his jaws vibrating, teeth clacking hard. He shook his head and, in spite of his fear, stuck out his chin obstinately.

"No?" The man shrugged indifferently. "Well, then…*Hadi biraz eğlenelim.*"

He reached into a pocket of his camo pants, took out a pack of

Marlboros and a Bic, extracted a cigarette and put it between his lips. Lit up, pocketed the tobacco and lighter, and puffed, the smoke curling in front of his face giving him a ghoulish visage. He stepped up to Niles, pinched the cigarette butt with his thumb and forefinger, took it from his mouth, and poked the smoldering end into Niles' bare stomach.

Niles let out a yowl but quickly stifled it, sucking in his cheeks, hands clenching and unclenching in the shackles over his head. He was singed a few more times, each burn eliciting an inward garble of pain.

Dropping the cigarette to the floor and mashing it with a heavy work boot, the man turned his attention to the device on the dolly, unfurling the connected cable, which had a rod on the end. He flipped some switches and adjusted some dials.

Niles had seen enough movies to know what this was and what was about to happen. Hysteria rushed through his mind like a torrent of flood waters, taking his terror to higher ground and, before he could begin any spiritual appeal or gird himself for bravery, the cyborg-like brute stuck the rod in Niles' armpit.

Niles screamed as jolts of electricity racked his body, circulating and searing in a shock wave of unimaginable agony. His muscles spasmed violently and his heartbeat ramped up so hard and fast he thought it might burst from his chest. What scarce amount of urine was in his bladder drizzled from between his spread-eagle legs.

The man followed the application with another just like it, but this time the convulsive jerking was that of a lifeless form, as Niles had passed out. This was addressed by a knee to the testicles, wrenching Niles from his blackout in an explosion of excruciating pain, possibly worse than that of the electrocution. He shrieked and wrestled against the restraints, saliva and blood from where he'd bitten his tongue spilling from his mouth.

Be brave, be brave, be brave, he desperately urged himself.

Now cyborg man was at the metal cabinet again, selecting from his à la carte menu of torture choices. He returned with a hammer.

In the minutes that followed, Niles screamed so much his throat went numb.

*   *   *   *   *

LISTENING TO THE BLOODCURDLING screams, muted though they were by walls and distance was, in itself, utter torture for Falcone. It might as well have been him bearing the brutality for all the vicarious suffering it was causing, his brain a firing range of incoming mental battery that struck as viscerally as the actual assaults to Niles. He had not moved from the mattress, his arms covering his head as he rocked back and forth, cringing with every outburst and, in the throes of his distress, momentarily anesthetized to his own injuries.

The only positive he could cling to was that, as long as he could still hear Niles, he knew he was alive, though Niles might be wishing not to be at this point.

And then, he stopped hearing him. There had been some breaks from his outcries, but now the silence stretched beyond several minutes.

Falcone got to his feet, wincing as his ribs and hips and knees and ankles twinged and throbbed from the movement and pressure from standing. He listened, frantically willing any kind of sound that he could associate with Niles. Finally, after what seemed like an hour but was in reality about twenty minutes or so, he heard scraping and the thump of boots. Saw the iron-barred square of the cell front fill with the midsection of a guard. The door panel was opened, the limp and listless body of his friend dragged inside by two of the men, and callously dropped on the other mattress. His gold J. Crew shirt and shorts, the palm tree pattern barely recognizable from the sordid stains of body and confines, were tossed in after him.

When the guards had retreated, Falcone limped quickly to Niles and eased down beside him. The damage he saw was extensive and unimaginably horrible, but the first thing that got his attention was one of Niles' hands. It was covered in blood and still bleeding, gruesomely swollen. Worst of all, it looked as if it had been disassembled and put back with the pieces in all the wrong places.

Horrified, Falcone whispered, "Oh, Curran…oh my God…" He felt a dam of tears break like an aneurism from somewhere inside his head.

With red spittle oozing from his misshapen mouth, Niles muttered, "Think my fucking hand is broken…" He coughed, spit blood, and gurgled, "But…didn't tell him a fucking thing." A look of defiance, contorted by the mask of cuts and bruises and abrasions, twitched in his cheeks and mouth. It quickly collapsed, and he broke into ragged sobs.

Falcone put his arms around Niles, holding him wordlessly.

With one arm, he tried to gently slip Niles' arms into the sleeves of his open-front shirt, and saw the burn marks in his armpits, then the cigarette singes dotting his sides. Felt the roll of rage fire through his chest.

Motherfuckers.

Thirty minutes later, the guards returned for Falcone.

54

IN A CITY OF more than five million people spread over an area of roughly a thousand square miles, Jake and the others had an overwhelming amount of ground to cover in Ankara but, with the help of Tashkiran, Kipnis had done a good job of whittling it down to what was on their list. Still, those targets were enough to make for daunting days of canvassing, and they had no particular indication that they were even searching in the right city or region. They also had no expectation of a red-carpet greeting at any of the facilities where they could make inquiries, with off-grid digs being even more restricted, in that accessing them would require the tactical skills and experience acquired in their collective operational backgrounds.

Dmello flew them into Esenboğa Havalimani, a suburban international airport seventeen miles northeast of the capital, parking the Pilatus in one of the private hangars that Tashkiran had arranged. In anticipation of their extended time in Ankara, the Turk had also enlisted a trusted comrade he knew from his military service to babysit the plane, freeing Dmello to accompany them on the road.

When everyone had loaded themselves and their arms and gear into the rental, another Mercedes Vito van, Remington making the dogs reasonably comfortable in the rear, they headed for their first stop, a removal center a few miles from the airport. While they had all but eliminated these kind of detainment depositories, this one was close and had been linked to controversial detentions, so they'd decided to make a visit.

They headed south along the Ankara-Çubuk road and then east on Mareşal Fevzi Çakmak and north on Çankiri boulevard, traversing a mix of manufacturing and farmland, Kipnis checking his phone for any intel updates and Jake checking for any texts from home.

He'd made calls earlier that morning, speaking with Kent Sanborn to get a status report on all things security related, Jesse Segura to get his take on household matters—which included his input on Callie—and then Camilla for the more personal aspects. His house manager and housekeeper had been unified in assuring him that Callie was doing well, but Jake's keen ability to read voices and word choices, facial expressions and body language, told him they were massaging the truth. While he always demanded full honesty, he understood and appreciated their intent, which was to lessen his concern so he could keep his mission focus. FaceTiming with Callie afterward gave him the real picture, confirming what he'd already guessed; she still wasn't sleeping and was reeling from the trauma of being shot. But her wounds were looking slightly better, which was a great relief.

"Wonder how long before Ignat's guys pick up on us here?" Jake asked. The observation of Callie's shellshocked demeanor and gunshot wounds fresh in his mind, he thought, *And when they do, I've got something for them.*

Dmello said, "Kip and I checked the plane thoroughly, inside and out. All clean."

From the front passenger seat, Kipnis amended, "What we can control. We do not know what kind of information network they have in-country. I have no doubt it is substantial and would not be surprised if we are already on their radar here. It goes without saying, we must remember who we are dealing with."

By now, everybody was abundantly clear on that.

Arriving at the removal center, which was near the small village of Büğdüz in the Akyurt district, they found a modern complex that more closely resembled a museum or mall, round and fronted with geometrical pillar beams and plate glass windows. But the perimeter fencing and concrete walls encircling the property tended to confirm its actual purpose, which was to confine and retain its occupants.

After explaining the nature of their inquiry to security personnel, they were actually allowed entry, and parked in one of the marked spaces. A red sign over the glass doors at the center of the building was inscribed in Turkish, a white dove and star emblem paradoxically added to lame effect. Tashkiran, joining Jake and Remington inside, translated for them. "Provincial Directorate of Immigration Management Repatriation Center." Repatriation being the favored term instead of removal or detainment.

Repeating their inquiry at the reception counter, they were asked to take a seat and wait. As they did, they watched others come in and go out, some in decidedly tense exchanges with personnel, nobody looking at all happy.

A thin, middle-aged man with scant wisps of dark hair combed over his scalp and a thinly suppressed inhospitable expression, approached to greet them. He wore a simple black suit, hands at his sides.

He said hello in English, and began, "I am told you look for two men…European?"

"American and British," Jake clarified.

"This is not typical, so I can tell you that yes, we currently have such two men. But you cannot—"

"*What?*" Jake's voice was so coarse and vehement that the man took a step back and people around them sidled away, glancing over their shoulders.

In a more reasonable tone, Remington corrected, "Not European. American and British."

The suited man, whose name badge identified him as Furkan Gökçe, an intake administrator, was confused but adamant. "Western, yes, but you cannot see them."

Jake put his hands on his hips, eyes drilling into those of the administrator. "Names or images," he snapped bluntly. "Right now."

Tashkiran put out a hand in placation and conducted an exchange with the administrator in their shared language. Turning to Jake, he said, "The two men were brought in this morning, and the only reason he knows about it is, as you already know, Westerners are not at all common. But Jake…" He paused sympathetically. "These guys are older, and from what he is telling me, it is not them."

Jake blew out a frustrated breath. "So let's just confirm that." He glared at the administrator. "I want names."

Gökçe considered the request, which was more a demand, seemed to size up Jake's stance and level of intensity, and muttered something to Tashkiran. He withdrew from them, disappearing into an office behind the counter.

Tashkiran told them, "He said he will see what he can do."

Arms now crossed, Jake stewed, not as much out of annoyance with the administrator as from the letdown he suspected they were about to receive.

When Gökçe returned, he said, "Understand, we normally—"

Jake rolled his hand, indicating he did not care what they normally did or did not do.

"The men are Henrik König and Jannik Rechtman. Ages…"

Remington interrupted to stop him. "Germans. They're Germans. Come on, let's go." He thanked the administrator, and the three of them left the building.

"Fuck this," Jake said dryly. "Kip's right. They're not going to be in these places. We need to stay on the black sites."

FOR THE REST OF the day and the next two, the group traveled a broad expanse of territory, looping around the nucleus of city center and venturing into the outer environs, much of which was agricultural or barren steppe land. As had been the case in Izmir, their quest turned up sites that were either currently inactive or appeared to be long-abandoned and, after all, what made black sites secretive and elusive in the first place was their transience. Any that were employed for a longer term tended to be exponentially more covert and challenging to infiltrate.

There were only a handful of hotels within close proximity of the airport but, in a countersurveillance move with their Mykonos engagement in mind, reservations had been made at all of them under cover names, their actual stay being at the Holiday Inn Express.

On their second night in Ankara, Kipnis got the location of a black site where intel indicated current or recent activity and, astonishingly, it was right in the heart of the city, a stone's throw from the Beştepe neighborhood in the Atatürk Forest Farm that contained the Presidential Complex.

Studying the site on satellite imagery and assessing the acreage of flat, wide open terrain surrounding it, the decision was made to conduct surveillance and, potentially infiltration, at night. Evaluating possible ingress points, Jake noted that they were realistically limited to two. The dedicated access road was obviously out, which left them a gas station on Anadolu Boulevard, approximately five hundred meters from the complex, or driving off a frontage loop from the Ankara highway. The latter was not much farther to hike and was riskier; a vehicle parked in an uncultivated field would arouse suspicion if spotted, especially by law enforcement, but the gas station with its lights and twenty-four-hour service was too high-profile.

Shortly after midnight, they set out on the forty-minute drive south from Esenboğa via the Özal Bulvari highway, crossing the O-20 Ankara beltway that ringed the city. Five miles in, they merged onto the east-west Turgut Özal, streaming with traffic even at the late-night hour and, from there, took a number of turns dictated by the Mercedes' navigation, winding up on Ankara Boulevard.

While they drove, Jake and Remington reviewed the sat images on Remington's Toughbook. Covering about four square miles, the site was encased by security fencing, access road off the boulevard controlled by a lift arm barrier a hundred feet from the main entrance gate. In some of the images, there were several vehicles lined up on a parking pad just inside, a sure sign of attendance and activity; another sign lending credence to some degree of regular use, was a cluster of satellite dishes. There were a few small outbuildings and a couple of larger red-roofed structures, one of which was hemmed in by dense woods on all sides.

Just beyond the Anadolu Boulevard overpass, they came alongside a railyard and exited the southbound artery of the highway for a parallel secondary road that led to the frontage loop west of the site. Here, they drove onto a dirt track that wound across flatland with little or no vegetation, leaving them open to exposure. But they were untracked in the desolate fields as there was nothing around in any direction. They got to a stand of trees about five hundred feet from the site perimeter and pulled into their cover.

Climbing out of the van, everyone strapped on packs, checked and readied their weapons, and began the hike to the compound. The five were clad in tactical black, the Malinois also geared up and eagerly leading the way. Kipnis had brought *Habari*'s tiny Teledyne FLIR Black Hornet drone, Tashkiran and Dmello scouting with FLIR Recon night vision binoculars. They crossed another dirt track, made their way through low-standing scrub, and stopped within a hundred feet.

Crouched down together, they passed the binoculars around, all seeing a roughly surfaced road outlining the compound and edged by metal and wired fencing. Although the security barrier was not particularly high, the configuration left little doubt that it was electrically charged and probably motion-detecting as well.

Remington said, "Let's get our spy up, see what we've got."

Kipnis removed the kit from his pack and put the self-contained pouch around his neck. Opened it, took out the controller, flipped down the display. The black drone—militarily referred to as a personal reconnaissance device—looked a bit like a toy helicopter, weighing less than an ounce and fitting in the palm of his hand, but it was a serious piece of technology, with EO and IR capability and a range of just over a mile and thirty minutes.

Lifting his palm and working the controls on the remote, Kipnis launched the Hornet into the air, Jake and Remington watching the display screen with him. When the drone was flying over the gated entrance, a single pickup truck could be seen on the parking pad, prompting Remington to say, "Looks like somebody's minding the store."

Enabling the thermal imaging, the display screen lit up with blots of color and Kipnis replied, "Yep…looks like one guy in the guard house." He saw movement, adding, "Make that two guys."

Jake felt a spike of adrenaline but kept his hope in check. He waited as Kipnis maneuvered the drone over the other buildings and, moments later, felt the suppressed hope plunge.

Kipnis gave him a somber look, "No heat signatures. They are most likely not here, Jake."

Or they're dead, thought Jake despondently. The dead did not give off heat signatures. He said, "Okay, well, we're here now and there are guys here guarding something, so let's verify."

Looking at the fencing, Remington asked, "How do you want to do this?"

"I can get us in that way," Kipnis told them, "but it will take more time. I say the direct approach."

They all knew what that meant and, after a beat of consideration, there were nods of agreement all around. Kipnis brought the drone back, put the kit in his pack, and took out his handheld electronic jammer, saying, "This should work on the motion detection and CCTV cameras that I am sure are around, but if those guys are awake and alert, it may draw them out to investigate."

Instructing the Malinois, Remington said, *"Zwijg…zoek…bewaken,"* which was effectively telling them to track silently and be on guard— not that he ever had to add the last command. That came naturally to the canines. He had again presented Falcone's t-shirt to them earlier that day, another thing he knew was unnecessary at this point but, as operators, they all embraced redundancy.

Each of the five were armed with their Glocks and M4 carbines equipped with SOCOM suppressors and FLIR MilSight sights, the rifles being what they were holding at the ready as they began the advance north and then east, moving along the fence line. When they were halfway to the entry area, the two men whose heat signatures had been visualized by the drone's thermal imaging burst out of the guard house, armed and coming toward them.

"Auf!" Remington ordered, and the Malinois halted, dropping flat to the ground.

The men from the guard house had automatic rifles and were also hugging the fence line, making both sides essentially equal targets, a factor Jake, Remington, and Kipnis addressed immediately. The three of them popped off shots, aiming to disable with the intention of extracting information, easily striking their marks from the approximately three-hundred-foot distance. But the guards did not go down and did not manifest surrender, getting off a rattle of fire that went wide as they were thrown off balance by their injuries.

"Okay then," Kipnis blurted and aimed, taking the man on the left while Jake took the one on the right. Both nailed their shots, and the men flew backwards and hit the ground.

The five hustled forward and, while the others kept watch, Jake and Remington inspected the bodies. There was no need to verify fatality—the 5.56 rounds had obliterated their faces—so they searched the pockets of their overshirts and pants, finding cigarettes and lighters, chewing gum, keys, and little more. No IDs. But Tashkiran, who was standing over them, recognized bits of an emblem patch on one of the guard's torn shirts.

"These guys are military intelligence." He took out his phone and snapped pictures of the bodies.

"Well," Remington said, "we're gonna need to get the fuck out of here pretty quick."

Jake held up a key card he'd plucked from one of the pockets. "Not before we go through this place."

Remington looked pointedly at the two-way radios clipped to the waists of the dead guards and said, "We don't know if they called this in."

"Remy, I need to know if they were here, or…" He cut the rest of his sentence, looking off toward the trees at the back of the property.

Remington nodded and replied, "Of course. Let's go."

IN A DEMORALIZING OUTCOME resonating with déjà vu, the Malinois signaled a scent hit as soon as they started down the path to one of the two primary buildings. Tashkiran and Dmello maintained cover outside while Jake, Remington, and Kipnis went inside, entering the room where Falcone and Niles had been invasively strip searched, the dogs highly reactive to the lingering smells, though the surfaces reeked of bleach. They found and combed the cell and torture chamber, each of which had also been disinfected and completely cleared out; gone were the bedrolls from the cells and the tools and instruments of sadism from the chamber.

But they saw enough to know what the room was for, to know what had probably taken place there. Saw the metal shackles and chains and hooks and floor drains. And no amount of emptiness or chemical sanitization could expunge the tangibility of that.

Jake stared at the walls, at the floor, his head feeling as if cement had been pumped inside his skull, his throat tight and dry. If it had all hit him in the gut at the other site where he'd seen some of their blood and inhaled their bodily odors, standing here in the dungeon that had been crudely scrubbed and depersonalized, he felt cleaved.

Remington muttered, "Christ Almighty."

The three of them turned and walked speechlessly from the building, emerging out of the trees to a more open stretch of grass and crossing to the other larger building within the compound. It contained a block of cells, several utility rooms, some office spaces with desks and chairs, a kitchen and eating area, and a few bathrooms. It, too, was vacant, with nothing left out that looked worth rummaging. And the Malinois were not picking up anything here, so they didn't linger.

Not much was said until they had trekked back to the Mercedes van. As Tashkiran took the dirt track to the highway, Remington put a hand on Jake's leg. In the seat beside him, Jake flinched, his mind still locked down in anguish.

"Hey. We're getting close, brother."

They rode in silence for a while, and then Jake remarked somberly, "All that bleach…do you think they were killed?"

Though everyone in the vehicle knew it was a distinct possibility, Remington replied, "We go until we know."

55

FOR ALL HIS EMPHATIC admonitions against communicating with their captors, Falcone wound up being the one to renege, his strategy shattering on seeing what had been done to Niles. So, when he'd been dragged into the torture chamber shortly thereafter, he was not thinking about what new brutality awaited him at the hands of their tormentor…he was thinking of what else might be in store for Niles, whose hold on survival, he believed, was thinning like a frayed thread.

Before the guards could put him in the shackles, Falcone had demanded to see the man in charge and was led to the interrogation room. Some twenty or thirty minutes elapsed, and the superior had appeared, folder in hand. He'd fastidiously unbuttoned his suit jacket and taken the chair opposed to Falcone, regarding him with the same banal, non-expression he'd consistently maintained.

Falcone licked his chapped, swollen lips and said, "Look…you have our passports. You know our names and our nationalities. We are not goddamn spies. We are photographers and filmmakers…creatively, not politically or to incite or to…to…whatever it is you think. We have done nothing wrong." His voice had cracked with a splinter of angst as he added, "We're just fucking *tourists*."

The man continued to look at him for several moments, had opened his folder and taken out a printed document. Slid it across the table with a pen. And said, "You sign."

Falcone had glanced at the printed words, none of which were in

English, and said, "We are not signing anything, but you now have our statement. I speak for both of us."

Without saying another word, the man had reached for the document and pen, signed it himself, and placed it back in the folder. Stood and left the room.

Falcone's new tact had worked, at least in the only way that it was ever going to, the two of them being spared further sessions with cyborg man. But Falcone had spent a dreadful night, watching over Niles with grave concern as his friend drifted in and out of consciousness, wondering if he had, in fact, executed their death warrant.

The following morning, they had once again been zip-tied and hooded and loaded into the back of a transport van. A thirty-minute drive later, they were hauled out and handed over to another party. Standing on pavement, they heard the van's engine start up and the sound of its motor recede as it drove away. Heard the slide and clink of metallic gates and muffled exchanges between several men. They were then escorted into another facility, their hoods removed in a holding room much like the one at the previous site.

And, once again, they were subjected to the humiliation, indignity—and now painful—violation of a strip search; just the act of being bent over and positioned made both of them cry out as their battered frames responded in agony. Once they'd managed to put their clothing on, they had been led down a long, dim corridor, followed by another, and another. By the time they had passed through a succession of electronically locked railed panels, Falcone realized the very prediction he'd warned of and then, in making his statement, halfway hoped for, had come to be.

They had been moved to a prison.

The last part of their procession had taken them across a passageway that spanned a vast, three-level open space, the perimeter of which was lined with steel-barred cells. And suddenly, they had entered a raucous cacophony of noise—bellows, whistles, spewed tirades, shouted profanities in English and other languages, floor stomping, rattling bars—a churning sea of men in orange jumpsuits behind the bars, many others roving the common space in between. Peering down in stark evaluation, Falcone had put the number of incarcerated in the hundreds, his head spinning as the reality set in. Stumbling along behind him, being held up by two guards, Niles had audibly gasped and then heaved.

A large part of Falcone's change in strategy had been the prospect of improved conditions of confinement, regular food and water, some hygiene and, most of all, medical attention for Niles. He could use some, too—he was pretty sure they had both sustained bruised, if not fractured ribs; they had innumerable cuts and lacerations, bruises and abrasions and burns; possibly infected wounds—but it was Niles' hand that worried him the most. In the hours since his friend had been returned to their prior cell with his horribly damaged limb, the disfigurement, swelling, and coloration had worsened substantially, his pain so severe it was causing wholesale motor and mental impairment.

As it had turned out, those hoped-for betterments did come with the new accommodation though, as it turned out, they proved negligibly remedial.

Now, as they took in these confines, Falcone was starting to doubt his choice.

The medical care they had received was hardly worth the risk he'd taken. A doctor—if the surly young attendant even was one—had barely given their surface defacements a good look, let alone clean or bandage them, had not otherwise poked, prodded, or palpated any bodily parts, or bothered to inquire about any specific concerns. Instead, he gave them a cursory inspection, scribbled some notes on a chart, and offered up aspirin or ibuprofen. As for the treatment of Niles' hand, the whitecoat had simply wrapped it in gauze, and not very well.

Their cell was an improvement over those from the previous, but just barely. It was furnished with cots, which at least got them off the ground, but the bedding was as squalid and threadbare as what they'd had before. The walls and floor were concrete and dingy, lined with cracks and stains that had probably been there for decades. They had a ceramic sink and toilet, pitted and chipped and turned nearly the same color as the concrete. There were no windows, and the front was walled solid with a secured door, only a small pass-through ledge in the center.

An hour after being deposited in the cell, the pass-through panel was opened, a guard announcing, *"Yemeğiniz."*

Falcone took the two plastic trays and water bottles the guard presented and walked over to Niles' cot. He set one of the trays next to his listless form, nudging lightly. "Hey, bud. They brought us food. Sit up, okay?"

Falcone looked bleakly at the slop in the sectioned platters, which contained meager portions of rice, some kind of slimy vegetables, a stew that resembled cat food, and stale pieces of bread, reminding himself that, awful as it was, it was still calories—something they'd not had in days.

"Come on," he said, "we need to eat."

Groggily and with great effort, Niles drew himself into a sitting position on his cot, a feeble smile pulling at his scabbed lips. "Don't s'pose it's fish n' chips?"

Falcone forced a chuckle to encourage him. "Sorry, no, but it's carbs." He gave the meal selection another look, adding dismally, "I guess."

The first sustenance turned into a hard fought struggle to consume and digest; mouths and jaws and throats were cut and sore and, worse, stomachs were as tempestuous as a choppy sea, roiling with the introduction of the ghastly fodder. Falcone gagged but was able to keep his down; Niles, not so much.

When the guard came for their food trays, they were given sets of clothing that consisted of loose-fitting gray pants and overshirts, t-shirts, underwear, socks, and rubber slides. Falcone helped Niles with his, and by the time he'd finished dressing himself, Niles had dropped back down on his cot and either dozed off or passed out.

Grateful as he was for the fresh clothes—their own were incredibly rank at this point—Falcone wondered why they had not been issued the standard prison-orange one-pieces the other inmates wore. He also wondered why they had been put in segregated cells, but he was certainly glad they'd been kept together and, whatever the reason, glad they were not in the riotous mix of general population. He glanced up as Niles moaned in discomfort, swallowing against a knot of raw emotion.

Falcone lay on his cot, staring into the deepening gloom until his own eyes closed, bringing a nocturnal highlight reel of the horrors that had been inflicted upon them in the days past. He was jolted awake sometime later, in pitch black, with a hair-raising scream from somewhere outside the cell. It was repeated several times before dying off after a commotion of heavy footfalls and raised voices.

Oh God, Falcone thought, were they just in a bigger hellhole?

SHORTLY AFTER WHAT PASSED for breakfast the next day—runny porridge of an unknown grain source, a greasy glob of something bordering on rancid, the same kind of stale bread from dinner, strong and bitter-tasting tea—they were led from the cell. Terror-stricken at first, guessing they were about to be interrogated or tortured, they were surprised to instead be brought into to a small, paved courtyard. No larger than a thirty-by-thirty-foot space, a scant amount of daylight leaked in from a half-dozen high window slits, casting stingy icicles of pale shadow in an otherwise murky room.

They were not alone, joining a group of four other men. Two appeared to be in their thirties, one perhaps forty to forty-five, and the fourth well into his sixties, maybe seventies. All were clad in the gray shirts and pants, shuffling or standing still with the stooped posture and lackluster demeanors of long-timers. The younger two were dark-haired with beards, the growth of which was neither short nor long; the older two were gray- and silver-haired, also bearded, their hair lengths approaching that of Harry Potter wizard territory.

Falcone absently ran a hand over the coarse stubble on his face, considering how scruffy and unkempt he must look by now.

Nodding to the four men sharing the communal space, he said, "Hi."

His greeting was returned with reciprocal nods but no words. The men were looking at them blankly; if they were at all shocked by the severity of Falcone and Niles' conditions, they did not register it. Possibly, Falcone thought, because they had either seen it before or had themselves been in similar shape.

"Uh…English?" Falcone asked.

The elder in the group extended his hand and gave them a sad smile. Making introductions in accented English, he said, "I am Gustl Afritsch, and"—he indicated one of the thirty-somethings—"this is Siemon Ehlers. We are from Germany." Gesturing to the second younger man, followed by the middle-ager, he continued, "Duje Milić, Croatia…Karel

Hořava, Czech Republic."

Falcone shifted uncomfortably, hesitating.

Recognizing his reservations, Afritsch said, *"Kein problem*...no problem. First names?"

"Eddie...Curran."

"Nice...meet you, Eddie and Curran." He held out his hand to Niles and then, getting a closer look at the Brit's grotesquely mangled appendage in its crude wrapping, pulled it back and just nodded.

Afritsch went on with his gradually cordial preamble. "So...this is call West Wing, where prisoners of the West are kept, separate from the rest."

"How many?" Niles asked.

"Not sure," Afritsch replied. "But only this many here"—he waved an arm around to indicate the six of them collectively—"allowed a time." He searched for the words, adding, "In social space. One hour."

"One hour a day?" Falcone asked. "That's the only time we get out of the cell?"

Everyone nodded. The other German, Ehlers, said, "Well, also to shower...but one time in the week. Maybe in two week."

Better than nothing, Falcone thought, and really better than where they had just been.

For the remainder of their hour in the communal space, through halting English, Falcone and Niles learned that the four prison mates had been taken into custody and incarcerated for accusations ranging from political activism, the dissemination of propaganda for terrorist organizations, recruitment and membership of the same, and the publication of anti-government defamation and disinformation. Afritsch was a college professor; Ehlers, a post-grad studying theology; Milić and Hořava, journalists. More alarming than the so-called reasons for their detainment and subsequent internment, was the revelation that two of the three had been tried and convicted and were, by any rational standard, unjustifiably serving decades-long sentences; the other two were currently awaiting criminal trials.

Hearing that, alarms blared in Falcone's head. He asked, "You have lawyers?"

Duje Milić, the Croatian, said, "Not allowed."

"Embassy?"

"No."

"Shit," Falcone muttered.

Out of the corner of his eye, he noticed several guards on the approach and figured the designated social hour was coming to an end. He was loath to ask the next questions but could not stop himself and did not want the guards to overhear.

Thinking of the screams he'd heard overnight, he asked, "Do they…torture here?"

The four glanced at each other, no one answering. Falcone took the lack of response as an affirmative, and felt the muscles of his face go slack. He then asked, "How long have you guys been in here?"

Ehlers sighed and said simply, "Long time."

They were escorted back to their respective cells in pairs, Falcone and Niles being the first to be led out and, as they passed the open door panels along the corridor, peered in, finding the same seedy, bare-bones quarters. But something on the wall of one arrested their attention, both of them cricking their necks at the last moment to fully comprehend what they had glimpsed.

Scratched into the flaking paint were countless rows of tally marks, endless sequences in row upon row upon row.

When they were secured in their own cell, Niles sat next to Falcone on Falcone's cot, slumped forward, and cradled his head in the uninjured hand. "We're not going to get out of here, are we, mate?"

56

WITH THE PASSAGE OF several days, something of a routine began to take shape in the mundane fundamentals of three meals a day—mostly the same slop and undoubtedly recycled well past the use-by date—fitful sleep frequently interrupted by tormented screaming or wailing or incoherent jabbering that echoed from indeterminate directions and distances, the one-hour social recesses in the communal space and, for the first time since their arrival, a trip to the shower room.

Falcone had been looking forward to the opportunity to scrub the filth and stink from his skin and hair, with the added benefit of maybe easing some of the soreness steeped into his muscles and bones. But Niles was oddly resistant, and emitted a feeble whine when the guards came to get them, providing towels and soap.

"Come on, bud," Falcone encouraged, "it'll be good for you, make you feel a little better."

Niles did not readily budge from his cot, giving Falcone the wary and petulant look of a child wobbling on the line between protest and tantrum. But it was a fleeting cloud of demurral, one of the guards sternly ordering him, "You go."

They were walked down the corridor to a room with six open stalls, no privacy curtains, tiled walls yellowed with age and blackened with mold and mildew. Niles' unease seemed to lighten slightly on seeing that they were the only ones, but he kept glancing nervously around as they removed their clothing and stepped into the narrow stalls.

Falcone found himself a little on edge, too, eying the pair of guards stationed inside the room, one standing in the doorway and the other in front of the sinks directly behind them. On entering, he'd felt an unexpected trill of warning, and became more watchful and self-conscious himself.

He glanced over his shoulder, checking the position of the guards, and caught both of them staring with a little too much interest but unmoving. The two men were young, probably late twenties, clean-shaven with the facial shadowing that comes with darker coloring, hair close-cropped. They were slim and youthful-fit, clad in the prison uniform of black slacks and polo shirts that bore a red-and-blue emblem with an inscription that read: *JANDARMA*.

Reaching to turn the water on, Falcone and Niles exclaimed at the same time as the chill hit them, instantly dispensing any prospect of therapeutic warmth. Lathering up with soap and vigorously rubbing his shoulders and chest to offset the frigid stream, Falcone felt sorry for Niles who he knew would be struggling to bathe without the use of both hands.

But Niles had not even begun the efforts, picking up a faint combination of sounds that sent his heart and mind leaping into a maelstrom of panic. Just as he'd twisted the knob to start the shower, he had heard the light scuff of boot soles on the concrete floor behind him along with the subtle chink of a belt buckle, a rustle of material.

Before he could turn around, a scream erupted in the hollow of his throat but lodged without escaping. And then, in a rapid bolt of forward momentum, he felt the compression of body weight slam against his back, a knee pummeled up between his legs. Felt the hard, rigid protuberance jab him with a force that pushed him into the ceramic tile wall, busting his forehead and nose and stunning him with a blinding haze of concussive pain.

Falcone reacted even before cognizance took hold, whipping around and barreling through the second guard who had moved in to block the opening of Falcone's stall.

Grabbing the assaulting guard by his shoulders, Falcone wrenched the man from Niles, throwing him into the sidewall, shouting, "I will fucking kill you, motherfucker!"

The guard who had been in place to prevent Falcone from interfering was now trying to pull him off his coworker, but Falcone sent him tumbling backwards again with a wide sweep of his arm. Vulnerable in his nakedness to almost any offensive blow, Falcone made sure the man stayed down by delivering a powerful kick to the groin, causing him to shriek and curl up on the floor.

Turning back to the attacker, Falcone saw Niles recoiled in the corner of his stall, the shower water still spraying, blood trickling over his face.

The man's pants were unzipped, his penis exposed but not so distended now that the intent of the assault had been disrupted. He'd removed his leather belt, which he began snapping, thrashing Falcone's arms and torso. But Falcone was so enraged, he barely registered the licks, moving in with his fists and punching the guard in rapid-fire rounds to the head and midsection. He did not know much about anatomy, but he knew he needed to protect his damaged ribs, and he also knew that the pre-existing injuries Niles had incurred took him out of the fight.

"Amina koyayim," the guard growled. *"Orospu çocuğu."* Shuffling his feet and lashing the belt.

Falcone parried the flays and continued pounding away at the attacker, but by now other guards were rushing in, having responded to a call on the radio from the guard balled up by the doorway. A babel of excited voices and frenzied grappling descended, with Falcone and Niles surrounded by bodies and, after an outraged tirade from the attacker, several of the responders broke from their cordon, throwing Falcone and Niles to the ground.

Falcone yelled, "Hey! *They* did this! I was defend—"

But the uniformed corps were not paying him any heed, kicking at them both.

Falcone and Niles, naked and wet and bloody, tucked their arms and rolled to shield themselves as best they could from the assault by boots. A supervisor must have entered, because the group stopped stomping them and dispersed. A different pair of uniformed guards stepped in, got them to their feet, handcuffed them, and threw towels over their heads.

Then they were paraded back to their cell, uncuffed, and tossed to their cots.

*   *   *   *   *

AS HE LAY AWAKE IN the darkness that night, Falcone was berating himself for not having anticipated the attack on Niles.

Thinking back over the time they'd been in this wretched place, Falcone had taken notice of the guard who'd assaulted and attempted to violate Niles, caught the man eying him a little too fixedly on more than one occasion. He suspected maybe Niles had gotten some kind of a vibe himself, which would explain his unwillingness for going to the shower.

Earlier, after the incident, they had been left alone; to their relief, no punishment or torture was administered—at least, not so far—and no communal time was given, which neither were up for, anyway. But there was also no medical care offered, not that the prison's sorry excuse for a doctor would have done much to administer to their newly sustained injuries.

Falcone was, of course, more sore than he'd already been but, aside from the added abrasions and bruises, he believed he had avoided serious damage. Niles was a different story. He had taken a hard hit to the ceramic wall and likely had a concussion. And, for the second time in a few months, his nose had been broken—except this time, he didn't have Jake to treat and repair it. During the subsequent aggression of the respondent guards, Niles had done his best to protect his injured hand, but Falcone knew it had taken some rough jostling in the beatdown.

The physical destruction to Niles was certainly bad enough, but it was arguably the mental and emotional that worried Falcone the most. Since their return to the cell, Niles had regressed to his shut-down state, had not uttered a word. Now, as he murmured and moaned in his cot, Falcone could only imagine how his friend was suffering. And, remembering Niles' freak-out during the first strip search, he again wondered if there was something more to it that would make what had happened earlier even more traumatic.

ON THE SECOND NIGHT following the shower incident, Falcone found out his instinct was right.

Another long day had passed with minimal activity and communication, the two being offered but declining a return to the one-hour social period. Falcone had picked at the hideous food, Niles had refused to even look at it. Several attempts to interact with his friend went nowhere; except for the few times Niles had struggled to use the toilet, he'd remained withdrawn, huddled on his cot, facing the wall.

Sometime in the late or predawn hours when the cell was at its darkest, Falcone heard Niles crying softly, and went to him. "Curran, I'm here," he said, and sat on the edge of the shabby mattress, putting a hand on Niles' back.

Flinching, Niles did not turn toward him.

"Okay. I'm just going to sit here."

A few minutes passed, and Niles slowly rolled over, wincing sharply as tentacles of pain undulated throughout his frame. He huffed in an effort to clear the congestion in his sinuses and, failing, continued to draw breath from his mouth. Working to raise up slightly, he held his damaged hand and, even in the darkness, Falcone could see the agony in his friend's face.

"How bad is the pain?"

"Bloody disaster," Niles murmured hoarsely. "I think my nose might hurt even worse than my hand at the moment…feels like I snorted shards of glass."

He coughed weakly and Falcone reached for a bottle of water by the cot, uncapped it, and tippled some into Niles' mouth, much of it dribbling down his front because of the difficulty they both still had with lips and tongues and ingestion in general.

Thinking of the blow to his head, Falcone asked, "What about your head?"

"'Course…got a massive headache…" He leaned back against the wall and closed his eyes.

Falcone posed a few more questions relative to Niles' physical condition, but Niles did not respond and, after a while, it seemed as if he'd dozed off. Then, abruptly, he opened his eyes but did not look at Falcone, his head down.

When Niles finally spoke again, his voice was so faint and devoid of inflection that Falcone could barely hear him. "My first year in the biz—

this was before I wound up at Twisted Logic, the tour coordination gig—I was working at one of the top music management firms in the U.K. It was my bloody dream job."

Falcone knew a great deal about Niles' background, the two having had many discussions about the common denominator of the music industry that had initially bonded them, but he suspected he was about to hear something never intended for divulgement.

Niles continued, still not looking at Falcone. "I've told you about my infatuation with Esme Dane..."

Niles had, in fact, regaled him with a great many tales of his desirous ambitions on the woman who, by Falcone's judgment, had been an uppity bitch.

"She was one of the top execs there, and I was constantly trying to get her attention, to make a play...but also make my way up in the company, which meant impressing the head chap, Ian Ballard." At the mention of the name, which Falcone could not recall hearing before, Niles paused, swallowing. He went on, "Neither of them really paid me much mind, so when I was included in the group to attend one of the major awards events and the after-party, I was over the moon. To be honest, I thought maybe once she got some drinks in her...you know..."

"Uh-huh."

"Thinking about the potential for hanky-panky with her made me a bit of a nervous Nellie, so I was getting somewhat tipsy..." His voice seemed to vaporize in his throat, and it took him a few moments to go on. "But instead of making any headway with her, it was Ian who took a fancy, chatting me up about the music scene and upcoming projects and such." He paused again, but now, emotion bubbled up and choked his words, making them even more muffled. "I...I'm still not sure what he did...but think he drugged my drink. I got so dizzy I almost collapsed...next thing, I was in some back room with him. He...he..."

As he relived the memory, he hiccupped a strangled sound of anguish, using his good hand to swipe at the start of tears. "He had me over a chair and pulled my trousers off...he tried..."

Now Niles broke down, sobbing inconsolably. Falcone put an arm around his quaking shoulders and let him expel the deeply rooted despair. Knowing this egregious act had haunted Niles for years, Falcone sensed that it was best to let him navigate the narrative without any commentary or commiseration from him just yet, so he waited patiently, a well of empathy swelling.

Mucus and tears and flecks of blood leaked from Niles' crushed nose, and he dabbed it gingerly on a sleeve of his shirt. "I don't know how, but I got away from him…maybe someone came in, or maybe after I tried to resist, he left…I don't really remember. But he didn't…do it." He looked imploringly at Falcone in the dark shadow, his face full of despondency and shame. "So…you see…"

Quietly, Falcone said, "Yeah, I do, Curran. I do. All this has been triggering for you."

"The worst thing…well, not the worst, but…I had really respected him, wanted to make a good impression on him." He paused again, the more complex layers of the memory adding more depth and shadow. "I had a tough time after that in other ways. I left them, but Ballard fucked me over in the industry, also on a personal level, so I was on the outs for a long spell. And I always wondered if I somehow—"

"No," Falcone said fiercely. "No. And it was in no way your fault. No way. Jesus, I'm so sorry that happened to you, Curran. Fucking bastard. Goddamn."

They stopped talking for a while and then, his lips quivering, Niles asked, "What if that happens again? What if it…really happens?"

"We won't let it," said Falcone firmly.

"But what if—"

"*I* won't let it," he said, more forcefully.

"But what if they separate us, Eddie?"

Niles' fears were starting to stage an uprising, and Falcone knew he needed to cut them off at the pass, needed to keep his friend clinging to the ledge of hope—even if only by the flimsiest of fibers. He said, "I don't think they will separate us. I really don't."

Falcone was no more sure of that than he was of anything else here and, given what had happened the day before and the psychological demons it had unleashed on Niles' already fraught state, he was idealistically hellbent on them getting out. But, realistically, he knew their chances were decidedly slim, especially after hearing about the legal constraints of their fellow jail mates and their unthinkable criminal indictments and sentences.

Secretly, he'd been racking his brain for escape plots, and coming up empty. It was not like they could replicate a *Shawkshank Redemption* or *Prisonbreak* scenario, digging their way out behind a poster of Rita Hayworth or with an elaborately tattooed blueprint of underground passageways. There would be no opportunity to smuggle a utensil from the kitchen or hop into an outbound laundry truck. No, if there was going to be anything to take advantage of, it would be something wholly unexpected with the narrowest window of feasibility.

JUST SUCH A MOMENT presented itself the following day, every bit as serendipitously and spontaneously as Falcone had guessed.

They had been spending time in the communal space with the other Westerners, which mostly consisted of strolling aimlessly around, staring at the walls or wistfully up at the window squares, exchanging a few words here and there. When the allotted hour expired, the pair of guards who had escorted them in appeared at the entrance of the room to lead them out. But instead of initiating the procession of removal, the two men loitered, engaged in a lively discussion that involved spirited hand gestures and joshing—probably, Falcone speculated, the same kind of things most men bantered about. Sports, women, drinking, sex. In any case, the key was, they were distracted.

Normally, the guards just being distracted would not have provided anything worthy of exploiting to their advantage in a place so rudimentary and insular, but Falcone had observed something on their way in that had planted the seeds of an idea; in addition to the two-way radios all of them carried, one of these two had a cell phone on him today. It was the first time Falcone had spied one since they'd been here and, from the way the man kept it possessively close to his body, scrolling on the screen and offering sneak peaks to his work partner, Falcone deduced that the devices were probably prohibited. For good reason, he thought, his idea germinating and working around pitfalls.

As the guards remained preoccupied in whatever they were ogling on the phone, Falcone nudged Niles and asked, "You see what I see?"

Niles looked briefly over, quickly averting his eyes. The two guards involved in the assault had not been back, but all of them unnerved him now. He replied, "Yeah, bloke's got a mobile phone."

"Wait for my move…and snatch it."

Niles gaped at him, dumbfounded. *"What?"*

"Get the phone off him. But you need to be smooth…like a pickpocket. Can you do that?"

"No, no, can't do it, mate. Can't."

Whispering, Falcone urged, "Yes, you can."

"Dunno, Eddie. If I bugger it up…"

"Just try, okay?"

Niles hesitated but nodded, and they both watched as the guard who held the phone slid it into a pants pocket and started toward them, the second guard in stride beside him.

When the pair reached them, phone guy announced, *"Haydi gidelim,"* something uttered often enough to be interpreted as "let's go."

Niles positioned himself to the left of the guard which, fortunately, was the side for his good hand. He saw Falcone, on the guard's other side, begin to sway, clutching his stomach. Both guards' heads swung Falcone's way just as he retched dramatically, not bringing anything up but putting on a performance convincing enough to propel them to reaction. They were, Falcone knew, totally unconcerned for the onset of his affliction, interested only in avoiding the projectile path of vomit. The two men grabbed Falcone by the arms to keep him from veering in either of their directions, and Niles seized the moment, sticking his fingers into phone guy's pocket and extracting the device.

He slipped it inside the waistband of his pants and the front of his underwear. And tried to keep walking as if he'd done nothing out of the ordinary.

Minutes later, when they were locked in their cell, Falcone let out a soft whoop and thumped Niles lightly on the arm. "You did it, bud! I knew you could! Give it to me…quick, let me have it!"

Niles fished the phone out of his pants and handed it over, blowing out a shaky breath and feeling legitimately nauseous himself. Looking at Falcone, he asked, "How the bloody hell are you going to unlock it?"

Though he'd not been able to tell the model of phone from the way the guard had been concealing it, Falcone had seen enough to determine that it was not an Apple device and said, "It's an Android, so I actually know a way that should work."

Holding it out to show Niles, he went through the steps to do a hard reset, turning the phone off and then holding down the buttons to put it in recovery mode. Once he had selected the factory reset option, it rebooted and restarted. The core functions were still intact, enabling him to open the phone app.

"Holy shit," he exclaimed, "it worked!"

Giddily, he tapped out Jake's number from memory. Put the phone to his ear and listened as it made the connection and dialed. Once, twice.

At that instant, the access gate for the cell clanked open and the two guards charged in, lunging for Falcone and confiscating the phone. An angry scuffle ensued, with Falcone and Niles both being hit and thrown around.

And then the guards left them sprawled on the concrete floor.

<h1 style="text-align:center">57</h1>

FOLLOWING THE NEAR-MISS at the black site they'd hit in the heart of the capital, Jake and the group had spent the next few days covering hundreds of miles in an ever-widening circle, from Kirikkale to the east, Çankiri and Bolu to the north, and Eskişehir to the west. And, for all their travel, they had found no trace whatsoever anywhere else—in fact, they'd not come across a single site with evidence of recent occupation or use.

Jake remained determined, but his frustration and sense of futility was growing, knowing that the more time elapsed, the more their chances of finding Falcone and Niles dwindled. But he would not give up…it was just not in his DNA.

Deciding they had pretty much exhausted all feasible possibilities there, they moved on to Istanbul, taking a one-hour flight in the Pilatus and landing at Sabiha Gökçen, the smaller and less busy international airport twenty-five miles to the southeast on the Asian side of the city. After implementing the same musical-chairs tradecraft with hotel reservations, they checked into the Radisson Blu, and set off in another Mercedes Vito van.

They were headed first to Silivri in the northeast, where there were a few black sites on their list and also the massive Marmara Prison. Halfway along the ninety-minute drive on the O-7, Jake got an incoming call and checked the screen of his phone.

When he saw the number, listed as UNKNOWN CALLER, and noted

the foreign calling codes, he tapped his Bluetooth earpiece, curious but wary. As soon as he connected, the dial tone stopped, and he looked at the screen of his iPhone again.

Addressing Tashkiran, who was driving, Jake said, "I just got an in-country call, but it disconnected after a ring or two. We haven't given my number out to anyone here, so could just be a mistake, but…I don't know…isn't 312 the city code for Ankara?"

"It is," the Turk confirmed.

Jake was thoughtful for a moment, then extended his phone to Kipnis in the passenger seat. "I can't think of a reason anyone would mistakenly dial a U.S. number from Turkey. Can you find out anything on it?"

Kipnis took Jake's iPhone, tapped the number into his tablet, returned the phone to him, and went to work.

They continued to navigate the heavily congested highway, crowded on both sides with industry and commercial development and the borders of tight and extensive grids of housing. After several minutes, Kipnis spoke up, his voice elevated. "Jake, the number is tied to a guy by the name of Burak Aksoy. He is employed at Dursun."

"Dursun," Jake repeated. "As in the prison? Where we couldn't get any information or access?"

"Yes. I have been trying to ping it, but now it is off."

Jake contemplated that and said, "We've got to get back to Ankara."

Tashkiran said, "I will take us back to the airport." He added soberly, "But Jake…I sincerely hope that is not where they are. Dursun is a very bad place. People incarcerated there do not get out."

THEY MADE THE QUICK reversal and, by late afternoon, had landed again at the Esenboğa airport. The Turk fixer had worked his connections and levers of influence throughout the return flight and managed to get an administrative noncommittal from the facility, merely an agreement to receive them. This, they knew, could mean anything from being seen at the gates to speaking by phone while they stood on the outside to being allowed to meet in some capacity with a lower minion in the personnel pecking order; there was no preconception of penetrating the facility's wall of impregnability.

But Jake did not intend to be dismissed; every instinct he had was firing on high to indicate there was something significant to that random phone call. Ever since missing Falcone and Niles at the two black sites, he'd believed there was a strong probability of the two eventually being moved to a prison. So, prior to their departure from Ankara, Jake and the group had made contact, either in person or by phone, with all of the ones around the city, but Dursun had not even accepted a call.

They were able to lease a Ford Transit Tourneo—not as cushy as the Mercedes van, but with enough room for the five of them and the dogs—heading southwest from the airport and north of the city on the O-20. Now, amidst the end-of-day stream of business commuters, the sixty-mile trip took them nearly ninety minutes, putting them there just as the sun was beginning to set over the Ahir Mountains.

They were on the outskirts of Kahramanmaraş, situated at the edge of an agricultural plain below the higher terrain, northeast of Adana. Historically, the city had been the capital of the Hittite kingdom of Gurgum in the twelfth century BCE. It had been conquered by Romans and Arabs, occupied by Crusaders, incorporated into the Ottoman Empire, and taken by France before being returned to Turkey. More recently, it had been overrun by Syrian refuges whose settlements, along with much of the city, were destroyed by one of the most powerful earthquakes ever recorded in the region. From the highway, the remnants of widespread damage to buildings and housing developments could be seen, big construction machines clambering about like plundering dinosaurs.

On the north side of the city, near the encroachment of a forested park, they exited and made a series of turns onto rural roads that took them toward the hills, from which rose a stone fortress with towers that had been modified to house armed sentries. There were no directional signs, but a metal post with the now-familiar emblems for the Turkish Ministry of Justice and General Directorate of Prisons and Detention Houses (CTE) indicated the way to a long paved drive leading up to the property which, like Marmara, was enormous, the main structure imposing and draconianly sinister-looking.

As they made the approach, Tashkiran gave them a background, expounding on the prison's origins as a fortress from the seventh century

BC, passing from Persians to Romans and Byzantines and, finally, to Turks before being converted to a prison in the 1800s. He told them it was categorized as an F-type, explaining that these were the most extreme, high-security, closed institutions designated for political prisoners, members of armed organizations, those convicted of drug offenses, organized crime, and lifers—also, he added, for spies and foreign nationals. He went on to say that Dursun was notorious among penal colonies, having jailed a number of prominent politicians, activists, journalists, authors, poets, and artists; it was known for its deplorable and cruel mistreatment, squalid and unsanitary conditions, insufficient healthcare, abysmal dietary regimen, and lack of access to legal services and communications. And torture, with many documented cases of prisoners dying from the abuse.

No one could conjure anything to say, all focused grimly on the vision materializing before them.

The construction was a bizarre mix of the ancient and the new, with the stone-walled fortress and its square towers surrounded by high electrified fencing and concertina wire, the interior yard a conglomeration of many concrete buildings. The entrance was barricaded by a boom-gated drive-through with several glass-enclosed attendant stations, a red canopy bearing the official emblems and words in white lettering that read: *ADALET BAKANLIĞI DURSUN CEZA INFAZ KURUMLARI KAMPÜSÜ*. Ministry of Justice Dursun Penal Institutions Campus—the final word in the title making it sound absurdly like some kind of academic environment.

On pulling up to the boom gate, they saw that each station was guarded by armed gendarmerie units in military garb and manned, inside and outside, by several attendants wearing black slacks and white polo-style shirts with the facility's logo emblem, ID lanyards around their necks.

Powering the van's window down, Tashkiran addressed the attendant who had come to inquire about the nature of their business, presenting the card case with his credentials. They had a brief exchange and the attendant retreated to a station. A few minutes later, he returned with plastic wristbands, instructing that they be worn until departure. Next, they were asked to step out of the van, which was inspected with an undercarriage mirror by one of the gendarmes while another waved a metal-detecting wand around each of them.

Tashkiran announced, "We were confirmed as having a brief appointment with the assistant director."

"Wonderful," Jake said acerbically, but he was surprised at the ease with which the administration had acquiesced, not to mention that they were being given an audience with an official higher up the management chain.

They were provided a numbered parking pass and let through the barricade, navigating to the corresponding space in an adjacent lot. Dmello remained in the van with the dogs while Jake, Remington, Kipnis, and Tashkiran walked toward another station where they underwent a more thorough security check. After signing a log and having their wristbands scanned, they emptied their pockets and passed through a fixed screening arch, retrieved their belongings, and were then escorted to the main entrance.

At the early-evening hour, the property lighting had come on, low lights spraying across the ground and sweeping upward to the buildings' eaves, high-mast lights blazing from well above the roofs. Overhead, the darkening sky was filling with slate-colored clouds shadowed in deep blues and purples and backlit with the last blushes of day.

The exterior façade was made up of the original stone and in need of a good pressure wash, the gray surface stained green and black with a combination of moss and mold. Inside, the reception area exhibited equal signs of negligent upkeep with a cold, institutional atmosphere; the off-white plaster walls and linoleum floors were cracked and tinged with age, the air smelling of disinfectant that largely failed in cleansing or freshening the space. Unlike the removal centers they had visited, the few vinyl chairs lined along the wall were mostly empty.

Almost immediately, they were met by a harried-looking man in his thirties in wrinkled white shirtsleeves with a loosened collar and tie and belted suit pants. His slicked-back hair was starting to go its own way, and the lines in his forehead suggested a long and tedious day. Standing before them, he made a show of glancing at his watch, undoubtedly to signal both the lateness of the hour and the limited allotment of time he planned to grant them.

They were led into a cramped and dismal office, outfitted with a plain desk, Dell computer components, a worn swivel chair, an old wooden credenza, and two of the same lobby chairs for visitors. The assistant director, who had introduced himself as Samet Göçek, took a seat at his desk while Jake and the others remained standing.

As he had done on the numerous previous occasions, Tashkiran recited the facts of their inquisition in Turkish, the assistant director tapping on his keyboard and squinting at the monitor. After a few moments, he shook his head, looking from Tashkiran to Jake, who he'd rightfully pegged as the alpha in charge. Göçek muttered something, which Tashkiran repeated in English, saying, "They are not here."

But when Tashkiran had spoken their names during the inquiry, Jake thought he'd detected a tick of recognition from the assistant director. He glared at Göçek, then said to the fixer, "Neval, tell him about the call…tell him we want to speak to that guard."

Tashkiran did so, which initially got a nonplussed reaction, followed by a lengthy reply punctuated with a series of erratic changes in expression. Turning to Jake, Tashkiran explained, "He says he cannot account for the call at that time of day as phones are totally prohibited on the premises." He hesitated, knowing how Jake would respond to what he relayed next. "He says we are not allowed to speak with any of the personnel."

Jake's face darkened, his black eyes flaring. "Tell him we are not leaving until we speak to the guard. We want to see him face to face, get his explanation."

Tashkiran did as he was told, apparently adding some of his own persuasion as he tapped his chest, elaborating on some point he was making. When Tashkiran was done, the assistant director mulled what had been said, possibly deciding it might facilitate a quicker exit by the group in his office, and picked up the receiver of his desk phone.

Minutes later, a young guard appeared in the doorway, looking rattled and apprehensive. His boss addressed him in a condescending and accusatory tone, causing the gendarme to shift nervously and sputter defensively.

Tashkiran said, "He is saying that he does not know how you could have gotten a call from his phone as they are not allowed—"

Exasperated, Jake retorted, "Yeah, yeah, we know…but the fact is, I *did* get a call from his fucking phone." He flashed a look at the gendarme. "You're Burak Aksoy, and that was your number?"

Glancing uncomfortably at Jake, the guard nodded but blubbered, "No phone…no phone inside." He jabbed his hands in the pockets of his uniform pants.

Leaning close to Jake, Remington said quietly, "He's not going to incriminate himself, so we best move off that and hit harder on the pretense of the guys not being here."

The young guard disappeared before any further inquest could be leveled or retribution dispensed.

"Okay," Jake said sternly, gaze locked on Göçek. "Are you going on the record in maintaining that Eddie Falcone and Curran Niles are not— and have not been—incarcerated at this facility?"

Tashkiran repeated Jake's challenge, and there was the slightest wavering in the assistant director's response but, before Jake could press any further, a pair of security men stepped into the already crowded room, the purpose of their presence obvious.

The four of them accompanied the men, and left the building.

Minutes later, when they were back in the Ford van, Jake declared, "The son of a bitch was lying. Both of them were. Did you see their body language?"

"Sure did," Remington said.

"So how do we get them out?" Jake asked angrily. "I know they're in there."

Kipnis was studying his tablet, evaluating something that had been sent while they were inside. He said, "Actually…they are not."

"What?"

"They might have been here—in fact, I agree with you that the guard and the assistant director were not telling the truth—but they are not here now."

Jake and Remington leaned forward from their second-row seats to see the screen of Kipnis' tablet. On it was a high-quality satellite image, dated and time-stamped just hours earlier. In it were two figures being led by several others; from overhead, not much could be made out in personal identifying detail, but the figures in custody had their heads covered and their arms behind their backs. Kipnis zoomed out to show them the unmistakable layout of the fortress and red-roofed buildings comprising Dursun Prison which, by this scale, appeared to be a kilometer or so from the figures.

But what they were all riveted to was where the figures were headed…across a small, flat square of land where a black helicopter had landed.

58

BARELY AN HOUR AFTER Falcone and Niles had swiped the guard's phone, incredibly, they were moved again.

They had become increasingly fearful of the process, as each different destination brought an escalatory worse set of circumstances in one form or another—miserable conditions with little or no food and water; indignities and violations; various degrees of torture; imprisonment in an actual penitentiary with almost no chance of ever getting out. Except now, they *were* being taken out, but not because they were being released…no, they were once again restrained and hooded and loaded into the cargo hold of a truck or van. So they were naturally wondering, where could they be going that was more awful than where they had already been?

This time, after a very short ride, one which took only minutes, they were unloaded and stumble-marched across a grassy stretch, recognizing the *whap-whap* of helicopter blades coupled with the draft of rotor wash. Once they had been strapped into seats and the aircraft lifted off, the transport turned into a much lengthier one, lasting close to three hours. After landing and being manhandled from the cabin to the ground, they were walked across what felt like the slick wood floor of an interior, contradicted by the fresh air of a moderate breeze.

When their hoods were removed, they were stunned and utterly confused to find themselves just inside the entrance to a stairwell—a modern, elegant one with recessed lighting, polished wood treads, burled veneer sidewalls, and mirrorlike stainless steel handrails.

One of their handlers gave a laugh and said, by way of explanation, "We would not want you should fall. Watch step." His partner found this funny, too, and chortled.

Like most of the others that had preceded them, these two men were big and brawny and clad in black—chinos, pocketed button-up shirts, and tactical vests—but there was a different countenance about them, something that seemed to set them apart from the previous rank-and-file thugs, as if they were cut from a different kind of enforcer fabric. They were also equipped with a comprehensive array of armaments, including handguns, automatic rifles, ammo clips, tasers, and knives.

When Falcone and Niles did not move, dazedly looking at each other, one of the two men stuck out a booted foot and thumped Niles behind the shins, sending him tumbling down the stairs. With wrists zip-tied behind his back, all he could do to counter the fall was roll toward the sidewall. Prior to departure from the prison, they had been redressed in the clothing they'd been wearing when first abducted in Chios and now, as Niles toppled and skidded over the treads, both of his canvas slip-on shoes came off his feet and went bouncing down ahead of him.

"Hey, asshole!" Falcone yelled irately, which got him an elbow between his shoulder blades, pitching him forward in a similar fall.

The two landed in a pile on a platform at the bottom. Thumping down behind them in the stairwell, the handlers laughed boisterously, as if watching a stunt-gone-wrong on a bloopers reel.

The two men pulled them into standing positions, Niles wincing sharply as he maneuvered his feet to get his shoes back on. He muttered, "Think you've twisted my bloody ankle!"

"Keep going, *mudak*," one of the men ordered, turning them toward another descending set of stairs.

"Where the hell are we?" Falcone demanded, cautiously navigating the steps with Niles, who was leaning against the sidewall as he shuffled his way down.

His question got no response, only grunts and pushes.

They were moved another level below and then taken into a large suite dripping in opulence from every corner and surface. The floor was herringboned planks of polished teak accented with ornate Persian rugs;

groupings of chairs and sofas were plushly upholstered in camel- and cocoa-colored fabrics; wood tables were varnished and inlaid with etched gold leaf marquetry. The window panels were draped with gold silk shades and curtains; the trey ceiling was sectioned in woven cane squares and spaced with big, round light fixtures ringed in brass, supplemented by small recessed LED dots. A rippled wood bar with metallized resin and more gold leaf occupied a back corner, mirrored shelves fully stocked with bottles and crystal decanters; an opposite corner was furnished with a giant TV screen and a wall of built-in cabinetry decorated with high-end gallery art pieces.

But the side of the room to which they were steered was that of an office area, dominated by a big executive desk and a long conference table, both made of dark wood, carved and inlaid and gleaming in the soft light. The men seated Falcone and Niles in high-backed upholstered chairs on opposite sides of one end of the table, tied them down with thick nylon ropes, and then departed.

The psychological jolt of going from the unspeakably dreadful settings in which they'd been previously confined to such utterly improbable grandeur had an initially disconcerting effect, much like that of being unexpectedly dropped into a zero-gravity cabin. Taking in the luxurious furnishings and décor, Niles eventually remarked, "Remind you of something, mate?"

"Yeah…I think we're on a fucking yacht," Falcone replied unbelievably.

They were harkening back to the Colombian cartel's exhorbitant 140-foot vessel, *Javiera*, where they had conducted one of their first missions for Jake—and the first time they had nearly met their demise.

Their heads swiveled to an entry hall on the other side of the suite, watching as a man in a resplendent suit entered and stepped behind the bar, reached for a decanter, and poured a generous amount of what was most likely vodka into a cut crystal tumbler. With his back to them, he took a swig from the glass, topped off his pour, and turned.

Strolling leisurely toward them, the man was in his fifties, graying brown hair immaculately cut and styled with a light and precisely shaped layer of mustache and beard, and spa-pampered skin. The suit he wore was a wide-striped bespoke Brioni in navy, white silk dress shirt open several buttons. Expensive gold jewelry gleamed from his neck and hands; overlapping cable chains nestled amidst sprigs of chest hair, shirt sleeves were cufflinked with nautical knots, a wrist was banded with an ornate Patek Philipp watch.

As he got closer, they noticed a folder tucked under an arm and resigned themselves to the usual questions.

The man took a seat at the head of the table, placing the folder in front of him. He took another sip from his tumbler and set it down. Glanced sharply from Falcone to Niles, and flipped his folder open. In an accent that was distinctively Russian, he said, "I will get straight to the point of my business."

He slid a five-by-seven color photo from the folder to a space on the table between the two of them. Both immediately recognized the face of the man named Logan Hays. Neither could hide their surprise but said nothing.

The man tapped the photo with a finger, on which a pretentiously large gold ring bedazzled like the head of a royal scepter, a mound of small diamonds with a colossal gem in the middle. He said, "You know him. Where is he?"

Falcone and Niles exchanged flabbergasted looks, totally thrown by the line of questioning. But a slow, mental confetti of thoughts were beginning to flutter…the yacht that Jake and Remington had reconned, a photo of the vet who had seemed like such a deviant outlier produced by this ostentatious man with the Russian accent…and they realized where they were and who was holding court.

Regarding the man they now knew was oligarch Taras Ignatkovich, Falcone and Niles remained silent. The Russian rapped the knuckle of his ring finger on the table next to the photo, repeating, "Where is he?"

This time, Falcone quipped, "Your guess is as good as ours. Who is he, and who is he to you?"

Ignatkovich eyed him shrewdly, replying, "He was with your group, and now he is gone."

Since Falcone and Niles had already departed from Psara by the time the man known as Logan Hays had drugged Remington, stolen the jugs, and made his getaway, they were again caught off guard by this disclosure.

"Have no idea," Falcone responded. Across from him, Niles shook his head blankly.

The Russian leaned back in his chair with an expression of annoyance that segued to one of crafty calculation. He reached for his tumbler and held it up as if proposing a toast. "You know," he said airily, "you could have some cocktails, nice steak and potato…lobster maybe…or juicy cheeseburger." His lips curled into a taunting sneer. "Nice bath…popcorn and movie." He winked. "Sexy company."

Falcone and Niles, despite their best efforts to affect the restored decorum of impervious self-possession, could not help but feel the tug of temptation for such offerings, stomachs spontaneously reacting at the mention of the food. But even if they were willing to concede and yield anything, they had no knowledge of Hays' whereabouts if he was, as Ignatkovich alleged, gone.

Clearing his throat to cover the hungry rumbles from his gut, Falcone said, "Can't tell you what we don't know."

"What *do* you know?" Ignatkovich asked.

"Not as much as you do, apparently," Falcone said.

The Russian downed the last of his vodka with a big slurp, gripped the glass and stared at each of them. Then he collected the photo of Hays and the folder, removed them from the table, and stood up.

"Shame I cannot reward you," he remarked drily, and left the suite.

THE BELLICOSE PAIR OF handlers promptly returned for them, moving Falcone and Niles further down into the belly of the boat by a succession of stairs and corridors. They were each allowed to use a lavatory on the way to a mechanical area, where they were seated on a floor that was spotless and shined to a high gloss. The zip ties were removed, their wrists repositioned in front of them with a new set of restraints. They were securely tied to metal railings and left with bottles of water.

Quiet for several moments, they drank and visually explored their surroundings, the systems in their midst generating a whitewash of somewhat muted noises. It wasn't particularly uncomfortable, especially by comparison to where they'd most recently been, the air neither cold nor hot and smelling only faintly of plastics and metals and maintenance fluids. There was low light, no crawling things, and no tormented screaming.

In the moment, it felt like some kind of heaven.

Reflecting back on their last encounter with Hays and the man's unsavory behavior—especially toward Callie—Niles said, "I knew there was something dodgy about that wanker, Logan Hays. Who d'ya think he is?"

"Obviously not Logan Hays," Falcone said. "I couldn't tell if there was a name on the photo, but the printing was foreign, probably Russian. I'd say, unlike us, he's an actual spy."

"So he was in the vet group to spy on them? To spy on us?"

Falcone shrugged vaguely but said, "It could explain some things that happened, and I always felt there was a lot more we didn't hear about."

Niles gave that some thought and perked up. "If this is the oligarch and the boat Jake and Remy were going after, they might be able to find us!"

"That would be the hope," Falcone agreed but did not share Niles' enthusiasm.

As the time began to tick by, Niles, too, felt the air drain from his hopeful speculation, aware of the dull ache in his twisted or sprained ankle—one more affliction to add to his growing inventory of hurt. "What I wouldn't give for some ice," he murmured, rubbing it against his opposite leg since he couldn't reach it by hand.

"No shit," Falcone replied. "A whole bathtub of it. What I wouldn't give for that cheeseburger. Christ."

"When I was in the loo, I got a gander at myself…I think I've lost a stone…and I look like a punk that's been gang beat." Following the thread of teased indulgences—though neither actually believed the offerings would have been tendered—Niles remarked, "Wonder if those birds are on the boat?"

Falcone groaned irritably. "You mean bitches. Wouldn't surprise me a bit. I knew they weren't from Greece, and now that I think about it, their accents could have been Russian."

Sighing wearily, Niles said, "Well, at least we're out of that fucking hell we were in."

Falcone did not reply, his thoughts troubled. Being on a luxury yacht full of accommodations, any of which could have been used to confine them, and instead tied up in the bowels, did not bode well. Still, Niles could be right; knowing that Ignatkovich had been on Jake's radar, there was a chance, however slim, that he would track them down. Falcone cast a compassionate glance at his friend, really hoping that the Brit's optimistic conjecture would bear out.

Turning his head to meet Falcone's gaze, Niles leaned into Falcone's arm. A single tear ran down his cheek.

"Hey," Falcone said, "we're gonna survive this, bud. That's what we do."

Sniffling, Niles said, "Right, mate."

"And yeah, these digs aren't too bad."

Their reprieve was short-lived.

59

SINCE SEEING THE SAT images of the helicopter near Dursun, the group had pulled an all-nighter at their hotel in Ankara, Kipnis working his intel pipeline, on the phone much of the time with Sabine Brisepierre. Dmello took the Malinois with him to the airport hangar, where he fueled up the Pilatus, gave it an extra thorough inspection, and then flew Tashkiran back to Izmir. Their Turkish fixer had his own business to tend to but committed to remaining available and responsive to anything they needed at a moment's notice. Remington spent some of the time on a video call with his team at the Psara basecamp, being brought up to speed on operations and glad to hear there had been relatively few issues in his absence. Jake was likewise relieved to find his Costa Rican household holding up under the circumstances. The circumstances being that Callie could not stop worrying about Falcone and Niles, was anxious for Jake to come home, and increasingly distressed over the state of her gunshot wounds.

Speaking in soothing tones, Jake tried to reassure her as much as he could, saying, "It will be all right...everything just needs time to heal. Try not to look so much, love. Remember, I said it looks worse than it is. I took good care of you, so yes, I'm sure. Be good for me...do what Jesse and Camilla say, okay? I love you, sweetheart."

When she asked him if they were going to find Falcone and Niles, he could only assert, "We're doing all that we can."

During their prior time in Ankara, after staying the first night at the

Holiday Inn Express, Remington had moved them into the more palatable Anadolu, which was where they were now, Kipnis on his phone with tablet and laptop in front of him, Jake and Remington alternately sitting and pacing.

Pouring himself another cup of coffee, Jake retook his seat on one of two sofas, Remington on the other, stuffing the last of a sandwich into his mouth.

Jake said, "I still think we should have just headed straight to Bodrum. We were already running a couple of hours behind them, and now"—he glanced at his watch—"we're coming up on twelve hours. Fuck."

A few hours earlier, Kipnis had acquired additional satellite images that showed a helicopter landing on the *Gala* at sea. With the HawkEye 360 tracking technology, which he'd been accessing regularly, he had charted the vessel's position around the time of the helicopter's touchdown to just below Chios in the waters of the Icarian Sea. And while none of the subsequent imagery showed the two figures they were assuming to be Falcone and Niles, the group was adhering to the belief that it was them, being delivered to Taras Ignatkovich. *If* the landing helicopter was the same one that had taken off from the field near Dursun; despite the superb quality and level of detail in the sat images, the helo's tail number could not be seen from the overhead view, but it was black and the shape was consistent with that of the Leonardo.

"I feel your frustration, brother," Remington commiserated. "But that's only one of an unlimited number of possible locations, and we don't know for sure if—"

"But it's a hell of a lot better than just sitting on our asses here," Jake barked loudly and testily, causing Kipnis and Dmello, who had dozed off after returning from his Izmir flight, to look his way. The Malinois, sprawled on the king-size bed next to the Kenyan, hopped off and scampered over to Jake, nuzzling at his knees to solicit petting in an effort to cheer up one of the humans in their pack and, maybe, get offered a sandwich from the room service tray.

Kipnis joined them, taking a seat next to Remington. Placing his tablet on the coffee table so they could both see the screen, he said, "Looks like you are right, Jake. The yacht is berthed at Yalikavak."

Jake sprang from the sofa. "Goddamn it! I knew it." He looked at Kipnis. "How old is the intel?"

"As of a few minutes ago, it's still at the marina."

Remington queried, "Any word on whether Ignat's on it…or the guys?"

"Not yet," Kipnis replied, "but I would say now we *should* go."

Dmello rose from the bed and headed for the bathroom. The rest of them began gathering all of their belongings and gear while Remington called to notify the front desk they were checking out.

THEY LANDED AT THE Milas-Bodrum Airport just as the morning was overtaking dawn in a bright yoke of yellow, hangered the plane, and leased a Volkswagen Caravelle van. Dmello took the wheel and did his best to weave through the thickening traffic along the D330.

During the hour-long drive, they discussed their predicament.

"With the marina security, we won't be able to get close to the boat," Remington said, stating the obvious.

"I'm sure Ignat's security knows us by sight," Jake added, "so even if we could, it wouldn't be wise. As I remember from the last time we were there, it doesn't really have any access with a decent vantage for recon."

"No, it doesn't," Remington agreed.

"I doubt they would be taken off the yacht there," Kipnis ventured, "unless it was in the middle of the night."

Dmello had been quietly thinking and offered, "My face is probably not known to them…maybe I could find a way to get on the boat. Obtain a marina staff uniform, or—"

Remington stopped him. "No, Mellie, that would be too risky."

"Yeah, good thought, but it would also take too much time and effort," Jake said.

As they pulled into the marina and passed through the security check, they were all realizing why the oligarch chose to take haven in such a busy, public place—it provided every amenity, every service, and every luxury while keeping him effectively off-limits, his security able to see anyone or anything coming. The bastard was also arrogant enough to believe he was untouchable by the law, Jake thought, and, with his network of connections and influence, he probably was.

They parked and filed out of the van, Kipnis asking, "Want me to bring the Hornet?"

"Might as well," Remington replied. "Not sure if we should deploy it, though. In daylight, tiny as it is, there's a chance one of their security goons sees it. That could get it taken out and us exposed."

"If I send it, they will not see it," the Israeli assured them.

They strolled cautiously along the shopping concourse, ready to take quick cover should any of the oligarch's men appear in their path. The quay on the right was as populated by stately vessels as on their previous visit, even more pedestrian activity on the promenade with the added subset of early-day walkers and joggers and coffee klatches. The Malinois were briskly alert and stimulated by all the smells, human and otherwise, but did not seem to be especially piqued by anything they were picking up.

Commenting on this as they approached the end of the walkway, Remington said, "Keen as their noses are, I'm inclined to think our guys are still on the yacht…or not on it at all."

They stopped adjacent to Zuma, the restaurant with the stone tower and pool, and spotted the *Gala* in all of its massiveness at the end of the quay, some four hundred feet out, hemmed by the fleet of security tenders.

Jake peered through his Steiner binoculars, honing in on the yacht. After a few moments, he reported, "Not seeing much. A few sentries standing around. That's it."

"I'd expect some life about the exterior decks," Remington remarked. "Staff and crew moving around, others having coffee, breakfast…women in bikinis sunbathing on lounge chairs."

As they stood watching and pondering, Kipnis got an alert and checked his phone. "I have new intel coming in." He tapped his tablet and navigated to an email, opening the attachments. Then he said, "I think we can put an end to speculation as to whether the guys are on the boat."

JAKE, REMINGTON, AND DMELLO were locked in on the screen of

Kipnis' tablet, studying the sat images as he slowly swiped through the sequence he'd been sent. Once the entire set had been viewed, one image in particular was recalled and magnified.

In it was a speedboat, thirty to forty feet in length judging by the scale, resembling their Technohull RIB and the craft like it that had taken up defensive pursuit when they'd been surveilling the *Gala*. Other images in the sequence showed the boat in successive positions between the superyacht at sea as it was on the approach to Yalikavak, but this particular image was the ace in the deck—it showed the speedboat to the south of the marina, nosing toward an empty stretch of shore. Four passengers could be seen, two of which were hooded.

The image that bookended, far less provocative but much more impactful, was of the boat beached and devoid of its passengers. The capture did not include much of the surrounding land, but there were no figures visible anywhere in the frame.

Jake broke the silence, asking, "That's it? That's all the images?"

"Yes," Kipnis replied. "Maybe there will be more to come, but it might very well be all we get now that they are on land." He pointed to the edge of the last sat image. "That's Çökertme street, so my guess is they got into a vehicle."

No one said anything for several moments, Jake's frustration palpable. When he spoke next, his voice was flinty and resolute. "We need to fucking find Ignat. Find him, we find them."

"About all we've got to work with at this point," Remington agreed.

Jake said, "We know it's them, but let's take Luna and Solis to that spot, see if they get a hit. Maybe we'll get lucky and find something with the boat."

AS THEY WERE ALL expecting, the canines reacted as soon as they were let out of the van, charging through low trees and shrubs to the sand. But the boat was gone, leaving only light drag indentions that disappeared within the vegetation, the dogs letting them know that the scent trail abruptly ended at the road's edge.

Glancing in both directions of Çökertme and seeing several secondaries feeding to the next parallel road, Jake said, "I guess we go back to the marina, get a hotel, and dig into everything Ignatkovich."

Remington nodded. "That's what I was going to suggest. We'll start going through all of his known property, local haunts, anything we can find around here."

They made the short drive back, checking into the Yalikavak Marina Hotel, which was beach-front, just past the parking lot. The thirty-six-room property was brand new, gorgeous, and as appropriately luxurious as its namesake, with decadent suites affording panoramic views of sea and yacht basin. Just not, unfortunately, the section that extended out the farthest where the *Gala* was berthed.

After getting settled into their accommodations, Kipnis' suite again turned into a war room, with the electronic devices of all being multi-tasked and trolled for resources and data. Paper maps were spread over tables, folders and notebooks open with contents scattered. Pots of coffee were made, emptied, and regenerated as crosstalk filled the space in discussions, questions, information sharing, and phone conversations. By late in the day, they knew little more than their speculations.

Seated on the ecru-colored sofa, Jake gazed through the full-length glass panels, watching as the blues and lavenders of sky filled with the pinks and oranges of oncoming dusk, giving the sea a rose-gold glint.

Repeating what had already been deliberated several times since the morning, he said, "I don't really get what Ignat would want with them. He's been on us since before we even got here, so it's not like he's lacking intel and, as you said, Kip, apparently had that guy Vasić planted in the dig. Maybe he's going to leverage them in some way?"

"Maybe," Kipnis answered, "but I think you might have hit on the motivation…Vasić. He was embedded for a mission, which was to spy on us and report back. And then he took off. We were not done and he had not been exposed, so there would have been no reason for him to leave when he did. Except for the theft of our finds."

Remington tagged onto the hypothesis. "Yeah…I think you might be right, Kip. That suggests Vasić was acting on his own, maybe going rogue. If he stopped reporting in, that would certainly have fired up Ignat, and when he got word of our guys being imprisoned and knew he could get them into his custody, he might have thought he could find out what had happened with his operative."

"Any leads on where his properties here are?" Jake asked.

Kipnis, who was rarely challenged for long, gave a disgruntled sigh. "Not yet. I am making some progress getting past the firewalls of the shell companies, but I wish I could do it faster."

Jake looked around the room, taking note of the solemn, weary faces. "Anybody want to take a break?"

The other three shook their heads, but the fatigue factor was evident.

"Okay, let's freshen up, get some dinner, and we'll get back to it."

"Luna and Solis are ready for a walk, so yeah, sounds good," Remington said, and followed Jake and Dmello out of Kipnis' suite.

The Israeli said nothing, tapping keys on his Toughbook as he dove deeper and deeper into the murkier realms of the cyberverse.

WHEN THEY RECONVENED AN hour or so later, the hues of sunset had bled away save for a thin ribbon of crimson, the sky now royal blue in twilight and lit with a nearly full moon, rising over the sea like a golden pearl.

They had all showered and changed into fresh sets of black clothing. Brooding by the wall of windows, Jake's eyes scanned the horizon as if he could somehow bend its line to incorporate the end of the Alpha quay. Fuming, he murmured, "God, I would give anything to get on that boat, find the son of a bitch and rip his fucking balls out through his throat."

"I could get on board with that," Remington sneered.

"To that…do we want to run the risk of going out to dinner or order in?" Jake asked.

"Yeah, I thought about that, too. They've got some great restaurants here, but we know his mercs have wide latitude on terms of engagement and no qualms whatsoever about incurring collateral damage." Mentally reviewing the layout of the marina, Remington said, "A good spot to watch the forward of that dock might actually be the helipad lounge at the Russian restaurant…what's it called?"

"Novikov," Jake remembered. "Then again, it might also be a place he'd be drawn to, and I'm going to guess alternative exits would be limited. Kip, is Ignat known to be a social animal?"

Immersed in whatever he was mining on his laptop, Kipnis replied vaguely, "Sometimes…with his security force, of course."

Glancing around, Jake noticed they were missing Dmello, but before he could inquire, there was a rat-a-tat-tat rap on the door to the suite and he was let in by Remington.

The Kenyan was also clad in black, but his shirt was festively patterned in pink and gray flowers and leaves, untucked over the Glock in the waist of his cargo pants, high-top sneakers on his feet. Grinning, he quipped, "I have some intel." With his colorfully beaded dreads, naturally jolly demeanor, and accented sing-song voice, he could have easily been taken for a happy-go-lucky, reggae-loving Caribbean national instead of the former elitist of the Kenyan Air Force Rapid Deployment Squadron that he was. His look and geniality gave him the guise of an innocuous tourist out for a carefree stroll, which was precisely what he'd counted on and what had yielded his results.

Taking out his phone, he cleared the lock screen and swiped into his photos. Proudly displayed an image of a face that was burned into all of their brains.

"How did you get this?" Jake asked, staring at the profile of Taras Ignatkovich.

Using his fingers to zoom out, he saw the man in full, sportily dressed in a pale blue lightweight Brunello Cucinelli suit, the blazer's double-row buttons open to reveal a nautical-striped polo. Even with sunglasses, there was no denying the subject's identity, arrogant smile and cocksure gait captured in mid-stride. He was flanked on both sides by several voluptuous women skimpily swathed in stretchy fabric that squeezed breasts to maximum display and did the bare minimum to sheath regions to the south. Preceding him and bringing up the rear was an imposing entourage of security men, all in black jackets and slacks and shades, very much resembling a cortege of Secret Service agents.

Jake looked at him incredulously. "You took this pic?"

"Oh no," Dmello said, and explained, "I decided to get some intel the good old-fashion way…walking and talking." In his mellifluous cadence, he went on, "Just making curious talk with people, you know, about the colossal yacht at the end of the dock. Sometimes I showed a photo of Ignat that I had loaded on my phone, asking if anyone had seen him here. One guy immediately recognized my photo and showed me this that he had taken, which he agreed to share. With the delegation around him, he thought Ignat was a rock star."

"Good work, Mellie!" Remington lauded. "Did he tell you anything else?"

"Yes. He said some attendants followed with rolling carts of baggage and boxes."

"And when was this?"

"A few hours ago."

"Goddamn asshole skated right by under noses," Jake muttered disgustedly. "Okay, so he's disembarked for a stay somewhere inland or maybe he was going to be taken to the airport."

Kipnis had been listening with interest, glancing at the image of the oligarch on Dmello's phone, but he had also continued to tap keys and pore over data on his laptop. Now, he said, "Airport."

The other three heads turned in his direction.

"Not sure of the destination yet, but he departed on a private jet. Of course, he could be headed anywhere, but he does have an estate in Cyprus."

"Wouldn't he have sailed the yacht there?" Jake asked.

"Probably," Kipnis replied, "but there could have been a number of reasons for this marina. He obviously likes it, the yacht has been here other times. It could also have been for the helo to land with the guys."

Jake pursed his lips, forehead creased as he contemplated. "Do you think he's had them transported to his place in Cyprus? Do you know where it is?"

"I will know," Kipnis said. "Working on it. But more likely, a black site or a compound, and I do not believe that will be in Cyprus." Thoughtfully, he added, "I have a hunch there is something else, some other reason, an agenda and destination."

Dmello asked him, "Should I get the plane ready for us to go to Cyprus tonight or in the morning?"

It took the Israeli a few moments, his mind flickering on intel he'd been finding and perusing over the past few hours. "Yes." He pulled up the island on Google Maps. "Paphos or Larnaca, they are both about the same distance from Limassol, which is where most of the billionaires have property."

"Let's scramble up some food and drink," Remington proposed. "We need it. There's a couple of JD's definitely looking for me."

SEATED AROUND THE DINING table, a beautiful piece of blond woodwork matching the other Scandinavian-style furnishings of the suite, they were finishing off a spread of takeout from the Cookshop, throwing out possibilities and theories as Kipnis quietly worked while he ate. Knowing that the oligarch had left the marina, they had been tempted to take their chances at one of the onsite restaurants, salivating at the thought of world-class gourmet beef from the Nusr-Et steakhouse or Japanese cuisine from Zuma, but ultimately erred on the side of caution by dining in. With the oligarch boss away, it was highly probable some of those remaining aboard the *Gala* would take the opportunity to eat, drink, and be merry; Jake and Remington did not care to add murderous mayhem to the menu.

Pouring himself another generous splash from a bottle of Jack Daniel's, Remington remarked, "You know, there is some good news here."

Jake eyed him narrowly. "Yeah? What's that?"

"They're still alive."

Jake nodded but made no comment, mindful of the torture chamber at the Ankara black site.

Dmello cleared the table, Jake and Remington taking bottles and glasses into the suite's sitting area. Kipnis stayed in his seat, eyes riveted to the screen on his Toughbook. While the other three got comfortable in chairs and on the sofa and the Malinois plopped at their feet, the Israeli let out an uncharacteristic exclamation.

"Holy fuck!"

Joining them, he set his laptop on the coffee table, the screen displaying what looked like a message board, contents in multiple languages and set against a dark background. Jake, Remington, and Dmello regarded him speechlessly, waiting for the revelation.

It took him a moment as he continued to stare at the Toughbook screen, and then he said, "I know where Ignat is going…Syria."

Jake's jaw dropped. *"What?"*

"What's in Syria?" Remington asked, equally astonished.

"A terrorists' auction."

60

JAKE, REMINGTON, AND DMELLO knelt around the coffee table to study the site Kipnis had found after spelunking his way through a myriad of iniquitous rabbit holes proliferating in the Dark Web.

"I have been following the coded breadcrumbs for hours," he told them. "I know of many such sites, but this is the most notorious one, and it takes real cyber chops to find it and get in. It uses the most complex IP randomizing and cloaking and the URL is also constantly changing."

"What is it?" Jake asked.

"A marketplace for global arms trafficking, and I am not talking about the usual hardware. At Mossad, we were always monitoring it when we could snag it and work our way in. Here, the players are the worst of the worst bad actors, and the goods up for purchase or bid are the stuff of nightmares…bombs and explosives of every kind, toxins and nerve agents, nuclear devices…you just cannot imagine."

"Jesus Christ," Remington muttered.

"The posting I have here is listed as a special auction, the host going by the name of *Zvezda Smerti*. I know Russian, but I had to look that up. It translates as Death Star. The description is in English, Russian, Turkish, Arabic, Persian, and several other languages. Basically, it is offering the highest bidder access to the formula, source, and substance for quantum stealth."

"It's Vasić!" Jake declared.

"Has to be," Remington agreed. "Where and when is this auction?"

"The exact location has not been disclosed as yet," Kipnis said. "Only that it will be in Syria, in two days."

"How do we know if Ignat is aware of this and is going?"

"I got wind of something big blowing up in chatter, which is why I have been looking for this, particularly since a former Wagner Group top commander known to be working for Ignatkovich has been mentioned…so yes, he knows."

Jake and Remington exchanged charged looks, Jake saying, "We've got to go. It might give us our best shot at cornering Ignat and getting our guys."

Remington nodded. "Not to mention the chance to get the polymer and device back. The thought of that tech in the possession of an enemy nation or terrorist organization…"

He did not have to finish the sentence, everyone knowing the potential horrors of that scenario.

Jake said, "Okay, with this development, I think we have two near objectives…keep an eye on that listing and find a way to get into the auction and, before that, find Ignat's place in Cyprus and pay him a house call, whether he's in residence or not."

THEY MADE THE QUICK hop from Bodrum to the Larnaca airport FBO before dawn the next morning, leaving Dmello and the Malinois behind with the Pilatus and renting a Mercedes Tourer van; they did not really expect to find Falcone and Niles in Cyprus but wanted to be prepared just in case. None of them had gotten much sleep, least of all Kipnis, who had been glued to the auction listing on his laptop, monitoring for changes or updates while simultaneously working his tablet and phone to unearth the location of Taras Ignatkovich's Cyprus estate.

He found it as they were making the final approach to Limassol on the A1 Nicosia-Limassol highway. They had just passed the vast archaeological site of Amathous east of the city, sprawled over the hills leading down to the sea, when he was able to penetrate the layers of fabricated consortiums cloaking a property known as *Villa Alekou*.

To Remington, who was driving, Kipnis announced, "We need to get off at the next opportunity, then get back on eastbound. We want to take the E109 junction, about three kilometers back."

Following his directions, Remington turned onto the road, which passed over the mountainous topography they had been skirting all the way from the airport. The route took them to the village of Parekklisia, just over ten miles to the north, twisting around rolling countryside. Dictating navigation from Google Maps on his tablet, Kipnis steered them through the small town center with its scattering of modest businesses and housing, the two-lane road winding up toward the slopes of the Troodos Mountains that rose across the horizon.

The farther out they drove, the more spectacular the views became, Remington commenting, "If you've got all those billions and need some Cypriot real estate close to the urban beat but isolated in the hills, this would sure as shit be the place."

Lush, sun-drenched expanses of wine vineyards and olive groves swept by their windows, an occasional ranch in between. After taking several rural roads to the west, they wound their way to a gravel drive which ascended to a three-story mansion built of stone with a red tile roof. A wraparound terrace covered the lower level, part of which was a port-style garage, the upper two stories inset with big glass panels and connected by a large chimney and a hexagonal structure accented by tall arched windows. A pair of curved concrete steps led from the base level to the terrace, the stone court hardscaped with ornamental trees and shrubs. The acreage surrounding the mansion was full of fruit trees and vineyards with the majestic mountain panorama stretched across the backdrop.

Peering at the grandiose manor atop the hill, Remington whistled. "What do you think? Ten thousand square feet or so?"

"I found an old real estate listing," Kipnis told them. "Over fifteen. Another five thousand of terrace space and balconies. Eight bedrooms, twelve bathrooms, three kitchens, and—"

"Okay, okay," Jake scoffed. "Don't need the brochure sales pitch. The only thing that really matters is how we get in."

Prior to heading out, they had discussed the plan for ingress, Kipnis coming up with multiple options depending on what they encountered. The house was enclosed by black wrought-iron rail fencing which, at a glance, might seem more decorative than protective, but the oligarch had not managed to maintain such a degree of insularity by deficient defense measures. To the contrary, just as his comprehensive fleet of trained mercenaries and well-protected assets demonstrated, there would undoubtedly be multilayered and complex systems installed here and any other place he set foot in.

To this end, Kipnis had brought along his array of penetration gadgets, which he employed as soon as they stepped from the van. They had parked at the bottom of the gravel drive behind a low roadside line of evergreens and were now making their way along the sloping periphery, Kipnis studying the readings on a device that detected a variety of signals, including electronic, infrared, microwave, tomographic, Wi-Fi, and others.

For the daylight op, they were dressed in tactical khaki combat attire consisting of the usual pocketed shirts and cargo pants, pouched vests with body armor and accessories, elbow and knee pads, gloves, and boots; they were armed with their Glocks, knives, and a few other munitions, Kipnis also slinging one of the M4s. They had commed up, loaded and checked their weapons, and strapped on lightweight packs.

When they were close enough to get a good line of sight, they took up prone positions and surveyed the front and western side of the mansion, not seeing any immediate sign of activity. No vehicles were parked on the pavers, but the grilles of a car and an SUV were visible inside the open arch of the garage. Oddly, there were no sentries positioned or patrolling around the terrace.

Through his comm, Jake said, "Don't think he's here. If he was, we'd be seeing at least some personnel on the grounds."

"Agree," Remington replied. "Good for us…means less to deal with inside."

As they were making this observation, a lone man, dressed in casual wear but similarly vested with a holstered sidearm and a radio clipped to his belt, wandered out onto the front terrace, a coffee cup and cigarette in hand.

They watched him through binoculars until he retreated inside the house. Jake said, "Probably a skeleton crew."

"Let's hope," Remington said.

Keeping low, they moved closer, Kipnis starting to get readings on his detector. He palmed a second device and said, "Attempting to jam now. Depending on the systems in place and their configuration, what I am using may or may not work." After a few moments of watching his jammer cycle through various frequencies, he proclaimed, "Success. Watch for reaction."

Several minutes passed with no apparent response, Jake remarking, "Well, somebody's asleep at the switch."

They waited and watched a little while longer and then continued their advancement toward the rear of the property. Finding no human presence there, they crossed to the eastern side and dropped flat to covertly surveil. Again, they waited and, seeing no movement, crouch-walked through a thick grove of shrubs and small trees until they were at the front corner, where the terrace covered an open-sided outdoor dining space, which was their planned point of entry.

They paused to pull up cravats from around their necks to cover the bottoms of their faces, Remington with a ball cap to conceal his auburn hair, and crept forward into the shadows, stepping around patio furniture. Kipnis made a quick check of the glass doors, gesturing with his hand that they could proceed, and slid one of the panels open.

With Glocks at the ready, they entered into a high-ceiling interior dining area, the walls elaborately framed in moldings, painted in creamy tones, and accented with richly textured paper. The floors were highly polished marble, every surface spotless and gleaming, light flowing in from the multitude of windows on the back side. But they paid little attention to the furnishings, instead focusing on any sound from those in residence.

The first contact came in the form of a startled housekeeper, a young-ish woman in a gray smock-style dress emerging from a laundry room carrying a stack of folded white towels. Before any of them could get to her, she emitted a shriek, the cry sharper and more amplified in the capacious vacuum and, within instants, the heavy thumps and shuffling of feet could be heard from above.

Kipnis crossed to her quickly, snatching her by the waist. Remington already had a roll of duct tape out, tearing off a piece and applying it to her mouth as Kipnis cinched her hands in flex-cuffs. They sat her on the floor just as a trio of men came scrambling hastily down the stairs from the second level.

Jake directed, "Taking tango one…Remy, two…Kip, three." Spreading out, each fired multiple rounds at their targets as the men from upstairs bounded into the room, their own guns up and swinging to line up with the intruders shooting at them. Caught by surprise, their fire was off just enough, while that of Jake, Remington, and Kipnis, was dead-on.

Each of the three security men dropped, their blood oozing in dark red pools on the pristine cream-colored marble and matte paint and finely textured wallpaper.

In the aftermath, Jake called out, "Everybody good?"

"Just peachy keen," Remington quipped.

"Yep," Kipnis confirmed.

While Remington and Kipnis kept their guns up, pivoting in all directions while watching the stairs, Jake squatted by the housekeeper, whose eyes were darting wildly, squeaky wails muffled behind the tape on her mouth. "You understand English?" he asked her. When she did not react, he said, "We won't hurt you, okay? English?"

She gave a slight nod.

"How many are here besides you? Just the three, or more?"

He got a small head shake.

"So, just three?"

Again, she nodded.

He stood, and rejoined Remington and Kipnis, who were going through the men's pockets. They snapped photos of their IDs with their phones, then turned to Jake, who said, "She's indicating it's just these three, but let's make sure."

With all the square footage of the mansion, encompassing the many bedrooms and bathrooms, the multiple kitchens and dining rooms, several sitting areas on each level, entertainment and game rooms, a gym and spa, a wine cellar and tasting room, it took them a good thirty minutes to clear every space.

When they were satisfied with their search, they met up in what was the only room set up as an office. Rich wood paneling gave it a more masculine look, the large windows making it light. In addition to the traditional workspace, one half of the big suite was furnished as a living room, complete with sofas and chairs in velvety materials the color of steamed milk and modern glass-and-metal tables. On the office side, a zebra-patterned rug covered much of the floor, a wall of built-in shelves and credenza backing a wood slab desk with an acorn-brown leather chair. Full-length in the center of the shelving was a grayscale abstract print that was vaguely erotic, a latch to the side suggesting the possibility of a hidden safe room behind it.

But the only thing of interest to them now, primarily to Kipnis, was a Mac computer angled on one corner of the desk. While Jake and Remington rummaged in drawers of the credenza, he sat in the leather chair and edged up to the keyboard.

Riffling through papers, Jake said, "If Ignat's just been here, it's impossible to tell. This place doesn't have even the slightest lived-in look."

"Yeah, didn't see suitcases or clothing strewn about in the bedrooms," Remington remarked. "Bathrooms are all tidy." He leaned over Kipnis' shoulder. "Can you access?"

Kipnis' fingertips were already drumming over the keys, small lines of code scrolling rapidly on the monitor screen, which flashed several times and then revealed the unlocked desktop display. Jake stood at Kipnis' other shoulder, watching in fascination as he checked the contents of multiple folders.

After a few minutes, the Israeli said, "I did not really expect to find much on the local drive, and I did not…but I am going to access and clone the cloud drive. I have a high amount of confidence there will be something there."

"How did you—?" Jake began to ask.

Kipnis did not reply, tapping keys as more sequences of letters, numbers, and symbols rolled over the screen, followed by a blur of folders sliding in hyper-fast-forward speed from one source to another. Then, just minutes later, Kipnis unplugged a thumb drive he had attached to the Mac, stuck it in a pocket of his shirt, and stood up.

Remington said, "I think we're done here. Let's boogie."

Back downstairs, they removed the restraints and tape from the housekeeper, Jake letting her know that they were leaving, would not be returning, and that the estate's systems, including her cell phone, would remain disabled until they were out of range. Dispensing some parting advise, he suggested she go home, take the rest of the day off. He was guessing after this experience, the young woman would probably take the rest of her job off.

RETURNING TO LARNACA, THEY booked rooms at the Ciao Stelio, a boutique hotel on Mackenzie Beach just north of the airport. Dmello joined them as, once again, all assembled in Kipnis' suite while he accessed the oligarch's cloud account on his tablet and began delving into the content. At the same time, Jake and Remington were monitoring the auction on his laptop, not seeing any updates to the listing.

It was not long before Kipnis announced, "I have found logs of Vasić's surveillance reports to Ignat. They are in Russian, of course, so I will run them through a translator."

Jake and Remington bracketed him on the sofa, leaning down to look at his screen, Kipnis scrolling as they read the entries. A few moments in, Remington blustered, "Goddamn son of a bitch. No wonder they were on us just about everywhere. He was really up our asses, had a pretty damn good bead on our action."

"No shit," Jake said. "And looks like these also support your theory about the bastard going off the reservation, because if you'll note, the reports stop just before you were drugged."

Remington clawed at his beard, scratchy from a quick trim and coppery in the late afternoon light beaming in through the suite's sea-facing windows. "All right, well, this doesn't help much now…anything else, Kip?"

"There is still a lot to go through," he answered, and continued tapping and scrolling. Just then, his phone buzzed, vibrating on the coffee table. He picked it up, glanced at the ID, and put it to his ear. From the subtle change in the sternness of his expression, the others surmised that the caller was Sabine Brisepierre.

When he ended the call, Kipnis said, "I have the coordinates for the auction and some of the confirmed bidders that will be in attendance." He recited a list of names and organizations that comprised a who's who of terrorists and jihadists and failed-state radicals of every badland in the region. Concluding, he added, "And yes, Ignat is one of the confirmed."

Jake went back to look at the auction site on the Toughbook. A live clock on the site was the only thing updating, ticking down to just over twenty-four hours. Eying Remington staunchly, he said, "We're going to be crashing that party." To Dmello, he instructed, "Wheels up at o dark thirty."

"City?" the Kenyan asked.

Kipnis said, "Aleppo."

61

WRAPPED IN TOTAL DARKNESS, Falcone and Niles slumped, barely upright, against a gritty concrete wall. It was their third day in the new location, although they had no actual grasp of how much time had passed. And, as with the other places they'd been held in captivity, they had no real fix on their whereabouts; they had, of course, known they'd most recently been in a prison and then on the oligarch's yacht, but otherwise, for all they knew, they could either still be somewhere along the eastern Mediterranean rim, or in parts much farther in any direction.

After spending the night on the yacht, they had been taken ashore in a speeding boat that bounced roughly over the water, then loaded into the back of a truck or van and driven for what they estimated to be about ninety minutes. Give or take, because with the passage of days and nights, everything seemed interminable and blurred together in a disorienting jumble.

Their current chamber of confinement was indisputably the worst of anywhere they'd been held, though it was not as close-quartered as some, perhaps a twelve-by-twelve-foot area, and they were restraint-free. Otherwise, the conditions were about as dire as they could have imagined; the walls and floor were damp and dirty and windowless, the air stagnant and fetid, the temperature vacillating between uncomfortably sweltering and bone-achingly chilly. They had been supplied a single bucket for bladder and bowel evacuation, tossed bottles of water at random intervals, often with hours in between. Food offerings were even less frequent, in the form of either bread or bananas.

Next to him in the darkness, Falcone was listening to Niles weakly hum a Moody Blues song, recognizing it as *I Know You're Out There Somewhere*. But after a few strains, his friend slurred, "Jake's never…going to find us…here."

His own speech hoarse and labored, Falcone huffed, "Wish I could say…I disagree…but I don't. Who knows…where the hell this hole in the ground is."

"How long…d'ya think…we've been gone?"

Trying to mentally tabulate their stints at the various locations, Falcone mumbled, "Lost track…maybe…three weeks."

Niles shifted on his haunches, moaning miserably at the discomfort; here, they didn't even have bedding.

Since their arrival, they had been indiscriminately roughed up on a regular basis—not so much torture, as they were no longer being interrogated, but seemingly more as sport for the amusement of their captors. Even so, the abuse was no less cruel and damaging.

"How's…pain?" Falcone asked him, needlessly because he knew the answer if, by no other indication, the severity of his personal pain and suffering.

There was a long pause before Niles responded around a strangled whimper, saying only, "Everything…but fuck…my hand…"

Falcone's dry eyes burned with the emotion of tears he could not produce. He scratched at the scraggly growth of beard on his face. "Got to…hold on," he implored, even as his own will to hang on was rapidly disintegrating.

They both wilted into a bleak silo of silence, the only sounds those of the faint rasps of their breaths and, periodically, the echo of distant screeches and thuds from somewhere above. A rat the size of a squirrel climbed onto Niles' lap, prompting a momentary fluttering of eyelashes and a repulsed grunt, but the Brit lacked the energy to so much as swat at the rodent. Mercifully, after a few moments, it jumped off him and moved on.

Sobbing softly and piteously, Niles gasped again, "Never…going…to…find us…here."

*   *   *   *   *

DMELLO HAD LANDED THE Pilatus at Aleppo International Airport just past dawn on the day following their foray to Ignatkovich's Cyprus estate. Syria, like so many Middle Eastern countries, is not a place where unrestricted travel or quick entry is usually possible, so their short-notice clearance and on-the-ground logistics required extensive back-channel negotiations and private arrangements between Tashkiran and Kipnis from their side and key facilitators on the Syrian side, but ultimately, they had pulled it off.

Instead of a hotel, for tactical and security reasons, they had chosen to set up in a vetted safe house close to the airport and southeast of the city center, Dmello hunkering down with the Malinois while Jake, Remington, and Kipnis organized their gear and took off in a rented Jeep.

The coordinates for the auction location put it about ten miles from the city limits, and since the time of commencement was not until 6 PM that evening, their plan was to make use of the interim by conducting a reconnaissance excursion. Their objective was to get the lay of the land, mapping all of the routes in and out, find and surveil the site, and do a risk assessment. Kipnis had not been able to get much on the area where they were headed, other than some devastating images of the recent earthquake damage and prior ones very similar in composition dating back to the civil war.

The Battle of Aleppo, spanning 2012 to 2016, had seen the city of over two million, which is one of the oldest continuously inhabited in the world—then under rebel control—bombarded by Syrian and Russian forces, leaving its infrastructure in a war-torn shambles. Years later, as much of it was still being reconstructed, the city was rocked by the magnitude 7.8 earthquake that struck Turkey and Syria.

As they drove through small suburban towns and settlements, evidence of the destruction was everywhere, sides of buildings shorn completely off with gaping cavities, others structurally compromised and boarded up, just as many reduced to piles of rubble. Even so, basic commerce was limping its way back into existence, with the locals selling goods and produce in open-market *souks* strung along the main roads. Battered, dirt-encrusted cars and pickup trucks that looked decades-old ambled alongside horse-drawn carts and scooters, vehicles sounding anemic horns to disperse pockets of children at play.

Jake, who was at the wheel of their Jeep, came to a stop as a huddle of townspeople crossed in front of them. Some wore Western-style clothing, a few were cloaked in the traditional *thobes* and *keffiyehs*, full-length robes and headscarves. As he waited for them to clear his path, he pondered, "Why would Vasić choose Syria?"

From the backseat, Kipnis said, "He has connections here, but also I think he wanted to go somewhere that Ignat would not normally travel." As a footnote, he added, "But he was foolish not to anticipate Ignat finding out about the auction and who was conducting it."

"Syria is also obviously a hotbed of the terrorist demographic Vasić's catering to," Remington supplied.

They continued through what was left of the town, spotting no less than a half dozen banners and billboards plastered on virtually anything still standing, all with the red, white, and black country flag and the ubiquitous headshot of Bashar al-Assad, Syrian president since the year 2000. As the dusty road took them into the outskirts and then the rural countryside, the day brightened, a hot sun quickly warming the dry steppe land, spread with scrub vegetation and scattered groves of trees. It did not appear to have rained much in recent weeks, the grasses tinged in yellow and gold.

After passing through several more towns, they came to the one that contained the coordinates for the auction site and drove slowly down the main street, its paved surface riddled with long fissures and gutted with sinkholes, chunks pushed up by the powerful seismic implosion. Monitoring a GPS device, Remington directed Jake to turn onto a dirt road, which took them through a ramshackle neighborhood of simple stone and concrete houses. Some were intact enough to be passably occupiable, but the majority had sustained severe damage with sides and roofs collapsed and in crumbled piles. Like the previous town, a few markets and businesses had regenerated and were offering their materials and services in the most fundamental way, set up outside or in temporary shelters amidst the ruins.

Jake had driven the length of the road when Remington announced,

"You should be almost—" and looked up, the rest of his sentence severed at the sight framed by the Jeep's dust-coated windshield. "The fuck?" Twisting around to address Kipnis, he asked, "Are you sure you gave me the right coordinates?"

Kipnis replied, "I did. This is the location."

Peering forward, Jake said incredulously, "It's a *mosque*. Surely this isn't where he's going to hold his event."

The Israeli checked his Toughbook and said, "I do not have a good connection, so I am unable to refresh the listing, but unless anything has changed, this is the location."

The ancient building just ahead of them had taken a hard hit, whether from battle or natural disaster or both was impossible to say. The fortified wall across the front was broken up as if a demolition crane had crashed through the stone, and the decapitated minaret tower had wide cracks running the height of it.

Remington said, "I can see some logic to the choice. There's not much concealment, for one thing, giving the host that advantage. Also, being a mosque, no weapons are allowed."

"But is it in service?" Jake asked.

"Guess we'll find out."

"Okay, let's go ahead with our recon," Jake decided.

They drove around the corner and, forty to fifty yards from the site, came to what had been a limestone and concrete-block building. It had sustained similar damage to the other town structures but half of the walls were partially intact, supporting what remained of the roof. Jake pulled off the road and found a spot to park on the far side that would not be visible from the mosque. They made an inspection and then began a cautious ascent to the top, using climbing gear and some lumber stacked nearby to set up a watch platform by laying boards across a corner of the exposed rafters.

After observing for over an hour from their perch and, with the exception of a few casual pedestrians, not seeing any significant activity, Jake said, "I'm ready to risk a look inside."

Kipnis, who had managed to get a good connection for his Toughbook using an Iridium GO satellite device, let them know, "The auction details have been updated, but the location and time is the same.

Apparently, those who have signed on to bid have been sent correspondence with special instructions via an encrypted app."

"Well, we can't sign up," Jake said, "so let's hope it's nothing vital. Maybe it has something to do with payment terms. Kip, you want to keep overwatch while Remy and I take a stroll?"

"Affirmative," he said, peering through the Leupold Mark 5 HD scope of his Barrett M82 rifle.

"We'll try not to stir up any trouble this early in the day," Remington told him.

JAKE AND REMINGTON MADE a preliminary circuit around the perimeter of the mosque, and discovered that there were several small roads running behind it. The upside was additional options for infil and exfil; the downside was…additional options for infil and exfil.

"This isn't good," Jake remarked.

"No, it's not," Remington agreed. "At least one of us will need to be positioned back here somewhere." He turned in each direction, seeing mostly flat ground covered with overgrown grass and shrubs. There was an occasional tree, more often than not either uprooted and cracked apart, a few buildings in total ruin.

Picking his way through the debris and vegetation, Jake said, "I want to take this side. It's the most likely point of entry. You can have the rest, Kip should stay up top."

Returning to the front, they paused at the arched entrance, over which was a calligraphic engraving in Kufic script; an ornate polished-stone plaque, inscribed in Arabic and English identified the mosque as *Shukri el-Matar*. Stepping inside the portal to the reception hall, they were prepared to remove their footwear to honor the Muslim custom but, as it became immediately evident, there was no need. The entry and the interior courtyard beyond was heavily littered with broken rock and stone, stacks of it cascading from shattered walls, the destruction pervasive. The pavers looked as if they had been jackhammered, marble benches and the ablutions fountain in the center completely destroyed.

Surveying the extensive damage, Remington said, "Wow."

"Yeah, what a shame. But safe to say there are no services going on here. Guess that's why Vasić chose it, but still seems odd to me." Jake glanced around quizzically. "I mean, where is he going to set up and hold the event?"

"Maybe the prayer hall is in better shape," Remington speculated, and they made their way through the debris field toward the rear.

The prayer hall was fronted by a series of arched doorways with the grand entrance peaked and crowned by a metal dome coated in gold. It, too, had been cracked and, as they entered the hall, the debris extended, now over what had once been an elaborately patterned and vividly colored carpet. In here, some scaffolding had been erected, but it did not appear that much, if any, restorative work had been done. They continued to the *Qibla* wall niched with a marble *Mihrab*, which was the Mecca-facing point of prayer, finding it amazingly unscathed, but the *Minbar* pulpit and staircase beside it was totally destroyed, decorative ceramic tile in shards on the ground.

Assessing what they were seeing, Jake said, "I'm just not visualizing a spot in here that's viable. Are you?"

Remington shook his head but said, "These places usually have a basement, but you gotta think it's collapsed beneath this wreckage." He looked at Jake. "Going with what we've got…how do you want to roll?"

Jake took a few moments to think, then replied, "Vasić will have armed guys for security, but also to disarm everybody else prior to their entry. I say we wait until all the bidders go in and things get underway, then maybe we can take out the security and stage an ambush."

"Yeah, that's the gist of what I'm thinking, too, but what's to say one of the other players or groups has the same plan?"

Jake put his hands on his hips, made another pan of the demolished mosque. "We'll just have to execute and adjust on the fly, like always." He eyed his friend earnestly. "But Remy, we've got to get Ignat. We may not have another chance. I'd love to recover the polymer jugs and mechanism, get that motherfucker Vasić, too, but we *have* to get Ignat, and take him alive."

"With you on that, bud."

HOURS LATER, FROM HIS position at the rear of the mosque, Jake was watching as a steady stream of men began to arrive on the scene. After their walk-through of the premises earlier, the rest of the day had passed tediously uneventful, but by midafternoon, the inertia shifted to heightened vigilance and analysis, the roads in front and back of the property starting to see the crawl of telltale traffic. Trucks and SUVs prowled the neighborhood, some aged and generic but battle-resilient, many others reinforced with ballistic armor and dark-tinted glass. Men in pairs and trios were dispatched to explore in and around the site just as they had done, making no attempt to pass themselves off as anything but what they were—bodyguards who were well-armed and clad in dark tactical wear, let out to conduct an advance scout.

By four o'clock, a van had pulled up and parked on the rear grounds, expelling four men armed with semiautomatic rifles. After a quick assignment discussion and radio check, they fanned out, each doing a patrol before taking posts at corners of the mosque.

Jake and Remington had both been able to construct covert hides using broken tree limbs and brush, going undetected even as the men passed within a few yards of their position.

Jake reported, "Sentries are in place…any eyes on Vasić?"

He got a negative response from both Remington and Kipnis, who informed them, "I am running a facial rec app on those I can visually capture, and so far we have some AQ and Isil, Al-Shabaab, Al-Nusrah, Jama'at Nusrat al-Islam, Ansar Bayt al-Maqdis, Hamas, Hezbollah, some freelancers and—"

"Wonderful," Jake interrupted. "The only one I want to hear about is the Russian asshole."

Their comm talk went quiet for a while, then Remington spoke up, saying, "Pretty sure I've got eyes on Ignat's detail on my side. They look the part and I think I recognize one of the guys."

"What about Ignat?" Jake asked.

"Negative. Maybe an advance team."

"Shit," Jake muttered irritably. "I hope to hell he's not sending some proxy. And where the fuck is Vasić? He's got to already be here somewhere…how did he get by us?"

He raised his Steiner binoculars and maintained surveillance of the ongoing activity.

At five o'clock, the two rear-corner sentries met up in front of an entrance at the back of the mosque, where they did exactly as predicted, screening each arriving attendee for weapons, disarming any individuals who had not followed protocol and checking their hardware at the door like a restaurant valet, tagging and arranging pieces in a large, heavy-duty plastic bin. When the parade of men entering the mosque seemed to have ceased, Jake again inquired about a sighting of Vasić or Ignat, his agitation growing.

"I have seen neither of them," Kipnis responded, "but my thermal optics are losing capture shortly after each body enters."

"Somewhere below, something underneath," Remington remarked. "We must have missed an entry or portal somewhere in there. Shit. What do you want to do?"

Jake said, "Go with the plan. Wait fifteen past eighteen-hundred, then we take out the sentries."

"Roger that," Remington said, Kipnis echoing the confirmation from his roost atop the block building opposite of the mosque.

JAKE HAD JUST SEEN the second hand of his Garmin tactix Charlie watch flick to 6:15 PM and was about to broadcast the go-hot order, when bedlam broke out from within the mosque and, quickly thereafter, from their targets outside.

The totally unexpected sound of gunfire popped, muted by the depth from which it originated, somewhere underground. As if this was not startling enough, the sudden blaring of the Call to Prayer, resounding loudly from still-functional and connected speakers in the minaret, wailed over the start of the chaos.

Jake froze for an instant, looking on as the sentries reacted, hoisting their rifles and swinging the barrels wildly in every direction as attendees began to pour out like a pod of spiders, racing for and snatching up weapons from the plastic bin.

"Breach now!" Jake shouted through comms, the ruckus from men yelling amidst the amplified *Adhan* permeating the air making it hard for him to hear himself or think clearly. But he quickly locked back in to his planned execution, coming out of the crouch he'd been in from the concealment of his lair, M4 rifle now the weapon of choice instead of knife or silenced Glock.

Some of the fleeing attendees had begun shooting, but their aim was erratic as they were mostly laying down preemptive fire in order to escape. Jake dodged their shelling, getting off shots when any of the shooters came close, and charged for the back entrance to the mosque, which was no longer being guarded. He was almost knocked over by a couple of men barreling across the threshold, babbling heatedly in Arabic.

In his ear, he heard Remington's raised voice. "I'm in at the front…moving to the prayer hall!"

Kipnis followed with, "Also moving…exterior."

Jake met up with Remington inside, both sprinting through the arches and heading toward the *Mihrab* dome, where light was spilling out into the shadows of evening that filled the open-air space.

"Where the fuck did that shooting come from?" Remington asked. "I thought everyone was disarmed."

Leading the way into a corridor that had somehow been obscured during their prior canvass, Jake said, "Somebody must have threatened Vasić…hopefully it's Ignat. I still don't know how either of them got in here…I thought we found every way in."

Pivoting back and forth behind him, Remington replied, "Well, we obviously missed one."

At the end of the corridor, which was lit with LED lanterns spaced along the ground, was a stairwell going down to a lower level. Descending cautiously, they advanced to an open doorway, and paused. The shooting had stopped moments ago and they'd not passed any attendees on the retreat since making their entrance, but now they could hear the echo of footfalls and muffled voices some distance away. They stepped through the doorway and came into a large room, also lit with the lanterns, but many had been knocked over in the commotion. A few dozen plastic chairs were strewn and toppled in a cluster at the center, fresh blood spray dripping from many.

A couple of bodies lay sprawled in the midst of the tangle, but Jake and Remington did not stop to look them over, rushing to an opening on the far side of the room. It was from this direction they could hear the sounds, rapidly fading, of several men.

Passing through the doorway, they entered another passageway, this one framed by support beams with mud walls surfaced in concrete, light-bulbs strung along the top, and they realized they were in a tunnel.

"Shit," Jake muttered. "*This* is how they got in without us seeing them."

"And how they're getting out," Remington said.

"Not if we can help it," Jake snarled.

They ran, the scuffle of their boots loud in the hollow enclosure. The sounds of talk and movement they'd heard became more distinct as they closed the gap. When they had jogged several hundred yards, the space lightened, sidewalls taking on the chalky sheen of moonglow. They reached a second set of stairs and pounded to the top, emerging from a hatch just in time to see three men hefting rucksacks into the cargo bed of a van that was tucked between rows of an olive orchard.

All wore black and at least two were slung with rifles.

Hearing Jake and Remington some twenty yards behind them, the men turned and took up their weapons, unleashing a barrage of fire from within the trees. As they did, the third man scurried beneath the over-hanging branches to get into the van, glancing once over his shoulder. Jake and Remington were charging into the orchard, returning fire but also having to duck and cover as bullets flew around them, shredding leaves and bark over their heads and into their faces, so they were unable to get more than a brief look at the third man. But for Jake, it was good enough.

"Motherfucker!" he screamed, and ran for the figure he'd recognized as Ignatkovich, the oligarch disappearing into the van. Doors slammed behind the pair of shooters, and the driver gunned the engine, taking off in a cloud of dirt and exhaust.

Jake's and Remington's bullets pinged impotently off the ballistic steel of the vehicle as it receded into the orchard, both cursing furiously as they continued shooting even as they knew it was pointless.

Kipnis swerved from around a corner at the wheel of their Jeep, dust whirling into the night air. Jake and Remington hurriedly yanked doors open, got in, and they sped off between the row of trees, coming out onto a dirt road. They had barely driven two miles before it dead-ended into a junction of several paved roads going in different directions, and Kipnis brought the Jeep to a halt.

"Which way?" he asked.

Next to him in the passenger seat, Jake muttered, "Fuck!" He slammed his fists on the dashboard in fury. "Fuck! Pick one, I guess."

Twenty minutes later, it became obvious they had picked the wrong one.

DESPITE HAVING HIT SPEEDS that far exceeded what was reasonably intended for the narrow road and pulling around every vehicle in their way, they never came up on the van. Turning around in the next town, they had driven back to the mosque, which was entirely vacated and silent.

Now, inside the lower-level chamber, the three of them pushed chairs apart to inspect the dead, finding a pair of Islamic men, both shot in the chest and surrounded by voluminous blood pools.

At the front of the room was an elevated platform and a long, cloth-covered table, on which had apparently been the jugs and geared device; in the melee, some of the pottery had been chipped, leaving a dusting of small fragments. Behind the table, they found another body, face up, eyes wide and fixed, a mass of blood and flesh and tissue splattered from a crater in the hollow of the neck.

Looking down at the gory mess of Kirill Vasić, Remington said, "At least one son of bitch got what was coming. Just goddamn wish it had come from me."

62

FOR LACK OF A known destination, the decision was made to go back to Bodrum where, once again, they booked in at the Yalikavak Marina Hotel. Normally, as a precautionary measure, they would have switched to different accommodations, but in this case it was the best location for keeping tabs on the *Gala* which, as they found on return, had not budged from its marina berth. Nor had there been any change in the minimal and low-key presence of personnel observed about the exterior decks; Ignatkovich had clearly not reboarded.

Now, late evening on the second day, Jake, Remington, Kipnis, and Dmello were gathered in the sitting area of Kipnis' suite, winding down after more long and frustrating sessions of trolling for new intel and parsing through every bit of data they had amassed so far.

Draining the last of his drink, Jake set the glass on the coffee table with a heavy clink, and rose to pace. "I can't help but think that might have been our last and only window of opportunity," he said dismally, running a hand through his hair.

"Maybe," Remington said, "but we're not giving up."

"Hell, no," Jake snapped, a little more fractiously than he'd intended. Moderating his inflection, he amended, "Of course not. But God, I feel like we're practically back to square one. And now that Ignat has what we found and Vasić is dead, he may not feel the need to keep the guys alive."

Not for the first time since their raid on the would-be auction,

Remington remarked, "We just need to figure out Ignat's next move and get to him *before* he makes that decision."

Kipnis, who had kept his primary focus on the copious amount of content stored in the oligarch's cloud drive, announced abruptly, "He has made his next move."

Jake and Remington both turned to look at him, their mouths agape.

"More importantly, I know where he is holding the guys."

IT TOOK ANOTHER DAY to acquire satellite images and detailed mapping of topography ninety miles to the northeast just beyond Muğla. The sat images showed what Kipnis had identified as Ignatkovich's primary Turkish command center, a massive compound surrounded by forests and mountains. And, unlike the oligarch's yacht and his estate in Cyprus, there was evidence of significant and ongoing activity; many trucks and other vehicles were scattered about the property, as well as a considerable presence of personnel distributed throughout. There were numerous rows of barracks and warehouse storage depots, training grounds and firing ranges, vehicle shelters and hangars, and a big primary fortress of a building.

What led Kipnis to the discovery were, among other things, shipping documents of military equipment and arms listing the location, but the real find was a set of blueprints for renovations that had been done less than a year ago, when Ignatkovich had taken over the abandoned base.

Now, as they all studied the layout from the aerial images, Jake said, "The terrain between here and there is rough, but we could still make it by road in a few hours…faster by air."

"We would need to find a landing zone," Dmello reminded him.

Jake tapped the screen of Kipnis' Toughbook. "Yeah, they have their own airfield…we couldn't use that. But that isn't the biggest issue." He pointed again, saying, "There is only one road in and one road out."

"Strategically, it's a solid place for a compound," Remington agreed.

Dmello pulled up an app on his phone that he often used when searching for off-grid landing zones. Within a few minutes, he beamed, and showed them what he'd found. "There…it would be a hike to the compound, but I could land right there. It is long enough and wide enough."

Jake had been thinking, a plan beginning to form. "That's good, Mellie. But I have a better idea."

DURING THE DRIVE TO the Bodrum airport that evening, their cell and sat phones began to blow up, virtually all at once.

Dmello, the only one not engaged in conversation, pulled into the hangar where the Pilatus was parked, surmising from the seriousness of expressions, terseness and pitch of voices, that something of major consequence was happening.

All of them hopped out of the Jeep, Dmello heading for the plane, the rest breaking off to continue their phone conversations.

Jake, who had been speaking with Bachman because the MVAA leader could not get through to Remington first, asked the others, "Are you getting what Caspian just told me?"

Remington and Kipnis both nodded gravely, Remington saying, "I was on with the lieutenant colonel, and the Med is on the brink of going into the red zone. It's a lit fuse, the coalition exercises about to turn into live action. The Ford strike group is already here for Aegean Forge, and now the Eisenhower group is deploying."

Jake said, "Oh shit. Well, Caspian is preparing to bug out, but I talked him into temporarily hunkering down in-country in the hope this blows over."

"Good, that's good," Remington mumbled distractedly. "But not sure this is going to blow over, at least not quickly. I need to call Luther, make sure he's got everything handled." He glanced at Kipnis. "What the hell brought this on? Did you get anything?"

"I did," the Israeli answered solemnly. "Earlier today, the missile deal between Russia and Turkey got derailed."

"In what way?" Remington asked.

"Reports are that a group of Greek commandoes of unknown ideology stormed in and blew it up…and made off with the missiles."

"*Greeks?*" Jake blurted, and then his eyes rolled skyward. "Ignat's behind it." He cast a shrewd look toward Kipnis. "Sabine Brisepierre's intel about the undersea cable tapping."

Kipnis nodded vaguely but did not reply, his mind thick with thoughts. He joined the rest in transferring bags and gear to the plane, taking a seat aboard and returning his attention to his tablet.

Getting the Malinois settled, Remington said grimly, "Whoever or whatever it is, the Turks *and* Russians are amassing forces at sea and starting to fill the skies. We could be looking at a goddamn NATO war."

JAKE'S IDEA WAS TO make a night jump from the plane.

For stealth, a HALO jump—which stands for High Altitude Low Opening—would cover the Pilatus' noise signature and allow them to make a quick insertion close to target; the single roads leading into and out of the compound property were heavily patrolled and would have made for a long trek. And, time had never been at a higher and more critical premium.

Just a few minutes into the flight, Jake and Remington had connected to the aircraft's oxygen and were going through preparations for their descent, which would be a seventeen-thousand-foot plunge through darkness to the Turkish countryside. They did a jumpmaster checklist on each other, both affirming all was in order.

Harnessed in RA-1 Ram Air parachute rigs and wearing helmets with Gen 3 AN/PVS-31 white phosphorous night optics, they wore layers of tactical black, fortified by body armor and hitched up with rucksacks and weapons cases, the combined weight of their clothing and gear coming in at about a 120 pounds. Kipnis and Dmello had also donned oxygen masks, Kipnis making sure the Malinois kept theirs on until Jake and Remington had exited and the cabin could be repressurized.

Within ten minutes, Dmello lowered the Pilatus' altitude and reduced its speed from cruise to 120 knots. As they approached the coordinates for the drop zone, he twisted around in his cockpit seat to make a final visual status check while communicating through comms, then giving and getting thumbs-up all around.

Remington and Jake disengaged from the plane's oxygen and connected to their O2 bailout tanks.

"Ready, partner?" Remington asked Jake.

"Let's rock and roll," Jake replied tightly, and the two made their way to the aircraft's jump door, which Dmello remotely opened, a gale of frigid air blasting inside.

Jake had done enough of these jumps to be fully confident, but he still got a rush of exhilaration as he gripped the sides of the door, wind buffeting his helmet and body, the starlit sky awash in the gray tones of his NODs. He pushed himself through the opening and felt the adrenaline surge as he began his free fall, arms outstretched, the wind whipping him about a time or two before he stabilized, glancing upward to see Remington airborne right behind him.

Though the movies often make these maneuvers seem much longer and more aerobatic, in reality, most are over in minutes, but the temperature extreme from space to ground was akin to taking a polar plunge. When Jake had achieved terminal velocity at 126 miles an hour, his digital wrist altimeter and the audible one inside his helmet indicating a level of three thousand feet, he deployed his nine-cell canopy. As the nylon blossomed overhead, slowing his descent, he floated toward the ground, working the toggles to steer. The automated voice continued to count down as he drifted lower, his eyes on the opening in the trees where they'd chosen to set down. It was a mile or so from Ignatkovich's compound, but it was the widest opening in proximity to allow for some displacement in landing.

Before touchdown, he released the snap links for his rucksack and weapons case, and they dropped to the ground just ahead of his landing. He flared his chute and, shortly thereafter, his boots made contact with the ground and he went into a light jog, the canopy deflating in his wake. He turned to watch Remington's landing, a little less graceful as a tree limb snagged some of his suspension lines. Remington wrestled them free and the two shucked harnesses and began gathering, folding, and tucking everything into their rigs.

"Hell, yeah!" Remington exclaimed, grinning. "Was it good for you?"

Jake grinned back, then panned the tree line around them. Reaching Kipnis through comms, the reception surprisingly good, he reported, "Made the DZ, ready to advance…do you copy?"

Affirming, Kipnis relayed, "We are secure at our LZ and standing by."

Jake and Remington took a few minutes to reorganize weapons and gear, extracting their handguns and rifles from the cases and strapping on their backpacks. After consulting the GPS data from their watches, they headed into the woods, hiking to the northeast. The air was crisp and cool, apertures of sky in the treetops bright with stars and moon, the foliage glistening like frost through their lenses. They moved quietly and, for the first twenty minutes of their trek, the only sounds were the light crunch of their footfalls and the soft chirr of insects.

When the forest thinned and GPS confirmed they were approaching the outer radius of the compound property, they heard voices in the distance. As they crept closer, now just barely concealed by trees, the chatter became more distinct. Casual, chummy, unconcerned.

Peering through the pine branches, Jake saw a grouping of four men standing around with their rifles loose on slings, smoking and drinking something hot from a thermos, little wisps of steam curling over their cups. Checking his watch again, he saw that they were coming up on an hour change, and held his wrist out to show Remington, who nodded. They waited the few minutes and, as they'd assumed, the four men reached for their radios and called in their status.

Jake and Remington positioned themselves several yards apart, flipped their NODs back to sight through the night vision scopes on their rifles, and took aim. Two bursts from each, muted by the SOCOM suppressors on their M4s, and the four men dropped to the ground.

They moved swiftly forward, dragging the bodies into the woods. Next, they initiated the first phase of their infiltration plan, stepping over to the area where the men had been stationed. Enclosed by razor wire-topped fencing were attached metal units, each with padlocked double doors and stacked on a platform. On the opposite side of the enclosed area was a row of satellite dishes.

Remington had already fished out a bolt cutter from his pack, and broke the lock securing the entry gate. Entering the enclosure, they took out canvas pouches, from which they selected pre-configured explosive charges, activating the timers on all and affixing one to each metal unit. They did the same for the satellite dishes.

Leaving the power and communications substation, they resumed their march toward the interior of the compound. Familiar with the layout from intensive study of the blueprints Kipnis had found, they knew the likely locations for a security presence and were able to take them out with relative ease, catching most completely by surprise. Reaching the main building, the big, multistoried stone-walled fortress, they halted. Checked their watches, glanced at each other, and waited.

Several moments passed, and then the charges they'd set detonated in one loud, powerful explosion that shook the ground and shattered the quiet night with a deafening blast. Instantly, the low floodlights spaced around the building and the high spotlights from its roofline all went dark.

Remington said, "Okay, brother, let's go get our guys."

63

THERE WAS A FRENZIED eruption of reaction in the immediate aftermath of the substation explosion, men trampling over each other as they raced toward the scene of flaming demolition and, more advantageously, others streaming out of the fortress. Jake and Remington's execution had accomplished both of their objectives, the first being to wipe out all light, power, and communications capability, and the second to provide a distraction requiring responsive involvement.

Now, Jake and Remington crept forward in the darkness, their paths illuminated and defined through the AN/PVS-31 NODs. They spotted a single man guarding the entrance at the building's perimeter wall, and he was keyed up, his weapon—which appeared to be either an MPT-55 or KCR-556, both Turkish assault rifles—aimed and fire-ready. Signaling for Remington to go left, Jake went right, and when they were on either side of the sentry, Remington gave a whistle. The man jerked in his direction, and Jake took him out with a shot center mass.

Entering the inner court of the compound, they encountered two more men on the run in their direction. As the men got closer, moonlight revealed Jake and Remington to them in silhouette, and rounds rattled in their general direction. They dodged the shooters' fusillade and returned fire, dropping the pair and moving on toward the main dwelling.

Inside, they stood at the front of a large, tall-ceilinged hall, doorways spaced along every side. From what they'd committed to memory from the blueprints, they knew most of the rooms served basic functions and would be empty at this hour, but they proceeded to clear each one. They made their way down a series of corridors, hearing muted noises coming from stairwells overhead as, apparently, a few slower-to-rally men were coming forth to investigate the fray outside. Jake and Remington continued to a rear antechamber where they expected to find another set of stairs, these going to a lower level below ground.

But before heading down, they were stopped by a room running the length of the back wall. On the plans, it had been labeled as a library, but one glance inside revealed it to be something else. After making sure no men were present, Jake and Remington ducked in for a quick survey of what was obviously a command center; the stone walls had been plastered over and were papered with maps and various schematics, printed photos, and satellite images. A lot of it was directly related to them and their operations, and Jake felt a wave of déjà vu, remembering his breach of the Valentín hacienda in Colombia when he'd come upon a room with photos of him and Callie from extensive—and intimate— surveillance.

Remington had taken out his phone and was snapping pictures, but Jake put a hand on his shoulder, saying, "Come on, no time, we've gotta move." And then something caught his attention.

Following his gaze, Remington muttered, "Son of a bitch. Greek commandos my ass."

Hanging from a free-standing rack were dozens of uniforms, patterned in green, gold, and brown army lizard camouflage, patches of the Greek flag stitched on the upper sleeves. As they stood gaping at the appropriated battle wear, yet another revelation kept them from moving on.

A leather-bound portfolio lay open on a big table near the rack.

They stepped over to see what it held, which were pages of computer-generated print in Russian. Their proficiency in the language was enough that, after a few moments, they both had a grasp of the content, their jaws slack with astonishment.

"Holy fuck," Remington muttered. "This is a goddamn manifesto and battle plan for a false flag op…that's what is about to go down, if it hasn't already. I've got to get this to Atticus!"

"Okay, let's grab it and whatever else we can, but we've gotta go *now*," Jake urged.

Remington stuffed the portfolio into his pack and took pictures of the camo uniforms while Jake tore some material from the walls and scooped up handfuls of documents. With his phone in hand, Remington tried to place a call to Lieutenant Colonel Merriweather, but could not get a signal. He then tried to reach him on his sat phone. Again unsuccessful, he blustered, "Goddamn it!"

Leaving the room and hurrying toward the back stairs, Jake reminded him, "We took out all the commo…not to mention these thick walls."

In response, Remington blew out an exasperated breath, and the two of them gripped their rifles and descended to the underground level where the blueprints had shown a dungeon to be.

ON TURNING THE CORNER at the base of the stairs, the change in atmosphere was stark; the coolness more of a permeating chill, the air unmoving and acridly foul with the decay of organic matter and the pervasive stench of bodily malodors and, possibly, the decomposition of death.

They pulled cravats up from their necks to cover their noses and advanced along an earthen passage that was immersed in total darkness, their paths lit by the NODs over their eyes, which were beginning to water from the overpowering fetidness. The passageway intersected with another and, as they paused, looking and listening, Jake picked a direction, proceeding to the right. Remington followed, walking sideways with his rifle aimed behind them.

At the far end of this passage, they came to a long section of concrete block, inset on one side with a series of iron-panel doors, each with a narrow, slitted grate midway and a pair of industrial eyebolts on either side of the jamb. As Remington continued to watch in their wake for any threats, Jake moved to the only door panel with chains looped and locked through the bolts.

Remington handed him the bolt cutter from his pack, and looked on tensely as Jake snapped through the metal links in several places, chains dropping to the ground with a thud. He tugged the heavy door open, recoiling and gagging as he stepped forward, his knees involuntarily buckling.

A weak cry gurgled deep in his throat and, beneath his cravat, he rasped, "Oh God." And thought: *We're too fucking late.*

IN THOSE FINAL MOMENTS, Eddie Falcone and Curran Niles had slipped away in a dreamy fog, their physical pain and suffering, mental and psychological anguish, fading into the gray abyss until it all went to black.

Falcone was at the wheel of his vintage '65 Mustang convertible, top down, its poppy-red paint gleaming in the afternoon sun as he sped south along highway 9 toward Atlantic City. The sky overhead was as bright and blue as the pigments in a Van Gogh painting, the sweet, sad, and jazzy sound of Springsteen's *Jungleland* interlude serenading him as the breeze combed through his dark hair, the sensation reminding him of the long, tantalizing fingers of a certain Jersey girl with the sass and figure and fashion sense of a brunette Barbie. As the music played, every stroke of the violin, every note of the piano, every wail of the Big Man's saxophone, reached deep into the core of his soul, evoking tears from a swirl of joy and sadness, of fulfillment and regret, of wants and needs and dreams that would never be consummated.

He had driven down to the expressway, oddly devoid of any of the usual traffic, just an empty ribbon crossing the marshes, and he could even see the herons and egrets plundering through the lime green grasses and taking off in flight with their big wings aflutter like the skirt of a summer dress. He had glimpsed the shore skyline ahead, but the road stretched on, and he never made it to the Boardwalk.

For Niles, bewilderingly, his retreat had not taken him through the uproarious euphoria of a jam-packed club rocking out in a gyration of candy-colored lights to the edgy pop-grunge of the latest Clash incarnation. Instead, he was strolling along the banks of the Thames in the cool night mist, all alone, not another soul in sight, the moon following over his shoulder like a spotlight. He could not recall ever having walked by the river at night, wondered why he did so now. And why was he back in London? Something felt wrong about that, something not quite aligning. But he did feel a sense of peace, even if sorrowful, an aching loneliness casting a shadow over the serenity.

As he walked, he realized there were no boats sailing or moored, and no swans gliding through the water. In the soft glow of amber lantern lights, its dark surface rippled like black velvet and, glancing up, he saw the iconic Tower Bridge with its grand, Gothic spired columns, and a gust of nostalgia swept through him and he felt so incredibly lonely…and cold…he was really cold.

Shivering, he looked off in the distance, the cobblestone path shimmering in the damp night, and suddenly tears sprung from his eyes and he wept at the sight of his best mate in the whole world. It seemed to take an impossibly long time to reach the spot where Eddie Falcone was standing, but Curran Niles got there.

The two friends stood together, both smiling with the guilelessness of little boys.

Falcone extended his hand, took Niles' broken one in his and, at that moment, it didn't even hurt.

He grinned and said, "Hey, bud."

64

SQUATTING BY THE LIFELESS forms that barely resembled the two individuals he had come to know and love, Jake rotated the tubes of his NODs away from his eyes, removed his MTP gloves, and unclipped a Nitecore penlight. Wanding the light over them, he fought back a gasp of abject horror and devastation, taking in the battered and debilitated condition of their bodies. They were filthy from head to toe, their hair tangled and matted, scraggly whiskered faces gaunt and blanched and bruised, tattered clothing soiled and blood-stained.

They looked and smelled of death, a voracious armada of flies buzzing around them.

Standing behind him, Remington whispered, "Oh sweet Jesus…are they…?"

Jake reached to the closest ankle, feeling for a tibial pulse, then scooted up to try the popliteal behind a knee. He was not detecting anything, and reached for a wrist, now noticing that the two were holding hands. He felt the strangle of emotion tightening in his throat but kept his focus honed and hardened.

Placing his fingers on each wrist of the loosely clasped hands, he abruptly bounced in his crouch and began to apply painful stimuli to their sternums, leaning over the pair.

"Hey!" he barked, and continued to rub the knuckles of his hands on their upper chests. "Eddie! Curran!" He rubbed harder, kept calling their names.

Remington bent down. "They're alive? What do you need me to do?"

Jake was working frantically now, flashing the penlight to check their pupils, his hands and fingers probing and palpating around their bodies, peeling fabric from skin to assess what he could. "They are," he replied, but thought grimly, *barely and maybe not for long.* To Remington, he said, "As much as I could use the help, I need you to keep watch and be ready."

After a few minutes, Jake managed to get some negligible signs of life but was unable to get any water into them as they were semiconscious at best, nor could he get them upright. Their pulses remained extremely weak but, with his stimulation, had become slightly more discernible. In a low voice, he told Remington, "They need emergency evac, but obviously that's not possible. The only way we're going to get them out of here—and it's not a great option—is to haul."

"Yeah, I can see that. Wouldn't be such a challenge if it weren't for those stairs and the asshole mercs running amuck out there."

Taking items from the small medical kit he had prepared for their op, Jake said quietly, "They need fluids—bad—but I already know, dehydrated as they are, they're gonna be a tough, if not near-impossible stick. They've also got a *lot* of hurt that's going to start screaming as soon as we move. One of Curran's hands is"—he grimaced with the acknowledgment—"crushed."

"Jesus Christ," Remington murmured.

He went on, "They've been beaten to hell, got bruised or fractured ribs and every kind of wound imaginable, most infected to some degree. I'll dose 'em with a small bump of ketamine, more when I can stabilize and get those IVs going."

In anticipation of such a situation—though he'd hoped it would not be as dire as this—Jake had added lightweight litter rolls to their kit, which they now slipped from pouches attached to their vests. Remington kept up his overwatch but helped Jake unfurl the rolls, lift Falcone and Niles, and securely strap them into position.

Squatting by their heads, Jake tried again to solicit responsive eye contact, lightly brushing hair back from each of their foreheads, thumbing their cheeks. Niles' eyelids twitched imperceptibly; Falcone's did not move, but tears leaked from the corners. Projecting confident optimism he did not fully feel, but which was necessary for the will of his critical patients to live, he said, "Okay, guys…gonna give you something to help with the pain and then we're getting you out of here!"

He injected them, checked their pulses once more, and let out a heavy breath. Then, he dug into his pack for two sets of the extra Invisio earbuds he always carried, plugging the ears of Falcone and Niles as some protection from the concussive noise of the gunfire they were sure to draw on exfil.

"Okay, Remy, let's move."

JAKE AND REMINGTON TETHERED the litters with Falcone and Niles to their belts, pulling them along the ground as they started back the way they had come. But when they reached the intersection, a stack of armed men were trotting toward them, tactically vested with pouches full of extra ammunition, the darkness no longer a detriment as now they, too, were equipped with NODs.

Jake and Remington fired multiple rounds on them and made a dash for the opposite side of the intersection, running down the passageway as fast as they could with the added weight and drag of Falcone and Niles in the litters.

Both knew this was a worst-case scenario because, not only did they have a limited range and speed of movement with which to flee or fight, they also had no idea where the passage led, or if there was any kind of alternate way up or out. For all they knew, it could dead end, trapping them without a means of escape and making them easy pickoffs. Fortunately, as they soon found, another junction gave them a left or right directional choice. This time, they chose left, and could hear the pounding of boots and shouts not far behind them. They kept running, this corridor much longer than the others, turned a corner, and were rewarded by another stairwell.

After making a quick check to ensure their cargo was still securely strapped in, they huffed up the steps and emerged back on the main level of the building.

And here, in what the blueprints had labeled the great hall, they encountered a whole battalion of the compound mercenaries. The men were scattered about the space in search mode, combing the peripheral rooms, but there were enough of them of them assembled in the middle of the hall to spot Jake and Remington as they entered.

Reaching into a pouch on his vest, Jake gripped an M18 cannister, pulled the tab, and tossed it toward the closest cluster of men. White smoke billowed high and wide, forming a thick cloud that filled much of the space, effectively obscuring the field of fire. That did not stop the combatants from doing so, but their shots were mostly skewed. Beside him, Remington had also palmed a grenade, but his was a round one which, shortly after he'd thrown it, produced a sizable bang and spewed more smoke and a shower of metal fragments. There were screams and shouts, more weapons firing indiscriminately.

With the cover and temporary pushback, they sprinted for the entry foyer and raced through the open doorway, sweeping their M4s as they expended what remained of the thirty-round capacities. They popped new magazines in on the run, chambered rounds, and continued firing at the growing number of mercs in pursuit.

"We really stirred up the fucking hive!" Remington yelled.

"Yeah, and there's a lot more hornets in it than I would have thought," Jake replied. Up ahead, he spotted what they had seen in the sat images —a line of parked pickup trucks—and said, "Hey, there's our ride outta here! Lay down some hate while I get these guys loaded up, then I'll cover you."

"Roger that!"

Selecting the nearest vehicle, a Toyota 4x4, Jake let the truck's tailgate down and detached both of their litters as Remington stood firing his rifle. Jake was relieved to see that Falcone and Niles were still alive; they were now moaning and thrashing weakly against their restraints in reaction to the pandemonium of being dragged and bumped over ground, smoke and dust filling the air and, though somewhat buffered by the earbuds, the cacophony of gunfire. He hoisted each of the stretchers and shoved them into the cargo bed, lashing them down with elastic cables that were fortuitously already connected to the sidewalls. He hopped up between them and braced his carbine against his shoulder, firing at the combatants coming their way.

Remington pivoted, reloading his M4 as he did, and ran for the driver's seat. When he was tucked in with the door slammed shut, he thumped down the visor and was elated to have keys fall into his crotch. "Hooyah!" he exclaimed, prompting a grin from Jake in the bed of the truck. Before he could comment, Remington had started up, gunned the engine, and stomped on the gas.

The Toyota fishtailed as they sped off, Remington's voice filling their comms as he began trying to reestablish contact with Dmello and Kipnis. He drove out of the compound, but before they had traveled a few hundred yards, they sighted a roadblock consisting of two trucks nose to nose across the dirt track. There were thick trees on either side, so the only way past it was through it. Though Remington was driving with headlights off, they were close enough for their engine to be heard, and the group of men manning the barricade had also obviously been alerted and were in a state of readiness, guns aimed.

"Got techs up ahead!" Remington declared, indicating rear-mounted machine guns.

"Fuck," Jake sputtered.

"Hold on, partner!"

Jake instinctively knew what the play was and, having executed variations of it times too numerous to count as an operator in South America and Africa, prepared by spreading his legs and wedging his feet at the sides of the pickup, propping his rifle on top of the cabin. He had to lean forward and push his weight hard against the truck's rearview window panel to keep from tumbling backwards as Remington accelerated, barreling straight for the roadblock.

A mix of 5.56, 7.62, and .50 caliber rounds pelted them, rattling the air, pinging and thudding against and into the Toyota's frame. A few bullets landed inside the pickup's bed while shell casings from Jake's M4 clattered around, worrying him that Falcone and Niles would either be hit or burned by the hot metal, but there was nothing he could do about it.

That particular concern was short-lived as they made impact with the roadblock, Remington pushing the Toyota to its maximum speed and smashing through the vehicles, free-standing shooters diving to get out of the way, gunners behind the heavy mounted weapons propelled into the air. At the last moment, Jake had clutched his rifle and dropped to the pickup's bed, laying on top of Falcone and Niles.

Within instants of clearing the impasse, Jake dug out another grenade, pulled the pin, and flung it like a Major League fastball, blowing up men and guns and trucks, the blast bumping their tires off the road and causing the Toyota to swerve. Remington recovered control and bounced off the dirt track and nosed into an opening in the tree line. Minutes later, he was rumbling along a shallow ravine. If the pickup had sustained much damage in the collision, it was not enough to impede its drive, the only hint of vehicular disfigurement a scraping noise in the vicinity of the front bumper and vague gnashing sounds from the undercarriage. There was a reason why Toyota trucks were the transportation of choice for militias and guerillas the world-over.

Dmello's voice soon broadcast through their comms, letting them know they were back on network and not far from the plane. He supplied the coordinates, which Remington tracked with GPS.

"Copy you Lima Charlie," Jake relayed and, though he'd not seen any other vehicles on their tail since the now-annihilated roadblock, he added, "Might be coming in hot, so be ready."

They heard Kipnis ask, "Sitrep?"

Knowing what he meant, Jake replied avidly, "We've got 'em." With more gravity in his tone, he added, "Kip, I need you to prep the way we discussed." Meaning, as he had laid out to the Israeli prior to their flight, to have specific supplies organized from his big medical kit and IV setups in place.

As Remington drove toward the coordinates, Jake returned his attention to Falcone and Niles. Sitting cross-legged between the two litters, any buoyancy he had allowed himself to feel on getting them out of the compound's dungeon and through the barrage of gunfire and explosive ordnances evaporated. If anything, their conditions had worsened; the subliminal adrenaline that had coursed their systems during the action was now in abatement, their vitals deteriorating.

Giving both of them a vigorous rub, he said, "Okay, guys, we got you out of the worst of it. You've got one last mission here…don't piss me off." He thought he saw Falcone's mouth twitch upward at the corners, but he couldn't be sure.

*　　*　　*　　*　　*

AFTER PASSING OVER SOME rough and rutted terrain, they made it to the LZ without any further obstacles, Remington pulling up to the side of the Pilatus in a plume of dust, braking hard and jumping out of his seat in almost a single motion. Jake had already been unlashing the litters and also sprang from the pickup, M4 slung over his back as he slid them out over the tailgate.

Waiting outside the plane, Dmello and Kipnis hurried over to assist in transferring Falcone and Niles from the truck, Dmello then climbing through the cargo opening of the plane to receive each litter. In preparation for the transport, several seats inside the Pilatus had been removed and stored in the rear to allow ample space for both stretchers.

Jake was pleased to see that Kipnis had followed his directives to the letter; IV stands were set up and hung with bags of the fluids that he had requisitioned and a full array of specific items and supplies were organized, including bandages, saline and antiseptics and antibiotics, equipment for vital monitoring, and his AED—automated external defibrillator kit. He really hoped the latter device would not be necessary, but if so, it was one of the best.

At the sight of Falcone and Niles, both Dmello and Kipnis had been visibly shocked but, to their credit, they kept their reactions in check and joined in the group effort to make the two as comfortable as possible. The Malinois, who were not as concerned about outward deportment, hovered anxiously, Remington having to finally admonish them with a stern command to stay back. They grudgingly complied, whining as they lay by Falcone and Niles, snouts close to their heads.

When Dmello inquired if he should prepare for takeoff, Jake quickly told him no, and went about establishing the IVs. As expected, what was normally a smooth and expedient procedure for him turned into a real challenge; severe dehydration had, in fact, caused vein collapse. It took a number of attempts on both but, ultimately, with patience, seasoned skill, and a knowledge of lesser-known methods, he was finally successful getting the needles in at the underside bend of their arms.

While Jake continued to work on Falcone and Niles, Remington took out everything they'd brought from the compound, spreading the materials out for Kipnis to review. As the Israeli scanned through the documents and then got to the oligarch's manifesto, Remington placed a sat phone call to Lieutenant Colonel Merriweather.

The call was intercepted by a lower-ranking officer, who answered, "We're a little busy here," letting him know that multinational combat brinkmanship in the Mediterranean was in full-blown escalation with some aggressive harassment by both air and sea already happening.

"That's why I'm calling," Remington asserted. "I have critical intel. I need Atticus—the lieutenant colonel—on the line right the fuck now!"

There was a muffled bit of protest between the subordinate and someone else, then Merriweather bristled onto the phone. Remington gave him a brief summary of their operations, telling him about the deadly raid at the Syrian mosque, their failure to catch up to Ignatkovich in Cyprus, Syria, and Turkey. By that point, the lieutenant colonel was becoming testy and understandably eager to get back to his command, but when Remington began sharing the narrative of their discoveries inside the oligarch's compound and connecting it to the intel surrounding the sabotaged missile deal, Merriweather's demeanor abruptly changed.

"Holy shit, all this is over a false flag?"

"Yep," Remington replied.

"All right, well, I'm going to need what you've got in my hands as proof. How fast can you get it to me? We're literally on an Armageddon clock here."

Remington glanced over to Jake, who was so steeped in his medical care of Falcone and Niles that he had not been following the conversation. The creases in his forehead and perspiration coating his face showed the extent and seriousness of his efforts.

Cupping a hand over the phone, Remington asked him, "What are we doing?"

Jake's head snapped up, giving him a strained look. "What?"

"What are we doing?" When Jake did not reply, Remington said, "Ignat's got those missiles...pretty sure we know what the fuck he intends to do with them."

Jake's expression shifted to one of anguished dilemma, and now all eyes were on him, awaiting his verdict. And he was wrestling with the torment and potential repercussions of his decision, one that weighed personal and moral responsibility, emotional involvement, and operational obligation to act with selfless valor for the greater good. As he struggled to calculate what he would be risking in not making the flight, he was surprised by a firm hand on his shoulder.

Kipnis said, "Jake, I do not have anywhere near your level of medical training, but I have this."

Jake stared at him, his mind still grappling and his heart still stubbornly refusing to let go of the control he needed to hold onto. He gazed down at the pale, skeletonic faces of Falcone and Niles. He had them mostly stabilized, but their conditions remained serious and, when every moment was precarious and vital, a lot could go sideways during an hour-long flight. But an hour or more out of this theater could very well squander any chance of stopping a madman on a mission to launch war on a massive scale. A madman who had, in one way or another, caused grievous damage and near death to him and everyone he held dear…Remington, Callie, Falcone, and Niles.

He looked back at the two of them, felt his chest heave. God, they had been through hell—maybe not entirely at the hands of Ignatkovich, but Jake had no doubt the monster would have eventually killed them. He bowed his head, agonizing, and felt a faint nudge by the side of his wrist. Turning, he saw that it was Niles' pinky finger—from his damaged hand—and wondered if he'd imagined it. And then it happened again, the finger barely moving, but lifting and dropping.

Kipnis saw it, too, and repeated, "I have got this," his face as earnest as Jake had ever seen, which was saying a lot since it was practically the Israeli's default expression.

Expelling a deep sigh, Jake said slowly, "Okay, Kip…okay. I'll give you a hardcore primer on everything you'll need to know and do." He looked at Remington. "Make sure Atticus lines up the best fucking trauma hospital in Athens and has them on top-priority standby."

The lieutenant colonel, who had overheard his vehemence, told Remington, "That's affirmative. My next call will be to the 401 Military Hospital." He paused. "My proof?"

"Coming to you, on the plane."

"And you?"

"We're going after Ignatkovich."

JAKE SPENT THE NEXT fifteen minutes going over all the medical contingencies that came to mind, explaining and showing Kipnis what to do in each situation. The more bad hypotheticals he premised, the worse he felt about leaving Falcone and Niles, but during the time he took to prepare Kipnis, he was encouraged by their relatively steady respirations and heartbeats, even if on the lower end of the threshold.

Just before deplaning, he leaned close to them and said, "You're going to be fine. Rest easy, boys…you're safe now."

And then he said a fervent prayer—for them, for Remington and himself, and for humanity.

65

WHEN JAKE WAS AS assured of Falcone's and Niles' parting conditions as he was going to be and reluctantly ready to cede control of their care to Kipnis, he had given the okay for Dmello to take off. Now, with the Pilatus in the air and bound for Athens, he sat in the passenger seat of the Toyota 4x4 pickup as Remington drove them back toward the oligarch's compound.

It was still night-dark, but dawn was not far off, the moon hanging lower in the sky. Running without headlights, they were watching the route through the lenses of their NODs, for the time being finding everything eerily still, even as they approached the location where the roadblock had been.

Observing Jake as he drove and seeing him constantly checking the screen of his phone, Remington said, "It's gonna be all right, partner."

"Yeah. I just hate that we'll be out of commo for a while and not be able to know when they've landed and get updates on the guys."

"Have faith. That's what you always tell me."

Jake forced a tight smile. "I do."

Remington said, "I've been thinking about that manifesto…also about the state of the compound." He paused reflectively. "There were a couple of dates mentioned in the timeline, but the last one was today's date. Did you see that?"

Jake nodded. "I'm tracking. I think today's the intended missile launch. But from where and to where? We don't know."

"I have an idea," Remington replied. "Think about the staged Greek commando raid."

Jake pondered that for a minute, then said, "Well, the Turks have been looking for a reason to take their disputes with Greece to full-on war for a long time, so now they have one, going on the presumption that the Greeks blew up their arms deal with Russia *and*—as far as they know—got the missiles."

Remington continued, "And Russia can be on board because it gives them a reason to join in the fight, even take the lead, because they lost billions in the deal and all the military tech, particularly those microchips and drones."

A new thought struck Jake, like a fresh lightbulb flaring brighter in a lamp socket. "Those hypersonic missiles are allegedly able to defy any kind of radar or surveillance technology but, as I understand, they are also capable of being programmed to show their point of origin as coming from anywhere…as originating from Russia, for instance. Historically, the Russians and Greeks have been aligned religiously and culturally, but of course, Russia's war against Ukraine has shaken that alliance. So this? A hypersonic missile strike on Greece, ostensibly from Russia? Fuck us. We could be hours, maybe minutes, from what would one hundred percent give justification for a NATO war against Russia, in defense of Greece."

Remington said, "I believe we're right about today being the day. If Ignat had been at that compound, or if the missiles were still there, his mercs would have been at a more heightened state of readiness than they were. We probably just missed him—again—and they were winding down, getting some rack."

"Okay, let's go to his airfield. That's most likely where the missiles would have been. Maybe we can find out something there, shake out some intel from whoever is on-site."

When they came to the stretch where the roadblock had been, all that remained was the detonated wreckage and carnage of metal and men, scattered and smoldering along the roadsides. Remington drove on, looking for and finding a half-hidden cutaway that led to another road. A mile or so farther brought them to a large fenced field, part dirt and grass, part asphalt. There were a number of signs posted, which read: *ASKERI GÜVENLIK BÖLGESI GIRILMEZ*; others with the single word, *DUR*. While they were not totally sure what the former stated, the one-word signs were familiar, and translated as STOP.

Referring to the multiple-worded postings, Jake ventured, "Pretty sure those are designating this as a restricted military zone."

Remington scoffed, "An oligarch's military zone."

He parked the truck well back from the chain-link fence, and the two of them got out, strapping on their packs, shouldering their rifles, and moving forward with Glock pistols in hand. Remington also had one of Kipnis' jamming devices, which he turned on as they approached. The entire enclosure was mostly dark and appeared to be quiet, but there were several metal hangars on the far side with security lights installed and illuminated at the roof corners. Being some distance from the compound, either the airfield's power was separately sourced or, possibly, backed up by a generator.

"Shit," Jake muttered. "I guess I knew we wouldn't find the missiles here—too easy—but it looks like there's nobody here, either."

"We'll see," said Remington, adding, "at least we're not up against a whole brigade. There's only so many times we're going to come out on the sunny side of those situations."

"No kidding."

There was a guard shack at the gated entrance, two pickup trucks parked side by side inside the fence. Jake and Remington advanced slowly, waiting for the jammer to knock out the Wi-Fi connected to the motion sensors and security monitoring. And, in moments, they knew they had succeeded, a pair of sleepy-looking men in camouflage wear stumbling from the shack, fumbling with their rifles.

Jake and Remington crouched down, shrouded by the darkness, and watched as the guards spread out to investigate. They were conversing in Turkish, the inflection of their voices raised in tense puzzlement. When the two met by the gate, Jake tossed a rock just past it, causing the men to freeze for an instant, and then one called out, *"Sen Kimsin?"*

There was a mumbled exchange between the two, followed by a chink and rattling of metal as the gate was opened, one man stepping to the right, the other, to the left. Jake tossed another rock, landing it in the middle of the gate opening. Predictably, the two guards swung around, back toward each other, and Jake and Remington charged at them.

They got control of the men quickly by grabbing them across the chests, covering their mouths and shoving the suppressed barrels of their Glocks into the sides of their necks. The guards initially reacted by thrashing in an attempt to free themselves and their guns, but loud and menacing rebukes from Jake and Remington stopped these efforts, Jake commanding, *"Susmak!"* It was Turkish he knew, meaning be quiet.

They complied, Jake and Remington disarming them of weapons and confiscating their radios. Next, they walked the pair through the gate and pushed them against the guard shack, Jake pointing his Glock while Remington zip-tied their wrists.

Gesturing for the men to sit on the ground, Jake flipped his NODs up so he could look at them directly and asked, "English?"

At first, the two said nothing, but now that they were closer, their faces seen more clearly, Jake and Remington realized they were quite young, and scared, so Jake adjusted his approach to one less threatening in demeanor.

"We will not harm you if you cooperate," he said reasonably. "Do you understand me?"

The two nodded nervously.

"Okay, good. Is there anybody else here?"

Neither spoke or reacted, which Jake took to indicate they were alone. Now, he got right to the point. "Were the missiles here?"

A harrowing look crossed their faces, confirming to Jake and Remington that they had been right. When the men nodded again, Jake continued, prodding, "When?"

The younger of the pair said, "Two…three hour?"

"Where are they now?"

Neither of the guards wanted to say anything more, their shoulders stiffening, chins down.

Jake bent closer, his tone hardening again. "Where?"

The younger man bit his lip and stuttered, "W-west."

"They're on the move west?" Squatting in front of them, Jake took out his phone, pulled up Google Maps. He found the airfield's location and widened the view. After studying possible routes and not really seeing one that was obvious, he got within reach and said, "Show me."

Lifting his cuffed hands, the man who had answered used a finger to trace a route that actually went south before twisting to the northwest through the mountains.

Following the trajectory, Jake asked, "Aydin?"

"*Evet*…yes."

"Okay, this is very important. Tell us the truth and we will leave you and be on our way." He paused, eying both sternly. "Is the boss with them?"

This question apparently struck a chord of fear in the young men and, just when Jake thought he was going to have to take action to get a response, the second guard sighed and replied, "Yes."

Jake and Remington got the two men on their feet and accompanied them into the guard shack. They inspected the small confines and disabled the communications setup by cutting the wiring and removing batteries, then tied them into their chairs, positioning them close enough to the desk to reach the sodas they had been drinking. Keeping their weapons and radios, they locked them in and left.

Lastly, after comparing the guards' two pickups—both of which were also Toyotas—they selected the one with the fullest fuel tank and slashed the tires on the other. They pulled up next to the truck they had been driving, transferred all their gear, weapons, and ammunition, and slashed its tires.

A few minutes later, they were making their way south toward the D585 highway as the predawn sky began its transition to sapphire.

LIKE MOST OF THE state roads in the country—or, in any given country for that matter—conditions ran the gamut from well-maintained and smoothly paved to dilapidated and in poor repair, and this route, known locally at the southern end as the Kuyucak-Tavas Yolu, was no exception. It had started out as a civilized four-lane, split by a dirt-and-grass median and lined on the sides by stretches of evergreens, low vegetation, and open fields, alternating with rural settlements with an emphasis on the rural. But the farther out from Tavas they got and the closer they traveled into the mountains, the more its condition deteriorated.

They knew from the briefing Kipnis had given them on his intel, that the missile deal was believed to consist of six new variants of the hypersonic Kinzhal, also known as Dagger. Russia had been testing them in Norway's Svalbard Archipelago, part of their ongoing military buildup in the Arctic, proclaiming complete success, although the precedent Kinzhals had performed with mixed results. The novel variation was purported to have speeds of up to Mach 10, or over seventy-six hundred miles per hour, a range of at least fourteen hundred miles, and could carry both conventional and nuclear warheads; able to launch from ground or air, it could easily strike Greece from western Turkey—or, ostensibly, southwestern Russia.

Hypersonic missiles are considered a major threat because of their insane high speeds, ability to fly at lower altitudes, maneuverability in flight and, perhaps most of all, because they are nearly impossible to detect, track, or intercept.

And the vindictive oligarch now had possession of a half-dozen of them—there was an awful lot of catastrophic havoc he could wreak with such an arsenal.

Cell service was sporadic, and Jake was unable to get through to Kipnis for an update on Falcone and Niles, but he did manage to pull up a list of military installments, deciding that Ignatkovich was headed for an air base outside of Aydin where the missiles could be loaded onto F-16s.

As the Toyota pickup bounced and bumped roughly over what had become a rutted two-lane without a median, Jake remarked, "Why in the hell would he have chosen this way? This road is awful. There's another one that runs east-west that would have been a straighter shot and, from what I could tell on Google Maps, it's a much better highway."

"Probably because this is a more low-profile route," Remington guessed.

"That's for sure. You think we have a chance of catching up? If he got a lead of a couple of hours…"

"I think so. You've got to figure, as much weight as those missiles are, and on this road, they've got to be rolling slow." He glanced at the truck's speedometer, the needle ticking eighty to eighty-five miles an hour, and grinned. "Yeah, I'm gonna say we'll catch 'em."

At this hour so early into the new day, there were virtually no other vehicles to contend with except the very occasional car or cargo truck, all of which, upon seeing the Toyota 4x4 gunning up their tails, pulled aside to let them pass. They had traveled through a few built-up areas, the first being west of Tavas and the next as they crossed into Aydin province but, for the most part, the roadside towns were tiny hamlets of old board and stone houses, farms with tractors and animals, and modest little businesses; for mile upon mile in between, there was nothing but the rural landscape of the foothills scaling up to the higher elevations. The moon had all but disappeared, taking its constellation of stars with it and casting a low glow at the horizon line, but there were still a few hours of semidarkness remaining. It was in that diminishing window that Jake and Remington hoped they would make their interdiction.

They were about an hour and eighty miles along the D585, approaching a stretch that ran parallel to a body of water known as the Dandalas Stream, when they were astonished to actually find themselves coming up on what was unmistakably a military utility truck—in front of which lumbered a massive transport vehicle wide enough to overtake both sides of the road. Because of the transport's girth, they could not determine if there were any additional vehicles in front, but it seemed highly likely that a lead truck would most certainly be the one occupied by Ignatkovich.

"Holy shit, Batman," Remington marveled.

In the passenger seat beside him, Jake got on his sat phone, connecting to a special number Lieutenant Colonel Merriweather had given them. When the call was answered, Jake recited the coordinates of their current location.

THEY DROPPED BACK, TRAILING at a subtle distance for a while, and considered their options. Studying the remainder of the route to Aydin on his phone, Jake remarked, "We've got about fifteen miles to the junction of the E87 which is part of a much more prominent, international highway or, a few miles north of that, the intersection with the D320, a state road. From there, it's about thirty or so miles to the air base."

Watching the sway of the thirty-five-foot HEMTT—Heavy Expanded Mobility Tactical Truck—Remington said, "I don't think we can hold off that long and let them get to a more heavily trafficked highway."

"No, we can't," Jake agreed. "Anything could happen before then, and we should act while we have the advantage of at least some remaining darkness."

In the miles and minutes they had been following, the road edges had expanded and curved enough in a few places for them to get a look at the full convoy. In a conventional military procession for missile transport, there is typically a march unit or column consisting of multiple armored vehicles that may include local and federal law enforcement, emergency services, fuel tankers, and wreckers, all coordinated with great precision. Fortunately for them, this was not the case with the oligarch's missile transfer; it was comprised of only the big tactical carrier and two utility vehicles, the one they were behind and the one escorting at the front.

"So, how do you want to do this?" Remington asked.

"Well, simply put, we need to stop them and either contain or take out the personnel...and Ignat."

"This stretch we're on, the transport takes up the whole width of the road, and there's not enough room on the sides to go around," Remington said. "I'd say, the first opportunity we get where there is a flat expanse of field, we overtake them, block the road, and engage. If we hit hard and fast, take out Ignat, the driver, and riders in his vehicle, then we might be able to get the rest to surrender. Did Command give you any kind of ETA on their response time?"

Jake replied, "They just acknowledged and said deployment was imminent." He knotted his fists, rage coiling like a cobra in his gut. "I want this motherfucker."

Feeling his own wrath, Remington's jaw hardened. "Copy that, my brother."

THEY WERE STILL DRIVING a segment with the narrowest of sidelines and maintaining their distance when the trail vehicle in the convoy suddenly began to take shots at them.

A dirt and rock embankment rose to their left, a fairly steep drop-off on their right, below which were perhaps twenty small houses and farms clustered in the village of Güzelköy. The barrel of an assault rifle poked out of a window on the utility vehicle's passenger side, that of a handgun appearing from the driver's side. Spotting the weapons in time to take evasive measures, Remington dropped further back and zigzagged the Toyota pickup as rounds split the air.

"Fuck!" Jake exclaimed, and lowered his window, bracing his M4 on the frame and aiming at the man on his side. After a brief exchange, he hit the passenger shooter, the man's rifle slipping from his grasp and tumbling to the road.

Remington's fire on the driver was a little more challenging, as he kept ducking in and out, dividing his efforts between steering and shooting. But a round eventually nailed the target, the utility vehicle veering to the right and rolling down the slope.

With the big HEMTT now directly in front of them, they began to take fire from it, too, which was a problem; with it carrying the missiles, they did not want to force it over the cliff in the same manner, but they needed to stop or disable it. The engagement was forcing their hand and necessitating a quicker confrontation, one they would have rather been on the front end of rather than at the back.

Evaluating the rear assembly of the carrier, which was configured with the outriggers for a handling crane, Jake asked, "Can you get close enough for me to climb on?"

Remington's initial reaction was one of dumbfounded incredulity but, with a few moments' theorizing, he was riding the same wavelength. "Yeah, yeah…that might be the way to do this."

The two of them continued returning fire, bullets slashing by on both sides of the Toyota pickup and a few striking the frame, but Remington gradually moved up behind the carrier until their front bumper was within a few feet of it.

Jake got a paracord from his pack, knotted it to a carabiner link that he clipped to his belt, tethering the other end to the door handle. Then he pulled himself into the window frame and onto the Toyota's hood, sliding to the grille and reaching out until his gloved hands could grasp part of the carrier's assembly. Unsnapping the paracord link, he quickly climbed to the top of the vehicle and flattened out.

As he crawled forward, feeling the force of forward momentum and air rush flowing over him, he was reminded of another time he'd per-formed this type of maneuver, though the circumstances had been quite different and, honestly, a lot more dangerous.

On that occasion, Jake had been in the throes of a raging battle in Sierra Leone between rebels and the government forces. An evac mission of wounded and deceased had been perilously subverted by a swelling swarm of desperate and hysterical villagers who stormed the bus in his protection, emaciated men, women, and children monkeying their way onto the rooftop and hanging off the sides. The driver had screamed at Jake, refusing to leave with all the surplus human cargo, forcing him to make an unconscionable decision; he'd climbed to the top and begun shoving people off until the bus started moving. Jake had never forgotten the wails of sorrow and outcries of anger from those jettisoned and left behind to certain massacre.

Now, as he slithered toward the front of the carrier, M4 rifle bumping his back, Glock in hand, he was about to climb down the passenger side when he heard something that was about to change his degree-of-danger assessment.

He twisted his head and glanced skyward, and thought: *Are you fucking kidding me?*

66

JAKE FELT THE VIBRATION of the carrier thrumming over the rough road in his chest, stomach, and groin, the mechanical grumble of its engine in his ears, but now he also heard the distinctive drone of a helicopter approaching.

When he glimpsed up, he could hardly believe what he saw and yet, how could he have not anticipated it? Of course there would be a helo scouting the route ahead of the convoy, he thought, and now it was circling back to provide air defense. The sky had still not lightened much but it was just enough for Jake to make out the color of the bird—black—and recognize the shape of the Leonardo. As it got closer, the throp of blades became more audible, the blinking white and red lights giving him flashes of its nose and side.

"Shit."

Through comms, Remington asked him, "What's happening?"

"Fucking helo…the fucking black helo. Can you hit it?"

"Do my best. Still taking heat from your ride."

The carrier slammed a pothole, bouncing Jake on the roof shell and causing him to grapple to keep his balance and not slide off. He had regained his stability and was edging back toward the side of the vehicle when the helicopter opened up on him, raining down 7.62 machine gun rounds that pelleted the top of the carrier like hailstones.

"Fuck!" Jake yelled. "Taking fire!"

He scrambled over the side, hanging onto the vehicle frame, the sound of bullets whanging and thumping across the roof, ricocheting like popping corn in every direction, a couple just missing his head and face. One nipped right by a gloved hand and he instinctively let go, dangling by the other hand and swinging next to one of the rolling front tires. His right leg bumped up against the rotating tread once, twice, and he almost lost his grip.

The carrier's passenger had not yet seen him and, when he leaned out of the window to fire his rifle just then, was taken by surprise at having Jake almost in his face, giving Jake the advantage he needed to reach out, grab the barrel of the merc's gun, and rip the weapon from his grasp. Jake drew his Glock and shot the man in the head, the round punching through his face, spraying blood and brain matter.

Almost simultaneously, he heard Remington scream in his comms, "RPG!"

What the fuck?

The animal reaction and adrenaline fuse it lit sent a frenzy of directives, the first and most insistent being to leap from the moving vehicle and roll as far away as momentum would take him; a more rational voice instantly overruled, reminding him that unarmed missiles were not subject to combustion by an artillery strike. Of course, a direct hit to even a heavy vehicle such as this one could cause a lot of other problems. Before he could debate further, a projectile whistled from the sky, invisible but for a plume of smoke, arcing down in their direction.

In the Toyota truck, Remington had dropped back from the carrier's rear to have the best position and angle from which to keep firing at the driver and also take aim at the helicopter. He had switched from the Glock to his M4 rifle, bracing it against his ribs and clutching it with his left hand as he held onto the pickup's steering wheel with his right. Being right-handed, he knew his aim would not be great, but if he could just land some shots anywhere around the helo, that would help deter them long enough for Jake to get off the carrier's roof.

But when he saw the big barrel of the rocket-propelled grenade launcher protrude from the Leonardo's open door, aimed not at the carrier but at himself, he pointed his rifle at the gunner and pulled the trigger.

His shot missed the door gunner but hit the tail rotor, skewing the aircraft and throwing off the gunner's aim and, as a result, the trajectory of the fired warhead. He did not see the helicopter slowly spiral as it fell from the sky, his focus instead riveted on the road in front of the Toyota's windshield and on the carrier.

The warhead that had been meant to blow up the Toyota and him in it struck the road next to the HEMTT, detonating in a powerful tsunami of dirt and dust and chunks of asphalt.

WITH THE IMPACT OF the RPG warhead, Jake was thrown from the carrier as it rocked and tilted sideways over the edge of the road. He tumbled backwards, somersaulting, rolling, and then sliding down the steep elevation. As he slid, his hands were clawing and clutching for anything to stop his plummet, or at least slow the rate of descent, boots trying to dig in for anchorage. Dirt blew into his face, grit scraping and shredding his skin, tendons and muscles burning from the strain of resisting against gravity.

All of it happened so fast that he did not immediately see the bigger peril.

The power and placement of the RPG strike had managed to dislodge one of the missiles from the carrier, the force of the blast propelling it through the roof shell, the size and weight taking it over the slope right behind Jake. Now, as he fought to control his slide, he looked up to see the thirty-foot-long, nine-thousand-pound hypersonic rolling down above him. Not far below, the ground shook with the crash of the helicopter, followed by a succession of explosions involving fuel and munitions. The acrid smoke of burning kerosene quickly filled the air.

Jake coughed as the first bites of it invaded his lungs. "Oh God…oh fuck, oh God. Remy…Remy, do you copy?"

He got no response, his head jerking left and right as his out-of-control descent continued, and he fought back panic as he sought a way to get out of the path of the missile almost on top of him. Its rate of roll was accelerating, and he knew if he didn't get clear of it in the next few seconds, it would crush him.

He looked down the slope, saw that there was a long way left to go and, on the way to wherever the bottom was, the inferno of helicopter wreckage. He looked back overhead and saw that the missile was just a few feet from him and still rolling.

Fuck me.

But no…he was not ready to die…but if he was going to go, it would by God be fighting to live until the final microsecond. He knew he could not survive being hit or crushed by the missile, and he could not survive a leap down the steep hillside—but if, by some miracle, he did survive that and maybe break bones in his limbs and spine—he would very likely be consumed by the fire that was directly in the path of his slide. His only hope was to somehow scrabble sideways, which was proving nearly impossible. The vegetation and brush covering the incline was thin, the surface here mostly soil and rock.

He was at the last-ditch point of taking a chance on that life-endangering leap downward when his hand snared a vine of some kind. He swung his other hand to it and pulled, but as he did, it dislodged from the ground, came totally loose, and he went sprawling.

But this time, the momentum took him in a different direction. He was sliding again, but the behemoth of a missile pounded just past him and continued its downward roll.

He redoubled his efforts to find traction and, after falling another dozen or so yards, hit a shallow ridgeline with a fringe of scrub. Using the breakpoint to maneuver sideways, he eventually reached a vertical trail of immature evergreens with sufficient rootstock to provide the means for him to make a climb back to the road.

As he grabbed handfuls of the brush and worked his way up the slope, he again tried to establish comm contact with Remington, but to no avail and, for the first time, it registered that his friend might have been critically injured or killed by the RPG strike.

JAKE CAME OVER THE road edge, where he found himself by the canted side of the HEMTT, next to the big front and rear tires. He could hear the grinding sound of the engine trying but not quite engaging, inner mechanicals resistant but grudgingly collaborating. His mind was running a dual track between getting to Remington—first and foremost—and getting to Ignatkovich.

Crawling carefully around the carrier's tires, he saw their Toyota 4x4 about twenty yards away, flipped on its side, cracked and cratered asphalt spread from the RPG warhead's point of impact. Crouched down, he scanned the environs for any sign of Remington while also keeping an eye out for the oligarch, for any movement from the front of the carrier.

Jake immediately realized that he'd lost both his handgun and rifle during the plunge down the slope and was mentally inventorying his other weapon options. Unless they had also become separated from him, he had another Glock and a few knives; the 43 9mm strapped above his boot, a fixed-blade KA-BAR and a Spyderco Paramilitary folder on his belt, and the Leatherman tool in a pocket.

Before he was able to verify the retention of any of those weapons and get at least one in his hand, the barrel of a rifle was jabbed into his back.

A Turkish-accented voice commanded, "Get up…slow…hands out."

Jake did as he was told, eyes still searching the periphery for Remington. The undercarriage of their overturned pickup was all he could see, so he had no idea if Remington was still in the vehicle, trapped or wounded or dead or if, hopefully, he'd walked away mostly unscathed and was covertly watching and waiting for a moment to strategically interject himself.

At gunpoint, Jake was vigorously patted down, all of his hardware removed. The Turk with the rifle ordered him to turn around and, when he did, Jake found himself face to face with the merc bodyguard, clutching an MPT-76, and Taras Ignatkovich.

The bodyguard, tall and raw-boned, was clad in black-and-gray camo with the full complement of tactical gear and had the imperial air of an elite combatant.

Ignatkovich, dressed in Brioni—fitted jeans, a dove-gray cashmere t-shirt, charcoal silk jersey blazer, and suede boots—looked more like he was on his way to a private club brunch than a military base for a missile launch. The oligarch stepped closer, his flinty eyes coolly studying Jake, chiseled features of his face framing an expression that was, on the surface, inscrutably impassive. But Jake noted the rigid set of the man's jaw, the tautness of tendons in his neck, and recognized an underlying anger.

"So…Jake Tyler," Ignatkovich mused. Though his Russian accent was pronounced, his English was exceedingly good, cultivated by a combination of the best state university education and decades of international business. "It would seem I was right in my risk assessment of you and your team. I will say that you even exceed your reputation. You have presented quite the challenge." A snide smile creased his lips. "But…" He paused, as if considering an evaluation, finishing snarkily, "I win."

The oligarch waited for a response but did not get one.

Jake was giving Ignatkovich the perception of captive listening while his mind worked out the aspects of his situation. Unless one or more mercs were holding Remington somewhere—and he believed if that were the case Remington would have been trotted out as further conquest—Ignatkovich and the bodyguard were the only members of the convoy remaining. Another observation supporting this was the absence of anemic engine noises, suggesting that it had been either the bodyguard or Ignatkovich himself trying to restart the carrier moments ago.

He had not seen evidence of a weapon on the oligarch, but he had to assume he was concealing a handgun or knife.

Jake had also been watching the bodyguard, whose attention was laser-focused on him; he'd not so much as twitched, eyes holding Jake's. This made what Jake liked to think of as the squirrel ploy, the perfect move. He rolled his eyes very deliberately, peering off to a space behind his two opponents, both of them doing exactly as predicted—turning their heads to see what, or who, Jake was looking at. Which was, of course, nothing.

The split-second diversion of focus was all he needed to seize the MPT-76 from the merc's grasp, flip it around, finger the trigger, and aim it.

"*Siktir!*" the merc shouted, and launched himself at Jake, grabbing the rifle barrel. Jake got off a wild burst of shots that punctured the ground and sliced through the air, the two men wrestling for control of the weapon.

As the fight continued, the merc jabbing him with his elbows and kicking out at his legs, Jake shuffled backwards past the HEMTT, dragging the merc along until they were scuffling by the road edge. Planting his feet, Jake violently wrenched the rifle up and down, offsetting the merc's balance, and swung him around as if they were square dancing partners.

The merc bodyguard went flailing over the slope, his screams trailing off as he fell. To keep from falling with him, Jake had to let the rifle go and had also been unable to recover any of his own weapons, all of which had been pocketed by the merc.

Turning back to the road, Jake was immediately fired on by Ignatkovich, pistol in hand. Ducking, Jake kept his eye on the oligarch's aim as he advanced on him. Ignatkovich continued shooting, stepping backward as he did, withdrawing a sat phone from one of his pockets, working it one-handed and putting it up to an ear.

He's calling for reinforcements, Jake thought.

They were now in front of the carrier and the lead utility vehicle, Jake bobbing and weaving as rounds popped, whizzing through the air or chinking on the vehicles' metal panels. Again, he glanced back, hoping to see Remington, but did not.

Jake was pretty sure the oligarch had either an MP-443 Grach or GSh-18, both of which were standard Russian military sidearms with an eighteen-round capacity. He'd been trying to keep a count of the number of shots fired and had tallied at least a dozen, so hopefully the gun would soon be empty.

As if on cue, the shooting abruptly stopped and Jake saw Ignatkovich shove the pistol into the waistband of his jeans, meaning he did not have a spare magazine on him. For a volatile instant, both stared at each other, and then Ignatkovich bolted up the road.

Not far behind, Jake chased him along the interior embankment until it leveled out and opened into an expanse of field, the oligarch leaving the road and bounding through low vegetation to a ramshackle old barn, timbers decaying, rotted, or missing altogether. He disappeared inside, Jake following after him.

Twilight filtered in through the many gaps in the structure's wood frame, but it somehow seemed darker and took Jake a few moments for his eyes to adjust. The interior that materialized had the look and feel of the set of a horror flick, openings overgrown with thatches of grass and weeds, thick swaths of cobwebs strung from every corner, damp ground layered and ripe with decomposed hay and manure and other organics. The carcass of a long-defunct tractor and spindly plow sat off to one side of the barn, rusted and corroded tools hanging or leaning on some of the timbers.

Ignatkovich was standing near one of the double-gated entrances, the planked panels of this one closed but not latched, so he could have shoved his way through and made another run. But the oligarch did not seem inclined to bail at this point, apparently deciding that the two of them were on equal footing.

A few feet inside the roadside entrance, the gate panels for which had been haphazardly broken apart as if kicked in by some headstrong mule, Jake was about twenty feet from Ignatkovich. Even from that distance, he could see the smirk curling around the oligarch's mouth, the arrogance in his expression, and Jake felt the rage building in his chest, boiling behind his eyes.

He took several slow steps forward. "I don't care who or how many you have coming, motherfucker," he said, his voice thick with malice. "Right now, it's only you and me…and you're done."

Ignatkovich took the same number of steps toward Jake, his grin widening wolfishly. "I do not think so."

The two continued their intentional advancement, closing the space that separated them.

At a gap of ten feet, Ignatkovich said, "What I am doing was always going to happen eventually. History repeats, but the ones who reenact it on their own terms control the outcome and harness the supremacy. Putin is doing it all wrong, using up all his own soldiers and resources. I knew the better way."

Jake said, "Spoken like a true delusional despot…but one who greatly overplayed and underestimated."

With four feet between them, they stopped, glaring at each other like two bulls about to charge. Feet set, arms out, postures stiff. Jake waited, his black eyes piercing into the oligarch's pale irises, knowing the Russian would make the first move.

And he did.

Just as Jake had suspected, Ignatkovich was harboring a knife, a Kizlyar-bladed one with ornate engraving that appeared to be a Gurza, withdrawn from one of the oligarch's suede boots in two quick movements. He pounced on Jake, immediately going for the jugular, angling the blade across his throat. For a moment, Jake could feel the sting of the steel cutting into his flesh, the searing pain like a live electrical wire, but he was able to get his hands up, knocking the knife free and sending it flying off somewhere into the gloom.

Without the lethality of weapons, it was a new fight now, and Ignatkovich opened with a jab at Jake's upper body, but his dominant fist was already targeting the lower region, swinging from the side where organs like the kidneys and liver would incur major pain and, potentially, incapacitating damage if struck with enough force and accurate placement.

But Jake's gaze had shifted just before the strike, watching for and interpreting the subtle movements of his opponent so he could anticipate and react accordingly. As Ignatkovich threw his punches and executed his kicks, Jake was able to successfully obstruct and counterstrike, but as the pace and intensity of battle escalated, he grew increasingly surprised at how well the older man moved and also the grade of his fitness; the oligarch had the brawn and dexterity of one that trained at a master level and probably to the point of obsession. He was proving a formidable foe.

Several times, Jake thought he'd set Ignatkovich up for the finish—with leg- or body-lock takedowns, choke holds, and the gold standard of dirty fighting, hard knee to the groin—but the man kept rebounding and coming back for more. Jake found himself in a couple of seemingly inescapable locks and chokes himself, almost blacking out once, and took a number of well-timed, crushing blows to his body and hammering assaults to the head and neck. His face was already a mask of blood, but a wicked sideswipe across his jaw—the massive diamond ring on the oligarch's finger slicing into his skin—opened a gash that bled copiously.

While much of the fight was close-quartered, the Russian pranced and parried to stage more athletic attacks, one of which sent them both crashing through a section of timbers into a thicket of tall grass and then wrestling and grappling their way back inside.

Soon, they were both exhausted but, apparently, equitably damaged.

Which led to a consequential change of tactic.

Backed against the side of the barn littered with tools, Ignatkovich reached around and grabbed a pitchfork, first gripping it with both hands and squaring off like a *Bōjutsu* stick fighter and then wielding and jabbing it at Jake, who danced out of the path, huffing breathlessly. After throwing the forked end and just missing Jake's head, Ignatkovich snatched a shovel and, with grunting exertion, began swinging back and forth.

Goddamn, Jake thought, frankly astounded at the Russian's stamina and resilience. In the amped-up, rapid pace of hand-to-hand combat or, really, most kinds of fighting, there was rarely time or mental aptitude to think reflectively, but Jake was slowing down and tiring, fury burning a hole in his heart, and he saw and heard the fearful cries of Callie when she'd been shot.

He twisted around and snatched the first thing he could get his hands on—a long-handled axe. Like the rest of the tools, it was coarsely encrusted with rust, but its blade was heavy and sharp enough. Turning, Jake caught Ignatkovich on a downswing, bent over, both arms gripping the shovel, and he rotated his arm.

Ignatkovich glanced up at the last second and his pale eyes went wide, bloodied mouth forming an O like an oxygenating fish. Jake slammed the axe blade into the oligarch's wrist, completely severing it. Geysers of blood as red as chili peppers spurted as Ignatkovich screamed, a string of shrill, incoherent Russian mixed in with the bellowing. Stunned, he gaped at the flow of blood pulsing from his stump of wrist, then at the detached hand on the ground in front of him.

Jake reared back and swung again, the second blow identical to the first, severing Ignatkovich's other hand. It flopped to the dirt, garish diamond ring looking more like a cluster of rubies in all the blood. Jake tossed the axe aside, exhaled breathlessly, and said, "That's for all of us, for every fucking thing."

He turned on heel, stopped, looked back, and said dryly, "You lose." He walked off, leaving the Russian to bleed out.

JAKE FOUND REMINGTON IN the Toyota truck, slumped across the front seats. The windshield was spiderwebbed, pebbles and shards of shattered glass covering him, a slice the size of a pie wedge sticking out of his back shoulder. Jake placed his fingers on Remington's neck, felt for a pulse.

Then he grasped him by the arms and eased him over. "Remy…hey!" More forcefully and closer to his face, he said, "Remy…Remy!"

Nash Remington's lids batted and then fluttered, unshuttering his olive-green eyes. He moaned and tried to straighten up.

Jake put a hand on him. "Whoa, partner. Glad you're back in the dance, but let me check you out."

He spent the next few minutes doing a basic assessment, deciding that his friend was mostly okay after being knocked unconscious by the RPG hit and the battery sustained in the rollover of the pickup. He dug for his medical bag and checked Remington's vitals, the pupillary response test suggesting Remington could have sustained a mild concussion.

As Jake was removing the chunk of glass from Remington's shoulder, cleaning and bandaging the laceration, his friend took notice of Jake's extensive collection of injuries for the first time; the sum total was every bit as bad, if not worse, than the fight the two of them had engaged in with some of Ignatkovich's thugs all those weeks ago in Izmir.

"Holy mother of God, what the fuck happened to you?"

"You remember what we were doing before your lights went out?" Jake asked him, the answer to which would help inform his medical evaluation.

A perplexed look slid over Remington's face and, after a few moments of rumination, he murmured dimly, "Going to pick up the dogs…"

Jake regarded him, concerned for a beat and then, catching the tickle of an impish grin on his friend's face, laughed. "You asshole."

"Ignat…you get him?"

"Oh yeah. He won't be waging any wars."

Studying Jake's face and what he could see from his ripped clothing, Remington told him, "You need some medical attention yourself, my man."

Jake turned a visor mirror down and peered at the mess reflected, grimacing vaguely. "You aren't wrong, but we'll put a pin in it for now." He spotted Remington's sat phone in the truck's footwell and picked it up. A moment later, after reading a text, he was smiling. "The guys made it to Athens and are at the hospital. Kip got everything to Atticus."

He looked up and cast a glance toward the HEMTT leaning sideways by the slope. "We've got another problem. Can you walk?"

With Jake's help, Remington climbed from the pickup and tested his legs. Pronouncing himself viable, he surmised, "We need to get that carrier away from the drop."

"Yep. And before I took him out, the son of a bitch put in a call for backup."

"Great."

They strode to the front end of the carrier.

Remington remarked, "Guess I'm not driving."

Jake hoisted himself into the driver's seat and keyed the ignition. The HEMTT's motor whined, stalled, whined again, sputtered, and then caught. Jake carefully maneuvered the vehicle forward until it was level on the road, steering it as far from the edge as he could get it.

He turned off the engine, slid out of the seat, and stood next to Remington. Their heads swiveled upward, the sky now an electric blue as dawn encroached, both hearing the throb of multiple helicopters just out of sight.

"God, I hope that's *our* cavalry," Jake said.

And then, the pounding rotors were obliterated by a seismic explosion from down below the hillside, rocking the ground under their feet as they grabbed the side of the carrier.

The fire from the Leonardo wreckage had blown up the missile. Dense black smoke rose and spread in a vast cloud, the already-burning slope turning into a sea of orange.

67

EIGHTY YEARS BEFORE, ALMOST to the day, a B-24 Liberator flew low and solo over the dark Aegean, its black shell effectively blending into the night sky. At just over 260 nautical miles out, the aircraft had cleared land and was nearing the halfway point of flight, its crew eager to complete their mission—so secret that the destination and details were known only to the pilot and navigator.

The four-engine, high-wing Consolidated B-24, was the most produced aircraft from its era and a mainstay in every battle and war therein, considered by most to be the workhorse bomber of its class. Often derided as the "Lumbering Lib" or the "Flying Coffin," it was ungainly and not particularly easy to handle, but what it lacked in grace and aesthetics was offset by ruggedness and versatility, able to fly a range of up to three thousand miles at a maximum ceiling of thirty thousand feet with speeds close to three hundred miles per hour.

But this particular plane was cruising far lower and slower than typical, at an altitude of about five thousand feet to evade detection and assault by anti-aircraft. It was also not configurated as bomber, camouflaged with more than five hundred pounds of the black paint and a specially modified interior, including the removal of the ball turret in the belly to construct a cargo hatch known as a "Joe" hole. Inside, on this flight, were three such men—the "Joes"—in padded jumpsuits and rubber helmets. They were part of the payload, which included one- to three-hundred-pound C and H containers of arms and ammunition, jerrycans of gasoline, bicycles and radio sets, and boxes of clothing, food, and medical supplies. There was also a large, multi-compartmented container filled gadgets and equipment for sabotage.

The young crew of eight, most in their mid to late twenties, were members of an OSS group—Office of Strategic Services—predecessor of the modern-day CIA, all of them either Greek American or Greek nationals from the U.S., and their mission was part of late-stage operations in the Allied efforts to defeat the Axis forces in the Mediterranean theater. Recruits were not only physically fit, intelligent, and motivated, they were also trusted and resourceful, with the added advantage of knowing the language and culture of the region. As high-value assets, it was rumored that Hitler had put a capture reward on them equivalent to their weight in gold.

Much of the time, they flew sorties over the Greek mainland in support of resistance fighters on the ground that were blowing up supply lines and railways and bridges, but their assignment tonight was to drop the supplies and spies—the Joes they were strictly prohibited from talking to—into German-occupied Rhodes.

The airship they flew, unlike other warplanes with more creative or quirky names, such as *Ford's Folly* or *Filthy Annie* or *American Beauty*, was inscribed with the moniker *Black Olive*, in a nod to the nation of their heritage.

After making it through an initial gauntlet of night fighters and enemy flak concentrated in the skies over the mainland, the flight had been mostly clear and smooth, the crew members watchful and anxious in their respective positions. The navigator and bombardier, both 1st lieutenants, were holed up in the nose; the captain and pilot, also officers, were behind them in the cockpit; the radio operator in the upper fuselage and the top turret gunner-engineer in the bubble dome above, were both technical sergeants; the remaining gunners behind the wings and in the tail, were all sergeants or corporals.

With air blowing through every turret opening of the non-pressurized cabin, the fur-lined sheepskin jackets the young flyers wore provided little comfort against the numbing cold, their teeth often chattering as they conversed through the aircraft's interphone system by push-to-talk throat mics.

This night was no different, and the army aviators were doing their best to break up stretches of monotony and ease nerves by making light of their discomfort.

One of the gunners, a corporal named Nick Pappas who hailed from Upper Saddle River, New Jersey, was keeping lookout for any spec in his vector that could conceivably be an enemy aircraft while trying to peel an orange, muttering, "This friggin' thing is frozen solid as a baseball…I bite into it, I break my teeth."

His counterpart nearby, Costas Kavourhas, another corporal, laughed and said, "Yeah, my sandwich was kinda crunchy." His speech crackled around the wad of Wrigley's gum he was chomping to compensate for the constant popping in his ears.

Through the comms, the bombardier chimed in, "You guys are pussies…you got it good, I'm freezing my fuckin' nuts off up here. Probably have to thaw me out when we land."

Listening to the banter, the pilot smiled but did not join in. He was preoccupied with the mission course and asked his navigator for an update. In the swivel seat behind the bombardier, the 1st lieutenant checked his compass and charts and the readings of his instruments and gave a report. Satisfied with the information, the captain, a second-generation Greek American named Michalis Philippedes whose parents immigrated to the U.S. from the island of Samos, thought about their ultimate objective.

When it came time to line up for their drops, Philippedes and the bombardier would be working in tight, coordinated tandem. On approach to the designated target, usually about thirty or so miles out, communication would be made with partisans on the ground for final drop instructions. Just prior to takeoff, the B-24's radio operator had received the mission flimsy, which included details of the signals, code letters, ground challenge and reply. Contact would be made by S phone, a short-range, ground-to-air radio, and they would lower to between four and six hundred feet, slowing to 130 miles an hour or less—a precarious maneuver, as the speed was just above stalling, their height over ground chancing collision with mountains. But the speed and height were calculated risks to reduce the opening shock of parachutes and lessen the potential for damage to the containers and agents. As the aircraft circled and lined up for the drop zone, they would be looking for a prearranged pattern of beacons—usually high-powered flashlights pointing skyward—and, on confirmation, the bombardier would execute the cargo release with the push of a button; parachutes attached to the containers and Joes would open as they floated to the DZ.

Back toward the rear of the plane, the gunners continued their wise-cracking, needling Pappas. The corporal was growing increasingly apprehensive as he peered through the Sperry K-13 Compensating Sight of his .50 caliber machine gun, gazing down at a sea black as oil, its surface faintly gleaming in the moonlight.

Costas Kavourhas sneered, "What's the matter, Nicky? Worried we're gonna drop into the drink?" Addressing the radio operator, he said, "Hey, Johnny…what did you say our odds of successful mission were?"

Chuckling through his comms, the sergeant named John Saralis, who was known to be a mathematics nerd and who constantly ran probability calculations, retorted, "Last I checked on my slide rule, it was like five, ten percent."

Others laughed at the ribbing, but the tail gunner broke through the heckling and said, "Stop it…you're getting him all worked up for nothing. We'll be fine."

Nick Pappas wiped his runny nose on the sleeve of his jacket. Teeth clicking, he said, "You know how scared I am of the water. I just…I just always have been." His face was wan with unease in the red glow of ambient cabin light, gloved hands rubbing the frozen orange.

The crew and clandestine passengers of the *Black Olive* flew on without incident for another fifty nautical miles, and then what every wartime aviator feared—and pretty much expected—came to bear.

From his dome overhead, the gunner-engineer suddenly declared, "We've got a squad of Messers coming up twelve o'clock, both sides!"

He was referencing Messerschmitt Bf 109s, single-piloted fighters that were the backbone of the *Luftwaffe*'s force. Though limited in range, they were lightweight with speeds of up to 450 miles per hour, and well-armed with 20mm cannons and 13mm machine guns, and they were just about the worst thing an Allied plane could find in its midst.

The Liberator's gunners immediately went to work, firing on the advancing fleet of fighters, the collective rattle of their 12.7mm Brownings loud in the belly of the plane. A flurry of frenzied communications went back and forth between the crew as they locked in on targets.

"I'm on the three o'clock bastards! Nicky, you got the nine's?"

"I got 'em! Sons of bitches!"

The two midship gunners swept their weapons wide over the airspace multiplying with German warships, raking the predators with unrelenting fire, expending looping belts of .50 caliber bullets as scorching shells popped and filled up the floor.

From the tail, another corporal gunner, Jerry Brady, suddenly cried out, "We're hit! We're hit!"

From his high vantage in the upper dome, the sergeant gunner-engineer, Gust Vellios, confirmed, "Right stabilizer's hit…it's on fire!" And, moments afterward, he saw one of the four Pratt & Whitneys sprout flames and spew thick curdles of smoke. "Oh shit, engine four is hit!"

Next to the captain, copilot Dino Babalis said, "Shutting down four."

Vellios next relayed that they were losing engine three, either from an unrelated malfunction or collateral damage or from a strike, and the pilots were struggling to keep the plane flying as level as possible under the circumstances. Captain Philippedes glanced to his copilot and said, "We might have to bail soon."

Hearing this, gunner Nick Pappas whined, "Oh God, no…not over the water!" In a voice that sounded like a child's, he pleaded, "Please, not over the water! Please!"

The navigator, Steve Agelopas, weighed in, telling the pilots, "Make a fifteen degree adjustment, south-southwest, and if we can stay the course another fifteen miles, we'll be over an island." As he continued to relay his readings and recommendations, activity in the belly and tail of the plane was growing frantic.

A Bf 109 had blown past the Liberator at more than twice the speed and fired off a 30mm cannon, blasting a hole through the fuselage, which caught fire. As the gunners tried to keep up their machine gun defense while trying to extinguish the fire, Costas Kavourhas was hit in the shoulder, the force slamming him against the aircraft's frame and almost knocking him out.

Seeing the horror flare over his comrade's face, he said, "I'm okay,

Nicky. We'll be okay."

But from the top turret, Gust Vellios was beginning to see parts of the Liberator cracking, wings wobbling, and somberly reported, "Time to bail, guys."

"Noooo," Pappas whimpered feebly.

Philippedes said, "Hold on, Nicky. I'll get us over that island. We're almost there."

His eyes flicked to the worn black-and-white photograph of his wife which he tacked up in the cockpit of every plane he flew. Her name was Sofia, the image taken during a barbecue with his entire family clan, all assembled in his Youngstown, Ohio backyard. In that moment, he thought about her and he thought about his crew. He surveyed his instrument panel, none of the indicators looking good.

The hum of the Liberator's two working engines were fading out to a fuzz in his head, as if a colony of bees had burrowed deep inside a hive.

He then sounded the emergency bell, three short rings which signified *Prepare to bail.* All around him—in front, overhead, and behind—his crew was reaching to the racks for their chutes, attaching and checking each other and moving to their bail-out positions in the aircraft. For the navigator and bombardier, this would be the nose wheel bay; for the gunners, the belly hatch and rear bomb bay; for the rest, including himself, it would also be through a bomb bay, accessed by crouching on the narrow catwalk in the middle.

As part of the emergency exit procedure, Philippedes heard each of his crew acknowledge on the interphone, some voices sounding stoic, others terrified. The Joes, who would be the first to bail from their cargo hatch, also acknowledged.

Through his glass enclosure, the pilot was eying the small bump of land coming into view in the black sea below…waiting, waiting…*got to get just a little closer,* he told himself. Next to him, copilot Lambros Babalis was securing his parachute and looking to ensure Philippedes had done the same.

And then the Liberator went into a spin, its body coming apart at the wings and tail section, engulfed in flames and smoke. Philippedes hit the bail-out bell again, this time in a single, sustained ring, prompting the bombardier to open all of the bay doors and the rear hatch.

Doing their best to remain upright, the three gunners stood close together, spent shells rolling around their feet and flying through the air. The orange Nick Pappas had been trying to peel thumped over his boots, and he almost bent to pick it up.

Facing the front of the plane, tail gunner Jerry Brady lunged forward from the yawning hatch, head tucked, Costas Kavourhas and Nick Pappas stumbling and lurching behind him as the aircraft's plummet picked up speed. Kavourhas, whose shoulder was missing a chunk and bleeding liberally, turned and gave Pappas a heartening smile just before the two of them bailed.

"See…we made it to land, buddy. You're gonna be fine."

They tumbled out of the hatch and were embraced by the frigid atmosphere. Above them, the *Black Olive* broke completely apart and exploded, pieces of its big Davis wings and fuselage and tail thundering down like flaming asteroids.

68

THE DAY WAS WARM and rippled with salt breezes that caressed and curled the fabric of the two flags flying, one bearing the red, white, and blue stars and stripes of the U.S and the other, the blue and white cross and stars of Greece.

Standing in front of the flags, at the head of a wide circle of men and women, was Caspian Bachman, dressed in a black MVAA t-shirt, khaki slacks, and Western Ariat boots, Ray-Bans shielding his eyes from the bright afternoon sun. The t-shirt was new, both it and his slacks clean, without the soil or perspiration of a day's dig activities; the boots were a dressier pair, shined, made of top-shelf ostrich leather and decoratively stitched.

In Bachman's open, outstretched hands were two sets of dog tags. Their silver metal alloy was corroded and discolored green and brown, outlines pocked and misshapen. But the engraved names were legible.

One read NICK PAPPAS, the other, COSTAS KAVOURHAS.

Bachman had been telling their story as he knew it, some from family annals and anecdotes, some from military records, some construed from transcripts of radio communication. Eleven souls were thought to have perished that fateful night, and ossified remains had been recovered here, but the pair of dog tags in Bachman's hands were the only IDs that had been found.

Hours earlier, in the morning, Antipsara had been swarming with people—far too many for the limited inhabitable spaces scattered along the trails and pooled from within the valleys of the little island—everyone buzzing with the prominence of the occasion.

In that mix were high-ranking figureheads from the archaeological sphere, which included the Greek Ministry of Culture and Archaeological Service, the Archaeological Society of Athens and Ephorate of Underwater Antiquities, and esteemed administrators and academics from several Greek universities. On the military side, a full investigative unit from the Defense POW/MIA Accounting Agency had joined the representative already embedded with the dig team and were now set up to oversee the processing and finalization of localized recovery; the transition to off-site work had already begun and, on the more comprehensive scale, full analysis would take years. There was also a contingent from the U.S. and Greek Aegean Forge military coalition, led by lieutenant colonels Atticus Merriweather and Thanos Koukodimos. Local law enforcement from Psara and Chios were in attendance, as well as the same government and regional dignitaries that had been on hand to welcome MVAA when they'd first arrived. And, of course, there was an abundance of media from all over—not only those who had been covering the excavation but, in the wake of the bellicose buildup in the Mediterranean, a slew of international mainstream news outlets and journalists.

Now, at Bachman's respectful but firm insistence, those present had been pared down to the more intimate group surrounding him. Loosely assembled off to one side of the circle were the archaeology experts and students that had taken part in the dig, the members of Remington's *Habari* team on the opposite side with Merriweather and his sergeant major.

The horizon beyond them was a vast canvas of vivid turquoise blue where sky and water came together in an almost invisible seam, the sky feathered with clouds as light and gossamery as dandelion fuzz. The sea, which only seventy-two hours ago had been clamoring with NATO-alliance ships and an aggressively advancing front of Turkish and Russian forces, had reverted to its serene beauty, empty of visible craft save for the USS Gerald R. Ford carrier and the Greek HS Psara frigate holding court in the far distance.

While war had been forestalled with the relay and presentation of the authenticated proof of conspiracy discovered by Jake and Remington, their interception of Taras Ignatkovich and the missiles solidified its dis-solution. As the two of them had stood next to the HEMTT on that day and looked to the sky paling with the onset of dawn, the helicopters they'd seen approaching were, in fact, their cavalry—U.S. Air Force coming from Incirlik Air Base in Adana.

Before the helos touched down on the highway, Jake had returned to the barn and set it alight; he knew torching the oligarch's body would make for a less complicated post mortem, hopefully eliminating any le-gal or political repercussions. He'd also figured the fleet of firefighting units responding to the rapidly spreading mountainside blaze could han-dle one more upslope.

As for the missiles, Jake and Remington were only too happy to let their military sort all that out, and hitched a ride on one of the birds back to Incirlik while the others blocked the road on either side of the HEMTT. In the hours that followed, a tactical convoy from the air base was dispatched to the scene, the missiles transferred to a U.S. carrier.

After a long initial debriefing with Merriweather via video confer-ence, Jake and Remington had been flown to Chios and then on to Psara.

Today, they were all standing next to the dig site, the core group of veterans—less the one who had not been a veteran nor an American—all wearing t-shirts that matched Bachman's. The tee bore the standard MVAA logo imprinted below the collar on one side of the front, larger and centered on the back—but with it were the words B-24 LIBERATOR and ANTIPSARA, GREECE.

Missing from the *Habari* crew were Falcone and Niles, still hospital-ized in Athens. On Remington's instruction, while in flight Kipnis had contacted Amelia Keogh, who'd arranged for two of the best specialty surgeons in the world—orthopedic and vascular surgeons, ironically from Istanbul's Hisar Intercontinental Hospital—to travel to the Athens Military Hospital. Niles had undergone several complicated surgeries on his horrendously damaged hand, both doctors pronouncing a successful outcome and favorable prognosis for functionality.

Back in Turkey, U.S. Special Forces, joined by the CIA, had swept Ig-natkovich's compound, while Sabine Brisepierre's clandestine team was on the ground in Cyprus scouring the oligarch's estate; custody of surviving mercenaries were ceded to the Turks, but all the material evidence had been extracted and retained by the U.S. operatives.

Which, luckily, included the jugs and the Antikythera mechanism-like device. Their custody was more of a gray area, one that had engendered a considerable amount of conversation and some debate as to who would take possession. Ultimately, an accord was worked out between the Greek authorities and archaeologists and the U.S. military, allowing for the Greeks to select a small group of highly credentialed personnel that could be vetted for the necessary security clearances. The group would be granted limited, supervised access to do their own analysis of the artifacts, but the military's testing—primarily of the polymer substance—would be conducted under strict, classified protocols, the details and process of which would not be shared.

Nor was it likely that any determinations or prototyping would be made known. On the contrary, as had been done numerous times in the past, any real potential for dynamic development would be skeptically downplayed, even mythified in the manner of a militarily programmed killer robot. Except, with the rapid advancement of Artificial Intelligence, technology of that type was not so farfetched anymore, and neither was that of the polymer's composition and potential applications.

It was also likely that Antipsara and its coastline would be under more carefully controlled "ecological" protection.

Standing next to Remington, Lieutenant Colonel Merriweather, his salt-and-pepper hair precisely buzzed close to the scalp, was clad in an immaculately pressed green-and-brown camouflage ACU, cap, and sand combat boots. He commented, "You two look like you've been in a John Wick marathon death battle." He leaned forward, appraising Jake with his keen slate-blue eyes. "Especially *you*. Goddamn."

Jake slid Merriweather a sidelong glance from behind his iPhone, which he held up with its camera aimed at the gathering; with Falcone and Niles absent, he'd decided to film as much as he could to top off what the two had already documented. Thankfully, all of the footage they'd shot—and lost in their capture—was backed up on a cloud drive.

Jake and Remington were both nearly out of clothing that had not been indelibly stained or torn or slashed, but today they were wearing clean pairs of their least battle-ragged khakis and button-up shirts.

Despite Jake's best efforts at grooming, maneuvering a razor over the lacerated minefield of battery covering his face had proved challenging, to say the least, and he had nicked several of his scratches and scrapes and cuts in the effort. The skin around his eyes was smeared with shades of blue and purple, his mouth sporting a few scabs, the line where Ignatkovich's Gurza had been pressed against his throat looking like that of a red Sharpie.

Catching Remington smirking at him, Jake scowled. "What?"

"I would not want to be you when your little sweetie gets the up-close-and-personal on that mug and body. You FaceTime her?"

Wrinkling up his mouth and eyes, Jake muttered, "God, no."

For the next few minutes, they listened in silence as Bachman continued to speak of the Liberator's flight and crew.

He was saying, "Though they were unable to complete their mission, from what was chronicled of the radio transmissions, it seems the pilots were doing their best to bail over land…you could speculate that, had they bailed a little sooner, over water, they might have survived and been rescued. Of course we don't know, but what has been theorized is that, on breakup, the parts of the plane came down and struck the parachutes…eradicating crew members." Nodding to the sets of dog tags in his hand, he said, "Except, maybe, for these two."

He inhaled deeply. "We have accomplished something special here, something for which you can take great pride." He paused pensively. "Hopefully, it will bring some closure to these two families and, eventually, all of the rest." Bowing his head, he prayed, "We thank you, God, for allowing us to partake in the privilege of this recovery, for all that we honored in the undertaking and outcome, for the enlightenment and healing, for the spiritual growth and nurturing of self-worth…for the shared experience and what each of us will take from it going forward."

Bachman looked up, earnestly eying each of the veterans and staff members in the circle. "I give all of you my respect and gratitude and hope this experience is something you will cherish and draw upon, possibly pursue in further projects with us."

Operations manager Shelby Hoskins passed him a small box, into which Bachman reverently placed the dog tags. He then said, "Corporal Nick Pappas…Corporal Costas Kavourhas…you're going home."

Around the circle, hands snapped up in salute.

On cue from Bachman, two of the vets moved to the pole hoisting the American flag, took a few moments to lower it and complete the ceremonial folding.

Moments later, after the box with the dog tags had been handed off to one of the DPAA team members, the assembly stirred out of formation, vets conversing and embracing, many holding back tears or letting them flow, emotions that did not normally come readily on full display.

Among those sharing fond sentiments and physical affectations were Kirk Perry and Daniel Rodriguez, the pair of vets that had been baited into the baseless scuffle by Kirill Vasić in the guise of Logan Hays; the two men had forged a bond during their time on the dig and were planning to stay in contact afterward.

Earlier, before the dedication and benediction, Bachman had invited the vets to share their thoughts, and the words spoken and emotions expressed reflected the profound impact of the project and mission and camaraderie shared. Jake and Remington soaked it all in with a swell of gratitude for having been a part of it. Aside from the parallel drama and danger, tragedy and trauma, peril and brink of war, lives had been changed here.

They stepped away from the group, accompanying Merriweather and his sergeant major along the trail to the island's floating wharf where an army patrol boat was docked. The vegetation that spread out from the sandy path was yellow and gold in the sunlight, copper-colored butterflies flittering close to scattered batches of nettles. The pair of Malinois were bounding back and forth in spirited play, biting each other and then, distracted by the butterflies, darting off in pursuit.

When they had reached the dock, the lieutenant colonel remarked, "I wouldn't be at all surprised to see a medal or two awarded to you both."

Remington's face registered mild surprise, but Jake reacted with a look of uneasy humility. "An honor, to be sure, but I'm not much on that."

"Understand," said Merriweather, "but what you guys did cannot be overstated. You might have to suck it up." He grinned.

Jake said, "Well, I know a couple of brave guys who, in my humble opinion, deserve it at least as much."

They all shook hands, Jake and Remington watching as the lieutenant colonel and his sergeant major boarded the patrol boat, giving them a parting salute as the motor was engaged and the vessel churned out to sea.

JAKE STOOD ON THE cliff overlooking the caves where the jugs had been found. The sun was lower in the sky, giving it the rich hue of melting butter, shadows stretching back across the meadow, and he was recalling the day when he and Callie had strolled through the grasses. Thinking of those moments, enraptured by the memory of her with him here, he was all at once overcome with yearning for her and for home.

He did not hear Remington behind him, and hitched at the sound of shuffling as his friend sidled up next to him, silently taking in the magnificent vista beyond the cliffs, their rock and soil the colors of nutmeg and cinnamon. The water was now a deeper blue, the surface crinkling in the breeze, clouds hovering above the horizon line and looking more like broad strokes of whitewash rather than feathers, appearing so close that they could almost touch the Aegean, backlit with the faintest touch of pink. It reminded Jake of the inside of a conch shell, and again, he felt the rising tide of emotion welling inside.

Remington put a hand on his shoulder. "We'll get things wrapped and packed. It's time for you to go home, brother."

"Yeah, Remy…yeah, it is."

69

WHEN JAKE LANDED AT Athens *Eleftherios Venizelos* International Airport the following day, he was expecting to lease a car and make the forty-minute drive to the 401 Military Hospital, where he would talk with Falcone and Niles' doctors and then get them discharged. Instead, as Dmello taxied the Pilatus to the FBO ramp, Jake heard the Kenyan's happy, melodic voice report over the intercom, "Looks like they saved you a trip!"

Standing in the aisle, Jake bent down and peered through one of the porthole windows, both dumbfounded and mildly annoyed at what he saw. A grin broke over his face, despite the irritation. His hand automatically went to his ear, reaching for the Bluetooth earbud but remembering he'd lost it sometime during the confrontation on the Turkish highway. Sliding his iPhone from his pocket, the screen showed several missed calls from a Greek number he recognized, at least a dozen more from one he did not—the hospital and, probably, a burner phone.

He waited for Dmello to park the plane, then met him at the cockpit for a farewell embrace. "Thank you, my man."

Beaming, brown eyes alight with the usual animation, Dmello hugged Jake carefully, mindful of all the injuries he'd sustained. "Always my pleasure," he quipped brightly. "Safe travels home… *tuonane inshallah.*"

In response to the Swahili expression for "we will see each other again God willing," Jake replied, "I'm sure we will. You take good care,

Mellie."

They exchanged a final smile and Jake stepped down the airstairs and strode slowly across the tarmac toward the access doors for Universal Aviation. Waiting for him there, fidgeting in a couple of plastic chairs an agent had brought outside, were Falcone and Niles, Falcone clutching a cheap-looking flip phone.

Forehead creased, Jake approached with hands on his hips. Sternly, he asked, "What the hell are you knuckleheads doing here? I was coming to the hospital to consult with your doctors and arrange for proper transport." He glanced around, adding, "You're not supposed to be out here on the apron, either."

But as he looked down at the two, a thought occurred to him from out of the blue: *They're afraid of being left behind.*

Painstakingly rising from the chairs, Falcone and Niles flung their arms around him, all of them grimacing with the soreness of physical contact. They held onto him for a few minutes, and Jake let them. When they finally released him and stepped back, their eyes were glistening.

Really registering Jake's appearance for the first time, Niles murmured, "Bloody hell...are you all right?"

"Yeah, yeah, I'm fine," Jake answered dismissively. "Just the usual battle wear and tear."

"Looks like a bit more than that, mate."

Jake did not reply, turning the scrutiny on them. They were dressed in slacks and shirts he'd ordered in their sizes and had delivered to the hospital, but the clothing hung on their emaciated frames as if draped from wire hangers. Both of them were easily twenty pounds lighter. They were moving gingerly and stiffly, as if one wrong move might cause a vertebral collapse like a misplaced block in a Jenga game, their skin the pallor and laxity of raw oysters. Niles had a cast wrapping his hand, interwoven around his fingers and extending halfway up his arm, which was elevated by a sling.

Even so, with the hospital's care, they presented a far cry better than when Jake and Remington had rescued them three days ago, and Jake remarked, "You look good, all things considered. Just need to get some meat back on those bones."

"Yeah, wouldn't recommend the thirty-day dungeon weight loss plan," Falcone said dryly.

A uniformed Universal agent came through the doors and did a quick pre-board check-in. While they had been reuniting, Dmello, in the Pilatus PC-12 NGX, had unloaded Jake's gear and taken off without further ado. Not long afterward, their outbound plane—the Gulfstream G650ER—taxied in, the thrum and whoosh of its Rolls-Royce engines causing them all to look up.

"Oh my God," Niles gasped. "We get to fly on your Gulfstream?"

"Well, it's not *my* Gulfstream," Jake corrected. "But yeah, we do."

The three of them were met and escorted to the aircraft by Captain Lee Monty as a ground handler drove up in a baggage cart, most of the contents belonging to Jake. If Monty or any of his crew were shocked by the rough appearance and shape of their passengers, they did not show it, professionalism prevailing; introductions were made, all crew members as welcoming and genial as ever. Jake watched Falcone and Niles reacting to the grand jet's interior and amenities, the tiniest hints of their personalities flickering from behind their eyes as they marveled over the cabin's elegant finishes and entertainment choices.

But the prisms that refracted the depths and dimensions and colors of their unique spirits were shrouded by a heavy veil, the stems of their vitality burrowed deeply, as if rooted by an anchor burrowed in a dark, subterranean trench. Like zombies hiding beneath human forms.

Once all three had settled into cushy leather club chairs, Monty and flight attendant Tabetha Radecki lingered for a few minutes. The sandy-haired pilot in command favored them with an engaging smile and said, "You guys will be getting the full rock star treatment." He winked at Jake. "Sound good?"

Falcone and Niles nodded but said nothing. When the pilot had retreated to the cockpit, Radecki to the galley, they lapsed into uncomfortable silence, eyes alternately roaming over the luxurious cabin and peering through the large oval windows. It was midday, the sun flaring off the Gulfstream's wings like the yellow and white of a freshly cracked egg.

After a few minutes, the aircraft's engines began to power up to a robust hum as the G650ER navigated the turns to the runway. Glancing away from his window, Jake caught Niles' eyes holding on him, liquid with an indeterminate emotion. He leaned forward and met his gaze, hands clasped together. "What is it, bud?"

Awed, Niles asked, "How did you ever find us?"

Jake replied softly, "I had faith, Curran…I didn't give up. You know I never quit."

Now tears pooled in the Brit's gray eyes, beading and breaking from the corners. His lips quivered and he swiped at his face with his uninjured hand. "I…I thought we'd never be found."

Jake put a hand on Niles' thigh, gave him a warm smile. "As long as you're with me, you won't ever be left behind. Not ever."

They fell into silence again, feeling the build of speed as the aircraft rumbled and then roared down the runway, tilted up, and lifted smoothly into the air. Watching the vast city spread of Athens shrink and blur into a palette of urban grayscale daubed here and there with browns and greens, the outline of the Greek peninsula gave way to the royal blue-and-teal brilliance of the Saronic Gulf.

"Greece is a beautiful place," Falcone mused moodily, "but I don't think we'll ever be coming back."

"I hear you," Jake said. "Can't blame you."

More somber silence ensued, and Jake leaned forward again. "Hey…we're going home."

When neither Falcone or Niles had anything to say, Jake sat back in his seat and got lost in his own reflection for a while, thinking about how much the harrowing experience had altered the two, about the extensive road of healing ahead of them—a road Callie was still struggling with.

Looking over at the pair, trying to read their faces, he said, "It's a really long flight. We can talk about things. Or not. Whatever you feel comfortable with."

Neither responded to that, but a few minutes later Niles quipped, "I want a massive cheeseburger with every bloody thing they've got on it."

Jake felt his heart tick a little lighter.

FOR THE DURATION OF the nine-hour portion of the flight, there was very little talking, and almost none of it about anything related to their ordeal. But Falcone and Niles did eat, enjoying hamburgers that were thick and juicy and piled high with ingredients that slid from between the fresh-baked buns oozing with catsup and mustard and steak sauce; later, they feasted on Kobe beef filets and stuffed baked potatoes and ice cream. Though they were still on some pain medications, Jake let them have limited amounts of beer which, combined with the food and lounging in front of the large-screen TV served to induce hours of sleep.

For destination, Jake had given them options, offering to put them up near him in Dominical for as long as they liked, but they'd chosen New York, their home base. At the last minute, as the Gulfstream had begun its descent to JFK, they seemed torn and conflicted, but did not change their minds.

On landing, Jake followed them off the plane and stood on the tarmac to say goodbye. In gaining hours on the Atlantic crossing, locally it was almost the same time they had departed Greece, but the skies were overcast here, ashen clouds rolling and a light drizzle beginning.

It was an emotional parting, especially for Falcone and Niles, who felt like an avalanche of broken rock had tumbled from an overhead ledge, the weight breaking after so many days and nights of being held back by a dam of manufactured bravery.

Blinking in the rain, his voice cracking, Niles said, "Thank you for getting us, Jake."

"Of course," Jake replied evenly. He gave each of them a long hug, Niles once more swiping tears from his face.

"Bollocks…sorry, sorry," Niles blubbered.

"Nothing to be sorry about," Jake said kindly. "It's a lot. If you ever want or need to talk, if you need anything at all…you know where I am."

The two nodded, turned, and started to amble toward the FBO, then stopped and looked back. Falcone said, "We never gave them anything."

Jake felt his throat constrict and when he spoke, his own voice was like gravel. "If you had, it would have been okay. You just do your best, and whatever that is, it's okay. But I'm proud of you…really proud."

He watched them resume walking, their gaits rickety, watching until they disappeared through the glass doors, and then reboarded the aircraft.

It pained Jake to see them that way, to know what they'd been through, and he had spent some of the four hours of flight time between New York and Costa Rica pensively thinking about the hurt and misery, the trauma—and worse—that those he cared about, those he loved, endured by being close to him and in his life. But he also knew with conviction that his friend Remington, Falcone and Niles, and certainly Callie, were in it with him for the long haul, whatever that brought and however long that was. All he could do was his best to prepare, protect, preserve, and fiercely hold them dear in his fold.

On landing in San José, Jake caught a Sansa flight to the Quepos airport, where Jesse Segura had dropped off his Jeep Rubicon earlier in the day. He was anxious to get home, shaving ten minutes from the thirty-five-minute drive along the Costanera Sur, even though it was clotted with evening-commute traffic.

He crossed the Rio Barú bridge, driving past the town's commerce and turning into the hills canopied with emerald-green rainforest. The Jeep's windows were down and, as he drove, he began to hear the chatter of monkeys, the squawks and calls of birds, and felt his heart fill with the happiness of homecoming.

When he pulled into the drive, he took a few moments to savor the image of the lovely stucco villa with its terra-cotta and cream coloring and red clay roof, its Spanish architecture with accent railings and arches, its landscape full of every kind of palm and lush greenery and splashes of bright florals, and said a silent prayer of gratitude. He thought, whatever the trials and uncertainties the universe put in his path, as long as all roads led back here, to Callie and home, it was all worth whatever he had to do.

He bounced from the Jeep, grabbed two of his rucksacks, and strode briskly across the crushed shells to the arched front porch.

And made his entrance.

CALLIE WAS WITH CAMILLA, helping the housekeeper with dinner. Jake had called ahead, requesting anything but seafood—as much as he loved it, he'd had more than enough for at least a day or two—and as soon as he set foot inside the foyer, the piquant spices of seasoned chicken wafted from the kitchen.

Hearing him come through the front door, Callie hurried from the kitchen, but when she caught sight of him, she gasped, halting in her tracks. This was the one moment Jake had dreaded, and he was quick to make reassurances.

Dropping his bags, he extended his arms, saying, "I'm okay…I'm okay. Looks a lot worse than it is, I promise."

Callie, dressed in a simple, sleeveless white dress with a shirred ruffle hem above her knees, looked like a confectionary vision of everything pure and blissful, and he wanted nothing more than to rush over and scoop her up. But, even as his heart was galloping in his chest with excitement, he tamped down his desire, and blew out a breath. Approached her slowly, smiling ruefully.

All the joy had drained from her face, hands over her mouth.

"I'm okay," he repeated soothingly.

Close now, it was his turn to be stunned, his dark eyes bugging. For an instant, he was gobsmacked, the connective strands of comprehension flailing in his head like loose, live wires.

What the hell?

He fought to keep his expression neutral and reached to Callie's neck, lightly fingering the string of tiny seashells encircling it. "Where did you find this?" he heard himself ask, the words seeming to float from some indeterminate point. His heart was thudding now, but not from excitement—from the internal alarm blaring in his brain.

One of Callie's small hands came up to her neck self-consciously, her face flushing. "Oh…I…it…I found it in the nightstand, by my side of the bed. I was sure I had lost it." She glanced back to Camilla in the kitchen, the housekeeper's face also registering shock on seeing Jake's appearance.

"Miss Callie thought maybe I found it when I was cleaning," Camilla supplied, wiping her hands on a dish towel and coming through the kitchen's bricked archway into the living room where Jake and Callie stood. Dressed in a yellow peasant blouse and full skirt paisley-patterned in red, yellow, and orange, her eyes locked on Jake's face, and she exclaimed, "*Ay, ay, ay, Señor* Jake!"

He gave her a quick shake of his head to discourage making any kind of a fuss over his state.

Camilla read his signal, mustered a smile, and said, "I have never seen the necklace, but it is so pretty!" She shrugged. "Who knows how things turn up?"

Though the housekeeper knew some of what had happened to Callie in South America—Jake had told all of the household team what they needed to know in order to understand and best care for Callie—Camilla did not know the background of the necklace. So she could not know that it was impossible for it to just randomly turn up.

No…someone had placed it in the nightstand so Callie would find it and, he was sure, as a message to him.

Callie was beginning to pick up on his sense of unnerve, her beautiful brown eyes wide with worriment.

Jake forced a new smile and said, "Well, it's nice you found it."

The worry lingered on her face, and she asked, "Are Eddie and Curran all right?"

"They will be." He drew her into his arms and kissed her. "God, I'm glad to be home. I've missed you, baby."

In his ear, she whispered, "I love you, Jake."

"I love you, angel," he said and, as he nuzzled her neck, felt the tiny shells press into his skin.

70

SOMETIME AFTER MIDNIGHT, JAKE lay awake in their bed, staring up at the wooden fan rotating overhead. The French doors to the balcony were open, a cool breeze blowing in, the air from both creating a comfortable temperature and a perfectly Zen sensation for sleep. And, any other time, after returning from a lengthy and grueling mission, sapped by the jet lag from a transoceanic flight, physically and emotionally spent in post-coital euphoria, he would have passed out and been practically comatose. He was exhausted.

Instead, he was wide awake, his mind a bedlam of troubling thoughts.

He rolled onto his side, gazing at Callie who, amazingly, *was* asleep. In fact, he was glad to see that she was deeply asleep, probably the most sound sleep she'd had in a while, her precious face a picture of calm. Propping himself up on an elbow, he studied her in the subdued glow of the room's LED night-lights. She lay facing him, her skin as pale and smooth as a pearl, blond curls coiled and swirled around her neck and over her forehead and cheek. He loved watching her in sleep when she was peaceful like this, which was rare, and the sight never failed to smitten him all over again. He loved her more than anything he could ever know in this world.

Earlier, their lovemaking had been everything it always was. Even with his soreness, he was not going to begrudge himself the physical and emotional ecstasy he craved and the expression of conjoined intimacy that elevated them together to that extraterrestrial level of internal oneness.

She had been even more tentative than usual, acutely aware of her gunshot wounds which, he was pleased to see, had healed nicely. The in-and-out holes to her arm were now small divots the color of bubblegum, and they would shrink and fade even more with time. Ten days after she'd returned home, he had instructed and supervised Jesse Segura in removing the stitches from the incision he'd made to extract the bullet fragments from her side, his suture skills leaving only a couple of thin, pink lines.

She had also been worried about his injuries, which were fresh and still painful, her fingertips delicately touching the scratches and abrasions and bruises on his face and body. But the mechanical and neural and sensual parts integral to his libido were working just fine, and he had managed to allay her concerns as soon as he was moving inside her. Losing himself to the primal rhythm and pace that took over, feeling the maddening graduation of resistance and yielding, the opening and elastic connection like that of the deepest, most passionate kiss. Then, the breaking rapture that was like shooting up the face of a waterfall with the sound of its rapids thundering and drowning out all else but pounding heartbeats, diving unbridled over the edge and straight down into the hot, steaming oasis on the other side, into a place of dripping greenery and glowing cavernous walls and the fragrant ambrosia of a million flowering vines…and finally, the slow, warm serenity of an Earth at the edge of creation, feeling as if no one else had ever set foot on its soil.

But now, he could not enjoy the same peaceful sleep that was cradling Callie.

He carefully eased himself up and off the bed, going to the window seat where his clothes were strewn. Slipped on his briefs and cargo pants and t-shirt. Jabbed his feet into his Hoka running shoes. Picked up his Glock 43 and stuck it in the back of his waist. And headed downstairs.

JAKE TOOK OUT HIS iPhone, opened the app for the security suite and made the necessary adjustments so he could move about without tripping anything. Not long after his arrival from the airport, he had met with Kent Sandborn and Jesse Segura, who led him around the property and inside the villa, showing him all of the systems put in place by the design and direction of Kipnis after the break-in had occurred. The level of protection was impressive, even if arguably a bit extreme and constrictive for his liking but, given everything that had happened and what was now heavy on his mind, totally warranted and necessary.

He crossed the living room and stepped through the French doors off the dining room, standing on the rear patio just below the balcony of their bedroom. The wide, circular sweep of pool was its usual luminant aqua, the surface rippling ever so faintly in the breeze. He strode around the pool's edge, glancing up to the balcony railing, his heart pulsing with the frenetic scramble of thoughts that had been cascading in his head ever since he'd laid eyes on the seashells around Callie's neck.

He stuck his hand into a pocket of his pants and took out the tiny piece missing from the center of the necklace—the opal heart he carried with him always, as symbolic and permanent as his wedding ring—and remembered with vivid clarity when and where and how he'd come upon it, separated from the strand of seashells…and from Callie.

He'd been searching one of the Valentín cartel estates to the north of Bogotá after she'd been abducted. There was no sign of her presence in the mansion, other than a minute speck of blood on a bedroom rug, and he'd been about to leave when something on the floor had caught his eye. Almost hidden by the bed's dust ruffle were fragments of crushed shells and the heart-shaped opal. Finding that one thing confirmed his worst nightmare and his world had imploded.

Now, he held the stone in the palm of his hand for several moments as the scene and horror replayed in his mind, then he touched it to his lips and put it back in his pocket.

He walked beyond the patio and pool, across grass that was soft and damp underfoot, the scent fresh from an afternoon cut. He strolled along the perimeter of shrubs and ornamentals and trees and palms, listening to the faint trill of insects and the occasional rustle of night birds in the high branches. The sweet aromas of plumerias, ylang ylang, ginger, and jasmine perfumed the air and, as he came to Callie's roses, he got a whiff of their delicate bouquet. With only a sliver of moon, the night was dark, the span of ocean below the hills barely visible, like a sheet of black velvet. The tide was going out, the wash of waves hushed and somnolent in their ebb.

He thought about the sequence of events, starting with the sniper's missed kill shot on his wedding day. The persistent and intensive surveillance and many deadly encounters and attacks for the entire time they'd been in the Greek Isles. The breach into the villa and injury inflicted on Camilla. And there had been one more thing, disclosed to him by Captain Monty during the second leg of the flight home. Monty had described the suspicious run-in with a Latino man at the San José airport FBO, letting Jake know that he'd quickly concluded the man clad in a pilot's uniform was an imposter, recounting the inappropriate and intrusive questions the man had peppered him with. Monty assured Jake that he'd not responded in any kind of compromising way.

But, even more prescient than that, were the incidents here at home while he was on-mission in Africa—incidents that still haunted Callie, who was the only one to witness them, like the man on the beach and the man by their pool. A man who, by Callie's description, looked exactly like Adonís Valentín, the vile monster who had brutalized and violated her.

He knew that was not possible. Valentín was dead, killed by his own hands.

And, up until now, he'd been adhering to the theory that the attempt on his life here and, most likely, the break-in of the villa, were executed as a result of the Dark Web contract that had been posted on him—a posting that Kipnis had yet to determine the origin of.

The seashell necklace materializing changed everything.

There was only one place it could have come from, as impossible to imagine as that was. It had come off Callie's neck, forcefully or accidentally, in South America. She'd been practically naked when he'd rescued her, the necklace not on her.

Jake shuddered, his skin tingling as if chilled liquid was circulating beneath it, the eerie feeling of an invisible presence in his midst. He pivoted slowly, peering into the darkness, eyes panning the grounds, the trees and vegetation in deep purple-black silhouette. He gazed out to the horizon, as if some spectral beast might emerge from between the lines of a metaphysical realm.

Banishing such thoughts, he inhaled the fragrance of the flowers and grass and rainforest and ocean, walking back to the patio. But the weight of his unease remained. He paused to glance up to the balcony, and felt his heart flood with love, his protective instincts in overdrive.

IN THEIR BEDROOM, JAKE was relieved to find Callie undisturbed in sleep. Standing by the bed and leaning against the headboard, he resisted the urge to stroke her hair, her face, delicately kiss her slightly parted lips and the breath she drew in and out. He watched her for a while, mesmerized by the fineness of her eyelashes and the silky strands of hair tickled by the swirl of the fan overhead.

Then his eyes drifted to the bedside table next to her, to the shell necklace that should not, by any account, be laying there.

He rose, went to the window seat, removed the Glock from his waistband, kicked off his running shoes, stripped off his pants and shirt, and shucked his underwear. He took the Glock and padded back to the bed, sitting on the edge.

Opened the drawer of his nightstand to place the handgun inside.

In the dim, ambient light, his eyes instantly landed on something he'd not put in there, something that did not belong. His heart lurched, thumping rapidly, his pulse audible in his ears. The air went out of his lungs.

He reached in and, using a handkerchief, picked up the object. It was just over four and a half inches in length, just over a half inch in diameter, tapered to a point on one end and coated in copper.

It was a .408 cartridge, the same caliber as the round fired at him on the beach.

Staring at the projectile, he felt a whole other barrage of emotions—disbelief, horror, anger, dread…and the roaring ignition of vengeance, like the torch of a flamethrower. He could not, would not, keep layering the property and villa with one high-tech security measure after another, making it into a veritable fortress. And, even with the comprehensive and cutting-edge applications and systems in place, someone had penetrated without alert, without detection, had invaded the most intimate room and space in his home.

But he also could not let an assassin, or assassins, keep coming for him, putting Callie in constant danger.

It was time for him to take it to them.

Jake wrapped the cartridge in the handkerchief and stuck it in the drawer, setting his Glock down on top of it.

Then he blew out a breath and lay down on the bed, his head on the pillow. But his eyes did not close for a long time. When they finally did, Callie had moved, tucking into his side. He slipped his arm around his wife and, concentrating on the soft sound and rhythm of her breathing, fell asleep.